THE THIRST THAT NEVER DIES

The shots whistled high over the boy, striking the man in the face and throat. Papa screamed – a resounding scream of rage – as he was flung backward to the floor where he lay with his face in shadow and his boots in red embers.

And then a slow, scraping noise from the other side of the room.

The boy spun round to look.

Papa was rising to his feet. Half of his face was gone, leaving his chin and jaw and nose hanging by white, bloodless strings. The remaining teeth glittered with light, and the single pulped eye hung on one thick vein across the ruined cavern where the cheekbone had been. White nerves and torn muscles twitched in the hole of the throat. The man staggered up, crouched with his huge hands twisted into claws. When he tried to grin, only one side of the mouth remained to curve grotesquely upward.

And in that instant both boy and woman saw that he did not bleed .

They Thirst

ROBERT R. McCAMMON

SPHERE BOOKS LIMITED

SPHERE BOOKS LTD

Published by the Penguin Group
27 Wrights Lane, London W8 5TZ, England
Viking Penguin Inc., 40 West 23rd Street, New York, New York 10010, USA
Penguin Books Australia Ltd, Ringwood, Victoria, Australia
Penguin Books Canada Ltd, 2801 John Street, Markham, Ontario, Canada L3R 1B4
Penguin Books (NZ) Ltd, 182–190 Wairau Road, Auckland 10, New Zealand

Penguin Books Ltd, Registered Offices: Harmondsworth, Middlesex, England

First published in Great Britain by Sphere Books Ltd 1981
10 9 8 7

Copyright © Robert R. McCammon 1981
All rights reserved

Made and printed in Great Britain by
Richard Clay Ltd, Bungay, Suffolk
Set in Times

For Sally, who helped me reach

It was midnight in Topanga
I heard the DJ say
"There's a full moon rising
Join me in LA. . . ."

      —Warren Zevon

I'd kill for love
I'd kill for love
As sure as there's a God above
I'd kill for love

      —Rory Black

Shadows shifting everywhere;
Very thin and very tall,
Moving, mingling on the wall,
Till they make one Shadow all

      —Augustus Julian Requier

I'd like to express appreciation to a number of people who helped me in researching this book and putting it all together: W. B. McDonald, M.D.; James R. Fletcher, M.D.; Gunnery Sergeant Larry Rocke, USMC; Captain Paul T. Taylor, USMC; Detective Sergeant William Ludlow; Radu Florescu and Raymond T. McNally for keeping the legends alive; and Mike and Elizabeth.

R.M.

Prologue

Tonight there were demons in the hearth.

They spun, arched, and spat at the eyes of the boy who sat at the fire's edge, his legs crossed under him in that unconscious way children have of being incredibly supple. Chin supported by palms, elbows supported by knees, he sat in silence, watching the flames gather, merge, and break into fragments that hissed with secrets. He had turned nine only six days ago, but now he felt very old because Papa wasn't home yet and those fire-demons were laughing.

While I'm away, you must be head of the house, Papa had said as he coiled a line of thick rope around his bear's paw of a hand. *You must take care of your mother and see that all goes well while I and your uncle are gone. Do you understand that?*

Yes, Papa.

And see that you bring in the wood for her when she asks and stack it neatly along the wall so it can dry. And anything else she asks of you, you'll do, yes?

I will. He could still see his father's fissured, wind-ravaged face towering over him and feel the rough-as-hearthstones hand on his shoulder. The grip of that hand had conveyed an unspoken message: This is a serious thing I do, boy. Make no mistake about that. Watch out for your mother and be careful.

The boy understood, and Papa had nodded with satisfaction.

The next morning he watched through the kitchen window while Uncle Josef hitched the two old, gray and white horses to the family's wagon. His parents had drawn away, standing across the room near the bolted slab of a door. Papa had put on his woolen cap and the heavy sheepskin coat Mama had made for him as a Christmas present

1

years before, then slipped the coil of rope around one shoulder. The boy picked listlessly from a bowl of beef broth and tried to listen, knowing that they were whispering so that he would not hear. But he also knew that if he did hear, he really wouldn't know what they were whispering about, anyway. *It's not fair!* he told himself as he dipped his fingers into the broth and brought out a chunk of meat. *If I'm to be the head of the house, shouldn't I know the secrets, too?*

Across the room Mama's voice had suddenly surged up out of control. *Let the others do it! Please!* But Papa had caught her chin, tilted her face up, and looked gently into those morning-gray eyes. *I have to do this thing*, he'd said, and she looked like she wanted to cry but could not. She'd used up all her tears the night before, lying in the goose-down bed in the other room. The boy had heard her all through the night. It was as if the heavy hours were cracking her heart and no amount of time on the other side of twilight could ever heal it again. *No, no, no,* Mama was saying now, over and over again as if that word had some magic that would prevent Papa from stepping out into the snowy daylight, as if that word would seal the door, wood to stone, to keep him within and the secrets out.

And when she was silent, Papa had reached up and lifted the double-barreled shotgun from the gunrack beside the door. He cracked open the breech, loaded both chambers with shells, and carefully laid the weapon down again. Then he had held her and kissed her and said *I love you.* And she had clung to him like a second skin. That was when Josef had knocked at the door and called out, *Emil! We're ready to leave!*

Papa had hugged her a moment longer, then gripped the rifle he had bought in Budapest, and unlatched the door. He stood on the threshold, and snowflakes flew in around him. *André!* he had said, and the boy had looked up. *You take care of your mother, and make sure this door stays bolted. Do you understand?*

Yes, Papa.

In the doorway, framed against a bleached sky and the purple teeth of the distant mountain ranges, Papa had turned his gaze upon his wife and had uttered three softly spoken words. They were indistinct, but the boy caught them, his heart beating around a dark uneasiness.

Papa had said, *Watch my shadow.*

When he stepped out, a whine of November wind filled the place he'd left. Mama stood at the threshold, snow blowing into her long dark hair, aging her moment by moment. Her eyes were fixed on the wagon as the two men urged the horses along the cobbled path that would take them to the others. She stood there for a long time, face gaunt against the false white purity of the world beyond that door. When the wagon had lumbered out of sight, she turned away, closed the door, and bolted it. Then she had lifted her gaze to her son's and had said with a smile that was more like a grimace, *Do your schoolwork now.*

It was three days since he had gone. Now demons laughed and danced in the fire, and some terrible, intangible thing had entered the house to sit in the empty chair before the hearth, to sit between the boy and woman at their evenings meals, to follow them around like a gust of black ash blown by an errant wind.

The corners of the two-room house grew cold as the stack of wood slowly dwindled, and the boy could see a faint wraith of mist whirl from his mother's nostrils whenever she let out her breath.

"I'll take the axe and get more wood," the boy said, starting to rise from his chair.

"No!" cried his mother quickly and glanced up. Their gray eyes met and held for a few seconds. "What we have will last through the night. It's too dark out now. You can wait until first light."

"But what we have isn't enough . . ."

"I said you'll wait until morning!" She looked away almost at once, as if ashamed. Her knitting needles glinted in the firelight, slowly shaping a sweater for the boy. As he sat down again, he saw the shotgun in the far corner of the room. It glowed a dull red in the firelight, like a watchful eye in the gloom. And now the fire flared, spun, cracked; ashes churned, whirled up the chimney and out. The boy watched, heat striping his cheekbones and the bridge of his nose, while his mother rocked in the chair behind him, glancing down occasionally at her son's sharp profile.

In that fire the boy saw pictures coming together, linking into a living mural: he saw a black wagon drawn by two white horses with funeral plumes, their cold breath

coming out in clouds. In that wagon a simple, small coffin.
Men and women in black, some shivering, some sobbing.
Others following the wagon, boots crunching through a
crust of snow. Muttered sounds. Faces layered with secrets. Hooded, fearful eyes that stared out toward the
gray and purple rise of the Jaeger Mountains. The Griska
boy lay in that coffin, and what remained of him was now
being carried by the procession to the cemetery where the
lelkesz waited.

Death. It had always seemed so cold and alien and
distant to the boy, something that belonged not to his
world, nor to the world of his Mama and Papa, but rather
to the world that Grandmother Elsa had lived in when
she was sick and yellow-fleshed. Papa had used the word
then—*dying. When you're in the room with her, you must
be very quiet because she can't sing to you anymore, and
all she wants to do now is sleep.* To the boy death was a
time when all songs ceased and you were only happy
when your eyes were closed. Now he stared at that funeral
wagon in his memory until the log collapsed and the
tendrils of flame sprang up in a different place. He remembered hearing whispers among the black-garbed villagers
of Krajeck: *A terrible thing. Only eight years old. God
has him now.*

*God? Let us hope and pray that it is indeed God who
has Ivon Griska.*

The boy remembered. He had watched the coffin being
lowered by a rope and pulley into the dark square in the
earth while the *lelkesz* stood intoning blessings and waving
his crucifix. The casket had been nailed shut and then
bound with barbed wire. Before the first shovelful of dirt
was thrown, the *lelkesz* had crossed himself and dropped
his crucifix into the grave. That was a week ago, before
the widow Janos had disappeared; before the Sandor
family vanished on a snowy Sunday night, leaving all
their possessions behind; before Johann the hermit reported that he had seen naked figures dancing on the
windswept heights of Mount Jaeger and running with the
big timber wolves that stalked that haunted mountain.
Soon after that Johann had vanished along with his dog,
Vida. The boy remembered the strange hardness in his
father's face, a flicker of some deep secret within his eyes.
Once he had heard Papa tell Mama, *They're on the move
again.*

In the fireplace, wood shifted and sighed. The boy blinked and drew away. Behind him his mother's needles were still; her head was cocked toward the door, and she was listening. The wind roared, bringing ice down from the mountain. The door would have to be forced open in the morning, and the hard glaze would shatter like glass.

Papa should be home by now, the boy told himself. *It's so cold out tonight, so cold . . . surely Papa won't be gone much longer.* Secrets seemed to be everywhere. Just yesterday night someone had gone through the Krajeck cemetery and dug up twelve graves, including Ivon Griska's. The coffins were still missing, but it was rumored that the *lelkesz* had found bones and skulls lying in the snow.

Something pounded at the door, a noise like a hammer falling upon an anvil. Once. And again. The woman jumped in her chair and twisted around.

"Papa!" the boy shouted joyfully. When he stood up, the flame-face was forgotten. He started toward the door, but his mother caught his shoulder.

"Hush!" she whispered, and together they waited, their shadows filling the far wall.

More hammering on the door—a heavy, leaden sound. The wind screamed, and it was like the wail of Ivon Griska's mother when the sealed coffin was lowered into the frozen dirt.

"Unbolt the door!" Papa said. "Hurry! I'm cold!"

"Thank God!" Mama cried out. "Oh, thank God!" She moved quickly to the door, threw back the bolt, and flung it open. A torrent of snow ripped at her face, the wind distorting eyes, nose, and mouth. Papa, a huddled shape in his hat and coat, stepped into the dim firelight, and diamonds of ice sparkled in his eyebrows and beard. He took Mama into his arms, his massive body almost engulfing her. The boy leapt forward to embrace his father, grateful that he was home because being the man of the house was much more difficult than he had imagined. Papa reached out, ran a hand through the boy's hair, and clapped him firmly on the shoulder.

"Thank God you're home!" Mama said, clutching onto him. "It's over, isn't it?"

"Yes," he said. "It's over." He turned and closed the door, letting the bolt fall.

"Here, step over by the fire. God in Heaven, your hands are cold! Take off your coat before you catch your death!"

She took the coat as he shrugged it from his shoulders, then his hat. Papa stepped toward the fire, palms outward to receive the heat. Flames glittered briefly in his eyes, like the glitter of rubies. And as he passed his son, the boy crinkled up his nose. Papa had brought home a funny smell. A smell of . . . what was it? Think hard.

"Your coat is filthy!" Mama said, hanging it on a hook near the door. She brushed at it with a trembling hand. She felt the tears of relief about to flood from her, but she didn't want to cry in front of her son.

"It's so cold in the mountains," Papa said softly, standing at the rim of the firelight. He kicked out with the toe of one scarred boot, and a log shifted, revealing a finger of flame. "So *cold*."

The boy watched him, seeing a glaze of ice from Papa's snow-whitened face begin to melt in droplets. Papa suddenly closed his eyes, inhaled deeply, and shivered. "Ohhhhhhhh," he breathed, and then his head came around, eyes opening, looking into his son's face for silent seconds. "What are you staring at, boy?"

"Nothing." *That smell. So funny. What was it?*

Papa nodded. "Come over here beside me."

The boy took a single step forward and then stopped. He thought of horses and coffins and sobbing mourners.

"Well? Come over here, I said."

Across the room the woman was standing with one hand still on the coat. There was a crooked smile on her face, as if she'd been slapped by a hand that had snaked from the shadows. "Is everything all right?" she asked. In her voice a note quavered like a pipe organ in the Budapest cathedral.

"Yes," Papa said, reaching out for his son. "Everything is fine now because I'm home with my loved ones, where I belong."

The boy saw a shadow touch his mother's face, saw it darken in an instant. Her mouth was half-open, and her eyes were widening pools of bewilderment.

Papa took his son's hand. The flesh was hard and welted with rope burns. And so terribly cold. The man drew him nearer. Nearer. The fire undulated like a serpent uncoiling. "Yes," he whispered, "that's right." His gaze leaped upon the woman. "You've let it get very cold in my house!"

"I'm . . . sorry," she whispered. She began to tremble

now, and her eyes were deep pits of terror. A low whine came from her throat.

"Very cold," Papa said. "I can feel ice in my bones. Can't you, André?" The boy nodded, looking into his father's shadowy firelight-sculpted face and seeing himself suspended within eyes that were darker than he remembered. Yes, much darker, like mountain caverns, and rimmed with eruptions of silver. The boy blinked, dragged his gaze away with an effort that made his neck muscles throb. He was trembling like Mama. He was beginning to be afraid but didn't know why. All he knew was that Papa's skin and hair and clothes smelled like the room where Grandmother Elsa had gone to sleep forever.

"We did a bad thing," Papa murmured. "Me, your uncle Josef, all the men from Krajeck. We shouldn't have climbed into the mountains . . ."

"Nooooooo," Mama moaned, but the boy couldn't turn his head to look at her.

". . . because we were wrong. All of us, wrong. It's not what we thought it was . . ."

Mama moaned like a trapped animal.

". . . you see?" And Papa smiled, his back to the flames now, his white face piercing the shadows. His grip tightened on his son's shoulder, and he suddenly shivered as if a north wind had roared through his soul. Mama was sobbing, and the boy wanted to turn to her and find out what was wrong, but he couldn't move, couldn't make his head turn or his eyes blink. Papa smiled and said, "My good little boy. My good little André . . ." And he bent down toward his son.

But in the next instant the man's head twisted up, his eyes filled with bursts of silver. "DON'T DO THAT!" he shrieked. And in that instant the boy cried out and pulled away from his father, and then he saw that Mama had the shotgun cradled in her shaking arms, and her mouth was wide open and she was screaming, and even as the boy ran for her, she squeezed both triggers.

The shots whistled high over the boy, striking the man in the face and throat. Papa screamed—a resounding scream of rage—and was flung backward to the floor where he lay with his face in shadow and his boots in red embers.

Mama dropped the shotgun, the strangled sobbing in her throat turning to stutters of mad laughter. The recoil had nearly broken her right arm, and she had fallen back against the door, her eyes swimming with tears. The boy stopped, his heart madly hammering. The smell of gunpowder was rank in his nostrils as he stared at the crazed woman who'd just shot down his father—saw her face contorting, lips bubbling with spittle, eyes darting from shadow to shadow.

And then a slow, scraping noise from the other side of the room.

The boy spun around to look.

Papa was rising to his feet. Half of his face was gone, leaving his chin and jaw and nose hanging by white, bloodless strings. The remaining teeth glittered with light, and the single pulped eye hung on one thick vein acrosss the ruined cavern where the cheekbone had been. White nerves and torn muscles twitched in the hole of the throat. The man staggered up, crouched with his huge hands twisted into claws. When he tried to grin, only one side of the mouth remained to curve grotesquely upward.

And in that instant both boy and woman saw that he did not bleed.

"*Szornyeteg!*" Mama screamed, her back pressed against the door. The word ripped through the boy's mind, tearing away huge chunks that left him as mute and frozen as a scarecrow in winter. *Monster,* she'd screamed. *Monster.*

"Oh, nooooooo," the hideous face whispered. And the thing shambled forward, claws twitching in hungry expection. "Not so easily, my precious wife . . ."

She gripped her son's arm, then turned and unbolted the door. He was almost upon them when a wall of wind and snow screamed into the house; he staggered back a step, one hand over his eye. The woman wrenched the boy out after her into the night. Snow clutched at their legs and tried to hold them. "Run!" Mama cried out over the roar of the wind. "We've got to run!" She tightened her grip on his wrist until her fingers melded to his bones, and they fought onward through whiplash strikes of snow.

Somewhere in the night, a woman screamed, her voice high-pitched and terrified. Then a man's voice, babbling for mercy. The boy looked back over his shoulder as he ran, back at the huddled houses of Krajeck. He could see nothing through the storm. But mingled with the hundred voices of the wind, he thought he could hear a chorus of hideous screams. Somewhere a ragged cacophony of laughter seemed to build and build until it drowned out the cries for God and mercy. He caught a glimpse of his house, receding into the distance now. Saw the dim red light spilling across the threshold like a final dying ember of the fire he'd so carefully tended. Saw the hulking half-blinded figure stumble out of the doorway and heard the bellow of rage from that mangled, bloodless throat— "I'LL FIND YOU!" And then Mama jerked him forward, and he almost tripped, but she pulled him up, urging him to run. Wind screamed into their faces, and already Mama's black hair was white with a coating of snow, as if she'd aged in a matter of minutes, or gone mad like some lunatic in an asylum who sees nightmares as grinning, shadowless realities.

A figure suddenly emerged from the midst of a stand of snow-heavy pines, frail and thin and as white as lake ice. The hair whipped around in the wind; the rags of its worm-eaten clothes billowed. The figure stood at the top of a snow mound, waiting for them, and before Mama saw it, it had stepped into their path, grinning a little boy's grin and holding out a hand sculpted like ice.

"I'm cold," Ivon Griska whispered, still grinning. "I have to find my way home."

Mama stopped, screamed, thrust out a hand before her. For an instant the boy was held by Ivon Griska's gaze, and in his mind he heard the echo of a whisper. *Won't you be my playmate, André?* And he'd almost replied, *Yes, oh yes,* when Mama shouted something that was carried away by the wind. She jerked him after her, and he looked back with chilled regret. Ivon had forgotten about them now and began walking slowly through the snow toward Krajeck.

After a while, Mama could go no further. She shuddered and fell into the snow. She was sick then, and the boy crawled away from the steaming puddle and stared back through waving pines toward home. His face was seared by the cold, and he wondered if Papa was going to be all right. Mama had no reason to hurt him like that. She was a bad woman to hurt his father who loved them both so dearly. "Papa!" he called into the distance, hearing only the wind reply in frozen mockery of a human voice. His eyelashes were heavy with snow. "Papa!" His small, tired voice cracked. But then Mama struggled to her feet, pulling him up again even though he tried to fight her and break free of her grip. She shook him violently, ice tracks lacing her face like white embroidery, and shouted, "He's dead! Don't you understand that? We've got to run, André, and we've got to keep on running!" And as she said that, the boy knew she was insane. Papa was badly hurt; yes, because she had shot him, but Papa wasn't dead. Oh, no. He was back there. Waiting.

And then lights broke the curtain of darkness. Smoke ripped from a chimney. They glimpsed a snow-weighted roof. They raced toward those lights, stumbling, half-frozen. The woman muttered to herself, laughing hysterically and urging the boy on. He fought the fingers of cold that clutched at his throat. *Lie down*, the wind whispered across the back of his head. *Stop right here and sleep. This woman has done a bad thing to your papa, and she may hurt you, too. Lie down right here for a little while and be warm, and in the morning your papa will come for you. Yes. Sleep, little one, and forget.*

A weather-beaten sign creaked wildly back and forth above a heavy door. He saw the whitened traces of words: THE GOOD SHEPHERD INN. Mama hammered madly at the door, shaking the boy at the same time to keep him awake. "Let us in, please let us in!" she shouted, pounding with a numbed fist. The boy stumbled and fell against her, his head lolling to the side.

When the door burst open, long-armed shadows reached for them. The boy's knees buckled, and he heard Mama moan as the cold—like the touch of a forbidden, loving stranger—gently kissed him to sleep.

I

Friday, October 25
THE CAULDRON

ONE

A star-specked night, black as the highway asphalt that bubbled like a cauldron brew beneath the midday sun, now lay thickly over the long dry stretch of Texas 285 between Fort Stockton and Pecos. The darkness, as still and dense as the eye of a hurricane, was caught between the murderous heat of dusk and dawn. In all directions the land, stubbled with thornbrush and pipe-organ cactus, was frying-pan flat. Abandoned hulks of old cars, gnawed down to the bare metal by the sun and occasional dust storms, afforded shelter for the coiled rattlesnakes that could still smell the sun's terrible track across the earth.

It was near one of these hulks—rusted and vandalized, windshield long shattered, engine carried away by some hopeful tinkerer—that a jackrabbit sniffed the ground for water. Smelling distant, buried coolness, the jackrabbit began to dig with its forepaws; in another instant it stopped, nose twitching toward the underside of that car. It tensed, smelling snake. From the darkness came a dozen tiny rattlings, and the rabbit leaped backward. Nothing followed. The rabbit's instincts told it that a nest had been dug under there, and the noise of the young would bring back the hunting mother. Sniffing the ground for the snake's trail, the jackrabbit moved away from the car and ran nearer to the highway, crunching grit beneath its paws. It was halfway across the road, moving toward its own nest and young in the distance, when a sudden vibration in the earth froze it. Long ears twitching for a sound, the rabbit turned its head toward the south.

A gleaming white orb was slowly rising along the highway. The rabbit watched it, transfixed. Sometimes the rabbit would stand atop its dirt-mound burrow and watch the white thing that floated high overhead; sometimes it was larger than this one; sometimes it was yellow; sometimes it wasn't there at all; sometimes there were tendrils across it, and it left in the air the tantalizing scent of water that never fell. The rabbit was unafraid because it was familiar with that thing in the sky, but the vibration it now felt rippled the flesh along its spine. The orb was growing larger, bringing with it a noise like the growl of thunder. In another instant the rabbit's eyes were blinded by the white orb; its nerves shot out a danger signal to the brain. The rabbit scurried for safety on the opposite side of the highway, casting a long scrawl of shadow beyond it.

The jackrabbit was perhaps three feet away from a protective clump of thornbrush when the night-black Harley-Davidson 750cc "chopper," moving at almost eighty miles an hour, swerved across the road and directly over the rabbit's spine. It squealed, bones splintering, and the small body began to twitch in the throes of death. The huge motorcycle, its shocks barely registering a shudder of quick impact, roared on to the north.

A few moments later a sidewinder began to undulate toward the rabbit's cooling carcass.

And on the motorcycle, enveloped in a cocoon of wind and thunder, the rider stared along the cone of white light his single, high-intensity beam afforded, and with a fractional movement he guided the machine to the center of the road. His black-gloved fist throttled upward; the machine growled like a well-fed panther and kicked forward until the speedometer's needle hung at just below ninety. Behind a battered, black crash helmet with visor lowered, the rider was grinning. He wore a sleek, skin-tight, black leather jacket and faded jeans with leather-patched knees. The jacket was old and scarred, and across the back rose a red Day-Glo king cobra, its hood fully swollen. The paint was flaking off, as if the reptile were shedding its skin. The machine thundered on, parting a wall of silence before it, leaving desert denizens trembling in its wake. A garishly painted sign—blue music notes floating above a pair of tilted, red beer bottles, the whole thing pocked with rust-edged bullet holes—came up on the right. The rider glanced quickly at it, reading JUST AHEAD! THE WATERIN' HOLE! and below that, FILL 'ER UP, PARDNER! *Yeah*, he thought. *Time to fill up.*

Two minutes later there was the first, faint glimmer of blue neon against the blackness. The rider began to cut his speed; the speedometer's needle fell quickly to eighty, seventy, sixty. Ahead there was a blue neon sign—THE WAT RIN' H LE—above the doorway of a low, wooden building with a flat, dusty red roof. Clustered around it like weary wasps around a sun-bleached nest were three cars, a jeep, and a pickup truck with most of its dull blue paint scoured down to the muddy red primer. The motorcycle rider turned into a tumbleweed-strewn parking lot and switched off his engine; immediately the motorcycle's growl was replaced with Freddy Fender's nasal voice singing about "wasted days and wasted nights." The rider put down the kickstand and let the black Harley ease back, like a crouching animal. When he stood up and off the machine, his muscles were as taut as piano wires; the erection between his legs throbbed with heat.

He popped his chin strap and lifted the helmet off, exposing a vulpine, sharply chiseled face that was as white as new marble. In that bloodless face the deep pits of his eyes bore white pupils, faintly veined with red. From a distance they were as pink as a rabbit's, but up close they became snakelike, glittering coldly, unblinking, hypnotizing. His hair was yellowish-white and closely cropped; a blue trace of veins at the temples pulsed an instant behind the jukebox's beat. He left his helmet strapped around the handlebars and moved toward the building, his gaze flickering toward the cars: there was a rifle on a rack in the truck's cab, a "Hook 'Em Horns!" sticker on a car's rear fender, a pair of green dice dangling from the jeep's rearview mirror.

When he stepped through the screen door into a large room layered with smoky heat, the six men inside—three at a table playing cards, two at a light bulb-haloed pool table, one behind the bar—instantly looked up and froze. The albino biker met each gaze in turn and then sat on one of the bar stools, the red cobra on his back a scream of color in the murky light. After another few seconds of silence, a pool cue cracked against a ball like a gunshot. "Aw, shit!" one of the pool players—a broad-shouldered man wearing a red checked shirt and dusty Levis that had been snagged a hundred times on barbed wire—said loudly with a thick Texas drawl. "At least that screwed up your shot, didn't it, Matty?"

"Sure did," Matty agreed. He was about forty, all arms and legs, short red hair, and a lined forehead half-covered by a sweat-stained cowboy hat. He was chewing slowly on a toothpick, and now he stood where he could consider the lie of the balls, do some more chewing, and watch that strange-looking white dude from the corner of his eye.

The bartender, a hefty Mexican with tattooed forearms and heavy-lidded black eyes, came down the bar following the swirls of a wet cloth. "Help you?" he asked the albino and looked up into the man's face; instantly he felt as if his spine had been tapped with an ice pick. He glanced over toward where Slim Hawkins, Bobby Hazelton and Ray Cope sat in the third hour of their Friday night poker game; he saw Bobby dig an elbow into Ray's ribs and grin toward the bar.

The albino said quietly, "Beer."

"Sure, coming up." Louis the bartender turned away in relief. The biker looked bizarre, unclean, freakish. He was hardly a man, probably nineteen or twenty at the most. Louis picked up a glass mug from a shelf and a bottle of Lone Star from the stuttering refrigerator unit beneath the bar. From the jukebox, Dolly Parton began singing about "burning, baby, burning." Louis slid the mug across to the albino and then quickly moved away, swirling the cloth over the polished wood of the bar. He felt as if he were sweating in the glare of a midday sun.

Balls cracked together on the green-felt pool table. One of them thunked into a corner pocket. "There you go, Will," Matty drawled. "That's thirty-five you owe me, ain't it?"

"Yeah, yeah. Damn it, Louis, why don't you turn that fuckin' music box down so a man can concentrate on his pool playin'! "

Louis shrugged and motioned toward the poker table.

"I like it that loud," Bobby Hazelton said, grinning over kings and tens. He was a part-time rodeo bronco-buster with a crew cut and a prominent gold tooth. Three years ago he'd been on his way to a Texas title when a black bastard of a horse called Twister had thrown him and broken his collarbone in two places. "Music helps me think. Will, you oughta come on over here and lemme take some of that heavy money you're carrying around."

"Hell, naw! Matty's doing too good a job at that tonight!" Will put his cue stick away in the rack, glancing quickly over at the albino and then at Bobby. "You boys

best watch old Bobby," he warned. "Took me for over
fifty bucks last Friday night."

"Just luck," Bobby said. He spread his cards out on
the table, and Slim Hawkins said in his gravely voice,
"Shee-yit!" Bobby reached for his chips and gathered
them in.

"Dumb luck my ass," Ray Cope said. He leaned over
the table, and Slim Hawkins said in his gravelly voice,
empty paper cup. "Jesus, it's hot in here tonight!" He let
his gaze shift past the red cobra on that kid's jacket.
Goddamn biker, he thought, narrowing ice-blue eyes
rimmed with wrinkles. *Don't know what it is to work for
a livin'. Probably one of those punks who robbed Jeff
Hardy's grocery store in Pecos a few days back.* He
could see the kid's hands as the albino lifted the beer mug
and drank. Under those gloves, Cope thought, the hands
were probably as white and soft as Mary Ruth Kennon's
thighs. His own large hands were chunky and rough and
scarred from ten years of ranch work.

The Dolly Parton song faded. Another record dropped,
hissed, and crackled for a few seconds like hot fat on a
griddle. Waylon Jennings started singing about going to
Luckenbach, Texas. Matty called for another Lone Star
and a pack of Marlboros.

The albino downed the rest of his beer and sat staring
into the mug for a moment. He began to smile slightly,
as if at a private joke, but the smile was cold and terrible,
and Louis winced when he happened to catch it. The
albino swiveled around on his stool, reared his arm back,
and flung the mug straight into the jukebox. Colored glass
and plastic exploded like several over-and-under shotguns
going off at once; Waylon Jennings's voice went into an
ear-piercing falsetto for an instant, then rumbled down to
a basso as the turntable went crazy. Lights flickered; the
record droned to a stop. There was utter silence in the
bar, broken only by the sound of pieces of glass clinking
to the floor.

Louis had raised his head from where he'd bent down
for Matty's beer. He stared at the ruined jukebox. *Madre
de Dios!* he thought, *that thing was three hundred dollars
almost five years ago!* Then he looked over at the albino
who was watching him with a death's head grin plastered
across his unholy face. At last Louis got his tongue work-

ing. "You crazy?" Louis screamed. "What the shit you do that for?"

Chairs scraped back from the poker table. Immediately the place was filled with the ozone smell of danger and hot tempers.

With eyes like solid chunks of blood-veined ice, the albino said, "I don't like that shitkicker music."

"You crazy, man?" Louis shrieked, sweat popping out on his face.

Bobby Hazelton, his hands curled into fists, said between clenched teeth, "You gonna pay for that machine, freak."

"Sure as hell are," Ray Cope echoed.

The albino turned on his stool very slowly and faced the men. His smile froze everyone but Will Jenks, who stepped back a pace. "Got no money," the albino said.

"I'll call the sheriff then, you *bastardo!*" Louis started to move down the bar toward the pay phone on the wall, but instantly the albino said "No you won't" in a softly chilling voice. Louis stopped where he was, his heart hammering.

"No call to bust that machine," Matty said and picked up a pool cue from the rack. "This is a peaceable place."

"Was," Bobby said. "What're you doin' around here anyway, freak? Lookin' to rob somebody maybe? Have some fun with somebody's wife or daughter when the man's gone to work? Huh?"

"I'm heading through. Going to L.A." The albino, still smiling faintly, glanced at each of them in turn—the track of his gaze freezing Ray Cope's veins, making Will Jenks's temples throb, sending a shudder along Slim Hawkins's spine. "Thought I'd stop to fill up, like the sign says."

"You're gonna pay," Louis threatened, but his voice sounded weaker. There was a shotgun under the bar, but to get it he'd have to step nearer to the albino, and something within him warned him not to.

"Nobody asked you to stop here, cottonhead!" Ray Cope steeled himself and began to move around the pool table toward the albino. "We don't like you biker freaks around here!"

"I don't like shitkickers either." This was said calmly, almost offhandedly, as if the albino had just said he didn't particularly care for the dry tang of the Lone Star beer, but instantly a surge of electric tension ringed the room. Bobby Hazelton's eyes bulged with anger, the sweat stains under his arms growing larger in circumference. The albino slowly began to unzip his jacket.

"What'd you say, freak?" Bobby hissed.

The albino, his stare impassive, whispered, "Shit . . . kickers."

"You sonofabitch!" Bobby shouted and then leaped toward the biker with fists swinging. But in the next instant the albino's jacket came open; there was a terrifying roar, a burst of blue smoke, and a hole where Bobby Hazelton's right eye had been. Bobby screamed, clawing at his face even as the wadcutter slug tore away the back of his head and spattered the men behind him with bits of bone and brain. He pinwheeled across the poker table, crashing down on kings and jokers and aces, and on the floor the legs of the corpse kept jerking as if Bobby were still trying to run.

The albino, blue smoke wafting between him and the other men, had withdrawn from the inside of his jacket a pistol with a long, thin barrel, a squarish black body, and a grip that resembled a sawed-off length of broom handle. The deadly muzzle was drooling smoke. The albino stared, his eyes slightly widened, at the contorted corpse on the floor.

"You killed him!" Slim Hawkins said with incredulous wonder, clawing at the droplets of Bobby's blood across the front of his gray cowboy shirt with the pearl-stud buttons. "Jesus God, you killed him . . ." He choked, gagged, and started to throw up through his hands.

"Godawmighty!" Will said, his mouth hanging open. He had seen a piece like the one that kid held once before, at a gun and knife show in Houston. It was an old automatic the Germans had used back in World War II—a broom-handle Mauser, he thought it was called. Ten slugs to a clip, and the damned thing could fire faster than a man could blink. "Bastard's got a machine-gun pistol!"

"Yeah," the albino said softly, "that's right."

Louis, his heart beating so hard he thought it would explode through his chest, took a breath and dove for the shotgun. He squawked with terror as his feet slipped out from under him on a wet spot. But even as his hands curled around cold iron, the albino had whirled around, eyes brimming with bloodlust. Louis looked up into two bullets that sheared off the top of his head. He crashed backward into a shelf of beer mugs, his brain exposed to the world; the corpse uttered a soft, eerie sigh and crumpled into a heap.

"*Oh . . . God . . .*" Will breathed. Bile rose to the top of his throat, and he almost strangled on it.

"Hold on now, fella . . . just hold on now . . ." Matty was saying over and over again, like a record that had gotten stuck on the jukebox. His face was now almost as white as the albino's, and his cowboy hat was splattered with Bobby Hazelton's blood. He put his hands up as if begging for mercy, which he was because in that terrible instant the men knew they were going to die.

The albino stepped through a churning curtain of smoke. He was smiling like a child at Christmas who wanted to see what would spill out when the packages were ripped open.

"Please," Will said hoarsely, his eyes wide circles of terror. "Please don't . . . kill us . . ."

"Like I said," the biker replied evenly, "I stopped in to fill up. When you boys get to Hell, you tell the devil Kobra sent you. That's with a *K*." He grinned and opened fire. A bloody cowboy hat sailed up toward the ceiling; bodies writhed and spun and fell like marionettes on crazy strings; a few teeth torn from a blasted mouth rattled to the floor; fragments of a gray shirt with pearl-stud buttons floated toward the rear of the room on the breath of a volcano.

Then—but for the soft dripping—silence.

Kobra's ears were ringing. He flipped the Mauser's safety and laid it on the bar where it gleamed like a black diamond. For a few minutes he stood motionless, eyes sated and lazy, examining the specific postures of death each corpse had taken. He breathed deeply of the bloody smell and felt electric with life. *God, it was good,* he thought. *So damned good!* His erection was gone. He walked around the bar and drew another bottle of beer from the refrigerator, downing it in a couple of long swallows and then tossing the bottle toward the other discarded containers. *Maybe I ought to take some with me,* he thought. *No. Don't want to weigh myself down. No room anyway. Want to be fast and free.* He returned to his weapon and slipped it into the special leather holster sewn into the inside of his jacket. *Little bitch had cost a lot of money in Salinas, but she was worth it,* he told himself. He loved that weapon; he'd bought her from a canny old trader who'd sworn she had actually been used by Nazi security units and wasn't just a gun shop antique. The magazine had jammed a couple of times but otherwise the weapon was perfectly responsive. She could cut a man down to bone pretty damned fast. He zipped up his jacket. The pistol burned its imprint into his side like a passion mark. He breathed the smell of blood until his lungs felt swollen with hot, sweet copper. Then he went to work, first going through the cash register. There was a little over forty dollars in ones, fives, and tens. The change he didn't care about. He rolled the corpses over and dug into their pockets, careful not to leave a bootprint in any of the puddles of thickening blood. In all he came up with about two-hundred dollars. He was about to rise up from the body of the first man he'd shot when he saw that gold tooth shining like a mother lode in the half-open cave of the mouth. He knocked the tooth out with the butt of his Mauser, replaced the gun in its holster, and put the tooth in his pocket.

And now he was ready to go.

Outside the desert air smelled weak and impure to Kobra as compared with the rich death smell within the Waterin' Hole. In both directions the highway vanished into darkness; he saw his shadow, thrown blue across the earth by the neon sign over his head. *Someone would find the shitkickers soon,* he told himself. *All hell would break loose. No matter. I'll be on the road to L.A. and a long way from here by the time the troopers show up.* Kobra turned his face toward the black western sky, his flesh faintly tingling.

The feeling was stronger than it had been in Ciudad Acuna, stronger than in Sonora, stronger even than in Fort Stockton just a few miles back. Like the prick of needles and pins, like a quick rush after a snort of coke, or the delicious, tormenting anticipation when watching a spoon of sugar-fine horse begin to cook. And getting better all the time, slowly increasing as he moved west. Sometimes now he thought he could smell blood when he faced west, as if the whole Pacific had turned crimson, and you could wallow in it all you liked until you got drunk with it and fell down and drowned in it. It was like being fed the greatest drug in the world drop by drop, and every mile Kobra traveled he grew more maddeningly eager for the whole kick in his veins.

And there was the dream, too; the recurring thing that had drawn him back into the States from Mexico. He'd first had it a week before and for three nights in a row, everything exactly the same and so damned . . . spooky: he sat astride his chopper in the dream, on a long, curving highway with high palm trees on each side and a lot of tall buildings. The light was funny—it seemed all reddish and murky as if the sun had gotten stuck on the horizon. He wore his black jacket, his jeans, and his black crash helmet, and behind him rode an army of outlaw bikers on every kind of chopper and hog a tormented mind could imagine—firebreathers with chrome shining bright red, metal-flake paint glittering purple and neon blue and gold, and engines roaring like dragons. But the army of outlaw bikers who rode in Kobra's wake looked strange and skeletal, white-fleshed things with shadow-rimmed eyes that did not blink in the miasmic light. There were hundreds of them, a thousand maybe, their bleached flesh covered with the remnants of buckskin jackets, tattered jeans with leather knee patches, Army surplus jackets burned sickly green by the sun; Day-Glo painted crash helmets, Nazi helmets, cracked and battered skid lids rattled around some of the grinning skull-like heads. Some of the things wore goggles. They began to chant, eerie braying voices from between clicking rows of teeth, louder and louder: Kobra, Kobra, KoBRA, KOBRA, KOBRA! And in the dream Kobra had seen a white sign way up in the hills above the sprawling city: HOLLY-WOOD.

Spooky.

And two nights ago he'd begun to sleepwalk. Twice he'd opened his eyes in the hot, dry house before dawn and found himself standing—actually goddamned s'and-ing!—outside the pitiful wooden shanty of a house that he'd been hiding in for the past three weeks since he'd left the country after that little party near New Orleans almost a month ago. What had awakened him both times was the weary voice of the thirteen-year-old prostitute he was living with, a frail girl with black hair that shone like oil and eyes that looked forty years old, calling from the dark doorway. *Señor? Señor?* But in the instant before her voice registered in his blurred brain, he thought he'd

heard a voice as distant and cold as a Canadian wind
whispering through his soul. And what it had said was
Follow Me. He was facing west when his eyes had opened
both nights.

Kobra blinked. A sudden gust of desert wind had blown
grit into his face. It was time to be moving. *And when I
get where I'm headed,* he told himself as he walked across
the lot to his chopper, *there's gonna be one hell of a party.*
He sat astride the Harley and slipped on his helmet, fastening the chin strap and lowering the visor like a demonic
knight readying for battle. He kickstarted the engine and
wheeled the rumbling machine out of the parking lot, leaving the silent Waterin' Hole with its last customers behind.
His belly felt gorged.

On the highway he accelerated to just below eighty. He
was going to have to follow the worst of the desert roads
to avoid the state troopers. *Have to be real careful,* he
warned himself. *But I have to hurry.*

Because of one thing he was certain.

He was following Death's keen promise.

TWO

When Andy Palatazin opened his eyes in the cool darkness of his bedroom, he had a single, chilling thought:
the Roach is here. He lay perfectly still, his bearlike body
swaddled in blue sheets, and waited for his heartbeat to
settle down. He listened to the quiet nighttime noises: the
creaking of a stair down the hallway, the muffled humming of the refrigerator downstairs, the ticking of the
alarm clock on the little bedside table, assorted cracks and
whispers and rustles. He was reminded of the tales his
mother had told him as a child about the elves who crept
out at night, riding on the backs of mice to have a festive
celebration, then disappeared by dawn. Beside him, Jo
stirred and drew closer to him. *What woke me?* he wondered. *I never wake up like this!*

He lifted his head a few inches to look at the clock. It
took him a minute to make out the little luminous numerals—eleven-fifty. *No,* he told himself, *the Roach is not
here. The Roach is out somewhere in Los Angeles doing*

those things he likes to do. His stomach crawled with dread and disgust at what the morning might bring. He eased over on his back, bedsprings sagging and whining like poorly plucked harp strings. He expected to feel the sharp jab of a spring cutting into his back or buttocks at any moment. The mattress was thin and worn from years of supporting his weight, which ranged annually from 210 during the summer when he played some golf with a few of the other detectives to 230 around Christmastime when he gorged himself on Jo's beef-and-sour-cream casseroles.

He stared up at the ceiling and heard a car taking the corner down on Romaine Street. Headlights flickered overhead, then faded away. *Very soon now another day would break,* he told himself. October in Los Angeles. Not quite like the Octobers he'd known as a boy. Those Octobers had been *real,* full of wild winds and erratic snowfall, cold gray skies and a dance of hail across the windowsills. These California Octobers were false, hollow, somehow unsatisfying: a chill in the morning breeze and again at night, but hot sun at midday unless the sky was cloudy, which was very seldom indeed. But it was difficult for him to believe snow was falling anywhere in the world when he could see people wearing short-sleeved shirts on the streets of L.A. It was the city of perpetual summer, the land of golden youth. Sometimes his heart ached for want of a single flake of snow. Oh, he could see the autumn and winter snowfall on clear days when the purple rise of the San Gabriel Mountains wasn't obscured by fog or smog, but somehow the palm trees waving everywhere you looked didn't seem to fit. It had been over sixty degrees on Christmas Day last year. Palatazin recalled boyhood Christmases of ten and twenty below zero when the windows were caked with ice and snow and Papa had to hack the door free with . . . Abruptly his mind went blank. He turned his attention to what he thought had wakened him: Roach. The *taplo* was out there somewhere, crawling through a city of over eightmillion people, waiting to strike. Or perhaps striking even now. It was Friday night, and the young prostitutes would be lining Sunset and Hollywood boulevards. *Perhaps he'll make a mistake tonight,* Palatazin told himself. Perhaps he'll try to lure one of the policewomen tonight, and then the nightmare would be over. Four young girls in two weeks, all strangled to death by powerful hands, according to the coroner's report, then raped. And the notes this hideous animal left on the corpses! They were rambling hand-scrawled messages that in one sentence talked about the divine plan of God and then said the prostitutes—"bad girls," the notes said—were liars and hellish angels who could only be led to peace through death. Palatazin could recall most of the notes word for word. He'd been studying them continually since the morning of September 27, when a surf fisherman in Venice had found the body of Kitt Kimberlin, a nineteen-year-old divorcée with two kids, beneath a rotting pier.

"God called me in the night," the note had read. "God is here among us right now, and out of all the people in this city He's called me to do His work!" That first note, hastily written in blue ink on ordinary drugstore typing paper, had been unsigned. It had been a Venice police officer named Duccio who'd found that the young woman's mouth had been crammed full of dead roaches; the story had leaked to reporters, and it was the *Los Angeles Tattler* that first printed a front-page article, by Gayle Clarke of course, with the headline, WHERE WILL THE ROACH STRIKE NEXT? Several photographs at the death scene by somebody named Jack Kidd were splashed luridly across the page, and Palatazin knew that the rag had probably sold a million copies that week. When the next woman, a Chicano barely sixteen years old, was found under a tarpaulin in an empty lot in Hollywood, there were the dead roaches again, and the other papers picked up on it.

The third letter was signed, "Roach. Ha ha. I like it." The latest note, found on the corpse of a blond, blue-eyed runaway from Seattle, was the most disturbing of the lot: "The Master calls me. He speaks to me by name now, and I have to answer. He tells me he needs me, and my head stops hurting. He says I'm doing it wrong, that he'll teach me things I never dreamed of. You won't hear from me again." It was signed "Roach," and the girl's mouth had been jammed full of them.

That had been on the tenth of October. Thirteen days now with no trace of him. Where was he? What was he planning? Waiting, biding his time, laughing as the LAPD ran to ground every possible lead, rumor, or bar and pool hall story about somebody knowing somebody who knew a guy who'd been drunkenly bragging about snuffing out

a girl and getting away with it, every pimp's tale of the
night this really weird customer with strange, flaming eyes
said he had a few roaches for Kitt Kimberlin, every
after-midmight telephone call from frightened wives who
whispered that they didn't know what was happening to
Harry or Tom or Joe but he was acting very strange and
not coming home until almost dawn. Palatazin could hear
the collective "Yes, ma'am, thank you for calling, we'll
check it out," being spoken by a dozen different police
officers across the city right at this very moment.

Of course every newspaper from the *Times* to the
Tattler was zeroing in on the Roach murders. The nightly
television newscasts always brought him up in some insinu-
ation or reference. The flesh traffic on Sunset and Hollywood had started to thin out for a while after midnight,
but now it was swinging back to business as usual. But
no one had forgotten: it seemed to be a big joke to some,
that the L.A. police couldn't even find a roach. Those
were the words that haunted Palatazin, that sat on his
forehead at night chuckling and lay like a moldering
corpse beside his bed for him to trip over on the way to
brush his teeth in the morning: *Find the Roach.*

How? The man was crazy, of course. An animal, a
fattyu, a maniac. But careful and cunning, too. And the
city was so big, so sprawling, so full of potential killers.
How? It was a question Palatazin wrestled with daily because, as Detective Captain of Homicide at Parker Center
in downtown L.A., he was in charge of the investigation.
He saw the fear, the mistrust in people's face now as they
stood talking in groups on the boulevards, as they pondered the fickle turnings of life and death in smoky bars.
The sheer ugliness of this maniac's methods surpassed
anything the Hillside Strangler had ever done. But if there
was anything that riveted the attention of L.A., it was the
horror show.

A sickening thing, Palatazin thought as he stared up at
the ceiling, trying to picture in his mind what the man
must look like. Judging from the bruises on the throats
of his victims, his hands would have to be abnormally
large and very strong; probably his forearms and shoulders would be well-developed, too. He would also probably have very fast reflexes—only one of the women had
gotten her nails into his flesh—but from that tiny bit of
tissue the police lab technicians had determined that the

Roach was a dark-haired Caucasian, most likely under forty. He was a very sadistic, sick man who seemed to be enjoying his newly found publicity. But what had made him go underground? What had made him decide to stop killing just as quickly as he'd begun? *Thirteen days,* Palatazin thought. *The trail's getting colder and colder. What is he doing? Where is he hiding?*

And suddenly Palatazin was aware of another noise in the room. The noise, he instinctively knew, that had awakened him.

It was a slight, soft creaking, as if someone were walking on the floorboards down at the foot of the bed. Beside him Jo stirred and sighed, locked into sleep.

Palatazin's blood turned icy. He lifted his head.

At the foot of the bed, over where the window looked down onto Romaine Street with its old, wood-framed houses standing shoulder to shoulder like aged friends, Palatazin's mother Nina sat in her rocking chair, slowly rocking back and forth. She was small and wrinkled and weary-looking, but her eyes blazed fiercely in the darkness.

Palatazin's heart thudded in his chest. He sat upright in bed and heard himself whisper first in the language of his native Hungary, "*Anya* . . . Mama . . . my God . . ."

His mother's stare was unyielding. She seemed to be trying to speak; he could see her lips moving, the sunken cheeks quivering with the effort. She lifted a frail hand and motioned with it, as if she wanted her son to get up and hurry, lazybones, you'll be late for school.

"What is it?" he whispered, his face gone ashen. "*What is it?*"

A hand gripped his shoulder. He gasped and looked around, his flesh crawling. His wife, a small, pretty woman in her early forties with bones like fine china, was looking up at him through deep blue, blurry eyes. She said thickly, "Is it time to get up yet?"

"No," he told her. "Go back to sleep."

"What do you want for breakfast?"

He leaned over and kissed her cheek, and she settled back down into her pillow. Almost instantly her breathing shallowed. He looked back to the window, beads of cold sweat on his face.

The rocking chair, over in the corner where it always sat, was empty. For a few seconds he thought it was moving, but as he stared at it he realized that the chair wasn't rocking at all. It never had been. Another car moved along the street, casting quick reflections of light that chased the clinging shadows along the ceiling.

Palatazin watched the chair for a long time, then eased himself back down in the bed. He pulled the sheet up to his neck. The thoughts whirled wildly through his mind, like remnants of tattered newspaper. *It's the pressure, of course, FIND THE ROACH, but I did see her, I did! Tomorrow more legwork and interviews and telephone calls. FIND THE ROACH. I saw my mother sitting in that chair . . . the day starts early so you must get your sleep . . . close your eyes . . . I saw her . . . close your eyes . . . yes, yes I did!*

Finally his heavy-lidded eyes did close. Sleep brought on a nightmarish shadowy shape, pursuing a small boy and a woman across a plain heaped with high snowdrifts. His last coherent thought before he began to run across the snowfield in his mind was that his mother had been dead since the first week of September.

THREE

Mitchell Everett Gideon, forty-four-year-old entrepreneur supreme and newly elected vice-president of the Los Angeles Millionaires' Club, was lighting up a dark-leafed, two-dollar Joya de Nicaragua cigar with a gold Dunhill lighter at about the same time that Andy Palatazin was staring at an empty rocking chair. A short, feisty man with a spreading belly and a face that would have been as innocent as Humpty Dumpty's except for the dark, deep-set eyes and the thin-lipped, callous mouth, Gideon sat in the gold-carpeted office of his Spanish pueblo-style mansion in Laurel Canyon staring at a half-dozen invoices spread across his antique mahogany desk. The invoices covered shipments of the usual items: a couple of freight-train loads of unfinished oak planking cut into prespecified lengths and widths, delivered to the factory in the Highland Park district; crates of varnish and stain; several dozen bolts of silk from Lee Wong and Company over in Chinatown; bales of cotton ticking; six drums of embalming fluid. "The robbers!" Gideon muttered, betraying his

New York upbringing with a single flattening of the tongue. "The dirty, rotten robbers! Especially Lee Wong. Been doin' business with that old chink for almost fifteen years," Gideon told himself as he bit down on his cigar, "now the old bastid's raised his prices for the third time in a year! Christ!" And the same with the others, too. The oak was costing an arm and a leg these days, and just last week Vincenzo at the Gomez Brothers Lumberyard had called Gideon to tell him what a terrific sacrifice he was making to sell the material that cheaply. *Sacrifice my ass!* Gideon thought, chewing on the cigar. *That's another goddamned robber!* "Well, contract renewal time's comin' up in a few months," he told himself. "Then we'll see who wants my business and who don't!"

He sucked in a mouthful of smoke and spewed it up toward the ceiling, sweeping aside the invoices with a diamond-ringed hand. "Overhead is killin' me this year!" he told himself. About the only thing that hadn't sky-rocketed in price was the embalming fluid, and the DeWitt Labs people were making threatening noises about that, too. *How the hell can a man make a decent livin' these days?* Cigar gripped between his teeth, Gideon stood up from his desk to pour himself a solid shot of Chivas Regal from a decanter taken from across the room. He wore a pair of crisply pressed tan slacks, a flaming red shirt open at the chest with several gold chains dangling, a pair of brown Gucci loafers on his feet. The shirt's pocket was monogrammed—MG in white letters. Gideon took his cigar and shot of Chivas out through a sliding glass door and onto a long terrace with a wrought-iron railing. Directly beneath him there was a fifty-foot drop into shrub- and tree-studded darkness, and off to the left, just faintly visible through a thick wall of pines, were the lights of another canyon dweller's house. Before him, like so much gaudy jewelry flung out on a black velvet-covered table, was a dazzling panorama of multicolored lights—Beverly Hills and Hollywood and L.A. from right to left as far as he could see. The tiny headlights of toy cars moved along Hollywood, Sunset, and Santa Monica boulevards; neon pulsated to private rhythms above discos and bars and rock clubs on the Strip. The rolling streets of Beverly tain Avenue traffic light the size of a pinhead turn green. many stars fallen to earth and slowly sputtering to death. Parks and cemeteries were dark squares in the electric

tapestry. Gideon drew on his cigar and watched a Fountain Avenue traffic light the size of a pinhead turn green.
He turned his head a fraction of an inch and saw a dust
speck of flashing blue veer up a ramp and onto the
sweeping line of the Hollywood Freeway; it sped south-
ward toward L.A. *Millions of people down there,* Gideon
thought, *right now they're sleeping, drinking, fighting,
talking, screwing, being screwed, loving, and hating. And
sooner or later they're all going to need what I sell.* That
thought made him feel a little better. *The world turns and
turns,* he told himself, *and spins off a few more unlucky
folks everyday. Auto accidents, suicides, murders, plain
old Nature taking her course. I know what you need,
baby, and I'm the man with the plan.*

Sometimes he felt like a god up here on Sky Vista
Road; sometimes he thought he could stretch his arms
and touch the heavens, take a piece of chalk and write
MITCH GIDEON up on that huge blackboard for all the
old bats at the public school (especially Four-Eyes Grimes
who said he'd never amount to anything but a hoodlum)
to see. Of course, they were all dead by now—*and buried
I hope,* he thought, *in pine boxes that leaked water on
their dead gray heads*—but he hoped that somehow all
those people who said he'd wind up in the juvenile home
or in the Tombs knew that now he was on top of the
world, now he had a million-dollar Spanish mansion on
Sky Vista Road, now he smoked two-dollar cigars and
wore Gucci shoes, now he drank Chivas Regal from a
crystal shot glass and watched the little people racing
around down in the valley. Now he was Mitch Gideon,
Mortuary King of Los Angeles.

A chill breeze came up the canyon, shaking pine
branches before it, and swirled around him, knocking
off a dangling inch of cigar ash. The dark brown hair of
his toupee remained glued in place above his long, gray
sideburns. In that breeze he thought he could smell the
rich aromas of mellow oak, woodstain, varnish, shellac
and clumps of wax caught in old, tattered rags, raw saw-
dust and chewing tobacco—the aromas of his youth, spent
between the juvenile home and his apprenticeship with
Jacob Richwine the Brooklyn coffin maker. Those were
the days. . . .

He stabbed his cigar out on the railing until the sparks
were gone and then thumped the butt out into the night.

He was about to step back into the warmth of the house
when his head turned to the right and he found himself
staring off into the distance, past the scatter of white lights
from Nichols Canyon and toward the slabs of darkness
that were the hills just above the Hollywood Bowl.

He could feel the magnetic pull of the Kronsteen Castle
as if he were the needle of a compass; he knew his eyes
had locked upon it across two miles of pine trees, pal-
mettos, rooftops, and naked rock. It was there, like a scab
where the earth had blistered into a peak, at the end of
Blackwood Road where it had brooded for over forty
years. And for the fifth time in as many days, Mitch
Gideon felt the sudden strong urge to leave his house,
get in his chocolate-brown Mercedes, and drive up along
that broken, godforsaken road to that huge, gothic cathedral of stone. He moved along the terrace as far as he
could go and stood with one hand gripped around the
cold railing, staring off into space. Another chill breeze
swept across him, raising bumps on his exposed flesh, and
as it whispered past his face, he thought he heard his
name called as if from a vast distance. His eyes seemed
so unfocused, as if he were staring through a huge, rain-
smeared, plate-glass window; the lights from Nichols Canyon distorted into elongated streaks of white and yellow.
He felt a slight throbbing at his temples, as if an invisible
hand were slowly caving in the sides of his head. And
Gideon thought for an instant that he could actually see
the looming, hundred-roomed Kronsteen Castle in the far
distance with the white candle of the moon above it,
guttering behind clouds of Spanish lace. His fingers gripped
tighter around the railing, and now he was watching a
river of plain, unfinished caskets come floating toward
him along the banks of a wide, black conveyor belt. There
were other people around him, too, both men and women
and even some small children, but the shadows were
thick, cobwebbed things that kept him from seeing their
faces clearly. The conveyor belt rolled the caskets along
to a loading dock where the trucks waited with engines
rumbling. Everyone seemed to know each other, but for
some reason no one spoke. Overhead the long banks of
fluorescent lights were burning at less than half-power,
and people moved around Gideon like sleepwalkers,
shadowy things without faces. The conveyer belt whirred
faster and faster, bringing more and more caskets to be

loaded onto the trucks. Gideon had a shovel in his hands. As a casket neared him, the worker just in front of him would lean forward and throw the lid back. Gideon then scooped up a shovelful of brown, sandy earth from a huge heap behind him and dumped it in; the next worker did the same, as did the next. Further down the line the lid was closed again, and a forklift rumbled forward to hoist it to the trucks. Gideon realized that the front of his shirt was dirty.

Quite close to his ear someone said, "Mitch!"

He heard something crash to the concrete, and at first he thought it was his shovel. *I'll get behind! Got to hurry!* he thought. But then he felt the October wind on his face and smelled Chanel; Estelle Gideon, a sweater thrown around her shoulders above a silver-colored gown that did not quite hide the stomach and hips that years of gourmet dining had given her, stood beside her husband, her dark brown eyes slightly puffed from sleep. Her face, unfortunately toadlike, was layered with green and white beauty creams from Elizabeth Arden's on Rodeo Drive. Gideon blinked and looked down at his feet where the crystal shot glass had shattered. "Oh," he said softly, "dropped it."

"What are you doing out here, hon?" his wife asked. "It's cold!"

"I was . . ." He thought for a minute, *What was I doing?* "I was working," he remembered. "In the office." He rubbed his eyes and glanced toward where he knew the Kronsteen Castle perched in the darkness. A shiver rippled up his spine, and he quickly looked away. "I just stepped out for some air. Can't you sleep?"

"I was sleeping," she said and yawned. "I got hungry for some ice cream. When are you coming to bed?"

"Just a few minutes. I've been going over some bills. That bloodsucker Wong's on my ass again." He looked out over the shimmering city and thought, *Someone's dying out there right now. Tell you what I'll do—I'll give you the special rate for that shaded plot and the silk-lined, oak, conquistador-style casket, and I'll throw in the Golden Eternity service gratis.* He smelled polishing wax, sweet and sour. He looked down at the hand that had guided the shovel.

"You've made a real mess here," the woman said, making a clucking sound with her tongue. "How many have you had?"

"Huh? Oh, just one. Watch your feet, babe. Shit, leave it for Natalie in the morning. She's got to have somethin' to do besides dumpin' out ashtrays and watchin' her goddamned soap operas!"

Estelle looked at him in silence for a few seconds. "You look funny, Mitch. Everything okay?"

"Funny? How?"

"Bothered, worried, I don't know. If business was bad, you'd tell me, wouldn't you?"

"Sure I would." *Like hell I would,* Gideon thought. The last time he'd tried to tell her about a business problem she fell asleep on him, still vacantly nodding her head. No one seemed to be interested in his problems anymore except Karen, Gideon's twenty-year-old mistress who lived out at Marina Del Rey. She made him feel like a kid again, but there were many nights spent just talking instead of fucking. Estelle had her lovers, too; Mitch could always tell when a new one had leeched onto her because she would always start taking exercise classes at the Beverly Hills Health Club again. They were always young men with tans—tennis players, lifeguards, beach bums. He didn't mind because he knew Estelle was smart enough not to let them get too near her purse. It was a good arrangement: he had his, she had hers. But in their own way they loved each other, even if not physically. They were good friends. And a divorce settlement would carve him too close to the bone because he'd built his business on the strength of her father's old New York money.

"It's cold out here," Estelle said. "Come on to bed."

"Yeah, yeah, I will." He stood motionless and felt the Kronsteen Castle at his back, tugging him like a magnet. "It's spooky . . ." he whispered.

"What's spooky? Mitch? You heard something on the radio about another one of those Roach murders?"

"No, not that. Damn it, what the hell happened to Mitzi? You'd think we would've heard something by now!"

She shrugged. "Dogs run away."

"Watchdogs aren't supposed to! I paid over three-hundred bucks for that bitch! You're telling me she ran away after *four years?*"

"So maybe somebody stole her? I've heard of that before. Dognapping. They like to get Dobermans."

"Dognapping my ass! Mitzi would've chewed the fuckin' arms off anybody who tried to throw her into a car! It's just not safe in this fuckin' city anymore! Burglars breakin' into houses all up and down the canyon, nuts like the Roach runnin' around; the cops don't know which way to turn!" His eyes darkened. "And you remember what happened up at the Kronsteen place."

"That was eleven years ago," she reminded him.

"Eleven years or eleven minutes, it still happened, didn't it? Christ, I should know! I saw the old man's body . . . what was left of it." 'There was a thick dryness at the back of his throat and a taste similar to the smell of embalming fluid. He wished he hadn't broken that shot glass because he badly needed another sip of Chivas. He resisted the impulse to turn his head and like a man transfixed, stare off into the night, toward that huge pile of stone and concrete two miles away. If there was any other place that had a better view of L.A. than mine, Mitch thought, then the castle was it. *"The cops never found the maniacs who did it either. Probably never will."*

"That's California for you," Estelle said quietly. "The land of nuts and fruits."

"The land of maniacs and murderers. I don't know, babe, I'm feeling awful damned strange these days. Spooked or somethin'. Scared." He ran a hand over his forehead; his fingertips were numb, like in that old game Dead Man's Hand where you squeezed a thumb until the blood drained out of it and it became so cold and alien that it hardly felt human at all. "Somethin' like what happened to old man Kronsteen could happen to us. It could happen to anybody."

"He was a loony," she said and shivered. "That was one loony killing another loony. Let's get in out of this wind."

"Mitzi," Gideon whispered. "What the fuck happened to my dog?"

"You can buy yourself another one." She reached out and took his arm. "Come on, let's go to bed."

Her hand felt deliciously warm against his. He looked at her, started to open his mouth to tell her about the strange feelings he was having lately—the weird visions of himself working on a conveyor belt where the caskets just kept coming one after the other as far as you could see—to tell her about how he thought he heard his name whispered in the wind when it came roaring through the canyon in the late hours of the night, to tell her that even during the day at any one of his six mortuaries scattered across the city he would find himself standing at a window, looking up into the hills where the horror actor's castle stood silent and impassive to sun or wind or rain. He wanted to tell her he was more afraid than he'd ever been in his entire life.

But Estelle's eyes were glazing, the lids already coming down like fleshy curtains. She smiled sleepily, and the mouth in that whitish-green face said, "Come on, hon. Beddy-bye time."

"Yeah," he said and nodded. "Okay." As he stepped into the house and turned to lock the sliding glass door, he thought, *Imagine me, Mitch Gideon the Mortuary King, ruining good merchandise by throwing in shovelfuls of dirt. Christ, what a sin!* He drew the curtains and followed his wife into the house, the golden chains around his neck clicking together like the rattle of dry bones.

And the dark shape that had been crouched on the roof just above Mitch Gideon's terrace, took to the air on widespread, gleaming black wings.

FOUR

"Ohhhhhhhh," Gayle Clarke said, staring up at the apartment ceiling, sweet fire bubbling in her veins. "That feels sooooooo nice."

"Knew you'd like it," the man who lay at the V of her thighs said softly. He caressed her stomach with slow swirls for a moment, then leaned forward to continue what he was doing. His tongue darted and teased; she gripped his shoulders tight, tighter, fingers digging into the flesh. He finished her off with an excruciatingly slow figure eight, and she shuddered with pure delight as the third orgasm of the night rolled like a tidal wave through her body. "Oh God," she said, "it's . . . it's . . ." And then she couldn't say anymore because the weakness had spread to her tongue, and she felt like a leaf that had been blown to this bed by the force of a hurricane.

After a moment more Jack Kidd came up beside her

and held her in his strong, lean arms. Gayle nuzzled his chest, drawing closer to him as she always did in the warmth aftermath of their love making. The dark hairs tickled her nose.

Jack kissed her forehead and then leaned over for the bottle of Chablis in the plastic cooler beside the bed. The ice was all melted now. He poured wine into a glass and sipped at it, then licked softly at Gayle's ear until she stirred and said, "What do you think you're doing?"

"Wine and ear lobes. Great combination."

"I'm sure." She reached up, took the glass, and sipped. "Wow, I'm tired. Thanks to you."

"You're welcome. Always willing to be of service."

"Pun noted, recorded, and rejected." She yawned and stretched until her joints popped. Her body was lithe and supple, though she was a small woman—only about five feet tall—who sometimes gave in to overwhelming urges for Oreo cookies and Mars candy bars. She played a lot of tennis, jogged infrequently, and spent time listening to Jefferson Starship and reading Franz Kafka when she was alone; she had turned twenty-two in September, and if she wasn't exactly a California beauty because of an overly wide mouth and dark brown eyes that always seemed to hold a hint of anger, she might be called, at the very least, vivacious. Long chestnut-brown hair, shimmering with auburn highlights, curled around her shoulders and was cut in bangs at her forehead. "What time is it?" she asked.

"Not midnight yet," Jack said.

"Yeah, but eight comes awfully early."

They were silent for a long time, their bodies side by side, then Jack said quietly, "It was important to me that you liked the whale flick. Really."

She lifted her head and ran a finger along his dark beard and mustache. "I do. The editing's tight, the narration's terrific . . . you're not worried about it, are you?"

"No, but . . . if I can get national distribution on this one, maybe it will be the break I've been looking for. Hell, if I could sell it to the networks. I'd be happy!" He frowned slightly. "No, cancel that. They'd make it look like the Greenpeace people are fanatics or something. I don't want anybody else screwing with my film."

"So what's to worry about? Friedman can get some immediate campus bookings, can't he?"

"Yeah."

"The national angle will take care of itself. Besides, the film's hardly out of the can. And speaking of film, have you taken care of the assignment that Trace gave you?"

Jack grunted. "Finishing it up tomorrow. I hope. Got some nice shots of Clifton Webb's old house today. In the morning I'm heading out to Hollywood Memorial, and I hope that'll be the end of it."

"I can see Trace's headline for that piece right now." Gayle held up two fingers as if straightening the type across a front-page layout. " 'Does Clifton Webb Haunt Hollywood Cemetery?' And maybe a teaser line, 'Only the *LA Tattler Knows!*' Catchy, huh?"

"Like the plague." He was silent for a moment, and Gayle could almost hear the gears clicking in his head. "You know what I've been thinking of doing next? A film on the homes of old movie stars. Not the new houses, but the mansions with *history*, know what I mean? Webb's is one; you can feel Old Hollywood oozing out of those walls. Flynn's is another. Valentino's, Barrymore, and . . . oh God, *yes!* . . . the Kronsteen castle! That would be a hell of a place for atmosphere!"

"What's so special about it?"

"Unsolved murder, babe. Old Kronsteen got his head chopped off up there a few years back, the place has been empty ever since. It's a real medieval castle, walls and towers and everything. High school kids go parking up there now. Jesus, I could do a whole film on that place alone!"

"Never heard of it," Gayle said.

"Before your time, babe. Mine too, but I drove up there once with a friend and a couple of chicks from Hollywood High. Many moons ago, that is, so don't get your feathers ruffled."

"Don't worry."

"Chuck knew the place, I didn't. Seems we went a hell of a long way up Outpost Drive and turned off onto a narrow road that went right up to the sky. Blacktree, Blackwood, something like that. Spooky as hell. I did some acid up there, and I swore I could hear that Bald Mountain thing from *Fantasia*, thought I saw demons flying around, all kinds of incredible colors. Strange trip."

"I'll bet. Before you start playing young Coppola again, you'd better wrap up those pictures for Trace. I've got a feeling he doesn't think the *Tattler* should arrange its deadlines around your film-making sessions."

"Why does he always give me the shit detail?" Jack frowned. "Last week it was a stunning photo-piece on vandalism out at the Wax Museum. Somebody carved his initials on Farrah's tits, knocked Elizabeth Taylor's head off, and played tic-tac-toe on Yul Brynner's skull. Christ! If I could just get a little bit ahead, maybe get somebody interested in my films or . . . I need a break, that's all. It'll happen, I know it will."

"I know it will, too, but a little patience wouldn't hurt. So what's all this junk about Cliff Webb's ghost being seen roaming around the cemetery?"

"Oh, every year a few people say they see somebody who looks like Webb strolling around Hollywood Memorial. It's nothing new. Last week a watchman thought he saw him . . . or it . . . in the cemetery after midnight . . ."

"Of course," Gayle said. "What ghost would be out before the witching hour?"

"Right. Well, Trace gets a wild hair and wants me to do the pictures for Sandy's story. The hell if I know what the story's going to say; I'm just clicking the shutter."

"So?"

"So what?"

"So what about the ghost? What happened after that watchman saw it?"

Jack shrugged. "I suppose it did what all ghosts do. It melted away or broke up into a thousand shimmering lights or . . . *heh heh heh* . . . turned toward the watchman's flashlight with a cold, red glare in its eyes. You don't really believe in that stuff, do you?"

"No, not at all. Now can we change the subject, please?"

He smiled and licked her arm, sending up a rash of goosebumps. "Gladly, Miss Clarke . . ." He lifted the sheets slightly and began to nibble on her right breast. The nipple hardened quickly, and Gayle began to breathe faster. "Better than ear lobes any old day," Jack managed to say.

Then suddenly from beyond the closed bedroom door came the sound of frenzied clawing.

Jack lifted his head from Gayle's breast and stared at

the door for a few seconds. He said loudly, "Cut it out, Conan!" The clawing went on and with it an occasional low whining.

"He's jealous," Gayle said. "He wants to come in."

"No, he's been acting crazy for a couple of days now." Jack stood up from the bed, took his bathrobe from where he'd laid it over a chair, and put it on. "He's clawing at the front door," Jack told her. "Maybe he's got a girl friend of his own. Back in a minute." He crossed the room, opened the door, and passed through a short hallway decorated with some of his framed photographs. In the small living room furnished with a brown sofa and a couple of wicker chairs, Jack found his three-year-old boxer clawing hunks out of the front door. The dog, large enough to place his paws on his master's chest when he stood on his powerful back legs, looked as if he were trying to burrow through the wood. Splinters were flying around the dog's head.

"Hey!" Jack said and swatted at Conan's rump. "Stop that!"

The dog didn't even look back. The frantic clawing continued.

"Damn it, what's wrong with you?" He reached down to pull Conan away from the door, and it was then that the dog whirled around, growling very softly, showing his teeth. Jack froze, his heart skipping a beat. Conan had always been a gentle dog, and lately Jack had been teaching him to catch a Frisbee out in the courtyard of the Sandalwood Apartments. Now Jack stared at those teeth and felt cold fear roiling in his stomach. The dog's eyes were unblinking, challenging the man to move.

"It's me," Jack said softly. "Conan? It's me, boy. I'm not going to hurt you."

The dog turned again, claws gouging at the door. The wood looked like a scarred battlefield.

Quickly Jack reached out and unbolted the door. Conan heard the click and stepped back, panting. When the door came open, the dog slipped through noiselessly and ran off across the courtyard toward Lexington Avenue. Jack stared after him, unable to believe that his pet had actually turned and snarled at him. Outside the fronds of palm trees stirred in the wind like lazy fans. At the base of the trees were multicolored lamps, and it was by the green light of one of these that Jack saw Conan's running shape, lengthened by its powerful strides, disappear from sight.

Gayle, now dressed in her tight Jordache jeans and checked blouse, stepped out of the hallway shadows and said, "Jack? What was that all about?"

"I don't really know. Conan just . . . went wild. He snarled at me. Actually showed his teeth! He's gotten feisty before, but he's never acted like this."

She stepped beside him and peered through the door. The rest of the apartment complex was utterly quiet. "Maybe it's the mating season or something. He'll be back."

"I don't know. You think I should go looking for him?"

"Not at this time of night." She glanced quickly at her wristwatch and made a face. "I've got to be getting home, Jack. Ace *Tattler* reporter has to have her head on straight in the morning when she goes to see the cops."

Jack stared out into the courtyard for another moment, hoping to see Conan bounding back, and then turned toward her. "Why don't you stay? I'll spring for breakfast."

"The last time I stayed for breakfast, I ended up burning the eggs. No thanks."

"Well, wait a minute while I get dressed. I'll drive you."

"What, and leave my car here overnight? Mr. Kidd, what would your neighbors think?"

"Screw 'em." He took Gayle in his arms and closed the door with his foot. "Who do you have to see tomorrow?"

"My favorite homicide squad captain—Palatazin. I imagine it'll be the same old 'no comment' session." She traced a line in Jack's forehead with a finger; she could feel his body beginning to respond beneath his thin robe and her own answering. "I have the feeling he thinks the *Tattler's* stories are a little on the sensational side."

"Imagine that." Jack nuzzled her neck and began to lick the base of her throat in slow circles. "Long live yellow journalism."

She made a noise between a grunt and a sigh and felt the feather of need tickling at her thighs. *It's soooooo chilly outside,* she thought. *And soooooo dark. Oh, that feels good.* Jack took her hand to lead her back to the bedroom, and she said softly, "Breakfast at eight?"

FIVE

Leaking blue exhaust fumes, a gray Volkswagen Beetle with a crumpled rear fender moved along Outpost Drive and up into the stark dun-colored hills above Hollywood. As the road steepened, the Volkwagen's engine began to rattle with a faint, evil, metallic chuckling. The headlights, slightly cross-eyed, threw wild shadows behind wind-stirred pines and granite boulders with edges as sharp as butcher knives. Low, rambling, glass and redwood houses on each side of the road lay in darkness, and only occasionally did a car pass on its way down to the city. The Volkswagen turned off Outpost Drive onto a narrow road of broken concrete that curved like a snake's spine and climbed upward at a forty-degree angle. Forbidding heaps of cracked granite loomed on the right-hand side of the road; on the left, where the road fell off abruptly into a series of ravines, stood a few hundred gnarled, dwarfish, dead trees.

Though there was no sign or road marker, the driver had made the correct turn onto Blackwood Road.

His name was Walter Benefield, and on the seat beside him, head lolling with every lurch of the car, was a twenty-year-old Chicano girl named Angela Pavion. Her eyes were half-open, the whites showing, and every once in a while she whimpered softly. Benefield wondered what she was dreaming about.

Wafting through the car's interior was a thick, almondy, slightly medicinal odor. Beneath Benefield's seat was a wadded cloth that had turned brown after being soaked in a solution of chemicals that he'd stolen from work. His eyes, behind thick, black-framed glasses, were watering slightly, though he'd rolled down the window only seconds after the girl had gone to sleep. *At least this had been better than those first few times*, he told himself. The first time the girl had died because the mixture wasn't diluted enough, and the second time he had to lean out of the car to throw up, and his head ached all the next day. He was getting faster with it, though he missed using his hands. They were large, fleshy clamps

40

that he exercised with stiff-springed handgrips. He often thought that he could squeeze those grips forever as he lay on his back in bed, staring at the pictures of posed musclemen with rippling backs and chests and arms taped to the walls, scissored from the pages of *Strength and Health* and *Strongman* magazines. And across the room the cockroaches scuttled in their wire-mesh cages, mating and fighting and sleeping. At the last count there'd been over a hundred, and some immense, cannibalistic bulls that had grown to three inches long.

He'd picked this girl up on the lower end of Sunset Boulevard thirty minutes ago. At first she'd been skittish about getting in the car, but he'd flashed a well-worn fifty dollar bill—kept just for the occasion—and she'd slid in as if her ass had been greased. She didn't speak or understand English very well, but that hardly mattered to him. She was pretty in a hard, coarse way; she was also one of the few desperate women who still walked the streets these days. *Too bad for her,* Benefield thought, *she should read the papers.* He had taken her to a deserted supermarket parking lot and unzipped his trousers. When the girl had leaned forward to do what he'd asked, he'd struck, too quickly for her to scream or evade him. The chemical-soaked rag was out from under the seat and pressed tightly against the girl's face, Benefield's other hand like a vise at the back of her neck. *It would be so easy, so easy,* he'd thought. *I could just squeeze a little bit—hardly an effort—and watch her eyes pop out of their sockets, like Bev's had. But no. That was not what the Master wanted done, was it?*

Her thrashing was over in a few more seconds. He'd put the cloth away, positioned the girl so she wouldn't slide down onto the floorboard, and then drove north toward the foothills of the Santa Monica Mountains, the high crests that split L.A. in two. He was breathing hard with exhilaration. The girl had managed to scratch his right hand, and two lines of blood welled from the flesh. He was following the Voice of God, the holy will of his Lord and Master, and now Benefield peered into the darkness beyond the range of the headlights and told himself, "Hurry. You've got to hurry, he doesn't like to wait." His voice was small and breathless, as excited as a child's at the prospect of a reward for a deed well done.

The road had leveled a few degrees but still took the

Volks higher. Occasionally Benefield could see the city below, glittering off toward the horizon where the half-dirt half-broken-concrete road wandered close to a drop-off. He had driven this way many times before in the last two weeks, but it was a tricky, treacherous way; the first time, when he'd brought a pretty, red-haired girl who couldn't have been over sixteen, he'd gotten lost and had driven in circles until the Voice of God had guided him back to the path.

Now the Voice was speaking to him again, whispering softly in the rush of the wind, calling his name. Benefield smiled, tears of joy in his eyes. "I'm coming!" he called out. "I'm coming!" A gust of wind hit the car's side and rocked it slightly. The girl whimpered once, something in Spanish, and then was silent.

The car's headlights glinted off a new chain strung across the road from tree to tree. There was a metal sign: PRIVATE PROPERTY—NO TRESPASSING. Benefield, his heart pounding, pulled the car to the side of the road, cut the headlights and waited. The Voice was like a cooling balm on the fever blister of his brain; it came to him almost every night now as he lay in that gray place between sleep and wakefulness on the mattress of his efficiency apartment near MacArthur Park. On those terrible anguished nights when he dreamed of his mother lifting her head from that man's lap, the throbbing penis as big as a python in her grip, her mouth opening to shout drunkenly, "YOU GET OUTTA HERE!", the Voice whispered like a sea-breeze around his head, enveloping him, protecting him. But some nights even the Voice of God couldn't stop the garish unreeling of the nightmare through his brain: the stranger grinning and saying, "The little bastard wants to watch, Bev. Come 'ere, Waltie, look what I got!" And the child Walter, standing trans-fixed in the doorway as if nailed there by hands and feet, his head thrashing in agony while the stranger pushed his mother's face down until her laughter was muffled. He had watched it all, his stomach and groin tied into one huge knot, and when they were through his mother— *Good old Bev never says no, never says no, never says no*—swigged from the bottle of Four Roses that sat on the floor beside the sofa and, hugging the stranger, said in a thick slur, "Now you take care of me, honey." Her dress, the one with the white dots on it, had been pushed

up over her large, pale thighs, and she wore no under-
wear. The child Walter could not tear his gaze away
from the secret place that seemed to wink like a wicked
eye. His hands had dropped to his cro ch, and after another moment the stranger laughed like a snorting bull.
"The little bastard's got a hard-on! Little Waltie's carryin'
a load! Come 'ere, Waltie. COME HERE, I SAID!"

His mother had lifted her head and smiled through
swollen, glazed eyes. "Whozzat? Frank? Is it Frank?"
His father's name, old Frank. Out the door and gone so
long ago all Waltie could remember of him was how
hard he swung his belt. "Frank?" she said, smiling. "You
come home, baby? Come gimme a great big kiss . . ."

The stranger's eyes had glittered like dark bits of
glass. "Come 'ere, Waltie. No. *Frank*. Come 'ere, Frank.
It's Frank, baby. It's your man come home." He laughed
softly, his gaze bloodshot and mean. "Drop your drawers,
Frank."

"Honey?" his mother had whispered, grinning at him.
"I got something needs you soooooo bad . . ."

"Come give your baby a great big kiss, Frank," the
stranger had said quietly. "Oh, Jesus, this I gotta see!"

When those dreams came, even the Voice of God
couldn't calm the fever. And he was grateful, so grateful,
when the Voice told him it was all right for him to go
out into the night in search of another laughing Bev, to
take her away from the dark-grinning strangers and bring
her to the holy mountain.

He winced as those bad things danced through his
head. His temples were aching, and he wished he had a
Bufferin. Sometimes when the Voice spoke to him he
felt as if a cauldron was being stirred in his brain, a thick
mixture of magic that had changed his life into something
with real purpose and meaning—service in the Master's
name. Turning his head to the left, Benefield could look
down upon the shimmering city. He wondered if there
were any others down there who were part of the cauldron brew, who were ingredients in the magic that now
rippled through his soul and his being and set him aflame
with sweet, cold fire. Of course, it was magic—*the way
of God is righteous, and He shall brighten the City of
Night with magic and kill all the Bevs in that bubbling
cauldron brew*—because what else could it be?

A car was coming. Benefield could see the flicker of

headlights off in the distance, coming down the mountain toward him. He got out of his car, went around to the other side, and opened the passenger door. The dazed girl almost tumbled out, but Benefield reached down and picked her up in his arms like so much deadwood. Then he turned to face the approaching car.

It was a long, black Lincoln polished so highly the sides and hood shone like glass. It stopped ten feet from the chain, its headlights centered like greedy eyes on Benefield and the offering he held in his arms.

He smiled, his eyes filling with tears.

The driver left the limousine and approached him, followed by a young girl that Benefield immediately recognized. Her long hair was blond and wind-tossed, and her dress was dirty. Benefield saw that the driver was the Servant of God—an old man in a brown suit and white shirt, his long, white hair flowing in the wind, his darting, ferret eyes sunken deep in a pale, wrinkled face. He limped as he walked and was slightly stooped, as if shouldering a backbreaking burden. When he reached the chain, he said to Benefield in a halting, weary voice, "Hand her over."

Benefield lifted her up. The blond-haired girl grinned and took her effortlessly, crooning like a mother to her child.

"Go home," the old man told Benefield. "Your work is done for tonight."

Suddenly the blond girl's eyes flashed. She stared at Benefield's injured hand, then lifted her gaze to his face. His smile cracked like a mirror. He blinked and started to lift his hand toward her.

"NO!" the old man said and held his arm back as if about to strike her. She flinched and scurried toward the car with her prize. "Go home," he told Benefield and turned away.

The limousine backed up to a wide spot, made a tight turn, and disappeared up the mountain.

Benefield longed to follow, but the Voice was whispering softly to him now, making him feel warm and needed and protected, taking his headache away. He stood where he was for a moment, the wind whipping and shrilling all around him, then walked back to his car. Driving down the mountain, he turned the radio to a station playing religious songs and began to sing along, happy and confident that the Master's will would be done.

II

Saturday, October 26
THE RESTLESS

ONE

The sun came up over the San Gabriel Mountains like a reddish-orange explosion, turning the sky a steely gray that would slowly strengthen to bright blue as the morning progressed. Tendrils of yellowish smog hovered low to the ground, clinging like some huge octopus between the glass and steel skyscrapers, throbbing concrete-walled factories, and serpentine meanderings of halfadozen freeways already clogged with traffic. Chilly shadows, remnants of the night, scurried away before the marching sunlight like an army in retreat.

Andy Palatazin stood before the open closet in his bedroom and deliberated over which tie to choose. He was wearing dark blue slacks, slightly tight around the midsection, and a light blue shirt with a neatly ironed but fraying collar; he chose a green tie with little flecks of blue and red in it, then walked out into the hallway and leaned slightly over the stairway railing. He could hear Joanna down in the kitchen, and the mouth-watering aroma of frying sausages and potatoes drifted up to him. He called out, "Jo! Come look at this!"

She came in another moment, her graying hair pulled up into a tight bun. She was wearing a dark green robe and slippers. "Let's see it," she said.

He held up the tie and raised his eyebrows.

"Iszonyu!" she said. "It's hideous with that shirt. Wear the dark blue tie today."

"That has a spot on it."

"Then the redandbluestriped one."

"I don't like that tie."

"Because my brother gave it to you!" she muttered and shook her head.

"What's wrong with this one?" He held out the green tie and made it wiggle like a snake.

"Nothing—if you want to look like a clown. Go on, wear it! Look like a clown! But . . . it . . . does . . . not

46

. . . go!" She sniffed the air. "The potatoes are burning! See what you've made me do!" She whirled toward the kitchen and disappeared.

"Your brother has nothing to do with it!" he called down to her; he could hear her mumbling but couldn't tell what she was saying, so he shrugged and stepped back into the bedroom. His gaze fell upon the rocking chair over by the window, and he stood looking at it for a moment. Then he walked over to it, placed a thick finger against one of the arms, and pushed. The chair creaked softly as it moved back and forth. *Was that a dream I had last night,* he asked himself, *or did I really see a* megjelenes, *an apparition, sitting here in this chair? No, a dream, of course! Mama is dead and buried and at peace. Finally.* He gave out a long sigh, looked down at the green tie in his hand, and stepped back to the closet. He hung it back on the rack and looked at the striped one Jo's brother, a lawyer who lived in Washington, D.C., had given him on St. Stephen's Day. *Never!* he thought stubbornly. He sighted a tie he hadn't worn in several months; it was bright red with big, blue polka dots, and it was buried so deeply on the rack he thought that Jo must've surely hidden it on purpose. *Someday,* he thought grimly, *she's going to burn them all up like she's been threatening!* As he slipped it on, he looked up at the top shelf and saw a flat box half-hidden under a couple of battered hats with small, sad feathers glued to their bands. He quickly looked away and closed the closet door.

In the small, cozy kitchen at the rear of the house, Jo was putting the breakfast plates on the little table that overlooked her backyard garden when her husband came in, smelling of Vitalis and Old Spice shaving lotion. She looked up, started to smile, and winced instead when she saw what was hanging around his neck. "Eat your sausages," she said. "You might have a hard day at the circus."

"Gladly. Ah, this looks delicious!" He sat down at the table and started to eat, taking in huge, sloppy mouthfuls of sausage and potatoes. Jo set a cup of hot, black coffee beside him and took her seat on the other side of the table. "It's good," he said with food in his mouth. "Very good."

"Slow down," Jo said. "You'll have an attack."

He nodded and kept eating. When he stopped to drink some coffee, she said, "Andy, you should take a Saturday off once in a while. You should relax, all this working and worrying isn't good for you. Why don't you call and tell them you're staying home today? We can go for a nice drive to the beach."

"I can't," he said, washing potatoes down his throat. "Maybe next Saturday."

"You said that last week."

"Oh. Well, I meant it, but . . ." He lifted his gaze to hers. "You know why I have to go in. Someone might turn up something."

"They'll call you if they do." She watched him, her eyes bright and blue and alert. She was also worried about the dark hollows that had now appeared beneath Andy's eyes, about the new lines that had begun to snake across his face. He didn't sleep so well lately either, and she wondered if even in his dreams he thought of stalking that awful killer through the dark canyons of the city. She reached out and touched his rough bear's paw of a hand. "Please," she said softly. "I'll make a picnic lunch for us today."

"They expect me to be there," he said and patted her hand. "Next Saturday we'll have a nice picnic. Okay?"

"No, it's not okay. They're working you to death! You leave early in the morning and don't come home until late at night. You work Saturdays and most Sundays, too! How long is it going to go on?"

He wiped his mouth with a napkin and dug his fork into a mound of potatoes. "Until we find him," he said quietly.

"That may be never. He may be out of the city now, out of the country even. So why are you the one who has to work like a dog and answer all the questions and be on the front page of all the newspapers? I don't like what some people are saying about you."

He raised his eyebrows. "What are they saying?"

"You know. That you don't know what you're doing, that you don't really care about finding that man, that you're not a good policeman even."

"Oh, those things." He nodded and drank down the rest of his coffee.

"You should tell them all to go to the devil!" she said fiercely, her eyes shining. "What do those people know about how hard you've been working, day and night like a Trojan! They should give you a medal! You've spilled

coffee on your tie." She leaned forward with her napkin
and dabbed at it. "If you keep your coat buttoned, it
won't show."

"All right," Palatazin said. "I'll try to." He pushed his
plate away and put a hand on his expanded stomach.
"I've got to go in a few minutes. That Clarke girl from
the *Tattler* is coming to the office this morning."

Jo made a disgusted face. "What—to write more slime?
Why do you even talk to that woman?"

"I do my job, she does her job. Sometimes she gets carried away, but she's harmless."

"Harmless? Ha! It's stories like hers that make people
so afraid. Describing what that awful *gyilkos* did to those
poor girls in such terrible detail, and then making out that
you don't have sense enough to find him and stop him!
She makes me sick!" Jo stood up and took his plate over
to the sink; she was shaking inwardly and trying to control
it, trying not to let her husband see. Her blood, the Hungarian gypsy blood of a hundred generations, was singing
with anger.

"People know what that newspaper is," Palatazin said,
licking a forefinger and rubbing the coffee stain. Defeated,
he let the tie drop. "They don't believe those stories."

Jo grunted but did not turn from the sink. A new mental picture was forming in her brain, something that had
gradually grown there over the past few weeks: Andy,
armed with a gun, moving through the dark corridors of
some unknown building, seeking the Roach all alone; and
then huge, grasping hands reaching for him from behind,
clamping around his throat, and squeezing until the eyeballs popped out and the face turned purplish blue. She
shook her head to rid herself of the nagging thought and
said softly, "God have mercy!"

"What?"

"Nothing," she said. "I'm thinking out loud." She
turned back to him and saw that his face was not purplish
blue, nor were his eyeballs popping out. His face, on the
contrary, reminded her of that dog in the Hush Puppies
ads, all jowls and sad eyes under bushy, gray-flecked
brows. She said, "You're not going to do anything dangerous today, are you?"

"Of course not." He thought, *Am I? How can I know?*
This was a question she asked him every morning and an
answer he gave in kind. He wondered how many wives of

policemen asked that question, how many cops replied as he had, and how many ended up dead from the burglar's or the rapist's or the junkie's gun. Far too many, he was sure. He wondered how George Greene had answered that question on a July sixth morning over twelve years ago. Greene had been Palatazin's first partner, and on that terrible day he was shot four times in the face while Palatazin watched it all through the window of a pizza parlor, buying a twelve-inch mushroom and black olive to carry back across the street to the car. They'd been staking out a suspect in the robbery-murder of a black heroin dealer, and much later, after the shooting was all over and Palatazin had vomited the last stink of gunpowder from his nostrils, he realized that the man must've figured out he was being watched and panicked, shoving his stolen .45 right through the passenger window into George's face. Palatazin had chased him over five blocks, and finally on a tenement stairway, the man had turned to make his stand. Palatazin had blasted him away with a pizza-smeared trigger finger.

His mother had cried for a long time when he'd told her that he thought he'd felt a bullet hiss past his head. She'd said she was going to the commissioner to have him given safer duty, but of course that didn't happen. The next day she'd forgotten everything he'd told her, and she was talking about how beautiful the summer flowers must be along the streets of Budapest.

Now Palatazin found himself staring at the hand that had held the gun that July 6. *Anya,* he thought: the Magyar word for mother. *I saw my mother's ghost last night.* He looked up into Jo's eyes. "I had a strange dream last night," he said and smiled slightly. "I thought I saw Mama sitting in her rocking chair in our bedroom. I haven't dreamed about her for a long time. That's strange, isn't it?"

"What happened?"

"Nothing. She . . . motioned with her hand. Pointed, I think. I'm not sure."

"Pointed? At what?"

He shrugged, "Who knows? I can't read dreams." He stood up from the table and looked at his wristwatch; it was time to go. "I have an idea," he said, putting his arms around his wife's waist. "I'll come home early and take you to The Budapest for dinner. Would you like that?"

"I'd like for you to stay home today, that's what I'd like." She thrust out her lower lip for a moment and then reached up to brush the half-halo of gray hair at the crest of his head. "But The Budapest would be nice, I think."

"Good. And music! Fine *ciganyzene!* Yes?"

She smiled. "Yes."

"We have a date then." He patted her rear affectionately and then pinched it. She made a mock clucking noise with her tongue and followed him out to the living room where from a closet he took his dark blue coat and a black hat that had seen its day years before. She held his coat for him while he strapped on a black leather shoulder-holster, all the time staring distastefully at the .38 Police Special it held. Struggling into the coat and crowning himself with the ragged-looking hat, he was ready to go. "Have a good day," he said on the front porch steps and kissed her cheek.

"Be careful!" Jo called to him as he walked to the old white Ford Falcon at the curb. "I love you!"

He raised a hand and slid into the car. In another moment it was rattling away down Romaine Street. A brown mongrel darted out from a hedge to chase it until it was out of sight.

Jo closed the door and locked it. *The Roach!* she thought and felt like spitting because even the sound of that terrible word made her sick. She moved back into the kitchen, intent on washing the dishes, sweeping and mopping the floor, then doing some weeding in the garden. But she was bothered by something beyond the Roach, and it took her a few minutes to find it lurking within herself. Andy's dream about his mother. Her gypsy instincts were keen and curious. Why was Andy thinking about her, dreaming about her again? Of course, the old woman had been insane, and of course, it was better now that she was dead and not wasting away day by day as she had been in that bed in the Golden Garden Home for the Aged. "I don't read dreams," Andy had said. *But perhaps,* Jo thought, *I should ask someone who does? It might be an omen of the future.*

She turned on the hot water tap and for the moment closed the mental cupboard on the age-old art of dream-reading.

TWO

Jack Kidd's black Chevrolet van, a darkroom on wheels airbrushed with sword-wielding barbarians and half-naked damsels *a la* Frank Frazetta, stopped at the gates of Hollywood Memorial Cemetery. The gates were wide open, and Jack could see a light burning in the watchman's station, though it was now almost eight-thirty and the sun was glaringly bright across the rolling, green cemetery lawn. Jack, a Canon hanging around his neck, hit the horn a couple of times, but no watchman came out to greet them. On the seat beside him Gayle yawned and said, "No one's home. Let's drive on through."

"I need to talk to this guy first." He pounded the horn again. "Maybe he's curled up somewhere, sleeping off whatever makes him see old Clifton roaming around out here, huh?" He gave her a quick smile and opened his door, stepping out onto the pavement. "Back in a minute," he said and walked across to the little white concrete watchman's station with the red-tiled roof. He could look through the window that faced the cemetery gates and see the whole interior at a glance. A lamp was burning on a blotter-topped desk, the chair pulled back slightly as if someone had just stood up. Atop the desk there was an open *Sports Illustrated*, a half-full coffee cup, and an ashtray littered with cigarette butts.

Jack tried the door. It opened easily. He stepped inside, checked a small bathroom, and found it empty, then walked back out to his van. "He's not there," he said, climbing up to his seat and starting the engine. "That's a hell of a note! The guy knew I was coming out this morning. How am I supposed to find old Clifton's grave?"

"Listen, can you wrap this up in a hurry and get me over to Parker Center?" She tapped the crystal of her wristwatch impatiently.

"Okay, but first I'm going to drive through and try to find the guy. It'll just take a few minutes. Three shots of a headstone, that's all I need." He drove into the cemetery, passing beneath towering Washingtonia palms. Marble gravestones, mausoleums, and angelic statues were

scattered on each side of the winding main road, all surrounded by huge oak trees, palms, and decorative clumps
of palmetto; the bright green grass sparkled with early
morning dew, and a thin sheen of haze clung low to the
ground. Gayle could see the stout white buildings of Paramount Studios over on the far side of the cemetery, so
close that any strung-out, bleary-eyed, hopeless kid who'd
just flunked a screen test could just stumble on over and
fall into a grave. It was odd, she thought, that most of the
major studios in Hollywood overlooked a cemetery.

Which reminded her of a rumor she'd heard around the
Tattler offices a few days before. "You know what some
people believe about Walt Disney?" she said, glancing
over at Jack. "This his ashes aren't really in Forest Lawn,
that his body's being preserved in liquid nitrogen so he
might be revived someday. Trace wants to do a story on
it."

"That figures."

"It is a little strange, though. Disney's plaque is the only
marker in the whole cemetery that doesn't have any
dates on it."

"What have you been doing—your cemetery history
homework?"

"No, but that story beats this bullshit about Clifton
Webb, doesn't it?" She looked over at Jack in time to
see his eyes widen. "Christ!" he said and hit the brakes so
hard the van's tires burned rubber. "What is *that?*" He
stared directly ahead.

Gayle looked and drew in her breath with a shudder.

Lying in the road was a skeleton wearing a long, pastel
green dress. Clumps of brownish hair still clung to the
shattered skull; both legs and an arm were broken off
like thin white pieces of gnarled driftwood. The remaining hand clawed toward the sky. On both sides of the
road, scattered across neatly trimmed grass and decorative clumps of sharp-tipped palmetto, were the fragments
of more skeletons. Skulls and arms and legs, spines and
hipbones littered the cemetery. *A boneyard,* Gayle
thought suddenly, a pulse pounding at her temples. She
could not tear her gaze away from the obscene and casual
lay of those skeletons. There were whole skeletons dressed
in grave suits and dresses, lying atop each other as if
they'd been dancing at the stroke of midnight and had

collapsed with the brutal coming of dawn. There were also worse things—new corpses that weren't quite all bone yet, covered with black flies. Gayle could see that dozens of headstones had been thrown over and the graves dug up, mounds of dirt standing over ragged, empty holes.

"*JeeeeSUS!*" Jack said, catching a bit of the breeze that carried with it the green smell of rot. "Somebody's torn the hell out of this place!" He popped the lens cap off his Canon and climbed down from the van.

"Jack!" Gayle called after him. She felt cold and clammy, like an old wet rag. There was something lying in the shadow of a tree, perhaps ten feet to her right, that she couldn't bear to look at. She thought she heard the high buzzing of interested flies. "Where the hell are you going?"

Jack was already snapping pictures. "Trace is going to want some shots of this!" he said; his voice sounded electric with excitement, but his face had gone as pale as paste and his finger was trembling on the shutter. "How many graves would you say are open? Twenty? Thirty?" She didn't answer. The shutter clicked, clicked, clicked. Since he'd signed on with the *Tattler,* a little more than two years ago, he'd taken pictures of freeway wrecks, suicides, gunshot victims, once even a whole family of Chicanos who'd been fried to black crisps in a gas-leak explosion. Trace had printed the pictures because he was true to the *Tattler*'s motto: We print it as we see it. Jack had gotten used to those things because he was a professional and he needed the money for his documentary film work. The *Tattler* was one of the last of the "bucket of blood" tabloids, and sometimes what Jack was required to photograph was pretty damned grisly indeed, but he'd learned to grit his teeth and shoot on muscle reflex. "If it's part of the human condition," Trace always said, "there's a place for it in the *Tattler*." *But this was different,* Jack thought as he took a couple of pictures of the green-clad skeleton lady, *what had been done here was just pure, plain old evil. No, check that. It was Evil, about as damned black as you could get.* A shiver went through him. *Welcome to the Twilight Zone.*

When Gayle came up beside him and touched his arm, he jumped so violently that he took a picture of clouds. "What happened?" she said. "What . . . did this?"

"Vandals. Maybe bikers or a devil cult or something. Tore the hell out of the place, whoever they were. I've seen cemetery vandalism before—you know, headstones kicked over and that sort of shit—but never anything like this! Christ, look at that!" He made a wide detour around a couple of broken skeletons and reached a massive, ornately carved stone vault. Its entire top had been torn off. He peered in and saw nothing but a little dust and some scraps of dark cloth down there at the bottom. A mossy odor, as if from an empty well, came floating up to him. *Whose vault was this?* he wondered. Tyrone Power's? Cecil B. DeMille's? Whoever it had been was just a handful of gray dust now. He stepped back to take a picture, almost tripping over a grinning skeleton in a dark suit at his feet.

A few yards away, Gayle stood staring down into an open grave. In ornate script the headstone read, MARY CONKLIN. Scattered in the dirt at the grave's bottom were yellow bones held together by cobwebs of wispy lace. "Jack," Gayle said quietly, "I don't think this is just vandalism."

"Huh? What did you say?"

She looked over at him, only vaguely aware of birds singing in the high treetops around her, oblivious to mortal concerns. "The coffins," she said. "Where are they?"

Jack paused, lowering his camera. He stared at the heavy concrete plate that had been shifted—*how many hundreds of pounds did that thing weigh?*—from the vault where Old Dusty lay. No coffin in there either. "Coffins?" he said, a trickle of sweat like ice water running down his side.

"There aren't any. I think . . . these remains were dumped out, the coffins stolen."

"That's crazy," he replied softly.

"Then look in these empty graves, damn it!" Gayle was almost shouting now, nausea roiling in her stomach. "Find me a coffin in any one of them! Go on, look!"

Jack didn't have to. He gazed across the green, sun-dappled landscape; the place looked like an ancient battlefield, all the soldiers left to rot where they'd fallen, left for the vultures and the scavenger dogs. No coffins? He let the Canon dangle down around his neck; it felt heavy with the evidence of some hideous, awful Evil. No cof-

fins? "I think . . . we'd better call the cops," he heard
himself say and, backing away from that violated tomb,
he stepped on a disembodied skull that cracked with a
noise like a tortured shriek.

THREE

"Do you mind?" Palatazin asked the young blond girl with
the glittery eyeshadow who sat on the other side of his
desk. He held up what had once been a perfectly white
meerschaum pipe, now a scarred lump of coal.

"Huh? Oh no, man, that's okay." Her accent was reedy
Midwestern.

He nodded, struck a match, and touched the bowl with
the flame. The pipe had been a gift from Jo on their first
wedding anniversary, almost ten years ago. It was carved
in the likeness of a Magyar prince, one of the wild
horsemen-warriors who'd swept bloodily down into Hungary in the ninth century. Most of the nose and one eyebrow were chipped away, and now the face more closely
resembled a Nigerian prizefighter. He made sure he blew
the smoke away from the girl. "All right, Miss Hulsett,"
he said and glanced quickly down at the notepad before
him; he'd had to clear away an armload of newspaper
clippings and yellow folders to make room for it. "This
friend of yours was walking to work Tuesday evening on
Hollywood Boulevard, and a car pulled to the curb. Then
what?"

"There was a guy in the car. A strange-looking dude,"
she said. The girl smiled nervously at him, fidgeting with
a small purple suede purse that she'd positioned in her
lap. Her fingernails were chewed down to the quick.
Across the office in a chair near the door, Detective Sulli-
van Reece, as chunky as a fireplug and dark as the ebony
Magyar pipe, sat with his arms crossed and watched the
girl, occasionally glancing over at Palatazin.

"How old did this man appear to be, Miss Hulsett?"

She shrugged. "I don't know. Not as old as you. She
said she couldn't really tell because, you know, the lights
are so bright and weird on the boulevard at night. You

can't tell anything about people until they're right up in your face."

He nodded. "Black, white, Chicano?"

"White. He was wearing real thick glasses, and they made his eyes look huge and funny. He was . . . my friend Sheila said . . . a chunky guy, not real tall or anything, but just . . . thick-looking. He had black or dark brown hair, cut almost to a stubble. He looked like he needed a shave, too."

"What was he wearing?" Reece asked, his voice powerful and gravelly. When he was a kid at Duke Ellington High School, he'd carried the bass line in the choir and made the auditorium floor vibrate.

"Uh . . . a blue windbreaker. Light-colored pants."

"Any mongrams on the windbreaker? Company emblem?"

"No, I don't think so." She looked back at Palatazin and shivered inwardly. Being so close to cops unnerved her; Lynn and Patty had told her she was a fool to go walking into Parker Center, to offer information to the cops because, after all, what had they ever done for her except bust her twice on soliciting charges? But she thought that maybe, if they ever busted her again, this sad-looking cop in charge might remember her and make things easy. The muffled noise of ringing telephones and clattering typewriters outside the office was beginning to grate on her nerves because she'd had to force herself to stay straight—no coke, no hash, no pills—when she came to see the heat. Now she was so nervous she could hardly stand it.

"All right, Amy," Palatazin said softly, sensing her uneasiness. She was beginning to look like a deer who'd caught a whiff of gunmetal. "What about the car? What kind was it?"

"A Volkswagen Bug. Gray or greenish gray, I think."

He wrote both colors on his pad. "What happened next to . . . uh . . . your friend?"

"This guy opened the door and leaned out and said 'Are you selling?' " She shrugged nervously. "You know."

"He was trying to proposition your friend?"

"Yeah. And he flashed a fifty, too. Then he said something that sounded like Wally's got something for you . . .' "

"Wally?" Reece leaned forward slightly in his chair, his

high-cheekboned face glowing like burnished mahogany in the sunlight that streamed through the open blinds behind Palatazin. "You're sure that was the name?"

"No, not sure. Listen, all this happened to my friend Sheila. How am I supposed to know anything for sure, man?"

Palatazin wrote WALLY? And below that, WALTER?

"And then?" he said.

"He said, 'You won't have to do much. Just get in and we'll talk.'" She paused, staring at the buildings of L.A. through the window behind him. "She almost went. A fifty is a fifty, right?"

"Right," Palatazin said. He looked into her troubled eyes and thought, *Child, how do you survive out there?* If she was over sixteen years old, he'd dance the *csardas* for the entire homicide squad. "Go on, please."

"She almost went, but when she started to get into the car, she smelled something . . . funny. It smelled like medicine, like the stuff . . . uh . . . Sheila's dad used to wash his hands with. He's a doctor."

Palatazin wrote DOCTOR? and followed it with HOSPITAL STAFF?

"So then Sheila got spooked, and she got out of the car and walked away. When she looked back, the dude was driving off. That's all."

"When did your friend start thinking this dude might be the Roach?" Reece asked.

"I've been keeping up with the papers. Everybody has, I mean. Everybody on the boulevard talks about it all the time, so I thought you cops should know."

"If this happened on Tuesday, why did you wait so long before reporting it?"

She shrugged and bit at a thumbnail. "I was scared. Sheila was scared. The more I thought about it being *him,* the more scared I got."

"Did your friend happen to see the license plate number?" Palatazin asked, pen poised. "Anything else about the car that stood out?"

She shook her head. "No, it happened too fast." She looked up into the placid, gray eyes of this heavyset cop who reminded her so much of the juvenile officer back in Holt, Idaho. Except this cop had a funny accent, he was almost bald, and he had a coffee stain on his loud red tie with the blue dots. "It couldn't have really been him, do you think?"

Palatazin leaned back in his swivel chair, tendrils of blue smoke wafting around him. This young *prostitualt* was like any one of dozens who'd been interviewed in the past few weeks: jaded and frightened, with enough street-sense to stay alive but not enough to break out of The Life. They all seemed to carry the same expression in their eyes—a sharp glimmer of contempt that masked a sad weariness somewhere deep and close to the soul. Over the last weeks he'd had to hold back his impulse to shake some of these street survivors and shout, "Don't you know what's waiting for you out there? The murderer, the rapist, the sadist . . . and worse. Things you never dared think about for fear that they would drive you mad; things that lurk in the shadows of humanity, that wait on the nightmare fringe for their chance to strike. Things of the basest evil that must spread evil and consume evil in order to survive. . . ."

Enough, he told himself. He was knotted inside and realized he was stepping too close to the edge. "Yes," he told Amy. "It might have been."

"Oh Christ," she said, the blood draining out of her face until she looked like a Kewpie doll, all paint and no insides. "I mean, I . . . I've had some dates with weird dudes before, but nobody's ever tried to . . ." She touched her throat, seeing in her mind's eye the way that creepy dude had grinned when she'd slid into his car.

"Amy," Palatazin said quietly, dropping the pretense, "we have an artist here who can put together a composite picture of the man who tried to pick you up. Now I'm not saying that this man *was* the Roach, only that there's a possibility. I'd like for you to go with Detective Reece and give a description to our artist. Anything you can remember—his hair, eyes, nose, mouth. All right?" He rose to his feet, and Reece stood behind the girl. "Also I want you to think about that car. I want you to see it in your mind and remember as much as you can about it. Especially think about the license plate. You may have seen it and gotten a number inside your head without realizing it. Thank you for coming in to talk to us, Amy. Sully, will you take her up to see Mack?"

"Sure. Come on with me, Miss Hulsett." He opened the office door for her, and the noises of the homicide-robbery

squad room tumbled in—shrill telephones, a couple of
typewriters being beaten mercilessly, file cabinets being
opened and closed, the monotone chattering of a Telex
machine. The girl stopped on the threshold and turned
back to Palatazin. "Something else I do remember," she
said. "His hands. They were . . . really large, you know?
I could see them where they were gripped around the
steering wheel."

"Was he wearing any rings?"

"I . . . no, I don't think so."

"All right, fine. Sully, as soon as you get that composite
bring it down to me, will you?" Sully nodded and led her
off across the wide, linoleum-floored room jammed with
file cabinets and desks. Palatazin, the heartbeat of hope
pounding at his temples, worked his way through the
maze of desks to where Detective Brasher sat waiting for
an informant's return call. Brasher, a young man with
sandy-brown hair and deep-set, green eyes that were already becoming hard, had met his match in this morning's
Times crossword puzzle. He shoved it aside quickly when
he saw the captain moving toward him.

"Brasher," Palatazin said, "you don't look too busy. I
need some files collected. Anyone we've been talking to
in connection with the Roach killings who owns a Volkswagen, also anyone who goes by the name 'Wally' or
'Walter' or uses that as a nickname or alias. I want you
to go through the rape and assault files, looking for the
same thing. Follow those back about three months."

"Yes, sir." He scribbled down the information on a
notepad and rose from his desk. "I was waiting for a call
from a pimp I've been talking to."

"Have Hayden answer your phone." Palatazin motioned to the man at the nearest desk. "I need those files
as soon as you can get them." He turned away from
Brasher in time to see Gayle Clarke come striding into
the squad room; he felt a quick surge of anger and irritation. She was over an hour late, and right now he didn't
feel like putting up with her inane questions. On the couple of occasions he'd refused to see her and had sent her
down to Press Relations, the *Tattler* had then run cheap-
shot editorials about how Captain Andrew Palatazin was
dragging his feet on the Roach investigation. He wouldn't
have minded at any other time, but right now all the city
papers were pressuring the mayor, who in turn pressured

the police commissioner, who jumped with both feet on Chief Garnette, who came to Palatazin chewing a toothpick and demanding to know why this thing wasn't cracked yet. Palatazin could only chew Tums and hulk around the squad room like an injured, dangerous bear; he knew his men were working as hard as they could, but the politicians in high places were getting nervous. So there had been a firm directive from the commissioner: Cooperate with the press.

It's not enough to be a policeman, Palatazin thought sourly as he moved toward Gayle Clarke. *Now you have to be social worker, psychologist, politician, and mindreader all rolled up into one!* "You're late," he told her tersely. "What do you want?"

"Sorry," she said, but her expression didn't show it. "I was held up for awhile. Can we talk in your office?"

"Where else? But please make this fast. I have work to do." He ushered her in, closed the door, and sat down at his desk. The name "Wally" buzzed in his brain like a hornet. "I'll tell you what I told the *Times* and the *Ledger* this morning: we're still without a prime suspect, but we do have several people under surveillance. And no, I'm not aware of any similarities between the Roach and Jack the Ripper. We've boosted the number of decoys on the streets, but I wish you'd keep that off the record. Will you?"

"Should I?" She raised an eyebrow, taking a Flair pen out of her purse.

"Miss Clarke," Palatazin said quietly, shoving aside his pipe and folding his hands together atop his desk. *Take it easy,* he told himself. *Don't let her bait you, she's good at that.* "In the past few weeks you and I have had the misfortune of having to work in close proximity. I know you don't like me, and I couldn't care less. I have nothing but the lowest regard for your newspaper." He turned and rummaged through a stack of papers; when he found last week's *Tattler,* he pushed it across the desk toward her. The front-page headline in blood-red type screamed, WHERE IS THE ROACH? WHO WILL BE NEXT TO DIE? Her thin smile wavered a fraction but held.

"You'll recall that I told you two weeks ago I was putting decoy policewomen on the streets to act as prostitutes. I told every newspaper in this city the same thing and asked all of them to keep that information off the record. You'll recall I asked you to do the same. Why was it then that on opening your paper to read your story my eye was caught by a headline that read, 'Policewomen May Trap The Roach?' He hasn't struck since that information was made public. Although I'm not assuming that he is sick enough to be a reader of your paper, I *am* assuming that he has found out about the decoys and has decided to go into hiding. It may be months before he surfaces again, and by then his trail may be very cold indeed."

"I tried to keep that out of the story," Gayle said. "My managing editor said it was news and should go in."

"Oh. Then perhaps your managing editor should have my job since he knows so much about police procedure?" He rummaged again, found another *Tattler*, and pushed it toward Gayle like a piece of rotten meat. The headline blared MASS-MURDER RAMPAGE. There was a picture in gory detail of Charlene McKay being pick up by the men from the morgue. Other headlines tried to scream each other out: HAVE UFOs LANDED NEAR L.A.? NEVER GROW OLD—THE AMAZING SEAWEED DIET; HOW TO MARRY A ROCK STAR. Palatazin snorted with disgust. "Do people actually subscribe to this thing?"

"Three-hundred-thousand by last year's figures," she told him coolly. "I would tell you I was sorry about that decoy thing getting in, but I don't think it would do any good."

"You're right, because I have the feeling that if we were to do it all over again, nothing would change. Don't you realize how much harm these wild stories about the Roach do? They frighten people; they make people suspicious of each other, afraid to even go out at night. And they don't help our investigation very much either." He picked up his pipe and clamped it between his teeth, almost biting through the stem. "I thought I could trust in your professionalism. I see I was wrong."

"Damn it!" she said suddenly and so forcefully Palatazin thought she was going to leap over the desk at him. She leaned forward, her eyes fierce with anger. "The stories I wrote are good! Damned good! I can't help what the headlines say, and I can't tell my managing editor what's right or wrong to print! Okay, I know the

Tattler's milking this thing for all it's worth, but so is every other paper in town! The bottom line is cash, captain, selling papers, and anybody who says differently is either a liar or a fool. But if you read my stories, you'll see I'm a damned good writer, and I've told people the truth as I see it!"

Palatazin was silent for a moment. He lit his pipe and regarded her through a haze of smoke. "Why do you waste your time with the *Tattler?*" he asked her finally. "It's beneath you. Couldn't you work somewhere else?"

"I'm making a name for myself," she said, the redness slowly subsiding from her face. "It's a living. Most women two years out of the UCLA School of Journalism are sitting on their asses doing rewrites, or editing somebody else's copy, or going down to the corner for coffee and ham sandwiches for the real reporters. Working for the *Tattler* may not be a dream job, but at least I'm gathering a following who buy papers to read *my* copy."

"Some following. The kind of people who like to stare at traffic accidents."

"Their money's as good as anyone else's. Better than most. And don't downgrade them, captain; they're the great American middle class. The people who pay your salary, by the way."

Palatazin nodded thoughtfully. Gayle's dark brown eyes still held a hint of anger, glittering like deep pools of water disturbed by the casual throw of a stone. "Well," he said, "I'd better get to work and earn that salary. Just what is it you wanted to see me about?"

"Never mind. You answered my questions already. I was going to ask you why you thought Roach had gone into hiding." She capped her Flair and dropped it back into her purse. "You might be interested to know that he won't be the lead story next week."

"I'm relieved."

She stood up from her chair and slung the purse over her shoulder. "Okay," she said. "Off the record. Are you any closer to catching him than you were last week?"

"Off the record? No. But we may have some new leads."

"Such as?"

"Too premature yet. We'll have to wait and see."

She smiled thinly. "Don't trust me anymore, do you?"

"Partly that. Also partly that we're working on some information that came off the street today, and you of all people should know how reliable that can be." He stood up and went with her toward the door.

She stopped with her hand on the knob. "I . . . I didn't mean to lose my cool. But I got involved in something that was pretty hairy today. Something weird. You must think I'm pushing pretty hard, don't you?"

"Yes, I do."

"That's because I don't want to stay on the *Tattler* all my life. I have to be there when you get him, captain, because riding this story to the ground is the only way I'm ever going to move up. Okay, I'm ambitious and opportunistic as hell, but I'm a realist, too. Something as big as this comes along for a journalist only once in a blue moon. I'm going to see that I take advantage of it."

"We may never find him."

"Can I quote you on that?"

His eyes widened slightly; he couldn't tell if she was kidding or not because her expression was serious, her gaze sharp and piercing. "I don't think so," he said and opened the door for her. "I'm sure we'll be talking again. By the way, what knocked Roach off the front page? Something about a little old lady who found Howard Hughes's will in her attic?"

"No." A chill passed through her; she could still smell the rot of those corpses in the cemetery as if her clothes were full of it. "Grave robbers over at Hollywood Memorial. That's why I was late; I had to call the story in and talk to the Hollywood cops."

"Grave robbers?" Palatazin said softly.

"Yeah. Or rather *coffin* robbers. Whoever it was ripped about twenty caskets out of the ground and left . . . everything else lying around."

Palatazin took the pipe out of his mouth and stood staring at her, a dull pulse beating at the base of his neck. "What?" he said in a strange, hoarse voice that sounded more like the croak of a frog.

"Yeah. It's weird." She started out the door, but suddenly Palatazin's hand was gripping her arm just short of painfully. She looked at him and blinked. His face had gone waxen, his lips moving but making no sound.

"What do you mean?" he said with an effort. "What are you talking about? When did this happen?"

"Sometime during the night, I guess. Hey, listen . . . you're . . . you're hurting."

He looked down at his hand and instantly released her. "I'm sorry. Hollywood Memorial? Who was first on the scene?"

"I was. And a photographer from the *Tattler*—Jack Kidd. Why are you so interested? Vandalism isn't your detail, is it?"

"No, but . . ." He looked wan and confused, as if he might suddenly collapse on the floor in a limp heap. The set of his eyes with their glazed intensity frightened Gayle so much she felt a quick shiver ripple up her spine. "Are you all right?" she asked him tentatively, and for a moment he didn't reply.

"Yes," he said finally, nodding. "Yes, I'm fine. I'm fine. I'd like for you to go now, Miss Clarke, I have work to do." He held the door open, and she stepped out into the squad room. She turned toward him, intending to ask him to keep her in mind if and when they did get a solid lead on Roach. The door closed in her face. She thought, *Shit! What's his problem? Maybe what I've been hearing is true. Maybe the pressure is starting to crack him wide open.* If so, that would make for a juicy human interest story. She turned away and left the squad room.

And behind that closed door, Palatazin was gripping his telephone with a white-knuckled hand. The police operator answered. "This is Palatazin," he said. "Get me Lieutenant Kirkland, Hollywood Division." His voice was urgent and full of terror.

FOUR

The sun reached its zenith and instantly began to fall, deepening the shadows that clung like a precious autumn chill to the eastern facades of the massive stone and glass buildings at the center of Los Angeles. In the slow decay of hours and light, the sun shone red on the smooth lakes of MacArthur Park; clear, golden beams wafted through the windows of shops and boutiques on Rodeo Drive in Beverly Hills; dust stirred lazily in the air among the cramped, boxy tenement buildings of East L.A., and clothes strung on lines from window to window caught bits of flying grit; the Pacific surf that rolled up to the

edge of the Venice Beach boardwalk, where the kids
darted and spun on roller skates like human tops, slowly
turned orange, then red deepening toward purple; lights
began to glimmer like hot jewels along Sunset and Hollywood boulevards; the San Gabriel Mountains were jumbled piles of light and darkness, the western face of stone
glowing red, the eastern exposures almost black.

And above the whole metropolis with its eight million
separate lives and destinies sat the Kronsteen Castle on a
throne of rock. It was a huge, sprawling edifice of black
weather-beaten stone with high turrets, arched Gothic
roofs, broken gargoyles leering from towers or contem-
plating the patchwork of humanity in the valley below.
Many of the windows had been shattered and replaced
with boards, but some of the windows at the higher elevations had survived vandalism, and those that were of
stained glass glowed red and blue and purple in the
strong, hard light of the setting sun. A chill gathered in
the darkening air and began to grow vicious. The wind
hissed and whispered around stone battlements like a human voice through broken teeth.

And many in the city below thought for just a cold,
eerie instant that they heard their names called from behind the falling curtain of night.

FIVE

Rico Esteban's brain was scorched with hot neon. Around
him there was the thunder of engines, the crisp notes of
electric music rippling through the air. He thought he
should say something to the dark-haired girl who sat
pressed against the other side of the car, but he could
think of only one thing and saying it wouldn't be right—
Holy Shit. Beyond that crude summation of his feelings,
his brain buzzed with overloaded circuits.

He thought, *Prenado? Did she say she was pregnant?*
Only a few minutes before, he'd pulled his fire-engine-
red Chevy lowrider in front of Merida Santos's apartment
building on Dos Terros Street in the dark, tenement barrio of East Los Angeles. Almost immediately she'd come
running out of the hallway, where a single, dim light bulb

exposed a shaky set of stairs and walls layered with spray-painted graffiti, and slid into his car. As he kissed her, he'd thought that something was wrong; her eyes looked funny, they were a little sad, and there were the beginnings of dark circles underneath them. He'd started the Chevy, filling Dos Terros Street with a rumble that shook window panes and brought a couple of shouted complaints from the old folks, and then had screeched off toward Whittier Boulevard. Merida, her long black hair cascading in waves around her shoulders, sat away from him and stared at her hands. She was wearing a blue dress and the silver crucifix on a chain that Rico had bought for her birthday the week before.

"Hey," he'd said and leaned over to tilt her face up with a forefinger beneath her chin. "What's wrong? You been crying? That crazy *perra* been beating on you?"

"No," she'd replied, her soft voice trembling slightly. She was still more a little girl than woman. At sixteen her flesh was smooth and tawny, her body as tight and lean as a colt's. Usually her eyes sparkled with shy, laughing innocence, but tonight something was different, and Rico couldn't figure it out. If her crazy old mother hadn't been beating on her again, then what was wrong? "Did Luis run away from home again?" he asked her. She shook her head. He leaned back, cushioned in the cup of his red bucket seat, and brushed a lock of thick black hair off his forehead. "That Luis better watch out," he said quietly, swerving around a couple of drunks who were dancing together in the middle of the street. He hit the horn, and one of them shot him the finger. "The kid's too young to be running with the Homicides. I told him once, I told him a hundred times not to get mixed up with those *ladrones*. They're going to get him in trouble. Where you want to eat tonight?"

"It don' matter," Merida said. Rico shrugged and turned onto the boulevard, where a gaudy carnival of neon pulsated over porno movie houses, bars, discos, and liquor stores. Though it was just past six-thirty, the low-riders were already jostling for position, chugging like streamlined locomotives. They were painted every color of the rainbow from electric blue to Day-Glo orange and outfitted with zebra-striped tops or leopard-skin upholstery or radio antennae that seemed as tall as towers. The mass of cars moved at a crawl, bouncing and swaying like

wild bucking horses along the boulevard, which was lined
with hordes of Chicano teenagers looking for fun on a
Saturday night. Music from transistor and car radios
blared at each other, the tumultuous frenzy of rock and
disco overpowered only by the thundering bass lines that
prowled out through the open doors of the bars. The air,
sweet and hot with exhaust, cheap perfume, and marijuana, crackled with tinny voices. Rico reached over and
turned his own radio up loud, his brown face split by a
grin. The growl of KALA's Tiger Eddie became a hypnotic chant—". . . gonna TEAR this town down tonight,
gonna lay it to WASTE, 'cause we're the BEST, beatin'
all the REST on a SAT-UR-DAY night! Mighty KALA,
comin' at you with The Wolves annnnddddd 'Born To Be
Bad'!"

Merida had turned the radio off. The Wolves wailed
on anyway from a dozen other sets of speakers. "Rico,"
she'd said, and now she was looking him straight in the
eyes, and her lower lip trembled. "I found out I'm pregnant."

He thought, *Holy Shit! Pregnant? Did she say pregnant?* He'd almost said, "Who did it?" but stopped himself cold. He knew she'd been sleeping only with him for
the past three months, even after he'd gotten his apartment down on the low, poor end of Sunset Boulevard.
She was a decent, good, loyal woman. *Woman?* he
thought. *Barely sixteen. A girl, yes, but a woman in many
ways, too.* Rico was too stunned to speak. The waves of
lowriders before him seemed to undulate, an ocean of
metal. He'd used rubbers most every time and thought
he'd been careful, but now . . . *What am I going to do?*
he asked himself. *Your big macho prick has gotten this
woman in trouble, and now what do you do?*

"You sure?" he said finally. "I mean . . . how do you
know?"

"I . . . didn't have my time. I went to the clinic, and
the doctor told me."

"Couldn't he be wrong?" He was trying to think—
*When did I not use protection? When we were drinking
wine that night, or when we were in a hurry . . . ?*

"No," she said, the finality in her voice started a dull
throbbing in the pit of his stomach.

"Does your mama know? She'll kill me. She hates my

guts anyway. She said if I saw you again she was going to shoot me or call the cops . . ."

"She don' know," Merida said softly. "Nobody else knows." She made a little choking sound like a rabbit being strangled.

"Don't cry!" he said too loudly and too sharply, and then realized that she was already crying, her head bent and the tears rolling down her cheeks in large drops. He felt protective of her, more like a big brother than a lover. *Do I love Merida?* he asked himself; the question, so simply stated, baffled him. He wasn't sure he knew what love would feel like. Did it feel like good sex? Or was it like knowing somebody was there to talk easy to you? Or did it feel awesome and silent, like sitting in church?

"Please," Rico said as he stopped at a traffic light with a row of other lowriders. Feet punched accelerators, challenging him, but he paid no attention. "Don't cry, okay?" She stopped after another moment but didn't look at him, then fumbled in her purse for a tissue to blow her nose. *Sixteen!* Rico thought. *She's just turned sixteen!* And here he was like all the rest of the strutting, Saturday night boulevard crowd, dressed in his tight chinos and pale blue shirt, gold chains and a tiny coke spoon dangling from his neck like a macho stud, going to take his woman to get something to eat, hit a disco or two, and then return her to his bed for a quick sex session. Only now there was a very big difference—he had gotten Merida pregnant, filled up a child with a child, and now he felt weighed down with age and the serious concerns he'd never dreamed about even in his worst nightmares. He imagined that if he could see his face—lean and high-cheekboned and handsome in a dark, dangerous way because of a nose that had been broken twice and set badly both times—he would be able to see faint lines around his eyes and crinkling in his forehead. In that instant he wanted to be a little boy again, playing with red plastic cars on a cold wooden floor while his mother and father talked about Mr. Cabrillo running off with Mr. Hernandez's wife as his big sister sat spinning the dial of her new transistor radio back and forth. He wanted to be a child forever, without worries or weights around his neck. But his mother and father had been dead for almost six years now, killed in a fire that had started from a spark from bad electrical wiring; the fire had roared through

the tenement building like a volcanic whirlwind, and
three floors had collapsed before the first of the fire engines arrived. Rico had been running with a street gang
called the Cripplers then, and was huddled under a stairway, drinking red wine with three buddies, when he'd
heard the fire engines screaming; it was a noise that even
now sometimes awakened him and made him break out
in a cold sweat. His sister Deanne was a model up in San
Francisco now, or so she said in her infrequent letters.
She always wrote that she was about to do a shooting for
some magazine or other, or that she'd met a man who
was going to get her into commercials. Once she'd written
that she was going to be the June Playmate, but of course
the girl in that month's Playboy was blond and blue-eyed
and worlds away from the barrio. He hadn't seen his
sister in two years, and the last letter had been over six
months before.

The traffic light flickered to green. Around him the
lowriders screeched off, leaving thick trails of rubber. He
realized he was gripping Merida's hand very tightly.

"Everything's going to be okay," he told her. "You'll
see." And then she quickly slid across the seat to him, as
close as a second skin, and if love felt anything like pity,
then yes, Rico loved her. "Listen, you want a hamburger or something? I can stop there." He motioned
toward a Fat Jim's burger stand, a huge, livid, neon hamburger floating in the sky. She shook her head. "Okay.
We'll eat later." He took his pack of Winstons off the
dashboard and lit a cigarette. A black and white prowl
car went gliding by in the opposite direction, the eyes of
the cop at the wheel meeting Rico's for one glacial, heart-
stopping instant. Rico was carrying a few grams of coke
and some nickel bags of fine Colombian Red in a box that
rested in a cavity cut beneath the rubber padding of the
trunk. That was his business now, supplying coke to the
kids who hung around the rock clubs on Sunset Strip.
Though he was just a nickel-and-dimer, he was making
enough money to keep himself in good threads. And his
supplier, a bald guy who wore Pierre Cardin business
suits and called himself Gypsy John, said he had the
nerve and ambition to be big in the trade someday. Not
as big as Gypsy John, of course, but big enough. Rico let
his gaze coolly slither away from the cop's and jockeyed
into position behind a Thunderbird painted in tiger

stripes. Someone called him from the curb, and he glanced over to see Felix Ortega and Benny Gracion standing with two fine-looking foxes in front of the Go-Go Disco. Rico raised his hand and shouted, "How's it goin', *amigos?*" but did not stop because they were walking reminders of his time with the Cripplers.

And finally Merida asked the question Rico had dreaded. "What are we going to do?" Eyes shining, she watched him carefully for any sign of betrayal.

He shrugged, cigarette dangling from his lower lip. "What do you wanna do?"

"It's your baby."

"It's yours too!" he said loudly, anger first filling his face with blood—*why hadn't she been on the pill or something!*—and then the flush of shame spreading hotly across his cheeks. "Oh, Jesus," he said hoarsely. "I don't know what I'm supposed to do!"

"You love me, don't you? You said you did. If you hadn't said that, I wouldn't have let you do it to me. You been the first and the only."

He nodded grimly, remembering the first time he'd taken her. It had been in the backseat of his car in a drive-in out near Southgate. He'd felt proud after it was over because she was his first virgin, and he knew you weren't really a man until you'd broken in a virgin. He remembered what Felix Ortega had told him once in the abandoned warehouse the Cripplers used as headquarters—"Fuck a virgin, man, and she'll love you forever."

Oh, Christ! he thought. *Forever? With just one chick? I got a business to think of. I could be buying myself silk shirts pretty soon, and alligator shoes, or a fine, black Porsche. I could get one of those penthouse apartments like the movie stars have. I could really be somebody in this town, I could be bigger than Gypsy John even!* But now he saw his path, and it wound straight back to the black, bitter heart of the barrio. In ten years he would be working in some garage and coming home at five to a two-room apartment where Merida and two or three kids waited, snotty noses and all; his hands would be black with engine grime, and his gut would be spreading from all the beer with the boys on Saturday nights. Merida would be haggard, the kids underfoot all the time and the close confines of the tenement making her nervous and jumpy, different from the beautiful girl she was now. They would argue about his future—why he couldn't find a better-paying job and why he had no more ambition—and life would start to close in around his throat, choking him to death. *NO!* he told himself. *I CAN'T DO THAT!* He reached down and turned the radio up loud so he couldn't hear himself think.

"Merida," he said, "I want you to be sure. I mean . . . I want you to be for certain that . . . you know . . . the kid's mine . . ." He was groping, looking for something to put between himself and the decision that had to be made. Instantly he felt like a traitor, a coward to the very pit of his soul. But he knew the truth—he didn't love her enough to change his life for her.

She turned her face away from him and very slowly straightened her spine so that she was sitting totally upright and not slumped as she had been a moment before. She moved away from him, her hands clenched in her lap.

So, Rico told himself. *Now she understands. Oh, Christ, this is shitty, man! You're treating her like common pussy, some Crippler groupie, or the neon-daubed hustlers who call out their rates from each side of the boulevard.*

And then Merida, a sob bursting from her throat, leaped from the Chevy before Rico knew what was happening. She ran down the street in the opposite direction, lowriders swerving around her, drivers cursing or calling out rude invitations. "Merida!" Rico shouted. He twisted the wheel, ran up onto the curb, then jerked the keys out of the ignition. Then he was out and running along Whittier, trying to find her among the hundreds of glaring, white headlights that stared impassively back at him. "MERIDA!" he called, braving a green Ford whose driver invited him to stick his head up his ass. He ran on through the traffic, being cursed in a variety of languages and inflections, but he didn't care. Merida was too young, too innocent, to be alone on a Saturday night on this neon hell of a boulevard. She didn't know the potential dangers, she was too trusting. *After all,* he thought bitterly, *she trusted me, and I'm the worst kind of rapist—I took her soul.* Half-blinded by charging headlights, he continued on, leaping aside as a burly, red-bearded biker swept past him on a blue chopper. Something shimmered on the pavement, and Rico bent to pick it up. It was Merida's silver crucifix, his birthday present to her. The clasp was broken where she'd ripped it off her neck; the necklace was still warm from her body heat.

"Merida!" he shouted, staring into a blaze of lights. "I'm sorry!"

But the night had swallowed her up, she was gone, and he knew that even if she did hear him calling over the tumultuous noise, she wouldn't turn back. No, she had too much pride for that, and in comparison to her, Rico felt slimy, covered with contagious sores.

He saw the blue light of that prowl car approaching, sliding through the lowriders. He was pierced by cold panic as he thought of his merchandise sitting in the Chevy's trunk, an easy score for the cops if they decided to see what he was carrying. Whirling around, he ran for the sidewalk, shoving people aside in his race with the prowl car. Pimps in peacock suits and their hot-pants clad hustlers slipped into doorways as the cops drove past. The blue light was going around and around, filling the air with electric resentment, but the cops weren't riding their siren. Rico slid behind the Chevy's wheel, jammed the key into the ignition, and backed off the curb, then spun the wheel sharply and merged with the slow, westbound traffic. About a block ahead he saw that two lowriders had slammed together in the middle of the boulevard, and a couple of guys were scuffling, urged on by a tight ring of onlookers. As Rico swerved past them, he heard the heart-stopping shrill of the police siren and, looking into his rearview mirror, he saw the prowl car stop to break up the fight. He punched his accelerator and slid smoothly around the slower cars. *No cops giving me hassles tonight,* he told himself. *Shit, I've had hassles enough!*

And then he remembered Merida, alone on the boulevard. He couldn't leave her for the mass of predators who were all looking for fresh meat. He found a clear spot, made a fast U-turn, and drove back past the prowl car, past where Merida had leaped out into the street. Figures that had vanished into dark alleys and doorways were now reemerging to hawk their wares. The sidewalks were crowded with hungry humanity, and in that jostling crush one skinny, pregnant, Chicano girl would hardly matter. Rico was frightened for her; he held the silver chain and crucifix clenched in one hand, and though he was not a particularly religious man, he wished she'd kept it on for good luck. He thought, *I'll find her. If it takes me all night, I'll find her.*

His Chevy moved on into the night, borne along and finally lost in the sea of metal.

SIX

Palatazin was standing at the locked iron gates of Hollywood Memorial Cemetery as Merida Santos was leaping from the red Chevy on Whittier Boulevard. His hands had closed around the bars, and he stood staring in as a chill evening breeze clattered palm leaves overhead. It was almost seven o'clock, and he realized that he'd told Jo on the telephone that he would pick her up at six-thirty for their dinner at The Budapest. He decided to tell her that something had come up at the office, to keep this cemetery thing to himself. Because what if he was wrong? That would make him as crazy as Lieutenant Kirkland had thought he was. *Stake out a cemetery?* Kirkland had asked incredulously over the telephone. *What for?*

"Because," he'd said, "I asked you to. That should be enough."

"I'm sorry, captain," Kirkland had replied, "but I'll have to have more than that. Saturday night in Hollywood can be pretty damned rough, as you well know. Now what exactly does this have to do with the vandalism?"

"It's . . . it's very important that you do as I ask." Palatazin knew he was sounding crazy and that his voice was high and nervous and that Lieutenant Kirkland was probably grinning at one of his detectives, making a circular motion at his temple with his forefinger. "Please, lieutenant. No questions, not just yet. I'm only asking for a man or two out there tonight."

"Captain, Hollywood Memorial has their own watchman."

"But what happened to the watchman who was out

there last night? Has anyone found him? No, I don't think so."

"Sorry." Kirkland had let a hint of irritation creep into his voice. "Why don't you send some of your own men if you want the cemetery watched so badly?"

"All my men are working day and night on finding the Roach. I can't ask any of them to . . ."

"Same here, sir. I can't. It's not justified." Kirkland had laughed softly. "I don't think those stiffs are going to be causing any trouble out there tonight, sir. I have to go, captain, if there's nothing else."

"No. Nothing else."

"Nice talking with you, captain. Sorry I couldn't help you out. Good hunting to you. Hope you nail that guy pretty soon."

"Yes. Good-bye, lieutenant." And Palatazin had heard Kirkland hang up his phone.

Now, for the second time today, he stood at the gates of the cemetery. This afternoon he'd watched the officers from the Hollywood Division walking around out there, stepping over skeletons; then the insurance and mortuary people had come in, followed by the dump trucks and work crews. Now the place looked serene again with the grassy knolls whitened by moonlight, the new mounds of dirt the only reminder that something terrible had happened here last night.

"Can I help you?" someone said from the darkness on the other side of the gate. A flashlight was flicked on, the beam directed into Palatazin's face. Palatazin reached for his wallet and showed his badge. "Oh. Sorry." The flashlight beam dropped, and a watchman in a dark gray uniform materialized from the night. He was a tall, white-haired man with friendly blue eyes. He wore a Hollywood Memorial badge on his shirt. "I'm Kelsen," he said. "What can I do for you?"

"Nothing, thank you. I just came to . . . look."

"To look? You should come back on Monday and take the tour—they show you all the celebrity graves." Kelsen smiled, but when Palatazin didn't respond, the smile faded. "Looking for anything in particular?"

"No. I was here earlier this afternoon when the officers were investigating."

"Oh, so that's it. Damndest thing I ever heard tell of. I didn't exactly see any of it, but I heard about it when they called me in. I don't usually work on Saturday nights. My wife pitched a fit."

"I imagine she did," Palatazin said quietly. "The man who worked last night. I understand his name was Zachary?"

"Yeah, old Zack." Kelsen leaned against the gate; behind him light streamed through the window of the watchman's station. "He usually has the weekend shift. Now he turns up missing, so they call me in." He shrugged and smiled again. "I don't care, I need the money. Listen, you people don't think Zack had anything to do with what happened here last night, do you?"

"I don't know. I don't work in the Hollywood Division."

"Oh." Kelsen frowned and swung his light up toward Palatazin again. "So why are you interested? I mean, it's damned strange and all, but I thought the cops wrapped it up today. Vandalism, right? Some cult kids who maybe needed coffins for . . . whatever it is they do. I heard the same thing happened over at Hope Hill Cemetery last week; somebody clipped the lock on the gates, tore up a few graves, and made off with five or six coffins. Hope Hill's a small cemetery, you know, and they can't afford a watchman, so nobody knows what happened. Just crazy kids, I guess. It's a crazy world, right?"

"Yes. Crazy."

"Listen, do you want to come in or something? Take a look around? I've got an extra flashlight."

Palatazin shook his head. "No need for that. I wouldn't find anything." He stared at Kelsen, his eyes going dark and cold. "Mr. Kelsen," he said, "is there a lock on the door of your little house there?"

"Yeah, there's a lock. Why?"

"Because I'm going to suggest that you do something, and I want you to listen to me very carefully." Palatazin's hands curled tighter around the bars. "If I tried to explain to you why I want you to do this, you wouldn't understand. So just listen, please."

"Okay," the watchman said, but he stepped back a pace from the man at the gate whose gaze had gone so hard and chilling.

"If anyone else comes to this gate tonight—man, woman, or child—you should lock your door and draw the blinds. If you hear this gate opening, you should turn up your radio very loud so you can't hear. And you should not come out to look. Let whoever it may be do as he or she pleases. But do not—*do not*—come out to try to stop them."

"That's . . . that's my job," Kelsen said softly, a crooked grin frozen on his face. "What is this, a joke? *Candid Camera?* What's going on?"

"I'm deadly serious, Mr. Kelsen. Are you a religious man?"

This guy's not a cop! Kelsen thought. *He's a freakin' nut!* "I'm a Catholic," he said. "Listen, what's your name?"

"If and when someone comes to this gate tonight," Palatazin continued, ignoring the question, "you should pray. Pray very loudly, don't pay any attention to anything they say to you." He squinted when the watchman's light hit his face. "Perhaps if you pray hard enough, they'll leave you in peace."

"I think you should go, mister," Kelsen said. "Get out of here before I call a *real* cop!" His face was contorted, and his once friendly eyes turned mean. "Go on, buddy, get out!" He started for the telephone on his desk. "I'm calling the cops right now!"

"All right," Palatazin said, "all right, I'm going." Kelsen stopped and looked back; the flashlight in his hand was shaking. "But remember what I've told you. Please. Pray, and keep praying."

"Yeah, yeah, yeah! I'll pray for *you*, you crazy freak!" Kelsen disappeared into his station and slammed the door behind him. Palatazin turned, walked quickly to his car and drove away; he was trembling, his stomach churning slowly. *Hope Hill Cemetery, did the man say? This has happened before? Oh my God,* he thought, trying to keep down a rising wave of nausea. *Please, no. Don't let it happen again! Not here! Not in Los Angeles!*

He hoped he was crazy; he hoped the pressure of the Roach killings was beginning to get to him, that he was seeing grinning shadows where nothing existed but the warped antics of . . . What had Kelsen said? . . . kids who belonged to some crazy cult? A hundred cults, a thousand of them, would be easier to deal with than what he was beginning to fear had ripped those coffins out of the ground. He had been sleeping in his bed less than six blocks away when it had happened, and perhaps when he'd awakened from the dream about his mother, the things were here at work.

Too late, Palatazin realized he'd turned off Santa Monica Boulevard and driven right past Romaine Street, heading south on Western. He touched the brakes for only an instant and then drove on because he knew where he was going.

The gray-bricked building on First Street was empty now—it had been condemned years ago—and the broken edges of glass gleamed in the windows. It looked desolate and forlorn, as if it had been abandoned for a very long time; the walls were smeared with old graffiti —he could see one faded white declaration that read *Seniors Fine in '59.* Somewhere in that graffiti would still be two painful statements scrawled by the hand of a vicious child—*Palatazin Sucks 'em* and *Old Lady P. Is Gonna Burn In Hell For Crazy People.*

He lifted his gaze to the top floor windows. All broken now, all dark and empty; but for an instant he thought he saw his mother up there, much younger of course, her hair almost fully gray but her eyes not nearly as haunted and wild as he remembered them at the end. She was peering out onto First Street, watching the corner where little André, now in the sixth grade, would cross carrying his green Army backpack filled with notebooks and pencils, math texts and history homework. When he reached that corner, he always looked up, and his mother would always wave from the window. Three times a week a woman named Mrs. Gibbs would come by to help him with his English; he was still having difficulties, though most of the teachers at his elementary school spoke Hungarian. Up in that small, dark apartment, the extremes of temperature had been almost unbearable; at the height of summer the place was an oven even with all the windows open, and when a cold winter wind blew down from the mountains and shook the ancient window frames, André could see the faint, wraithlike plume of his mother's breath. Every night, no matter what the season, she peered fearfully down onto the street, checked and rechecked the three dead-bolt locks on the door, and paced the floor muttering and crying until the downstairs neighbors slammed the ceiling with a broom and shouted, "Go to sleep, you witch woman!"

André was never liked or even tolerated by the other

children in the neighborhood, a hodgepodge of Jewish, Hungarian, and Polish families, because their parents were afraid of his mother, because they discussed the "witch woman" over their dinner tables and told the children they'd better stay away from her son, he might be crazy in the head, too. His friends were those awkward, shy, or backward children who do not quite fit in with the others, who can find no place to exist except on the outer rim and consequently play alone most of the time. On some occasions when he grew nervous, André the witch woman's son lapsed into speaking Hungarian with a thick accent. Then he would be chased home from school by a pack of children who threw stones and laughed whenever he tripped and fell.

It was very hard for him, because home was no refuge. It was a prison where his mother scrawled crucifixes on the walls and windows and doors with red Crayola crayons, where she shrieked out in the night from the images that seared her brain, where she sometimes lay in her bed for days at a time, curled up like a fetus, staring blankly at a wall. It became progressively worse and worse, and even Uncle Milo, his mother's brother who had immigrated to America in the late thirties and owned a successful men's clothing store, began to stop in and ask her if she would like to go someplace where she wouldn't have to worry about anything anymore, where there were people to take care of her and keep her happy. *No!* she'd screamed during one terrible argument that kept Uncle Milo away for weeks. *No! I won't leave my son alone!*

What would I find up there if I went in? Palatazin asked himself, staring up at the front room. A few newspapers all cut in pieces, lying in a thick sediment of dust? Perhaps an old dress or two hanging in a closet? Things best forgotten? Some of the crucifixes might still be scrawled on the walls, close to the nail holes where the religious pictures had hung in their gaudy gilded frames. Palatazin, grown-up André, looked up to the window where he thought he saw the pale, ghostly face of a woman waiting for her son to come home. He didn't like to think about those last months; putting her in Golden Garden and leaving her there to die had torn him to pieces, but what else could he have done? She couldn't take care of herself anymore; she had to be fed like a baby, and very often she spat up her food like a baby or soiled the awful rubber, diaperlike thing she wore. She was wasting away to nothing, alternately praying and crying. Her eyes had become the largest thing about her. As she sat in her favorite rocking chair day after day and stared down upon Romaine Street, her eyes became luminous, as large as pale white moons. So he'd sent her away where the doctors and nurses could take care of her. She'd died of a stroke in a small room with forest-green walls and a window that looked out on a golf course. She'd been dead for two hours before a nurse came in to check on her at six o'clock in the morning.

Palatazin remembered her last words to him, the very night before she died. "André, André," she'd said softly, reaching up her frail, white hand to grip his arm. "What time is it? Is it day or night?"

"Night, Mama," he replied. "It's almost eight o'clock."

"Night comes too fast. Always too fast. Is the door locked?"

"Yes." It wasn't, of course, but when he told her that it was, he could see that it comforted her.

"Good. My good André, you must never forget to . . . to lock the door. Oh, I'm so sleepy. I can hardly keep my eyes open. I heard that black cat scratching on the front door this morning, so I shooed it away. They should keep that cat in their apartment."

"Yes, Mama." A black cat had belonged to their next-door neighbors in the First Street apartment building; after all these years it must surely be dust.

And then his mother's eyes had clouded over, and for a long time she'd stared at her son without speaking. "André, I'm afraid," she'd said finally, her voice cracking like old, yellowed paper. The tears glimmered in her eyes, and Palatazin had carefully wiped them away with a handkerchief when they started to roll down her cheeks. She'd gripped his hand tightly, her flesh as dry as leather. "One of them . . . one of them followed me when I came back from the market. I heard him walking behind me, and when I . . . turned I saw his grinning face. I saw his eyes, André, his terrible burning eyes! He wanted me to . . . to take his hand and go with him . . . because of what I did to your papa . . ."

"Shhhhhh," Palatazin had said, wiping tiny beads of perspiration off her forehead. "You're wrong, Mama. There was no one. You were only imagining it." He remembered the night she was recalling, she'd dropped a sack of groceries and run home, screaming. It had been the last night she'd ever left the apartment. "They can't hurt us now, Mama. We're too far away for them to ever find us again."

"NO!" she'd said, her eyes widening. Her face was as pale as a china plate, her fingernails digging half-moons into his hand. "DON'T YOU EVER BELIEVE THAT! If you don't watch for them always . . . ALWAYS! . . . they can come for you and find you. They're always there, André . . . you just can't see them . . ."

"Why don't you try to sleep now, Mama? I'll sit here with you until I have to leave, all right?"

"Leave?" she'd said, suddenly panicked. "Leave? Where are you going?"

"Home. I have to go home. Jo's waiting for me."

"Jo?" She'd looked at him suspiciously. "Who's that?"

"My wife, Mama. You know who Jo is, she came with me to see you last night."

"Oh, stop that! You're just a little boy! Even in California they don't let little boys get married! Did you get that milk I asked you to bring on the way back from school?"

He'd nodded and tried to smile. "I brought it."

"That's good." And then she'd settled back and closed her eyes. After another moment her grip on his hand had loosened enough for him to pull away. He'd sat and gazed at her for a long time; she looked so different, but still there was something there of the woman he'd known a long time ago, the one who'd sat in the little stone house in Krajeck, knitting a sweater for her son. When he'd stood up very quietly to leave, his mother's eyes had opened again, and this time they burned through to his soul. "I won't leave you, André," she'd whispered. "I won't leave my son alone." And then she was asleep again, just that quickly, her mouth half-open, and the breath rustling in and out of her lungs. There was an odor in the room like lilacs on the edge of decay.

Palatazin had slipped out of the room, and a doctor named Vacarella had called him just after six the next morning.

My God! Palatazin thought suddenly and looked at his wristwatch. *Jo is waiting at home!* He started the car, glanced up once more at the top-floor window—now empty, the broken pane catching a little leftover light from someone else's house—and drove toward Romaine Street. When he stopped at a traffic light two blocks away, he thought he heard dogs howling very far away in a strange close harmony. But when the light changed and he drove on, he didn't hear them anymore—or perhaps he was afraid to listen. Thoughts of Hollywood Memorial loomed up too quickly for him to cut them off. His hands began to sweat on the steering wheel.

They can't hurt us now, he thought. *We're too far away. Too far away. Too far away.*

And from the depths of his memory, his mother's voice answering, *Don't you ever believe that. . . .*

SEVEN

Merida Santos had run a long way from the noisy tumult of Whittier Boulevard, and her legs were beginning to ache. She stopped and leaned against a half-demolished brick wall to rub her calves. Her lungs were burning, too, her eyes felt gummy with tears, and her nose was running. *Damn Rico!* she thought. *I hate him, HATE HIM, HATE HIM!* She thought of what she should do to him: Tell Luis he'd beaten her up and raped her, so the Homicides would go after him and cut him to pieces; tell her mother he'd gotten her drunk and had his way with her, so she'd call the cops on him; call the police herself and tell them she knew somebody who was selling cocaine to kids on the Strip and ask them if they would like to know his name.

But in the next instant her plans of vengeance broke apart in a single sob. She couldn't do any of those things. She couldn't bear to see him hurt; she would rather die than think of him being beaten up by the Homicides or put in jail. From a bitter spark of her anger and hurt, the hot flame of love—and of need, both physical and emotional—leapt up, its crazy brightness making new tears stream down her cheeks. She started trembling and couldn't stop. A hole had opened up somewhere in the pit of her stomach, and she felt she was in danger of being swallowed into it, turned inside out, and then all the world would see the tiny fetus just beginning to take form within her. She hoped that the baby would be a boy with the same coffee-and-cream eyes that Rico had.

But now what was to be done? Tell Mama? She shivered at the thought. Her mother hadn't acted right since Papa died last year; she was suspicious of every move Merida made—doubly suspicious of what Luis did, and that just made Luis stay away from home more—and lately had begun awakening Merida in the middle of the night to question her about the kids she was running around with, about what they did. Smoke that filthy weed? Get drunk on wine? Luis had told Mama that Merida had been seeing Rico and that Rico was a big man in the coke trade up on Sunset Boulevard. Luis, only twelve, was running with the Homicides almost every night now, and the barrio toughs hated Rico because he'd once been where they were and had made it out. Merida's mother had gone into a screaming fit, threatening to lock Merida in a closet or turn her over to the social worker lady if she kept seeing "that Esteban *mugre.*" Now what would happen if she told her mother she was carrying his baby in her belly?

Or she could go to see Father Silvera first, and perhaps he could help her talk to her mother. Yes. That was the thing to do.

Merida wiped her swollen eyes and looked around to get her bearings. She really hadn't noticed where she was running. The narrow street stretched out before her, lined with brown brick buildings that were gutted and desolate, bombed and burned out by the hands of the arsonist or feuding street gangs. Mounds of rubble glittered with bits of broken glass; layers of yellow mist hung over empty lots where a rat as big as a gopher occasionally scurried from shadow to shadow. Some of the buildings looked as if they'd been split right down the middle by a huge axe, the tiny rooms and hallways exposed as were the metal twistings of pipes, the toilets, and the tubs. And everywhere was the wild spray-painted scrawl: ZORRO '78; L.A. HOMICIDES (and beneath that in a different color, SUCK); RAPHAEL HIGH CONQUISTADORS BEST; GOMEZ WAS HERE; ANITA DOES 69. There were also drawings of crude sexuality interspersed. On the side of a wrecked apartment building, staring impassively down at Merida, was a huge face,

drawn in red with blood dripping from both corners of
the mouth.

Merida shivered; it was getting colder, wind twisting
savagely through the maze of wreckage as it sought a way
out. And now she realized that she'd run too far. She had
no idea where she was. She could turn around and see
lights in the sky from Whittier Boulevard, but in this silent place the boulevard seemed a hundred miles away.
She began to walk hurriedly, new tears wetting her eyes;
she crossed the street and moved along another that became narrower still and was rank with the odor of old,
charred brick. Of course her street, her apartment building, couldn't be too far away; it would have to be only a
few streets over. Mama would be waiting, wanting to
know where she'd been.

She was wondering what she was going to say about her
swollen eyes when she heard the footsteps behind her. She
caught her breath and whirled around; something dark
scurried for the shadows like a rat, but whatever it was
was big enough to be a man. Merida narrowed her eyes,
squinting to get a better look, and she stood very still for
what seemed like hours. Then she started walking again,
faster, her heart hammering in her chest. *A young, pretty
girl like you can get raped out there,* she remembered her
mother saying. *Raped or much, much worse.* She walked
faster, and at the next desolate corner she turned again
toward the distant lights of Whittier. She looked back and
saw two figures this time, both leaping for the cover of
open doorways. Merida almost screamed, but forced
down the sound. She thought she'd seen a face as white
as gossamer and within it a pair of eyes that shone in the
dark like a lowrider's headlights. Footsteps clattered
somewhere close to her, echoing between the brick walls
like muffled explosions.

Merida began to run, the breath bursting from her
lungs in a high whine. When she dared to look over her
shoulder, she saw five or maybe seven figures, running
silently like a pack of wolves; they were gaining on her,
and the one in the lead had a face like a grinning death's
head. She tripped over debris in the street, cried out, and
almost went down. Then she was running as fast as she
could, her mother's warning echoing in her head—*Raped
or much, much worse.* She looked back again and

screamed in cold panic. They were almost upon her; one of them reached out to grip her hair.

And from the darkness of the street, three more of the things emerged before her, waiting for her. She recognized one of them—Paco Milan, one of Luis's friends from the Homicides, except now Paco's face was as pale as the belly of a dead fish, and his fiery gaze crackled through Merida's skull. She thought she heard him speak, though his mouth didn't seem to open, "No more running, sister," he whispered, the sound like a wind through dead trees. "No more place to go." He held his arms out for her and grinned.

A clawlike hand gripped Merida around the neck and jerked her head backward. Another clamped her mouth shut, freezing fingers digging into her flesh. The figures danced around her as she was dragged toward a doorway.

And in a crumbling hulk of brick, she learned that there *was* something worse than rape. *Much, much worse.*

EIGHT

It was almost midnight, and the party was just getting started. The hospitality bowls that had been brimming with Quaaludes and amphetamines, Black Beauties, Bennies, and uppers of a hundred different sizes and colors were now almost empty; the silver trays that had been crisscrossed with white lines of fine, pure cocaine were now only dusted with the traces of it, and the ceramic vases that had held dozens of red-striped McDonald's drinking straws now contained only a few. But the house was still filled with people of all ages and in all manner of dress from Bill Blass suits to Yves St. Laurent disco dresses to denim cutoffs and T-shirts advertising Adidas or Nike running shoes. The huge sunken living room to which most of the party had gravitated was heavy with several layers of sweet, thick pot smoke; the beige, deep-pile carpeting had started catching cigarettes when the ashtrays had overflowed, and now the dime-sized burns looked like a natural pattern. Someone was hammering at the grand piano over by a plate glass window that looked out over the blue-lit swimming pool; someone else was playing a guitar and singing, all this plus the cacophonous noises of a hundred people battling the thunder of Bob Dylan's voice from a pair of thousand-dollar Bose speakers. The house throbbed with bass guitar and snare drum backbeat; the picture windows shivered every few seconds. Somebody in a cowboy hat was trying to climb on top of the grand piano urged on by a stunning blond wearing a tight black dress. A few women had stripped off their blouses, proud of what they had, and moved through the crowd pursued by young men with bulging crotches. Older men in suits, confident of the power in their bulging wallets, were content to wait. Dylan's voice became a shriek when the stereo's needle dug a trench across it; he was replaced by the Cars.

Damn it, Wes Richer thought. *I like Dylan. Why'd somebody want to go and do that to my record?* He smiled and took a drag off the fat joint that was slowly burning down between his fingers. *Doesn't matter,* he reassured himself. *I can buy another one tomorrow.* He looked around the room through glazed blue eyes. Stellar. One fucking whale of a stellar party. Tonight he felt he had the answer to a question that had plagued him for most of his twenty-five years. The simple question was addressed to God: *Whose side are You on, anyway?* As he regarded the glowing eye of his joint, he knew he had the answer right in his back pocket, just arrived in a Cosmic Fortune Cookie: *Your side, Wes. God is on your side.*

But He hadn't always been, Wes thought. *Damn straight.* He fashioned an image of God in his mind—an elderly, slightly doddering being in a white London Fog overcoat with a gold muffler to chase away the chill of the high altitude. God would look suspiciously like Wes Richer in his "old man in the park" bit, and—*yeah, give the bit a kick*—God might talk a little like a tired Jewish, vacuum cleaner salesman: "Wesley, I got a lot to do, I can't get around to everybody! Who do you think I am, Santa Claus? There's this guy over in New Jersey wants to get away with a little cheating on the taxes; a lady in Chicago keeps after Me to send her lost dog home, but the mutt got run over by a bus; a pimply kid in Des Moines wants to pass a history test or he's completely *vermisched;* this fella in Palm Springs wants Me to keep his wife from finding out he's got three women on the side . . . everybody wants something, Wes! And that's just right down there in the US of A! What am I, Dear Abby? And you, Wes! You keep wanting to know whose side I'm on, and why your last pilot went down the tubes, and why you can't win anymore at the blackjack tables! *Gevult,* what a mess down there! I slap My own hands! Okay, okay, so maybe if I help you out, you'll quit bugging Me so I can get on to bigger things? Okay, boom, there you go! Happy now? So enjoy it already!"

God had come through for him today; this afternoon he'd won over two-thousand bucks betting on Alabama over USC, and the premiere of his new show, "Sheer Luck" looked good in its seven-thirty spot on ABC. At least everybody here had laughed in the right places and applauded when it was over. And then the party had *really* started.

The Cars were thundering away now, and from his chair Wes could see some people swimming bare-assed down at the pool. He laughed out loud, his bright Midwestern face crinkling with mirth; he was a medium-sized man with a curly thatch of reddish-brown hair and thick eyebrows that also seemed curly, set high over light blue eyes that, when not totally bloodshot from drugs, seemed more like a kid's eyes. He had a healthy, friendly, innocent look—a "safe look" one of the ABC executives had dubbed it. It was a look that drew teenie-boppers and at the same time assured Mom and Dad that he was really an okay guy, probably a class cut-up but nothing to worry about. Like the assessment from another ABC brain— "an All-American comedian."

Someone jostled his elbow, spilling ashes onto the dirty carpet. Wes looked up and smiled but couldn't tell who was standing there. He thought for an instant that it was his father because the man had a mane of silver hair, but of course it couldn't be his father—he was back home in Nebraska, fast asleep at this hour. "There you are, Wes!" the man said. "I've been hunting all over this place for you! I missed the show, but I heard you were really great in it." A hand found Wes's and squeezed it. "The show's got *stellar* written all over it, boy. Good to see you again."

"Who are you?" Wes asked, still smiling and thinking about those fools in the pool who were freezing their nuts off because no one had turned on the heat.

The man's head was split in half by teeth. "Good to see you again, Wes. Great party!" And then he was gone,

swallowed up into the crowd that swirled around the chair
where Wes sat smoking.

I don't know that guy, do I? he wondered. *Jesus! Where
did all these people come from?* He looked around but
didn't seem to recognize any of them. *Who were they?
What the hell. They were all friends, or friends of friends.
Or somebody's fucking friends!* In another moment a couple of young women were standing over him, one in a violet dress, her breasts spilling over the top. He stared at
those breasts, still smiling easily, while the two girls chattered on about how good "Sheer Luck" had been and how
they'd never ever been to a party anywhere near this fine,
not even at Hef's place. *Who the hell were these girls?*
One of them—he wasn't sure which—put a hand on his
knee and slipped a little white card into the pocket of his
blue Ralph Lauren cowboy shirt. He knew it would have
her name and phone number on it in elegant black script;
everybody carried those around these days, it was essential to the wardrobe.

He caught a glimpse of her Ultra-Brite smile before the
party closed in around him again. A group called 1994
hammered away on the stereo now, Karen Lawrence's
lead vocals making the windows shake. *Christ, what a set
of pipes!* Wes thought languidly. He stared down at the
reefer and said to himself, "You've hit, Wes. You've come
back. God . . . is . . . on . . . your . . . side."

"Wes?" someone said, gripping his shoulder. He looked
up and saw his manager, Jimmy Kline, standing over him;
Jimmy's broad face looked beatific, his dark eyes shining
like little black buttons behind his wire-frame glasses.
There were two older men with Jimmy—Wes recognized
one of them as Harv Chappell, an exec at Arista Records.
Wes tried to stand up, but Jimmy pushed him back down.
"Stay right there, my man," Jimmy said in his thick
Brooklyn accent. "You know Harv Chappell, don't you?
And Max Beckworth? They liked the show, Wes. Every-
fuckinbody liked the show!"

"It was great, Wes," Harv said, smiling.

"Fantastic. Three seasons at least," Max said, smiling.

Wes nodded. "Hope so. You men need a drink, something to get mellow on?"

"We're going to be talking record contract with Arista
on Monday," Jimmy said, his eyes getting brighter and
brighter. The Hawaiian print shirt he was wearing, a wild

mixture of purples and oranges, seemed to glow in the dim, living-room light. "How's that grab you?"

"Great, just great."

"Of course," Jimmy turned to smile at the Arista execs, "we'll be negotiating with Warner's and A&M, too. You know Mike Steele over at A&M, don't you, Max? He's talking six figures on a single record deal with options."

Max shrugged. "Comedy records are risky," he said, glancing around the room to take stock of who was there. "Only Steve Martin and Robin Williams turn a profit these days, sometimes Richard Pryor if his material appeals to the kids. It's just too easy to take a bath with comedy these days.

"Baths? Who's talking about taking fucking baths? I'm talking about mass appeal, man, everybody from Farmer Jones to the punk crowd. Wes covers all the bases."

"We'll see, Jimmy. Let's wait for the ratings on 'Sheer Luck,' shall we?"

"Yeah, yeah. Uh . . . Wes, where's Solange?"

"I don't know," Wes said. "She was here a few minutes ago."

"The hospitality bowls are going dry. I'm going to get Joey to fill 'em up, okay?"

Wes smiled and nodded. "Sure. Anything you want to do. 'Sheer Luck' was pretty good, wasn't it?"

"Good? It was terrific! It'll be leading the schedule in three weeks!"

Wes reached up and caught Jimmy's arm as he and the Arista men started to move away. "Don't bullshit me," Wes said quietly. "It *was* good, wasn't it?"

"Stellar," Jimmy said; he flashed a quick smile and was gone.

God is on my side, Wes thought, relaxing again. And then: *Solange? Where the hell is she?* He rose unsteadily from the chair, and immediately a path cleared before him. Hands clapped him on the back, faces mouthed words he couldn't hear. He wandered around looking for Solange, the last of his reefer crumbling in ashes to the floor.

A moment later he found her, sitting with a group of people on the long, dark brown sofa near the center of the room. She was drinking white wine from a crystal goblet, her long brown fingers curved delicately around the stem. On a low table in front of her, three candles burned in

brass holders, the golden light setting amber fire to her
skin, glittering in the black pools of her slightly almond-
shaped eyes. A backgammon board and a huge vase of
dried flowers had been cleared away to make room for a
Ouija board; Solange was staring at the white planchette
as she drank her wine, her gaze at once vacant and intense. A few people sat around her, smoking pot and
drinking wine, looking from Solange's beautiful, sculpted,
Oriental-African face to the board. "Come on, Solange,"
Wes heard one of the men say. "Do it for us. Call up . . .
oh . . . call up Marilyn Monroe or somebody."

Solange smiled faintly. "You want party games. You
don't want to be serious," she said in a voice as cool as
the October wind.

"We'll be serious," the guy said, but he was smiling too
widely. "Promise. Come on, call up . . . Sharon Tate . . ."

"Oh, Christ, no!" a girl with long, shimmering waves of
blond hair said, her eyes terror-stricken; Wes recognized
her from the current NBC hit, "Skate Fever."

"How about Oswald?" somebody else said, blowing on
a stick of jasmine incense just to make the sparks fly.
"That fucker'll talk to anybody."

"Clifton Webb." The NBC starlet slid over closer to
the Ouija board but seemed afraid to touch it. "I hear he's
prowling around again."

"No." Solange looked into a candle, her cat eyes narrowing. The candle flame flickered very gently. "I don't
think I want to do this tonight. Not here, not with everyone standing around." The light glittered off the hundred
or so tiny brass beads strung in the tight braids of her
ebony hair. "The spirits won't answer if the mood isn't
right."

"What's wrong with the mood?" the guy who wanted to
talk to Oswald asked; he waved the incense stick around,
his glazed eyes hypnotized. "Seems fine to me. Do it,
Solange. Call somebody up for us."

"The spirits don't like to be laughed at." She sipped at
the wine but did not move her gaze from the candle's
flame. From where he stood, Wes could see the flame undulating very slowly, and a sudden chill skittered down
his spine. It was the same kind of chill he'd felt when he'd
first looked into Solange's eyes in the Presidential Suite
of the Las Vegas Hilton almost a year ago.

"I've got it, luv," the thin young man sitting on

Solange's left said. He was Martin Blue, the British whiz-kid who'd produced Wes's first comedy album for Warner's over three years ago. Blue smiled like a fox. "Conjure up . . . oh, what was his name? . . . Kronsteen. Orlon Kronsteen."

The NBC starlet—Missy something, Wes thought her name was—laughed nervously. There was a moment of silence while the party swirled around the group at the table; Wes thought they looked afraid, all except Solange who wasn't smiling anymore.

Time to save her ass, he thought and stepped forward into the candlelight. "What is this?" he said, his voice somewhat slurred. "Ghost stories? It's not Halloween yet, kiddies."

"Hi there, Wes," Martin Blue said. "We're trying to get your woman here to conjure us up . . ."

"I don't conjure," Solange said softly.

"Yeah, I heard all this bullshit." Wes plopped himself down on the sofa and stretched. "You want to talk to Kronsteen so bad, Martin, why don't you hike on up to that little fortress he built and give out a yell? He'll probably come floating out with his head in his hand."

"Oh, don't!" Missy said and squirmed in her seat. "Wasn't he that old actor who . . . ?"

"Horror flick actor," Wes corrected her. "Made about a hundred of 'em. Enough to get rich on, at least. They still play some of them on Creature Features."

"What happened to him?" she asked, looking at Martin and Solange, then back to Wes.

"Kronsteen married a European heiress he met on location. It turned out she had cancer, leukemia, something like that; after she died, he went a little nuts and used the rest of their money to bring that castle over from Europe. About ten or eleven years ago, somebody stripped old Kronsteen naked up there, tortured him with cigarettes and a hot poker, and hung his corpse up from a chandelier when they were through. Oh, yeah, whoever did it cut Kronsteen's head off with a rusty hacksaw and took it with 'em when they left. One of the legends of Hollywood, my dear, guaranteed to send you out shopping for an electrified fence or a couple of guard dogs."

Missy shivered, and the guy next to her, the incense waver, took her hand.

"So you see?" Wes continued, his eyes scanning the

group, "there are a lot of Roaches in this town, a lot of homicidal nuts, and some of them would just love to go running around up here in Bel Air with a machete or an icepick. Sooner or later all us celebs have to wall ourselves in."

"You're kidding me. That's not true about Kronsteen . . . about his head."

"God's truth, luv," Martin said with a pleasant smile. He turned back to Solange, who was passing a finger back and forth through the flame. "Let's hear from Orlon, luv. *If* you can do it. *If* you're really a medium."

"Knock it off," Wes said. "This is a party, not a god-damned séance."

"Oh, but séances can be so much fun. And so informative. Maybe Orlon can tell us who the Roach is. A ghost can see everything, can't he?" He glanced at his gold Rolex. "Two minutes until midnight. The witching hour, eh?"

"Martin," Wes said sourly, "you've got your head up your ass." But when he looked at Solange, she was staring intensely, right through him.

"There is no need to call those who are already here," Solange whispered.

"Huh? What'd she say?" Martin leaned forward, but for a minute or so Solange didn't speak. Finally she whispered softly, "You're a fool, Martin. You want to play games with something beyond your understanding. The spirits see and know everything, and they are always here—in the shadow of a candle, at the center of its flame, stirring like smoke through the air. They are always trying to break through, to speak to those of us on this plane. Though most often we would not like what they have to say." She turned the full force of her gaze on Martin Blue.

"Well," he said, but his voice had climbed a pitch. "What are we waiting for? Let's find out who the Roach is, shall we? Or at least what happened to Mr. Kronsteen's head."

Solange glanced at Wes through heavy-lidded eyes. "Very well," she said softly. "Wes, will you sit beside me and help me guide the planchette?"

"How about letting me?" Martin asked quickly. "I've heard tales of your being able to do this sort of thing, but . . . I'd like to be sure it isn't faked. No offense of course, luv."

"Of course. None taken. Then slide over here so you'll be touching me, thigh to thigh. Now place your fingertips on the planchette opposite mine. That's too heavily, you have to let your fingers just graze the top of it. Ah. Better." She closed her eyes and smiled slightly. "I can feel the electricity already."

"I don't feel a fucking thing," Martin announced to the others.

"Solange," Wes said, "you don't have to prove . . ."

"I think I do. You're pressing again, Martin. Let your fingers relax."

Wes looked around; for the first time he realized that a lot of people had gathered around them and were watching with interest. The thunderous sound of the stereo had quieted to a dull rumble; the grand piano was silent.

"It's too loud in here. I can't concentrate," Solange said. A mumble rippled through the audience, and the stereo went off. Wes could hear drunken laughter from the pool. He leaned back on the sofa, watching Solange's brown face turn dreamy; Martin was smiling, mugging at people who stood around him.

"I don't think I like . . ." Missy began nervously. But Solange hissed, "Quiet!" From somewhere in the distance Wes thought he could hear the shrill pipings of wind through the Bel Air streets, over the manicured lawns and brick walls and wrought-iron gates, around the sharp angles of the million-dollar mansions. Solange's eyes had narrowed into slits; they rolled back until Wes could see the whites, and her mouth slowly opened. Missy gasped suddenly, and the gasp was repeated through the room. Wes felt his heartbeat quickening and wished he had another joint. "My mind is open," Solange said in an odd, faraway tone just above a whisper. "The pathway is open. Use us as your voice. My mind is open. The pathway is open. Use us as your voice . . ."

"Shall I intone anything?" Martin said. He laughed, but no one paid any attention.

". . . pathway is open. Use us as your voice. My mind is . . ."

Martin's eyes were getting larger, and if Wes hadn't been so tense, he might have laughed at the sight. "Jesus!" Martin said. "How long does this go . . . SHIT!" He jumped and pulled his fingers back from the planchette.

". . . us as your—*Martin, don't break the contact!*—
voice. My mind is open . . ."

He touched the planchette again but gingerly, his hands
trembling. "I thought I felt it . . . CHRIST! IT MOVED!"
But this time he kept his fingers on it, and as the planchette moved a tentative inch or so, another murmur went
through the onlookers. Wes leaned forward, his heart
pounding. The planchette stalled, then began to move
again smoothly now across the board. "We've made a contact," Solange whispered, her eyes still closed. "Let it flow.
Martin, you're trying to slow it down."

The planchette began to make long, slow circles. "Who
are you?" Solange asked. The planchette slid quickly over
to YES. She repeated the question, and it lay still for a
moment, then dropped toward the lines of black letters
imprinted on the board. "Read the letters off to me,"
Solange said.

Wes slid across the sofa so he could see the board better. "B," he read. "O . . . B . . ." The planchette dipped
and swirled as if riding on a waxed surface. "Another
B . . . Y . . ." The planchette stopped. "Bobby."

"Bobby will act as our guide, then," Solange whispered.
"The contact is strengthening now. It's becoming very
strong . . ."

"My fucking fingers are burning . . ." Martin croaked.

"What did you do in life?" Solange asked.

The planchette started to spell again, faster than before. Wes read, "M . . . E . . . S . . . S . . . A . . .
G . . . E . . ." That word was repeated twice more, faster
each time.

And then another word took shape. "E," Wes said.
"V . . . I . . . Evil. It's spelling *Evil.*"

"Is that your message?" Solange's voice was a quiet
murmur in the silent room. "What does it mean?"

The planchette spun in a mad circle, dropped back to
the letters. E, V, I, L, E, V, I, L.

"Are there others with you?"

YES.

"Who?"

S, A, M, E, L, I, K, E, M, E.

"Christ!" Missy breathed and reached for her wineglass.
She spilled some on her designer jeans before it reached
her mouth.

"Who's the Roach?" Martin blurted out. "What's his name?"

The planchette was still. Solange repeated the two questions slowly, and almost immediately the planchette haltingly spelled out—E, V, I, L, U, S, I, N, G, H, I, M.

"Using him?" Wes said. "What's that supposed to mean?"

"There is one among us who would reach Orlon Kronsteen," Solange went on, in a whisper. "Is he with you?"

Immediately, YES.

"Then let him come forward."

There was a long pause. The planchette seemed to be dead. And then suddenly it almost leaped off the board. Martin said, "SHIT!" as the thing spun from side to side, from YES to NO to MAYBE and back again, three or four times. "Unfocused energy," Solange said calmly. "Quiet, quiet. Do you have a message?"

"This is even better than the *Crosswits*," Wes said under his breath; Martin glanced at him and giggled nervously.

But then the planchette dropped to the bottom of the board so quickly it seemed only a blur. It began to race along the lines of letters. Wes leaned forward. "E, V," he read. "EVIL. EVIL. It's repeating the same thing over and over again."

"Is this Kronsteen?" Solange asked.

YES. YES. YES. Then, EVIL. EVIL. Again and again.

"Quiet, quiet. What's evil? Can you tell us?"

The planchette vibrated, seemed to spin in midair. Then it moved again, gathering speed until it had spelled out a new word so quickly Wes barely had time to read it. "T, H, E, Y." The planchette stopped, and Wes looked up at Solange. "THEY. Fine message from the spirit world, huh?"

Solange opened her eyes and said quietly, "It's moving again." Wes looked back to the board. The planchette moved to the T again, then to other letters, faster and faster. "THIRST," Solange said. The planchette had begun spelling out THEY again. "THEY THIRST is the message. It's repeating the words now . . ."

Wes said uneasily, "What's it supposed to mean?"

"Do you have more to tell . . . ?" Solange began, and suddenly the planchette stopped. She narrowed her eyes, and for an instant Wes saw something there that seemed a

mix of bewilderment and fear. "Bobby?" Solange asked.
"Who's there? Who wants to speak?"

And slowly, with terrifying purpose, the planchette
spelled out a new word.

"FOOLS," Wes said. "Now what in the name of God
is that s . . ."

Solange gave out a piercing scream. The planchette
darted from beneath her fingers and came up off the Ouija
board, its sharp, triangular point flying like a missile at
Wes's right eye. He was able to throw up a hand in time;
the planchette struck his palm and bounced off, then fell
to the carpet like the dead piece of plastic it was. Someone else in the room screamed, the scream was echoed
from two or three more throats. Solange leaped to her
feet. "Wes! Are you all right?"

"Sure," he said nervously. "Sure. I'm fine." He stood up
on shaky legs and stared down at the thing that had almost gouged out his eye. "Little bastard tried to get me,
didn't it?" He laughed and looked around, but no one
else even smiled.

"I think . . . I'm going to be . . . sick," Missy said, her
pretty face having taken on a yellowish cast. She stumbled
toward the bathroom, and her boyfriend followed.

"It . . . moved!" Martin was saying, shaking his head
back and forth. "It really did move!"

"That's enough." Solange took Wes's hand and mas-
saged his palm. "You wanted party games, and that's what
you got."

"Yeah." Martin looked around for a drink. "Party
games."

Soon the life drained back into the party, but it wasn't
the same. Already people were leaving. A cold wind
seemed to be trapped within the living room, trying to
batter its way out through the walls. The stereo came
thundering back, Alicia Bridges begging for some body
heat. But nothing was the same as it had been.

"I'm okay, baby," Wes said and kissed Solange on the
cheek; her skin tasted of pepper and honey. She was looking into his eyes, her high brow furrowed, and he could
feel her shaking. "Martin," he said finally, "you sure
know how to fuck up a good party. Now why don't you
get your ass out of here?" Wes felt like stomping on the
planchette, breaking it into a hundred pieces of cold plastic. But he didn't; he didn't because for just an instant it

looked like the white head of a cobra there on the floor, and no way—*no way!*—was he ever going to touch that sonofabitch again.

Solange bent down, touched it tentatively, then picked it up and returned it to the Ouija board.

The music stopped, the guests left, and very soon the party was over.

III

Sunday, October 27
THE NIGHTWALKERS

ONE

The last of the big green trucks had hauled away Saturday's litter, and now the gently rolling knolls overlooking the green swan pool near Disneyland's Sleeping Beauty Castle gleamed with bright droplets of dew. White rocket boosters aimed toward cold stars from their pads in Tomorrowland; the Skylift was still; the Mark Twain Riverboat lay at the dock, dark water as smooth as a mirror beneath its hull; on flower-festooned Main Street gas lampposts burned low, casting just enough golden light for an occasional security guard in his electric cart to see by. It was just before three o'clock in the morning, and the huge Disneyland complex lay silent.

Except for the muffled noise of footsteps at the center of Fantasyland. A thin shape moved through the darkness, pausing for a moment alongside the docked Peter Pan Pirate ship, then moving away toward the high, white concrete Matterhorn Mountain. It was a dark-haired young man wearing a black velvet suit, black Gucci loafers, and a light blue Beach Boys T-shirt. Though his sharply chiseled, fine-boned face was unlined, there were subtle swirls of yellowish white in his hair, particularly at the temples and running along the neat side part. The whites of his eyes were the color of old yellow dust, veined with red. He was very thin and slight, standing several inches under six feet; he looked like a seventeen-year-old boy made up to play Henry Higgins in a high school production of *My Fair Lady* except that the pupils of his eyes were as green as Pacific Ocean shallows and slitted like a cat's. A network of blue veins throbbed slowly at his temples as he regarded the strange wonders of Fantasyland.

He crossed the path and stood staring at the dark, octopuslike ride, the arms of which were connected to grinning Dumbo elephants. He thought it looked sad and unnatural in its stillness, all the magic drained out of it.

He made a quick circle in the air with the index finger of his left hand, and the pupils of his eyes narrowed in concentration.

An engine began to whine. Sparkling white lights stuttered once and then flickered brightly. The machine began to turn, the grinning Dumbos bouncing gently up and down in the air. He smiled, entranced, wishing that someday he could meet the one who had built this magnificent place; he thought that if he owned this place, he would never grow tired of playing here, not in the whole eternity of existence that lay before him. But after a few minutes of watching the machine turn, his attention wandered. The white bulbs dimmed and went out; the Dumbos slowed and finally stopped. There was silence again.

He walked along the path toward the Matterhorn, peering up at it, thinking of home. The false mountain looked cold, coated with thick snow, and there were concrete icicles clinging to some of the ledges. They made him yearn for the blizzards of his youth, for the wild, screaming winds that drove the snow along craggy passes where no human dared to walk. It was too hot here in this land called California, too full of the sun; but he had vowed to walk where his teacher called, and there would be no turning back. He closed his eyes; a quick whirlwind of icy air shrilled around him, refreshing him before it died.

He had come out here from the city to be alone, to think about Falco. The man had aged. It was time to come to a decision because Falco was now unsteady and tired; and worst of all the spark of remorse Falco had carried within him for almost fifty years had now burst into the gnawing flame of despair. *Falco is like all the others,* he thought as he moved reluctantly away from the Matterhorn. *As he grows old, he grows soft and seeks an escape, and now in his bed he wonders whether praying will save him. If he prays,* the boy decided, *I shall kill him. Like the others.* The boy didn't want to think about that; his head had already been stung once this night by the name of God, spoken in a whisper from the mouth of a fool.

His skin suddenly tingled as he neared a cluster of trees on the far side of the Matterhorn. There were a couple of brightly painted benches beneath those trees, and in the darkness the boy could see the Headmaster sitting on one of them, waiting for him. He stopped and stood perfectly still; he realized with sudden shame that his brain had been too clouded to sense the presence of his Lord, his King, his strong and willful teacher.

"Conrad," the thing on the bench said in a soft, velvety voice. "One comes seeking from the south. You have called him, and he answers."

The boy closed his eyes for a second, concentrating: he distantly heard the roar of an engine, smelled oil and hot pavement. "The snake man," he said, opening his eyes when he was sure.

"Yes. Your lieutenant. He has come a very long way, following your command. Soon it will be time to act."

The boy nodded. "Our circle grows now." His eyes were bright green and luminous with eagerness. "We're stronger every night."

The thing on the bench smiled faintly and crossed one leg over the other; it folded a pair of hands like black talons on one knee. "I've spent much time with you, Conrad. I've taught you the arts of the ages, and now you stand poised to use your knowledge in my name. The world can be yours, Conrad. You can stride across it like Alexander."

Conrad nodded and repeated the wonderful name, "Alexander."

"Alexander had a marvelous thirst, too," the thing whispered. "Your name will be written in the history books of a new world. *Our* world."

"Yes. Yes." His gaze clouded, the problem of Falco streaked through his brain. "Falco is old now, much aged since we talked last. He knows too many of my secrets, and he grows weak."

"Then find another to aid you. Kill Falco. There's one near you now who has broken his ties with humanity, hasn't he?" In the darkness the thing's eyes, like white-hot circles, bored into the boy's face.

"Yes," Conrad said. "He brings the offerings of flesh."

"And in so doing, betrays his race for the sake of the new world yet to be. You are his king, Conrad; make him your slave." The thing regarded him in silence for a moment, a grin splitting its face. "Tread surely, Conrad. Use what I've taught you in my name. Carve your legend in the annals of the new race. But be wary—there are those in this city who know your kind, and you must strike soon."

"Soon. I swear it."

"In my name," the thing prompted.

"In your name," Conrad replied.

"So be it. Faithful servant, student, and right hand, I leave you to your task." The thing, still smiling, seemed to melt away into the darkness until all that was left was the mouth, like the grin of the Cheshire Cat; then it too vanished.

The boy shivered with delight. Touched by the Headmaster! Of all of his kind who walked the earth or hid in mountain caves or stalked in city sewers, he alone had been touched by the Headmaster! He concentrated on the snake man now, the one the Headmaster had told him long ago would be perfectly suited to the task ahead. He turned inward to search and saw the snake man on his motorcycle, reaching the distant limits of the great sprawling city. He thought, COME TO ME, and then visualized the black castle—so much like his own far away— perched on its cliff above Los Angeles. He was putting together a picture of the mountain road in his head when suddenly headlights blazed behind him.

Conrad whirled, hissing. A man driving an electric cart shouted, "Hey! What're you doin' here, kid?"

The security guard suddenly stomped on the cart's brakes and screamed in terror. The kid wasn't there any-more; he had changed into something large and horrifying that leaped into the sky with a leathery rustle of black wings. The cart skidded along the path and left tire marks on the newly cut grass. The man's bladder quickly drenched the inside of his trouser legs. He gripped the wheel and stared straight ahead, his teeth chattering. When he finally got out of the cart and looked around, there was nothing there at all, nothing. The place was si-lent and dead, just like any other Sunday morning at Dis-neyland. Suddenly his nerve broke like a frayed line; he leaped back into the cart and drove as if he'd had an early glimpse of something from Hell.

TWO

Kobra could barely see straight; his head felt like a blacksmith's anvil being beaten with a hammer. Somewhere at the center of his brain pulsed the red-hot, fading echo of the voice that had roared through him a couple of miles back—COME TO ME. He'd heard it distinctly, shatteringly. It was like standing right in front of the booming speakers at the Stones show at Altamont. He had been flying northward on the Santa Ana Freeway, keeping his speed just under sixty, when the voice had hit him. He'd opened his mouth and shouted in surprise, and the black chopper had veered across two lanes before he could get a handle on the bastard. Now, roaring across the dark network of streets in Buena Park with Disneyland just behind him, he knew he was going to have to pull off soon for some coffee, whiskey, speed, or whatever he could find to quiet the thunder between his temples. There seemed to be something burned on his eyelids, too, because when he blinked he thought he saw a picture outlined in electric blue against the darkness—some kind of big fucking cathedral, a place with towers and stained-glass windows and doors that looked like nine-foot slabs of redwood.

He thought he had to be flying on nervous energy because he'd been on the road now for ten hours straight with just a barbecue sandwich and a couple of ampules of amyl nitrate to keep him going. But he didn't care now whether he was hallucinating or not; below and around him there were scattered fireflies of lights, an occasional blinking neon sign or amber traffic signal. Ahead there was a dull yellow glow in the sky that meant the end of his journey. *Or maybe,* he told himself, *it was really just starting. Going to see what Fate, that phantom on a golden Harley chopper whose face can look in all four directions at once, has in store for old Kobra. Going to race that grinning sonofabitch to the finish line.*

The steady blink of red neon off to the right of the freeway caught his eye: MILLIE'S—FINE FOOD—STEAKS—BREAKFAST SERVED 24 HOURS. *Get me some eggs and coffee,* he thought as he took the next exit,

104

*get my fuckin' head to stop ringing. Maybe pick up a little
traveling cash, too.*

Millie's was a square little box of white-painted brick
with cactuses growing underneath the windows. The air in
the parking lot smelled greasy from a thousand steaks,
bowls of chili, and plates of eggs passed over a chipped
Formica counter. But there were two old Harley-
Davidsons parked in the lot up close to the building's side,
and Kobra took a minute to inspect them before he went
in. They both bore California plates, and one of them had
a red swastika painted on the gas tank.

Inside there was a line of stools along a low, white
counter and a couple of rows of booths in the back. Behind the counter an old man with a face like a piece of
crumpled sandpaper was cooking two hamburgers. He
looked up, eyes glittering with disdain, as Kobra stepped
through the door and unsnapped his black helmet. Kobra
took a seat on one of the stools at the end of the counter,
where he could whirl toward the door suddenly if he had
to.

There were two guys at the back, sitting across from
each other in a booth. They were both wearing biker
jackets—one of faded brown leather and the other a tattered, olive-green Army surplus thing. Kobra stared at
them for a few seconds as the old man came walking along the counter, stopping once to hawk and spit into
a Mason jar. The bikers in the back looked like total op-
posites, an outlaw Mutt and Jeff—one husky and broad-
shouldered with wild, curly red hair and a beard that
reached almost all the way down to where his beer belly
displayed a FUCK YOU T-shirt; the other cadaver-
ous and totally bald, wearing a gold earring in his right
ear lobe. The bikers stared back at Kobra. The air sim-
mered between them.

"What'd you want, buddy?" the old man said. As
Kobra turned slowly to face him, the old man's eyes widened slightly, as if he'd recognized the presence of walking
death.

"You Millie?" Kobra asked quietly, reaching for a
greasy menu.

"That's my wife." He tried to laugh, but it came out in
a croak. "Everybody asks that."

"Uh-huh. Well, Millie, how about some ham and eggs
and a cup of black coffee? Make 'em sunny-side-up."

The old man nodded and moved away quickly. He took the burgers back to Mutt and Jeff, then scraped charred bits of beef off the grill with a spatula and broke a couple of eggs onto it. Kobra watched him work, then took a glazed doughnut out from under a clear plastic cover on the counter and ate it greedily; the doughnut crunched between his teeth and tasted like plaster. And while he was chewing, he thought about the voice he'd heard, the single powerful command that had almost split his head in two. He could still see that blue-glowing cathedral, as if it had been seared into the back of his brain. *What the fuck was that?* he wondered. *Road fever?* Or the voice of Fate calling to him from the west? Was it the same voice he'd heard whispering through the still, humid Mexican night? Through the heavy air that hung around the bar on that Texas desert highway? Something was here for him in L.A.; he felt certain of it, at least as certain as anything he'd ever seen or felt or known in the twenty years of a life that had thrown him in with biker gangs, dope dealers, and murderers from California to Florida. *Or maybe,* he reasoned, *it wasn't Fate calling at all. Maybe* —and he smiled thinking about this—*it's Death calling.* Plugging in the phone line that led to Kobra's brain, dialing his number with a finger of bone, whispering for him, *"Got something for you to do out here in California, Kobra. Got something big for you, something I can't trust anybody else with. Want you to pack your chopper and come on out, maybe throw me a little scrape along the way. I'll be expecting you."*

Yeah, maybe so. But fuck, what's the difference between Fate and Death anyway? They both take you to the same hole in the ground.

The old man slid Kobra's coffee across the counter, his hand trembling. Kobra looked up into his face with the stare of Medusa and froze him. "Hey, old man," Kobra said, "I'm looking for a place, might be around here, might not. It's real big, could be a church or something. Got towers and stained-glass windows, and . . . I don't know . . . seems like it's on a cliff maybe. Any place around here look like that?"

"Presbyterian church three blocks west got stained-glass windows," he said. "Got a steeple. I don't know." He shrugged, his eyes suddenly zigzagging to the left. Kobra, still smiling, began to unzip his jacket because he felt those two bastards coming up behind him. He slipped his hand in and got hold of the grip, eagerness rushing through him like sweet, fiery cocaine.

"What'd you say, man?" a voice behind him asked.

Kobra turned. It was the red-headed one who had spoken; there were pieces of bread and hamburger in his beard. His eyes were deep-set and black and fixed somewhere on Kobra's forehead. The bald biker—an older guy, maybe in his forties or so—stood beside his friend, a rod of flesh beside a cannonball. The bald dude's gaze was vacant, as if speed had burned out his brain.

"I don't recall saying anything to you," Kobra said.

"Hey now," Millie's husband said, "let's don't have no trouble. I run a . . ."

"Shut your fuckin' face." The bald dude spoke hoarsely, like somebody had tried to slash his throat but only gotten a hunk of vocal cords.

"I asked you a question, whitey. Let's hear it."

Kobra almost squeezed the Mauser's trigger then, having gotten the gun twisted in its holster, but he paused with a quarter of an ounce of pressure left to go. "I'll tell you what you're going to hear, you big piece of shit. You're going to hear a couple of Mauser slugs sizzle your face off—DON'T MOVE!—'cause that's what I got my finger on right now. Want to test me?"

"Please . . ." the old man whimpered.

The bearded dude stared at Kobra for a few seconds and then smiled, showing a mouthful of broken teeth. The smile widened until it seemed about to crack his face. "Hot shit!" he growled through an explosion of laughter. "I knew it was you when you walked in! Hell, I ain't never seen anybody looked like *you* before, so I knew it had to be! Kobra, right?"

"That's my handle." He kept his finger on the trigger.

"What's wrong? You don't recognize me? Well, I guess not. I growed this beard and belly a couple of years ago after that little la-de-dah between the Angels and the Headhunters up in Frisco. I'm Viking, man! Don't you remember?"

"Viking?" The name rang a faraway note in his head, but he connected it with a Hell's Angel who was slim and wiry and carried a pair of pliers around to yank out teeth with. Still, it seemed that Viking had been red-haired and could put away a couple of six-packs of Bud before you

could crack your third. Of course he remembered the
showdown between Angel and Headhunter troops because
then he was eighteen and ready to burn his name into Angel history. He'd sent two Headhunters to hell with a
Luger and kicked the nuts off another one in that empty
lot in the middle of the night with the chains and
the knives swinging. "Viking?" Kobra said again and realized that he'd been ready to waste a brother. He took
his finger off the trigger. "Christ! Viking? Man, you carrying a horse inside there?"

"Old brew kinda caught up with me," he said, affectionately patting his stomach. "Hey, I want you to meet
my ridin' buddy, Dicko Hansen. Dicko, this albino sonofabitch here can catch bullets between his teeth and fire
'em out his ass!" He laughed long and loud; Kobra and
Dicko shook hands, grasping each other's thumbs palm-to-
palm and squeezing so hard the knuckles cracked. "Jesus
Jumpin' Christ!" Viking said. "Where you been keeping
yourself?"

Kobra shrugged. "Around. Been doing some traveling."

"I heard a few months ago you were ridin' with the
Lucifer Legion, got yourself wasted in a little fracas down
New Awleens way."

"Nope. It was me did the wasting. That's why I've been
in Mexico for a while."

The old man behind the counter was now as pale as
Kobra. He slinked away trembling and hoped they'd forget about him.

"Bring this man's food back to the booth," Viking
called after him, making him flinch. "Come on, bro, we
got a lot to catch up on."

Kobra ate his ham and eggs, listening to Viking talk;
Dicko sat beside Kobra because Viking took up most of
one side of the booth. "Me and Dicko ride with the Death
Machine now," he was saying between swigs of beer. "I
had to change the way I look, see, 'cause the cops were
after my ass. A lot of brothers split from the Angels,
formed their own clubs or joined up in other states. Shit!
The Angels ain't like they used to be, Kobra. They're re-
spec-table, can you dig it? They wear fuckin' suits and
take up donations for fuckin' orphans! Makes you sick to
your stomach to see them old boys kissin' cop ass! I don't
know." He tilted his bottle and drank it dry, smacking his
lips noisily at the end. "Those old days, they were good,

weren't they? Hundreds of Angels out on a run, takin' up the whole highway, and nobody darin' to pass us! And God, did the booze and brew and high times flooooow! Those Angel bashes up in Frisco would keep your hair curled for weeks, man. Aw, shit." He uncapped another bottle and started in on it. "Well, times change don't they? It ain't like it used to be. People too interested in boogie and hard cash to think about how it feels to ride at the front of the pack, to feel that good, raw wind across your face at ninety miles an hour. And territory? Nobody cares about territory. Bunch of Chicano and nigger punks fight over some dry chunks of ceement up in L.A., but nobody carves out land like we used to." He pulled at the beer again, and droplets of foam glittered in his beard. "Nobody gives a shit about nothin'. Except the Death Machine, o' course. Now there's a good bunch of brothers. Old Dicko and me just got back from a San Diego run. You shoulda been there and seen the looks on these fucker's faces when thirty Death Machiners come runnin' right through their campground, scatterin' picnic baskets and tables all to hell and back. Yeah, it was allllright. Wasn't it, Dicko?"

"Sure was."

"So what about you, Kobra? What's the story?"

"Nothing much to tell," Kobra said. "I hooked up with the Nightriders up in Washington for a while, started getting road fever, and moved on. I guess I've ridden with nine or ten clubs since I left the Angels."

Viking leaned closer, his eyes glimmering with low, beer lights. "Hey," he whispered conspiratorially. "Who'd you waste in New Awleens? What was the action?"

"Couple of Dixie Demons trashed a buddy of mine. I killed 'em as a favor."

"How'd you do it? Fast or slow?"

Kobra smiled. "The first one I shot in the kneecaps. Then the elbows. And I tossed him into the mighty Mississippi. Fucker flopped around like a frog for a while before he went under. The second one I caught in a gas station toilet. I made him lick the johns clean and then . . . pow! . . right through the old beanbag. Bled like a swamp." His gaze clouded slightly. "Too bad he was working with the cops, about to turn state's evidence on some Demon dirt. All kinds of pigs were hunting me from FBI on down. That's the luck of the draw, right?"

"Right." Viking leaned back and let out a satisfied belch.

Kobra drank his coffee and felt it roiling around in his stomach. He could feel Dicko's stare on him, like a leech clinging to the side of his face. "Viking," Kobra said after another moment, "is there any action going on in L.A. I might be interested in? Anything big?. You know, maybe some down-and-dirty, or somebody in bad need of an out-of-town shooter?"

Viking looked at Dicko and then shook his head. "Don't hear anything. Well, the Knights and the Satan Stompers are having a little war over in La Habra, but it'll blow over in a few days. Why?"

"A feeling I've got. Like something's about to break."

Dicko's ferret eyes gleamed. "What kind of feeling? Sorta weird, like you can feel power hummin' inside you?"

"Yeah. Sort of like that. Only it's getting stronger all the time, and a little while ago I thought I heard . . . you guys know of a place something like this—real big, maybe on a cliff, and it's got high towers and stained-glass windows, could be a church?"

Dicko looked startled. "Uh . . . on a cliff? Way up over L.A.? Jesus! A castle, maybe?"

Kobra nodded.

Viking barked out a laugh. "A fuckin' castle? Sure, old Dicko knows it! You talkin' about the Kronsteen place? That's where Dicko and a bunch of freaks stoned out of their gourds on LSD and mesc had a party about . . ."

"Eleven years," Dicko said quietly. "It was eleven years ago we did that."

"Did what?" Kobra asked. "What're you talking about?"

"You want to go up there?" Dicko's gaze was dead again. "Why?"

Kobra said, "Maybe it's not the place I want to go. I don't know. But I'd like to see it. How far is it from here?"

"It's way up in the Hollywood Hills. But we could make it before sunrise if you want to see it. I hear somebody's moved in up there."

"Who?" Kobra asked. *How do you like that,* he said to himself. *A castle, not a church.*

Dicko shrugged. "Some foreign fucker. There was a piece in the paper about a month ago. I saved it."

"Okay. What the hell, I got nothing better to do. Let's burn on up to this joint and take a look at it." Kobra was suddenly eager to get under way. *Is my trip over?* he wondered. *Or has it just started?* His blood seemed to be boiling in his veins.

"Let's git gone!" Viking said and shoved his bulk away from the booth.

THREE

Out of the dead, blue darkness, three moons rose in the hills above the Hollywood Bowl. Kobra rode on Dicko's left flank, following the twistings of the road with an almost extrasensory knowledge. They had made good time from Millie's, even though Viking—riding on Dicko's right, his bike wheezing like an old, used-up horse—had to stop and take a beer piss every few miles. Now they were climbing at an incredible angle, their engines cracking the silence with pops and growls. Dicko made a quick turn onto a narrower road lined with hundreds of dead trees. They continued to climb, the wind swirling like whirlpools around them.

And then they came to a chain across the road with a sign on it. PRIVATE PROPERTY—NO TRESPASSING.

"We'll see about that," Kobra said; he got off his chopper and moved toward a tree on the left side of the road. The chain had been wrapped around the trunk and secured with the kind of padlock you couldn't even shoot through. Kobra touched the chain and pulled at it. It was tighter than a cock ring, and there was no way to go around it either—the left side of the road pitched off into empty space, while the right was blocked by a boulder as big as a house. "Gonna have to walk the rest of the way," Kobra said and started to step over the chain. He heard a sudden, faint click, and the chain slithered to the road.

"Alllllright!" Viking said, revving his engine. "How'd you do that?"

"I . . . I don't know." He backed away a pace and bent to look at the open prongs of the lock. They were polished and new. "Rusty lock," he said and rose to his

feet. *What's waiting for me up there, Fate or Death?* He
went back to his bike and stepped on, his knees beginning
to shake a little but damned if he was going to show it.

"You sure you want to go up there?" Dicko asked him;
in this faint light there were deep, blue hollows beneath
his eyes, and his mouth was twisted like a gray worm.

"Yeah. Why shouldn't I?"

"Roads tricky as hell higher up. I ain't been here in
a long time. I hope I don't take us right over the edge and
down to L.A."

"You want to turn back, Dicko?" Viking asked with a
soft laugh, his eyes mocking.

"No," Dicko said quickly. "I'm able. But . . . you
know . . . I think about that night a lot. It was a freak
named Joey Tagg did the cutting."

"That's not what I hear," Viking said, but then he
kept quiet. Dicko roared on across the chain, and Kobra
followed closely. Higher up they had to swerve around
slabs of rock that had fallen from ledges just above their
heads. The road turned at an eighty-degree angle as they
neared the top, and through a cut in the trees Kobra could
see the whole glittering valley below from Topanga Canyon to Alhambra.

And then there it was, perched at the top like a stone
vulture. The thing was enormous, much larger than
Kobra had envisioned. He felt doused with ice water.
This was the place, no doubt about it. Black towers jutting into the sky, high pointed roofs like dunce caps, the
soft glimmer of a blue window sixty feet off the ground.
The whole place was surrounded by a ten-foot high stone
wall with coils of barbed wire strung along the top. The
huge wooden slab of a gate hung wide open, and Kobra
could see along a weed-infested driveway that led across
a barren courtyard to a series of stone steps. At the top
of the steps was a front door as big as a drawbridge.
Should have a moat with fucking crocodiles, Kobra
thought. "Who built this bastard?" he asked Dicko.

Dicko cut his engine, and the others did the same. In
the silence they could hear the wind rippling through the
foliage below them; the wind touched Kobra's face like
cold fingers exploring his features. "Crazy old movie star
name of Kronsteen," Dicko replied softly, getting off his
bike and letting it rest on its kickstand. "He brought this

thing over from Europe piece by piece. You ever seen any of his flicks?"

Kobra shook his head.

"Monster flicks," Dicko went on, his gaze following the sharp angles of towers and parapets. "They drove the old dude crazy, I guess. You see all those dead trees we passed? Kronsteen hired a bunch of guys to spray them with black paint, just covered 'em with the shit, like something from a horror flick set."

"How long's it been here?" Kobra asked, stepping off his chopper.

"A long time. I think he built it back in the forties. But it's old. It must've been in Europe for hundreds of years."

"But old Kronsteen wasn't near as rich as you dudes thought he was, huh?" Viking asked, grinning; he belched and muttered.

Dicko didn't answer for a long time. Then he said, "Hardly had a stick of furniture in there. Wasn't no gold statues, wasn't no chests full of money. Wasn't nothing but a lot of empty rooms." He turned to Kobra. "You've seen it. Let's go."

Kobra had taken a few steps along the driveway, gravel crunching under his feet. "Wait a minute." *What's here?* he wondered. *What called me?*

"Come on, bro," Viking said. "Let's git . . . HEY! YOU SEE THAT?" He pointed, and Kobra looked up to the right.

In one of the tower windows a candle was flickering, the light made orange by the stained glass. From the corner of his eye, Kobra saw another candle begin to burn off to the left behind another window. And now there were more candles glittering, from almost every window in the place. The tiny flames glowed green, blue, and white behind colored glass, candles burning like lanterns to welcome the hunter home.

The front door silently opened. Kobra felt a surge of joy and fear course through him, like a charge between opposite poles. His legs moved slowly, as if he were crawling across flypaper. "Where you going?" Viking called behind him. "Kobra? What you doin', man?"

"It wants me," he heard himself say and looked back at Viking and Dicko standing at the far end of the driveway. "Come on," Kobra said, a wild grin rippling across his face. "Come on with me. It wants us all."

Neither of them moved.

The castle loomed above Kobra, dwarfing him. Through the huge, open doorway he could smell the guts of the place—dry, cold, maybe as old as time itself. At the threshold he paused to look back at his friends, and a voice like a cool wind wafted through his brain—COME TO ME. As he stepped into the darkness, he heard Viking shout from a world away, "KOBRA!"

He stood in a womb of darkness, a place without ceiling or walls or floor. There was a distant noise like water dripping onto concrete, or muffled footsteps. When he started walking again, feeling his way, his boots clattered like a toss of bones across the floor of rough stone. Echoes converged and passed each other like riptides with Kobra at the center. His eyes were getting used to the blackness now, and he could see smooth stone walls around him, a geometric pattern of rough-hewn rafters perhaps twenty feet overhead. An old, rusted metal chandelier hung crookedly from that ceiling, still holding two light bulbs that looked like teardrops. From the depths of the place, a candle flame flickered, far away; Kobra followed its light, his fingertips grazing the wall. He was in a long, high corridor that seemed to go on forever, like the trick done with mirrors in the carnival funhouses. Half of him cowered in fear like a mongrel dog; the other half lurched with drunken glee, and it was this half that kept his legs moving. *I'm in a haunted house at the New Orleans fairgrounds,* he told himself; *I'm walking through the Madman's Maze. Going to feel cobwebs in my hair in a minute, going to see a dummy dressed up in an ape mask.*

He reached the candle. It sat in a gleaming brass holder on a long table of dark, shining wood. He couldn't see beyond the range of the light, but he had a feeling the room was as large as a cavern, maybe with stone stairs that wound around and around and out of sight. He could hear the wind whistling through broken windows very high above him.

Off to his left he saw another candle, moving in mid-air, carried by a ghost. But then he saw the quick flicker of pale light on the face of a girl. She had a long sweep of ebony hair, sensual pouting lips, a face as beautiful as the moon. There was another candle now, on his other side. This one was held by a young man in a Kiss T-shirt. He had a lean, sharp-boned face and predatory eyes. Then a third candle, behind Kobra. A tall, smiling girl, her red hair cascading in disarray around her shoulders. Then the others: Kobra saw a couple of Chicano girls, a black dude wearing a headband, a middle-aged man and woman who looked at him lovingly, as if he might be their long lost son. Candles burned in a silent circle around him.

And then a hand as cold and hard as a chunk of ice touched Kobra's shoulder. He whirled, ready to go for his Mauser. But the hand moved in a white streak and caught his wrist, not hurting him but only holding him where he was. In the golden candlelight Kobra could see the face of someone who looked at once very young and very old.

There were no lines on the white face, but the eyes seemed ancient and wise, ablaze with powerful secrets. Where the hand touched him, Kobra tingled with electricity; the feeling slowly spread until he thought he must be plugged in to the same socket that supplied power to the universe. He felt like he was going to explode with fear and exhilaration, that he should kneel down there on that cold stone floor and kiss the wintry hand of Death.

Death smiled—a boyish smile—through an old man's eyes. "Welcome," he said.

For a long time Viking and Dicko waited outside, but Kobra didn't come back. The first tentative rays of gray light were creeping across the eastern horizon. After they had called him a few times, unsuccessfully, Viking unsheathed a hooked hunting blade from a leather holder at his side. "Somethin's happened to Kobra," he said to Dicko. "I'm gonna find out what. You comin'?"

Dicko paused, then reached to the small of his back and took out the .45 from its black holster. "Yeah," he replied. "I'm in."

They moved into the castle and were swallowed up by darkness.

The sun gradually strengthened its hold on the horizon, chasing shadows in its path. Sometime before dawn the door swung closed, and a bolt was thrown

FOUR

Sunday morning dawned bright and warm. Bells chimed from a hundred church steeples across L.A. The God of Light was worshipped in as many different ways, from formal services to the simple act of prayer on Malibu Beach by the Pacific Ocean Church. Incense cones were burned by the Holy Order of the Sun, Catholic masses were being said. Buddhists bowed before their altars. The city seemed quiet, at rest, the planet spinning in an ordered universe.

From his Laurel Canyon terrace Mitch Gideon watched a flock of birds moving gracefully across the sky as if in slow-motion. He stood in a warm splash of sunlight, smoking a cigar and thinking about the dream of coffins on a conveyor belt. He'd had it again last night and had sat up in bed so violently Estelle almost had a heart attack. That dream had been peculiar at first, something to laugh about. Now it was terrifying, the details gradually becoming clearer and clearer. Last night he'd been able to see the faces of some of his co-workers. They'd looked like grinning dead men, and the cold whiteness of their flesh had been so real, so close, that Gideon had just fought his way out of the dream as if up from the bottom of a deep, green pond. He was playing golf this afternoon in a foursome at the Wilshire Country Club, and he hoped hacking at a Slazenger would take his mind off a dream that was really turning shitty.

Andy and Jo Palatazin sat in their usual places at the Hungarian Reformed Church on Melrose Avenue, just a few blocks from their house. She gripped his hand and squeezed it, sensing his preoccupation. He smiled and pretended to be paying attention, but his mind was seesawing back and forth between two dark concerns: the Roach, whose presence in the city now seemed as intangible as a ghost's; and whatever had ripped through the Hollywood Memorial Cemetery. The artist's composite of the man who had tried to lure Amy Hulsett had been printed up by the dozens for detectives and uniformed officers to use in their conversations with street people. Of course, the man might not have been the Roach after all, just a guy out to buy a good time, but it was an angle that had to be pursued. All that Brasher's hard work had turned up was one suspect who owned a dark blue Volkswagen, and the man was almost the total physical opposite of the young prostitute's description. Palatazin had put an officer on surveillance to be certain.

The second concern made him more uneasy. He'd driven past Hollywood Memorial on the way to church; everything had looked okay, and Palatazin had caught a quick glimpse of the watchman, Kelsen, unlocking the front gates for the Sunday morning visitors. *Had it only been mindless vandalism after all?* He was hoping it was. The other answer—the one that lurked deep in the back of his mind—might drive him mad.

And in a huge circular bed in his Bel Air home, Wes Richer stirred, reaching across to touch Solange's cool brown flesh. His fingers gripped the edge of the sheet where she should have been lying. He opened his eyes and winced; the light was buffered by thick beige curtains, but it was still bright enough to make his optic nerves sputter like severed live wires. He turned over on his back, his palms pressed against his eyes, and waited for the first wave of the crashing headache to pass. "Solange?" he called out, the sound of his voice making his eardrums throb. There was no answer, and finally Wes sat up on the edge of the bed. "Solange," he called again irritably. *Damn! Where is she?* he thought. His sinuses were clogged with the mingled odors of marijuana and jasmine incense with a cold dash of cocaine in there for good measure. *How was the show?* he wondered suddenly. *Was I good? "Sheer Luck" strikes again. Alimentary, Dr. Batson.* Wes stood up and struggled into his Fruit of the Looms.

When he walked into the living room and looked around, he swore loudly. He saw the ruined wall-to-wall carpet, a mahogany coffee table scarred like a K-Mart reject, a shattered piece of Inca pottery that he'd been too high to notice the night before, the empty hospitality bowls that had been brimming at least five times last night, the silver cocaine trays snorted clean, the bits of glass that glittered in the carpet between all the stains and crushed butts, the heel marks—*heel marks, for Chris-*

sake?—atop the grand piano, the . . . *oh, to hell with it!* he thought. The wreckage was consummate.

And sitting there in the middle of it was Solange, wearing her long white robe cut low to show the soft dark swelling of her breasts. She was sitting on the sofa, her arms crossed tightly as if she were chilly. She was staring at the Ouija board.

"Morning," Wes said and plopped himself down in a chair. An instant later he stood up to remove the filled ashtray he'd sat down on. There was a ring of ashes on his ass. "Christ!" he said softly, surveying the damage. "If the guys at the Domino Club could only see me now. As they say." He saw she was not paying attention; her eyes were fixed on a spot at the center of the board. "I didn't feel you get out of bed. What time were you up?"

She blinked and glanced up at him as if just now aware that he'd walked into the room. "Wes," she said. "I . . . I've been up for a long time. I couldn't sleep after the sun rose." She looked at him for a long time and then smiled appreciatively. "You look like someone hit you with a *nganga*."

"A nuhwhat? What's that?"

"An evil spell. A big one." Solange frowned slightly and turned back to the board. She picked up the planchette and examined the bottom of it with a fingertip.

"Better watch out for that bastard," Wes said. "It might bite you. I'm going to kick Martin Blue's ass the next time I see him. He could've put my eye out!"

She replaced the planchette. "What are you saying, Wes? That Martin was in control of what happened here last night?"

"Sure he was! I saw his hands! He skidded that thing right off the board!" When Solange didn't reply, he walked over to the picture window and looked down at the swimming pool. A bright yellow and greenstriped lawn chair was floating in it; there were some Coors cans at the deep end. "All right," he said finally. "I know that silence. What are you thinking?"

"Martin didn't do it," she said. "He had no control over it, and neither did I. Something very violent and very strong was here . . ."

"Oh, come on! Listen, I can take that mumbo stuff when we're at a party, but when we're alone, I wish you'd forget the spirit world!"

"You don't believe?" she asked coolly.

"Nope."

"Do you pray to God?"

He turned from the window to face her. "Yes, but that's different."

"Is it? Think back. You were playing high-stakes poker in a room at the Las Vegas Hilton nine months ago. You were playing against some very influential and wealthy men."

"I remember."

"Do you remember the final hand? You closed your eyes for a second before you picked up that last card. To which spirit were you praying?"

"To . . . I was wishing for an ace from Lady Luck. That's not a spirit."

She smiled faintly, her nostrils flaring. "I say it is. All deities are spirits, and all beliefs can become deities. Oh yes, Wes, you believe." She regarded the board again. "You saw. You spelled out the words."

"What words? It was gibberish!"

"It was a message," Solange said quietly. She shivered and lifted her gaze to him. "The spirits are troubled, Wes. There's a great, terrible *nganga* in the air. If you had Bantu blood in your veins, you could feel its vibrations, or smell it like the reek of old vinegar. The spirits know every mystery; they see the future and try to protect us from harm, if we will only listen to what they say." Wes smiled slightly, and Solange's eyes snapped with anger. "I've never felt a power before like the thing that was here last night! It simply silenced the beneficent voices; it brushed their spirits away with as much effort as it takes to flick a fly away! That was the thing that spelled out the final message, the thing that took the planchette into its power and . . . ."

"Stop it," Wes said abruptly.

Solange's face tightened. She stared at him for a few seconds with what Wes sometimes referred to as her "molten ink" eyes, and then she rose gracefully. "I didn't mean to upset you . . ."

"I'm not upset!"

" . . . but I wanted you to know the truth . . ."

"Oh, for Christ's sake!"

" . . . about what happened last night. I *have* told you the truth."

"And the truth shall set us free." His grin spread. "Seems like I've heard that before."

"Wes!" Tension was stretched tight in her voice now. "You can stand on your stage and make your little jokes for other people; you can contort your face and voice and make the people think you live for their laughter, but don't think for an instant that you can put on your disguise in front of me! Sometime the jokes will have to end; the laughter will die. And you'll have to face the world on its own terms without falsehood."

"What world are we talking about, dear? The spirit domain, I assume?"

Solange had already turned away. She crossed the living room, her white gown swirling behind her, and disappeared into the far hallway. He heard the faint sound of a door closing. *Her problem is, she can't take a joke,* he thought.

He rose to his feet and went through the living room and the short, connecting hallway to the kitchen, where copper cooking utensils hung from an overhead rack and African woodcuts decorated the walls. He found a carton of orange juice in the refrigerator and took a variety of plastic bottles from the vitamin cupboard. As he downed his breakfast, he was aware that his pulse was kicking hard. He'd been thinking of that planchette coming for his face like a runaway Nike missile, and he knew that there was no damned way Martin Blue could've done it. *The bastard had been scared witless. So what, then? Spirits, like Solange said? No, that was bullshit!* When Solange got started, she could really lay it on thick, stuff with crazy names like *Santeria, brujeria, nkisi, makuto.* Once he'd peeked inside the ornately carved wooden box she kept under the bed. There was a strange collection of peacock feathers, seashells, black and red candles, corn husks, white coral, and some kind of weird iron nails wrapped up with string inside. Wes tolerated her beliefs, but he had drawn the line several months ago when she'd wanted to put a twig tied with a red ribbon behind every door in the house.

He'd never known her last name; the man who'd lost her to him in the Vegas poker game hadn't known it either. She told Wes she was born in Chicago, the daughter of a woman who'd been a classical actress in Japan and an African man who was a practicing *santero,* a good

magician. She was born, she said, on the seventh day of
the seventh month at exactly seven o'clock in the evening. On the day before her birth, her father had dreamed
of her sitting on an ivory throne with seven stars moving
about her head like a glittering tiara. Which seemed to
be a damned good omen, the way Solange had explained
it. It was supposed to mean that she had inherited her
father's powers of white magic, that she was to be considered a living talisman. Solange didn't talk about the
things she'd learned from her father in her formative
years, but Wes figured she must've been pretty important.
Solange recalled that people always came to their door,
wanting to touch her, or ask her about problems they
were having with love or money.

When she was ten years old, walking home from school
with the snow falling softly, a car had pulled up to the
curb, and two black men had stuffed a rag into her mouth
and thrown her onto the backseat. She was blindfolded—
she could vividly recall the coarseness of the cloth against
her face—and the car traveled all night. They went fast,
over all kinds of roads. When the blindfold was taken
off, she was at a big house with snow-filled woods all
around. For several days she was locked in a beautifully
furnished bedroom with windows that looked down on an
ice-glazed lake and fed by a black man in a white suit
who brought her food on a silver tray. On the third day
she was taken to a glass room full of jungle vines and
blooming red flowers, where a large-bellied black man
who wore a gray-striped suit and smoked a cigar waited.
He was very nice to her, very friendly, and offered her a
lace handkerchief to wipe her eyes when he told her that
she wouldn't be going home again because this was her
home now. His name was Fontaine, and he said there
were some things Solange was going to have to do for him.
She was going to have to give him good fortune and protect him from evil. Or something might happen to her
mother and father.

It was only gradually, she'd told Wes, that she learned
he was a bad man, a gangster who controlled most of
the Harlem rackets. His power was slipping, and he'd
heard about her through some of his people in South
Chicago. In a period of four years, during which Solange
did very little but read the lines in his hand and touch
photographs of different men to feel their weaknesses,

Fontaine never came to her bedroom, never laid a hand
on her. He left her alone, first because he was beginning
to fear her all too accurate predictions of the future and
the incantations that caused his enemies to suddenly
wither from health to sickness; also, his brain was steadily
being gnawed away by syphilis. Many nights she could
hear Fontaine roaming the long hallways of the mansion,
howling like an animal in mad rage. In the end it was
the syphilis, not his enemies, that crept up on him with
a deadly hand, and none of Solange's incantations or
poultices could halt its advance. Fontaine was locked
away behind a massive oak door, and soon after that a
couple of well-dressed white men came to the house,
paid Fontaine's business manager a great deal of money,
and took Solange with them to the west.

Her new owner was an elderly Mafia *capo* who
wanted her around for good luck; he'd heard of what
she'd been doing for Fontaine and knew that Fontaine's
business had shown an eighty-percent increase while
she'd been with him. He never touched her either, but a
couple of his hired men did come to her room one night.
They said if she ever dared to tell what they did, they'd
cut her throat. That went on for a long time, until Solange
fashioned corn husk dolls of them and set them on fire.
They died when their Lincoln Continental slammed into
the rear of a Sunoco gas truck on the San Diego Freeway.

And so it went on, year after year, a succession of
powerful and greedy men. Another Mafia lieutenant,
then a motion picture studio head, then a director, then
a record company executive who was robbing his part-
ners blind. She was with him when she met Wes, who
was doing a show in Vegas. It wasn't much money, but
at least it would take him through the bad period after
his second series had been canceled. He was looking for
private action, too, so he'd gotten himself invited to this
poker game at the Las Vegas Hilton with a group of big
money players, Solange's record exec among them. During the long, grueling game Solange had sat behind the
man; Wes remembered she had had a bruise on her cheek.
Anyway, the guy's luck had started turning bad and
went downhill; after he'd lost the first thirty thousand or
so, he'd taken Solange into a back room and whaled the
shit out of her, then brought her in again and shoved
her back in her chair. Her eyes were swollen and red;

the record exec was really starting to sweat. After another three hours the game had pared down to just the two of them: there was a stack of red chips in front of Wes and a look of animal fear on the record exec's face. But he'd wanted to play on, and so it continued until he had no more chips, nor money, nor keys to his robin's-egg blue Cadillac. Wes was willing to leave it there. "SIT DOWN!" the man had screamed. "I TELL YOU WHEN TO LEAVE!"

"You're through, Morry," one of the onlookers said wearily. "Give it up."

"SHUT UP! Deal the cards . . . COME ON!"

"You're cleaned out," Wes said. "The game's over."

"No, it's not!" He'd turned and gripped Solange's arm with a crushing hand. "I'm putting her up as security!"

"What? Forget it!"

"You think I'm kidding, Richer? Listen, punk, this bitch is worth her fucking weight in gold! She can suck your cock right out of the roots; she'll fuck your eyeballs out with tricks you never even heard of!"

"Now listen, I don't think . . ."

"Come on, you lousy little punk! What do you have to lose? You're floating in my cash!"

It was the second use of that word that got to Wes. He paused for a moment and looked at the beautiful, battered woman behind him. He wondered how many times she'd had to endure this man. Then he said, "I'll accept her as security on five hundred dollars." Solange had responded with a slight nod.

And ten minutes later it was all over as Wes sat facing a beautiful royal flush. The record exec had leaped to his feet and grabbed Solange's face, squeezing her jaw so hard she whimpered. "Back off, you sonofabitch!" Wes had said quietly. "You're marking up my merchandise."

Then the guy had really turned ugly, making all kinds of threats about how Wes would never have a series again because he had connections with all three networks, and as for recording, forget it! Someone gave the poor bastard a drink and ushered him out of the room. For a long time Wes sat looking at Solange across the poker table, not knowing what the hell to say or do. She broke the silence: "I think he chipped my tooth."

"You want to find a dentist?"

"No. It's all right. I've seen you on television before. You're the comedian," she went on. "I remember now, I saw your face on the cover of *TV Stars.*"

He nodded. "Yeah, I made that cover and a lot more. There was an article on me in *Rolling Stone,* too. I've got a couple of comedy albums out." He stopped, feeling foolish for tooting his horn in front of a woman whose right eye was swollen and blue and whose left one was an odd shade of yellow. Still she was beautiful: it was an exotic, cool beauty that had made Wes's pulse gallop ever since she'd walked in.

"You're working here now?"

"That's right. But my agent's hot on a deal for a new series next season, and I may do a bit in the next Mel Brooks flick." He cleared his throat nervously. "How long have you been . . . his mistress?"

"Almost a year. He's a very unkind man."

"Yeah, well, I guess I cleaned him out, didn't I?" He stared at the wad of bills and the big money IOUs that sat in front of him. "Christ. There's a lot of dough here."

"It's late," Solange said. "Why don't we go to your room now?"

"Huh? Oh. Listen, you don't have to . . ."

"Yes I do. You own me now."

"Own you? Abe Lincoln freed the slaves in case you . . ."

"I've always belonged to someone," she said, and Wes thought he heard fear in her voice. "I made his luck go bad. I can make yours good."

"Huh? What do you mean?"

She stood up and reached out her hand for him. He took it. "Your room," she said.

That had been almost a year ago. Wes put the orange juice back into the refrigerator. He knew he should be getting dressed because Jimmy might be coming over this afternoon to talk over some figures on that Mel Brooks movie, a spoof on trendy department stores called *Quattlebaum's.* When he walked into the living room, Wes paused over the Ouija board for a moment, wondering how he could get away with throwing the thing in the garbage. He didn't believe in those spirit tales that Solange liked to tell, but one thing had bothered him ever since he'd brought her back to Hollywood with him. Less than a week after he'd made the down payment on

this house, he'd seen Solange at the pool in the middle
of the night, slowly twisting the arms and legs of a GI
Joe doll. Then she'd dropped it into the water and held
it under for several minutes. Two days later her old record exec was found drowned in his own kidney-shaped
pool. *Variety* ran a short squib on his death; the doctor
who'd examined the body said the guy's muscles were
all cramped up into knots.

I'll throw you out later, you bastard, Wes mentally
told the Ouija board, and then he went back to his bedroom to put on some clothes.

FIVE

Palatazin was in the den, watching the Steelers crawl all
over the Forty-Niners at two o'clock when the telephone
rang. Jo got up to answer it. "Come on, get him!" Palatazin said to the television screen as Terry Bradshaw
evaded not one but *two* stumbling linesmen and cocked
his arm back like a piston to pass. "Don't let that guy
score again! Oh, for . . . !" He slapped his thigh as the
pass was completed for thirty-four yards.

". . . yes, I'll get him," Jo said from the kitchen.
"Andy?"

"Okay." He hauled himself out of his La-Z-Boy and
took the receiver from Jo. "Yes?"

"Lieutenant Reece, captain. We've got somebody in
here who's seen the guy on that artist's composite."

"I need more than that. Maybe he just likes hookers."

"I've got more. The young lady in here says he told
her he was going to take her to a motel but stopped instead in a vacant lot on Yucca Street. She got scared
and took off, but he chased her in his car. The car was a
grayish Volks, and she remembers part of the license
plate."

"Keep her there. I'll be down in fifteen minutes." He
felt Jo's disapproving stare as he replaced the receiver.
"I have to go," he told her as he started for the front
door.

"I heard. Will you at least be home for supper?"

"I don't know." He shrugged on his coat and kissed her cheek. "I'll call."

"You won't be home," she said. "And you won't call." But by then he was already out the door and gone.

SIX

As Palatazin was hanging up his telephone, Rico Esteban was climbing a long series of stairs in an East L.A. tenement, where sunlight took on a muddy pallor as it streamed hotly along the hallways through dirty windows. The steps creaked underfoot, and in some places there was no railing; Rico could look down four floors to the cracked yellow tiles in the entrance hall. Garbage had spilled from cans on the stairway landings, a sheen of smelly liquids making the stairs as slick as if they were carved from ice. Rico still wore the same clothes he'd been dressed in the night before, only now the back of his shirt was damp with sweat. His eyes, now somewhat sunken due to lack of sleep, were veined with red. Around him the building swelled with clashing noise—a toilet chugging as water strangled a clogged pipe; a man and a woman both shouting in Spanish, trying to outcurse each other; a baby howling to be fed and a mother's desperate *"Quieto!";* someone coughing violently, the cough finally falling to a rattle of phlegm; transistor radios and televisions battling for dominance with the thump-thump of disco, a Spanish news broadcast, or the gunshots from a cowboy or detective movie.

Along the fifth floor hallway the heat was sickeningly oppressive. Rico's shirt was glued to his chest and back like a second skin by the time he'd stopped before the door he sought. He paused, his heart racing. He was afraid of the woman who lived in that apartment; she was crazy, there was no telling what she might do to him. Once old lady Santos had sworn to get a gun and blow his balls off if he ever got her daughter into trouble. So now he hesitated, unsure whether to knock or just retrace his steps out of this sweltering pigsty. *What if Merida had gotten back last night and told everything to her mother?* he wondered. *Then there would be hell to pay.*

But what if Merida hadn't come home at all? What if something had happened to her on the jungle strip of Whittier Boulevard? The uncertainty filled him with a dull sense of dread. *That Roach dude was still on the loose, wasn't he? And there were plenty more dudes a whole lot meaner than Roach, too.* Or, on the other side of the coin, Rico could find Merida inside with tear-streaked cheeks and an enraged madwoman with a Saturday Night Special aimed at his groin. *Madre de Dios!*

But he couldn't leave without knowing; he couldn't stand it for a minute longer. He reached out, balled his fist, and knocked on the door. Almost immediately another door down the hallway opened, and an elderly Chicano man stared out suspiciously.

"Who's there?" The words spoken in strident Spanish made Rico jump.

"Uh . . . it's me, Mrs. Santos. Rico Esteban."

There was a long, uneasy silence. *Shit!* he thought, suddenly overcome by panic. *She's gone for her gun!* He was going to run when she said from behind the door, "Eh? What do you want, you little bastard?"

"I'd like to talk to Merida. Please."

"She ain't home."

A knot of tension burst like shrapnel in his stomach. He could sense Mrs. Santos behind the thin layer of scarred wood with her ear pressed to the door. "Do you know where she is?" he asked.

Then the door came open, and Rico took a startled step backward. The woman peered out through a crack, her black, snake eyes staring at him disdainfully from a leathery, deeply creased face. "What do you want to know for?"

"I have to find her. It's important." He couldn't see her hands and thought she might have a damned gun behind her.

Mrs. Santos regarded him in simmering silence for a moment. "I know she's been sneakin' around behind my back, thinkin' she's gettin' away with somethin'! I know she's been seein' you, filth! I figgered when she didn't come home last night she was with you."

"I . . . picked her up in front last night," he said with an effort. "On Whittier she . . . she jumped out of my car, Mrs. Santos, and I tried to find her all night, I went everywhere I could think of, I only got about two hours sleep in the back of my car, and I don't know where else to . . ."

"WHAT?" she screeched, her eyes going wide and wild. "My Merida's been out on the boulevard all night? You bastard, you let my Merida stay out there *all night?* I'm callin' the cops on you right now, you don't get outta here!" Her eyes blazing with black heat, she started to slam the door in his face. But instantly he braced it with a hand. She looked at him open-mouthed, fear beginning to glimmer deep in her gaze.

"You're not listening to me!" he said, almost shouting. "If Merida didn't get home last night, I don't know where she is! She could be in trouble!" *She's already in plenty of trouble,* he thought grimly. "Where else could she have gone?"

Mrs. Santos was frozen, and he knew what she was thinking—*Merida was a good girl, loyal to her mother; she'd never stayed away from home all night before, and she wouldn't run away either.*

"I'm afraid for her," Rico said softly.

Her voice began in a whisper and started to rise. "I told you to leave her alone, didn't I? I warned my Merida about what was out there! You're trouble and you always been trouble, even when you was a smart-assed punk runnin' with the Cripplers! Now only God knows what badness you're doin'!"

"Look, I didn't come here to fight. I don't care what you think about me. I just want to make sure Merida's okay . . ."

"Why? 'Cause you tryin' to talk her into walkin' the streets for you? Everythin' you touch turns filthy! You touched my Merida, and God saw it, and because He knows you're filthy evil He . . . wait a minute! You just wait a minute!" She spun away from the door, and Rico started in after her, his face flaming with anger. She crossed the cramped, dirty apartment and opened a drawer next to the sink and hot plate. "You just wait a minute, you filth!" she shrilled, and then she turned upon him with a butcher knife clamped in her hand. "I'll kill you for what you done to my baby!"

"Please!" he said, backpedaling for the door. "I only want to find . . ."

"This is what you goin' to find!" she shouted and came toward him with the knife aimed for a killing blow.

"You crazy old . . . fuck!" Rick yelled back at her; he wheeled through the door and was able to slam it shut before she could get to him. Then he was running headlong down the hallway, hearing the dry, amused chuckle of the old Chicano man. Rico got to the stairway and started down; behind him the building seemed filled with Mrs. Santos's screams and threats. Her screech of a voice —*just like an old harpy's,* Rico thought—drowned out transistor radios, squalling babies, and marital cursing bouts. But then it began to grow faint, and Rico knew with a surge of relief that she wasn't following him from the fifth floor. Still he hit the entrance hallway at a run. When he got outside, sweat was rolling off his face. A couple of small kids were trying to pry off his wheelcovers, and he sent them running with a kick and an oath. They stopped in the middle of the street to give him the finger, and then they were gone.

He was about to go around to the driver's side when a cool, childish voice said, "Hey, Rico! You shoulda let those punks alone, man!"

Rico turned. Merida's twelve-year-old brother, Luis, was sitting in shadow on the steps of the tenement building next door. There were two other kids with him, neither older than eleven, but already their eyes seemed hard and haunted. They were playing cards, and Luis was smoking a hand-rolled cigarette. "Yeah?" Rico said, walking back to the curb. "Why?"

"They need the bread they coulda sold those shoes for on the street. Two cards." He picked up the two cards dealt to him and snorted with disgust. "Their old man's got a fifty-dollar-a-day habit, gettin' worse all the time. You think just 'cause you move up to the Strip everythin' changed around here, man?"

The words, spoken so calmly from the mouth of a child, stung him. "What do you know about anything?" Rico said. "You're just a kid yourself."

"I know a lot of things." He looked up from the game. "Like my sister was with you last night, and she never came home. My old lady's been pacin' the floor all day. She says she's thinkin' about puttin' out a contract on you with the Homicides."

"Who's going to cut my throat? You, Luis? For how much? Five bucks? Yeah, you're even beginning to think like a Homicide, aren't you? Man, you keep hangin' around those dudes you're going to wind up either gut-stabbed or in the slammer."

Luis dealt the next hand and smiled like a fox. "Too bad we all can't be big like you, Rico. Man, you so big you outgrown the barrio. You're a giant now up on Sunset Strip, ain't you?" He made a farting sound with his lips, and the other kids laughed. "Maven could tear your ass up with one hand! Why don't you get off this street? You don' belong here no more!"

"Maven? He's still prez of the Homicides?"

"That's right. Dealer takes one. Allllright, *amigos!*" He disregarded Rico until the hand was over, and the next cards were dealt. "What're you doin' comin' outta my buildin', man? You let my old lady see you, she'll come after your ass."

"I already saw your mother," Rico said. "She's ready for *la casa de locos*. I'm trying to find Merida, Luis. I don't know where the hell your sister could be!"

Luis looked at him sharply. "What do you mean, man? She was with you all night!"

"No, she wasn't. That's what I was trying to tell your mother. Merida jumped out of my car on Whittier and ran off. I looked for her almost all night. Now where else could she be?"

"You left her *alone?*" Luis said incredulously. "Out on the boulevard all by herself?" The cards dropped from his hand, a couple of grinning kings and a joker. "Man, you livin' so far away from here now you don' know what's goin' on? The Vipers are tryin' to move into Homicide territory! Three blocks from here it's a god-damn battle zone! The Vipers are hittin' on every Homicide they can find. Last week they got Hotshot Zasa, Paco Milan and Juan Morales!"

Rico's heartbeat quickened. "Killed them?"

"Nobody knows. They just vanished . . . poof! . . . and Maven figures the Vipers ambushed 'em and dragged the bodies away somewhere. On Friday Maven's girl Anita was missin', and yesterday Paulo LeGran's little brother, Benny."

"Jesus!" Rico said, fear crackling through his brain. "You think maybe . . . the Vipers got Merida?"

"They woulda known she was my sister." Luis rose to his feet, his gaze smoldering; his face was that of a battle-hungry man, but his chest—bare behind a cheap leather vest—was that of a child's, his skinny ribs jutting. He ran the back of a hand across his mouth. 'Yeah, they could've got her. They could've been waitin' for her in an alley and jumped her. Sonsofbitches could've raped her right there and dragged her off somewhere."

Rico's stomach throbbed; he thought he was going to have to lean over and vomit.

"They could've already killed her," Luis said quietly and turned the full force of his gaze onto Rico. "If she's dead, then you helped kill her! You put her right in Viper hands, *bastardo!*"

"We don't know what happened to her!" Rico said. "We can call the cops and let them . . ."

"NO COPS!" Luis shouted. He was trembling, trying to fight back tears. "This is business for the Homicides, for my brothers. Come on," he said to the other boys, and instantly they stood up from the steps. "We got to go find Maven and tell him!" They started off along the street, swaggering like little roosters. But suddenly Luis turned and pointed a finger at Rico. "You better hope my sister's okay!" he shouted, and then his voice cracked. "You just better hope and pray, man!" Luis turned away from him, and the trio of boys vanished along the street.

Rico watched them move out of sight. A surge of vomit came up from his stomach, and he stood in the mouth of an alley with his head bent, but he couldn't throw up. *Dead?* he thought. *Merida dead?* Killed by the Vipers, a bunch of war-happy punks who were just kids when Rico was running with the Cripplers? A rain of slop came spattering into the alley from a window high overhead. and as Rico jumped away, he heard thin, vicious laughter. Dazed and prickled with cold sweat, he made his way to his car and quickly drove away from the hellish barrio.

SEVEN

"That there's the dude." The black prostitute with heavy-lidded, sensual eyes and orange-streaked hair slid the printed composite portrait across the interrogation-room desk to Lieutenant Reece. "I'd know him anywhere. Tried to run my ass down on Yucca Street. Tried to kill

me. Oh yeah, that's him." She inhaled deeply on a Cigarillo and blew the smoke from the corner of her red-
slashed mouth.

"Did he mention a name to you, Miss Connors? Anything like Wally or Walt or Walter?"

"No. He didn't say a word except to ask my . . . uh
. . . price. Now look here." She glanced nervously at the
slowly turning reel of the tape recorder on the end of the
desk. "You aren't going to try to trick old Lizz now, are
you? I don't like my voice going into that box, you
know?" She looked over her shoulder to where Officer
Waycross and Captain Palatazin sat watching. "You
promised me," she said to Waycross. "You didn't drag
me down here to trap me on a soliciting charge, now did
you?"

"No one's trying to trap you," Palatazin said quietly.
"We're not interested in what you do for a living. We're
interested in the man who picked you up Wednesday
night. One of the problems we've faced during this thing
is that you ladies usually don't like to talk to us."

"Well who's to blame for that? John Law comes down
hard on the sisters. We gots to make a buck, too, you
know." She returned her languid gaze to Reece. "There's
plenty of worse ways to get by."

"I guess there are," Reece agreed. "But you're sure
about these numbers? Two and seven?"

"Yeah. The last number might have been a three . . .
or maybe a five. I don't know." Reece nodded and looked
over the report sheet he'd filled in as the girl talked.
"What about the letters? You think the first one was 'T.'
What about the second one?"

She shrugged. "I didn't have no time to stand there
and read the man's plate, you know. I was tryin' to save
my ass." She blew out another plume of smoke toward
the offending tape recorder. "I figure I did pretty good
to remember anything at all."

"Dave," Palatazin said to Waycross, "why don't you
take the report and get started on the license trace right
away? Ask McCullough and Price to give you a hand as
soon as they're free."

"Yes, sir." Waycross took the report from Reece and
left the room.

"Can I go now?" the girl asked. "I've told you all I can
remember."

"In a minute," Palatazin replied, leaning forward in his chair. "You said—if I can use your exact word—that you were 'jumpy' with this man. Why was that?"

"I usually don't care who I date," she said, "but this dude gave me the creeps. He seemed okay at first, kinda quiet and all. I figured a quick date at the Casa Loma Motel, and then I'd be on my way with fifty bucks. Easy cash because I don't do any specialties, you know?" She raised her eyebrows and waited until Palatazin had nodded. "But his eyes were real funny, and he kept cocking his head to the side like he was having a nerve spell or something. But later on I thought about it, and it seemed he was . . . like . . . listening, you know?"

"Listening? Was the radio on?"

"No. It was like he was listening to something I couldn't hear, and once I saw him smile this weird, peculiar little smile. Anyway, he turns off Hollywood about two blocks before we get to the Casa Loma, and I ask him where does he think he's going, but he don't answer. Just kinda nods. Weird. So then he pulls into this lot where a Seven-Eleven used to be, and he cuts the engine. I figure he wants me to do him right there because he's grinning like a goon. He . . . uh . . . starts to unzip his pants. I was getting kinda jumpy then, but I figured what the hell? So I . . . uh . . . started to lean over and I see his hand drop down off the seat real fast. That's when I got a whiff of stuff, like alcohol but a lot stronger. I didn't know what it was, but old Lizz sure didn't want none of it. I jumped out of that bug and started runnin', and then I hear his engine start, and I say, 'Oh God, that creep's comin' after me!' It was then that I thought about the Roach. But you know, nobody's been trashed by the bastard in a long time, so most of my friends and me figure the guy got his kicks and crawled back under a rock. I made it to the corner, and the Volks peeled right on past me, made the next right, and was gone. I walked to a pay phone and called my man, Tyrone. He came and picked me up."

"This substance you smelled," Palatazin said. "You said it had the odor of alcohol? Could it have been turpentine? Something like that?"

"Can't really say." She crushed out her Cigarillo in an ashtray. "But it was a sharp smell. I was so close to whatever was under that seat that my eyes started to burn. Whatever it was, it was *wicked* shit." Reece smiled in spite of himself, then cleared his throat and looked away when Palatazin glanced at him.

"All right, Miss Connors. I think that's enough." Palatazin rose from his chair and switched off the tape recorder. "You're not planning on taking a trip any time soon, are you? In case we need you for a positive ID?"

"Nope. My stompin' ground's right here in L.A."

"Good. Thank you for coming in. And if I were you, I'd suggest to my friends that they keep their dates platonic until we have the Roach in a jail cell."

"Sho' nuff." She gathered up her handbag, gave a little twitch of her tail to Reece and went out the door and into the squad room. Palatazin sat down again, took his pipe from beside the chair, and lit it. "What do you think?" he asked Reece. "Does that sound like our man?"

"Hard to tell. If this is the same guy who tried to pick up Amy Hulsett, he's not showing the same *modus operandi* as Roach. There's been no attempt at either rape or strangulation."

"If this *is* our man, why would he change his pattern? I don't know, something's strange. That's twice we've heard about a strong odor in this man's car. What could it be?"

"Any one of a number of things from spilled gasoline to cleaning fluid."

Palatazin sat for a moment, smoking his pipe in silence. Reece was reminded of a new TV show he'd seen last night, "Sheer Luck," about some nutty private detective who thought he was the reincarnation of Sherlock Holmes and ran around L.A., trying to solve mysteries with his psychiatrist, Dr. Batson. It had been pretty funny. "The ME went over those four corpses as thoroughly as possible, didn't he? Would he have found swelling or inflammation in the mucous membranes of the nose, or possibly in the eyes?"

"Sure."

"But he didn't, did he? That is to say, no unnatural inflammation other than what would come as a result of the strangling. Right?"

Reece nodded. "What are you getting at?"

"Suppose the Roach *has* changed his MO. Perhaps he didn't like the way those girls clawed at him as they were dying. Perhaps he wanted to keep them from struggling so much. How could he do that?"

"Bop 'em over the head with a hammer, I guess."

"Granted. But suppose he misses with the first whack and the girl starts screaming? Now remember, Miss Connors said that he was reaching for something under the seat and that the strong odor was coming from under there. What does that suggest?"

"Oh," Reece said, "a drug, maybe. Something like . . . ether?"

"That or a similar substance. But in any case it would have to be strong enough to knock out an adult with just a few whiffs. Then the Roach could rape her, strangle her, do whatever he wanted for as long as he wanted."

"What's that stuff they used to use in the mad scientist flicks? You know, they always waved a bottle or a rag under a cat's nose, and then the thing keeled over? Chloroform."

"Possibly. But as far as I know, chloroform can't be purchased over the counter. Maybe it's still used in hospitals. But it would have to be strong, maybe even a concentrated liquid or powder. And where would our man get it?" He blew a long tendril of blue smoke toward the ceiling and watched it swirl in front of the air-conditioning duct. "Something you said a minute ago." He narrowed his eyes. "What *about* gasoline?"

"Whiffing gas might make somebody upchuck all over the place, but I think it would take a while for gasoline fumes to knock you out."

"Right, and we're talking about something that could act in less than a minute." He shrugged. "I don't know. Will you do me a favor? Since you're going to be working this evening, why don't you call some hospitals and pharmacists and get the names of whatever might do the job? I think we'll be looking for a substance that's available over the counter, but it wouldn't hurt to check hospital inventories of ether-related drugs." He rose from his chair and moved toward the door. "What Miss Connors smelled was probably *szeszes*."

"Huh? What's that?"

"Hungarian white lightning." He smiled wanly and then picked up the composite picture from the table. His smile faded as he looked into that chunky, squirrelish face. The eyes, so vacant and detached behind those thick glasses, were what bothered him the most. *Where are you?* he asked silently. *If you're still striking, why haven't we*

found any more corpses? Palatazin was well aware of an
unfortunate fact: It was the corpse, or in this case the
trail of them, that eventually pointed to the murderer, in
the fragment of cloth clutched in a death grip, in the
tissue and hair beneath the fingernails, in a telltale
matchbook or printed napkin found in a handbag or
pocket. Any homicide squad was practically powerless to
stop a murder; all they could do was clean up and piece
together the ugly jigsaw puzzles of passion. And without
fresh corpses, great fragments of the puzzle were missing.

Palatazin pushed the picture back toward Reece. "It's
time we released this to the papers. Will you get it down
to Press Relations for me?"

"Yes sir, I'll take care of it."

Palatazin left the interrogation room and walked back
across the squad room—very quiet today, only a few
detectives working—to his office. He glanced at his wristwatch—five-twenty. The sun was beginning to slide down
across the sky, leaving cold, gray shadows in its track. It
was time to get home to Jo, to try to get himself ready
mentally for the next day's work. Tomorrow morning there
was going to be a meeting with the chief of detectives and
the commissioner, and the caseload of non-Roach-related
homicides was getting heavier day by day: a Chicano
man found bludgeoned to death in a downtown alley;
a pretty teen-aged girl found stuffed into the trunk of a
stolen car with her throat slashed from ear to ear; a
middle-aged woman shot on the sidewalk by someone in
a passing car; a three-year-old child battered beyond recognition and stuffed into the bottom of a garbage can.
Palatazin was a reluctant witness to a daily sideshow of
horrors. Some days, of course, were worse than others:
on the worst of them, usually at the height of the summer,
his nightmares were vivid with the heat-swollen corpses of
men, women, and children, all of them holding out their
arms to him and begging like lepers for a cure. And the
means of murder in this city were terrifyingly infinite:
Baseball bat, pistol, broken bottle, poisons from a dozen
different countries, knives of all description and purpose.
coat hangers, clothesline cord, barbed wire, and even in
one instance a brass ball fired from a slingshot. The motives for murder were just as complex: Vengeance,
money, freedom, hatred, and love. The City of Angels?
Palatazin knew differently.

When he was fourteen years old, his Uncle Milo had gotten him an afternoon job sweeping up at his neighborhood police precinct station. He'd been fascinated with the cops-and-robbers shows he'd seen on the television in the window of the Abrahms Brothers Appliance store a block from the apartment, and he was thrilled to imagine himself as part of that world with its blue-uniformed policemen, sleek cars, and crackling, urgent radios. The officers liked his interest, and they went out of their way to explain the details of their jobs to him. For several years he was the willing recipient of every chase and shoot-'em-up story the cops could dish out, and those ran into the hundreds. Only it was years later, when he himself wore one of those crisp, blue uniforms, that he realized the world was not quite as black and white as the TV shows had depicted. He'd been walking his beat along Fountain Avenue when a fat, red-faced man in a white apron had started shouting about a robbery in his grocery store. Palatazin had seen the suspect—a thin black man in a long, tattered coat—running in the opposite direction with hands clamped around a couple of loaves of bread and a Polish sausage. He'd given pursuit—he'd been much thinner in those days and fast on his feet—and had caught up with the guy easily, grabbing his flagging coat from behind and yanking him to the ground. The food had scattered into the street and was smashed into pulp by the next passing car. Palatazin had wrenched the arms back, snapped cuffs on the wrists, and turned the man over.

It wasn't a man; it was a woman, terribly thin, her stomach swelling in the sixth month of pregnancy. "Please," she'd begun sobbing, "please don't make me go to jail again. Please don't make me . . ." Palatazin was stunned and ashamed; the red-faced man, who had as much beef in his belly as on his racks, came up and started shouting about "this whore, this filthy whore" who had come in and stolen right off his shelves in broad daylight and what were the cops going to do about it? Palatazin couldn't answer; the cuff key in his hand burned like a white-hot flame. But before he could say or do anything, a police car came cruising up to the curb, and the shouting man turned his attention to the arriving officers. As they put the woman into the car, her sobbing had stopped, and her eyes looked like the empty windows of a long-abandoned building. One of the officers clapped Palatazin on the shoulder and said, "Good job, this broad's been hitting stores all up and down Fountain for the past two weeks." As the car pulled away, Palatazin stared at the paste of bread and sausage in the street. The red-faced man was bragging to a group of onlookers about how nobody could rob him and get away with it, *"nobody!"*

Now a world away from Fountain Avenue, Palatazin felt a wave of regret pass over him. He took his coat from the back of a chair and wearily shrugged into it. Why hadn't things worked out as he'd planned so many years before? His dream had been to take his wife and son up to a little town north of San Francisco where the climate was cooler and head a small police station where the most serious crime was kids stealing from a pumpkin patch. He wouldn't even need a car, and he would know and be liked by everyone in town. Jo could open that florist shop she was always thinking about, and his son would be quarterback on the high school football team. He buttoned his coat and let the dreams drift away, like so much shimmering dust. After the second stillbirth Jo's doctor had told her it would be dangerous for her, both physically and emotionally, to try again. He suggested adoption and left it at that. And Palatazin had been caught, as everyone is, in the huge whirlpool of events that takes you down once, twice, a third and final time. He knew he would probably remain in this city until he died, though sometimes late at night he thought he could close his eyes and see that little town, full of white picket fences and clean streets and chimneys that puffed white plumes of cherrywood smoke in the long winters.

Time to go home, he thought.

And something rustled very softly behind him.

Palatazin, startled, whirled toward the door.

His mother was standing there as substantial as any flesh he'd ever seen. She was wearing the pale blue gown she'd worn the night she died, her skin wrinkled and white over frail, sharply jutting bones. Her eyes were fixed upon his face, terribly intense. One arm was thrust out, as skinny as a pole, the finger pointing toward the window.

Palatazin, the blood drained out of his face by the shock, took a step backward and collided with the sharp edge of his desk. His pipe rack toppled over, as did the framed photograph of Jo. File folders drifted to the floor.

His mother opened her mouth, showing almost tooth-less gums, and seemed to be trying to say something. Her finger was trembling, her face contorted with effort.

And then Palatazin saw the outline of the door through her, saw the gleaming doorknob as if in a haze of gravish smoke. Her figure rippled like gossamer caught in a high wind. And was gone.

The breath exploded from Palatazin's lungs. He was trembling uncontrollably, his hands gripping at the desk behind him. For a long time he stared at the spot on the floor where his mother had stood, and when he finally waved a shaking hand over that spot, the air felt a few degrees cooler than the rest of the room.

He opened the door and thrust his head out so vio-lently that Officer Zeitvogel, who was at the nearest desk promptly spilled a cup of hot coffee into his lap. Zeitvogel cursed and leaped to his feet, drawing the attention of the other officers to Palatazin's pale, wide-eyed face. Instantly Palatazin retreated into his office but left the door open; he felt sick and light-headed, as if he'd just snapped out of a brain-burning fever. He stood staring dumbly at the folders on the floor, then bent and started picking them up.

"Captain?" It was Zeitvogel at the door, mopping his pants legs with a couple of paper towels. "You okay, sir?"

"I'm fine," he said, but kept his head away from the man so he wouldn't betray the fear that was still making one corner of his mouth twitch.

Zeitvogel looked down at his lap. *Christ!* he thought. *Wonder if I can make the department foot the cleaning bill? Fat chance! The captain has all those folders in his arms now, why won't he stand up?* "For a minute there you looked like you'd seen a ghost, sir."

"Did I?" Palatazin rose and dumped the folders onto his desk. He righted Jo's picture and the spilled row of pipes. Fishing for the keys in his pocket, he stepped out of his office quickly and locked the door. "Don't you have work to do?" he said tersely, and then he was mov-ing past Zeitvogel and out of the squad room, his shoes clicking on the tiled floor.

Weird, Zeitvogel thought. He shrugged at the other men, swabbed at the worst of the stain, and sat down at his desk again. Before he returned to work, he wondered whether what he'd been reading in some of the papers and hearing whispered around the building *was* true, that the captain was being squeezed over this Roach thing, and the pressure was starting to crack him. He continued typing his report on a young man found shot to death in bed that morning and thought, *Better him than me.*

EIGHT

Night had filled up the barrio like black rainwater filling a bomb crater, and what stirred in its depths was unnameable. Chill, tortured winds gnawed at the corners of silently crumbling buildings; in the narrow alleys rats scuttled in search of food, their eyes catching red pinpoints of light. And three Chicano boys clad in tight black leather vests and black headbands crouched behind a spill of dusty bricks and watched a dilapidated, graffiti-smeared building less than a hundred yards away. In the distance the tenement buildings seemed to be standing at odd angles, like crooked rows of gray tombstones.

"Ain't nothin' moved in there for over an hour, Maven," the boy on the left, as thin and dark as whipcord, whispered huskily. "Ain't nobody in there."

"I say they are." The one in the center was the largest of the three, his biceps and forearms bulging with muscles. On the left bicep there was a tattoo of an eagle clawing a snake and beneath it the name MAVEN. Jet black hair spilled over his headband, and his eyes— set in a square, large-jawed face—were tight slits of animal cunning. "Oh yeah," he whispered, "the *enemigo* is in there and tonight they gonna pay."

"They musta moved their headquarters," the thin one said. "The scouts musta been wrong."

"They're hidin'," Maven said, "because they're scared shitless of what we're gonna do to them." He gazed up at the surrounding rooftops; a few more Homicides were up there, keeping watch on the Viper headquarters. But Maven couldn't see them; they were hidden too well. He looked back to the building and shifted because the .45 in his waistband was beginning to cut into his stomach.

The other two, Chico Mapazan and Johnny Pascal, were equally armed: Chico carried a nine-inch blade and a pair of nail-studded brass knuckles; Johnny clutched a baseball bat with four-inch nails driven through it. "Who wouldn't be scared shitless," Maven said softly, "knowing the Homicides were huntin' for 'em?"

"Gonna clean those fuckers out," Johnny whispered, fingers clenching and unclenching around the bat. "Gonna make 'em pay."

"I get the first shot," Maven told him. "I get my revenge for what they done to Anita. Bastards probably raped her dead and dragged her body off to the garbage dump." A muscle in his jaw flexed. "They want to play rough, we'll show 'em what rough means."

"When do we go?" Chico asked, his gaze flaring with impatient fire.

"When I say so. Right now we wait."

In about fifteen minutes the building's front door opened. Maven tensed like a strip of barbed wire. Two boys—one in an Army surplus jacket and the other bare-chested, came out and sat on the front steps. They seemed to be talking, and in a swirl of wind Maven could hear their raucous laughter. "Bastards," he breathed. "Gonna make you pay." They sat there for a long time, then they both rose at the same moment and disappeared back into the building.

Almost immediately a small figure came scrambling across the lot, ducking low and keeping close to the thicker patches of shadow. It was Luis Santos. He hit the ground and crouched next to Chico. "Everybody's ready, Maven," he said. "Zorro's got some troops around at the back door."

"Good. He carryin' his momma?"

"Yeah." Zorro's momma was a sawed-off shotgun, stolen from a gun shop less than a month ago but already put to good use.

"He may need it when those bastards run out the back door." Maven took a breath and then said, "Okay. We go." He lifted his head, put two fingers in his mouth, and let out a couple of short whistles. "You goin' with me, little soldier," he said to Luis. "Make 'em pay for trashin' your sister, man." He handed Luis a carved ebony switchblade that could pass for a butcher knife. Maven whistled again, long and low, ending in an as-

cending note. Instantly shadows filled the lot and began
to move. Maven and the others got up quickly and began
to run through the darkness, crouched low and ready to
dive for cover.

Nothing moved, no one fired a shot, as they approached the building.

"Gonna catch 'em sleepin'," Maven whispered. "Gonna
wipe 'em out." He reached the building first with Luis
right behind him. Maven took one of his two black market
grenades from his belt, pulled the pin, and lobbed it
through the nearest window. Then he dove against the
building's side, flattening himself, and saw Luis do the
same.

When the grenade exploded with a hollow *whuuump!*,
blazing white fragments of metal came whining through
the window like hornets. In the next instant Maven was
charging up the steps, followed by a horde of Homicides.
He kicked in the door and leaped through, firing .45 slugs
in a red-hot arc. Luis clicked open the blade, feeling it
thrum up his wrist. He felt like the Ice Cream Soldier
to Maven's Sergeant Rock; his blood was boiling, his
brain crystal clear. He leaped through the open doorway,
followed by Johnny and Chico and the rest of the Homicide troops. Inside Maven was crouched on the floor in a
blue haze of gunsmoke. He could see the holes in the
hallway wall where his bullets had hit. But the entrance
hall and the dim corridor leading back through the building were empty. He heard nothing but the clatter of
Homicide boots, the fierce breathing of his soldiers.

"Ain't nobody here!" Chico wailed.

"SHUT UP!" Maven shouted and rose to his feet, his
finger twitching on the trigger. "They got to be here!
Where are you, fuckers?" He saw the outlines of more
open doorways further back along the corridor. "Bastards
are scared shitless!" he shouted. "Come on out! We're
gonna have a little party!" He fired into the corridor and
heard a rain of plaster. "Chico, you and Salvatore and
about six more go on up them stairs and check out
the second floor. Don't let 'em jump you. GO ON,
WHAT'RE YOU WAITIN' FOR? Everybody else stick
to me!" He started along the corridor, crouching like a
panther, peering into one empty room after another.
"Hey man," somebody said behind him, "I don't like
this . . ."

"Shut your mouth and follow me!" Maven said, but now there was uncertainty in his voice, and a couple of his men faltered. But Luis stuck close beside his Sergeant Rock. At the rear of the corridor, there was a padlocked door. Maven snarled a curse and stepped into the nearest room; he fired twice into a closed closet and then wrenched it open, expecting a couple of bleeding bodies to tumble out. But there was nothing but a clothes hanger dangling from a rod. Luis bumped into him, and Maven said, "Get back, kid!" He could hear the noise of boots overhead—his troops checking out the upper floor.

And then he looked up.

They were clinging to the rafters like bats.

Maven shrieked and lifted his gun as the bodies began to fall. His shot went wild as something landed on his back and grabbed his hair. He fell to the floor, hearing a hiss very close to his ear. And now all over the building, there were shrieks, cries to God, angered curses, the noise of falling bodies, and gunfire exploding into wood and plaster. A heavy form hit Luis's shoulders and drove him down, slamming his head against the floor. In a red-misted daze he heard Maven babble for mercy and then scream piteously, like a woman. A shotgun blast knocked the rear door off its hinges, and now Zorro's troops were streaming in. Dark figures leaped through the corridor to meet them, and a dozen separate battles raged in the darkness. Gunfire cracked, etching quick, hot veins in the air. Luis, his head pounding, tried to drag himself up off the floor and caught a kick in the ribs; he doubled up, tears blinding him, his fingers searching for the ebony blade. Someone else began to scream, and he scream was echoed all through the building. A body hit Luis and crashed to the floor. Luis heard a moaning sound followed by a strange and terrible . . . sucking. His brain flared, *I don't want to die like this! I don't want to die like. . . .*

An icy hand gripped his shoulder and turned him over like he was made of straw. A figure crouched next to him, eyes burning, pinning him to the floor. And then Luis saw that it was Hotshot Zasa, the Homicide lieutenant who'd supposedly been trashed by the Vipers. Relief coursed through him, and he said, "Hotshot?" He wasn't going to die after all, wasn't going to die, wasn't . . .

Hotshot grinned.

The four fangs in his mouth—two protruding from the upper gums and two from the bottom—were yellow and dripping with fluids. The lower fangs curved inward slightly, like fishhooks; the upper ones were slanted toward each other, making a hideously efficient *V*. Hotshot's face glowed white, like the moon; his fingers, skinny and clawlike, dug deep into Luis's flesh to keep him from twisting away.

And now Hotshot was bending forward, the eyes in that terrible face starting to roll up into the head with greedy expectation.

Luis screamed a single word, the word that had carved itself into his brain as if from a red-hot switchblade—*"Vampiro!"*

Above him Hotshot cackled and bent forward to his feast. The lower fangs pierced flesh and hooked. Hotshot twisted his head a fraction to hone in better on the flaming river of life that flowed just beneath Luis's chin. Luis's hands came up to push Hotshot's head away, but they moved too late with too little strength. When the *V* of Hotshot's fangs came down, blood spurted across his face. He blinked, shifted his position again, and as if from a great distance Luis heard his blood being sucked, the sound like someone sucking Coca-Cola through a straw or sniffing fine cocaine from a golden spoon. Luis's hands fluttered, one finger digging into the corner of Hotshot's eye. Instantly he heard a voice in his brain, something dreamy and soft—*Lie still, little brother. Lie very still.* Luis's hands fell to the floor like dead birds.

He was beginning to feel cold, really cold, but where Hotshot's lips were pressed against his flesh, an inferno raged. He lay very still while the arctic cold crept through his veins, inch by merciless inch. Winds were rising in his head, deafening him with their shriek. And by the time his jugular vein collapsed, as flat as a gutted worm, Luis was fast asleep.

Gradually the hideous sucking noises that echoed through the many rooms were quiet. But in a few minutes they were replaced by another noise—the sound of bodies being dragged across the floors.

NINE

Roach—much younger, but with an agonized madness already fermenting in his brain—pushed open the door.

In the small bedroom with its mustard yellow wallpaper and acrid smells of tobacco smoke and sweat, another stranger was astride his mother, riding her roughly with flesh-smacking thrusts. The man's buttocks and thighs tensed and untensed like the action of a mindless machine. Bev's hands gripped his shoulders, and the man's broad back was gridded with scratches. The bed trembled, springs squealing beneath their combined weight.

There was an empty whiskey bottle at the foot of the bed. Roach moved into the room, bent, and picked it up. He could see Bev's face—blank, drunken, bloated. She seemed to be looking right at him, her eyes lascivious and brimming with invitation. His groin was throbbing that hateful bass drum beat of desire. He lifted the bottle by the neck and stepped forward, already choosing the spot he would strike. As the bottle came down, he heard Bev scream, "NO!" And then it had crashed down not upon the stranger's dark-haired skull but across his right shoulder because he'd twisted with the scream. The bottle broke across a shoulder blade, jagged edges digging into the flesh. The man shrieked, "Goddamn it, you crazy little bas . . ." and then struck out with the back of his hand, hitting the boy across the nose and dropping him to the floor. Roach, blood stringing from his nostrils, scrabbled to his feet and, whining like an animal, rushed forward. The bottle was forgotten now, he was going to kill this man with his hands. The stranger twisted off Bev and drove a solid blow to the boy's chin that lifted him off his feet and then down again like a heap of laundry. "You stay away from me!" the stranger shouted, bending quickly to retrieve the broken bottle. "You stay away or I swear to God I'll kill you!"

Roach started forward again, his beady black eyes as dead as marbles, but then Bev shifted in the bed, and he stopped. Her thighs were exposed, and between them her sex glistened like a gateway to all the pleasures he'd ever

145

imagined in his tortured dreams. He turned toward her, the stranger forgotten now, and approached the bed on trembling legs. Bev's face flushed red. She closed her thighs and pulled the sheet up to her neck. Her son stood at the foot of the bed transfixed, his hand moving in slow circles at his crotch.

"My God," the stranger whispered, droplets of blood tapping to the floor. "My God . . . how long . . . has this been going on . . . ?"

"It's not what you think, Ralph!" she said, avoiding her son's languid gaze. "Please . . . !"

"You . . . and him?" The stranger's eyes moved back and forth between them. "Your own *son?*"

"Not long, Ralph . . . I swear to God, not long!"

He saw it all then. "You . . . you like it, don't you? Jesus! You like it with your own son?"

And suddenly it all came bursting out of her before she could stop it, the anger and fear and black guilt that was her legacy to her son. "YES, I LIKE IT!" she shrieked. "I like it when he touches me! Don't you dare look at me like that . . . get out of here! GO ON! GET OUT!"

The man was already struggling into his pants. He grabbed his shirt from the back of a chair and shrugged it on over his injured shoulder.

Bev was screaming now, a high, whiskey scream, "I'm *glad* we do it! He's more of a man at thirteen than you'll ever be . . . !"

"Sure, sure," he said, working his shoes on. "You're both nuts, aren't you? Christ, I knew *he* was off his rocker, but you, too?"

"GET OOOOOUUUUUUTTTTTT!"

The man paused at the doorway, fumbling with his wallet, and flung a few bills at her. They spun like dead leaves at the boy's feet. "Maybe they'll give you the same room at the nut house," he said and whirled out. A door opened and closed, and then there was silence but for Bev's harsh breathing. She stared at her son, tears beginning to slide down her cheeks. "It don't matter," she said softly. "Not a bit. We've got each other, don't we? We'll always have each other. They don't understand how bad it is to be alone, do they, Waltie? Nothing matters. Come on. Hurry."

And he did.

The bedroom and Bev and the mustard-colored walls

rippled like a pond into which a stone has been tossed. The ripples strengthened, moved faster and faster and suddenly the whole scene vanished as if it had been sucked to the dark depths of a whirlpool.

Roach rubbed his eyes and sat up in bed in his dank apartment. It was still very dark outside, and somewhere jukebox music was playing. He could hear the black cockroaches scrabbling in their cages. He stood up and went to the window, looking down on Coronado Street. Dreaming about his mother made him nervous; sweat had come up on his face. It made him angry, though he couldn't exactly figure why. Perhaps it was because he knew now how much of a liar she was; she *had* left him after all, and because she had, they had sent him off to a place—the Crazyhouse—where people laughed and shrieked all the time, where he had to take pills and drink a lot of water. Something within him needed but hated that need. When he found his mother, as the Master had promised him he would someday, he wouldn't have to fear going back to the Crazyhouse again. Everything would be all right.

He walked across the room to the table on which sat the little cages filled with roaches. Their backs glistened like black armor in the darkness. He picked up a matchbook, struck a match, and held it to one of the cages; the roaches scrambled away. When the flame died down to a red pinpoint, he could hear them scurrying back over each other again.

Walter Benefield was dead now. His name was Roach, and it was a name he liked. Ever since he'd gotten the job at Aladdin Exterminators four months before, he'd been studying them in their death agonies when he sprayed Dursban or Diazanon in cracks between floors and walls. Sometimes the roaches would flood out in a strange kind of dance, flopping and running and falling as the chemical began to drown them. Often there would be large, black roaches, the bulls of the nes , that would start to recover and scurry away; they were the ones he would catch by hand and drop into a plastic bag to bring home for his experiments. He was awed by their strength, by their sheer tenacity; very few things could kill a massive, three-inch bull. The diazanon might make them crazy for a little while, but without a good second spray they would recover. Even stomping on them couldn't do it; they played dead for a few seconds and then zipped away with their guts hanging out, like relentless tanks. They were so *fast,* natural survivors that had remained virtually the same for millions of years. Over the months he'd burned them, tried to drown them in the toilet, tried to suffocate them, cooked them in a pot of boiling water, and performed a dozen other experiments in death. Very few things worked. It had just been luck that he'd had a bag of them in his car the night he'd picked up that first girl. After she was dead, he wondered whether the roaches would suffocate inside her mouth, and so he went to work. They had, finally, and he'd been very pleased with himself. Doubly pleased when he realized the papers were calling *him* Roach. It was an honor to him, and so he continued doing it just for fun because the papers and the police seemed to expect it.

Now when he saw himself in a mirror, it seemed he was beginning to look like them. His shoulders were broad and slightly stooped, his hands and forearms as muscular and large as steel clamps; he had the heavy, dark-browed forehead and small black eyes that missed nothing. Once his hair had been black and curly, but when he started working for Aladdin, he cut it very short, right against a large, bulbous skull. Very small ears and jutting, bony elbows completed the image he had of himself—that he was undergoing an evolutionary change, crossing the line between man and insect, becoming stronger and smarter and almost invincible, just like them.

He untaped a corner of the waxed paper that covered one of the cages and reached down inside, grasping a roach between his thumb and forefinger. It got away, and it took him a few more seconds to get another one. Then he pressed the corner back so none of them could escape and, holding the squirming roach inside his balled left hand, he turned on the lights. The overhead fixture, an opaque umbrella of dirty glass, lit the room with a harsh glare that threw the man's huge shadow out around him. He went to the stove, turned on the gas flame, and dangled the roach over it. The insect scrabbled frantically at his fingers. He had the power of life and death over it, just as he did over those girls who were friends of Bev and who laughed at him when they thought he wasn't looking. Oh, he knew how they laughed; he was much smarter than he let on. Some of them he'd seen with Bev before, when he was just a kid and she used to walk the street. They were her friends, and they were hiding her from him.

It used to be he could fix them with his hands and stop them from laughing, but the Master had said that was a waste. The Master wanted them for himself, so he'd told Roach that he should take poisons from where he worked —liquids and powders—and use them on those girls to make them sleep for a while. Roach had taken some of them—Seven dust, V-1, Dursban, Diazanon and a few others—from the stockroom at work late on Saturday night; he knew very little about them except that Mr. Lathrup had warned him to wear his mask when he used them. So he did just that when he mixed the chemicals in bottles on his stove. Then he tore up an old towel and soaked the rags in the solution for a long time, pouring what was left—an oily, brown liquid—into an orange juice bottle which he stored under his sink. The first time he used it was the next Tuesday night, and the Master was very angry at him because the girl was dead when they reached Blackwood Road. After that he cut the mixture twice with water, and it worked just fine.

The roach caught fire. He watched it sizzle and then dropped it into the sink where it writhed and ran around in circles. He turned on the water, and the roach spun down the drain, still kicking.

He looked up suddenly, his eyes glowing. He thought he'd heard a faint whisper coming in through a crack in the window, filling the room. He stepped to the window and put his palms against the glass, staring out into the darkness. He listened, his head cocked to one side. The Master was going to need another one tomorrow night. Now he wanted Roach to sleep, to forget all the bad things, to think only of tomorrow and the new kingdom that was to be.

Roach pressed his forehead against the glass for a few minutes and then went to turn out the lights. When he was in bed again, he picked up his handgrips from the floor beside him and began to squeeze them, s ueeze . . . hold . . . release, squeeze . . . hold . . . release. He would do that twohundred times before he went to sleep. In the darkness the springs sounded like the rubbing of hungry mandibles.

IV

Monday, October 28
THE GRAVEDIGGER

ONE

It was twelve minutes before three in the morning. Noel
Alcavar had his feet propped up on his desk, and beside
him a transistor radio blared Latin disco loud enough to
wake the dead. *No, not quite,* Alcavar mused as he slid
his gray cap forward over his eyes. *At least the stiffs out
there weren't sitting up in their graves yet,* he thought. *If
they did, I'd kick 'em in their asses and send 'em back to
Hell. Ai-yi-yi, what a job this was!* He closed his eyes
and moved one foot to the disco beat, trying to forget
that there were about fifty stiffs lying out in the darkness
under huge, gnarled trees filled with the green drip of
Spanish moss.

For the last five nights Alcavar had been covering for
his brother Freddie, who held the dubious title of Head
Watchman for the Ramona Heights Cemetery in the
Highland Park district, dubious because Freddie Alcavar
was the only real full-time watchman, and he held rank
over one skinny Chicano kid who was mentally retarded
but smart enough to play sick most of the time. And now
Freddie had been hit by a virus that kept him in the bed
between dashes to the toilet, and the doctor had told him
to stay home and rest. So Noel was helping out, playing
loud disco so he could imagine that he was boogying with
the foxes at the Disco 2000 on North Broadway. Freddie
had told him he was supposed to take his flashlight, leave
the green-painted shelter, and stroll through the cemetery
every half-hour or so. Noel had done it twice since he'd
gotten here at ten, and that had been enough to leave him
with a lingering case of the chills. In every whisper of
wind he thought he heard the icy tinkle of ghostly laughter, and every mound of grass seemed to be pressing upward, about to split open for a skeletal hand covered with
mold. *This ain't a job for a young man,* Noel had told

himself as he hurried back to the shelter and turned the latch on the door. *Bet old Freddie's fakin'. Bet he's at home laughin' his ass off right this minute!*

If he hadn't felt sorry for Freddie because of the way his ex-wife had treated him during the divorce, Noel would never have volunteered for this graveyard shit. But as it was, he was going to be stuck with it until Freddie was back on his feet, which might be another day or two. Noel shivered when he thought about that and turned the radio a bit louder.

He was about to close his eyes again and drift into the spin of Disco 2000 dancers when he saw the two head-lights right up against the front gate about thirty yards away. Noel straightened up in his chair and peered out the window. *Now who the hell is that?* he wondered. *High school kids parkin', maybe? Doin' a little drinkin' or dope-smokin'? No, they wouldn't have their lights shining like that.* He stood up, moving to the window. In the dim backwash of the lights, he cou'd see that it was a large vehicle, some kind of truck with markings on it. The thing was just sitting there, and now Noel could see a couple of shadowy figures moving alongside the gate. One of them stopped and looked in through the bars. *What is this?* he asked himself and quailed at the thought—*Trouble? No way!* He remembered what Freddie had said just before he made a flying leap into the bathroom, "Is easy job, Noel. No trouble, nobody bothers you. You jus' make your rounds and look like you know what you're doing. Everything is okay. No trouble."

Now both figures were standing at the gate, peering through the bars; the headlights made their shadows thin and gigantic on the cemetery drive. They seemed to be waiting, taking their time. But suddenly one of them rat-tled the gate, and Noel felt his stomach roil.

He took his flashlight from atop the desk and went out-side, the single thought, *no trouble, no trouble,* repeating over and over like an incantation against harm. He neared the gate, the headlights blinding him, put a hand over his eyes, and switched on his own light. The large vehicle was a U-Haul truck, and the two figures were kids younger than he, maybe in their late teens. One was a black dude wearing a headband, the other was white with shoulder-length brown hair: he was wearing a T-shirt tha bore a cartoon, a Big Daddy Roth beach bum smoking a bomber joint over the message King Kahuna Wants You! Noel moved uneasily toward them and saw that they were both smiling. But their smiles hardly made him feel better because their eyes were as cold as those of a dead fish. Noel stopped and shone his light in their faces. "Cemetery's closed," he said stupidly.

"Yeah, *amigo*," the white one said. "We see that." He reached over, pulled at the gate's padlock, and grinned. "You got the key to this?"

"No." The key was in his breast pocket, but he didn't want these two to know. Somehow he didn't feel safe, not even with the gate between them.

"Yes you do," the black dude said very quietly, his gaze boring into Noel's skull. "You got the key, don't you? Got it right . . . right in your pocket. Yeah."

"No, I don't. I don't . . . uh . . . have . . . a key . . ."

"Open the gate." The black dude coiled his fingers around the bars. "Come on . . . Noel? Open the gate, Noel."

Noel shook his head. *My name? How does . . . he . . . know . . . my name?* He thought he could hear the blood rushing through his head; he felt dizzy, weak, confused. *What would be the harm in opening the gate, anyway?* he asked himself, and a smaller voice shouted, *You're not supposed to do that, no trouble, no trouble. . . .*

"Noel, we don't have much time, man. Step on over here . . ."

His right foot moved. He blinked, his brain full of disco thunder.

". . . let us in, okay?"

For an instant he thought he was strutting on the Disco 2000 dance floor with the foxiest chick there—Dianna Valerio maybe—and the mirrored ball at the ceiling reflected a thousand different colors, all as electric bright as exploding novas. The music stopped with a quiet *click!*

"That's good, man," the black dude said as he stepped through the opening gate. He gripped Noel's wrist with freezing fingers and took the key. "Who gets him?" he asked the white boy.

"The new girl's thirsty," he replied, and they led Noel around the rear of the truck, unlocked the doors, and lifted him up. Noel's face was frozen with a crazy, crooked grin, his heart about to beat its way through his chest. He thought it was quitting time, six A.M., and he was on the way home. *Made it through another night,* he told himself. *Wasn't so bad.*

"For the girl only," someone said.

The doors slammed shut behind him.

There were five or six people in the darkness, and one of them—a slender wraith of a thing—took his hand. He felt like he'd stepped into a meat locker. Then there were arms around him, enfolding him closer toward the heart of the chill. He stumbled over something—a pickaxe— and then a freezing mouth kissed his lips, darting tongue forcing its way in; the mouth kissed his cheek, his chin, his throat.

And became hideous.

In the darkness someone sighed and whimpered.

The truck's engine rumbled to life, and it moved through the opened gate into the Ramona Heights Cemetery while the boy in the Kahuna T-shirt stood watch on the quiet street. Deep within the cemetery it stopped. The rear doors were opened again, and now the figures came out—five of them because the girl was filled and lazy— carrying shovels and pickaxes. They scattered out beneath the trees and set to work on the graves, digging like well-oiled machines without pause. When the first coffin was struck, two others stopped their work to help; they dug it free in less than a minute and heaved it out of the ragged hole. Inside there was a skeleton in a black suit and yellowed shirt. The casket was quickly turned over to dump out the bones, then shoved into the rear of the U-Haul. There was a faint *clang!* as another coffin was struck. This one was small, cradling the brittle bones of a child. The bones were spilled to the ground and cracked underfoot like twigs as the coffin was loaded into the truck.

At the end of an hour almost thirty coffins were stacked in the rear of the U-Haul. Mounds of dirt and scattered bones littered the cemetery, and the clothes and faces of the exhumers were filthy. But still they worked on, until finally the black with the headband straightened up from the empty hole below him and said quietly, "Enough."

They returned their tools to the truck. The figures climbed in and the doors were locked. The truck backed up across the bone-littered grass and turned toward the gate, where the lookout was picked up. Then gathering speed, the truck pulled out of the cemetery and turned right along Aragon Avenue toward the commercial district of L.A.

TWO

Gayle Clarke, squinting in the bright, early morning sunlight, pulled her red Mustang into a public parking lot off Pico Boulevard and walked half a block to a small, gray building that had been, in previous incarnations, a karate school, a health club for overweight housewives, a Zen Buddhist temple, and a health food store specializing in varieties of kelp. Now the legend painted across the plate-glass window in bold, blue, scrolled letters said THE LOS ANGELES TATTLER. WE PRINT IT AS WE HEAR IT. WE PRINT IT AS WE SEE IT. There was what looked like a virgin in a tacky long dress beneath the words holding a flaming torch. *The ethics of corn,* Gayle told herself as she went through the front door.

Inside six desks were scattered across the room in various stages of disarray; there were stacks of old copies of the *Tattler* and other newspapers and magazines on the floor, a battery of dented file cabinets bought at a warehouse fire sale, a bookcase crammed full of decaying dictionaries and reference books either copped from the library or bought at flea markets. Across one wall was an air-brushed mural left from the kelp store days—spouting whales, sea otters playing happily in the kelp beds, the sun shining on a beach full of perfect, healthy bodies. She hated that mural because every time she went on a binge of Twinkies and Oreos, she had to come in on Monday morning and look at those disgustingly *healthy* figures. Holly Fortunato, wearing her usual skin-tight black dress, looked up from the reception desk which was about ten feet away from the closed door with the plaque that read, *Harry Tracy, Editor.* She smiled, "Hi, Gayle. Have a gooooood weekend?"

"Same as usual," Gayle said tonelessly, ready for the next line in the ritual.

"I had a kinky weekend,", Holly breathed. She was

wearing glittery eye shadow, and her breasts heaved like black melons. "Kay-ink-key! I was just telling Max . . ."

"Hi, Max," Gayle said to the studious-looking young man at the nearest desk. He looked up from his typewriter and smiled, the braces on his teeth showing. Then he went back to work without a word, and Gayle sat down at her own desk in the back beneath the precariously leaning bookcase. She hung her purse over the back of her chair and began straightening a morass of papers and magazines so she could have a clear shot at her typewriter, an old gray Royal with a mind of its own, usually malevolent.

"I met this guy at a party down at Marina del Rey," Holly was saying. "And you know what? He was a *director*. He did a movie a year ago called *Free 'n Easy* . . ."

"Sounds like porno," Gayle said.

"Oh, no! It was about a couple who meet in a nudist camp!"

"That's what I said," Gayle replied. "Porno." She crossed the room and poured herself a cup of coffee. She could hear Trace muttering through the tissue-thin wall.

"Anyway, it had a limited release, but he said he was working on another one, and he'd like for me to . . ."

Gayle tuned her out and nodded whenever she felt she should. In the meantime Bonita Carlin, a thin girl with crimped, red hair who favored punk outfits and covered what she called "the world of rock 'n roollll," came in carrying an armload of *Rolling Stones*, and immediately Holly began at the beginning with "Hi, 'Nita. Have a gooood weekend?"

"Shitty," Bonita said.

Gayle sipped her coffee and checked the assignment board. Beneath each name printed with a Flair pen on pieces of colored cardboard were index cards with the details of their stories for the week. She glanced over each one in turn to get an idea of what next week's *Tattler* was featuring: "Biology professor at UCLA—Dr. Peter Willingham—says eating eggs can cause sterility. Call 345-4949 ext. 7"; "Rod Stewart—Do married blonds have more fun?"; "Could Kim Novack cop this year's Oscar for Best Supporting? Her agent wants to talk"; "CHiPs may be Dips—motorist group charges Highway Patrol with reckless driving. Call Mrs. Jordan, 592-7008."

Oh God, Gayle thought as she came to her own name.

There were four words scribbled on her card, "See me. HOT! Trace."

She drank down half of her coffee before she knocked at his door. "In!" the voice behind the door said.

Trace was on the phone; he waved at her to close the door and sit in a chair next to his desk. A fresh copy of this week's *Tattler* lay open before him. "Okay, Warren, okay!" he was saying. "So I ruffled some big money birds with the story. So what? I mean, if the *Tattler* can't print the truth, who can?" He paused, his high forehead wrinkled; he was in his early forties, a hippie who'd never quite outgrown the life-style. He was almost bald except for the wild tufts of graying hair that stuck out from the sides of his head, and his thick-lensed glasses had slipped down on his severely hooked nose. As he listened, he unscrewed a bottle of Vitamin C and popped down a couple of orange pills, then offered some to Gayle, who shook her head.

"Fine," he said. "Warren, I don't give a shit! Those guys have built a condo that's going to go sliding into the Pacific the next time the San Andreas fault even *thinks* about moving! What are they going to do, sue the earth?" He listened again, his face beginning to redden. "It's structurally unsound, the engineering reports prove it! And I don't care if some people are moving out of their condos. Jesus, they *should* move out before the next quake hits! And everybody—all the national psychics— are predicting The Big One within five years! So let 'em get out while they can! Listen, Warren, I've got to go, I've got a paper to put out." He paused, his lips working, but no sound coming out. "What do you mean by that remark? My people can write rings around the *Talking Leaf!*" He slammed down the receiver so hard his desk trembled. "Wait a minute, Gayle," he said and began to breathe rhythmically. "Negative air floating around here. That was my silent partner, not so silent today." He shrugged and pushed the paper across to her. "Seen this yet? The front page is a grabber!"

She turned the paper around and opened it. There was one of Jack's photos of the skeletons at Hollywood Memorial; the picture took up the entire page and was bordered with red spot color. Above it, also in red, the headline screamed, "WHO IS THE GRAVEDIGGER?"

Beneath that in much smaller print, "See Gayle Clarke's shocking story, page three."

"The . . . Gravedigger?" Gayle said quietly, a knot of tension growing in her stomach. "Trace. What's this . . . this Gravedigger bullshit?"

"It's not bullshit," Trace said, looking genuinely hurt. "I thought the buildup would please you. Listen, the Gravedigger's going to knock Roach out of every paper in this town!"

"The Gravedigger," Gayle repeated, not believing what she was seeing. She felt like crawling into one of those ragged holes in Jack's photo. "Trace, I don't think the story merits a push like this. Okay, I admit it's a weird item. I don't think anything like it has ever happened before, at least not in L.A., but what's the bogeyman angle? I didn't imply anything like this in my piece."

"Roach is old news. The guy's gone underground. He's all used up. You know what sells papers, Gayle? Evil. That's right. People pick up a magazine or a tabloid or even the *Times* looking for evil, for something to blame for all the misery in their lives. And most of all they want a villain, a Nixon or a Dracula or a Hillside Strangler. The Roach has disappeared, so we've simply given the people what they want—another villain. And we can build this thing, Gayle, God can we ever! The Gravedigger, creeping through cemeteries in the dead of night, digging up coffins and scattering the bones . . ."

"Please," Gayle said and shivered. "I was there, remember?" She felt sick to her stomach, as if she'd had another whiff of the reek of rot in the hot, lazy sunshine. "The cops say it must've either been a death cult or kids on drugs, and that's what my story says, too. So how can we say anything that may be untrue?"

"Ah. You don't read your own copy, do you? Look at page three."

A surge of panic rushed through her. She opened the paper and saw a red-bordered box right in the middle of her story surrounded by more of Jack's gruesome photos. The headline of the story read, "Did The Gravedigger Visit Resurrection Cemetery?" "What is *this?*" Gayle said, her voice trembling between horror and fury.

"You think I don't have contacts too? I got interested in this thing and made a few phone calls over the weekend. The same thing that happened in Hollywood Memorial happened at Hope Hill and at Resurrection. Missing caskets and everything." He shrugged. "Friend of mine on the force owes me a favor, so I collected. I went over to the printer's Saturday night and typed the story right there."

Gayle quickly read through the article. It was written terribly but got its message across: Resurrection Cemetery had been vandalized in exactly the same manner a little more than a week ago. "So you see?" Trace said, lifting one eyebrow. "The Gravedigger makes the Roach look like an amateur, at least in the chills department."

"Christ." Gayle put the paper back down on his desk and looked at him in numb astonishment. "What's going on?"

"You're going to tell me. I want you to forget about old Roachie and concentrate on the Gravedigger. Maybe he struck somewhere else before he ripped through Resurrection, maybe he's done another job since Hollywood Memorial. I want as much as you can get, and I want it complete by Thursday afternoon. Can you handle it?"

"Trace, it can't be just one guy! Nobody could rip up a cemetery like that alone!"

"Maybe he's strong. Maybe he drives around in a custom-built bulldozer, who knows? Anyway, narrowing the angle to one weirdo sells more papers. Evil, babe, evil!" He caught the flicker of hesitation across her face. "Now what's wrong?"

"I'm so into the Roach thing, I . . . Trace, I don't think I should leave it just yet. I think it's way too early to write him off. Why not let Sandy take care of this?"

"Look," he insisted. "Nobody's seen the Gravedigger, and anyway you're about three times the writer Sandy is. Now go. Get started!"

Gayle reluctantly stood up. She said, "I'd like to stay with . . ."

"The Gravedigger. Out!"

She moved toward the door, unable to believe this wild turn of events. Her head was throbbing, her stomach roiled, she felt sick to her very soul. *This is bullshit!* she told herself. *The Roach is really important. Doubly important when you think about my career. But this is . . . bullshit!*

"Wait a minute," Trace said as she turned to go. "Have

you seen Kidd? I need him to get some shots of Miss California Redwoods this afternoon."

"No, not lately. We went to a Joan Baez concert Saturday night, but I didn't see him all day yesterday. He may have gone out to see the Greenpeace people."

Trace grunted. "That guy's spreading himself a little thin, isn't he? Listen, will you try his number for me when you get a minute? I really need him to come in early and set up the shot."

She nodded, still in a daze, and left his office. Outside Holly Fortunato was telling the sportswriter, Bill Hale, about the wide variety of whips her director friend kept in his closet. Gayle sat down at her desk, shuffled papers, and tried to think how she could get out of the story Trace wanted. Still, three cemeteries vandalized—no, not just vandalized, ripped to shreds—in less than two weeks. Possibly more. Who could she call to find out? She jotted down the names of several police force antivandalism squad members she knew. She thought Davis Tortirici was the captain of that squad, but she wasn't sure.

But there was something else bugging her that hadn't surfaced until Trace had pointed it out—where was Jack? He'd said he was going to splurge and take her to dinner at the Mandarin on Sunday night, but he'd never called. She'd spent her evening drinking white wine and reading a nasty little book called *Bethany's Sin*, which she'd tossed away in boredom after the fourth chapter. She wanted to be with Jack, really needed to be with him, and she'd dialed his number three or four times during the course of the night. Each time the phone had rung at least ten times before she'd put the receiver down.

So where was he?

What am I? she asked herself. *A mother hen?* But then her hand was reaching out, and she was gripping the telephone beside her. She dialed Jack's apartment again and let it ring.

No answer.

There were a dozen different places Jack could be; she'd gotten used to the fact that the only consistent thing about Jack Kidd was his inconsistency. That was due to his chart, he'd told her proudly, double Gemini.

She hung up the phone and wasted a few minutes making herself another cup of coffee, then wandered over to where Kenny Morrow was pounding out his health hints

column. This week his column opened up with a letter
from a Sacramento reader who thought the government
was controling his sex desires through the rays from his
color TV. She was looking over Kenny's shoulder when
her telephone rang, and she hurried back to answer it,
thinking Jack might be calling in.

"Gayle?" the man on the other end said. "This is Tom
Chapman from the *Times*. Remember? We met at Palatazin's last press conference?"

"Oh, sure." She faintly recalled the guy—stout and
balding, wearing a brown checked coat. "How are you,
Tom?"

"Fine. Better since I . . . uh . . . picked up your paper
and saw your piece on that cemetery business. I got
quite a kick out of that. Who came up with the 'Gravedigger' angle?"

"My editor."

"That was great. Really sell some papers that way . . ."

"Can I help you. Tom?" she interrupted because the
sarcasm in his voice was beginning to irritate the shit out
of her.

"Huh? Oh, listen, don't get sore. I was just kidding.
No, I thought I'd call to help you. Us journalists have to
stick together, right?" He paused for a few seconds. Gayle
was silent, her anger simmering at a low boil. "Our story's
already out on the streets, so I thought I'd pass the information along to you. We just ran a few graphs on
page eleven, but maybe you can . . ."

"Tom . . ."

"Okay, okay. Somebody dug up Ramona Heights Cemetery over in Highland Park last night. Stole about twenty
or twenty-five coffins, left the stiffs scattered to hell and
back. The watchman, guy by the name of . . . hold on,
I'm looking in the paper . . . Alcavar, is now on the
missing persons list. The Highland Park cops are checking out some tread marks they found in the grass. It
seems the Gravedigger drives around in a large truck.
Now don't say I never gave you anything."

Gayle had started scribbling on a notepad. *What the
hell is going on?* she wondered. For the first time a spark
of real curiosity crackled inside. "Do you have Alcavar's
first name and address?"

"Noel. Got his brother's address from the cops—he's
the regular watchman—909 Costa Mesa Avenue in High-

land Park. What are you thinking, that Alcavar loaded up those coffins himself? Why?"

"I'm not thinking anything. I'm just looking for a starting point. Thanks for calling, Tom. Incidentally, this doesn't mean I'm finished with the Roach."

"Yeah, I hear you've been sneaking in to see Palatazin when the rest of us had our backs turned. Well, anyway you can get it, I guess. Uh . . . listen, Gayle, you remember I told you about the situation with my wife? I've moved out of the house, sort of a free bird now. How about having dinner with me ton'ght? I've got a Playboy Club key, and you can take a look at my new apartment and tell me what it needs . . ."

"Tonight? Uh . . . no, Tom, afraid I can't . . ."

"Tomorrow night then?"

"My editor's calling me, Tom. I'll talk to you later. And thanks a bunch for the information. Bye-bye." She hung up the phone and read over her scribbled notes. *Ramona Heights? That made four cemeteries vandalized in less than two weeks? What kind of freaks would do something like that? Death cultists, Satanists, what?* The term *Gravedigger*, repellent only a few minutes before, now chilled her. She put her notepad and a couple of Bic pens in her purse and hurriedly left the office, bound for the Ramona Heights Cemetery.

THREE

Police Commissioner McBride sat reading Pala*azin's progress report on the Roach investigation at the far end of the conference room's polished oak table. Every few minutes he grunted, and when he did, Chief of Detectives Garnette glanced across the table at Palatazin with a look that said it all—*You'd better hope he's in a gracious mood, Andy, because there is nothing concrete in that report.*

Palatazin was well aware of the fact. He'd come in before seven that morning to finish typing the report and felt ashamed when he'd taken it to Garnette for a first reading. There was nothing in it but specu'ation, vague theories, and leads that went nowhere. He'd included the information from Amy Hulsett and Lizz Connors toward the end, and detailed the work Sully Reece and his team were doing to track down the gray Volkswagen, but even that looked woefully ineffectual on paper.

McBride glanced quickly up at Palatazin and turned a page. From where Palatazin was sitting, McBride was bracketed by an American flag and the California state flag, and golden sunlight seeped through the venetian blinds at his back. There were dark circles beneath Palatazin's eyes, and as he lit his pipe for the fourth time during the conference, his hand was trembling slightly. His night had been terrible, his dreams filled with shambling horrors coming for him out of a snowstorm, creeping nearer and nearer out of the windswept pines that circled him. He had seen their burning eyes, their mouths slashed like grinning sickles, and in those mouths the terrible, unholy teeth. And just when they were about to claim him, his mother had appeared, floating over the snow, and gripped his hand. *Run,* she'd whispered. *Run, André!* But he had left Jo waiting in a cabin, and he had to get back to her, but that meant running the gauntlet of the grinning terrors. *I won't leave you,* his mother had said, and at that instant the things had leaped for Palatazin's throat.

He had awakened cold with sweat, and this morning over breakfast Jo had wanted to know what he'd been dreaming about. Palatazin told her the Roach; he wasn't ready to tell the the truth yet.

At the end of the table, McBride closed the report and pushed it aside. Over the rim of his coffee cup, he looked from Garnette to Palatazin, his eyes stunned for an instant by the bright green striped tie Palatazin wore with a light brown coat. He put the cup down and said, "This isn't enough. In fact, it's little more than nothing. The *Times* is applying some pressure for a public progress statement. If I used this report as my basis, they'd be printing thin air. So what's the problem?" His icy blue eyes flared. "We have the best police force in this entire country! Why can't we find *one* man? Captain, you've had over two weeks to work on this thing with the entire force from helicopters to beat cops at your disposal. Why haven't you turned up anything more concrete than this?"

"Sir," Palatazin said, "I think we're making some progress. The artist's composite was printed on the front page of the *Times* this morning, and it'll be carried by the afternoon newspapers as well. We'll get it to the television stations in time for the afternoon and evening newscasts. Also there's the matter of the Volkswagen . . ."

"Slim, Palatazin," the commissioner said. "Awfully damned slim."

"I agree, sir, but it's more of a lead than we had before. The women—the street prostitutes—are wary of being seen talking to police officers. They're frightened of the Roach, but they don't trust us either. And that's how we're going to find the man, sir, through them. My men are working on finding a Volkswagen with a two, a seven, and a 'T' in the license number . . ."

"I suspect there may be several hundred," McBride said.

"Yes, sir, there will be. Possibly a thousand or more. But you have to agree it is a lead that merits investigation."

"I want names, captain, names and addresses. I want suspects in for interrogation. I want surveillances. I want that man caught."

"We all do, commissioner," Garnette said quietly. "And you know Captain Palatazin has been interrogating suspects daily and carrying out some surveillances as well. It's just that . . . well, sir, the Roach seems to have gone underground. Maybe he's left the city. Catching a hit-and-run killer like this, a psychotic without motive, is the toughest job there is . . ."

"Spare me, please," McBride answered. "I don't want to hear any confessionals." He returned his gaze to Palatazin, who was trying unsuccessfully to light his pipe again. "You're telling me that this Volkswagen license plate is the only real lead you've got, is that it?"

"Yes, sir, I'm afraid so."

McBride sighed loudly and folded his hands in front of him. "I don't want this thing to turn into another Hillside Strangler case, captain. I want this man—or men—caught quickly so we don't get our asses kicked by the public and the press. Not to mention the fact that as long as this bastard remains unidentified, someday we're going to stumble over another hooker's corpse. I want him canned, do you understand me? And I want him canned *fast!*" He took the report and slid it down the table to Palatazin. "If you can't find him, captain, I'll put someone in charge who can. All right? Now both of you get back to work."

As they waited for the elevator in the hallway outside the conference room, Garnette said, "Well, Andy, that wasn't as bad as I thought it was going to be."

"It wasn't? I was fooled then." His pipe had gone stone cold, so he shoved it in his pocket.

Garnette looked at him in silence for a few seconds. "You look tired, Andy. Worn out. Everything okay at home?"

"At home? Yes. Why?"

"You got a problem, you can tell me about it. I don't mind."

"No, there's no problem. Except the Roach."

"Uh-huh." Garnette was silent for a moment, watching the numbers advance above the elevator door. "You know, something like this could strain even the strongest ox of a guy. It's a hell of a responsibility. I'll tell you, Andy, you look like you haven't slept for two days. You . . . hell, you didn't even shave this morning, did you?"

Palatazin ran a hand across his chin and felt stubble. He couldn't remember if he'd shaved or not. No, he decided, he probably hadn't.

"I understand that your men are also beginning to see changes in you." The elevator arrived, and they stepped in. It began to descend. "That's not good. It weakens your leadership position."

Palatazin smiled grimly. "I think I know who you've been talking to. Officer Brasher, possibly? He's a lazy bum. And Zeitvogel? Who else?"

Garnette shrugged. "Talk gets around. You haven't been yourself for the past few days . . ."

"And so people have started pointing their fingers, have they? Well. It didn't take as long as I thought."

"Please, Andy, don't get me wrong. I'm talking as an old friend now, okay? Just what were you getting at when you called Kirkland at Hollywood Division and requested a stakeout on a cemetery for God's sake?"

"Oh," Palatazin said softly. "I see."

The elevator opened on a wide corridor floored with green linoleum. They stepped out and walked toward the homicide squad room, beyond two frosted-glass doors. "Well?" Garnette said. "What about it?"

Palatazin turned to face him. His eyes were dark holes

in his pale face. "It has to do with the vandalism over there . . ."

"I thought as much. But that's not your problem or your detail. Let the antivandalism squad over in Hollywood mop it up. You stick to homicide."

"Let me finish," Palatazin said, and in his voice there was a tremble that made Garnette think, *Andy's about to crack.* "You have to know that where I was born, in Hungary, people think differently about . . . many things than they do in this country. I m an American now, but I still think like a Hungarian. I still believe in the things that Hungarians believe. Call them superstitions or old wives' tales or whatever, but I accept them as the truth."

Garnette's eyes narrowed. "I don't understand."

"We have different beliefs about . . . life and death, about things that you would consider material for movies or bad paperback books. We think that not all is explicable by the law of God because the Devil has laws of his own."

"You talking about spirits? Ghosts? You mean you wanted Hollywood Division to stake out some ghosts?" Garnette almost laughed but didn't because the other man's face was so deadly serious. "Come on, is this a joke? What have you got, Halloween fever?"

"No, I'm not talking about spirits," Palatazin said. "And it is not a joke either. Fever, perhaps, but my fever is called fear, and it's beginning to burn me up inside."

"Andy . . ." Garnette said quietly. "You can't really be serious . . . are you?"

"I have work to do now. Thank you for listening." And before Garnette could stop him, Palatazin had gone through the doors into the squad room. Garnette stood in the corridor for a moment, scratching his head. *What was wrong with that crazy old Hungarian?* he thought. *Now he's going to have us running around after spooks in cemeteries? Jesus!* A darker thought stirred sluggishly in his brain, *Is the pressure making Andy unfit for duty? God,* he thought. *I hope I don't have to . . . do anything drastic.*

And then he turned away from the doors and made his way to his own office further down the corridor.

FOUR

The intercom on Paige LaSanda's desk crackled to life, "Miss LaSanda, there's a Phillip Falco here to see you."

Paige, a stunning, ash-blond woman in her early forties, looked up from a report on a piece of industrial property she was interested in purchasing on Slauson Avenue and pressed the Speak button. "He doesn't have an appointment does he, Carol?"

There were a few seconds of silence. Then, "No, ma'am. But he says it concerns money owed to you."

"Mr. Falco can make his payments to you, dear." She returned to the report. The property looked promising; it was underdeveloped and could support a larger factory than the one now on it, but the asking price might be a bit too. . . .

"Miss LaSanda?" the intercom voice said. "Mr. Falco wants to see you personally."

"When and who is my next appointment?"

"Eleven-thirty. Mr. Doheny from the Crocker Bank."

Paige glanced at her diamond-studded Tiffany wristwatch. Five after eleven. "All right," she said, "send Mr. Falco in."

After another moment the door opened, and Carol ushered Falco—a gaunt man with long white hair and deepset eyes—into the office. For a few seconds Falco stood at the center of the huge room, seemingly awed by its sumptuous furnishings, though he'd been to this office twice before. Behind her glass-topped, mahogany desk Paige said, "Please sit down, Mr. Falco," and motioned toward a brown leather chair.

Falco nodded and took his seat. In his rumpled, brown, pin-striped suit, he looked like little more than a cadaver, his flesh pale to the shade of gray, his wrists jutting from the coat sleeves. On a table beside him a burst of bright red roses made him look duller still. His eyes were never at rest; they moved across Paige's desk, across her face, the broad picture window that looked out over Wilshire Boulevard, to his own hands in his lap, back to her desk, and then to her face again.

Paige held up a carved, Dunhill cigarette case of lustrous black wood, and Falco took three cigarettes without apology, putting two in the breast pocket of his coat and lighting the third from the lighter flame Paige offered. "Thank you," he said softly and leaned back in his chair, smoke dribbling from his nostrils. "These are European cigarettes, are they not?"

"Balkan tobacco," Paige said.

"One can tell immediately. American brands are so dry and tasteless. These remind me so much of a brand sold in Budapest . . ."

"Mr. Falco, I presume you've brought me a check today?"

"What? Oh, of course. The check." He rummaged in an inside coat po ket and brought out a sealed and olded envelope. This he slid across the desk to Paige, who instantly used a twenty-four carat gold letter opener on it. The check was written against a Swiss bank account and signed by a smooth, graceful hand Conrad Vu kan.

"That's fine," she said, eyeing the amount with mental glee. "How long should this take to clear?"

"A week at most," he answered. "Prince Vulkan plans to transfer a large amount to a local bank shortly. Do you have any suggestions?"

"I suppo e the Crocker Bank's the most convenient. One of their vice-presidents is coming in at eleven-thirty. You might speak to him about it."

"There's something else in the envelope, Miss LaSanda," F lso said.

"Oh?" She opened it wider and turned it upside down. A small white card fell out; it was engraved with the words Requesting The Pleasure Of Your Company— Prince Conrad Vulkan. "What's this?"

"As it says. I've been instructed to invite you to dine with Prince Vulkan at eight o'clock tomorrow evening if that's convenient for you."

"Where?"

"Why, the castle, of course."

"The castle? Then I take it you've somehow convinced the power company to repair the lines running up there? That's more than I could ever do."

"No." Falco smiled slightly, but it was a smile of the mouth; the eyes remained vacant and faintly troubled. "We have no power yet."

"What's your prince going to do then, have something catered? I'm afraid I'm going to have to say . . ."

"Prince Vulkan is very interested in meeting you," Falco said softly. "He assumed the reverse would be true as well."

Paige regarded the man for a moment—*sad-looking guy*, she thought, *doesn't he ever see the sun?*—and then lit a cigarette of her own, placing it in a long black holder with a gold band. "I'll be honest with you, Mr. Falco," she said finally. "When you came to me in September, wanting to rent these pieces of property, telling me you represented Hungarian royalty, I was highly skeptical. Before the deal was signed, I made a few transatlantic telephone calls. I could find no one in the present Hungarian government who knew anything about a Prince Vulkan. So I was ready to pull out, until you made your first payment in cash. I may not trust very many people, but I do trust the dollar, Mr. Falco. My last husband left me with that philosophy. Yes, I am interested in meeting your Prince Vulkan . . . if indeed he is a prince."

"He is. Most definitely."

"Of a country that doesn't even recognize his existence? I don't think I'd be out of line if I asked where he gets his funds from, do you?"

"Family money," Falco said. "He's currently involved in selling some pieces from his very old and valuable art collection."

"I see." Paige ran a fingernail over the raised lettering on the invitation. She recalled what a Hungarian official had told her during the last of her overseas calls, "Miss Lasanda, we *have* found a Conrad Vulkan mentioned in a fragment of Magyar history dated around 1342, but that would hardly be the gentlemen you're seeking. This Prince Vulkan was the last of a long line of pretenders to the throne of the northern provinces. His carriage went off a mountain road when he was just seventeen, and it was assumed that wolves ate his body. As for someone passing himself off as Hungarian royalty, that's a different story indeed. We would hate for the name of our government to be involved in any . . . shall we say, unsavory practices?"

"For a man of royal tastes," Paige said to Falco, "this Prince Vulkan doesn't seem to care very much about his living conditions, does he?"

"The castle suits him perfectly," Falco replied, crushing out his cigarette in an onyx ashtray at his side. "He lives now approximately the same way he lived in Hungary. He needs no luxuries, no conveniences of a modern world. He's never used a telephone and never plans to. For light there are always candles, aren't there?"

"And he uses the fireplaces for heat?"

"That's right."

"Well, I've sold and rented both houses and commercial property to all kinds of people, but I'll have to say that your Prince Vulkan is quite a unique individual." She drew on her cigarette and blew smoke toward the ceiling. "I bought that old place for a song. At the time the Hilton people were thinking about converting it into a hotel, but the plans fell through for one reason or another . . ."

"The castle is built on unstable rock," Falco said quietly. "Prince Vulkan has told me he can feel the walls vibrate from time to time."

"Oh, really?" Paige's cheeks reddened a bit; of course, she'd already known that fact from the Hilton surveyors. "Well, it's stood for over forty years, and I'm confident it'll stand for another forty. At least." She cleared her throat and felt the old man's stare fixed to her. "But Prince Vulkan isn't involved in local commerce, is he?"

"No."

"Then why did you want those warehouses? Of course, it's none of my business. As long as he pays the rent, I don't care what he stores in there, but . . ."

Falco nodded. "I understand your curiosity, and so does Prince Vulkan. I would therefore suggest that you accept his invitation. All will be explained."

"I've never met a prince before," Paige said thoughtfully. "A couple of sheikhs and some rock stars, yes, but not a prince. Or an ex-prince either for that matter. How old is he?"

"Old enough to be wise, young enough to have ambitions."

"Interesting. Eight o'clock?" She picked up the card again and looked at it, then looked at the signature on the check. "I have a previous engagement for tomorrow night, but I suppose I could break it this once. Well, what the hell? I've never had dinner in a drafty old castle before. Tell him I'd be honored to have dinner with him."

"Very good." Falco rose to his feet and moved unsteadily toward the door. He put his hand on the knob and paused, standing still for a few seconds.

"Anything else?" Paige asked.

Falco's spine seemed to stiffen. Very slowly he turned to face her, and now his eyes had retreated so far back in his creased, weary face that they seemed no more than small black circles somewhere at the brain. "I've spoken for Prince Vulkan," he said in a soft, tired voice. "Now I'll speak for myself, and God help me. Turn down the invitation, Miss LaSanda. Keep your previous engagement. Do not come up that mountain to the castle."

"What?" Paige smiled uncertainly. "I've said I'll come. There's no need to twist the knife of suspense . . ."

"I mean what I say." He paused, staring straight at her so intensely Paige felt a chill run up her spine. "Now what reply shall I take to the prince?"

"Uh . . . I'll come. I guess."

Falco nodded. "I'll tell him. Good day, Miss LaSanda."

"Good . . . uh . . . good day."

And then Falco had slipped through the door and was gone.

"Now what in the name of Christ was that all about?" she asked herself. She held up the check—*I hope this bastard's good,* she thought grimly—and looked at the signature, trying to envision the man through it. The lines were thin and elegant, and under the name there was a looped, intricate flourish that reminded her of the signatures on old faded, yellowed documents. *Probably used a quill on this too,* she thought, *no Bics or Mark Cross for the prince. He would, of course, be dark, very tall, and a thin as a drawn rapier; he would be in his late forties or early fifties, and he probably had a list of ex-wives as long as Wilshire Boulevard. That's probably why he came to the States—to get out of alimony payments.* She wondered what to wear—her sensible gray business outfit? her sleek and sexy black dress? She decided to run over to Bonwit Teller during her lunch hour and check out the display windows.

The intercom crackled. "Mr. Doheny is here, Miss LaSanda."

"Thank you, Carol. Send him right in." She folded the check and, smiling dreamily, tucked it away in a drawer.

FIVE

A blood red Chrysler Imperial with a foxtail tied to the radio antenna pulled smoothly to the curb of Machado Street in East L.A., three blocks from the Santos's apartment building on Dos Terros. From the car a young black man wearing sunglasses and a pale blue suit emerged, at first glancing warily up and down the street and then swaggering toward an unpainted wooden bench a few feet away. He sat down to wait because he had just finished a deal up on Whittier and he was early.

Across the street, lines of multicolored clothing hung between the dark, brick buildings. Occasionally someone passed by a window—a woman in a printed dress, a man in a stained undershirt, a child with thin shoulders—and stopped to stare out vacantly at the rest of the world. From other open windows the black man could hear tinny transistor radios, the rattle of pots and pans, the long wail of a child, voices raised in feverish anger. Sometimes jammed in between the tenements were ramshackle houses with sagging front porches, hulks of cars, or remnants of washing machines in rock-strewn front yards. It was just after noon, and the sun was merciless, beating down like a hammer on the dry, flat streets; it seemed that everything trembled at the point of ignition, ready to flare into fire with each tick of the clock. The black man turned his head, beads of sweat glittering on his cheeks, and stared across at a clapboard bar decorated with white-painted music notes. It was, not surprisingly, called *El Musica Casino*. At the corner of Machado there was a flat-roofed grocery store, its windows plastered with Spanish signs. A slat-ribbed dog sniffed around garbage cans, stopped to stare balefully at the black man, then scurried away down an alley.

It was a neighborhood ripe for the dreams that Cicero sold.

When he looked to his left again, he saw a man and woman approaching, holding hands like frightened children. The man, a walking skeleton with deep blue hollows beneath his eyes, wore faded brown trousers and a

shirt with a green and brown floral pattern; the woman
would have been quite attractive but for the acne scars
on her cheeks and a feral look in her eyes. Her hair was
dirty, and it hung limply around her shoulders, and she
wore a bright blue shift that barely covered her swelling
belly. Their combined ages would hardly have added up
to much more than forty, but their faces carried ancient,
desperate expressions.

Cicero watched them coming, his teeth flaring white.
He hooked a thumb back toward that alley, and the two
figures hurriedly entered it. Cicero looked up and down
the street again. *Everything was cool,* he thought. *The
cops never prowled around here.* He got to his feet and
took his sweet time in going back to the alley where they
waited.

"Gimme," Cicero said when he reached the man.

He gave Cicero a coffee-stained envelope, his hand
trembling. Beside him the woman shivered; her teeth were
chattering. Cicero tore open the envelope and counted the
money very slowly, relishing the cold waves of need that
washed in off the two bodies. Then he grunted, said
"Lookin' good," and withdrew a small packet of white
powder from an inside coat pocket. He dangled the
packet before the man's face and saw him bare his teeth
like an animal. "Sweet dreams," Cicero whispered. The
man grabbed it with a soft moan and raced off along the
alley with the woman shouting at his heels. Cicero
watched them vanish around a corner and put the money
in his pocket. *Stupid shits,* he thought. *Fool didn't even
wait to check the horse. Junk's cut so much they'll barely
get a buzz, and before nightfall they'll be needin' again.
Well, they know where to find old Cicero . . . . .*

He laughed to himself, patted his pocket, and walked
back along the alley toward the street.

At the mouth of the alley, a hulking figure stepped into
his path. Cicero said "Wha . . . ?" and that was all because in the next instant a hand had slammed into his
shoulder, sending h'm flying back into the alley. Cicero
collided with a brick wall and went down to his knees, all
the breath squashed out of him. A hand with scarred
knuckles grasped Cicero's collar and wrenched him up
until he was standing on the toes of his gray alligator skin
boots. His sunglasses dangled from one ear, and his first
coherent thought was *Cop.*

The man who held him pinned against the wall was over six-four with wide shoulders that looked as solid as concrete. He was a Chicano, possibly in his mid-forties, dark complexion with fierce, black eyes under thick, gray-flecked brows. He wore a mustache, also flecked with gray, and there were swirls of gray at the temples in a head of hair so black it seemed to hold shimmers of blue. His eyes were narrowed into fierce slits above a craggy nose, and there was the faint, pinkish line of a scar running through his left eyebrow and up into the hairline. This man had a deadly look, and he was crowding Cicero too close for him to reach the ten-inch blade in his back pocket.

Not a cop, Cicero thought. *This fucker wants to rob my ass, maybe kill me, too!*

And then Cicero's gaze dropped to the man's throat. And the white collar he was wearing. A priest!

Cicero almost laughed as relief surged through his body in waves. But when he began to smile, the priest slammed him back against the wall so hard his teeth clicked. "Come on, man," Cicero said. "How's about backin' off, huh?"

The priest stared at him coldly, keeping that hand clenched on Cicero's shirt. "What kind of filth was in that packet?" he rumbled. "Heroin? Answer me before I break your neck, *culebra!*"

Cicero snorted. "You ain't gonna break no neck, Mr. Priest. That's against your re-ligion."

With a sharp twist of his shoulder, the man flung Cicero to the ground. "Hey!" Cicero squawked. "You crazy or somethin'?"

"How long have you been dealing heroin to Miguel and his wife?"

"I don't know no damned Miguel."

"Who else have you been selling to?"

Cicero started to get up, but the priest moved forward with fists clenched, so Cicero stayed where he was. "Sellin'? I ain't sellin' nothin'!"

"All right, suppose we let the police decide that, *sí?*"

Cicero's hand began the long creep back to his pocket. "Look, old white collar, you don't want to mess with me, understand? I don't want to hear no talk 'bout cops. Now you're gonna step aside and let me go on my way."

"Get up," the priest said.

Cicero rose slowly, and by the time he'd straightened, he had the blade hidden in the hand that dangled loosely behind him. "I said you're gonna let me pass!" he said hoarsely. "Do what I tell you!"

"I've been looking for you for a long time, ever since I knew Miguel and his wife were hooked on that trash. And you've been selling to Victor DiPietro and Bernardo Palamer, haven't you?"

"I don't know what the fuck you're talkin' about." Cicero grinned widely, and then the tongue of steel lapped at hot sunlight. "Move out of my way, man!"

The priest looked at the blade but didn't move. "Put that down or I'll make you eat it."

"I ain't never stuck no white collar before, but I will if you pushes me! And by God you're pushin' me right now! Ain't nobody pushes Cicero Clinton, understand?"

"Bastardo," the priest said quietly. "I'll stick that knife up your ass and send you running home to your momma."

"Huh?" Cicero said, stunned for a second by the priest's language. That second of hesitation spelled his doom for, right in the middle of it, the priest's fist came flying out of thin air and crashed against the side of Cicero's head. As Cicero staggered back, he flailed out with the knife, but his wrist was suddenly caught in a crushing vise; he shrieked in pain and dropped the blade. Then another fist filled his vision, bloodily knocking a few teeth into his mouth. Cicero started to go down, but then the priest grabbed him by the scruff of the neck and was dragging him along the alley. On Machado Street, in full view of a number of people who had watched the whole thing from their windows, the priest picked up Cicero and jammed him down into a garbage can.

"You ever come back to my streets," the priest said, "I'll have to get rough with you. *Comprendo?*"

"Yeth," Cicero croaked, spitting out blood and bits of enamel. When he tried to struggle out of the can, black waves crashed over him and sent him spinning down to the bottom of the sea.

"Hey! Father Silvera!" someone called out, and the priest turned. A small boy in blue jeans and scuffed white sneakers was running toward him. When the boy was near enough to see the arms and legs sticking out of the garbage can, he stopped and stared, open-mouthed.

"Hello, Leon," Father Silvera said. He rubbed the

skinned knuckles of his right hand. "Why aren't you in school today?"

"Uh . . . I don't know." He stepped back as one of Cicero's arms twitched. "I didn't do my homework."

"That's not an excuse." Silvera looked at him sternly. "Your father let you stay home from school?"

Leon shook his head. "I have to take care of my sister. Papa didn't come home last night."

"He didn't come home? Where did he go?"

"Out." The boy shrugged. "He said for me to stay home with Juanita, and he was going to play cards. That was last night."

"He didn't go to work today?"

Leon shook his head again, and Silvera's shoulders sagged forward slightly; he'd helped Sandor LaPaz get that job at the garage, he'd even vouched for the good-for-nothing *bastardo*. Now Sandor had probably lost a week's wages in a card game with the neighborhood hustlers, and he was drinking himself into a stupor in a bar. "Are you and Juanita okay?"

"*Sí*, Father. We're doing good."

"Did you eat anything for breakfast?"

The boy shrugged. "Taco chips. But I gave Juanita a glass of milk."

"Your Papa left some money for you?"

"A little bit in a drawer." His face clouded over slightly. "He's gonna come back home, isn't he?"

"Of course he will. He's probably home right now. You'd better get back there yourself and keep an eye on Juanita. She's too young to be left alone. Hurry now. I'll be by later this afternoon."

Leon beamed and started to turn away, then suddenly he heard a soft moan that didn't come from the man in the garbage can. When Leon looked back, he saw Father Silvera wiping sweat off his forehead with the palm of a trembling hand. "Father?" he asked. "You all right?"

"Yes. Hurry on now. I'll see you later. Go!"

The boy scurried on away. He felt better now that Father Silvera was going to come by to see him. If the *padre* said things were going to be all right, then they would be. And Papa would be home, too, just like he said. Truly, he was a miracle man.

Silvera was aware of the people watching him from their windows. *Not now!* he told himself. *Please don't let*

it happen now! When he let his hand hang by his side, it
jumped and twitched with erratic spasms. He felt a boil
of anger at the pit of his stomach, and suddenly he kicked
over the garbage can, spilling Cicero out over the curb
into the gutter. Cicero stirred and began to stagger to his
feet. "Remember," Silvera said. "Don't come back around
here. I'll be looking for you."

Cicero struggled behind the wheel of the Imperial and
started the engine. Then he spat blood toward Silvera and
shouted, "I'll get you, cocksucka!" Then the car roared
away from the curb, leaving a blue haze of exhaust and
scorched rubber.

Silvera thrust his hands in his pockets and began to
walk away from those watchful eyes. He'd made it
around the corner when the bile came up volcanically
from his stomach; he leaned over and threw up against a
wall, and as he was heaving, he could feel both hands
jittering in his pockets as if pulled by unseen strings. He
took them out, leaned his back against the graffitied wall,
and watched the fingers jerk, the veins twitching under
the flesh. They seemed to belong to someone else because
he had no control over them anymore, and he never knew
when the spasms would start or stop. The spasms hadn't
yet begun their slow creep up his forearms, as the kind
doctor at County General had told him they would. But it
was just a matter of time. The death dance of the muscles, once begun, was irreversible.

After a moment more he walked on, past more sun-
burned apartment buildings and more low, dusty houses
jammed in between brick walls. The barrio seemed to go
on forever, one narrow garbage-strewn street after another. The place smelled of rotting, stifled souls to Silvera,
the reek of corpses that had died at the dead-ends in the
huge, tangled maze of life. *There is so much to do,* he
told himself as he walked. *So much to do and so little
time.* He was going to have to find Miguel and Linda and
get them off that hellish junk, but it would be hard.
Once hooked, it was easier to drift in that limbo of
heroin-induced dreams than to face the stark reality of
life. Silvera knew; he had the needle track on the insides
of both his elbows to show for two years of life on the
edge of bestiality. *So much to do and so little time. God
help me,* he thought. *Please give me strength. And time.
Please.*

At the end of the block, he could see the bell tower of his church pressed close between tenement buildings. The tower was painted white, and through the open shutters the large brass bell caught a shard of golden sunlight. Silvera had found that beautiful bell in the abandoned mission of a town called Borja, near the Mexican border. The town had been almost deserted, and it exuded a strange aura of old evil. One of the remaining residents had told Silvera that several years before a man who'd called himself Baal had come to the town and since then Borja had been tainted. Silvera had brought that bell back from the desert in a pickup truck over a hundred miles of winding, sun-scorched road. He'd rigged a hoist and with the help of a few neighborhood men had lifted the bell to the tower. He'd worked on it many weeks, polishing away the last of the corrosion, and now it sang —joyful and clear to beckon all to Sunday Mass or announce Saturday weddings, quietly mournful tolling over a funeral procession—as a symbol of the Church of Our Sainted Mary. Not very long ago a crack had appeared at the very top of the bell and now was gradually snaking its way down to the rim. The bell's destiny was clear, and yet it had so much more work to do. Silvera smiled when he thought of what Leon and several of the other children called it—Mary's Voice.

Father Silvera reached his church and climbed a few rickety, wooden steps to the front door. He was feeling better now; he'd stopped sweating, and his hands weren't trembling nearly as much as they had been. It had been the strain of throwing that heroin dealer around that had done it. He knew better than to do things like that, but he was still a bullishly strong man, and in this case his temper had gotten the best of him.

Inside, the church was almost claustrophobic with the wooden pews packed closely together, and a wine-red runner spread along the narrow aisle from front door to altar. Atop the altar stood a heavy brass crucifix, brightly polished, on an ornate base. Behind that altar with its chipped, ceramic statue of Mary cradling the Christ child in her arms was a large, oval, stained-glass window that split the light into a kaleidoscope of white, azure, violet, umber, and emerald green. In the window's center was a representation of Jesus carrying a staff and behind him a green knoll dotted with sheep. On sunny days His eyes

were circles of kind, warm, brown light; on cloudy days
His gaze turned stormy, the light stern and grayish. It
intrigued Silvera to watch those changes and reminded
him that even Jesus Christ has His bad days.

Silvera walked through the church to his living quarters, his steps sounding hollow on the wooden floor. It
was a single room, painted white, with a thin-mattressed
bed, a chest of drawers, a reading lamp, and a sink in
the corner. There was a shelf of hard-cover books, most
of them more political and sociological than theologic:
Future Shock by Alvin Tofler, *The Politics of Evil* by
James N. Virga, *Drawing Down the Moon* by Margot
Adler. On another, lower shelf was a toaster and a hot
plate, neither of which worked particularly well. The
walls were decorated with crayon drawings given to him
by some of the younger children in his parish—sailboats
skimming a green ocean, stick figures waving from windows, rainbow-colored kites among the clouds. There
was a ceramic crucifix hanging near the door, a bright
travel poster that said See Mexico's Wonders, and a
framed painting of a fishing village featuring nets drying
in the sun. It reminded him of the village he'd been born
in, Puerto Grande on the Gulf of Mexico. Another door
led into a tiny bathroom with a noisy toilet and a stuttering shower.

He crossed the room, drew water from the sink into a
drinking cup, and gingerly tasted it. *Not so bad today*,
he thought. He drank it down gratefully, only spilling a
few drops on his shirt because his hand wasn't trembling
quite so much. And then he listened; he thought he'd
heard the front door open and close. Yes, there was the
noise of footsteps now. He put the cup aside and hurried
out.

There was a young man standing at the altar, staring
up at the stained-glass window. He wore a pale blue shirt
and faded, tight-fitting denims. His eyes were dark and
haunted, very tired-looking. Silvera stopped and looked at
the young man, hardly recognizing him. "Rico?" he said
quietly. "Is that Rico Esteban?"

"Yes, Father," Rico said. "It's me."

"Good God, how you've grown!" The priest stepped
forward and shook Rico's hand in a firm, dry grasp. "The
last time I saw you was . . . well, I hate to think how

many years have passed! But you're a man now, aren't you?"

Rico smiled and shrugged. He thought, *Father, if you only knew . . .*

"So I've heard you've moved out of the barrio. You're living on Sunset Boulevard?"

"I've got an apartment on the Strip."

"I'm glad to hear that. Where are you working?"

"For myself," Rico said, and when Silvera's gaze sharpened, he added, "Doing this and that. I'm trying to start my own messenger service."

Silvera nodded. Of course, he knew that Rico was probably selling drugs or pimping, possibly both. Rico's hands were too smooth, and he'd never had the education for a desk job, though as a child playing around this very church Rico had shown a healthy curiosity about life that Silvera hoped would blossom into a quest for real knowledge. A stab of sorrow and pity caught Silvera in the heart. *The waste,* he thought, *the terrible waste.*

"I'm making out okay," Rico said. He'd sensed what was going on in the priest's head, behind those black, fathomless eyes.

Silvera motioned toward the front pew. "Please, sit down." Rico did, and Silvera sat beside him. "You look fine," he said, which was a lie because Rico looked as drained as an empty bottle and much thinner than he ought to be. He wondered what Rico was selling, *Cocaine? amphetamines? angel dust? Surely not heroin. Rico was too smart to get involved with junk, and he probably recalled how the addicts had screamed from their windows when they'd injected themselves with a hit cut with baby powder or sugar.* "It's been too long," Silvera said.

"A long time since I've been inside here, yeah." Rico looked around the church, his gaze coming to rest on the window. "I'd almost forgotten what it looked like in here. What surprises me is that your window hasn't been broken yet."

"It's been tried. I've been having some trouble with the Homicides."

"They're a bunch of punks. You should call the cops on them."

"No. It's neighborhood business and nothing that I can't take care of. Your attitude about the police seems to have changed since you were running with the Cripplers."

"You're wrong, Father. I still think the cops are good-for-nothing pigs, but you can't handle the Homicides by yourself. They'll cut your throat as fast as anybody else's. Maybe faster."

Silvera nodded thoughtfully, searching the younger man's eyes. A terrible bitterness seemed to be churning there, the look of a dog long deprived of food. And there was something else, too, something that lay much deeper and closer to Rico's soul. Silvera saw just a quick flash of it, like dark, glimmering quicksilver, and recognized it as fear—an emotion he'd seen in his own mirror eyes a great deal recently. "You come to see me for a reason, Rico. How can I help you?"

"I don't know. Maybe yes, maybe no." He shrugged, looked at the stained-glass window, and seemed to have a hard time saying it. "Father, has Merida Santos come to see you in the last couple of days?"

"Merida? No."

"Oh, Jesus," Rico said softly. "I thought she might've . . . you know, come here to talk to you. I've . . . I've made her pregnant, and now she's gone. Even her crazy mother doesn't know where she is, and I can't sleep at night not knowing what's happened to her . . ."

"Slow down," the priest said and gripped Rico's shoulder. "Take it easy and tell me everything from the beginning."

Rico took a deep breath. "I picked her up at her building on Saturday night . . ."

When Rico was finished, his hands were clasped tightly in his lap. "I called the cops this morning and talked to the missing persons guy. He said not to worry about it, that a lot of people disappeared for a couple of days at a time and then came back home. He said it's called running away from home, so I knew then that he wasn't taking me too seriously, you know? He said that if her mother wasn't concerned, I shouldn't be either. Good-for-nothin' pig! I don't know what to do, Father! I think . . . maybe something bad's happened to her!"

Silvera's eyes were black and brooding. In this neighborhood, he knew, any of a dozen terrible things could've happened to Merida Santos—kidnapping, rape, murder . . . He refused to think about that. "Merida's a good girl.

I can't imagine her running away from home. Still if you say she's pregnant, she may be afraid to face her mother."

"Who wouldn't be? She tried to chop me up with a butcher knife."

"That was yesterday afternoon?"

Rico nodded.

"Then maybe Merida's come home since then? Maybe she just stayed away from home overnight because she was afraid to tell her mother she was pregnant?"

"Maybe. I thought about calling the missing persons cops again and saying I was Merida's father or uncle, but you know what that *bastardo* told me? He said they were too busy to hunt down every little girl who decided to run away from the barrio. Busy doin' what? Ain't that a load of shit?" He stopped abruptly. "Oh. Sorry, Father."

"That's all right. I agree. It is a load of shit. But why don't we go see Mrs. Santos together? Maybe Merida's come home by now, or Mrs. Santos might talk to me more freely than she would you." Silvera rose to his feet.

"I love her, Father," Rico said as he stood up. "I want you to know that."

"That may be, Rico. But I don't think you love her enough, do you?"

Rico felt speared with guilt. Silvera's eyes were like hard bits of black glass, reflecting the secrets of Rico's soul back at him. He was shamed to silence.

"All right," Silvera said and clapped Rico softly on the shoulder. "Let's go."

SIX

"Here's what we've got," Sully Reece said as he laid a thick sheaf of white, blue-lined computer printout paper amid the general disarray on Palatazin's desk. "The people down in Vehicle I.D. are going crazy, but they're sending their computers back through the whole list of plate numbers again just in case it missed any the first time, which Taylor says is highly unlikely. As you can see, there are quite a few people in L.A. who drive a gray, white, or light blue Volks bearing a two, a seven, and a 'T' in some numerical combination."

"My God," Palatazin said as he unfolded the list. "I never knew there were so many Volkswagens in the whole state!"

"That's every combination the computers could come up with."

Palatazin bit down on his pipe. "Of course, he could be driving with a stolen license plate."

"Don't even think it, please. If that's the case, then you can just about triple the number of plates listed on that printout. And if that chick was wrong about even one digit, then the whole thing's screwed."

"Well, let's hope she wasn't." He glanced down the list, which contained a few hundred names and addresses. "These are grouped by area?"

"Yes, sir. Taylor thought the computers were going to blow up, but he programmed them to give us our information on the basis of twenty major areas. The first twenty-five or so addresses, for instance, are located in a grid from Fairfax Avenue to Alvarado Street."

"Fine. That makes it a little easier for the officers." Palatazin counted down twenty-eight names and tore them off the list. "Split whoever's available up into teams, Sully, and hand out as many of those names as you can. You and I will be taking these."

"Yes, sir. Oh, have you seen this?" He held up the morning edition of the *Times*. There on the front page in a black-bordered box under a headline that read "Do You Know This Man?" was the composite of the face they were seeking. "That should do some good."

Palatazin took the paper and laid it out on his desk. "I hope so. It's flashed through my mind that this man might be an insurance agent from Glendale—a wife, two children, and a cat—who likes a bit of action on the side. If that's the case, then we're back at square one." He looked up suddenly, as if he'd heard something, and stared intensely past Reece into the corner.

"Captain?" Reece asked after a few seconds. He glanced over his shoulder—nothing there, of course. But nevertheless he felt a chill ripple between his shoulder blades, as if he sensed someone standing right behind him.

Palatazin blinked and looked away, forcing himself to stare down at the list of names and addresses. *Garvin, Kelly, Vaughan* . . . he thought he'd seen something begin to stir in that corner . . . *Mehta, Salvatore, Ho* . . . where

the apparition of his mother had stood yesterday afternoon . . . *Emiliana, Lopez, Carlyle* . . . but before he
could focus on it, the faint movement like the sluggish motion of ripples through muddy water had ceased. He
glanced quickly up at Reece. "What . . . uh . . . about
that other thing I asked you to look into?"

"Not much luck there. There's nothing you can buy
over the counter that would cause the effect we're looking
for. One of the pharmacists I talked to said airplane glue
might smell like that and make you pretty drunk if you
were to inhale a concentrated dose of it, but it wouldn't
put you under right off. The same with some of the ant
and roach sprays on the market. Even hair spray."

"No, I don't think that's what we want. Maybe our
friend knows a druggist who's making him something special?" He dared to glance into that corner again. Nothing
there, nothing at all.

"Possibly. Another guy told me there used to be a salve
you could buy that had a chloroform base. A couple of
good whiffs and you were on your ass. But it's not sold
anymore."

Palatazin frowned. "We could be . . . what's the saying?
Singing in the dark."

"Whistling in the dark," Reece corrected him. He took
the rest of the printout and went to the door. "I'll get these
distributed. You eating lunch today?"

"From home." He motioned toward a paper sack half-
buried in file folders on his desk.

"Well, it's about that time. *Bon appétit!*"

"Thank you." Palatazin looked down the rest of his list.
He was certain many of these addresses would no longer
be accurate. Some of these people would be impossible to
find, some would probably have sold their cars. Regardless, the task had to be done, he had nothing else to go on.
He put the list aside for the moment, reaching for his
lunch and the *Times* Sully had left. Jo had made a ham
salad sandwich for him today; there was a dill pickle, a
nice red apple, and a can of V-8 juice. He knew his stomach would be roaring an hour after he finished eating, but
he'd promised Jo he'd try to stick to his diet for a while.
Last week he'd found himself slipping, sending out for
chocolate-cream doughnuts in the middle of the afternoon.

He looked again to the corner—nothing there, of course

. . . if there ever had been. He turned and opened his blinds, then began to eat his sandwich while he paged through the paper. It took him about fifteen minutes to reach page eleven, and when he did, the headline "Vandals Hit Highland Park Cemetery" jumped out at him. He read through the story twice, his heart beginning to beat like a blacksmith's hammer. Then he rummaged through a drawer for a pair of scissors and carefully cut out the article. In the middle of scissoring he remembered his mother holding a pair of scissors, too, going through the *Times* and the *Herald-Examiner* and the *National Enquirer,* the *Tattler* and the *Star* and *Fate* magazine and a dozen others, searching for articles she would clip and put away in a little metal box that now sat on the top shelf of his bedroom closet. He had brought it back to the house from Golden Garden after his mother had died. He read the story over once more, folded it, and put it in his shirt pocket. His temples ached with dull thunder; his stomach turned over when he glanced at his half-eaten lunch.

Because now he knew that *they* were here. Hiding in a city of over eight million, half the globe and many worlds away from Krajeck, Hungary. Lurking in the darkness, walking the streets and boulevards of Los Angeles in human shape, ripping through the city's cemeteries in search of . . . *My God,* he thought, a shiver almost splitting him in two. *What is to be done?*

Who would believe before it was too late? Because one of their greatest strengths, the strength that had kept them existing in a world that had come from ox cart to Cadillac and from slingshot to laser beam, was lack of belief in their existence. "Rational" thought was their shield of invisibility, because they stalked the land of nightmare fears.

What is to be done? Palatazin asked himself, panic bubbling like a cauldron's brew in the pit of his stomach.

There was a knock at his door, and Lieutenant Reece looked in. "Captain? The teams are organized. We're ready to move."

"Huh? Oh, yes. Of course." He stood up, shrugged into his coat, and took the list of addresses from his desk.

"Captain, are you all right?" Reece asked.

Palatazin nodded brusquely. "I'm fine." *What is to be done?* When he looked up into the other man's face, he saw that Reece's eyes looked concerned. *Now he thinks I'm cracking, too,* Palatazin thought, and then he heard the dark answer in his brain, *Well? Aren't you?* Reece turned away, and Palatazin followed him out.

SEVEN

The building cast a deep shadow along Dos Terros Street. In front of it, half up on the curb, was a rust-eaten old Ford standing on two flat shoes and two cement blocks. Overhead lines of clothes, stirred by a dusty breeze, hung from windows. As Father Silvera stepped out of Rico Esteban's car, he saw a shirt break loose from one of these clotheslines and flutter to the earth, arms waving in eerie futility.

On the front steps a thin, brown mongrel dog was sleeping, head resting on its paws. Rico stood on the sidewalk and looked up at the building. Several of the windows were open, but no faces peered down from them. "Mrs. Santos lives on the fifth floor, doesn't she?" Silvera asked as he went up the steps.

"Right. Fifth floor, Apartment D. Hey . . ."

Silvera, halfway up the steps, turned toward him. "What is it?"

Rico stared at the building. "I . . . don't know. Something's funny."

"Come on." Silvera took another step, and the dog's head instantly rose. Its eyes flared like bits of burning topaz. Rico said, "Father . . ." The dog stood up, turned to face the men, and bared its teeth with a low, vibrating growl. Silvera froze.

"Kick that damned mutt," Rico said, coming up to stand beside the priest. When Silvera didn't move, he kicked out toward the dog's side, but the mongrel simply dodged him, then stood its ground, the growl deeper and full of menace. "Get out of here!" he said. "Get away!"

"Whose dog is this?" Silvera asked. Rico shrugged. When the priest moved forward again, the dog crouched down in front of the door, ready to leap. "Whoever he belongs to, he doesn't want us to go inside, does he? I thing I'd rather try another door than risk having my leg chewed off."

"Ah, you shit!" Rico muttered to the dog and spat at it. The dog didn't move. Silvera was already at the alley beside the building, and Rico gave up after another moment to follow him.

They found a locked door that led down into the basement. Silvera was about to go around to the rear when Rico kicked at the basement door, splitting the rotten wood. The door sagged on its hinges. Silvera gave him a grave stare, but Rico shrugged and said, "Here's our way in, Father." He stepped into the musty, low-ceilinged basement.

It was almost totally dark inside, but in the murky light from the open doorway Silvera saw vague shapes— a tattered sofa lying on its side like a gutted hog, a couple of chair frames without cushions or backs, the shell of a television set, mounds of papers, and what looked like some rolled-up rugs and shower curtains. Cigarette butts and beer cans littered the floor. Rico and Silvera climbed a rickety, wooden stairway to another door, opened it, and found themselves in the building's entrance hall. They could still see the dog crouched on the steps, but the closed door stood between them. Now the dog seemed to be sleeping again.

They left the first floor and began climbing up, their shoes making the frail stairs whine. They had passed the second floor landing when Rico realized what was making the flesh on the back of his neck crawl—the place was as silent as a tomb.

"It's quiet in here," the priest said at almost the same instant. His voice echoed along the corridor. "How many people live in this building?"

"I don't know. Maybe fifty or sixty. Christ, just yesterday there was so much noise in here you couldn't think straight! Babies cryin', radios, people fighting . . ." He looked at the stairs that lay ahead. "Christ, where is everybody?"

In the third floor corridor Silvera knocked at a door that had "Diego" scrawled across it in green spray paint. The unlocked door creaked open a few inches, and Silvera peered inside. "Diego?" Silvera called out. "You home, man?" A table had been thrown over, and on the wooden floor flies crawled over the food that spilled from plates and glasses. Silvera felt his heart pound.

"Wait a minute," he said to Rico, stepping into the apartment. Newspapers had been jammed in around the windowsills and stretched over the glass; the sunlight was cut to a hazy murk. There was an unmade bed and a door leading to a bathroom. Silvera peered in and found himself staring at the shower curtain rod. It was bent, and several of the hooks lay scattered on the floor. The curtain itself was gone. When Silvera turned, Rico was standing right behind him.

"The apartment across the hall's open, too," Rico said. "There's nobody inside."

Silvera stepped past Rico and looked at the overturned table. "Diego *was* here, last night at least. That looks like what he must've been eating for dinner." He glanced at the newspaper-covered windows. "This place is already dark enough. Why did he try to cut the light?" He went out into the corridor and tried a few more doors; all of them were unlocked, the apartments empty but showing signs of recent life—cigarettes and cigars in ashtrays, dishes in sinks or on the tables, clothes hanging in closets. A few doors had been broken open, the wood splintered around the locks. Several of them seemed to have some kind of scratches imbedded deep in the wood, as if made by an animal's claws.

"Anybody here?" Rico shouted at the stairway. His voice rolled on through the building and was unanswered. He stared at the priest, his face paled by fear.

"We go up," Silvera said and started climbing the stairs again. The fourth floor hallway was as quiet as all the others. Rico could see doors standing open, and in the dim light he could make out the same deep scratches that they had seen downstairs.

Just above the fourth floor landing, Silvera stopped, his eyes wide, staring at the walls. New graffiti covered the old—HOTSHOT WAS HERE. VIPERS ARE KINGS. ZEKE SUX (HA HA). ALL FOR THE MASTER. BURN BABY BURN. Silvera reached out and touched the brown letters. "My God," he heard himself say, his voice hollow, as if he were speaking from the bottom of a well. "That's blood!" He continued upward, his senses coiled like a *culebra de cascabel*. For now his nerves were vibrating with the presence of something he'd felt a thousand times before—in a jail cell where two heroin addicts cut each other to pieces with razor blades; in a suffocatingly hot room where a drunken father had just beaten his three-year-old son to death with a baseball bat; in the smoldering, corpse-strewn ruins of a tenement razed by the arsonist's match; in the greedy eyes of Cicero, the dealer of demonic dreams. That presence was Evil, and now Silvera felt it as he never had before, so strong it was a tangible thing that clung to the walls, holding the odor of blood and brimstone. His heart was pumping hard, and before he reached the fifth floor he could feel the twitching—fibrillations, the doctors called them—begin deep in his hands.

The fifth floor corridor stretched out before them. Rico looked in through one of the open doors. The place was a wreck, and bits of a shattered mirror glittered on the floor like dusty diamonds. Silvera moved on ahead of him toward the Santos apartment and was about to push open the door—*scratches,* he thought, *there are scratches in this wood*—when something crashed violently behind a closed door on the opposite side of the hallway.

"What the shit was that?" Rico said, twisting around.

Silvera crossed the hall and put his hand on the doorknob. He paused for a moment, listening. From the apartment he could hear a muffled *thump, thump, thump* that was unlike anything he could identify. Then there was silence. "Who's there?" Silvera called out. But there was no answer. He started to push the door open.

"Father!" Rico said. "Don't . . . !"

But then Silvera started across the threshold, and something dark came flying into his face from the ceiling. He cried out, feeling a claw graze his cheek, and threw his hands up before his face. The thing tangled in his hair, then whirled off over his head like a swooping, gray leaf. Silvera spun around to watch it hit the corridor ceiling with that muffled thumping noise; it flew over Rico's head and disappeared into shadows at the far end of the hallway.

Silvera was shaken, but he felt like exploding with nervous laughter. *A pigeon,* he thought. *I was frightened by a single pigeon.* He looked back into the apartment and immediately saw the broken window where the thing must've flown in, on the floor a broken bottle and knickknacks spilled from a shelf that the pigeon had probably collided with. He went into the apartment, his hands shaking badly now—he wondered how he was going to keep Rico from seeing—and checked the bathroom. A mirror had been smashed, and Silvera stared at himself through a series of concentric cracks. Again he noted that the shower curtain was gone. The rod itself had been ripped out of the wall.

Across the hallway Rico was slowly pushing open the door to Mrs. Santos's apartment. He stood at the threshold and called out her name, but of course there was no answer, and neither had he been expecting one. It was just that he wanted to hear a voice in this place, something human in this silent vault. He stepped into the apartment, his heartbeat racing. A sheen of sweat clung to his face. He walked across the room and looked into the small, darkened bedroom. It was sweltering, the air hanging in heavy layers. Rico saw that the sheets had been torn off the bed. He felt the hair rise on the back of his neck suddenly and didn't know why. Quickly he left the bedroom and went back out to the hall.

Father Silvera had stepped into another room further along the corridor. In this apartment he found an empty cradle with several spots of blood on the infant's pillow. When he stepped into the bedroom, he immediately froze. On the wall over the bare bed, written in blood, was ALL FOR THE MASTER. Newspapers were jammed over the single window, reducing the light to a pale, smoky haze. Silvera ripped them away. The light immediately strengthened, and he opened the window for some fresh air.

And then something moved in the room—a bare whisper of a movement that made Silvera twist around from the window. But no one was there. The bedroom was empty. He listened, ignoring the increased muscle fibrillations that ran through his hands, making his fingers twitch like claws. Again that noise, somewhere close. A sliding, cloth-on-cloth sound. He stared at the mattress. No sheets. *Where are they?* he wondered. *Did these people leave their homes and belongings, taking with them only sheets and cheap plastic shower curtains?*

But when the noise came again—very softly—he knew where it was coming from, and something within him recoiled.

Under the bed.

"Rico!" Silvera called out, his voice sounding hoarse and hollow in the small room. When Rico came, the young man's eyes were haunted, gleaming bright with fear. "Help me," Silvera said and moved to push the bed aside.

Beneath it was an oddly shaped cocoon, the bed sheets wrapped tightly around what might have been the body of a two-headed man.

"What's that?" Rico said, his voice cracking. "What's that thing?"

Silvera bent and gingerly touched it. The form seemed to radiate a chill. He slowly began to work the sheets loose, and now Rico could see the disease in his hands, but he didn't care. The sheet caught, and Silvera ripped at it.

"Hey, Father," Rico said. "I don't like this, you know? I say we get out of here and call the cops. Okay? I mean, I'm not chickenshit or . . . WHAT'S THAT?"

A hand and arm, as bone white as marble and veined with blue, slithered out in front of Silvera. The priest checked his impulse to leap away and continued tearing at the sheet. In another moment he could see grayish hair and a pale, heavily lined forehead; then a second scalp, this one black-haired. He pulled the sheet free from the faces. It was Joe Vega and his thirteen-year-old son Nicky, entwined together. Their faces were as white as carved stone, but what made Silvera almost cry out with terror was the fact that he could see their eyes through the thin, almost clear membranes of their closed eyelids. The eyes semed to be staring right at him; they filled him with cold dread. He forced himself to reach down and feel the chests for heartbeats.

"They're dead," Rico said. "Somebody's killed them!"

Their hearts weren't beating. He felt for a pulse, found nothing.

"What killed them?" Rico was babbling. "Why do they look like that?"

"How do I know?" Silvera snapped. When he stood up, a shard of white sunlight fell across Vega's face like a stripe of hot neon. "I can't imagine what's happened here! We've got to check all the apartments. Maybe there are more corpses jammed under the beds. We'd better look in all the closets, too. God, what's done this thing?"

Behind him something rustled. Rico made a strangled sound, and Silvera turned.

Vega's corpse was moving. Silvera felt the hair rise at the base of his neck, but he couldn't look away from that unholy sight. Vega's legs were moving within the sheet, feet pushing against the floor, his arms tightly locked around his son. The gray-lipped mouth was twitching, as if a scream were about to burst free. The dead eyes blankly accused Father Silvera.

"He's not dead!" Rico said. "He can't be, not if . . ."

"They have no heartbeat!" He raised his hand and made the Sign of the Cross in the air. Instantly Vega's corpse-that-was-not-a-corpse opened its mouth and made a hideous, anguished moan that sounded like a low wind blowing through dead trees. The legs pushed frantically, and in another moment the two figures had squirmed back underneath the bed. They gave a couple of convulsive twitches and lay still.

Rico's face had gone almost as white as Joe Vega's. He turned and stumbled over his own feet trying to get out to the corridor. Silvera came out, walking unsteadily. "Let's get out of here, Father! Let's call the cops!" Rico pleaded.

"Did you look for Mrs. Santos?"

"Yeah. There's nothing in there . . ."

"Were the sheets on the bed?"

Rico went cold. "Sheets? No. But Christ, Father, don't go back in there!"

Silvera stepped into the apartment. He forced himself to look under the bed, but there was nothing there. He crossed the room to a closet, gripped the knob, and opened it. At the bottom there was a pile of old newspapers and clothes. Silvera stared at it for a few seconds, then probed it with his foot.

Something moved, shifting uneasily.

He slammed the door shut and hurried out to where Rico, his face a shade between white and green, waited. "All right," Silvera said. "Now we go for the police."

EIGHT

Palatazin and Reece came out of an apartment building on Malabar Street in Boyle Heights trailed by an elderly black man with a gnarled walking stick. The man's name was Herbert Vaughan, he was a retired L.A. police officer, and he owned a light gray '72 Volkswagen Beetle with license plate 205 AVT.

"You know Captain Dexter?" he asked Palatazin when they'd reached the dark blue car with the municipal tag parked in front of the building.

"Will Dexter? Yes sir, I did know him, but he retired about six years ago."

"Oh, Captain Dexter retired? He was a fine man, a real fine man. He could find this Roach fella for you if you got him out of retirement." The man's eyes snapped from Reece to Palatazin.

"I'm sure he could, Mr. Vaughan. He did a good job on the Chinatown killings back in '71."

"Uh-huh. Sure did. And I'll tell you what, Will Dexter could catch the Gravedigger, too. Could find that fella fast as you could say 'Jack Robinson.' "

"The Gravedigger?" Reece said. "Who's that, Mr. Vaughan?"

"Don't you boys keep up with anything anymore?" He cracked his stick impatiently down on the sidewalk. "It was in the *Tattler* this morning! The Gravedigger! That fella who's been goin' through cemeteries and makin' off with the caskets! Ha! That kind of shit didn't go on when I was on the force, I'm here to tell you!"

"The *Tattler*?" Palatazin said softly. "This morning?"

"Son, have you got wax in your ears? That's what I said. What kind of accent have you got? Italian?"

"Hungarian. Thank you for talking with us, Mr. Vaughan." Palatazin went around the car and slid in under the steering wheel. Reece climbed in, but Mr. Vaughan shuffled forward and gripped the door handle before Reece could close it. "You get Cap Dexter out of retirement, you hear? He'll find the Roach for you, and he'll put that Gravedigger in the nut house where he belongs!"

"Thank you, Mr. Vaughan," Reece said and gently closed the door. As they drove away Palatazin glanced in the rearview mirror and saw the old man leaning on his cane, watching them drive out of sight.

"Who's next?" Reece asked.

Palatazin checked his list. "A. Mehta, 4517–D, Arizona Avenue in East L.A. That's a white Volks with the plate 253 BTA. I hope the other men are having better luck than we are." He waited for a light to change and then turned right on Whittier Boulevard. He'd gone almost a block when an ambulance screamed up from behind. Immediately he swerved to the curb; the ambulance, white and orange lights flashing, careened through traffic and on out of sight.

"Gravedigger," Reece said quietly and smiled. "Christ! This city's full of nuts, isn't it? If it's not Roach, it's the Gravedigger, and if not him, it'll always be someone else tomorrow."

"Remind me to find a *Tattler* on the way in. I'd like to read that story."

"I didn't think you were a fan of that rag."

"I'm not. But Mr. Vaughan's right—we have to keep up with things, don't we?" In the distance he heard the shriek of another siren. He could look down the side streets off Whittier Boulevard and see a smoky haze hanging in the afternoon sunlight between buildings that looked like bombed-out hulks. He didn't often come into the poor black and Spanish sections of Boyle Heights, East L.A., and Belvedere Gardens. There were detectives, though, who been trained especially in dealing with the barrio population, and in many instances riot situations had been defused by a detective or a beat officer who'd been accepted into the barrio's fold. All others were *extraños*, strangers not to be trusted.

Reece glanced over at Palatazin, then back to the street. "Any particular reason you wanted to hit the street yourself on this one, captain? You could just as easily have handled it from the office."

"No, I wanted to get out of there for a while. I'm getting fat and lazy sitting around telling other people what to do. That's the trouble with promotions, Sully. You're rewarded for what you do best by being shoved upstairs to let younger men do the legwork. Of course, if what you do best is the legwork, then . . . well . . ." He shrugged. What he did not say was that he was becoming fearful of his own office, of the shadows and shapes he was beginning to think he saw within those four walls.

At the next intersection a third ambulance shrieked across, heading south.

"Wonder what's going on?" Reece said.

Their radio, which had been humming with codes and locations all across the city, suddenly came to urgent life. The dispatcher's voice sounded loud in the closed vehicle—"All cars vicinity of Caliente and Dos Terros Streets, East Los Angeles, see the senior officer at 1212 Dos Terros." The message was repeated again, and then voices from various cars confirming.

"That sounds hot," Reece said. He motioned toward the next street sign. "Caliente's coming up."

Palatazin's heartbeat quickened. A black and white roared past them, siren wailing, and turned left on Caliente with a screech of tires. "Let's see what's going on," Palatazin said. He swerved through traffic and raced after the prowl car as Reece hit the siren and clamped the flashing Magneto light to the cartop.

For a few minutes they wound through an area of narrow, pot-holed streets and crumbling tenements, until they came to a street that was already being cordoned off by a couple of uniformed officers. The prowl car was permitted to sweep on through. Palatazin applied the brakes and showed them his badge.

"What's happening?" he asked one of the cops.

"No one's certain yet, captain," the officer said. "They're bringing a lot of corpses out of that building over there, but . . . well, you'll have to see for yourself, sir."

"Who's senior officer?"

"Sergeant Teal. I believe he's inside."

Palatazin nodded and drove through. People were clustered around the stairs of a tenement in the middle of the block, and the police were trying to push them back behind sawhorse cordons. Four prowl cars were parked at different angles in the street with their lights spinning, and there were two ambulances parked close to the stairs. Palatazin whipped the car to the opposite curb and jumped out. Reece followed him across the street, and when they reached the stairway, they saw two white-uniformed ambulance attendants bringing down a stretcher with a woman's body on it. The white sheet pulled up to her chin matched the color of her flesh. From where he stood Palatazin caught a brief glimpse of those eyes staring through the closed lids. A shiver of horror went through the crowd of onlookers. The body began writhing in the sheet, the face contorting hideously, but no sound came from its mouth. The body was loaded into one of the waiting ambulances.

"I thought these were supposed to be corpses," Reece

said, watching the ambulance wheel away. "God, what was wrong with that woman's eyes?"

Palatazin was already moving up the stairs. He flashed his badge at the officer at the door. "Where's Sergeant Teal?"

"Third floor, captain."

He started to ascend the stairway, but suddenly his attention was caught by a small, yellow form shoved in a corner of the entrance hall. It was a dead dog. The teeth were bared; there was a bullet hole in the skull. Palatazin climbed the stairs, stepping aside as another stretcher was brought down, the pallid "corpse" twitching beneath the sheet. The hair rose on the back of his neck as he sensed the cold waves radiated by this thing. The dead eyes grazed his own. He turned away from it, bile raging in his stomach, and continued upward.

In a third-floor apartment Palatazin found Sergeant Teal—a large, curly-haired man with the physique of an ex-UCLA linebacker. He was talking to two Chicanos—an older man wearing a starched priest's collar and a boy whose eyes looked dazed and sick. Palatazin approached Teal and showed his badge. "Sergeant Teal? What's the situation here?"

The other man motioned Palatazin away from the two Chicanos. Palatazin's shoes crunched over bits of glass. He looked down to see the remnants of a broken mirror. *Yes,* he thought, suddenly calm and resolute. *Yes. They've been here.* "Those two over there, Father Ramon Silvera and Rico Esteban, found the first bodies. So far we've pulled thirty-nine of them out of closets and from under beds. They were all rolled up in shower curtains, rugs, and sheets. Thirty-nine of them." Teal's clear blue eyes were full of sick confusion. He lowered his voice. "You're going to think this is crazy, captain, but . . ."

"Go on."

"Well, I don't know whether to classify these bodies as corpses or not. Oh sure, they move a little bit, but it all seems to be muscle reflex, like some trick of rigor mortis. The hell of it is . . . the bodies don't have heartbeats or pulse rates. I mean . . . technically they're dead, aren't they?"

Palatazin closed his eyes for a few seconds, his hand coming up to his forehead.

"Sir?" Teal said. "They *are* dead, aren't they?"

"Any wounds on the bodies?"

"I've just looked closely at a couple of them. I saw some cuts and bruises. That's about it."

"No," Palatazin said quietly. Another stretcher passed the door. "That's not all."

"Sir?"

"Nothing. I'm thinking out loud. Where are the bodies being taken?"

"Uh . . ." He looked down at a notepad in his hand. "Mercy Hospital in Monterey Park. That's the nearest, and they've got the facilities to handle this mess." He paused for a few seconds, watching Palatazin's face. "What's wrong with these people, captain? Could it be . . . like . . . a disease or something?"

"If you think that, Teal, keep it to yourself. We don't want the neighborhood panicking worse than it probably has already. Did Mercy send a doctor over?"

"Yes sir. Dr. Delgado. She's upstairs right now."

"Okay, fine. Will you give me a few minutes alone with these two?" He motioned toward the priest and the boy across the room. Teal nodded and went out, closing the door behind him. Palatazin kicked at the shards of glass, glanced quickly around the apartment, and then returned his gaze to the priest who seemed to be in better shape than the boy. Except for one thing—his hands seemed to be trembling, clenching and unclenching. *A nervous reaction?* Palatazin wondered. *Or something else?* He introduced himself to the two men. "Sergeant Teal tells me you two found the first bodies. What time was that?"

"About one-thirty," the priest said. "We've told all this to the other officers."

"Yes, yes, I know." Palatazin waved a hand at him to quiet his objections. He walked past them and peered into the dim bedroom, noting the newspapers covering the windows. There was another shattered mirror in the bathroom. He came back out. "What do you think happened here, Father?" he asked the priest.

Silvera narrowed his eyes; the slight quaver in the policeman's voice put him on edge. "I have no idea. Rico and I came looking for Mrs. Santos, who lives . . . lived on the fifth floor. We found the building just as it is now."

"I want to get out of here," Rico said quietly. "I can't stand being in this place anymore."

"A little longer, okay?" Palatazin said. He looked back

to Silvera. "You saw the bodies. Tell me. Are they dead or alive?"

"Dead," Rico said.

Silvera took a while longer in answering. "I don't know," he said finally. "No heartbeat, no pulse . . . and yet they move . . ."

"Sergeant Teal tells me thirty-nine bodies have been found. How many people lived in this building?"

"Sixty or seventy, at least."

"But not all of the apartments were occupied?"

Silvera shook his head.

"All right. Thank you." Palatazin turned and started for the door, but Silvera's voice stopped him. "What's happened to these people, officer? What kind of thing did this to them?"

He almost answered, almost said the terrible word, but fear gripped his throat and squeezed it. He left the room without another word and stood outside, clutching at the stairway railing like a man on a heaving ship in a world that had suddenly tilted crazily on its axis and begun to spin backward in time. He was only dimly aware of someone—no, two people—coming along the corridor toward him. When he looked up, he saw that it was Teal and a middle-aged Chicano woman with haggard circles under her eyes. "Captain?" Teal said. "This is Dr. Delgado."

The woman extended her hand, and Palatazin shook it. Another body was carried past them through the corridor, and Palatazin cringed at the sight of those staring eyes. "Captain, to be perfectly honest with you, I don't know what in the name of God we have here," Dr. Delgado said in a soft, weary voice. "These are not corpses technically, yet there are no outward signs of life; no rigor mortis is setting in, and no fluids are collecting in the intestines or extremities. I pricked the finger of one of them, and do you know what came out? Absolutely nothing. The body was drained dry. I don't know about the others, but that body was totally bloodless. And yet when the ambulance attendants were strapping it to a stretcher, the body—what should've been a corpse—*moved.*"

"Jesus!" Teal said, his eyes icy blue circles.

"As I say, I don't know what we have. I may not *want* to know, but that's my profession. One of my colleagues at Mercy, Dr. Steiner, is on his way over right now. Possibly he can help . . ."

"Nothing can help," Palatazin said suddenly and realized it was all about to pour out, all of it like bile flowing up from the secret pit of terror, and he was going to be unable to stop it. He clenched his teeth, his eyes widening, but the torrent of words forced them apart. "It's too late, nothing can help. We've got to . . . got to leave all of them inside here and burn this building to the ground right *now* before the sun goes down! Then we've got to scatter . . . scatter the ashes and pour holy water on the ruins!" He looked from Teal to Delgado and back again —they were too shocked to speak. The priest and the boy were standing in the doorway of that room, watching him, as was a uniformed officer further along the corridor who stood staring at Palatazin in amazement.

"What are you all looking at?" Palatazin shrieked and felt something give way, like timbers exposed too long to vicious weather. "You've seen the bodies! You've seen what they can do! They can sweep through a whole building in less than one night! What will they do soon to whole streets? Neighborhoods?" He trembled, and a voice within him roared, "STOP," but he couldn't stop, he had no power now over the words tumbling from his mouth. Cold beads of sweat had popped up on his face, and the only sound in the entire building was his voice. "We can burn this building to the ground and kill some of them, because when these . . . when these wake up they're going to be thirsty, too!" He looked at Dr. Delgado, the raging fear in his eyes completely exposed. "You can't take them to Mercy Hospital! You can't let them get out into the streets!"

Someone gripped his shoulder. He spun around, panting.

Sully, his expression grave, said quietly, "Captain, come on with me. Let's get some fresh air, okay?"

"LEAVE ME ALONE!" He jerked free and shoved Sully away. His gaze fell upon the priest. "You! You of all people should realize the evil that's creeping up on this city! God in Heaven, can't you feel it in here? Tell them not to let these things wake up tonight!"

Silvera glanced quickly at Teal and then back to the police captain. He felt he was on the verge of madness himself, split between a shudder and a scream. Of course, he felt the evil; it was everywhere in this place, like viscous mist, but what was this man saying?

"Father," Palatazin said, and in his voice there was now something of a terrified nine-year-old boy. "Please don't let the *vampir* loose on the streets! Tell them we have to burn the bodies!"

Vampir? Silvera thought. The word struck him in the chest like a sledgehammer blow. *Vampire?*

And then Palatazin was suddenly drained, like a bottle whose contents had just spilled all over the floor. He blinked, looked around, and then staggered back against the railing. Sully and Teal both rushed forward to prevent him from falling. Palatazin's face was ashen, the sweat glittering on his cheeks and forehead. As Sully was helping him down the stairs, Palatazin lifted his head and looked back at Dr. Delgado. "Don't take them to the hospital," he said in a hoarse whisper. "Burn them. Burn them." His head slumped forward. "Come on, captain, take it easy," Sully said. "Watch that step now. That's right, real easy."

"Can I go now?" Rico asked Teal.

"Yeah, sure. But I may be talking to you again."

Rico nodded and hurried away without looking back. On the stairs he gave a wide berth to that big crazy cop, then moved past the dog the cops had had to kill because the damned thing wouldn't let them into the doorway.

"What *are* you going to do with them?" Silvera asked Dr. Delgado when the boy had gone. He was visibly pale and shaken, his hands twitching out of control, the fibrillations in his wrists now as well.

"They're going to Mercy, of course. Probably an isolation ward until we can . . ." She dropped her gaze to his sides and stared. "How long have you . . . ?" she asked softly.

"It started about three months ago," he replied. "It's getting worse all the time."

"You've seen a doctor?"

"I'm seeing Dr. Doran at County General."

The full impact of that took a moment to sink in. Dr. Delgado said, "Doran? Isn't he a specialist in muscular atrophy?"

"That's right." He held up his hands and smiled grimly. "Very nice, *sí?* They tell me it's what Lou Gehrig had."

"Gehrig's disease?" she said softly. She knew immediately what that meant—this broad-shouldered, healthy-

looking man would be dead in two to five years. "I'm
sorry."

"Dr. Doran's sentiments exactly. Now I'll leave you to
your work." He moved past her, went down the stairs,
and was gone.

NINE

Afternoon grayed into evening, and slowly the night approached from the east. Winds stirred lazily across the
Mojave Desert and chilled as they swirled across the
mountains into L.A. After nightfall dogs began to howl in
the hills—their music eerie and compelling, and pleasing
to twice as many as had listened the night before.

And in the sky, caught only briefly by shopping center
spotlights or the bright glow from Sunset Boulevard billboards advertising new albums by the Stones, Cheap
Trick, and Rory Black, the bats that had come from their
mountain caves spun like a whirlwind of dark leaves.

TEN

Gayle Clarke turned off Lexington Avenue into the parking lot of the Sandalwood Apartments, and immediately
saw Jack Kidd's airbrushed van in its usual place. *So,* she
thought, *where have you been hiding? I sure could've
used some pictures at Ramona Heights today!* She pulled
up beside the van and left her car, walking across the
courtyard with its green-spotlighted palm trees. Though
the lot was almost full, she noticed now that the apartments were dark. She reached Jack's door and saw that
his apartment was also dark. *Maybe he's gone out of town
with friends?* she wondered. *Where would he go? With
the Greenpeace people maybe? Promoting his film somewhere? If that was the case, Trace was going to hit the
roof.* Gayle found the key to Jack's door on her key chain
and was about to slip it into the lock when she realized
that the door was already cracked open about two inches.

Now that, she thought, *is strange. Jack doesn't trust people enough to leave his apartment door open.* She pushed it wider and called out, "Jack? You home?" When there was no answer, she frowned, stepped into the dark room, and felt along the wall until she found the light switch.

The living room coffee table was overturned, and on the floor was a candle in a puddle of wax, a broken Bong pipe, and a couple of books on Ansel Adams and David Hume Kennerly. "Jack?" Gayle called out again and then moved through the hallway toward his bedroom. The door was closed, and Gayle paused a few seconds, wondering what to do. The silence was thick and ominous; it reminded her of the silence at Ramona Heights Cemetery in the wake of what had been done the night before. She remembered the faces of the policemen out there; they'd been prepared to list it as just another case of vandalism, but when they'd seen those bones scattered in the warm, morning sunlight, their faces had turned alternately pale and greenish, and Gayle had overheard several of them speculating that a Satanic cult must be planning something really big, or some maniac like Manson was on the loose and doing this for kicks.

Good material for her story.

She opened the bedroom door and reached around for the light switch.

Something grabbed her hand and yanked at it; pain exploded across her knuckles and up her wrist. She screamed and wrenched her hand back. It was covered with blood.

And through the half-opened door came a crouching figure that stared at her with cold, hungry eyes. It was Jack's dog, and when it snarled Gayle could see her blood flecking the animal's teeth. She stepped away from the thing, backing into the wall. Two of Jack's framed photographs clattered to the floor.

Conan advanced, stalking her as he would a rabbit. The dog was hunched low to the floor, its back legs ready for the leap that would send his teeth directly at her throat. Gayle took her handbag from around her shoulder and—slowly, very slowly—coiled the strap around her uninjured wrist. She hoped that when the dog did leap, she could strike it in the face; although she didn't carry much makeup, she did have a book in there, as well as a wallet bulging with photos and credit cards. *Clout*, she thought suddenly and heard crazy laughter echo at the back of her head. *I'm carrying clout.* She looked quickly to her side along the hallway to the living room and wondered whether she could beat the dog to the door. *No way,* she decided. *He'd be on my back before I'd taken three steps. Christ!* She looked back and saw that Conan had crept closer. Now the dog's growling was low and guttural, full of real rage.

"Conan?" Gayle whispered, her voice shaking. "It's Gayle, boy. Stay back. Stay back." She raised her arm carefully to position the handbag for a blow.

The dog started to leap, then stopped less than a foot away from her. Its eyes had gone dull, and it was tilting its head like he was listening to one of those high-pitched whistles you get in pet shops. Without hesitation Conan leaped past Gayle, ran along the hallway, and squeezed out through the front door.

Relief flooded her. *God,* she thought. *That damned dog was going to tear out my throat!* She let her arm fall to her side and looked at the wound on her other hand. Conan had taken all the skin from her knuckles, and there were punctures and scratches on two fingers. Blood was still welling up, but at least the mutt hadn't pierced any of the large veins. *Christ, what was wrong with that damned dog? Jack should have the bastard shot!*

She turned toward the living room and had taken two unsteady steps when she heard a noise—a muffled, unpleasant sliding sound. She stopped, listening. The noise again—it was coming from the darkened bedroom. She reached around, her heart hammering, and hit the light switch.

The first thing she noticed was that there were no sheets on the mattress. Otherwise the bedroom looked as it usually did—slightly rumpled. She paused at the doorway and then stepped in. *What was that sound?* she wondered. *And where was it coming from?* She stopped next to the bed and listened. Silence. *You're imagining things,* she told herself. Her hand throbbed. *Fucking dog ought to have his ass kicked!*

And then something cold gripped her ankle.

She looked down, her mouth opening in dumb bewilderment.

A white, clawlike hand held her ankle like a freezing

vise; it had snaked out from beneath the bed. And then there was that sliding sound again, slow and labored. Gayle saw the fingers move. It was only then that she found her voice and screamed, instantly thinking *Scream, fool! What good will it do?* She kicked out, kicked again, and got her ankle free, then staggered backward while a shape wrapped in the white sheets writhed its way out with some difficulty. The free hand began to rip at the cloth, to work it loose from the thing that lay within. *Run!* a voice screamed in Gayle's head. *Run!* But she couldn't run. Her legs were made of rubber, and her mind had no control over them. She watched in horror as the hand began to wrench the cloth away from the head.

In another moment she could see dark, tousled hair, a mustache and a beard against a face so pallid it was almost transparent. The other hand worked its way free, and now both hands were ripping the cloth away. "Jack!" Gayle said when she found her voice. She stepped nearer, but when that head swiveled around and she saw those dead, glittering eyes, she stopped, a knot of panic filling her throat. "Jack?" she whispered hoarsely and thought, *It's a trick! He's trying on his Halloween makeup for me! That dirty sonofabitch!*

Jack— or the thing that had been Jack Kidd—shrugged off the rest of the sheets like a discarded snake skin and started to rise to his feet. His eyes were blazing, and suddenly a black tongue darted out and licked the lips. "Gayle . . ." Jack whispered, a sound like the quiet hissing of wind across newly fallen snow. It was the sound of that voice that snapped Gayle's nerve. She'd never heard anything like it before. She was filled with cold, consuming dread. Jack stepped forward, a quick grin flickering across his mouth.

Gayle turned for the door and ran. She could sense rather than hear him behind her; he seemed to be leaping for her through the air instead of running. She could feel his grinning face right behind her, radiating cold the way a radiator puts out heat. As she screamed and scrambled through the front door, she felt his hand grip her blouse. It tore, but Gayle kept running across the courtyard toward the parking lot. She was aware of shadow shapes lurking in the corners, of grinning faces daubed green by the spotlights. When Gayle dared to look back over her shoulder, she saw Jack's face only inches away, floating like a green-lit moon. She stumbled and fell to the grass. Jack leaped upon her, gripping her hair and forcing her head back.

"NO!" she screamed. "PLEASE NO!"

"Darling . . ." he hissed, his face coming toward her relentlessly. "My darling . . ." She heard the cold, wet sound of his lips parting.

Something dark whirled into Gayle's line of vision. She heard Jack grunt, and then his weight lifted off her. Replaced by that of another figure, a larger man with a heavy, jowled face that was as pallid and terrifying as Jack's; he leaned over Gayle and grinned, and within that grin Gayle saw the glitter of fangs that almost drove her over the brink into madness. She could smell a grave-rot about him. She screamed and twisted, trying to fight him off as those fangs moved closer to her throat. Before they could snap shut, Jack's arm gripped the man's throat, and he was hauled off Gayle. As she rolled away and got to her feet, she could see them fighting in the grass, their fangs snapping at each other like enraged animals.

They're fighting over me, she thought numbly. *Both of them want to . . . want to . . . what sort of thing has Jack become?*

She didn't wait to see who won. She turned and ran, losing a shoe. Something rustled in the bushes to her right, and off to the side she saw another figure—a woman in a glittery disco dress—steadily bearing down on her. Gayle reached her car, locked the doors, and started the engine. The woman, her hair dark and wild around a face that was fish-belly white, started clawing at the windshield, hammering at it with her fists. Gayle slammed the car into reverse and crashed into Jack's van as she accelerated. Then she was roaring across the parking lot, the horror in her disco dress running after her. She made the turn onto Lexington with a screech of tires and looked in her rearview mirror only after she was four blocks away. A surge of tears blinded her, and her lungs were heaving so fast she thought she wouldn't ever be able to catch her breath. She jerked the car to the curb, hearing horns blowing angrily, and sat with her face in her hands.

In another moment something tapped softly at her window, and Gayle cried out when she looked up into the face of a figure standing by her car. "What do you want?" she shrieked, cowering. "What do you want?"

"I want to see your license, Miss," the policeman said. "You almost caused a three-car pileup back there!"

ELEVEN

Jo was sitting up in bed, a copy of *The Thorn Birds* in her lap, watching her husband unknot his tie and wearily get out of his shirt. She knew there was trouble—he'd come home from the office just after three this afternoon, something he'd never done in the eleven years of their marriage. He'd picked listlessly at his dinner, sat with a black cloud on his shoulder, and didn't even watch Monday Night Football. During the course of the evening he'd hardly spoken to her, and though she was accustomed to his troubled silences when he was working on a difficult case, she could tell this was something bad; several times she caught him staring off into space as if dazed, or running a trembling hand across his forehead.

And now it was almost nine-thirty and a long time before morning. She knew him well enough to know he'd have more nightmares if he didn't talk to her about this terrible thing. Sometimes he confided in her things she didn't like to hear—finding a murdered infant or another of those Roach victims—but she steeled herself because she was his wife, that was his job and that was how the world turned.

"So," she said finally, putting aside her book. "Do you want to talk about it now?"

He placed his shirt on a hanger in the closet, then returned his tie to the tie rack.

"I'm waiting, Andy. It can't be that bad. Can it?"

He drew a long breath and turned toward her, and when she saw his eyes, she thought, *Oh, yes. Oh, yes, it can be that bad.* When he spoke, his voice was tired, but somewhere within it, Jo could hear a nervous tremble that set her own nerves on edge. "I should have told you long before this," he said softly. "I should have trusted you first, before all others. But I was scared. I *am* scared. I didn't know until today that what I was thinking was right. I'd hoped I was wrong, that I was seeing shadows where there were none, or cracking because of the pressure. But now I know I'm right, and soon not even God Himself will be able to save this city."

"Andy, what are you talking about . . . ?"

He came over and sat on the bed beside her, taking both her hands in his. "I want you to leave in the morning. I want you to get away as far as you can go. When you've found a place, call me, and I'll join you as soon as I can . . ."

"Andy!" she said, shocked. "Why?"

"Because they're going to be in the streets soon, going from house to house all across this city. And some night —possibly not tomorrow or the night after, but *some* night—they're going to come to our house." His voice cracked, and Jo squeezed his hand.

"What is it?" she pleaded. "Please tell me what's wrong!"

"All right. Yes, I have to tell you . . ." And then it all came out, from the incident at Hollywood Memorial to the living corpses found in East L.A. As he spoke, his voice became more and more frantic, more consumed with fear. Jo gripped his hands until she could feel the bones grinding. He finished by telling her of his outburst in the Dos Terros tenement, and how Sully Reece had driven him back to Parker Center in silence, glancing over at him once or twice as if he were one of those crazed transients who sleep on the grass under Beethoven's striding statue in Pershing Square.

He smiled grimly at her through haunted eyes. "My days on the force are numbered. I know that. I'm crazy, yes? Insane, just as they said my mother was. But my mother *knew*. For years I believed she shot my father because she was insane, but now I know differently. It took a great deal of courage for her to pull those shotgun triggers, but she *knew* that just because the thing looked like my father didn't mean it was truly him. She was trying to save our lives, and because I didn't understand that I . . . I hated her for . . . a very long time." Tears sprang to his eyes and quickly he wiped them away. "Now I see them coming again. I see them conquering this city just as they conquered Krajeck. And when they've finished here . . ." New terror choked him. "My

God, Jo! They'll number in the millions! No power on earth will be able to stop them . . . !"

"Andy," Jo said quietly, "when I was a little girl, my parents told me stories about the *vampir*. But those were legends, old tales that had been passed down from generation to generation. We live in a modern age now and . . ." she stopped, seeing the fury in his eyes.

"You don't believe either? Jo, can't you see? They don't *want* us to believe because if we recognize them in our midst, we can guard ourselves against them. We can hang garlic on the windows and nail crucifixes to the doors! They want us to laugh, to say 'that can never be!' When we close our eyes, we help them hide, and we help them come one step closer to our front door!"

"You can't be certain," she reasoned.

"I am certain. I saw those bodies today. They'll be awakening soon, and the only thing I can do is rant and rave like a maniac. Oh, I can take a can of gasoline and a torch and try to burn them before they escape into the streets, but then what would happen? I'll be locked away, and tomorrow there will be twice as many *vampir* as there are today."

"Have you told anyone else?"

"No. Who could I talk to? Who would believe? I see in your eyes that you don't believe either. You've always thought my mother was insane, that she shot my father in a fit of madness, and that whenever she rambled on about the *vampir*, they were the imaginings of a fevered brain. But it's the truth! I know that now. I see it clearly!"

The bedside telephone rang suddenly. Palatazin reached over and picked it up. "Hello?"

"Captain Palatazin? This is Lieutenant Martin. Detectives Zeitvogel and Farris just called in with a positive ID on that plate you were tracing. It's 285 Zero Tango Hotel, and it belongs to a guy named Walter Benefield, residence Number Seventeen Mecca Apartments, 6th and Coronado near MacArthur Park."

"They're at the scene now?" His heart was beating so wildly he could hardly hear himself talk.

"Yes sir. Shall I send a backup unit?"

"No, not yet. I'm going over myself. Thanks for calling, Johnny." He hung up and rose from the bed, taking another shirt from the closet and hurriedly putting it on.

"What is it?" Jo said tensely. "Where do you have to go?"

"Across town," he said, reaching up on the closet shelf for his shoulder-holster. He strapped it on, then shrugged into his brown tweed coat. Jo was putting on her robe, and she followed him downstairs.

"Is it something about the Roach?" she asked. "You will be careful, won't you? You're not as young as you used to be, Andy. You let the younger men take the risks. Are you listening to me?"

"Yes," he said. "Of course." But he wasn't really listening—he was thinking that he could hear a distant voice, speaking urgently in his brain . . .

"Be careful," Jo said, buttoning his coat for him. "Remember . . ."

. . . and the voice was telling him that after tonight things would never be the same in his life again because tonight he would take a step that would change the fate of a million people.

". . . let the younger men take the risks. Do you hear?"

He nodded, kissed her, and walked out of the house into the still, cool night. At the car he turned back and said to her, "Remember to lock the door." Then he slid behind the wheel, aware of the weight of the .38 beneath his left arm. He started the engine and drove away into the darkness.

V

Tuesday, October 29
THE DARK PRINCE

ONE

At twenty minutes after midnight Palatazin was sitting in his car at the curb of Coronado Street, two blocks from MacArthur Park. The sign MECCA ROOMS—DAY, WEEK, OR MONTH blinked in glaring blue neon in the middle of the block; the building itself was made of yellow brick with ornamental blue tiles that might have looked decorative twenty or more years ago. Now the whole thing looked cheap and tawdry; many of the tiles were cracked and blistered with spray-painted slogans in Spanish scrawled across the side of the building that faced a narrow service alley. Every so often a drunk would stagger out of the Club Feliz next door and barely make it into that alley before throwing up. Coronado Street caught some of the neon glitter from 6th Street and Wilshire Boulevard but was in itself essentially dark, its old buildings that dated from the twenties clustered together like a flock of black crows.

Across the street a match flared inside a parked white Chevrolet. Palatazin could see Farris's profile as he lit his cigarette. Farris was a big, bulky man whose favorite sport was professional wrestling; he had black, beetle-like eyes that could freeze a suspect a block away. Around Parker Center he was called The Wheel only half-jokingly because when he rolled over somebody, they didn't get up for a very long time. Palatazin could see the dark outline of Zeitvogel's head on the driver's side; he thought he could feel Zeitvogel watching him instead of the Mecca, but he brushed off the notion as paranoia.

When Palatazin had reached the scene from his house, Zeitvogel had briefed him on the situation: At around nine o'clock he and Farris had come to the Mecca to check the sixteenth name on their list. No one had an-

swered Benefield's door, but they'd run into the building's manager downstairs. He'd taken one look at the
composite picture and positively identified it as being the
man who rented Apartment 17. So Zeitvogel then ran
the name Walter Benefield through the Vehicle ID computers and gotten the tag number back on a '73 gray
Volkswagen Beetle. Then he'd called in to tell the night-
watch officer, Lieutenant Martin.

An hour before midnight, the manager, Mr. Pietro,
fumbled with his keys in the narrow, dimly-lit corridor
and finally slipped one into the door of No. 17. "I
wouldn't do this if I couldn't tell it was important," he
said to the three policemen standing around him. "I
mean, I know you cops wouldn't want to invade anybody's private property without good reason, huh?"

"We have good reason," Palatazin told him. "And
we're not invading, Mr. Pietro. We're simply going to
look around for a minute or two."

"Oh, sure, sure." The lock clicked open. Pietro
switched on the lights, and the men stepped inside. The
room was claustrophobic, and instantly Palatazin was
aware of a bitter aroma that might have been burnt al-
monds. Clothes were piled on a chair and scattered on the
floor, and the bed was unmade. Palatazin saw the pictures
of weightlifters taped up around the headboard. He had
started toward that corner of the room when he sensed
a scurrying motion from a battered old card table. He
stopped and stared at three wire-mesh cages filled with
huge, black roaches, tumbling and roiling over each other;
he drew his breath in sharply. "Look at that," he told the
others.

"Jeez!" Mr. Pietro said incredulously. "What's he doing with all those . . . *things* in here? Listen, I run a clean
place . . ."

"Yeah," Farris said and peered into one of the cages.
"Ugly little suckers, aren't they?"

Palatazin stepped away from the table and looked at
the pictures on the wall, then back at Pietro, who looked
thoroughly revolted. "Where does Benefield work, Mr.
Pietro?"

"Out in West L.A. He works for one of those bug-spray
companies, you know, exterminators."

"Do you know the name of the company?"

"Nope. Sorry." He glanced at the roaches again and

shivered. "Jeez, do you think Benefield's bringing his work home with him or something?"

"I doubt it." Palatazin looked over to where Farris was going through a chest of drawers. "Take it easy with that, Farris, we don't want to tear the man's furniture apart. Mr. Pietro, what time is Benefield usually at home?"

"All hours, in and out." Pietro shrugged. "Some nights he comes in, stays a little while, and then leaves again. I've gotten to where I can recognize all the tenants' footsteps now, you see. My ears are real good. Anyway, he don't keep no regular hours."

"What sort of person is he? Do you talk with him very much?"

"No, he keeps to himself. Seems okay, though." Pietro grinned, showing a gold tooth. "He pays his rent on time, which is more than you can say for a lot of them. No, Benefield doesn't talk too much. Oh, one time when I couldn't sleep and was listenin' to my radio, Benefield knocks on the door—I guess it was about two in the morning, couple of weeks ago—and he seemed to want to talk, so I let him in. He was real excited about something, said . . . I don't know, it was crazy . . . that he'd been out looking for his old lady, and he thought he'd seen her. Two o'clock in the morning." Pietro abruptly shrugged and turned to watch Zeitvogel rummaging under the bed.

"Old lady? Do you mean girlfriend?"

"No. His mom. His old lady."

Zeitvogel said, "Here's something," and pulled out a box of magazines from under the bed. It was an odd mixture of comic books, muscle magazines, and porno. Zeitvogel held up a couple of publications devoted to bondage, and Palatazin frowned with distaste. Lying on the bed were a pair of black handgrips used for strengthening hand and wrist muscles. Palatazin picked up one of them and tried to squeeze it, finding the resistance quite powerful. He made the connection between them and the crushing hands that had killed four young women and laid the grip back down where it had been. He checked the bathroom, finding a tub with a couple of inches of standing water in it. In the medicine cabinet there were bottles of Bufferin, Excedrin, Tylenol. It seemed that Benefield was plagued with headaches.

"Captain," Zeitvogel said, offering him a yellowing Kodak snapshot as he came out of the bathroom. The picture showed a blond, slightly rotund woman sitting with her arm around a young boy on a sofa. The boy wore thick glasses and had a crewcut, and he was smiling vacantly into the camera; the woman's legs were crossed, one fleshy thigh over the other, a crooked grin on her face. Palatazin studied the photograph for a moment, catching what he thought was a strange, glassy look in the woman's eyes, as if she'd been drinking too much. "Have you ever seen Benefield's mother, Mr. Pietro?" he asked.

"Nope. Never."

Farris was probing around the stove and sink. He bent down, opened a cupboard, and brought out a bottle half-filled brownish liquid. He unscrewed the cap and sniffed it, and in the next instant dark motes were spinning in front of his eyes. He jerked his head away and said, "Shit! What's this stuff?" He quickly capped it and coughed violently a couple of times, having the sensation of oil clinging to his lungs. His nostrils seemed to be on fire. Palatazin took the bottle from him and sniffed around the cap. "Mr. Pietro, do you know what this is?"

"Looks like old piss to me."

Farris caught his breath and looked under the sink again, bringing out a few dry rags. "Don't know what that is, captain, but it's *wicked*. The smell of it down here'll knock you out."

"Zeitvogel," Palatazin said quietly, "go down to your car and call in on our friend, will you? Let's see if he's got a rap sheet."

Zeitvogel was back in fifteen minutes. "Bingo, captain," he said. "Benefield's got a long record of assaults, a couple of molestation charges, a Peeping Tom, and an attempted rape. He spent eight years in and out of mental wards and did a stretch at Rathmore Hospital."

Palatazin nodded, staring at the cages full of scrabbling roaches. He put the bottle back where it had been and closed the cupboard. He wanted to shout, "YES, WE'VE GOT HIM," but he knew that wasn't the case. There was a long way to go yet in proving that Benefield had anything to do with the four murders. "We'll wait for him to come home," Palatazin said, trying to keep his voice steady. "Mr. Pietro, we're going to be outside in our cars.

I think the best thing for you to do is simply stay in your room. All right? If you hear Benefield come in, don't leave your room to be friendly."

"You going to arrest him? What's he done?"

"We just want to ask him a few questions. Thank you for showing us his room, Mr. Pietro. We'll take care of the rest."

And now Palatazin sat in his car, waiting. Several times he thought he saw a Volkswagen approaching down Coronado, but it never was. The faint odor of that liquid in the bottle stayed with him—bitter and almondy, slightly medicinal. In a rag, pressed up tightly against the nostrils, that stuff would probably act like a kind of chloroform; it was evidently some substance or mix of solutions that Benefield used at work. If he was the Roach—and those caged roaches indicated more than anything that he was—he had found a darker kind of work. But if he was the Roach, why had he changed his MO? He hoped that if Benefield was given enough rope, he might hang himself with it, or at least trip himself up.

The minutes crept into hours. Soon there were no more cars moving along Coronado, and the only movement at all was the quick flicker of a match as Farris lit another cigarette. *I can wait*, Palatazin said mentally. *You'll have to come home sometime. And when you do, Mr. Benefield, I'll be right here . . .*

TWO

Wes Richer woke up in the darkness, his head buzzing with Chablis and his stomach full of Scandia's Danish sole. At once he knew that Solange wasn't lying beside him, and when he looked up, he could see her figure outlined in moonlight, naked and chocolate brown, holding a curtain aside as she looked out of the window onto Charing Cross Road.

He watched her sleepily, the events of the night happily jumbling together in his head—the calls and congratulations from the ABC brass over "Sheer Luck"; a call from his father in Winter Hill, North Dakota, telling him how proud his mother would have been if only she were alive; Jimmy Kline calling to tell him that Arista was biting on the record contract hook and that the "Tonight Show" people were inquiring to see if Wes might guest-host after the first of November; a congratulatory call from Cher, whom Wes had met at a party for Gene Simmons; and then the dinner that evening with Jimmy, Mel Brooks, and Brooks's screenwriter, Al Kaplan. The part was being rewritten for him with a couple of added scenes to spotlight some of that "Goyem Klutz," as Brooks called it, that he showed in "Sheer Luck." At the end of the evening, Brooks had squeezed his cheek and said, "I love that face!" Which meant for Wes, as far as *Quattlebaum's* was concerned, money in the bank.

He blinked, rubbed his eyes, and said huskily, "Solange? What is it?"

She didn't move from the window. Her head was cocked to one side, a black statue, listening. Wes let his gaze roam appreciatively down her back, along the smooth curving spine, to the firm roundness of the buttocks and the swelling of her upper thighs. He'd been between those thighs less than an hour before; the sheets were still bunched at the bottom of the bed, the room filled with the peppery scent of desire. He could feel himself responding again, and he sat up, supporting his head on one arm. "Solange?" he said. "Come back to bed."

When she turned toward him, he saw her eyes—they were hollow pits in her fine skull. "I heard a scream, Wes," she whispered. "From across the street."

"A scream? You were probably dreaming."

"No," she said, her voice like velvet and steel. "I wasn't dreaming. I heard a scream. Who lives across the street?"

Wes struggled up out of bed and stood beside her, peering out into the night and feeling pretty stupid about going along with her even this far. "Uh . . . I think Dick Clark lives over there . . . no, wait a minute. It's Dick Marx. He produced the *Sea Wolf* remake with Richard Gere last year. I think." He couldn't really see the house, just the tops of trees and a chimney perched over a high brick wall. "I don't hear anything," he said after another moment.

"I think we should call the police."

"The police? Why? Listen, Dick Marx has a reputation for . . . you know . . . a little S&M thrills? Maybe he

just got carried away with his latest girl friend. Calling the
cops would be a *faux pas*, right?"

"I don't agree. What I heard was not a scream of pleasure. Will you call the police or shall I?"

"Okay, okay. Christ, when you get something on your
mind, you hang onto it until Hell freezes, don't you?" He
stepped over to the phone beside the bed and dialed 911.
When the operator answered, he said simply, "Somebody
screamed in Bel Air," then he gave the address, and hung
up. "There," he said to Solange. "Did I do my duty?"

"Come here, Wes," Solange said. "Hurry!"

He did. She gripped his arm. "I saw someone crawl
over the wall. Look! Did you see that?"

"I don't see a thing."

"Someone's in our yard, Wes!" she said, her voice rising as she gripped his arm tighter. "Call back. Tell the police to hurry!"

"Oh, shit! I'm not calling them again!" He leaned
closer to the glass and tried to make out a figure moving,
but it was pitch black; the arms of trees waved in the
wind. "There's nobody outside. Come on back to bed . . ."

He was about to turn away from the window when he
heard it. At first he thought it was the high wailing of
wind, but then the sound became higher and stronger, the
wail of a human voice—a little girl's voice—that ended
in a cascade of silvery laughter like water bubbling in a
fountain. "I seeeeeeee youuuuuuuu," the voice said.
"There at the winnnnnndowwwwwww." More childlike
laughter, and now Wes thought he *could* see a figure
standing down there on the neatly manicured lawn beside
a thin pine tree. He was almost sure he saw a white gown
being whipped by the wind, a long mane of reddish-blond
hair, a grinning moon-face staring up at him. But he
heard the voice again, and it seemed to be coming from a
different place entirely. "Come outside!" it called sweetly.
"Won't you come out and be my playmate?"

Wes narrowed his eyes. He was only marginally aware
that Solange's fingernails were digging into his arm. Something moved beside that pine tree, and now Wes was sure
he could see a little girl down there. She was barefoot and
carrying what looked like a Raggedy Ann doll. "Mister!"
she called out. "Please come outside and play with me!"

There was something in her voice that made Wes want
to go to that little girl. That voice was so sweet, so com-

pelling, so innocent. It rang in his head like Christmas
bells in the church at Winter Hill, and suddenly there
were six inches of new snow on the ground, and he was
ten-year-old Wesley Richer, stuck in his room with a head
cold the day after Christmas while all the other kids were
playing in the snow with their new sleds. He could see the
bundled figures of the big kids way out on the frozen,
milky surface of Massey Pond; they picked on him because he was sickly and skinny, but he'd memorized a lot
of jokes from a couple of books at the library, and now
even Brad Orr was beginning to laugh at them and call
him Funnyman. From his window he could see them skating around the pond, turning slow circles and figure eights
like people from those Currier and Ives pictures Mom
liked. And the sleds had already left a hundred runner
trails on Frosty Slope; ice glittered there in the weak, gray
sunlight like the dust of crushed diamonds, and a distant
figure raised a mittened hand to wave at him.

There was a pretty girl he didn't know, standing underneath his window. "Come outside!" she called, grinning
up at him. "Let's play!"

"Can't!" he called back. "Mom says no. I gotta cold!"

"I can make you all better!" the little girl said. "Come
on! You can jump right through the window!"

Wes smiled. "Aww, you're foolin'!" She was barefoot in
the snow, and maybe she was so pale because she was
really cold.

"No, I'm not! Your friends are waiting for you." She
gestured vaguely in the direction of Massey Pond. "I can
take you to them."

"Oh . . ." He was tired of staying in the house, he
wanted to get out and run in the cold wind with the
snow crunching underfoot, and maybe he wouldn't even
need any shoes either. Sure would be nice to do a belly-
flop down the Slope. "Okay," he said excitedly. "Okay!
I'll come out!"

The girl nodded. "Hurry!" she said.

And suddenly a strange thing happened. There was a
pretty chocolate-colored lady standing beside him, gripping his arm. She leaned forward and blew on the window, instantly fogging it. Then she drew a Cross in the
fogged part with her forefinger and mumbled something:
"Nsambi kuna ezulu, nsambi kuna ntoto!"

Wesley Richer said, "Huh?"

The little girl beneath the window screamed piercingly, her face contorting into a gray mask of horror. Instantly it all changed—Massey Pond and Frosty Slope and all the distant figures skating and sledding whirled out of Wes's brain like cobwebs caught in a high wind. The little girl staggered backward, gnashing her teeth. Solange shouted, "GET AWAY!" and fogged the window again, drawing another Cross and repeating the incantation again, but this time in English, "God is in Heaven, God is in Earth!"

The little girl hissed and spat, her back arching like a cat's. Then she ran across the lawn toward the wall. When she reached it, she turned and screamed, "I'll get you for that! I'll make you pay for hurting me!" And then she scrambled over the wall, her bare legs the last thing to disappear.

Wes's knees sagged. Solange caught him and helped him back to the bed. "What is it?" he said. "What happened?" He looked up at her through glazed eyes. "Gonna go skate," he said. "Snow fell last night."

She put the sheet over him and smoothed it down. She was shaking so hard her teeth were chattering. "No, no," she said softly. "You had a dream, that's all."

"A dream?" He looked at her and blinked. "Dick Marx lives across the street, that's who."

"Go to sleep," Solange told him, and in another moment his eyes closed. She stood over him until his breathing was even and deep, and then she returned to the window. The pine trees moved fitfully, as if the dull terror that gripped at her soul gripped the soul of Nature as well. She wasn't certain what the thing had been, but she knew from its violent reaction to the Cross and the name of God—a powerful talisman in all languages—that it was something terribly evil. She recalled with a shudder the messages from the spirit world as spoken through the Ouija board. Evil. They thirst. Evil. They thirst. She drew a chair up before the window and sat down to meditate. She did not move again before daylight.

THREE

"You want another cup of coffee, Miss Clarke?"

Gayle looked up. She was huddled on a bench in the main corridor of the Hollywood police precinct building where she'd been brought hours before, after she'd crumbled in hysterics in front of the officer who'd stopped her for reckless driving. She thought she might have fallen asleep for a few minutes or passed out because she hadn't heard the patient desk sergeant named Branson come up behind her. She didn't want to sleep; she was afraid of it because she knew she'd see Jack coming for her in her nightmares, those burning eyes set in a bleached skull, the fangs in his mouth making him look like some strange hybrid between man and dog. She shook her head, refusing the coffee, and hugged her knees to her chin. Her hand had been cleaned and bandaged, but the fingers still throbbed, and she wondered if she would have to get rabies shots.

"Uh . . . Miss Clarke, I don't think you have to stick around here anymore," the desk sergeant said. "I mean, I appreciate the company and all, but you can't stay here all night."

"Why not?"

"Well, why should you? You've got a place to live, don't you? I mean, it's quiet in here right now, but later on we're going to have hookers, hustlers, pimps, junkies, all kinds of low-life stumbling in here. You don't want to be around all that, now do you?"

"I don't want to go home," she said weakly. "Not yet."

"Yeah, well . . ." He shrugged and sat down on the bench beside her, making a big deal out of checking a scuff mark on his shoe. "It's safe for you to go home," he said finally without looking at her. "Nothing's going to get you."

"You don't believe me either, do you? That first dumb clod didn't believe me, neither did your lieutenant, and you don't either."

He smiled faintly. "What's to believe or not believe? You told us what you saw, and it was checked out. The officers found a lot of empty apartments and a couple of dogs running around . . ."

"But you'll admit it was goddamned strange that all those apartments were unlocked at eleven o'clock at night, won't you? That's not common in Hollywood, is it?"

"Who knows what's common or uncommon in Hollywood?" Branson said quietly. "The rules change every day. But this stuff about your boyfriend being some kind of . . . what did you say he was? Vampire or werewolf?"

She was silent.

"Vampire, didn't you say? Well, couldn't he have been wearing a Halloween mask maybe?"

"It was no mask. You people have overlooked the most important point—what happened to all those people in that apartment complex? Did they all step off into the Twilight Zone or something? *Where are they?*"

"That I wouldn't know anything about." Branson said, getting to his feet. "But I'd suggest you go on home now, huh?" He moved back toward his desk, feeling her stare boring into the back of his neck. Of course, he hadn't told her that Lieutenant Wylie was over at the Sandalwood Apartments right now with a team of officers, going over every room with vacuum cleaners and roping the place off from the street. Branson could tell that Wylie was more than a little worried. When Wylie's left eyebrow started to tick, that was a sure sign something was cooking. This Clarke woman had answered all the questions she could, and she'd put some questions of her own to the officers, who of course couldn't come up with any decent answers. Wylie had told him emphatically to get rid of her since she was a real thorn in the ass. Branson sat behind his desk, shuffled papers, and stared at the telephone, wishing it would ring with a good old-fashioned robbery or mugging. This vampire shit was for the birds. *No,* he decided, *make that for the bats.*

FOUR

Awaken, the voice whispered. Mitch Gideon heard it quite clearly. But he didn't have to open his eyes because they were already open; his head simply seemed to jerk backward, and his vision cleared as if he'd been looking through frosted glass. It took him a moment to fully realize where he was. When he did, the shock of it almost staggered him.

He was standing in the entrance foyer of the Gideon Funeral Home Number Four on Beverly Boulevard near CBS Television City. Behind him the heavy, chrome and oak doors stood wide open to the street; a cold breeze was rushing in around him. He heard a noise like the tinkling of Chinese wind chimes and looked to his side—he was holding his key ring with the key that unlocked the front doors still grasped between his thumb and forefinger. He was wearing brown bedroom slippers and his brown velour robe with the initials "MG" on the breast pocket over his usual white silk pajamas. *I'm in my pajamas?* he asked himself incredulously. *What the fuck's going on here? Am I dreaming, hypnotized, or what?*

Overhead a huge chandelier with electric candles lit up the entrance foyer with a rich, golden glow. He didn't remember flicking the wall switch. *Damn!* he thought, *I don't remember anything since I got into bed beside Estelle at . . . what time had that been?* He looked at his wrist but knew his watch was sitting on the chest of drawers in the master bedroom where he put it every night before going to sleep. He felt like shouting the two questions aloud: What am I doing here? And how the hell did I get down from Laurel Canyon to Beverly Boulevard in my *sleep* for Christ's sake?

Gideon turned and walked back out of the building into the parking lot. There sat his Lincoln Continental in the space marked, "Mr. Gideon Only." But there was another vehicle in the parking lot as well—a large U-Haul truck. He stepped closer to it but didn't see anyone sitting in the cab. And when he looked back at the Tudor-style funeral home, he saw a light burning in a window on the upper floor. *My office,* he realized. *Have I been up there working? How did I get out of the house? By sleepwalking? Didn't Estelle hear me leave?* He seemed to remember being behind the wheel of his car, the hot splash of headlights and traffic signals on his face, but he'd thought that was only a dream. He was grateful that tonight he wasn't dreaming of that conveyor belt full of coffins where the workmen were beginning to grin at him as if he were one of their own. His brain felt feverish and violated, as if someone or something had peeled back the top of his head and gone to work in there, fitting him with a wind-up key that could be turned to send him spinning madly in any chosen direction.

He whirled around and stared into the dark distance. *It was that goddamned house,* he thought suddenly, *that castle where some maniac had sawed Orlon Kronsteen's head off.* The place was preying on his mind, intruding into his thoughts both day and night, making him crazy. He thought he could see the castle even now outlined against the darkness in blood-red neon. *Crazy,* he thought, *I'm going fuckin' crazy!*

And from the corner of his eye, he saw the light go off in his office. Gideon stared at the black window, his heart beating rapidly. Chill bumps had risen on his arms and legs beneath the silk pajamas. *My God,* he thought. *Oh, my God . . . did I unlock the doors for someone else?* He walked back across the parking lot to the building's threshold. The only sound in the entire funeral home seemed to be the ticking of a large grandfather clock at the far end of the central corridor where a wide marble staircase with black, cherrywood banisters curved grace-fully up to the second floor. Gideon moved along that corridor until he could make out the hands on the clock—two-ten. He'd closed his eyes in his own bedroom at just after twelve o'clock.

From somewhere upstairs there came a muffled, soft *thump*. Gideon knew what that sound was from years of hearing it—the noise of a coffin lid closing, probably in the first of the three display rooms. He came to the end of the corridor, the grandfather clock ticking madly in his head. And he started up the long stairway, hand clench-ing the banister. There was another corridor on the sec-ond floor and several rooms on either side; at the corridor's end a shorter stairway led up to the third floor and the administrative offices. Gideon's searching hand found the wall switch, and instantly the corridor was lit by a dozen wall-mounted electric candles. On the first of the polished oak doors there was a golden plaque that said Blue Room, and underneath that in white plastic letters pressed against a black velvet background, Mr. William R. Tedford. Gideon opened the door and pressed another wall switch. A sapphire-colored chandelier blazed to life. Everything in the room was blue—walls, ceiling, carpet, sofa, and chairs. Blue flowers peeked from azure vases; a six-foot statue of a blue angel with unfolding wings stood in a corner; the guest book, powder blue, sat atop an indigo pedestal. But the room's main fixture, supported on a royal blue dais, was a closed ebony coffin containing the remains of a certain Mr. Tedford.

From further along the hallway came the quiet sound of a door closing. "Who's there?" Gideon said, his voice sounding weak and defenseless in the thick silence. He stood where he was for a moment, listening, and then moved forward past the Gold Room, past the Green Room, past the Amber Room. He peered cautiously into the Red Room, switching on a chandelier that lit up the place like the center of an inferno. He could almost smell the sulphur and smoke. But then he saw that the coffin's lid was propped open and, as he neared it, he realized with a start of alarm that the corpse—an elderly woman in a pale pink gown—was smoking a cigarette.

Or rather, a burning cigarette had been forced between the dead lips. It was almost out now because, of course, she wasn't inhaling. A few ashes lay on her cheek, gray against artificial peach. *Someone's playing a joke,* Gideon thought angrily as he plucked out the cigarette and tossed it aside. *It's not very funny. Not very funny at all!*

He was answered by a single peal of laughter from one of the other display rooms. He went back out to the corridor, trembling, wanting to run but knowing he couldn't hide. "Where are you?" he shouted. "What do you want with me?" There were two more rooms further along the hall—the Violet Room and the White Room. Gideon looked from door to door, his legs refusing to move. "What do you want?" he shouted again. "I'm going to call the police if you don't get out of here!"

Dead silence.

Gideon threw open the door to the Violet Room. It crashed against the wall, knocking down a gilt-framed picture of purple flowers in a dark green and lilac field. He approached the coffin and looked in, recoiling instantly. The corpse—a shrunken old man with sharply protruding cheekbones—had been painted to look like a clown. There were red spots of lipstick covering his cheeks and the bulb of his nose, the lips had been painted bright red and the sewn-shut eyelids as well. Gideon slammed down the coffin's lid and backed away into the corridor where he turned to face the White Room's door.

He stepped inside, holding his breath in this place of glacial, heavenly whiteness. In this room, the most expensive and ornate of all the display rooms, even the coffin was white with gleaming, gold-plated trim. There was a white grand piano with gold-plated keys replacing the black ones, and a long, black and white checked sofa. Two tall, golden candelabra stood on either side of the coffin dais, each holding six electric candles that now guttered with golden light. But there was no one in here, no one at all. Gideon, bloated with relief, turned toward the door.

And then the ice-white coffin began to open.

He whirled around, a long whine beginning in his throat. The coffin's lid rose, pushed by a bare arm. When it was fully open, the corpse sat up. It was a young Chicano boy with shining black hair, wearing a white T-shirt and dirty jeans. Gideon could see that he'd been lying on top of the other corpse in the coffin, a blue-haired society matron who'd kicked off in her sleep, and now the boy started to climb out of the coffin, his dark eyes transfixing Gideon. He reached out, felt the silk lining of the coffin, and grinned. "Real nice, man," he said softly. "You know how to make 'em real good, don't you?"

Gideon couldn't speak. Couldn't move. Couldn't think.

"Just trying it on for size, Mr. Gideon," the boy said, his gaze flicking to the corner.

And the black-haired girl who'd been standing there leaped for Mitch Gideon's throat.

FIVE

"Ah," Prince Conrad Vulkan said softly, pressing his white fingers to his temple. He opened his green cat eyes and looked across the room at Phillip Falco. "There. Mitch Gideon is ours. We can begin mass production tomorrow night."

"Sir, if you'll allow me," Falco began quietly, "you took a great risk in bringing him down from his home like that . . ."

"Risk? What risk?" Vulkan's eyes moved, green marbles in a pallid face, toward his servant. "If the police had stopped him, he simply would have awakened from his trance. That's all. We need the coffins; we need his factory. And what military leader in all of history has been a stranger to risks?" He sat motionless for a moment, then rose to his feet and moved across the stone-floored room to the huge fireplace. It was large enough to hold more than a cord of wood, but now only six or seven logs blazed in there, and the yellow-orange glow splashed across the vampire's face. There were crates scattered about the room, some of them open, with old, rare books spilling out. Beautiful paintings, many of them cracked and faded but obviously the work of masters, hung on the walls along with delicate fragments of rotted tapestries. At the center of the room there was a large, blue and red Oriental carpet and a long, polished table on which sat a silver candelabra and eight guttering black candles. Before Vulkan's black velvet chair were maps of L.A., Torrance, Glendale, Pasadena, Compton, and most of Orange and Los Angeles counties. Vulkan stared into the fire, his eyes glittering. Soon the servant who called himself Roach would be bringing him his food for the night, and the prospect of drinking hot blood made him eager and impatient. He had missed his feeding last night because he felt it unwise to use that human again so quickly. He'd been reading the newspapers Falco brought to him, and he knew that it would be foolish to do something that would call needless attention to his servant. "Roach will be here soon," he said, watching a log burst into flame. He pondered what had to be done tonight; fast or slow, that was the question.

"Master," Falco said, stepping closer. "That man is dangerous. He takes chances. He's going to cause you harm . . ."

"Why should *you* care?" the prince asked softly.

Falco paused for a moment, watching the slight figure dappled red and black by the flames. "I only mean to say, Master, that the police are bound to catch him sooner or later. I know you've chosen him because you found his mind most . . . receptive, but the time is coming for you to dispose of him. *I* could bring them for you. Why not let me?"

Vulkan turned toward the other man, smiling slightly. "Let you? Let you, Phillip? Time has used you all up. There's nothing left of you. You're old and weak, and the women would get away from you too easily. No. Roach is young, strong, and . . . new." Vulkan regarded him in silence for a moment, then shook his head. "No, Phillip. If anyone causes me harm, it will be you. Won't it?"

"Me?" A cold flame of terror flared in Falco's soul. "I don't understand what you're . . ."

"Oh, yes, you do. It's time to stop the charade. Do you think just because I sleep during the day I know nothing of what transpires? You sadly misjudge me, Phillip." Vulkan's voice had dropped to a soft, gentle whisper. "How unfortunate. The Headmaster visits me as I sleep, Phillip. He sees everything, even what hides in your heart and mind. That is how I know you've been thinking of betraying me . . ."

"No!" Falco said, his eyes widening. "No! I swear it isn't true!"

"Oh, but it is. Ever since we left Hungary, you've grown more and more . . . how shall I put it? . . . penitent? Now you sink to your knees and pray to a god who will have nothing to do with you. You pray, and you repent—for what good it does you. And you have been thinking of going to the police."

"NO!"

"The Headmaster told me, Phillip. And he never lies. Never." Vulkan turned his back on Falco and watched the fire burn. "I've given you a good life," he said after another moment. "Why did you want to hurt me?"

Falco trembled, his mind reeling. He put his hands to his face and drew in a tortured breath. Above him in the high rafters of the room, he could hear the wind moaning like a chorus of doomed souls. "It's . . . it's not right!" he blurted out, a strangled sob breaking from his throat. "It's perverted, unholy . . . !"

"You can do better than that."

"I . . . I remember in Budapest, when I was a young art dealer and . . . the old man came to see me . . ."

"Kovak," Vulkan whispered. "A loyal and true servant."

". . . with that priceless, Byzantine woodcarving, so beautiful it stunned me. And I remember he said there were more pieces of art like that one, hundreds more in a monastery atop Mount Jaeger. He said his . . . his Master had heard of the auction I'd arranged for the Koppe estate, and perhaps I could arrange an auction for Prince Vulkan as well." Falco's eyes grew cold. "Vulkan. The first time I ever heard your name I felt . . . contaminated."

"And of course, when you saw my collection . . . or, I should say, the collection my father began . . . you ceased to care what sort of creature I was. Even after I'd killed Kovak, you helped the others throw his body from the cliff. Do you remember that as well?"

Falco shuddered.

"Look around you, Phillip," Vulkan whispered softly. "Look at the beauty you sacrificed your soul to be near."

Falco blinked and looked at the walls where the medieval tapestries and the ancient works of Byzantine art hung. There were more modern works as well—pieces by Lorrain, Ingres, Delacroix, Nolde, Degas, Lorenzo Di Credi, and the Hungarian artists Laszlo Paal, Jozsef Borsos, and Simon Hollosy. In the dim firelight magnificent black horses leapt on their canvas fields; a peasant celebration, done in earth tones, swirled across a village square; a bright red Nolde demon giggled while a poet struggled with his verses; wind moved, cold and silent, across a gold and purple autumnal scene, sending a gaggle of black crows flying from an amber field; Degas ballerinas wearing pink masks pirouetted on a shadowy stage; the somber face of a Hungarian nobleman in black stared out from his canvas, a golden coronet around his head the only hint of light or color. The paintings filled the room, their subjects bright and dark, colors muted and sparkling. *The beauty,* Falco thought; *oh, the terrible beauty . . .*

Prince Vulkan took a step toward him, but his face remained in shadow. "It comes to an end, Phillip. The one who calls himself Roach is bringing me food tonight. He'll be staying here with me. In your place."

Falco's mouth opened. He whispered, "Please," then whirled away from the prince, racing across the huge room toward the slab of a door on the other side. Before he reached it, Vulkan raised a finger and formed a triangle in the air; Falco found himself grasping for a doorknob that was no longer there. Now a rough, stone wall stood before him. "Illusion!" Falco shrieked. "There's a door here! I know there is!" His fingers scrabbled over the stone frantically, and then he began beating at it with his fists.

Vulkan giggled—the giggle of a young, spoiled boy—

and called out in a high singsong, "Phillip can't get out, can't get out, can't get out . . . can you?"

"God help me!" Falco shrieked, his voice cracking. "God help . . ."

"STOP THAT!" Vulkan shouted, clapping his hands to his ears. His face had sharpened, the mouth half-open to show the vicious fangs. "I'll tear you to pieces for that!"

Falco whirled around, his back to the cold stone, and watched in horror as the prince approached. "Master!" he whispered hoarsely and began to sink to his knees. "Master, please, I'm begging you! I'm begging you! Don't kill me, don't kill me . . . make me like you! You said you would someday! Do it *now!* Make me like you!"

Vulkan stood over him, smiling slightly. "No, Phillip, you've aged too much to be of any further use to me. And you know too many of my secrets, too many of my plans . . ."

"Don't kill me!" the old man on the floor whimpered, tears streaming down his cheeks.

"The world belongs to the young," Vulkan said. "The old have no place in it. I give the gift of everlasting youth, and soon this world will be *mine.* Think of Alexander, Phillip. During his campaigns on Tyre and Babylon, he left behind the stragglers and invalids who would hold back his march. You are now worth as much to me as a straggler was to Alexander . . ."

Falco hid his face in his hands. "God save my sinning soul, I have sinned, Father, and I . . ."

"YOU FOOL!" Vulkan shouted and gripped his palms around Falco's temples. The fingers tensed; Falco's eyes widened in shock. There was a soft cracking sound and a fine thread of blood spread from the crown of Falco's head to the bridge of his nose. Vulkan's eyes blazed green, the pupils darkening.

Then Falco screamed, the scream echoing eerily against the walls as it was drawn up with the wind toward the high ceiling. Drops of blood were being squeezed from Falco's forehead, streaming down to the tip of the nose, spattering onto his shirt. The cracking noise grew louder, and Falco began babbling in terror.

Vulkan's wrists suddenly twisted. Most of Falco's face and the top of his skull caved in, blood exploding from the ruined nose and the crack that zigzagged from his forehead to the back of his head. The body began kicking frantically, eyes filling up with blood. Vulkan applied more pressure, and the head became a morass of flesh, bone, and brains. Vulkan loosened his grip, and the corpse gave out a soft sigh as it crumpled into a formless heap. Blood had splattered across the vampire's face, and now he took a thick drop of it on the end of a finger and licked it off. Then he waved that finger in a triangle opposite the first one, and the door reappeared like a photograph coming up on blank paper. The figures that had been pressed against it on the other side, listening and laughing softly, scurried away into the corridor's darkness when Vulkan opened the door. He called sharply, "Kobra!" and one of them stopped and came back along the corridor.

"Master?" Kobra said softly. The flesh of his face was tight and masklike, veined with blue at the temples. His eyes were as red as a rat's, his white hair matted and dirty. He stepped into the room, following Vulkan, and stared down at the bloody figure on the floor.

"Drink," Vulkan said, motioning vaguely toward the corpse.

Kobra's eyes blazed in anticipation. He gasped and went down on his knees, fastening his fangs in the throat and drinking greedily as his chest heaved up and down.

The prince walked across the room and sat back down in his chair, watching Kobra feast. Every so often Vulkan giggled. Kobra was young and inexperienced and didn't yet know the rich difference between living and dead food. These young ones were so easy to please and so eager to learn. Soon, though—very soon—he and the others would learn some of the secrets that Vulkan had kept for almost eight hundred years—how to summon dogs and rats, bats and flies in thick, noxious clouds; how to peer into the mind of a human and read the secret thoughts waiting to be tapped. How to tell from a single drop of blood how old a human was, or what his diet had consisted of—the tastes a hundred thousand complex variations of sweet and sour, coppery and salty, tart or flat, poor or fine like wine aged in old Belgian kegs. How to drain the blood from a living human to the dregs and in so doing transform that person into a brother or sister of the night. So many things to learn.

Vulkan leaned back in his chair. Kobra glanced up,

wasting the blood that dripped from his pale lips, and then returned to his work. *This one is dedicated. He actually loves me,* thought the prince. *What to do with Falco's carcass?* His gaze moved toward the huge fireplace. The logs had caught now, and the blaze filled the room with dancing orange specters. He wondered if the dogs in the castle's lower regions would like their meat roasted tonight.

And so he sat and waited for the Roach.

SIX

Startled, Palatazin raised his head and glanced at his watch. He'd fallen asleep for a few minutes. Three-twenty. Coronado Street seemed deserted. Even the Club Feliz had closed its doors and cut the lights. The two shapes in the parked car across the street weren't moving, and Palatazin wondered if they were sleeping, too. *Should've brought some coffee,* he told himself irritably. Then another thought—*what if this Benefield isn't the one we're looking for? The killings have stopped. Perhaps he's gone for good. Or have they stopped? Is the Roach just lying low?*

A car's headlights winked from the far end of Coronado Street. Palatazin sat upright, his heart starting to beat a little faster. The car approached very slowly, and in another minute Palatazin saw that it was a light-colored Volkswagen Beetle. His throat went dry. The car pulled up to the curb perhaps thirty yards away, and Palatazin ducked down in his seat. The headlights went out. A car door opened and closed. Footsteps sounded on concrete.

When he lifted himself up, he caught a quick glimpse of the man disappearing into the Mecca. *That's him,* Palatazin thought. *That's the man!* After a moment or so Zeitvogel came across the street and peered into Palatazin's car. "Do we go up after him now, captain?"

"No. Let's wait awhile and see what he does. If he comes back out, we'll follow him, and if he stays in, we'll have plenty of time to make the arrest."

"This is him, isn't it? The Roach, I mean?"

"We'll see. You stay alert."

Zeitvogel nodded and dashed back to his car.

Palatazin stared fixedly at the building's front door. When it opened again and Benefield stepped out onto the sidewalk, Palatazin felt his heart kick as if it had been given a charge of electricity. *The man was carrying a small paper bag—what could that be?* he wondered. *One of those rags soaked in that noxious brew? Then maybe he was going to strike tonight?* Benefield reached his car, looked up and down the street—Palatazin ducked his head so fast his neck cracked—and then got in. The Volkswagen's engine fired, the headlights came on, and the car pulled away from the curb. It moved slowly past Palatazin to the end of Coronado, then turned right on 6th.

Palatazin quickly started his engine, made a tight U-turn, and followed. He saw Zeitvogel's lights, about fifty yards behind in his rearview mirror. The gray Volkswagen turned on Western Avenue, and Palatazin realized the man was driving right up into Hollywood. His pulse was pounding, the palms of his hands sweaty against the steering wheel. He kept as far back as possible, driving with his lights out so Benefield wouldn't notice his tail. In a few minutes the Volkswagen turned onto Hollywood Boulevard, which was still ablaze with neon from the bars, discos, massage parlors, and porno bookstores. There was still a good deal of traffic on the boulevard, too, so Palatazin had to turn his lights on and speed up. He hung back a few car lengths behind the Volkswagen. From the sidewalks young girls in tight denims or slit skirts, T-shirts and halters called out invitations to the drivers, waving at them and holding up fingers to indicate their price. Most of the girls, hopeful starlets from every state in the country, were very pretty; perhaps they'd modeled once or twice or done bit parts or even starred in a skin flick or two, but now for a variety of reasons, their luck had just turned bad. They were the throwaways, the tissues some agent, director, or disco smooth-talker had sneezed into and then tossed out with the trash. All of them potential victims.

Up ahead under a huge red "X" that proclaimed a porno triple-bill, the Volkswagen swerved. The car plowed through traffic toward the curb.

SEVEN

His head was filled with the Master's voice, so he knew he had to hurry. He'd driven past several girls who'd tempted him, but tonight he was looking for one who was just right. There were so many to choose from—all colors, all sizes, the greatest candy store in the world. He had an erection already, but he wouldn't have an orgasm until he clamped the chemical-soaked cloth against her mouth and nostrils.

And then he saw her, standing beneath the red "X" of the Hollywood Adult Cinema. She had long waves of blond hair, lips pouting sensually in a face that looked more like a little girl than a woman. She was wearing a shocking pink dress and pink stockings, and best of all, she wasn't nearly as thin as the others. There was something about her eyes and her mouth that reminded him of Bev. Of course, all the girls did in one way or another, but this one . . . yes, this one *was* Bev! *It really was!* He thought he'd found her so many times, that she'd been sorry for leaving him and had come back, but always he realized that it wasn't her, that he'd been tricked again. And so he had to kill the nasty, evil bitches. They were helping Bev hide; they were laughing at him behind his back with their ugly, painted lips.

But this was her—he was sure of it. Oh, the Master would be so glad he'd found Bev!

Tears brimmed in his eyes as he pulled up to the curb and motioned the girl over. She looked around for something better and then shrugged as she stepped over to the Volkswagen, peering in at the man with her heavy-lidded, dark eyes. "I won't go for less than seventy-five," she said disinterestedly, in a thin voice. She had wanted to sing backup for somebody like Bob Seger, but it was really hard getting a gig in this town.

"Fifty," Roach said. He started digging for his wallet.

"You talking a quickie or what?" the girl asked.

"Yeah. A quickie."

"You want some lip service?" He looked like a creep, but fifty bucks would buy her those new shoes she'd been

234

wanting over at The Broadway. There was a funny smell in the car, too. Alcohol? Aftershave lotion? She'd just gotten a whiff of it, and now it was gone. *Well, what the hell?* She slid into the car. "My name's Vicki," she said and gave his thigh a quick squeeze.

He smiled and pulled back into the flow of traffic. "I know what your name is. You can't fool me."

"Huh?" Kim muttered. *Some nut. God,* she thought, *maybe he's the Roach.* The idea chilled her, but then she pushed it aside. Everything about the guy was little except his hands; his cock was probably as big as a shrimp. That made her giggle a little bit.

"What are you laughing at?" he said sharply.

"Oooooh," Kim said in a little girl voice, "don't bite baby's head off, sweetheart. Why don't you turn in that alley, sugar, and let baby give you what you need?"

"Okay," he said. "Yeah. Fine." He turned off the boulevard but drove right through the alley onto Franklin Avenue.

"Hey! Where are you taking me?"

"You'll see," he told her, cutting across Franklin and driving north toward Yucca Street. "You just sit quiet, you'll see."

"Stop the car!" Kim said suddenly. "I want to get out!"

"No, you don't. You'll run away. I've looked for you for a long time, Bev, and I'm not going to let you go again . . ."

Dull terror hit the girl. Her breath quickened. "Let me out," she whispered and whirled to open the door, but one of the man's hands flashed out and caught her by the back of the neck. "DON'T DO THAT!" he shouted. "THIS ISN'T THE WAY IT'S SUPPOSED TO BE!" He turned onto Palmero Street and followed it to a dead-end where a couple of dark apartment buildings stood. There was a mound of dirt and rubble piled at the center of a weed-infested lot. Kim was struggling, scratching at him now. "STOP THAT!" he shouted. "BEV, STOP IT!" She went limp for a second, and when his grip relaxed, she turned and dug her nails into his cheek, then leaped for the door again. He caught her hair and throat and pulled her back.

And then he realized the truth, as he realized it every time, every single time—this wasn't Bev. This was some-

body who'd tried to fool him, somebody who was laughing at him. This was someone who was wicked and who
could only be saved by the Master's touch.

"You're not Bev!" Roach said. "You're not, you're not,
you're . . ." He reached down beneath the seat for the
cloth and brought it quickly up into Kim's face. She gave
a muffled scream and fought harder, but he wrenched her
head back and pressed the wet cloth firmly against her
nostrils.

And then he was caught in a blaze of headlights.

EIGHT

Palatazin and Zeitvogel had hit their lights at about the
same time, and Zeitvogel shouted, "Police! Hold it!"

Benefield twisted around frantically. In the next instant
he threw open the passenger door and kicked the blond
out. She staggered to her knees and then pitched forward,
unconscious. The Volkswagen's engine roared as the car
plunged forward, then turned in a wild circle on the vacant lot and came screaming back along Palmero Street
toward the makeshift roadblock formed by Palatazin and
Zeitvogel's cars. The Volkswagen tried to turn aside at
the last instant, but Zeitvogel accelerated and slammed
into Benefield's side. The Roach scrambled out, his eyes
enormous circles of fear behind his glasses. He started to
run for the darkness as Palatazin leaped from his car and
drew his .38. "STOP OR I'LL SHOOT!" he shouted.
Benefield kept running. Palatazin fired into the air, and
immediately Benefield fell to the ground in a trembling
heap. Holding his gun at arm's length, Palatazin approached the man. "Hold it!" he said tersely. "Don't
move, not even a finger!" Behind him he could hear the
chatter of Zeitvogel's radio, and Farris came running up
beside him like a bull.

When he reached Benefield, Palatazin saw that the
man had contorted himself like a fetus and was sucking
his thumb. Farris hauled him to his feet, snapped hand-
cuffs on his wrists, and read him his rights. Benefield's
eyes were glazed and empty, and he kept staring up into
the hills.

Palatazin walked back to the empty lot and bent down beside the girl. Her breathing was ragged, but otherwise she seemed to be okay. On the ground near her there was a piece of cloth that smelled so strongly of the liquid substance they had found in Benefield's apartment that tears came to his eyes. Sirens were coming nearer. In another moment two prowl cars came roaring along Palmero Street, followed by an ambulance. One of the attendants broke open a plastic ampule under the girl's nose, and she began coughing; she sat up in another moment, rivulets of black mascara streaming down her face with her tears.

The night was filled with flashing lights and the metallic crackle of police radios. Farris was frisking Benefield at the side of a prowl car, and Palatazin put his gun away and came over to them.

The man was babbling like a lunatic, ". . . calling me, I hear him calling me, he's not going to let you do this, he's going to protect me, he will he will . . ."

"Sure he will," Farris said. "Now get in that car and shut your face."

But Benefield turned his full gaze onto Palatazin. "He won't let you put me away! He knows what you're doing! He sees everything, all the wickedness in the whole world!" He looked up into the night past Palatazin's shoulder. "Master!" he called out and began to sob. "Master, help me! My life is yours! My . . ."

"Get in!" Farris said, shoving Benefield into the backseat.

The cold slowly crept over Palatazin. Had the man said *Master?* Did he mean God or . . . something else? He looked through the window at Benefield, who had his face in his hands, as if ashamed. The prowl car backed along Palmero, turned, and then disappeared into the night, leaving Palatazin staring into the darkness. Slowly he turned and gazed up at the Hollywood hills, a cold wind suddenly rushing past him like something huge and invisible. From far away he thought he could hear a dog howling forlornly.

"Captain? You going back to Parker Center?"

Palatazin looked over his shoulder at Zeitvogel. "No. Let them put Benefield on ice for a while, and I swear if anybody calls the press in on this thing before morning, I'll have him walking a beat on Selma Avenue!" He ran a

hand across his forehead. "I'm going home to get some
sleep."

Zeitvogel nodded, started to walk away, and then
stopped. "Do you think we've got the Roach?" he asked
quietly.

"Your guess is as good as mine."

"I hope we do. If not, we sure busted our asses for
nothing. See you at the office." Zeitvogel raised his hand
in good-bye and walked away toward his now-battered
car.

"See you," Palatazin said. He gazed back into the darkness, feeling as though he were being watched by a presence that was slowly gathering strength. *Where was
it hiding? What was its strategy? When was it going to
strike? Could Benefield supply any of the answers to
those questions?* Palatazin paused a moment longer, feeling the hairs standing up at the back of his neck. Then
he walked to his Ford and drove away.

NINE

Mother of Mercy Hospital was an old, ten-story chunk of
brick and glass in Monterey Park about five minutes away
from the San Bernardino Freeway. At five minutes after
four A.M. the parking lot was quiet, and most of the
building's windows were dark. The last real trouble in the
Emergency Room had ended an hour ago, when the police had brought in eight or nine members of the Homicides and the Vipers who'd started swinging knives at
each other at the Matador Drive-In. Three of them were
cut pretty badly and needed whole blood transfusions,
but the rest were patched up with bandages and Mercu-
rochrome and hauled off in a police van. It had been an
easy night—a couple of traffic accident victims, one gunshot wound, a child who'd mistaken a jar of ant poison
for honey, assorted broken bones and sprains, nothing really out of the ordinary. But tonight the Emergency Room
staff wanted to stay busy so they wouldn't have time to
think about the gossip they'd been hearing all night from
assorted nurses and orderlies about those fifty-seven people lying in the isolation ward on the tenth floor. Nurse

Lomax said that not one of them had a drop of blood in their bodies. Paco, an orderly on the ninth floor, had said he'd seen some of those bodies twist and writhe like mad things, yet they had neither heartbeat nor pulse. Hernando Valdez, an aged janitor and a renowned voice of wisdom in the hospital, said their skin was like marble, and you could see the trails of collapsed veins beneath it. He said they were *maldito,* cursed things, and it would be best not to be around when they awakened from their evil sleep. Nurse Esposito said everything about them was dead except their brains—when electrode contacts were placed on their scalps, jagged spokes were displayed on the electroencephalograms.

The Emergency Room staff agreed—whatever was going on, it was *muy misterioso.*

So none of them spoke when Dr. Miriam Delgado, her eyes still puffy from a brief and uneasy sleep, came through the Emergency Room entrance and stepped into the elevator without acknowledging any of them. The lighted numerals at the top of the door advanced to "10."

Dr. Delgado had received a telephone call about twenty minutes earlier from Mrs. Browning, head nurse on the isolation ward. The woman sounded extremely puzzled. "Dr. Delgado, there's a change in several of the patients. We're getting increased EEG readings." Delgado was thankful to return to the hospital; in her sleep she'd dreamed of those terrible eyes staring at her through transparent, milky lids like the eyes of sleeping reptiles. They seemed to be surrounding her, spinning in a mad circle like the baleful lamps of some out-of-control carnival ride. When she awakened, she was shaking and could not seem to stop.

The elevator doors slid open on the tenth floor. Dr. Delgado stepped out and walked along the green-walled corridor toward the nurse's station. Her brain was still buzzing from her dream as well as from all the heated conferences she'd been involved in yesterday with everyone from Dr. Steiner to Dr. Ramez, the head of the hospital. The theories had flown hot and fast; diagnoses were formulated and then just as quickly discarded. The press had been nosing around, but the hospital's public relations man had been able to keep them at bay, for the time being at least. Which was a relief to Dr. Delgado for she needed time to find out just what they were dealing with here. A virus? A contaminant in the water pipes? Some element in the building's paint? In the air? One of the nurses had found precisely spaced puncture wounds on three of the victims, but not all in the same place. Two of them were wounded in the throat, a third at the crook of the elbow. The others were bruised and some had ragged cuts on their faces or at the backs of their necks just beneath the hairline. The nurse had offered a valid speculation—snakebite. But so far none of the victims had reacted to any antivenom serum.

Dr. Delgado reached the station, halfway between the elevator and the white door with the sign that said ISO-LATION—NO ADMITTANCE WITHOUT WHITE BADGE. The first thing she saw were case files scattered across the floor. A blue coffee cup had fallen from the desk and cracked into several pieces. On the desk itself there were coffee-stained papers, and a pencil holder had spilled over. *Damn it!* she thought angrily, staring at the mess, *what's going on here? How could these night nurses be so incredibly sloppy?* She tapped the little bell on the desk and waited, but no one came along the hallway to answer it.

"Ridiculous!" she said aloud and walked on past the station through the white door. The isolation ward con-sisted of a series of large rooms cut by a central corridor; there were large, plate-glass windows through which Dr. Delgado could see the mystery disease victims lying side by side, hooked up to IV tubes and bloodbags and as many electroencephalographs as Dr. Delgado's staff had been able to beg, borrow, or steal. She watched the green spikes jump and realized with a surge of excitement that most of them were showing almost double the amount of brainwave activity as they had when she'd left the hospi-tal last night. Were they finally reacting to the IVs and the blood transfusions? Was it possible they were beginning to come out of their odd comalike state? She walked to the door marked ISOLATION I and took a green surgical mask in a cellophane packet from a stainless steel tray. She tied the mask in place and then walked through into the ward.

The room hummed with electric circuitry and the chit-tering of the EEG monitors. Dr. Delgado stopped at each bed to watch the spikes gathering strength, though she was still unable to find pulses when she felt for them. Those eyes, like the forming eyes of embryos, seemed to be staring right at her through the closed lids.

And at the far side of the ward, she saw that five of the beds were empty.

She hurried over to them, her heartbeat racing, and saw the tangled mess of torn tubes and wires that had been ripped out of arms and scalps. A few bloodbags, totally dry, lay scattered on the floor.

"*Madre de Dios!*" she whispered, and was startled by the sound of her own voice. "What's going on here?"

She was answered by the rising noise of the EEGs, their thunderous chattering like a din of crickets, swelling to a hideous crescendo. She whirled around, somehow imagining she'd seen a furtive movement out of the corner of her eye. But the bodies in their white-sheeted beds lay motionless, the electroencephalograph noise now like eager communication between them. It was maddeningly loud, as if the bodies were shouting at one another. She clapped her hands to her ears and hurried for the door.

She had almost reached it when one of the bodies—a middle-aged Chicano man with a pendulous belly and rattlesnake eyes—sat up in his bed, ripping the electrode contacts from his scalp and the IV tube from his arm. He grabbed for her, yanking her backward by her coattail as she screamed in dazed horror. Across the room another body stirred and sat up. Then another, stretching as if waking up from a long *siesta*. A woman with gray-streaked hair plucked her bloodbag from its hanger and bit greedily into it, spraying blood in a thick arc. As the thing pulled Dr. Delgado toward the bed, she saw the pale-lipped mouth open, and in that dark cavern were gleaming fangs wet with hideous fluids. She almost fainted in shock, but she knew that if she did she'd never wake up again. She wrenched free, ripping one arm of her coat loose, and ran for the door. The things came after her, leaping out of their beds, their white hospital shifts flying around them.

Dr. Delgado reached the door and felt a clawlike hand grasp at her shoulder. She screamed and struggled away, feeling her flesh tear. Spinning around, she slammed the door behind her, but one of them crashed through the plate-glass window in a silver shower of fragments. Another followed that one through, and they stalked her as she whirled and ran along the corridor. Before she could

reach the white door, another of them—a young girl with
blood splattered across the front of her shift—came
through the doorway, blocking her path. The girl grinned
and came shambling forward, her eyes as black as evil itself. There was a closed door to Dr. Delgado's left, bearing the word Storeroom. She burst into the dark room and
braced her body against the door as one of the vampires
—*yes,* she thought, *vampires!*—struck it from the other
side, trying to break through. A fist hammered against
it; the door began to bulge inward. The doctor whined in
terror, keeping her shoulder pressed against the wood but
knowing it would only be a moment or so before they got
in. She reached out, feeling for the wall switch; the lights
came on, and the first thing she saw was Mrs. Browning's
open-eyed corpse—*or was it truly a corpse?*—lying at her
feet, its face a shade somewhere between white and yellow. On the wall above Mrs. Browning's head was a
square of metal with a handle on it. Dr. Delgado's heart
leaped. It was the laundry chute, a metal tube leading
down to the basement. She'd opened that chute a hundred
times before, and now she prayed that it was wide enough
for her. It would have to be.

The door was struck by a tremendous blow. She was
knocked backward, her shoulder blazing with pain, and
then the things leaped in. She only had time to scratch at
the eyes of one of them, then she threw open the chute
and tried to squeeze her shoulders in. "Please God!" she
heard herself scream, echoed by the tube's metal walls,
"Please . . . !"

But cold hands gripped her ankles and calves and pre-
vented her from getting down the chute. She kicked and
flailed, still screaming, but as they pulled her back, she
realized with maddening certainty that she could not escape.

The vampires fell upon her, clawing and fighting
among themselves over who would draw the first draught
of blood. When they were finished with her, they cast her
aside like an empty bottle and scurried off for more.
There were many rooms between them and the street,
and many patients in Mercy Hospital who would never
again awaken as humans.

TEN

Daybreak, cold blue shadows running from the sun.

Gayle Clarke tossed uneasily in the bed of her studio apartment on Sunset Strip. Two sleeping pills and a long swig of Smirnoff vodka would keep her knocked out until after noon, but they couldn't entirely erase the hellish memory of a Jack Kidd who looked like leering Death, chasing after her across that apartment courtyard.

In her Laurel Canyon bedroom darkened by heavy drapes, Estelle Gideon sat up suddenly and said, "Mitch?" There was no answer.

Father Ramon Silvera drew cold, rusty water into the sink of his room in East L.A., cupped his hands beneath the spigot, and splashed a few drops in his face. Murky sunlight streamed in through a single window that faced an alley wall of gray bricks. Silvera walked to that window and opened it, inhaling a lungful of air tainted with dust and smog. Down toward the mouth of the alley, he could see the words scrawled in black spray paint in the tough capital letters favored by the street gangs: FOLLOW THE MASTER. Silvera stared in silence, recalling the bloody graffiti on the walls of the Dos Terros apartment building. He remembered the expression on that policeman's face, the abject terror in his eyes, and the chilling urgency of his voice. *"Don't let them out on the streets,"* the man had said. *"Burn them while you can."* Silvera abruptly closed the window and locked it. *What was happening in this city?* The feeling he had now—and had had ever since he'd stepped into that tenement—was one of dread, impending doom, Evil rapidly gaining strength like a cancer running unchecked through a human body. He felt afraid—not of dying because that was a certainty and he had learned long ago to accept the will of God—but of being helpless in a situation where God might call on him to act.

Evil was on the march, an advancing army of the night;

Silvera was more positive of that now than he had ever been in his life. And who could stand in its path?

With these thoughts weighing heavily upon him, he dressed and went out to face the new day.

Wes Richer lifted his head and saw Solange sitting naked before the window, staring out onto Charing Cross Road. He said huskily, "Solange?" She didn't answer. "Solange? What is it?" She didn't move, didn't even acknowledge him. *Christ!* he thought, drawing the sheets around him. *She can really be weird sometimes!* As he closed his eyes again, he recalled the dream he'd had: A little girl standing in the snow beneath his window, beckoning him to come out and play. It had been a good dream, one in which he'd been tempted to step through the window as if it were Alice's Looking Glass, into a childhood world where he could skate and slide and be a kid forever, and not worry about things like tax shelters and house payments and . . . grownup stuff. He returned to sleep, hoping he'd find that little girl again. This time he'd go out.

ELEVEN

"I want you to look at some pictures, Benefield," Sully Reece said, taking four black and white prints from a manila envelope. "Examine these very carefully and tell me if you recognize any of them." He dealt them out one at a time onto the table in front of Walter Benefield, then arranged them in a neat row. Reece could see the corpses reflected in the man's thick glasses. Benefield looked at each one in turn, his expression not varying a fraction. He was still wearing the vapid half-smile he'd had on his face since he was brought into the interrogation room. "Well?" Reece asked, sitting down beside the man. "What about it?"

Benefield said, "I'm sorry, sir. I don't know why I'm looking at these pictures."

"You don't? Well, I'll tell you then. These are on-scene photographs of young women who were strangled to death and then sexually abused, Benefield. Four women in a period of two weeks. If you look very carefully, you can see the bruises on that one's neck. See? Right there at the edge of the shadow. I wonder if your fingers would make marks like that. Do you think they would?"

"Lieutenant," the gray-haired man in the dark slacks and light blue sportscoat said from his chair in the corner; he was a public defender named Murphy, and there was nothing he relished less than having to play watchdog as the cops grilled a suspect.

"I'm talking to Mr. Benefield," Reece barked. "I'm asking him a question. We're not in court now. This is *my* ballpark, right?"

"You don't have to answer any leading questions like that, Mr. Benefield," Murphy said emphatically.

"Okay." Benefield smiled. "I won't."

Across the room Zeitvogel muttered, "Bullshit!" and then he remembered the reel-to-reel tape recorder turning on the table several feet away from Benefield.

"We could do that, you know," Reece said. "We could see if your fingers fit those marks."

"Stop picking on me," Benefield whined, his smile finally breaking a bit. "When can I go home?"

"Picking on you? Man, I haven't even begun! You've been arrested for assaulting a young woman named Vicki Harris, Benefield. She's about the same age as those other women in the pictures. She even looks a lot like that one, doesn't she?"

"I guess she does, yeah."

"Where were you taking her? What were you going to do to her?"

He shrugged. "I was . . . I was going to park right there at the end of Palmero Street. She's a bad girl, you know that. I was going to . . . pay her to . . ."

"Were these bad girls?" Reece motioned to the photographs.

Benefield stared at them for a few seconds and then smiled again. "If you say they were."

"Do you think this is funny? Do you think what you were about to do to Vicki Harris was funny? How often do you cruise Hollywood Boulevard?"

"Once in a while."

"Looking for bad girls?"

Benefield glanced over at the attorney and shifted uneasily in his seat. "Yeah, I guess so."

"Have you ever heard of the Roach, Benefield?"

He shook his head.

"It's been in all the newspapers. Don't you read the papers?"

"No."

"But you know how to read, don't you? And you know how to write?"

"Yeah."

Reece nodded and reached for a smaller manila envelope at the edge of the table. He opened it and took out photostats of the Roach letters, placing them over the pictures in front of Benefield. "Have you ever seen those before?"

"No, sir."

"That surprises me. You remember how you wrote your name for us, once with the right hand and once with the left? Well, handwriting doesn't lie even when you try to distort it. You know what a graphologist is, Benefield? Two of them say you wrote these letters with your left hand."

"They're lying," he said quietly.

"Are they? They're experts on handwriting, Benefield. The judge isn't going to think they're lying. Neither is the jury."

"Leave me alone!" Benefield whined. "I never saw those letters before!"

"We talked to Mr. Pietro at your apartment house," Reece continued. "He told us that sometimes he hears you come in late at night and then you leave again. Where do you go?"

"Just . . . out. Places."

"What places? Hollywood Boulevard? Where else?"

"Just around. I like to drive."

"What about your mother? Do you go see her?"

Benefield's head snapped up. "My . . . mother? You leave her out of this, you black bastard!" He was almost screaming.

Reece smiled and nodded. He leaned back in his chair, watching Benefield's eyes. "We've got the evidence, Benefield. We've got witnesses who've seen you cruising Hollywood. We know everything we need to know. Why don't you tell us about those four young women?"

"No . . . no . . ." He shook his head, his face reddening.

"Four women." Reece's gaze sharpened. "Strangled

and raped, thrown away like garbage. And that thing with the roaches, that was real cute. Whoever did that is a very sick man, wouldn't you agree?"

"Leave me . . . leave me . . . alone . . ."

"Whoever did that was warped and belongs in a hospital. I've seen your record, Benefield. I know about Rathmore . . ."

Benefield's face went scarlet, his eyes bulging. He grabbed for Reece, snarling like an animal, and Zeitvogel was up in an instant reaching for him. Benefield got one hand clamped on Reece's throat. The three men struggled for a few seconds, then Zeitvogel got the man's arms pinned behind him and snapped cuffs on his wrists. "You . . . filth!" Benefield shrieked. "You dirty nigger filth! I'm not going back there! You're not gonna send me back!"

Reece stood up, his knees shaking. His throat felt bruised and contaminated. "I am going out for a cup of coffee," he breathed. "When I get back, you'd better be ready to talk to me, or I'll make it damn hard on you. Understand?" He stared at Benefield for a few seconds, then glanced over at Murphy. The attorney was sitting bolt upright, his eyes slightly glazed. Reece turned and stalked out of the interrogation room.

Palatazin was waiting outside, patiently going through the contents of another file. When he looked up, Reece could see the deep blue circles under his eyes. "How is he?" Palatazin asked.

Reece shrugged and rubbed his throat. "He's pretty worked up. I tried the line about his mother that you suggested and got a real rise out of him. How'd you know?"

"There's something strange going on. According to this," Palatazin waved the folder, "Beverly Teresa Benefield died in a fall down a tenement stairway in 1964. She was carrying a suitcase with her, evidently about to abandon her fifteen-year-old son, Walter. It was the middle of the night, the neighbors heard some shouting, but the coroner ruled the death accidental. Anyway, Benefield made a reference to his mother to Mr. Pietro not long ago. I figured we could probe that to good effect. Also . . ." He took his notepad from his shirt pocket. "He used a cloth soaked in a combination of chemicals from his extermination work on Miss Harris. The lab says breathing it like that in the close confines of a car would be just short of lethal. And an interesting point—they think Benefield had built up a resistance to the fumes, just like real roaches do. But now my question is—why go to the trouble of keeping them alive? If he *is* our man, why did he change his MO?"

"Because he's a nut," Reece said.

"Possibly, but even nuts stick to some kind of pattern. Well, I suppose it's my turn now. Let me borrow your cigarettes and matches."

Reece reached in his shirt pocket and handed him a pack of Kents and a lighter. "Good luck," he said as Palatazin entered the interrogation room.

Benefield was sitting with his chin slumped forward on his chest. Palatazin sat down beside him, pushing away the letters and photographs. He closed the ME's file on the death of Beverly Benefield and laid it on the table. "Would you like a cigarette, Walter?" he asked.

Benefield nodded. Palatazin lit it for him and put it into his mouth. "When can I go home?" Benefield asked.

"Not just yet, Walter. First there are some things we have to talk about."

Benefield's eyes narrowed. "I know you. You're the cop who shot at me."

"I fired a warning shot, yes. I was trying to protect you from the others. They might've killed you."

"Oh."

"Take the cuffs off," Palatazin told Zeitvogel. The detective started to protest, then he shrugged, took the cuff key from his pocket, came over, and unsnapped them. Benefield drew deeply on his cigarette and watched Zeitvogel carefully as the man took his seat again. "Are you comfortable now?" Palatazin asked.

"I'm okay, I guess."

"Good. I know Lieutenant Reece can be a bit too hard sometimes. Pretty overbearing. My name's Andy. Is it all right if I call you Walter?"

"I don't mind. Listen, I told that nigger a thing or two. He won't be bothering me anymore."

"I hope not. I imagine he came in here and talked about the Roach, didn't he?"

"Yeah. I told him I didn't know what he was talkin' about."

Palatazin nodded. "And why should you? The Roach is gone. Nobody cares about him anymore. The vice squad should probably thank him. How do you feel about prostitutes, Walter?"

He was silent for a moment, staring at the burning end of the cigarette. "They stick together," he said softly. "All of them do."

"Uh-huh."

"They laugh at you behind your back. They try to fool you."

"But they didn't fool Roach, did they?"

"Nope."

Palatazin was beginning to sweat under the stark fluorescent overheads; he loosened his tie and unbuttoned his collar. "You work for Aladdin Exterminators, right? Do you like that job?"

Benefield smoked his cigarette and thought about it for a minute. "Yeah," he said finally. "I do."

"I'll bet you're a good worker. What do you use, one of those metal spray cans?"

"A B&G sprayer, yeah. Shoots the Diaz right into the cracks."

"Tell me about Beverly," Palatazin said softly.

"Bev . . . erly?" Benefield's eyes glazed over immediately, and his mouth dropped open. He stared right through Palatazin as the cigarette burned down between his fingers.

"That's right. Your mother. Where is she?"

"She's . . ." His brow furrowed in concentration. "She's not here."

"She's dead, isn't she?"

"Huh?" Shock stitched Benefield's face. "No! You're wrong! She's hiding, they're helping her hide so I can't find her! Sometimes they can even make themselves look like her to fool me. Oh, they know all the tricks!" His voice dripped with bitterness now, and his eyes were hard and cold.

"She's dead," Palatazin persisted. "And after she died, you were sent to Rathmore State Hospital."

"NO!" His eyes flamed, and for an instant Palatazin thought the man was going to leap at him. "Rathmore?" he whispered and rubbed his forehead. "No. Bev went away, and because she left me, they sent me to . . . that place. It's not a *hospital*. Hospitals cure sick people. That place was a . . . a Crazyhouse. When I find Bev, things will be like they were *before*. I won't have to think about the Crazyhouse anymore, and my head won't hurt. But first . . . first I'm going to have to punish her for leaving me . . ." He crushed out the cigarette and dropped it on the floor. "She's somewhere in the city," he said. "The Master told me so."

Palatazin's heart began to pound. "The . . . Master?" he murmured softly. "Who's the Master, Walt?"

"Ohhhhh, no. You'd like me to tell you, wouldn't you? You'd like to know, but you can't."

"Who's the Master? Are you talking about God?"

"God?" Something about that word seemed to trouble Benefield. He blinked and ran his hand across his forehead. "He talks to me at night," he whispered. "He tells me what to do . . ."

"Where is he?"

"Can't tell. *Can't.*"

"He's here in L.A.?"

"He's everywhere," Benefield said. "He sees and hears everything. He knows where I am; he knows where you are. If he wants you, he'll call you in the night, and you'll have to go to him. *You'll have to.*" He looked up into Palatazin's face, his black eyes strangely magnified by the glasses. "He's going to be mad at me for not going to him last night. He's going to be mad at you, too."

"What's his name, Walt?"

"Name? He . . . doesn't have a name. Before he saved me, I was . . . paying them back for fooling me, but the Master said I was . . . I was wasting. He said he could use them and that I would be helping him win the great battle."

"What battle?"

Benefield looked at him and blinked. "For Los Angeles. He wants the city."

A cold terror spread through Palatazin. "Where is the Master, Walt? If I wanted to find him, where would I go? He's hiding in the Hollywood Hills, isn't he?"

"Can't tell," Benefield said.

"Where? A house? A cave . . . ?"

Murphy, across the room, cleared his throat. Palatazin glanced up and saw Zeitvogel staring oddly at him. *Let them think I'm insane!* he thought. *I don't care!* He returned his attention to Benefield. "I want to find the Master," he said urgently. "I have to. Please help me."

"Oh, no. He has to want you first. He has to call you, then you'll know how to find him."

Palatazin forced himself to calm down. His face seemed to be burning up with fever, his guts filled with arctic cold. "Are you the Roach, Walt?"

Benefield froze. Slowly his face contorted into a sneer. "You're just like that nigger, aren't you? Pretending to be my friend, and laughing at me all the time. You want to send me back, don't you? Back to that place! I won't let you do that. *He* won't let you!"

"WHERE IS HE?" Palatazin shouted suddenly and lunged for Benefield's collar. He slammed the man's face down on the table, then jerked his head up again. The man snarled and grabbed for Palatazin's throat, blood stringing from his nostrils. "WHERE IS HE!" Palatazin shrieked again, all control gone now, nothing but animal rage and fear left. Benefield grinned, and then Murphy and Zeitvogel were pulling him away. "No," Zeitvogel ordered, his gaze fixed on Palatazin. "Don't do that, captain."

"LET ME ALONE!" Palatazin fought free of them and stood up, breathing harshly. "Just leave me alone!" He started for Benefield again, but Zeitvogel blocked his way. "You don't understand," Palatazin said. "I've got to make him tell! I've got to!"

Zeitvogel shook his head. Benefield grinned and wiped his bloody nose.

"Get him out of here before I throw up," Palatazin demanded abruptly and brushed past Zeitvogel out of the interrogation room.

In his office he lit his pipe and tried to calm down. He couldn't get his thoughts organized. Of course Benefield was the Roach, and of course he knew where the Master was hiding. But how could he make him talk, how could he break the hold that evil force had on him? And then an even more terrible thought gripped him—how many were there now in this city who had heard the Master's voice? How many now walked at night, hungering for blood? A thousand? Five thousand? Ten thousand? It would happen insidiously, slowly, as it had happened in Krajeck so very long ago, until at the end the city would be at the mercy of the Master and his brood. He *had* to tell someone now, anyone who would listen. The newspapers perhaps? Chief Garnette? Maybe the National

Guard could be called out, and the things found, burned or staked before they grew stronger. Perhaps the city could be evacuated and firebombs dropped from helicopters. . . .

But no. They wouldn't believe. He felt a chill of dark madness cover him. Who would believe? *Who?* He remembered the doctor in that building on Dos Terros Street, Dr. Delgado. The bodies had been taken to Mercy Hospital. Perhaps she could be made to believe. Yes! He reached for the telephone, but it rang before he could pick up the receiver.

"Captain Palatazin," he said.

"Andy? It's Garnette. Would you come down and see me right away?"

"Yes, sir, I will. But first I have to make a . . ."

"Andy," the voice was sterner, cast a tone lower, "I'd like to see you right now." The phone clicked and went dead. Palatazin put it back on its cradle and then got up, moving as sluggishly as a zombie. He felt weary, drained, about to split apart at the seams. He walked along the hallway to the Chief of Detectives' office. When he rapped on the door, he heard Garnette say, "Come in, Andy."

He stepped into the office. "How are you feeling, Andy?" Garnette asked, motioning to the chair in front of his desk. "I understand you were busy last night."

"Yes, sir," he said and smiled wanly. "Quite a few of us were."

"I talked to Lieutenant Reece and Detective Farris. I'd say you did one hell of a good job. Now tell me about this Benefield character."

"Well, I believe he's the Roach, though we haven't got all the evidence we need to make an arrest stick, and I don't think we're going to be getting a confession from the man."

"But you're holding him on an assault charge?"

"Assault, reckless driving, resisting arrest—whatever we could come up with."

Garnette nodded. "Okay. But you think it's too early to tell the papers?"

"I think so."

"In your best estimation, that man you're holding *did* kill those four girls and wrote the letters signed by Roach?"

"Yes, sir. Possibly more than four girls. He changed his MO in the past two weeks and began using a chemical-soaked cloth to knock his victims out first. We're still questioning him about his procedure."

"I see." Garnette was silent for a moment, his hands folded on the desk. When he looked back at Palatazin, his expression was tough and direct. "You've worked long and hard to crack this thing, Andy. No one in the department appreciates that as much as I do."

"Thank you, but I'm afraid we have a long way to go yet before we can consider it closed."

"No matter. You're a good cop, Andy. You've been a good cop and a credit to this department ever since you joined us." He smiled slightly, his eyes warming up with memories. "You remember those old days? When you were a detective first-grade and I was trying to make sergeant? We were scruffy bastards then, weren't we? Out on the streets throwing our weight around, flashing our shields whenever we could, making a lot of noise about every goddamned thing. We had chips on our shoulders as big as redwood logs, didn't we? Those were the days. You remember that time we cornered the sniper on the fourth floor of the Alexandria Hotel? About fifty cops out in the hall shaking in their shoes, everybody afraid to breathe because the bastard had an elephant gun in there? And you just walked right up to the door and knocked on it! I almost dropped my teeth when that guy opened it and came out with his hands over his head! Shit! You remember that?"

"I remember," Palatazin said quietly.

"That took guts. And how about the time we were looking for the Chinatown Strangler? We were on rooftop stakeout with binoculars and a girl in one of the windows started doing a striptease? That crazy broad had the biggest set of oompahs I've ever seen. She could've made it in the movies. Things were better then, weren't they? We didn't have computers or sociologists or psychics trying to do our jobs for us. We got out in the streets and worked our asses off, and we didn't have to worry about a mountain of files and paperwork. Well, that's progress for you, right? Seems like you and I have gotten a little grayer and slower over the years. The pressure is so much tougher now. You have to contend with so many conflicting factors. It's not cut-and-dried anymore.

The psychiatrists and the ACLU people see to that.
Sometimes I just want to chuck this whole mess and take
the wife down to Mexico City or someplace like that.
Haven't you ever felt that way?"

"Of course I have," Palatazin said. "Everyone does."

"Uh-huh." Garnette nodded, placing his fingertips together and staring at the other man for a few silent seconds. "Okay, fine. I'm going to give you a chance to
take a little vacation, Andy. Two weeks with pay. How
about that?"

"A . . . vacation? Well, that's very nice, but I've got
to finish this thing first."

"No, you don't," Garnette said sternly.

"What?"

Garnette cleared his throat. "Lieutenant Reece is going to take over for you for the next two weeks, Andy. I
want you to take off."

"I . . . I'm afraid I don't understand."

"You're tired, Andy. You're overworked and worn
out. You deserve some time off, but I know you—if it
were up to you, Hell would freeze over before you left
your desk. So take advantage of this. You and Jo go
somewhere nice for two weeks . . ."

"What is this?" Palatazin demanded, his cheeks reddening. He knew exactly what it was, but he wanted to
hear Garnette say it. "What are you trying to tell me?"

"I . . . the department's giving you some time off . . ."

"Damn it!" Palatazin blurted out, getting to his feet.
A pulse was pounding at his temple, and he quavered
with confusion and anger. "The department's canning
me, is that right?"

"No, for Christ's sake! Two weeks, Andy! That's not
forever!"

"What is it? Who have you been talking to? Who's
been saying I'm crazy this time?" It dawned on him then
—it had probably been that outburst at the Dos Terros
tenement. Who had told Garnette? Sergeant Teal? One
of the officers who'd been working the scene? Surely it
hadn't been Sully Reece! "Do *you* think I'm crazy, Paul?"

"I think . . . you deserve a rest. It's long overdue.
You just go home and let your men finish this up."

"NO!" Palatazin shouted. "I WON'T DO IT! There
are some things I have to find out from that suspect.

Some very important things! I can't . . . I can't leave it now!"

"You're going to have to." Garnette forced himself to look away. He stared down at his hands. "You'll report back to work two weeks from today."

"I won't . . ."

"Is that understood?" Garnette said very quietly, and lifted his gaze.

Palatazin started to protest again, but he knew it was no use. He placed his palms on the desk and leaned forward, his eyes glimmering. "I'm not crazy," he whispered hoarsely. "I'm *not!* I don't care what you've heard. There's a good reason for everything I've done or said, and by God if you don't start listening to me, there's . . . there's going to be great evil in this city. There's going to be evil beyond your wildest nightmares!"

"Andy," Garnette stated firmly, "go home."

Palatazin straightened up, wiping his forehead with a trembling hand. "Go home?" he whispered softly. "Home? I can't . . . I . . . there's so much to be done." His eyes were wild and bloodshot, and he knew that he must truly look insane. "Shall I . . . leave my badge and gun with you?" he asked after another moment.

"I don't think that's necessary. This is a vacation, not a suspension. Now take it easy, Andy. And for God's sake don't worry about the Roach or anything else."

Palatazin nodded and moved dazedly toward the door. "Yes," he said. "All right." He heard himself speaking as if he were inside a tunnel. He felt the cold doorknob touch his hand, and he twisted it.

"Send me a postcard from Vegas," Garnette said as Palatazin stepped through the door. The captain's shoulders were slumped forward and he carried himself as if he'd just taken a hard blow to the stomach. Garnette started to say, "I'm sorry," but then the door closed. *God!* Garnette thought. *I hope two weeks makes a difference! If not . . . well, let that take care of itself. But anybody who wanted to burn bodies found in an East L.A. tenement—who* demanded *that they be cremated—was obviously in need of a long rest.*

Poor guy, Garnette mused and then forced himself to concentrate on other matters.

TWELVE

It was just after two o'clock when Jo heard the front door open and close. She came down the stairs hurriedly and found Andy in the kitchen, holding a paper bag. "What are you doing home so early?" she asked. "You scared me to death!"

He glanced at her quickly, then looked away. "I won't be going back to work for a while," he said quietly.

"What do you mean? What happened, Andy? Tell me!"

He began to take items out of the bag. There was a smaller bag inside with H. Shaffer and Son, Fine Jewelry printed on it. "I've been given a two-week vacation," he said and smiled grimly. She watched him open the bag and take out two identical white boxes. "Two weeks," he whispered. "Los Angeles might not even exist in two weeks." He gave her one of the boxes. "Put this around your neck. I want you to wear this all the time; don't take it off—not in the shower, not when you sleep."

She opened it with a trembling hand. It was a small gold-plated crucifix on a long chain. "It's beautiful," she said, "but . . ."

"Put in on right now," he said. He opened his box, took out the other crucifix and clasped it around his neck. "I want you to get used to wearing it," he told her, "so you won't forget it. I don't know how powerful its influence will be because it hasn't been blessed by a priest or sanctified with holy water, but it's better than nothing. Go on, put it on now." He went behind her to help her clasp it.

She watched him, dumbfounded, as he stepped back to the counter and reached into the bag again. *Oh, my God,* she thought suddenly as she looked into his face. He looked just like his mother did just before she went into the rest home. His eyes held that same fanatical, crazed gleam; his jaw was set with an unyielding determination. "Andy," she whispered as he took several cloves of garlic from the bag and laid them on the counter.

"We'll slice these and smear all the windowsills with

them," he said. "Then we'll chop some into pieces and
spread them on the front lawn. Mama said it would help
keep the *vampir* away because their sense of smell is
so strong and the odor reminds them of death." He turned
toward her and saw her face as pale as chalk. "Oh, I see.
You think I'm crazy, too, like everyone else, don't you?"

"I think . . . Andy, you're not in Hungary now! This is
a different place, a different time. . . ."

"There's no difference!" he objected sharply. "The
vampir doesn't care what place he attacks, so long as
there's an abundance of food! And time to his kind
means nothing! I tell you the *vampir* is here in this city!
And someone has got to find the Master, the king *vampir,* before it's too late!"

"You don't mean . . . Andy, what's come over you?"

"The truth," he said quietly. "Jo, I want you to leave.
I want you to take the car and drive as far away from here
as you can. Go east across the mountains. Will you do
that—for me?"

She took a step toward him and clutched his arm.
"We'll both go," she said. "We'll make a real vacation
out of these two weeks! We'll pack and leave in the morning, all right? We can drive down to San Diego or . . ."

"No. It has to be far from this city because when they
start spreading out, there will be no stopping them. I
want the mountains between you and L.A., and I want
you to leave now."

"I can't go without you," she told him, tears of despair
welling in her eyes. "I won't, damn it! No matter what
you say!"

He took her shoulders and looked deeply into her eyes.
"When they come, Jo—and they *will* come, it's only a
matter of time—I won't be able to save you. I probably
won't be able to save myself. But I have to stay here,
I have to try to . . . do something! Running doesn't do
any good. They just advance, and sooner or later all of
humanity will be pushed together in a tiny pocket, and
the *vampir* will come and then . . . that will be the
end, don't you see? The *vampir* will eventually destroy
themselves, but only after all of humanity is bled dry.
Someone has got to at least *try* to stop them!"

"You? Of all the people in the world, why you?"

"Because," he said quietly, fixing her with his gaze,

"I'm here. And I know their ways. Who else is there?"

"Let the police do it!"

"The police? Ah, yes. I know firsthand how efficient the police can be. No, it has to be me. Alone, if that's the will of God. Now go upstairs and pack your things." He turned back to the paper bag.

Jo did not move. "I won't leave," she protested. "You can't make me."

"You're a fool," he said.

"I love you."

Palatazin looked at her and grunted. "Twice a fool then. Haven't you understood a word I've said?"

"I understand my place is with you. I'm not leaving."

He stared at her for a silent moment, and she could feel the heat of his gaze. She returned it stubbornly. "All right," he said finally, "if you're going to stay until morning, you can help me prepare for them. Cut those garlic cloves into pieces." As she moved to get a knife, he reached into the bag and brought out a can of black spray paint. She didn't want to ask him what he was going to do with it.

He walked to the front of the house, shaking the spray paint, and opened the door. On the wood he sprayed a large, black crucifix and beneath it the Hungarian word OVAJODIK.

Beware.

THIRTEEN

The last bell had rung at Fairfax High School. The classrooms and halls were emptying rapidly. Toyotas and Triumphs squealed out of the parking lot onto Fairfax Avenue and left trails of rubber aimed toward the nearest McDonalds.

Tommy Chandler, one of the few eleven-year-old freshmen who had ever walked the not-so-hallowed halls of Fairfax High, carefully dialed the combination of his Yale lock, pulled it open, then opened his locker. Inside there were the usual American history, algebra, and Latin textbooks, a pack of Bic pens, and a few Nifty notebooks. Taped to the inside of the locker was a picture of Orlon Kronsteen in his Jack the Ripper makeup from *London Screams*, clipped reverentially from an old *Famous Monsters of Filmland* magazine. There was a picture of Raquel Welch in a bikini, too, but that took a lower place of honor. Tommy took out his history and algebra books and the corresponding notebooks. Mr. Kitchens would probably throw a sneak history quiz at the class first thing in the morning, and Tommy wanted to do some advance reading in algebra because what they were covering now was just plain *booooring*. Across the locker room Jim Baines and Mark Sutro were discussing the physical attributes of Melinda Kennimer, head majorette for the Fairfax High Marching Band and an untouchable but deliciously stacked senior.

"I saw her in the hall today, fifth period," Mark was saying as he gathered up a biology text and a geometry notebook. "God, I almost creamed my jeans! She smiled at me. Actually *smiled* for God's sake! She's got a smile like Farrah Fawcett."

"Better than Farrah Fawcett," Jim said. "More like Bo Derek. God, what a bod! I hear she's going with Stan Perry, the lucky asshole! Last week at the pep rally when she flashed those thighs and the drum corps was putting down a jungle beat, I thought I was going to shoot to the moon. It's unnatural for a girl to look so good. I'll bet she's got a mean streak in her."

"Who cares? I like 'em mean. Have you got a date for Homecoming?"

"Not yet. I'm going to ask Ronni McKay."

"Ha!" Mark slammed his locker door and spun the lock. "Too late! Johnny Jackson already asked her, and she said yes."

"What? Keerist! I had my lines all ready for her! Damn! Who are you asking, Selma Verone?"

Mark made a sickened face. "Are you kidding? Old Pizza Cheeks Verone? I'd rather go stag." He nudged Jim in the ribs with an elbow and motioned toward Tommy. "Bet Selma would go with Chandler if he'd ask her."

Here it comes, Tommy thought. *Hurry and get it over with.*

"Hey, Chandler!" Mark called to him across the aisle. "Why don't you ask Selma Verone to go to Homecoming with you? You like monsters so much, she'd be perfect for you!"

"I doubt it," Tommy mumbled. He heard the locker room door open and close, but he was concentrating on what the next jibe would probably be, so he didn't notice who came in. Tommy closed his locker, spun the dial, and turned right into a slab of beef wearing an Aerosmith T-shirt. A hand shot out, catching Tommy on the collarbone, and shoved him back against the lockers. He hit his head on metal, and his ears rang like a fire drill alarm. His eyeglasses dangled from one ear, but he didn't need to see to know who it was. He heard the raucous laughter like the snorting of pigs. Jim Baines and Mark Sutro were as quiet as the dead.

"You're in my way, Fuckface!" the slab of beef growled.

Tommy adjusted his glasses. There were three boys standing before him, Jules "Bull" Thatcher with his usual entourage of Buddy Carnes and Ross Weir. Thatcher's face was broad and ugly, as cratered and hostile as the surface of the moon. He had shoulder-length brown hair, a scar through one thick eyebrow, and black ferret eyes that radiated hatred. He towered over Tommy. Bull had been a pretty fair running back on the freshman football team until Coach Maxwell had caught him selling 'ludes in the parking lot about two weeks before. He should've been a junior, but the sixth and eighth grades had been beyond his capacity. Now he mostly cheated to squeak by. His eyes gleamed with bloodlust as he stared at Tommy. His face was slashed by a cruel, thin-lipped mouth, and Tommy could well believe the stories he'd heard about Bull's love of pure violence. It was his misfortune to have been assigned the locker right next to Bull.

"I said you're in my way . . . fuckface!" Bull said grimly, his hands on his hips.

"Uh . . . sorry," Tommy said, rubbing his collarbone. "I was just leaving."

"He was 'just leavin',' " Ross Weir mimicked Tommy's high, childish voice. "He sounds like a fairy. You a fairy, punk?"

"Don't you guys know?" Buddy Carnes said. "This here's the little brain. He's in my algebra class, gets *A*s on every goddamn test and fucks up the curve for everybody else. He's the reason I'm flunkin' my ass off!"

"Oh yeah?" Bull said quietly. "A brain, huh?"

"Looks like a fairy to me," Weir said and cackled.

Baines and Sutro tried to slip past the Unholy Three, but suddenly Bull's head turned, and Tommy saw his eyes gleam like Gort the robot's power blast from *The Day the Earth Stood Still*. "Where do you think you're goin'?" Bull said ominously.

"Nowhere . . ." Mark stammered. "We're just . . . nowhere . . ."

"Better not be!" Bull said and turned his attention back to Tommy.

Ah, yes, Tommy thought. *He needs an audience for his performance.* Over Bull's massive shoulders his cohort's faces looked like the half-human animals from *The Island of Lost Souls.* Tommy could feel his heart thumping against his thin rib cage. The "flight or fight" instinct was pumping adrenaline through his body—his head said fight, but his feet said flight.

Bull stepped closer and shoved Tommy against the lockers again. "You think you're smart, don't you? Don't you?"

"Not particularly, no."

"You callin' Bull a liar?" Ross Weir snarled.

Uh-oh, Tommy thought. Caught by the deadly triangle! His face flushed with a mixture of anger and fear. Bull reached out and plucked off Tommy's glasses. "Hey, don't!" Tommy said. "Those are expensive!"

"Oh yeah? You want 'em back? Come take 'em!"

"You're about three guys bigger than me."

"He's a chickenshit fairy, too," Weir said.

Bull narrowed his eyes into fierce slits. "I've seen you in here before, kid. You got the locker next to mine, don't you? I'm going to give you some advice. I find you in here tomorrow afternoon, I'm going to smear your little fairy ass up and down Fairfax Avenue, you got that?"

"Just give me back my . . ." Tommy began, but in the next instant a massive hand had grabbed his collar and was choking him.

"Maybe you didn't hear me," Bull said evenly. "I don't want to see you in here again. Understand?" He shook Tommy like a dog shakes a bone. "UnderSTAND?"

"Yeah," Tommy said, tears beginning to swim in his eyes. He felt more rage than fear, but he knew if he swung a blow, Bull would probably snap his arms out of their sockets. "Yeah, I understand."

Bull laughed, blowing fetid breath in Tommy's face. He flung Tommy back and sneered at Baines and Sutro. "You want some of it, too?" he growled. Their heads shook in unison.

"My glasses," Tommy said. "Give 'em back."

"Huh?" Bull glowered at him and then smiled. "Sure, kid." He held them out and dropped them to the floor as Tommy reached for them. "Sorry," Bull said. "I'll get 'em." He placed his boot on a lens and ground down on it. The *crack* sounded as loud as a gunshot. Buddy Carnes howled with laughter. "There you go, kid," Bull said, bending to pick up the glasses and then handing them to Tommy. "Put 'em on and let's see how they look."

Tommy was looking through one clear lens and one crisscrossed with cracks. The damaged side kept slipping off his ear, and he had to hold it in place.

"Looks real good," Bull said. His face contorted viciously. "Now get out of here, fuckface! And you don't come back, you got it?"

Tommy slipped past Bull and started for the door. He was almost there, thinking he was really going to make it, when Ross Weir stuck a leg in his path and pushed him. He went down in a tangle of arms and legs, his books falling everywhere. Laughter exploded as he gathered up his books again and hurried out of the locker room, leaving Jim Baines and Mark Sutro to their own unfortunate fates. Tommy walked across the empty parking lot and turned south on Fairfax, heading toward Hancock Park. His knees were trembling, and within him there was a great urge to turn around and shout, "BULL THATCHER SUCKS!" as loud as he could. But what good would that do? He'd only end up with a busted head and a mouthful of loose teeth. Soon he'd left Fairfax High behind and was out of shouting range. He wished he had muscles like Hercules; he wished he could deliver a flying kick like Bruce Lee. Then the Bull Thatchers of the world—and there were so *many* of them—would think twice before they bothered him. *Ah! The perfect fate for Bull Thatcher*. He imagined the boy running through the fog-shrouded streets of old London, fear glistening in his eyes beneath the whale oil lamps as he heard the approaching footsteps. Orlon Kronsteen's Ripper was afoot in the darkness, his three-foot sickle seeking new victims to behead. The Ripper's eyes would look like black holes behind a mask of gray cloth, and as those eyes made out the running figure of Bull Thatcher, the thin mouth would twitch into a cunning smile. *There's no where to run, boy!* The Ripper would call out. *There's nowhere to hide! Come, let Mary Death take a taste of your blood!*

Of course, he'd catch Bull Thatcher, and then . . . heh, heh, heh!

Tommy caught the smell of oranges and cloves in the breeze. It was the deceptively fruity smell which had lured thousands of prehistoric saber-toothed tigers, giant ground sloths, and mastodons into the clinging trap of the LaBrea Tarpits, over in the green, tree-studded expanse of Hancock Park. Tommy liked to roam around over there on Saturdays when his dad was working at the Achilles Electronics plant in Pasadena and his mom was out making telephone calls for whatever volunteer group she'd hooked up with this month. Last month it had been the Society to Aid Cambodian Orphans. Now it was the Save the African Elephant bunch. While his mother crusaded, Tommy would sit beneath a tree in the park and watch the roller skaters or read H.P. Lovecraft. He was accustomed to being alone.

He turned onto Lindenhurst Avenue, across from the park, and walked along a street lined with Spanish stucco houses that seemed to stretch on out of sight, hundreds of houses that looked similar except for the different colors of paint and different cars in the driveways. But, Tommy had noticed, there was even a pattern to the cars. Most of them were imports or economy cars, including his dad's Pacer and his mother's Toyota Celica. There were a few Porsches and Mercedes Benzes sitting around, too, but most of these were inconspicuously driven and usually covered over with protective canvas. It was a firmly middle-class neighborhood, complete with Boy Scout troop meetings and backyard barbecues on weekend evenings. It was quite similar to the neighborhood Tommy and his parents had lived in when his dad was working at the Achilles plant in Scottsdale, Arizona; and about the same as the one in San Antonio, Texas; and almost identical to the old neighborhood in Denver, Colorado. Actually they'd lived in a small town just outside Denver, and that place had been Tommy's favorite—streets lined with elm trees and white picket fences, chimney smoke stirring in a crisp, northerly breeze, people wearing sweaters and raking leaves into orderly piles. That had been a really neat place. California was different. Everybody was wacky, everybody had ulterior motives. It wasn't the moving that bothered Tommy so much because he knew his father was being promoted gradually through the Achilles corporation. It was changing schools so much and leaving behind whatever few friends he'd managed to make. In his experience real friends were few and far between. But there was one definite advantage to L.A., though. So many monster flicks were shown on the tube! Almost every weekend on Creature Features or Horror Hotel, he got to see an Orlon Kronsteen, Vincent Price, or—very rarely—a Todd Slaughter flick. At the end of the summer, he'd helped his dad attach a gizmo to the TV antenna that pulled in a couple of Mexican stations, and down there they really made creepy horror movies. So all in all, it wasn't too bad.

His heart suddenly gave a kick. A silver Vega was parked in the driveway of the house across the street from his. *Her* silver Vega. *Her* name was Sandy Vernon, the daughter of Pete and Dianne Vernon, and she was a sophomore at UCLA. Tommy had fallen in love with her while watching her mow the lawn on a Sunday afternoon, clad in tight, denim cutoffs and a dark blue halter. She was tanned and blond and . . . *stacked!* She made Melinda Kennimer, Farrah Fawcett, Bo Derek and Raquel Welch look like Selma Verone. He'd melted into a little puddle, like the goo that comes out of a chocolate-covered cherry, when he'd seen the tight muscles of her thighs and buttocks as she shoved a sputtering, red Toro mower back and forth across the lawn. He would have offered to help, but then he would've been deprived of watching that heavenly body. So he'd sat on the front steps, leafing through an *Eerie* magazine and not making a bit of sense out of the stories.

And when she'd finished, she'd cut the mower and then turned toward him, that mane of blond hair flowing like hair does in shampoo commercials. Even from across the street Tommy had seen that her eyes were a bluish violet. "Hi there," she'd said and smiled.

"That's a pretty neat lawnmower you've got there," was the only thing he could manage to say.

She'd smiled wider as if she could read the thoughts—
STUPID! ASSHOLE! STUPID! ASSHOLE!—that were
battering against the walls of Tommy's brain. "Thanks.
It's my dad's. What they need to invent is one that does
all the work by itself."

"Uh . . . yeah. I think somebody's come up with a robot
mower. It runs along a wire you put down in the grass.
My name's Tommy Chandler."

"I'm Sandy Vernon. Your folks just moved in?"

"Since July."

"That's nice. What grade are you in?"

"Uh . . . I'll be a freshman at Fairfax High. In September. You sure did a good job on that lawn." *STUPID!
ASSHOLE! STUPID!*

"Thanks. I'll be seeing you, Tommy." And she'd
pushed the mower away, her cute little behind moving as
if on ball bearings.

Tommy's body, in the bewildering throes of change, was
never quite the same after that Sunday afternoon meeting.
Once he woke up in the middle of the night, looked down
at his pajama bottoms, and almost passed out thinking he
had some hideous kind of VD. But that was impossible
since he'd never had the opportunity to dabble in the mysteries of the opposite sex, and he decided that it was one
more of nature's tricks to make sure he was ready
for manhood.

Now as he stood in front of his house and looked across
Lindenhurst at the silver Vega that meant *she* was home,
he saw a collie sitting on the steps in front of the Vernon's
door. *Whose dog is that?* he wondered. *Maybe the Vernons bought it in the last couple of days?* It was a large,
beautiful dog, and right now it seemed to be sleeping. Tommy strolled out into the street and said, "Hi, boy!
Hi there, fella!"

The dog didn't move.

What's wrong with it? he wondered. *Is it sick?* He
crossed the street and stood on the sidewalk. "Hi, fella!"
He clapped one hand against his leg, but the collie didn't
react. When Tommy placed one foot on the Vernons'
lawn, the dog's head came up, the eyes staring blankly at
him. "Hi, boy!" Tommy said. "Whose dog are you, huh?
Are you Sandy's dog?" *Dogs have all the luck!* he thought.
He took another step closer, and the collie bared its teeth,
growling very softly.

Tommy froze. The collie slowly rose to its feet but didn't move from in front of the door. A drop of saliva fell from its lower lip and spattered onto the walkway. Tommy backed away, very carefully, and the collie immediately curled up again. On the other side of the street, Tommy stopped and stared across, knowing that Bull Thatcher was going to growl like that when he stepped into that locker room again tomorrow afternoon. It was either that or carry all his books around all day. He wondered if a kid could buy a can of Mace. *Funny the way that dog acted,* he thought. *I always heard that collies were friendly. Well, after all, I guess I was invading his territory or something.*

And then he remembered that "The Invaders" was on television in fifteen minutes, so he dug the key out of his pocket and hurried inside so he wouldn't miss the first part where the saucer comes down.

FOURTEEN

Darkness. Twenty minutes before eight o'clock.

Paige LaSanda cursed as her pale blue Mercedes crashed over yet another pot-hole on serpentine Blackwood Road. *God!* she thought. *Why did I ever tell that Falco character I'd come up this mountain in practically the middle of the night? Why didn't I make him send a car to pick me up and take me back home? If that Prince whatever-his-name-is can afford to rent that castle, then by God he could afford to send a limo to pick me up!* She could hear the wind whining through the dead trees out there, so she turned on her radio and searched for music. She came across the tail end of a newscast from KMET. ". . . registered 3.4 on the open-ended Richter scale, but San Diego residents did suffer some broken windows in a series of aftershocks . . ." *Another earthquake,* she thought. *Christ! If it's not forest fires or mudslides, it's earthquakes!* She turned the dial and found a song she liked, the new Rory Black single. ". . . I'm not the kind of guy who gets a second chance with pretty girls like you;/I'm not the kind of guy who gets a second glance from pretty girls like you. . . ."

She was wondering what this Prince what's-his-name

would look like when she realized that there was something out there in the dark, running alongside her car.

A couple of dogs, caught in the backwash of the headlights, were running on either side like royal escorts.

She shivered, wondering what dogs were doing way up here, and accelerated to leave them behind. In another few minutes she turned a corner, and there was the massive hulk of the Kronsteen castle. There were candles in some of the windows, shining with different colors. She had to admit that if the place was not quite attractive, then at least it was mysteriously appealing.

She drove through the open gate, parked her car in the driveway, and walked up the stone stairs to the front door. She was wearing a sleek, black dress and a silver necklace with diamond stars clustered around a gleaming half-moon, and she knew she looked stunning. She was going to knock the prince's socks—or whatever they called them in Hungary—off tonight. She knocked on the front door and waited.

It opened almost immediately, and standing there was a young Chicano girl in a long, white gown.

"Hi," Paige said. "I'm Miss LaSanda, and Prince Vulkan expects me."

The girl nodded and motioned for her to enter.

She stepped across the threshold. The door was closed behind her. She followed the servant girl—*her makeup is atrocious,* Paige thought—under a chandelier studded with gleaming candles. Paige glanced up at it, realizing that it was where the cops had found Orlon Kronsteen's headless body. It was as cold as a refrigerator inside the place, and above her head Paige could hear the whine and moan of conflicting winds across the high ceilings. They moved down a long hallway lit by more candles, then up a curved, stone stairway that had no banister. On the second floor the servant girl motioned Paige through a rough-hewn door into a huge room with two roaring fireplaces on either side of a highly polished, gleaming black dining table. More candles guttered from a chandelier overhead and the two silver candelabra set equidistantly on the table. There was only one place setting, at the head of the table, with a silver dish and gleaming silverware. A crystal decanter half-filled with red wine and a single goblet were set beside the dish, both catching golden light from the fireplaces.

"Where's Prince Vulkan?" Paige asked the servant girl as she sat down.

The girl poured a glass of wine for Paige but didn't answer. Then, without a word, she moved like a wraith to the door and vanished.

What's this guy going to do? Paige wondered. *Make a grand entrance or something?* She sipped the wine and asked herself what the hell she was doing there; then she looked up, startled. She thought she'd seen a face way down at the other side of the room, floating in the shadows that had gathered at the limits of the firelight. Now it was gone, but she was left with the distinct impression of white flesh, white hair, and . . . red eyes. Now there was nothing there at all. She looked away quickly and thought she heard footsteps echoing off stone in the distance, not walking but . . . scurrying. Voices seemed to be whispering all around her, and she was almost certain she heard a cold chuckle.

Maybe, she thought, *just maybe I ought to call this whole thing off. Maybe I ought to get my little ass out of here right now because there's something definitely screwy about this whole thing.*

She drank down another swallow of the wine and started to rise from her chair.

And that was when the hand came down very gently on her shoulder.

Paige gasped and turned her head. She was staring into a pair of green cat eyes set in a pallid, high-cheekboned face.

"Miss LaSanda," he said and slightly bowed his head. "I'm Prince Vulkan."

"Prince . . . Vulkan?" she said in a whisper.

"That's right. I'm sorry you had to wait. There were some things I had to take care of before I could come." He walked around from behind her and stood beside the table, staring down at her with a piercing, intense gaze.

"You? You're the prince?" She almost laughed, but the shock was too great. All her Omar Sharif fantasies were shredded like so much rotten tapestry. She looked at him wide-eyed, thinking that his flesh might well have been sculpted from white marble. "You're . . . you're just a boy!" she finally managed to say.

He smiled slightly, his eyes sparkling with firelight. "Am I?"

"I was expecting someone older . . . in his forties at least!"

"Were you?" He nodded. "Forty years old? I'm sorry I disappoint you."

Paige saw the yellow streaks in his hair and stared at them. *What sort of kid was this anyway?* His face looked like a seventeen-year-old's, but there was something in his voice, his manner, his eyes that seemed much, much older. "Is Mr. Falco your guardian?" she asked.

"Falco is . . . *was* . . . in my employ. I saw fit to terminate his services last night."

"Oh. But what about your parents? Surely you didn't come all the way from Hungary without *somebody!*"

"I'm not a child, Miss LaSanda," he said, his lower lip curling. "I'm not! I can take care of myself!"

"Well, sure. I just thought, you know . . ."

Vulkan leaned over the table toward her, and she found herself inwardly cringing. "You're disappointed, aren't you? You wanted me to be older. You wanted me to be handsome and wealthy, didn't you?"

"No, not at all. I'm just . . . surprised." She tore her gaze away from his with an effort that made her neck muscles thrum like bad guitar chords. She was afraid to look at him again, but when she looked into his eyes, she felt there was a cauldron bubbling at the center of her brain. "Listen, Your Royalty or Your Highness or whatever, I think this has all been a big mistake. I really shouldn't be here. It's late, and I have some work to do at home, so . . ." She started to rise.

"You'll stay where you are," he whispered.

Instantly her back was rigid against the chair, her hands gripped tightly around the arms of her chair. She felt as if a seat belt had suddenly been drawn tight around her stomach. She gasped for breath.

"There," he said. "I don't want to hear anything else about your leaving. I've got too much on my mind tonight to worry about you, Miss LaSanda, so please sit quite still. I've been planning to entertain you for some time, and I don't want you spoiling the evening. Drink your wine."

She shook her head and gasped, "No . . ."

"Drink it," he said, his eyes boring through her skull.

Her hand went out, obediently grasped the crystal goblet, and tilted it to her lips, then returned the glass to the table. Her eyes were shining with fear, and a pulse ticked at her right temple. The prince picked up the glass, swirled the wine dregs around for a silent moment, then sniffed it and slid it back to her. He smiled. "You're a very attractive woman, Miss LaSanda. Very attractive indeed. I'm sure you have many suitors. Don't you?" When she didn't reply, he leaned forward and touched her throbbing pulse with a cold finger. Then he brought the finger back and passed it under his nose a couple of times. "Very attractive," he whispered.

"Please," she said, her jaw muscles aching with the effort, "let me go home. I don't . . . I don't care who you are. Just . . . let me . . . go . . ."

"That would spoil everything. You want to stay here with me. Don't you?" His eyes widened slightly.

Her head nodded involuntarily, like a marionette's.

"Good." He regarded her for a moment in silence, then walked across the room to one of the fireplaces where he made a gesture of warming his hands. "I'm cold," he said softly. "I've been cold now for several nights, and I can't stand it any longer. But you wouldn't understand that, would you? When you're cold, you simply turn up the heat. You don't know pain, Miss LaSanda, that pain that roars through the body like a blizzard." He looked over his shoulder at her. "I'm glad you're here tonight. I needed somebody to be with me, to talk to. Sometimes I get lonely for people . . ."

The woman's mouth worked, but no sound came out. Two tears trickled down her cheeks, leaving twin mascara trails.

Vulkan stared into the fire. "It was only a matter of time before you found out. My checks are worthless. My bank account in Switzerland has been closed for a long time. I didn't know how much you knew about me. So it was much simpler, you see, to bring you here. To me."

"I don't . . . I don't know . . . anything . . . about you . . ." she whispered.

"Ah, but there are things you might have found out." He turned back to her, rubbing his palms together. "You might have called the police. You might have hurt me before it had even started."

"Started? What . . . ?"

"*Everything!*" he exclaimed, making a sweeping gesture with his arms. "The *future!*"

Paige heard the door open. Vulkan glanced up. "Here's

your meal," he said. "It's a true Hungarian beef *gyulash*. I had it made just for you." A girl in a white gown brought in a silver bowl brimming with a thick-looking broth in which bits of potatoes, beef, and carrots floated. She set it down in the plate before Paige and left the room. Paige stared at it but didn't move. "I want you to eat it," Vulkan said quietly.

Paige's arms were still pinned to the chair, and tears were dripping from the point of her chin. "Eat your meal," Vulkan said as if he were speaking to a small child. Her right hand whipped out, grasped a large spoon, dipped it into the bowl and brought it to her lips. Her mouth jerked open. The spoon returned to the bowl. Then again. "Swallow it or you'll choke," he warned her. "That's a good girl." He stood over her and watched. "There are so many things I want to know about this land called California," he said eagerly. "You can help me. You can tell me everything. Like . . . who are these?" He touched the T-shirt he wore, printed with a picture of the Beach Boys. "Are they religious figures, like the movie stars? I have to know about the music I've heard playing. What instruments are those? Lutes? Harps? The world changes so fast. The years pass like days to me, the days like minutes. It becomes more crowded and complex. Every time I leave my refuge, I find myself in a different world . . ." He squinted suddenly, hearing something (MASTER!!) but he tried to force it away. Waves of need crashed through him as he stood in the hot presence of Paige LaSanda. But there it was again (MASTER HELP ME!), urgent and compelling. He touched his forehead, eyes rolling back, and tried to focus on where that thought had come from. And then . . .

. . . he could see the detectives in that large, rectangular building with all the windows, bringing his servant Roach into a room where they were going to ask him questions. Roach sat at a table, and one of the detectives —a black man—switched on a tape recorder. "All right, Benefield," the black man said. "We're going to ask you a few more questions."

"Questions? (MASTER HELP ME!) When can I go home?"

"Remember the photographs I showed you this afternoon?" the black man said. "The four bad girls?"

"I remember them," Roach said.

"Good." The detective opened a folder and looked through some papers. Then he shivered and glanced up at a larger man who sat across the room. "Does it feel cold in here to you, Farris?"

"Yeah, kind of," the one called Farris said. "A little chilly."

"Chilly, my ass! Feels like a north wind blew in!" He shivered again and then returned to the folder. "What were you going to do to Vicki Harris after you knocked her out with that stuff, Benefield?"

"Nothing."

"Really? Let me read you something from your rap sheet. Do you remember a young woman named Gilly Langford from August of '76?"

"No. (MASTER HELP ME!)"

"That's odd because she knew you when she picked you out of a lineup in an attempted rape case. She said you tried to strangle her, and she had the bruises on her throat to prove it. Then there was a little girl, Janis Chessler, eight years old. November 1977. Do you remember her?"

Roach closed his eyes tightly, clenching his hands into fists. (SAVE ME MASTER! THEY'RE GOING TO TRY TO MAKE ME TELL!)

"Do you remember Dr. Carl Friedman, Benefield?" the black man asked. "He was the State Mental Health Board psychologist assigned to your case after your molestation sentence was suspended. We've been in contact with him. Shall I tell you what he says about you?"

"Lies," Roach. "Everybody lies about me."

"He says you're what's called a paranoid-schizophrenic," the black man said. "That things get mixed up in your head sometimes and you lose track of past events. He says you complain of severe headaches and you have abrupt mood changes. Dr. Friedman says you show hostility to women. Are those lies, Benefield?"

"Yes . . ."

"I'll ask you again. What were you going to do to Vicki Harris?"

Roach trembled and whispered, "He . . . doesn't want me to tell . . ."

"He? Who are you talking about?"

"The Master." There were beads of sweat on his face. "He says I'm not supposed to . . ."

Prince Vulkan broke mental contact with Roach and looked over at Paige LaSanda. Her spoon was scraping the bottom of the silver bowl; her chin dripped with beef *gyulash,* and it had splattered down onto her dress. The woman's eyes were glazed, brimming with tears and totally insane.

"That's enough," Vulkan barked. Immediately Paige's hand opened, and the spoon clattered to the floor. He turned his gaze away from her, looking inward again. He wasn't certain how strong Roach's will was and how long the man could bear this sort of questioning. The night before, Vulkan had made the castle tremble with his screams of rage when he'd realized Roach had been caught. The man was bringing his offering—and Vulkan's food—up the mountain. But Roach was a loyal servant and could be put to future use, so now he had to be saved from the den of the enemy. Vulkan put a hand to his left temple and looked deep into the night, concentrating on what he wanted done. His dark essence, like a formless shadow, left his body and traveled upward, squeezing through a chink in the wall and moving outward; it was something the Headmaster had taught him to do. All of the city gleamed underneath. In just a moment he could see the bats spinning in the black sky like a mad whirlwind, hundreds of them flying from their caves in the San Gabriel and Santa Monica Mountains, gathering directly above Parker Center in downtown Los Angeles. They churned there, a squeaking cyclone of wings, awaiting his next command. When the sky was filled with them, he watched in his mind . . .

. . . the bats dropping lower, still spinning in a huge circle, hovering like a black noose around the gray-green building. They began to split formation and fly into the walls and windows. Those that didn't smash themselves to death flew a distance away and then came back to strike again . . .

Vulkan shifted focus, linked with Roach again and saw . . .

. . . the black detective looked up suddenly from the folder. He glanced at Farris, his brow creasing. "What was that? Did you hear something?"

"Wait a minute," Farris said, listening.

Roach's eyes were full of tears. He smiled as he heard something shatter glass outside beyond the door. "The Master!" he shouted joyously. "It's the Master come to take me home!"

"Shut up!" the black man said, rising from his chair. More glass broke, and now there were people shouting in the corridor. "What the hell's going on out there?" He opened the door and stood on the threshold, transfixed by what he saw. Windows exploded like gunshots. A dozen bats flew over his head into the room, and Roach laughed as Farris ducked away from them.

The black detective suddenly shivered and took a step backward.

"Reece?" Farris shouted.

The one called Reece staggered back, a ragged cry torn from his throat. He whirled around, his face covered with bats. A storm of them swept into the room, darting into Farris's hair, catching onto his shirt. Roach clapped and shouted, "YES! YES!" None of the bats touched him; they attacked the other two men, covering their bodies like a crawling tide. The walls were covered with bats, and they spun around the room like bits of black paper caught in a high wind . . .

"Roach," Vulkan said softly, speaking through his mind. *"Come to me."*

"YES!" the man shrieked. He leaped up from the table and ran past the black man's body, which was twisting on the floor in agony. He ran into a larger room where there were other men trying to fight off the creatures, but the bats numbered in the thousands now and were still coming in through the broken windows. Roach passed a man whose head and back were swarming with furry bodies; another man ripped blindly at his shirt, his eyes reduced to bleeding holes. The bats parted to let Roach through and closed in his wake. He ran into the corridor, which was also filled with bats, and on to the elevator. A few bats tangled in his hair, but they felt the Master's presence on him and flew away. When the elevator came, he stepped in, escorted by two dozen or more swirling protectively around him, chittering and squealing. On the first floor he ran toward the main doors where a uniformed officer shouted and drew his gun. A phalanx of bats whirled away from Roach and shredded the policeman's face.

Roach burst through the doors and ran into the night along a wide avenue bordered by huge buildings. "Thank you, Master!" he shouted. "Thank you, thank . . ."

Prince Vulkan brought himself back and opened his eyes; the pupils were tightly slitted and seemed to be glowing with green fire. He thought *Kobra* and in another moment Kobra stepped through a door at the far side of the room. "Roach is coming to join us," Vulkan said. "Take a few of the others and go down to help him. Hurry."

Kobra left to find Viking and Dicko and any other members of the Death Machine who'd already awakened. It would be good to ride his Harley again, to feel the cold wind in his face, to see the stars burning savagely in the night. He'd been right—this was the greatest drug there was.

When Kobra was gone, Vulkan turned his attention back to the madwoman in the chair. He approached her, saw her eyes moving feebly toward him, her mouth opening in a soundless "no." He took her hand and felt the blessed heat flowing like volcanic currents beneath the flesh. As he kissed the back of her hand, he could smell the sweet, delicious blood millimeters away from his fangs. He kissed along her arm, pushing the sleeve back, licking with a black forked tongue.

Paige LaSanda shuddered, her eyes rolling back to white. "Boogeyman, Mama," she said in a little girl's voice. "Boogeyman . . . boogeyman . . ."

When he reached the pulse at the crook of her elbow, the coldness within him turned unendurable. His head snapped forward, his fangs piercing the flesh. A bubbling fountain filled his mouth, and he drank with great, thirsty heaves.

In a few minutes Paige whimpered, her face chalky yellow, and then she was silent.

VI

Wednesday, October 30
THE HEADMASTER'S GIFT

ONE

Rico Esteban, hands thrust deep into the pockets of a silver jacket and head bowed in thought, was walking home along Sunset Boulevard. Around him the boulevard swirled with nightlife—the sidewalks were crowded with rockers in sleek, black jackets, their hair cut rooster-style and dyed in a variety of outrageous colors; transvestites hung around the entrances of the El Lay Club and the Disco 2001, hoping to be escorted in by some unaware stud; teen-aged girls in jeans so tight they deadened the ass stood in groups on the corners, talking among themselves about shoes and records when they weren't trying to flag down the driver of a passing Jaguar or Porsche; furtive older men stopped to ask them what time it was or how to find a good disco, and when the laughter hit, they hunched down and scurried off into the shadows; pimps in long Cadillacs cruised up and down the Strip, diamond rings flashing on their hands, their eyes alert for action or trouble. Music crashed around Rico like throbbing, electric thunder from a dozen rock clubs; the lightning was blue and white and green neon, pulsating like silent fury.

He'd made some good sales tonight—a couple of grams of coke in front of the Whiskey a Go Go, some Colombian Red inside Disco 2001. Now there were a couple of ounces of Red left in the lining of his jacket, and he knew he could've sold that too if he'd stayed around the disco any longer. But he'd gotten a creepy feeling in there just as the Jets were singing "Body Heat" and the strobe lights had started flashing so fast everybody looked like windup dolls gone berserk. The walls had started closing in around him, reminding him too much of the feeling he'd had in that building on Dos Terros Street. As he'd rushed out, shoving through a knot of people who stood around a couple writhing on the floor, urging them on, a girl with bleached blond hair and glitter on her cheeks had gripped his hand and whispered, "Come home with me, baby." He'd seen something horrible moving behind her vacant gaze, and her hand was as cold as death. Suddenly the girl on the floor whimpered—Rico heard it quite clearly, though no one else seemed to—and when he looked down, he thought he saw the boy astride her, his lips pressed against her throat. Rico jerked free and ran.

He walked on, keeping his head down to avoid eye contact. Things were going crazy. Everything was falling to pieces. He almost bumped into a skinny kid with a crew cut. When he looked up, Rico saw that the kid wore a T-shirt with WHO IS THE GRAVEDIGGER? scrawled across it in red crayon. The kid cursed and stumbled on, his eyes aflame with uppers. Rico hurried away, the gold chains around his neck merrily tinkling against each other. In another moment he felt himself being watched and looked up again. On the corner there were two teen-aged girls, one in a wrinkled, violet dress and the other in a pink satin jacket and dirty jeans. They stared at him with hunger in their eyes, their childlike faces vulpine and as pale as the ashes of a long-dead fire. Rico shuddered and found he could not look away. The girl in the violet dress smiled and motioned for him to come over. He had almost reached them when a blue Porsche with two guys inside swerved to the curb. One of the guys said, "Want a ride, baby?" and the girls climbed in without hesitation. The car roared away, and Rico felt cold beads of sweat trickling down into his eyebrows. He went on, walking much faster now.

It seemed to him that the endless party had gone on much too long, and now it was out of control. Something unspeakable had invited itself in because here the door was always open and everyone was too stoned or crazed to guard the entrance. Rico shivered; someone had just walked past him who gave off cold like an icebox. He was afraid to see who it was. He kept moving, the blare of music from the Mad Hatter's Tea Party almost blasting him out into the street. Someone else bumped into him—an older man in a white shirt. Rico felt those waves of cold gnawing at him again. Lifting his gaze high enough to see brown spots on the front of the man's shirt, he suddenly pushed a couple of kids out of his way and was running,

hearing a long shriek behind him that turned into a chilling howl of laughter.

He thought he could hear the noise of boots striking the
concrete, chasing after him. He seemed to be at the center
of a din of screams and laughter rising like a dark wave,
crashing over the music. A girl's hand clutched at his
sleeve. He cried out and pulled away, almost tripping in
his haste to escape. It was only two blocks later that he
dared to slow his pace and look over his shoulder. There
was no one following him, no one at all. Just figures moving along the sidewalks and back and forth across the
boulevard, bathed in cold neon.

What's wrong with me? he thought. *I'm cracking up or
something!* He walked another block, then turned into a
doorway centered between the Temple of the All-Seeing
Eye and the Rubens Nude—Fingerpaint a Real Live Nude!
—Art Studio. He climbed a narrow, dimly lit stairway and
stood in the hall. His was the third door on the right; he'd
been lucky to find an apartment with a view of Sunset
Boulevard. He switched on the lights and locked the door
behind him. It was a one-room with a kitchenette and
cracks in the ceiling that sometimes leaked brown drops
of water. There was a long mirror on the wall beside the
door, and now Rico peered into his face to see if he
looked crazy. His eyes were a little bloodshot from the
smoke at Disco 2001, but otherwise he looked okay. He
walked across the room, his weight making the loose
floorboards squeal, and looked out a small window onto
Sunset. A few figures were running along the sidewalk;
one of them, a woman, tripped and fell. A man stopped
and helped her to her feet, then they all ran out of Rico's
field of vision. In another few seconds a pack of grinning
teen-agers passed, running in the same direction. A car's
tires screeched far in the distance. Somewhere a siren
wailed like the voice of a woman, rapidly fading.

Someone knocked at Rico's door.

He whirled around, his heart racing with fear. For a
long time he stood where he was, staring across the room
at that door. In another moment the knob rattled.

"Go away!" he shouted and instantly thought, *Oh, God!
Now they know I'm here!*

The knocking was repeated. Then a voice in an urgent
whisper—"Rico! Open the door! It's me!"

"Who . . . ? *Merida?*"

"It's me, Rico! Hurry! Open the door!"

He let out his breath, almost overcome by dizziness. *God in Heaven! Merida!* He stepped to the door, unlocked it, and threw it open. Instantly she leaped forward into his arms, burying her face in his shoulder. "Merida!" he said. "Where have you been? I've been . . . I've been crazy looking for you!"

"Don't say anything, please," she whispered. "Just hold me. Tight. Tighter."

He squeezed her against himself, feeling her cold lips against his cheek. Tears threatened to spill from his eyes, and he realized then how very much he did love her. She was shivering, and her flesh was so . . . so cold . . . Something dark stirred in the pit of his belly. "You're freezing!" he said. "Where have you been? God, I'm so glad to see you!"

"Don't talk," she said, burrowing closer. "Just love me . . . make me warm . . ."

And it was then that Rico turned his gaze toward the mirror.

He was embracing an empty dress, wrinkled where it might have been pulled by the movements of a human body. But he knew, and the knowledge almost made him scream, that what he was embracing was no longer human . . .

She lifted her head, her dark eyes swirling with tendrils of red and silver. "Make me warm, my darling," she whispered. "Make me warm." Her mouth opened. The fangs slid out like a rattlesnake's.

"NOOOOOOO!" he screamed, pushing her away and taking a step backward. He tripped and crashed down against the wall, cracking his head on the edge of a junkshop table. Through a red mist of pain, he saw her approach as silently as a puff of smoke. "Ricooooo," she whispered, her eyes yearning. "I've come back to you. I've come back . . ."

"Get away!" he gasped, trying to scrabble to his feet. They wouldn't work; his brain spun between poles of frost and fire.

". . . for you," Merida said. "Now we can be together forever . . ."

"NO! NO!" His voice cracked, his eyes about to pop out of their sockets. Deep inside himself he heard the first faint chucklings of mad laughter.

"Yes," the vampire whispered. "Forever and forever and forever." She reached toward Rico, her eyes glimmering like Sunset Strip neon. He screamed and thrust out his arms to protect himself, to give himself a few more seconds of life. Merida grasped his right arm, grinned, and sank her fangs into a vein at his wrist.

He was shot through with pain, and now he could hear her sucking the life out of him. He tried to strike at her with his other hand, but she grabbed that wrist and held it with extraordinary strength. Her fangs plunged deep, not missing a drop. Her eyes began to roll back in her head with pleasure, and Rico began tumbling down into a dark place that was so terribly cold, so . . . terribly . . . terribly . . . cold. . . .

When she was finished, she let his arm drop to the floor. She crouched down on all fours and licked up the few red spots of blood that she had missed. Then she crawled over to Rico and cradled his head against her bosom, gently rocking his cold body back and forth. "Now," she said. "Now, we'll be together for always. We'll always be young . . . and we'll always be in love. Sleep, my precious. Sleep." She held him awhile longer, then she went to the unmade sofa-bed and pulled off the sheets. She laid the sheets down on the floor, dragged him into the middle, and wrapped him up. *Now,* she thought as she finished the task, *you can sleep undisturbed until the Master bids you to awaken.* She knew he'd be filled with hunger when he got up and might not be able to hunt for himself, so she would come back to help him. Her love knew no bounds. She dragged Rico's shrouded form into the closet, piled a couple of cardboard boxes around him, and closed the door. Now the sun, that hated bringer of pain, couldn't get to him.

The Master would be pleased with her work.

She left the room and raced along Sunset Boulevard to help the others in the hunt. She was getting quite good at following the blood scent.

TWO

"Arista wants you, Wes," Jimmy Kline was saying as he drove along Sunset, disregarding the kids who were stalking the sidewalks in what seemed to him record numbers for this hour. "They'll kill to get you after the Brooks deal is hammered down. And that is when our price goes *up*. Waaayyyyy up. Hell, they can't afford not to grab you up while you're hot!"

Wes sat in the back seat of Jimmy's custom-built, white Cadillac, his arm around Solange. The evening had been too much for her, and now her head was nestled on his shoulder. "That Chuck guy was pretty funny, wasn't he?" he said. "What was his last name?"

"Crisp or Kripes or something like that. I'll tell you how I'm going to play Arista, Wes. Long and cold. I'll give 'em the old baleful stare when they quote facts and figures to me. Ha! I'll have 'em climbing the walls ready to sign anything. 'Sheer Luck' is going to be a hit for ABC, and the record companies are going to come crawling to us on their fucking knees! You want to hear a tape or something?"

"No," Wes responded quietly. "I'm fine."

"Okay. Hey! How'd you like to do a couple of Vegas dates? We could write our own ticket!"

"I don't know. I've got bad memories of Vegas. Maybe I should just keep a low profile for a while and see what develops."

"Low profile?" Jimmy said as if Wes had uttered the ultimate profanity. "Did I hear you right, man? *Low profile?* The only people keeping low profiles in this town are the has-beens! We've got to strike while the iron's hot. You know that as well as I do. Christ!" He suddenly twisted the wheel to the right, swerving to avoid a group of spaced-out kids who'd run out into the street right in front of the Caddy. "You fucking jerks!" Jimmy shouted, giving them the finger as he drove past. They scattered, grinning and jeering. "Bunch of freaks!" Jimmy said, his face flushed. "Christ! We almost killed us about four punks back there. What an item for Rona's column, right?"

"Yeah, right," Wes said nervously. He glanced back and saw the kids leaping out again in front of a Spitfire convertible. The car screeched to a halt, and the kids moved forward. Then he turned away and didn't look anymore because suddenly he was filled with dread.

"Where do all these freaks live?" Jimmy said, glancing around at the people hanging out in front of stores and bars. "What do they do, just come out at night or something?"

Solange suddenly sat up as if she'd never been sleeping at all. "What's happening?" she said, her tone of voice alert.

"Nothing. Jimmy's driving us home. Go back to sleep."

"No." She looked around. "Aren't we there yet?"

Wes smiled. "We just left the Improv about fifteen minutes ago. I suppose you don't remember the three glasses of Chablis you put away?" He looked into the rearview mirror at Jimmy's eyes. "What'd you say that guy's name was again? Chuck what?"

"Kreskin. No, that's not it."

"He's a good comedian. His material's really sharp. The audience liked him too."

"I guess they did. Of course, everybody knows you could get up there on your worst night and blow him or anyone else right off the stage. Cream rises to the top, Wes. That's why he's working the Improv and you've got an ABC contract."

"Footsteps," Wes said quietly.

"What?"

"Footsteps," he repeated. "Footsteps in the dark, coming up behind you. You can run your ass off, run until your heart's about to burst, and then when you slow down, you think you won't hear them, but there they are right behind you."

"Solange, what's our crazy golden boy talking about?"

"Sometimes I wonder," Wes mused, "what would've happened to me if I hadn't stepped up on that stage for the first time. It was right there in the Comedy Store on a Monday night—amateur night—and I was just off the bus from Winter Hill and scared shitless. I was supposed to meet an old frat buddy at the Greyhound station, but the bastard didn't show up, so I started walking, lugging suitcases. Jesus! I must've dragged those things twenty blocks. I didn't even know where I was going. Anyway, I saw this poster tacked up—Monday Night's Potluck at The Comedy Store. The Stage Is Yours! I found myself a motel room and started practicing in front of the mirror. Which had a big crack in it—I'll always remember that—and I was afraid it was going to be bad luck. But I figured somebody else broke it, so it was somebody else's bad luck. Right?"

"Definitely," Jimmy said.

Wes smiled at the flood of memories. It all seemed so very long ago, but then time in L.A. was deceptive. When you're riding high and surrounded with friends, time speeds up, turning the months and weeks into days and hours. But when you're down and all alone, every minute stretches into a poisonous eternity. "I never saw a stage as big as that one was," he said. "I never again saw one as big either. There was a long line of people waiting to go on in front of me. Some of them were really good; the others just slunk off stage when they were finished beating their dead horses. God, what a night that was! The guy in front of me was a short order cook named Benny . . . uh . . . Kramer, I think his last name was. He did sound effects—ray guns, flying saucers, machine guns, and bombs with a half-assed running commentary. He was a nice guy but as stiff as a board up there. El Stiffo. After they carried him out, somebody pushed me from behind, and I went stumbling out into the lights. Christ, they were . . . so bright." His voice had steadily become lower, his eyes glazed with remembrances. Jimmy glanced at him every once in a while in the rearview mirror. They were driving through Beverly Hills now, heading toward Bel Air. "So bright," he said. "They burned into you like lasers; they made the sweat pop out of your pores. I could just barely see the people sitting up close to the stage, but I was aware of the whole staring . . . *mass* of them out there. I could see light glinting off glasses and ashtrays, and it seemed like the whole place was full of noise—people coughing like they'd swallowed their dinners whole, talking back and forth across the room like I wasn't even there at all, hollering for a waitress. It was then that I knew I was a looooong way from fraternity parties and podunk clubs. This was the big time, and it was going to be *tough*." He paused, staring out the window.

"Were you good?" Solange asked, holding his hand.

"I was shitty," he admitted and smiled. "My timing was off, I blew most of the punch lines, and I stood like I had a poker up my ass. About two minutes into the act, the crowd started calling for my blood. It was Gong Show reject all the way. I forgot the rest of my jokes and went nuts, started blabbering on about growing up in Winter Hill and how funny my folks and friends had always thought I was. That drove the last nails into my coffin. I think I must've crawled off that stage on my hands and knees because I sure don't remember walking off. And that was my big debut in Hollywood." He squeezed her hand. "But I got myself a job selling shirts at the Broadway, and I went back the next Monday night. And the next, and the next. I found out that if you wanted God on your side, you had to work like a demon, and I did. I threw out all the jokes that had worked at the frat parties and started from scratch. After a couple of months of that, they wouldn't let me do amateur nights anymore. People were asking for me. I started doing shows on New Comedians Night. Sometimes I bombed, sometimes I won them over. But I always worked my ass off. And then one night this guy came backstage and asked me if I was interested in writing some material for the Carson show. Rags to riches." He pondered that for a moment and then added, "to rags to riches."

"Rags? Shit!" Jimmy said. "In your worst year, after 'Just You 'n Me' went under, you were clearing a hundred thou!"

"Which went just about as fast as it came in," Wes reminded him. "You forget how far a hundred thousand goes in this town these days."

" 'Tis true," Jimmy said. "Regrettably true."

Solange shivered and drew closer to him. "What's wrong?" he asked, "Are you cold?"

"I'll turn up the heat." Jimmy reached for the climate control.

"I'm all right," she said. "I'm only tired."

He looked at her closely. "You've been acting strange all day," he said softly. "You coming down with a cold or something?"

She shook her head. "I only want to get to sleep."

Wes saw there was something more to it than that, but he knew from experience that when Solange wanted to keep something to herself, nobody on God's earth could get it out of her. He remembered yesterday morning. It had taken him almost ten minutes to snap her out of the trance she'd fallen into. She'd been sleeping with her eyes open.

"So just think about a couple of Vegas dates, will you, Wes?" Jimmy said. They were driving along a curving boulevard lined with tall palm trees, and they hadn't seen another car for five minutes.

"Vegas?" Wes repeated. "I don't know . . ."

"Las Vegas?" Solange gripped his hand tighter. "Could you get a job there?"

"Babe, when 'Sheer Luck' starts rolling in the Neilsons, old Wes could get a job in Fairbanks!"

"That would be nice, Wes," she said, looking at him hopefully. "A week or two in Las Vegas maybe? Or a month? Why not?"

"I'm not ready for that right now. I want to take it easy."

"Easy, smeasy," Jimmy muttered.

"Why not do it?" Solange continued. "It might be good to . . . to get away from Los Angeles for a while. You could relax in . . ."

"Get away from Los Angeles?" Wes said. He'd caught the emphatic tone in her voice, and his eyes narrowed slightly. "Why? What's so important to you about going to Vegas?"

"It's not important to me. I just thought you might enjoy the change."

"I wouldn't. You know what I think about working in Vegas. It's an armpit town as far as progressive comedy goes. Those people just want somebody to ease them down after losing their shirts . . ."

"HOLY CHRIST!" Jimmy suddenly shouted.

Wes twisted his head around. He heard the high squeal of brakes and saw a gray car hurtle into the intersection on a collision course with the Caddy. Jimmy wrenched the wheel and slammed on the brakes, but Wes saw that the gray car, a Maserati, was coming too fast. He saw a face behind the wheel—eyes widened in horror, mouth opened in a soundless scream. He grabbed Solange, then the two cars hit in a jarring *whump* of rending metal. Glass shattered very close to Wes's ear; the interior of the Cadillac seemed to be filled with angry hornets. Solange

screamed. Wes's head rocked forward and hit the back
of Jimmy's seat, then he was thrown against the door with
rib-cracking force. For an instant the Cadillac seemed in
danger of going over on its side; the Maserati seemed to
keep on coming, its gray torpedo of a nose plowing into the Caddy's side. Then the Cadillac righted itself,
slammed against a palm tree, and was still.

The ticking of hot engines sounded like a bomb about
to go off. "Are you okay?" Wes said to Solange. "ARE
YOU OKAY?" She nodded, her eyes glazed, a blue
bruise coming up over her right cheekbone. "You crazy
or something?" he shouted at the Maserati's driver, but
all he could see was a shattered windshield. *The sonofabitch must've been doing eighty!* he thought. *Must've been
doing ninety fucking miles an hour when he came into
the intersection!* The entire right side of the Cadillac was
folded in, all sharp angles of leather and metal. The front
of the Maserati had been crushed like an accordion, the
hood almost ripped from its hinges.

"Jimmy," Solange whispered thickly.

Wes looked, his heart pounding. There was blood on
the steering wheel where Jimmy's forehead had cracked
half of it away. Jimmy was wedged under the wheel, his
left arm almost turned backward. His face was a sick,
purplish color, and blood was streaming from one side
of his mouth. He made a soft moaning noise, his lungs
sounding wet and clogged. "Jimmy!" Wes shouted and
started to lean over the seat. Jimmy's eyes opened. "Oh,
shit," he said softly. "Looks like somebody plowed our
asses, didn't they? Christ, my chest hurts!"

"Don't move. Don't move. I'll find a phone somewhere
and call an ambulance. Don't move." He had to shove
against the door several times to get it open because it
was jammed up against that palm tree. He squeezed out,
his ribs laced with pain. He fell to the grass and puked
like a hurt dog. Solange helped him to his feet. His head
was throbbing terribly; it felt like a balloon expanding.
"Got to find a phone," he told her. "Jimmy's hurt bad."
He looked up and down the boulevard for a pay phone,
but they were right in the center of Beverly Hills and
pay phones were as hard to find as Skid Row winos here.
Across the street there was a large, white, stucco house
with a wall around it. A light shone in an upper window,
and a head popped out. "Hey!" Wes shouted. "Some-

body help us! Call an ambulance, there's a guy hurt down here!" The person in the window paused a few seconds, then withdrew into the room. "The car may blow up!" Wes yelled suddenly to Solange. "We've got to get him out!"

"No, leave him where he is," she said. "Don't move him. Your head's bleeding."

"Huh? Shit!" He felt up at his hairline and looked at the red smear on his fingertips. He staggered, but Solange's firm grip on his arm kept him from falling. "I'm okay," he insisted. "How about you?" She nodded, and he walked around the crumpled Caddy to the remains of the Maserati. Oil and water were bubbling out of the engine block, hissing where they kissed hot metal. Wes couldn't see anyone inside the car. He stepped forward through a puddle of water and peered through the smashed window on the driver's side.

A mask of blood was suddenly thrust before his face. Before he could step back, a hand clamped his arm. The Maserati's driver was a man with silvery gray hair, now clotted with blood. His face was twisted with agony, the lips trying to squeeze out words. "Uhhhhhhh . . . they're coming!" he said in a frantic whine. "They took Denise, and now they're coming for me, they're not going to let any of us . . . uhhhhhhh . . . any of us get . . . get . . . get away . . . !"

"What's he saying?" Solange asked.

"I don't know. He's drunk or crazy," Wes said. He could hear a siren, approaching fast. *An ambulance. Thank God, that guy in the house must've called*. He started to pull away from the man, but the fingers dug deeper into his arm. "NO!" the man cried out. "No! Don't leave me! Please . . . please don't leave me!"

"You'll be okay," Wes said. "There's an ambulance coming."

"Don't leave me . . . don't . . . don't . . ." His voice died to a faint moan, and he slithered back down into the seat, his fingers dangling over the edge of the door.

Wes stepped away from the Maserati and peered into the Caddy where Jimmy lay crumpled against the wheel. "You're gonna be okay, Jimmy! Help's coming. You just hang on, buddy!"

"Right . . . hang on . . ." Jimmy whispered.

An ambulance, orange lights flashing, came roaring

around the curve and screeched to a stop on the other side of the Maserati. The two uniformed attendants, one a Chicano and the other a lanky, red-haired guy, got out and approached the accident, walking quickly.

"Jimmy's hurt bad!" Wes told them. "He's all crushed up in the front seat!"

"Yes, sir," the Chicano said softly. But then the other guy was pulling the Maserati's door open and reaching for the injured driver. The gray-haired man opened his eyes and babbled in terror.

"Hey," Wes said, "what's . . . going . . . on . . . ?"

The gray-haired man screamed. In the rippling orange light Wes could see the glittering fangs slide out from the jaws of the ambulance attendant. Solange made a soft sound of horror and gripped his arm. Wes could hear the chatter from the ambulance's radio— ". . . got a two-car collision, corner of Wilshire and Detroit, two people involved . . . hit-and-run, corner of Pickford and Orange, man's down on the scene . . . car hit a telephone pole, Olympic and Catalina, two victims pinned inside . . . the hunting's fine . . ." The voice carried a cold hiss.

Solange pulled at him. "Run!" she insisted. "We've got to run!"

The Chicano glared at her greedily and wrenched open the Caddy's front door. Then he reached in for Jimmy and began to pull his body out from underneath the wheel. Jimmy screamed in agony.

"Are you crazy?" Wes shouted. "You're killing him, you bastard!" He started forward to tear the maniac away from Jimmy, but instantly Solange grabbed his arm to hold him back. *"No,"* she said, and he stopped to look at her as if she were crazy, too. Her face was a grim-lipped mask, an African goddess with strange lights glimmering in her eyes. He could hear another siren approaching. The gray-haired man was on the ground now, his legs twitching as the attendant bent down over him. "Jimmy!" Wes cried. "Jim . . . my . . ." And then the Chicano was leaning over Jimmy. Wes saw orange light glimmer off the fangs as they sank into Jimmy's throat. As he drank with thirsty heaves, the Chicano's black eyes sought out Wes and Solange.

And then, as if something had collapsed at the center of his rational soul, Wes realized what kind of things they were. Solange shouted, "WES!" and pulled at him as the second ambulance rounded the curb, orange lights flashing. As they ran, Wes looked back to see Jimmy's body spread out on the concrete. It shivered as if it had been plugged into a high-voltage charge; then he couldn't look back again for fear of being caught by that thing's hot, Gorgon-like stare. In the next instant the second ambulance roared up onto the sidewalk behind them, headlights blazing.

Wes and Solange ran along a high, wrought-iron fence; beyond it was a sloping lawn and a dark, Tudor-style mansion framed with palm trees. The driveway, closed off from the street by a locked gate, lay just a few yards ahead. Wes could see that the bars had been forced apart as if with a crowbar. There might just be room enough for them to squeeze through—If they could get to that house and a telephone . . . ! But the ambulance was gaining on them, swerving around the high Washingtonia palms, clumps of grass flying up behind the tires. They reached the gate, and Wes shoved Solange through the bars. She tripped and fell on the other side, but he squeezed through and pulled her up, then both of them ran toward that house. The ambulance crashed into the gate behind them, knocking it open and smashing both headlights with a noise like a shotgun blast. Wes saw that some of the mansion's windows were broken out; it looked dead and desolate, and he realized with a surge of panic that *they* could already be inside. He looked back and saw the driver's pallid, grinning face streaked with the orange light. The ambulance was again almost on them. Wes wrenched Solange to the side as it roared past and up the hill, cutting them off from the house. It skidded up on the lawn, turning in a tight circle, and slammed into a palm tree.

They ran on, cutting across the lawn and past the house. Just on the other side of the hill's crest was a white, concrete structure that looked like a storage shed. A stone walkway led down through a landscaped flower bed, and below that was a swimming pool with a canopied bathhouse. Wes couldn't hear the ambulance anymore, but he knew they'd be coming soon. He tried the shed's door. It was locked, so he kicked it open. He stood among sacks of concrete mix and potting soil, various tools, a few large ceramic pots, and several cans of paint. Even before he heard Solange shout, he heard the

ambulance roaring across the lawn. He lifted one of the
paint cans and pried its lid loose.

"Stay here!" he yelled at Solange and ran down into
the flower beds where the vampires could see him. The
ambulance came for him, its grillwork grinning like the
mouth of a hungry ogre. He saw the flicker of recognition across the driver's face. Before the ambulance could
slow down, Wes heaved the paint can at the windshield,
then leaped to one side with Solange's scream ringing
in his ears.

The glass shattered, bright blue swimming pool paint
covering the interior of the ambulance and blinding the
things inside. It swerved, roared on past Wes through
the flowers, and pitched over a small brick wall that
separated them from the pool area. The ambulance nosed
into the deep end of the pool with a huge splash. Hot
metal hissed. The orange light grew weaker, casting rippled reflections.

Wes didn't wait to see if the things could get out. He
ran back up to Solange, and at the crest of the hill they
could both see the streaks of orange flashing out in the
street. Wes froze.

"The house," Solange said.

It was the only choice they had. They got in through
a pair of shattered French doors at the rear of the house,
which opened onto a large sitting room where furniture,
cabinets, and bookshelves had been overturned as if in
a mad fury. Wes fumbled through the debris, trying to
find a telephone in the dark. Solange picked up a lamp
and stood at the doors; her eyes were wide and shining
with fear but her hand was steady, with the lamp's metal
base poised as a weapon. In another moment she thought
she sensed movement outside. Wes did, too; he froze
where he was, crouched on the floor with dirt all over
his clothes and face.

Solange listened, her heart beating hard. They were
there, she was sure of it. And now she heard the wet
squeaking of shoes just beyond the doors. They would be
coming through any second now. Her grip tightened on
the lamp, though she was well aware she couldn't fight
them hand-to-hand.

And then in the distance, there were two gunshots. It
might have been from the house next door or from across
the street. The shots were followed by a woman's scream

and a man's rising, madly babbling voice. Another siren began to shriek. She heard the slapping squeak of the shoes running away from the doors, quickly fading. She exhaled and leaned aganst the wall, lowering the lamp. "They're gone," she said after she'd caught her breath again. "I think they found something better . . ."

Wes shoved aside an overturned coffee table and found lying underneath it an old black antique that Ma Bell herself must've used about a hundred years ago. When he picked it up, his heart sank—it had been ripped from its terminal. "Damn it!" he breathed. "We've got to call the cops!"

"There's no use in that," Solange said quietly. "The police won't be able to help. If they did come, they'd only . . . find those things waiting for them . . ."

"What about Jimmy?" It was all he could do to keep himself from shouting. His strained voice echoed through the room, many ghosts speaking at once. "What in God's name are they?" He knew the answer to that already, and there was no need for her to utter the awful word. "It can't be!" he said. "They're not real . . . not real . . . !" He steadied himself against an old sofa with red velvet cushions that had white music notes and lettering stitched on them, *The Sweetheart of Sigma Chi* and *Charleston, Charleston.* "Somebody must live here," he said. "They must be upstairs." He was afraid to shout, though, for fear those things outside might hear him.

"I think you're wrong," Solange said. Wes stared up at her. "Look around. I think the things have come here and gone."

He forced himself to look. The mangled burglar bars were bad enough; a large, gilt-framed mirror was smashed all to pieces and now hung crookedly over a cold fireplace. Antique lamps lay in fragments on the floor. A couple of bookcases had been overturned, scattering old volumes and little ceramic figurines. Solange bent and picked up one of the figures—it was the remnants of a ballet dancer, both legs and one of the arms broken off. The tiny painted face smiled up at her.

"There's got to be a working phone somewhere in this goddamned tomb!" Wes said and moved through a pair of sliding oak doors into a carpeted corridor that led to the front door. There were more smashed mirrors and framed posters of old movies—*One Night in Madrid,*

The Prince and the Showgirl, Hollywood's Heaven.
Through the front windows he saw the orange flicker and
thought he saw figures moving out on the lawn.

Solange was beside him. "An elevator," she said, and
Wes turned. Next to a stairway with thick, ornately
carved banisters, there was a wire-mesh elevator shaft.

"Yeah. Fine. So what?" he said irritably. He glanced
back toward the front door, a shiver rippling through
him. "Where did those things come from? What in God's
name *made* them like that?"

Solange said, "We're not safe yet. We've got to find a
place to hide in case they come after us again." She
started for the stairway, and he was about to follow when
a cold hand snaked out of the darkness and gripped his
wrist.

THREE

Roach was down on the cold stone floor, whimpering
like a dog at Prince Vulkan's feet. Vulkan, sitting in his
chair at the long, waxed table covered with maps and
diagrams, paid the human little attention. He stared
into the fire, his face caught between light and shadow.
The room still smelled of Falco's charred body; the dogs
in the lower basement had gone wild over the cooked
meat. *Dust to dust,* Vulkan thought, *and ashes to ashes.*
Over on the other side of the table, Kobra sat, his boots
propped up before him, and watched Roach through
narrowed, red-lit eyes; he held Falco's femur in his left
hand like a hideous scepter. Since after midnight couriers
from Vulkan's lieutenants had been coming up the mountain to report on the shifting concentrations of activity
—troops were now rampaging through Hollywood and
Beverly Hills and a great part of southern L.A., including
an area called Watts, which had already fallen. There
had been several skirmishes with police officers who'd
never known what they were chasing until it was too late.
The control tower at the Santa Monica Municipal Airport
had been overtaken, and some of the less-disciplined ones
had amused themselves by crashing a few private planes.
A military school in Westwood Village had been taken,

and along with it sixty-eight young boys who had been asleep in their beds when the attack came; they would make fine soldiers tomorrow night. But for the most part the action had been hit-and-run, which was how Prince Vulkan preferred it right now. Individual houses broken into, the sleeping man and woman and children quickly drunk dry and shrouded away from the sunlight to sleep awhile longer; cars flagged down on the avenues and boulevards, their drivers taken by surprise; apartment complexes taken silently, one cubicle after the next. Prince Vulkan had been in L.A. a little over a month now, and by his conservative estimate there were over six hundred thousand of his kind spread across the city. Moreover, the number doubled every night. His fangs had sired the beginnings of a new race.

He touched Roach's shoulder; the man looked up at him, his face as joyous and dumb as a devoted puppy's. "You're safe now," Vulkan said quietly. "You recognized your weakness down there, and you were wise to call for me . . ."

"I could've killed all those fucking cops," Kobra said. "I could've done it easy, the Death Machine and me, killed them all . . ."

"I didn't speak to you," the prince said, angered at being interrupted. "I didn't ask you to speak. Did I?"

"You don't need *him*," Kobra said, his gaze burning with a sullen glare. "You said I was going to sit at your right hand. You said that's why you called me from Mexico, because I was special . . ."

"I didn't speak to you!" Vulkan's voice was like hot steel.

Kobra stared back at him for only a second or so, then dropped his gaze and flung the bone into the fireplace. "I need both of you," Vulkan declared, "equally."

"Why do you need one of *them*?" Kobra said, and this time he looked away immediately because Vulkan's green eyes had flared like blasts of napalm.

"Because," the prince said, "we'll need a human to go before us when we've finished here. I'll need him to arrange passage, to care for the crates, to secure a proper dwelling just as my last servant did. And sometimes I forget how humans think, I forget what their needs are, what motivates them. Having one of them here is essential. Look on Roach as a . . . a mascot."

Kobra stared down at his knuckles.

"You are at my right hand, Kobra. You're inexperienced yet, but before we're through you'll lead my army to victory . . ."

Kobra looked up again, his eyes shining like headlights.

"Yes!" Vulkan said. "I called you from Mexico because I could *feel* your presence, and the Headmaster helped me find you. Even as one of *them* you knew how to use Death. You were a true brother, even as a human." He placed his fingertips together and looked from Kobra to Roach. "To each their special place. Think back to Alexander . . ."

"Who?" Kobra asked.

Vulkan looked shocked. "Alexander! The boy king, the greatest warrior this world has ever seen! Don't you read?" Don't you know anything about military strategy?" His lips curled in answer to his own question. "No, I suppose not. You'll have to be taught, won't you? Alexander the Great carried a full contingent on his campaigns—archers, infantry, carpenters, cooks, scholars, prophets, even women to serve the needs of his men. He left nothing to chance, and each man knew his proper role. Am I less than Alexander? Would I not follow his example? As I say, to each their special purpose."

Kobra shrugged. He didn't know what the Master was talking about exactly, but if the Master said it was important, then it was. The Master closed his eyes now, leaving Roach to fawn at his feet. Kobra didn't like that one. On the way up the mountain, the human had sat behind him on his Harley, grasping him with hot hands. If Kobra hadn't already fed tonight, he might've borne him down to the ground and . . . but no. The Master wouldn't like him even thinking like that; he wouldn't like it at all. But he still couldn't see what good that one was going to be. He would be slow and stupid, a lap dog trying to keep up with wolves. Already Kobra was delirious with the sense of power that coursed through him. Right after he fed, he felt invincible, tuned like a perfect 750cc flying along the hot currents on the highway, able to concentrate on the glittering plain of the city and pick up bits of a hundred thousand conversations going on all at once, like overlapping radio stations that faded in and out when the antenna moved. It must have been easy for the Master to find him just by concentrating on the *feeling* Kobra had in his brain, the dark attitude under the trapdoor of his soul. Every time he fed, the power was going to grow stronger; he was going to learn more, see more, know all the secrets in human hearts and minds. It would take time, yes, but he was going to be twenty forever, and time coupled with ageless youth was the great gift the Master had bestowed on him.

"Leave me," Vulkan said. He opened his eyes and stared at Kobra. "Take Roach to his quarters. See that no harm comes to him."

Kobra stood up. "Come on," he said to Roach. He motioned with his hand, and the man scurried after him. "No one is to touch him, Kobra," Vulkan ordered. "Do you understand that? He is to have free run of the castle, and the one who touches his flesh or blood will answer to me."

Kobra bowed his head slightly and ushered Roach through the door. It closed behind them with a hollow noise that echoed up toward the vaulted ceiling.

Prince Vulkan turned his head and stared into the fire. He thought he'd felt a cold breath stirring across the back of his neck, and his senses snapped on, vivid and aware. Paige LaSanda's blood thrummed in his veins; it had made him sleepy for a while, but now he sat straight-backed, the pupils of his cat eyes slowly widening. The red embers in that fire reminded him of the ironsmith's forge in his father's castle, a long time ago. He remembered watching the ironsmith—a huge bear of a man with gray hair on his arms and shoulders—hammering out the raw blades that the swordsmith would painstakingly fashion into rapiers that glimmered like blue lightning. And he recalled those afternoon drills in a dusty hall with the sunlight streaming in through high, arched windows. Forward and back, forward and back, parry, thrust, attack. His father had been proud of his progress and proclaimed him an even better swordsman than his own father, Simon Vulkan the Strong. Now his father had been dust for many hundreds of years; now the castle of his birth was so many broken stones on a mountain ridge; now the pieces of the carriage that had crashed over a serpentine road on that wild, windswept night lay in a Budapest museum along with other odd memorabilia of the Vulkan brood. That night—September 29, 1342—had forever changed him and forever kept him the same. He remembered the scene vividly, could recall it down to the finest detail simply by closing his eyes. His father, Jon the Hawk, sitting across from him in the swaying, gold and ebony coach, his father's wife Sonya beside her husband, pressed close to him because the storm made her fearful. Sonya the Barren, she was called in the village mead halls, though never loudly enough for any of the Hawk's mercenaries to overhear. Conrad knew she wasn't his mother. The Hawk was regaled by the minstrels for his prowess in bed as well as on the battlefield. Sonya bore him no grudge because the Hawk was aging now and had needed a son.

The land was a wild, crazy quilt of powers, men building mountain fortresses and calling themselves kings and hiring mercenaries to take the next man's land. The Vulkan province had spread in all directions as far as a horseman could ride in a day, encompassing a great deal of what is now the northern part of Hungary. It was a varied landscape of harsh rock citadels, sudden deep valleys of dense, unexplored woodland, grassy plains, and lakes that caught mirror images of the sky. The land was beautiful, though unforgiving, but never at peace; there were very few nights when the torches of some ragged army or another didn't burn along the strategic mountain passes. The Germanic tribes were always on the march, and if the Hawk was not battling them in the wild northern forests, he was faced with the crawl of the Huns or the mercenary army of some jealous neighbor.

As the Hawk grew older and slower, assassination attempts became bolder. Three nights before that fateful coach trip, returning from the new fortifications the Hawk had built on the eastern frontier where groups of barbarians had been seen gathering in the mountains for a raid, one of his most trusted advisors had been caught rimming a wine goblet with poison. The man's arms and legs were torn from their sockets, his mutilated torso thrown to the castle dogs. Such was the fate of all traitors.

Conrad Vulkan had been weaned on warfare, drilled in classical military strategy by such warriors as Jozsef Agna and Ernst the One-Eyed, taught to ponder the scope of his world by the philosopher Bran Lazlo, tutored in the myriad ways of man at the knee of his father. He was destined for greatness, the Hawk had always said. Conrad's mind had been steadily honed like the blade of a newly fired rapier. Even now, sitting in a high-backed chair worlds away from strife-torn Hungary, he recalled a favorite lesson his father had taught him: *Attack like the wind. Seem to be in all places at once. And never be there when the enemy turns to grasp at you.*

Before the coach incident there was only one moment of foreboding in Conrad's life. It happened during the celebration of his tenth birthday in the castle's great hall. One of the guests had brought, as a gift, a gypsy woman who read fortunes in the palm of the hand. In the ruddy light of hearth and torch, she had grasped his wrist and bent over to see, her toothless gums masticating raw tobacco. Instantly she'd recoiled and asked him—through a translator because she spoke only a crude, Germanic gypsy language—if he'd had those few hairs at the center of his palm since he was born. He'd nodded, and she'd begun clucking like a frightened hen. She'd dropped his hand and said something else, which when translated conveyed that she saw a great and terrible change ahead for him. His line of life had hardly begun when it seemed to disappear *under* the flesh and manifested itself in a thin, blue thread that curved around the base of the thumb and circled the wrist once, twice, three times, and again. She refused to read anything more and had been sent on her way with a loaf of black bread.

But it was that night in September that remained most prominent in his memory—that night of terror and magic. The coach was moving through the Keyding Pass escorted by four soldiers when the driver suddenly slowed. One of the soldiers had sighted huge rocks, fallen from the slab of stone overhead to block the road. Suddenly, as the horses pawed the earth wildly and the driver tried to calm them, figures leaped from the rocks and trees, attacking the mounted soldiers. The horses screamed and reared. They took off with the coach racing, and suddenly a filthy, grinning death's head of a face peered in at a side window. The horses broke their harnesses; the coach shuddered and pitched off the road, crashing over and over down a rocky incline into the cold arms of a mountain stream.

Conrad had opened his eyes inside the coach to see dark, ragged figures scurrying outside, breaking in through the shattered wood. His father and Sonya lay before him like broken dolls, and he knew at once that they were dead. He'd tried to fight off the things as they came swarming in, but one of his arms wouldn't work, and a hulking form covered with filth and lice grabbed him up like a piece of kindling and carried him off into the night. Others chased after, and he was flung aside several times as the things fought, rolling over and over on the ground, hammering at each other, hissing and snarling with demonic fury. Finally, a long way from the Keyding Pass, he was carried into a cavern that smelled of Death and vermin. The thing that held him threw him to the floor, and it was then that he saw the *vampir's* face and recognized it for what it was. The thing looked more like an animal than a man, with long, dirty black hair and a scraggly black beard. Its eyes glowed with bursts of red and silver, its fangs dripped saliva, and its fingernails were hooked like claws. The *vampir* had approached, whining in its eagerness to feed, and had leaped upon the boy like a leech.

And the following night Conrad Vulkan had awakened as one of the Undead.

For a while he'd lived as the rest of them did—in a series of deep, winding caverns cut through the mountains, feeding independently on whatever he could find, usually rats, boars, or an occasional human who'd taken the wrong road. He fought like an animal to defend his sleeping and eating spaces, losing both of them many times and always digging out new ones in the cavern's clay floors. Eventually he realized that several of them always followed him to the stream where he washed the lice and roaches out of his clothes. They watched him curiously and eventually began to do the same thing. Many of them babbled in strange tongues he'd never heard before, and most of them couldn't communicate at all. After a while he began to speak with several of them through a crude sign language and organized them into hunting parties. And then came the great realization of his new existence. He was, after all, a prince. Why could he not be a king to his new subjects? He organized the group into foodgatherers, scouts, and firetenders, and he began teaching them a common language. It was a slow process, but after a long while they began to trust each other, to see themselves as brothers and sisters of the night. They expanded their hunting range, raiding the nearby villages for children who would add the gifts of youth and speed to the collective. In those days Conrad knew very little of what he was or the powers he could control; he simply craved survival and recognized blood as Life.

And finally he was ready to return to the castle of his birth.

His scouts reported that it was in Germanic hands now. So this was to be a mission of warfare as well as a mission of survival. Vulkan contemplated the problem of taking the castle. He knew its interior as well as he knew the palm of his star-crossed hand, but its high, sheer walls would stop even an army of the Undead. And while he contemplated, he watched a rat scurrying back and forth from its nest down in the guts of the cavern where the rock was riddled with cracks and holes.

He began to stretch his power, to test its limits. He stared at the scuttling rat and, concentrating fiercely, made it freeze in mid-step. He made it turn, made it run backwards, made it spin like a child's top. Then he let it go deeper into the cavern, following it with his mind, and made it return to him day after day. Then he did the same to two rats. Three. Four. A dozen rats, spinning in circles before him while the other *vampir* looked on in amazement. He laughed and clapped his hands because now it was becoming effortless. He could feel his will build upon itself, like the dark stones of his father's castle piled one on top of another. Soon a hundred rats danced for him, chittering and squeaking in mindless ecstasy. When he could bring three hundred rats out of the cavern's bowels and control them with a mere squint of his mind, he sent his army out into the mountains.

The rats found it a simple task to squeeze through the holes and cracks in the walls of Castle Vulkan. It took less than a week for the plague to follow. Prince Vulkan could stand on a hillock, hidden by the forest, and see the dark plumes of smoke rising from within the castle keep —bodies were being burned by the dozens. The deathwagon rattled in and out of the castle every night with its cargo of corpses. He could hear the screams and moans of the dying, and the death song brought a smile to his face. On a cold, snowy February night, while the doors were unbarred to let the deathwagon out, he led his *vampir* army into the castle. They met no resistance.

Prince Vulkan opened his eyes. Again he'd felt a cold breath stirring at the back of his neck.

A bow sobbed across violin strings. The music echoed like a wail through the chamber.

Vulkan turned his head and saw the Headmaster stand-

ing before the fire, holding a bone-white violin beneath
its chin; a gnarled claw gripped the bow with cunning
delicacy. The Headmaster's eyes burned low, as deceptively cool as the last embers of the fire. The music went
on for a few minutes more and ended with a low growl
that sent vibrations shivering through the prince.

"My pupil, my favorite," the Headmaster said. "Your
army grows. How many?"

"More than sixhundredthousand." Vulkan replied.

"Ah, good. Very good. But we must have more, Conrad. And quickly. You recall our agreement: In return
for my services you must hand this city over to me on
All-Hallow's Eve. That time approaches quickly, Conrad.
I expect eight million in my service as my due by tomorrow midnight."

"We double in strength every night. How can I give
you that many?"

The Headmaster's teeth flashed. "An orgy of hunger,
Conrad. A celebration of power unlike any the world has
ever seen. Let them gorge and throw up and gorge again,
like a vast Roman orgy. Let them run wild and take as
many victims as they can. I've observed how you saw
fit to deal with the problem of your servant Roach. That
may have been less than wise, Conrad. You forget the
power of the media, and you also forget that special element that blinds the human race to your existence, their
dogged determination—no, let's call it hope—that your
kind doesn't exist. The element of surprise and confusion
may soon be gone. We have to act now, in accord." The
Headmaster's eyes closed for a few seconds. When they
reopened, they were as bright as blast furnaces, and the
prince could hardly stand to look at them for fear of
dwindling to a cinder.

"I hunger for souls, Conrad. I hunger . . ." The Headmaster held the white violin in its hands and very slowly
crumpled it into a ball as if it were paper. The claws
clapped shut. Vulkan stared, seeing something begin to
glow yellow-orange between the Headmaster's hands. The
Headmaster opened its hands as slowly as it had crushed
the violin. Something was taking shape between them,
glowing golden. When the brightness dimmed, the prince
saw it was a gold urn about two feet high, filled to the top
with coarse sand. "I give you this gift," the Headmaster

said softly and held the urn out to Vulkan. It radiated heat. "Take up a handful of sand."

The prince hesitated only a second, then scooped up some sand. It burned in his palm.

"Drop it back in," the Headmaster said. Vulkan did so, and the Headmaster leaned forward, blowing softly on the falling column of sand. It began to writhe, slowly at first, but rapidly gaining speed. The column stood upright, about six inches high like a small cyclone. Vulkan thought he could hear the distant shrieking of wind.

The Headmaster stepped past Prince Vulkan and set the urn at the center of the table. "Our powers are united. No one is to disturb this in any way, Conrad. Do you understand?"

He nodded.

"Good. The sun's graying the sky to the east; soon you'll sleep. Rest well and easy. When you awaken, you'll see that my gift has brought you the ability to move at will with your entire army throughout the whole of this city. And the humans will be powerless to run, powerless to escape in their cars or planes or boats. So sleep well, Conrad, there'll be much work for you when you awaken." The Headmaster stared at the urn again, grinned, and then began to fade away. The last thing to disappear was the terrible, fanged grin. Then it, too, was gone.

Prince Vulkan looked at the golden urn. The sand was twisting with more force now, a corkscrew of power. The cry of distant wind sounded like the droning of an insect, greedy and voracious.

The fire was almost cold now. Outside the hateful sun would be climbing the eastern peaks of the San Gabriel Mountains. It was time to rest, to plan, to prepare for the next night.

And oh, he thought, *oh, what a night that will be!*

FOUR

Palatazin awakened to the sound of something creaking. At least he thought he was awake because he could see the ceiling and feel Jo pressed against him. He'd been dreaming of a shadowy forest where hands seemed to snake out of the underbrush to grasp at him. The trees bent over from both sides, making the pathway ahead look like a narrow tunnel walled with thorns and brush. Pallid faces grinned, floating in the foliage like balloons from a Satanic carnival. Jo was with him, and they were running headlong through the tunnel when something hulking and monstrous stepped into their path, reaching out to welcome them with hooked claws.

And now he knew he was awake, and something was creaking softly in his bedroom.

He reached out for the lamp switch. The creaking stopped immediately. Palatazin later regretted not turning on the light, but instead he turned his head and peered into the darkness.

His mother was sitting in her rocking chair again, watching him; her face bore a stern, grim expression that reminded him of the times when she got so angry if he dared creep back into bed for a few extra moments of sleep before getting dressed for school. *Sleepyhead!* she'd chide, wrenching all the covers off the bed. And then, clapping her hands with the noise of righteous thunder: *Get up! Get up! Get up!* He didn't realize until later how she'd equated sleeping with death.

Palatazin stared at the figure in the chair. Her eyes were frightened but determined, too. They were the eyes of the woman who'd fired a shotgun at the unholy thing that wore her husband's flesh like a suit of clothes. She rose from the chair, and Palatazin could see the window— with its spray-painted cross at the center—through her form. She motioned to him, *Get up, sleepyhead!* He was frozen with wonder for a few seconds, but then he carefully rolled out of bed so as not to disturb Jo. She murmured something in her sleep, stirred slightly, and then was quiet.

His mother motioned him closer. He took a step forward; he could see the deep lines around her mouth and eyes as if they were superimposed on the wall. Then she turned and pointed past his shoulder. He looked and saw she was pointing toward the closet door. He glanced between her face and the closet, not knowing what she meant. Her face was clouded with despair, her mouth working but no sound coming out. Then, abruptly, she stepped past him—he felt a breath of air, and for a second he smelled the childhood aromas of cookies baking, the breeze through a stand of pines, a coat Papa had bought her in Budapest—and then she walked right into the closet *through* the closed door.

Like smoke that has whirled through an open window, she was gone.

Palatazin found himself unable to move for a moment. He realized he'd been holding his breath, and now he let it all out. He turned, switched on the bedside lamp and went to the closet.

"Andy! What is it?" Jo was sitting up in bed, her face as white as the sheets that were bunched around her.

"It's all right," he said, and heard his voice shake. "It's nothing." But no, he knew it was *something*. His mother had been trying to speak to him through the barrier between life and death, and he knew the message was of vital importance. He gripped the doorknob, turned it, and pulled open the closet door.

He didn't know what he'd expected to find—his mother's spirit standing in there, perhaps, staring at him through the clothes? The closet all torn up as if a violent storm had whipped through the walls?

But there was nothing. The clothes were undisturbed. On the top shelf cardboard boxes were stacked up just as they always had been.

"What is it?" Jo asked. "What are you looking for?"

"I . . . don't know," he told her. *What's in here? What is it that's important enough to disturb my mother's rest?*

"It's getting light outside," Jo said. "Can't you sleep?"

"No." He pushed the clothes back and forth for a moment, even felt the wall behind them. *What am I looking for? A secret passage in my own house?* He reached up to the shelf and moved a couple of the boxes around. Jo's skeins of wool and knitting materials were in one, some old shoes he'd even forgotten he'd had in another. There were some sweaters packed in mothballs. He was putting the boxes back when he saw the glint of rusted metal in the far corner behind a box he used to store his gun and holster.

The metal box his mother had saved all her newspaper clippings in. The box that had been at her bedside when she'd died.

Palatazin lifted it down from the shelf. "Andy . . ." Jo began to protest, but she was instantly quiet when she saw how tight his face had become and how his eyes had begun to shine with what looked like to her a maniacal fascination. She watched in silence as he sat on the bed, opened the old metal box, and began to look through the clippings, some of them so yellowed they were barely legible. She could see some of the headlines—Prominent College Prof Says Vampires Do Exist; What Strange Force Turned Lizbethville Into A Ghost Town?; Fourth Cow Found Killed By Vandals; Linc McRae, Powhatan Civic Leader, Still On Missing Persons List; Bats Plague Midwestern Town For Third Day. Most of them were cut from the *National Enquirer*, *Midnight*, *The Star*, and *Fate* magazine, but there were dozens clipped from the pages of the *Times*, the *Herald-Examiner*, a host of smaller L.A. papers, and whatever out-of-state papers Andy's mother could get her hands on. At one time her room in this house had been filled with old magazines and newspapers, and there were boxes stacked tall with them down in the basement. The silverfish had started coming in droves, and Jo had demanded that the papers go immediately. Andy had hauled them away but only to make room for the next batch his mother had begun saving. Jo had gone half-crazy trying to keep the place clean, always vacuuming and dusting and picking up scraps of newspapers. It had been the worst just before she'd gone into Golden Gardens.

Palatazin turned the box upside down, dumping all the clippings out in a thick pile.

"What are you doing?" Jo gasped. "You'll get the sheets dirty!"

He paid no attention to her. He began reading the clippings one by one. The first was ragged and yellow and bore the headline: Crate Filled With Dirt Found In NYC Hotel Room. The story from the *New York Times* was only two graphs long but went on to say that police had found the imprint of a human body on top of the dirt and speculated that it had served as some kind of strange, makeshift casket. The next item was also from the *Times* and was headed Rash Of Disappearances Continues—ConEd Exec Latest Missing.

Palatazin picked up the next yellowed item, a small squib with the headline Bats In NYC Subways? A workman inspecting a section of track had seen something large and black down there, clinging to a wall like a bat with enfolded wings. When the man had shined his flashlight, the thing had screeched and come swooping toward him, but he'd run like hell to the nearest platform. One of the man's quotes intrigued Palatazin—"Mr. Luftek told police, 'If it was a bat, it was one the size of a man! It'll be a cold day in hell before I go back down in that tunnel!'" Palatazin went through the next few stories, all about disappearances and prowlers in the New York City area, and found one that chilled his blood—Historic Cemetery Vandalized. It was dated August 24, 1948, and the cemetery was located near Martha's Furnace, Pennsylvania. There were more clippings of people missing, animals found drained of blood, most of them in the Pittsburgh area. Another cemetery was vandalized near Canton, Ohio. The town of Paulinwood, Indiana, had to be evacuated because of a siege of rats and flies. A banker and his family were missing from their home in Mt. Carmel, Illinois, and his neighbors were frightened because they'd heard insane laughter in the middle of the night. In May of 1950 the townspeople of Dean's Field, Illinois, vanished overnight; food was still on the table in farmhouse kitchens, sheets were turned down in beds that would never be slept in again, lights were on, and doors unlocked; the only sign of "foul play" were several shattered mirrors. The next few clippings concerned similar events in Missouri.

"My God," Palatazin said softly. "They've been moving westward all this time."

"What?" Jo's brow was furrowed deeply. She rose from the bed and put on her robe. "Do you want some coffee?"

He looked up at her, blinking heavy-lidded eyes. "My mother knew. All these years she knew they were slowly moving west. My God! She knew and had to keep silent because no one would believe . . ." He quickly turned through the rest of the clippings his mother had saved just before she died. The last one was an *Enquirer* article about a man in Caborca, Mexico, who'd murdered three women with a hatchet and drank their blood because, he told the police, he'd felt possessed by a *vampiro*.

"I'll make coffee," Jo said. "Do you want yours the usual way? Black with sugar and nails?"

"Yeah, fine," he said. She grunted, rolled her eyes and went out the bedroom door. He went back to his reading. There was an item from the L.A. *Times with the headline*

No Bats In Reno? Don't Gamble On It! The pilot of a
Delta jet, circling for a landing at Reno International,
had suddenly picked up a huge mass on his radar, closing in fast. The control tower had advised him to drop a
couple of hundred feet, and as the pilot started down, the
jet was engulfed by a cloud of bats heading westward.
Luckily none were sucked into the jet intakes, and the
pilot was able to bring his plane in. "Must've been hundreds of the things," the pilot said when he got his feet
firmly on the ground.

Do the bats precede the vampires, Palatazin wondered, *or do they follow?* In either case, their presence
had meant something to his mother in the days just before her death. He picked up the next item and saw with
some amazement that it was a Rona Barrett column
dated September 3. He read, ". . . a major Hollywood
studio is searching for a successor to the late JOHN
WAYNE in a planned remake of the Duke's classic *Red
River*. Mentioned most often are *Dallas* big daddy JIM
DAVIS and new face CLAY SANDERS. Watch for
CLAY in the new Paramount film *The Long Haul* . . .
for the fans who asked, JANE DUNNE is alive and well
and living in Beverly Hills. She'll be interviewed by this
reporter on an upcoming ABC special . . . more royalty's
moving to Hollywood. It's all very hush-hush, but rumor
has it that a European prince, no less, will soon be re-
modeling the Hollywood Hills castle that once belonged
to horror-film star ORLON KRONSTEEN . . . wedding
bells may soon be tolling for JOHN TRAVOLTA. The
lucky girl's name is still a secret, but this reporter hears
the church bells ringing on Christmas Day . . ." His
eyes snapped back to the reference to Orlon Kronsteen.
He'd worked briefly on that case about ten or eleven
years ago. He'd never seen the decapitated corpse, but
he'd seen the expressions of a couple of the officers who
had. Their faces were pale, and their lips drawn up into
grim, gray lines. That case had never been solved, he recalled. But what bothered him about those lines of type
were the two words *European prince*. Those were the
words, he was certain, that had caught his mother's attention. If this prince were the vampire king he sought, the
castle would be a perfect refuge, hidden away in the hills
and probably high enough to be a strategic observation
point as well. And now he recalled how the Roach had

stared up into those hills and begged his master for help.

His blood went cold.

Yes, he told himself. *This is what my mother wanted me to find.*

And now another question racked him—was this the same European prince and/or vampire king who had conquered the village of Krajeck on a stormy winter night so long ago? Was this the same creature who had taken his father?

He put the clippings back in the box and snapped the lid down. Rising from the bed, he stepped to the window and looked down on Romaine Street. The earth was still layered with blue shadows. The sky was a dull, slate gray, but he could see the faint pink light coming up in the east. There was a bitter, coppery taste in his mouth— the taste of utter dread at what had to be done. His fingers clamped on the windowsill; the black-painted crucifix was centered in his vision and seemed to be burned across his face. Terror writhed in his stomach. "I can't do it alone," he heard himself whisper. "Not that. I can't."

But then who will?

"I can't." He shook his head, his lower lip trembling. He would have to go to that crumbling old castle and find the vampire king to drive an ash stake through the thing's heart and sever the head from the body, then do the same to as many others as he could find. He would have to set the bodies on fire or drag them out to let the sun bake them into dust. God help him if he was caught up there when the sun went down.

He remembered his father's face, streaked with orange light from the hearth. Those gleaming, terrible eyes. Remembered the shotgun blasts and the hideous thing—not Papa anymore—that rose from the floor, its face ripped away and the long, glistening fangs exposed.

"I can't," he said to his reflection in the glass.

Then who will?

He didn't hear Jo call him from downstairs, finally yelling in exasperation, "You don't want coffee? You won't get coffee!"

Oh, God, why me? And then he answered the question himself. Because you know them. Because you ran from them once, never knowing they were following, day after day, year after year, all across the United States. And now they are here, and there is nowhere else to run.

If you don't do it, what will happen to this city? To the millions of people, all of them unaware? Los Angeles would eventually fall, just as Krajeck had fallen, and a tidal wave of vampires would move eastward across America, possibly to link up with other isolated pockets of vampires that awaited their coming. The entire world would lie before them, before their ravenous thirst.

In the window's glass his face looked thirty years older. His remaining hair seemed to have gone white all at once, like a man who has had a nightmare of grinning Death slowly stalking closer.

There was much to be done, and it had to be finished before dusk. But he knew he couldn't do it alone, and he was going to have to have protection. The taste of fear in his mouth was acrid.

Across the street and one house down, he saw a German shepherd settling itself on a front porch. He hadn't realized that the Zemkes had bought a watchdog. *Good luck to you,* he mentally told the sleeping family in that house. *You'll need every bit of it and more.*

He turned away from the window and began to dress hurriedly.

FIVE

"Blackberry brandy," the old woman in the wheelchair offered as she poured from a crystal decanter into three tulip-shaped glasses. There had been four in the set, but the fourth now lay in shards on the hardwood floor. "One hundred proof," she promised, winking at Wes. "Knock the fear of Satan right out of you. Here."

Wes handed one glass to Solange and sipped from the other one. His mouth instantly flamed, and he could feel the liquor spiraling down into his stomach where it seethed for a moment like lava. He drank down the rest of it, squeezed the tears from his eyes, and held the glass out again. "More," he said.

Jane Dunne smiled, the lines across her heart-shaped face deepening, but there was a center of cold fear in her brown eyes that refused to thaw. "Sure you can handle it, kiddo?" He nodded, and she poured again.

Solange stood on the other side of the wrecked room and drew aside a heavy, wine-red curtain to look out onto the lawn. The first trace of new light hovered in the sky. "The sun's coming up," she said softly. "It'll be daylight soon."

"Thank God," Wes breathed. "Any of them still out there?"

"No. At least I can't see any."

He came over beside her and peered out. The boulevard was deserted, the houses dark. Nothing moved. "I think they've gone. They can't stand light, can they?"

"I wouldn't be so sure about that, kiddo," Jane said, turning her wheelchair around to face them. She drank down her third glass of brandy. "I wouldn't be so sure of anything in this screwed-up world anymore."

Wes stepped away from the window and eased himself into an overstuffed, antique chair with one broken arm. A single candle burned on a coffee table beside him. Over near the door a grandfather clock had been thrown over on its side; the hands, frozen behind shattered glass, had stopped at ten minutes after one. Wes put his glass aside and wiped a cold sheen of sweat from his forehead. "We've got to find Jimmy," he said suddenly, looking up at Solange. She stared at him without speaking for a few seconds, then turned back to the window. "We've got to get the cops," he insisted. "We've got to get *somebody!*"

"When the sun rises," Solange said. "Not before."

"So you put two of the bastards in the swimming pool, did you?" The old woman let out a high-pitched cackle of glee. "Hot damn! I was about to drain the thing, too! Hope they weren't wearing their Mae Wests . . ." She laughed again and then stared into her glass. Her smile quickly faded, leaving her eyes dark and hopeless. She muttered softly and reached for the rapidly emptying decanter.

"The thing I can't understand," Wes said quietly, "is why they didn't . . . uh . . . get you after they'd broken into the house."

"Because I live right, that's why. Plenty of Johnny Walker Red and blackberry brandy—that'll keep you young forever." She patted the useless sticks that lay beneath a blanket on her lap, then looked back up at Wes. "I saw their faces," she said. "Two of them, both just kids. The girl had a safety pin through her ear. Rock and rollers, I guess. I took one look at them and thought, 'This is it, Janie. You've gone through four marriages, a string of box-office bombs, one hell of a smashup on the Pacific Coast Highway, and here's the finale—a couple of dope-heads who are going to kill you in the middle of the night.' I thought they'd come to steal my tons of paste jewelry." She drank from her glass.

"Then the boy came toward me, and he . . . it . . . opened its mouth. I could . . . see . . . those teeth. Fangs, just like in the Dracula movies, except there were a couple on the lower jaw, too, and they just slid out like a rattlesnake's does when it's about to strike. God!" She shivered and said nothing more for a moment or so.

"Then he stopped right beside my bed. He seemed to be . . . sniffing the air. I think I saw myself reflected in his eyes, and I . . . I realized how close Death stood to me. Then they were gone, just like that. I didn't even see them leave. Of course, they'd screwed up the lights and the phones, and I had to wheel around in the dark not knowing whether I'd run into one of them or not. When I was downstairs, I heard all the shouting and commotion, so I hid in here. I thought you two were . . . you know . . . like they were until I heard you talking." She swirled the brandy around her glass and drank it down. "I think what saved me is that I . . . smelled *old*. I'll be seventy-five in May and with busted gams to boot. I think they wanted younger blood."

"They got my friend," Wes said, glancing at Solange and then quickly away. "Christ, how many of the things are there? And where did they come from?"

"Hell, kiddo," Jane said. "Straight out of old Satan's black bag of tricks. I thought I'd seen everything this world had to offer up, but I see now I was way wrong."

Solange had gone cold. If there were vampires stalking the streets of Bel Air and Beverly Hills, too, and if there were so many that they could organize themselves to hunt humans at the scenes of traffic accidents, then there must be—and she shivered to think of the possibility—hundreds of them. Outside the light was slowly growing brighter, but there were still huge pools of shadow lying in wait like treacherous oil slicks. Or tar babies. She recalled the stories her father used to tell her—*Lemme go, Br'er Rabbit, lemme go!* Somehow her life had slipped away from

that bright childhood, and now she walked the dark side
of the moon.

". . . seen you on the tube," Jane was saying to Wes.
"That show you've got. You're pretty good."

He nodded, his shoulders slumped forward. "Thanks,"
he said, his mind sheered away from the image of Jimmy
screaming in agony, being pulled from that crumpled
car by a grinning vampire.

"Yeah, pretty good." She smiled, her eyes beginning
to glaze over now. "Not *great*, mind you. Jack Benny
was *great*. But you'll do. PBS ran a special on me last
month, showed clips from some of my hits. You catch it?"

Wes shook his head.

"Too bad. You know what they called me? America's
Girl Friend. I was wearing sweaters before Lana Turner
was even a gleam in her daddy's eye. I had good boobs,
too. Oh, Jesus." She looked over at Solange, where the
gray light was slipping in around the curtains. "Those
were the days. High noon, that's what I called it." She
returned her gaze to Wes, who was sitting slumped over
with his face in his hands. "High noon. You better enjoy
it while you can, kiddo. When that sun starts going down,
it can get mighty cold."

"There's a police car!" Solange said, and Wes's head
jerked up. He hurried to the window and looked out. The
prowl car was slowing, probably to investigate the smashed
cars on the curve of the boulevard. Wes ran out of the
room, unlocked the front door, and ran onto the lawn,
waving his arms. "Hey! Stop! Hey!"

The car slid to the curb. Two officers got out, one of
them dropping his hand to his holster as Wes came running down the driveway, shouting like a maniac. As Wes
neared the car, he abruptly froze. In the dingy light he'd
thought he might have seen the glitter of fangs. *Oh God*,
he thought, *not the cops, too!*

They came around the car, and Wes took a few steps
backward.

"He's scared shitless," one said to the other. Then to
Wes, "What the hell's been going on here, buddy?"

Solange stood in the doorway, watching as Wes began
talking to the officers, motioning with his hands. *How
defenseless he looks*, she thought. *How small . . .*

Jane wheeled up behind her. "What now, kiddo?"

"I don't know." Solange looked at the old woman over

her shoulder. "There are more of them. Many more. I think that soon they'll be all over this city."

"Does he think the cops are going to believe him?" she asked. "Do you really think anybody's going to believe any of us?"

"I don't know."

"Well, I wouldn't have believed it myself if I hadn't seen two of them. I may be a little on the senile side, but I sure as hell ain't crazy. Not yet, at least. But I will be if I stick around here." She turned the chair and started to wheel toward the elevator.

"Where are you going?" Solange asked her.

"To pack. Next stop, LAX. Like I say, I may be old, but I'm not crazy. Not by a long shot." She reached the elevator and closed the cage behind her.

"Good luck," Solange called after her, but the elevator had already started to rise. Solange left the house and began to walk down the driveway to Wes and the two policemen. A sudden cold breeze came at her, hitting her diagonally and rolling over like a great invisible wave. Something sharp speckled her cheek. She brushed it away with her fingers, then looked down at the bits of grit clinging to her skin.

Sand.

She walked down to where they were standing, the two officers staring incredulously at Wes. A great feeling of dread had suddenly leeched onto her back and seemed to be weighing her down with every step. The sun was coming up out of a red slash across the sky, but the sky itself seemed wicked—a patchwork of clouds that looked as thick as slate-gray bricks veined with purple. They were scudding fast, being driven westward over the sea. As Solange watched, she saw a cloud split apart by a cross-current of winds; its interior glowed red with reflected sunlight, like hot coals stirred by a demonic breath. When she reached Wes, she grasped his hand tightly, afraid to let go.

SIX

The telephone was ringing. Gayle Clarke, her eyes shadowed by sleeplessness, came out of her kitchen with a cup of Morning Thunder tea and stared down at the little black bastard on the telephone table. She was wearing a dirty pair of jeans—which she'd slept in—and a ragged workshirt she'd had since she was a high school sophomore. Her face was swollen, her entire body sluggish from the dangerous mixture of Valiums, liquor, tea, and coffee that she'd been putting away since that night at the Sandalwood Apartments. She couldn't seem to sleep, and then when she finally did, she couldn't wake up. She'd been walking around in a daze since she'd left the police station—kicked out rather, by a very irate lieutenant—and had even started taking 'ludes again. Now she kept all her curtains and blinds drawn, the door securely bolted with a chair next to it, ready to be used as a barricade. *This is what cracking up feels like,* she told herself repeatedly, but she didn't care. If Jack's hideous face hadn't sent her over the edge immediately, the recurrent nightmares of him chasing her across the apartment courtyard eventually would. She'd lost track of time. The kitchen clock said it was ten-twenty-five, but with the windows shrouded she had no idea whether it was night or day. The ringing telephone told her it was morning, and it would be Trace on the other end, wanting to know where she was for the second day in a row and why she wasn't working on the fucking Gravedigger story.

"Shut up," she said to the phone. "Just shut up and leave me alone." *Is this what cracking up feels like?* she wondered. *Not giving a shit about anything?*

The phone kept shrilling, like the nagging voices of her parents—Gayle, why don't you dress better? Gayle, why aren't you making more money? Gayle, you should be thinking about marriage. Gayle, Gayle, Gayle. . . .

"SHUT UP!" she said and lifted the receiver to slam it down again. *There. That fixes you, you bastard!* She walked over to a window, pulled aside the curtains and looked out. The sunlight was weak, hidden behind a

315

strange, violet pallor, but strong enough to sting her eyes. She dropped the curtains back and decided she was going to have to go outside today; she'd be okay in the daytime, the things couldn't move around when it was light. Or could they? *A 'lude,* she told herself. *That's what I need.*

She was heading for the medicine cabinet when the phone started ringing again. "DAMN IT!" she shouted, looking for something to throw at the thing. *Okay,* she thought. *Calm down. Calm down.* She was afraid of that phone. Last night—*or was it last night?* she couldn't remember exactly when—she'd picked up that receiver, said "Hello?" and had been treated to a long silence that was finally broken by a voice speaking a single word, *"Gayle?"* She'd slammed it down and screamed because it had sounded too much like Jack's voice, calling to find out if she was home so he could come pay her a nice, friendly visit, fangs and all.

Calm down.

If it was Trace, she knew he'd keep calling until she answered. She'd tell him she was sick, that she couldn't leave her apartment. She picked it up and said in a trembling voice, "Yes?"

There were a few seconds of silence. Gayle could hear her heart pounding. Then a familiar voice said, "Miss Clarke? I'd like to see you . . ."

"Who is this?"

"Andy Palatazin. Captain Palatazin, from Parker Center."

"What is it? What do you want?" *Calm down. You sound fucking frantic.*

He paused and then went on, "I need your help. It's very important that I see you as soon as possible."

"My help? Why? How did you find me?"

"I called the *Tattler.* A man there gave me your number. I need your help because . . . I'd rather not talk about this over the phone."

"I'd rather you did."

He sighed heavily. "Yes. All right. I'd like to tell you a story, and I'm hoping you'll believe it enough to write about it in your newspaper . . ."

"Why? I thought you called the *Tattler* a rag." She sipped her tea and waited for him to speak again.

"I can tell you who the Gravedigger is, Miss Clarke,"

Palatazin said. "I can tell you why those graves are being torn up. I can tell you all that and much, much more."

"Yeah? Well, I'm retired. I'm thinking about driving up to San Francisco for a while . . ."

"LISTEN TO ME!" he said so furiously Gayle jumped. She was tempted to hang up on him, but there was a pleading note in his voice that held her attention. "Yours is the only paper in this city that would even consider printing the story I'm going to tell you! And by printing it, you could save lives, Miss Clarke. Possibly millions of lives! I thought you told me you were a journalist. You said you were a good one, and I believed you. Was I wrong?"

"Maybe you were."

"Perhaps. But were *you?*"

She gripped the receiver. Her knuckles were white. She wanted to tell him to go to hell; she wanted to tell him to go over to the Sandalwood Apartments and help the other stumble-bum cops look for about twenty-five tenants who'd vanished overnight. Instead, she heard herself ask, "What kind of story is it?"

"One that you'll have to have courage to write. I think you have it, Miss Clarke. That's why I called you."

"Cut the bullshit," she said irritably. "Where are you? Parker Center?"

"No, I'm . . . at home." He gave her the address. "When can you be here?"

"I don't know. I . . . whenever I get there, I guess." .

"All right. That'll have to do. I'll be here all afternoon."

"Good-bye." As she was hanging up, she heard him say "Thank you." And his voice was so full of relief and real gratitude that she was momentarily stunned. The line went dead, and she slowly put the receiver down.

She drank the rest of her tea and went into the bathroom. Her face in the mirror looked awful. She opened the medicine cabinet and took out a small yellow bottle. There were three Quaaludes rattling around at the bottom. She shook one out into her hand and lifted it to her mouth; her hand was shaking, and she had to grasp her wrist to hold it steady. *Is this what cracking up feels like? Who said that?* She looked down at the pill. *No,* she told herself. *If I'm going to get back to work, I've got to stay straight.* She looked at the pill longingly for a while, then dropped it back into the bottle.

She turned on the cold water tap in the shower, undressed, stepped in before she could reconsider, and stuck her head beneath the torrent.

SEVEN

At twelve noon Bob Lampley stood next to the Hell's Hole Hilton and watched the sky. On top of the Hilton, enclosed by a chain-link fence, a great radar cup turned smoothly on its tower. In the space of a half-minute, a metal wind-direction indicator twirled, first due west, then west-northwest, due north, back to northwest, then slowly returned to due west where it hung steady. The winds swirled around Lampley as hot as the breath of a blast furnace. Every so often he felt the sting of sand on his face or hands, and his scalp itched. Thermals were coming up from the Mojave Desert, the strongest winds bringing sand with them. *That's odd as hell,* Lampley thought. *That's one for the record books, I guess.*

The Hell's Hole Hilton was a wood-framed weather station 5,012 feet up on Old Baldy about twenty-five miles from the heart of L.A. and sixty miles from what Lampley considered the fiercest place God ever created —the hot, sand-choked throat of the Devil's Playground at the center of the Mojave Desert. He'd tried to hike across that monstrous place a few years ago with some friends who were as crazy as he was. They'd wound up scorched to the bone, babbling with sunfever, packed into a Jeep racing toward a case of cold Coors in Ludlow.

But the weird thing about this new weather picture was that the sand was being blown such a long way. The weather station at Twenty-nine Palms had reported some strong winds this morning centered between the Cady and Providence Mountain ranges in the Playground, but any loose sand should've been caught miles back by the peaks that stood between the San Bernardino National Forest and the desert. If the winds were strong enough and high enough to carry the sand over those mountains, then by all the rules of weather forecasting they should

lose strength dramatically the further they got from the
center of strongest activity and dump the sand at the lip
of the forest. That wasn't happening, and this new change
in the rules was beginning to bother him. The hot winds
were melting snowcaps for miles in all directions, the
wind-direction indicator seemed to point due west most
of the time when it wasn't spinning around crazily to
show the progress of a sudden corkscrew, and Lampley
was getting sand in his face 5,000 feet up.

Won't do, he thought. *Nope. Won't do at all.*

Directly overhead the sun shone weakly through
chinks in cirrus clouds as thick and gray as an iguana's
hide. Those clouds were racing, tumbling over each other
in what seemed to Lampley like frantic haste away from
the storm center. And there it was—he'd finally allowed
the thought that had been lurking at the back of his brain
to come forward—a hideous pupil allowed to sit in the
front row. Storm center. *What storm?* he asked himself.
*Some high desert winds in the Playground sure as hell
don't constitute a storm, Lampley. You're thinking in
terms of tornado or a dust-devil, and neither of those
can be right. There's a pretty slim chance of a tornado,
and if this is a dust-devil forming, it's got to be the biggest
bastard of a dust-devil that ever spun out of a whirlwind.*

Okay, he thought. *How about a plain old sandstorm?*
They happen all the time, kicked out of the Mojave
Desert by two or more pressure ridges that meet and
don't like each other, stomping around trying to get out
of one another's way. The Mojave, like all the world's
deserts, crept. It already covered roughly 25,000 square
miles of southern California and still wanted more. Every
few years it lapped up to the back doors of some nearby
town, as slowly and innocently as a golden dog who
wouldn't bite you, not for anything in the world. But then
when the forty-five- and fifty-mile-an-hour winds came
screaming out of that furnace—always quite unexpectedly
—the golden dog turned into a ravenous beast who slithered over sandbag barricades and brick walls to leave its
shifting spoor.

Can't be a sandstorm, Lampley told himself. *There's
supposed to be a high pressure ridge sitting astride California and six other states in a slow eastward sweep, supposed to be clear skies with moderate westerly winds until
Monday.* And no storm that Lampley had ever heard of

or read about in his six years with the National Weather Service had ever shot tendrils of sand so high. It was as if the Mojave had decided it was better to leap than to creep.

Lampley watched the sky for a moment more and then walked up a slight grade to the Hilton. The place was weather-beaten outside and looked as old as the surrounding mountains, but inside it was quite comfortable with a woven, red and brown Indian rug on the floor, a couple of castoff but good chairs around a wood-burning heater, which was not needed now since the temperature up here had risen to the low sixties. There was a desk and a bookcase with dog-eared paperbacks set before a window that afforded a westerly view of the Mount Baldy winter sports area and Silverwood Lake. On the other side of the window was a battery of electronic equipment—wind-speed indicators, pressure gauges, and a radar screen that now showed the soupy, green clumps of the cloud masses moving overhead. A black telephone sat on the desk next to a photograph of Lampley's wife, Bonnie, and their two-year-old son, Chad. On the wall over a teletype machine, there was a red phone hooked up directly to National Weather in L.A.

Lampley sat down at his desk and dialed Twentynine Palms Weather on the black phone. In the distance he could see a ranger tower that looked like a spindly War of the Worlds Martian machine. "Hal?" he said when the phone was picked up about forty-five miles away. "This is Bob up at the Hilton. What are you showing down there?"

Hal's voice was weakened not only by the distance but also by the strange weather. "Still got some high winds on the Play . . . *crackle squeal* . . . Bob. Wait a sec. Let me check the figures. Okay. West and southwesterly . . . *squealllll* . . . from thirty to forty miles per hour, gusting to forty-five. Air pressure's dropped from . . . *crackle-crackle* . . . in the last ninety minutes. What do you have up there?"

"Cloud city," Lampley said. "Pressure's still hanging steady, though. I'm picking up some kind of electrical interference on this end, so you'll have to speak louder."

"What?" Hal said. "I didn't . . . all of that . . ."

"Talk louder!" he said. "I don't understand what's going on. Did a pressure drop creep in on us or what?"

"Not from Canada it didn't. Funny. Vegas weather . . . clear and sunny, high in the mid-eighties . . ."

"So whatever's happening is right over the Mojave?"

"Sorry . . . didn't hear . . ."

"I guess we've got a bad connection. Listen, I'll call you back around two. If those winds build anymore, give me a call."

"Sure thing. Talk . . . later . . ."

Lampley hung up and looked at the red phone on the wall. He'd feel like a fool calling L.A. National about some desert winds, no matter how hard they were gusting. *So it was an infant sandstorm, so what? LAX Weather would keep the planes out of trouble, and the mountains would take the brunt of the winds. Sooner or later the storm would spin itself out.*

But what if it doesn't? What if this bastard gets so big and wild it whirls all the way across the mountains and into L.A.?

Impossible, he reassured himself. *Los Angeles might get a little grit, but they needed the winds to blow off their smog cover anyway. Nothing to worry about.*

He stared at that phone for a few seconds more, looked out the window at the lizard-hide sky, and returned to the Mike Shayne mystery he'd been reading before he'd heard the grate of sand against glass.

EIGHT

Gayle Clarke pulled her Mustang up to the curb on Romaine Street and stared at the house with the black crucifix painted on the front door. There was a word written underneath it in a foreign language. Some of the windows were painted with crosses, too—the house looked like some kind of weird church. She glanced at the mailbox: Palatazin. Reluctantly she got out of her car and walked up the porch steps to the door. The black paint was new; she could see where it had dripped. She knocked on the door and waited.

It was almost one o'clock. It had taken her two hours to get out of her apartment, then she'd driven over to Pancho's and forced herself to eat two tacos before driv-

ing up through Hollywood. She wore clean denims and a
light blue blouse; her face was scrubbed and, if not exactly infused with a pink glow, much healthier-looking
than it had been this morning. There was still a glassy,
shocked look in her eyes that wouldn't go away. Behind
her, wind swirled through the trees and hedges along Romaine, making a noise like barely restrained laughter.

The door opened, and Palatazin looked out at her. He
nodded and without a word stepped back to allow her in.
He was wearing gray slacks and a white pullover shirt
that showed his belly in its full splendor; he looked oddly
vulnerable, just another human being when not seen from
the other side of a captain's desk at Parker Center. His
eyes were dark and troubled, and when they locked with
hers, she felt the skin at the back of her neck prickle.

He closed the door, locked it, and motioned toward the
sofa. "Please sit down. Can I get you something to drink?
Coffee? Maybe a Coke?"

She could still taste the tacos, and now her stomach
was doing flipflops. "Uh . . . a Coke would be fine."

"All right. Just make yourself comfortable." He disappeared toward the rear of the house, and she sat looking
around, her purse in her lap. It seemed to be a cosy
house, much warmer than she would have thought. It
smelled vaguely of onions and potatoes; probably some
kind of foreign dish he favored, she guessed. There was a
rusted metal box on the coffee table in front of her.

"So you're Gayle Clarke," someone said, and Gayle
looked up into the icy eyes of a gray-haired woman who
stood gazing at her from across the room. She was pretty
with high, sharp cheekbones, but now the flesh was
stretched tight to give her face a hard, masklike appear-
ance. "You're the one who wrote such awful things about
my husband."

"I didn't write anything . . ."

"Are you denying your trashy paper said he ought to
be fired?" Her eyes flared.

"Maybe it did, but I don't write editorials."

"Oh. Of course you don't," Jo said with a bitter edge.
"Do you realize the strain you've put on my Andy? You
and all the rest of the filthy papers in this city?" She
came forward a few steps, and Gayle tensed. "Well, you
got what you wanted. You can be happy now." Her
lower lip was trembling, and now tears of anger were

beginning to dance in her eyes. "Why did you want to hurt him?" she said quietly. "He never did anything to you . . ."

"What's this?" Palatazin said, coming into the room with Gayle's drink. He looked at Jo in bewilderment, then at Gayle. "What's going on?"

"Nothing," Gayle said. "Your wife and I were just getting . . . acquainted."

He handed her the glass and picked up the morning *Times* from where it lay in a chair. "Have you seen this, Miss Clarke?"

"No." She took it from him and looked at the front page. The headline was about the Mid-East situation, the talks breaking down again. But another story just above the fold caught her eye. The headline said "Bats Kept Coming," Says Shaken Officer. There was a shorter kicker line above it, Six Die At Parker Center. "What's this?" she said, looking up at Palatazin.

"Read it." He sat down in the chair and folded his hands before him. "Those men who were killed were my friends." His eyes seemed almost black. "When you're finished with that, I'd like you to look through the clippings in that box on the table."

Gayle read the article, feeling Jo Palatazin's gaze burning into her skull. "This says a suspect in the Roach killings got away. Is that right?"

"Yes."

"A suspect? Or the Roach himself?"

"It was him," Palatazin said quietly.

"My God!" She looked up sharply. "What is this all about? What's with the crosses scrawled on your doors and windows?"

"In time," he said. "There's someone else coming to join us. He should be here soon."

"Who?"

"A priest from East L.A. named Silvera."

"A priest? What's this going to be, a confession?"

Jo said coldly, "I think you're the one who has sins to confess . . ."

"Please," Palatazin said and touched his wife's arm. "She's a guest in this house, and she was very kind to come."

Gayle opened the metal box. When she saw what the clippings were about, she felt as if she'd been kicked in the head. She looked through them for a few minutes, her hands beginning to tremble.

There was a knock at the door. Palatazin answered it, and Father Silvera stood there staring darkly at the crucifix painted on the front window. "Come in, Father," Palatazin said. When Silvera entered the house, he instantly caught the same odor Gayle had smelled. He recognized it as the aroma of garlic. Palatazin introduced Jo and Gayle, and Silvera sat down on the sofa.

"Thank you for coming, Father," Palatazin said. "I appreciate your driving all this distance. Can I get you a cup of coffee?"

"Yes, please. Cream and sugar."

"I'll get it," Jo said; she glared once more at Gayle before leaving the room.

"Did you bring what I asked, Father?" Palatazin asked quietly, leaning forward in his chair.

Silvera nodded and reached into his coat. He brought out something wrapped in white cloth and handed it to Palatazin. "Just as you asked," he said. "Now I'd like to know what you need it for, and why you called me since there are maybe thirty Catholic churches within a five-mile radius of this house."

Palatazin was stripping away the white cloth. Inside was a small, corked bottle holding about two ounces of clear liquid. "I called you," he said, "because I thought you would understand the . . . gravity of the situation. You were in that tenement building in East L.A. You saw the bodies being carried out. I hoped you'd . . ."

"I see," the priest said. "So that's what this is all about —your belief in vampires. That's why you've painted crosses on your doors and windows. That's why you felt you needed a vial of holy water. Mr. Palatazin, I don't wish to seem . . . condescending, but I'm afraid vampires should be the least of this city's concerns. I still don't know what was wrong with those people, but I'm sure it's strictly a medical question and not one of vampirism." He glanced at the girl beside him, who was going through some clippings from a metal box. Her eyes were glazed, and she didn't even seem to realize he was sitting there. *Did I break my gasoline budget for the week for this?* he asked himself.

"I suppose you've called Mercy Hospital to check on those people?"

"Yes, I have."

"Then let me tell you what you found out. Absolutely nothing. I called Mercy this morning, and I was shuffled around from doctor to doctor until a press relations man told me no information was being given out about these cases. Is that what you were told?"

"Roughly," Silvera said. "But what does that prove?"

"This is not a matter of proof!" Palatazin said, his face flushing with sudden anger. "This is a matter of *knowing!* I *know*, Father! I've spent my entire life in their shadow, and now that shadow has fallen over this city!"

Silvera nodded and rose to his feet. "If you'll excuse me, I have to get back to my parish."

"No! Wait, please! You can't stand there and tell me you didn't feel the presence of evil in that tenement! You're shutting your mind to it, Father! You don't want to believe because you know that if you do, you'll realize how nearly hopeless this situation is and that perhaps you're not strong enough to face it!"

Silvera looked at him sharply. "There are many evils in this world, Mr. Palatazin. The heroin pusher, the child-beater, the homicidal maniac, the killer . . . as you well know. I think we both have enough work to do without . . . inventing more evils." A chill suddenly rippled through him as he remembered the blood-written graffiti on the tenement walls and the strange, almost transparent eyelids of those stricken people. *Can you really—logically—explain those?* he asked himself.

Gayle was fixedly staring at Palatazin. She looked up at the priest. "Father," she said, "he's . . . he's right."

"What?"

"I've seen them. He's right. They do exist, and they're here in L.A." She told them about the Sandalwood Apartments, the figure squirming beneath the bed, the dark things in the courtyard, and her own narrow escape. When she had almost finished, her voice cracked like a thin pane of glass. "I was afraid," she said. "I was . . . scared to death, so I locked myself in my apartment, and I didn't want to come out. I think I knew it would just be a matter of time before they found me . . ." She looked up. Jo was standing behind her husband, holding a cup of coffee on a tray. Gayle's eyes were wide and fearful. "They *are* here," Gayle told the priest.

Silvera's mouth had tightened; he seemed to have aged

ten years in the last few minutes. He glanced over his shoulder through the window at his car. Wind stirred the trees across the street. How easy it would be to leave this house, get in the car, and drive back to East L.A., pretend he'd never heard any of this, pretend he hadn't walked into that tenement with its living corpses jammed under beds and in closets. Pretend this evil did not exist. Easy? No. He felt himself poised on the point of an irrevocable decision. Slowly he looked back into Palatazin's face.

"Sit down," the policeman said. "Please."

Silvera took the coffee from Jo and drank most of it down in one swallow, wishing it were laced with whiskey. Jo pulled a chair up close beside her husband and sat down, as did the priest.

"How could you be so sure?" Silvera asked. "How did you know?"

"Because my . . . father is one of them," Palatazin said with an effort. "No, not my father. What used to be my father. I was born in a village called Krajeck in northern Hungary. There the people recognize and fear the *vampir*. They don't fully understand how the *vampir* comes to be, or why God allows such an evil to walk the face of the earth, but they know enough to mark their houses with crucifixes and garlic. They know that Satan gives power and unholy life to the *vampir*, just as God gives life to all the good things of this world. The *vampir* can never be satisfied. They will forever be thirsty, not only for human blood but also for land. Possessions. Power. They want to rule the earth, and I'm afraid that if this city falls, they will be well on their way to amassing an army large enough to take it. I'm not talking about three or four or fifty or even a thousand vampires, Father. I'm talking about *millions* of them. If Los Angeles falls to them, they will have increased their army by more than *eight million*. And no country on earth can withstand a force like that. You ask me how I can be so sure? I was given the . . . opportunity to see them at work. I know their signs, their track. I see them on the move everywhere now, and very soon they'll attack in earnest, going from house to house, street to street, all across L.A. Krajeck fell to them when I was a child, and I've seen the same things happening here that prefaced that terrible night." He looked at Gayle. "That wave of vandalism in some of the cemeteries, for instance. The *vampir* needed those caskets in which to sleep, and they needed native soil. They must sleep secure from all sunlight when the transformation from corpse to living dead is complete . . ."

"Just a minute," Silvera interrupted. "What do you mean by 'transformation'?"

"The creatures we saw in that barrio tenement were neither corpses nor *vampir*," Palatazin said. "They'd been bitten and drained and protected from the light as much as possible, though in that transitory stage I don't think the sun is as painful to them as it is later. When the last of their humanity dies within them, they awaken. Some sooner than others, I think. And they awaken thirsty. When they drink their first blood . . . then they're complete." He glanced over at Gayle again, then back to the priest. "Somewhere in this city, somewhere close to their Master, they must be hiding by the hundreds. It would have to be somewhere secure from both sunlight and intruders. I think it's probably in an abandoned building . . . possibly a warehouse or factory. Someone would have to lock them away at dawn and return to let them out at dust . . ."

"A human?" Gayle asked.

"Yes. I don't know what part Roach—Walter Benefield —plays in this, but he could be the human pawn used by the *vampir* king."

"The king?" Silvera's eyes narrowed. "You mentioned something about a master. Is that the same thing?"

Palatazin nodded. "The vampires see their Master— their king or maker or whatever you choose to call it—as a kind of savior figure. He commands their respect and loyalty, and they will do whatever he says."

"All right," Silvera shrugged. "Supposing I believe all this about vampires and caskets and kings. How can you be so certain they're being commanded by *anyone*? Couldn't they exist without a leader?"

"This is simply my opinion," Palatazin said, "but I think they need a strong guiding hand, an intelligence to lead the collective body. If the vampire king is destroyed and there's no one able to take his place, the resulting confusion might cause them to fight among themselves or to make mistakes. They might stray too far from their hiding places, for instance, and the sun might catch them out in the open. I don't know. But I want you to think about this: If the vampires feed just once every night—creating others of their kind by totally draining them and instilling that terrible hunger—then they're doubling in number every twenty-four hours. Some of them may feed three or four times in a single night. Again, I don't know. I'm speaking from things I've read and from the legends of my homeland. But of one thing I am certain—if we hope to stop them, we must destroy the king."

There was a long moment of silence in which they could hear the wind hooting around the house. Gayle peered uneasily out the window at the scudding gray clouds.

"Destroy," Silvera whispered. His throat felt dry, and he couldn't think beyond the memory of that graffiti in the alleyway just outside his window—Follow The Master. "How?"

"I'm not sure," Palatazin said grimly. "I can only suggest the methods used in Hungary, stakes and decapitation. The stake must pierce the heart, and decapitation both rids the vampire of his hypnotic gaze and . . . prevents regeneration."

"Regeneration?" Gayle asked sharply. "I thought they were like . . . ghosts or something."

"No. Unfortunately, they're very solid. They can be wounded, but if they haven't fed for a while, they won't bleed because evidently the blood is absorbed quickly into the tissues except for a reservoir within the heart. When they've just fed, their victim's blood would seem to circulate through the veins, and in that case they'll bleed until their regeneration ability heals the wound. I don't know whether they all have that power or not. I remember . . . in Krajeck, when my father touched me after he'd come back from Mount Jaeger. He was so . . . terribly cold. I think human blood warms them, keeps them supple and young in a way we can't understand. Whatever it is, it's the devil's work. Hungarian tradition suggests that they fear fire as well, and their eyes may be their weakest point. Blinding them would make them momentarily helpless, though whatever other senses they might have I dare not imagine."

"You talk about them as if they're another race altogether," Silvera said.

"They are. Their powers are superior to ours. They can

move faster, and they're stronger as well. They can live forever as long as they can feed on human blood." He looked from Silvera to Gayle and back again. "God made mankind," he said. "And Satan made the *vampir*."

Silvera leaned back. He was working the knuckles of his hands, aware of the spreading numbness.

"Please believe me," Palatazin said. "I know they're here."

"It's all so . . . strange. I mean, people have learned to scoff at such things. Anyone in this day and age who says he believes in vampires is, forgive me, considered insane . . ."

"The world may change, Father. But you and I both know that Evil remains constant. I think that for many years the *vampir* have worked quietly in this country, taking a village here, a town there. All very quietly. Now they want much more, and they feel strong enough to reveal their existence to the world, knowing it will soon be too late for us to fight back."

"Fight back," the priest repeated, his brow furrowing. "How do we? If you're right—and I'm not ready to say you are—what do we do?"

"We find the vampire king," Palatazin said. "And we do it quickly."

"Jesus!" Gayle whispered.

Palatazin's gaze darkened. "I think I know where their Master may be hiding. There's a castle up in the Hollywood Hills somewhere that once belonged to a horror-film actor named Kronsteen. He had the thing brought over from Hungary, and I imagine the vampire king would find it to his liking."

"Orlon Kronsteen?" Gayle said. "I remember reading about his murder, back in the early seventies, wasn't it? My boyfriend Jack . . ." she stopped herself, her face going pale. "A . . . guy I used to go with was . . . a documentary filmmaker. He wanted to do a film on the homes of old movie stars, and I think he mentioned something about that castle. It's supposed to stand on top of a cliff, isn't it? I think Jack . . . my friend said he drove up there a few years ago. He may have spent the night, knowing him . . ." She smiled painfully, her eyes clouding over. Which surprised her because up until that moment she'd never really admitted to herself that she cared anything for him. Her smile began to slip. *Too late now, kid,*

she told herself. No amount of caring would change him
back from what he became.

"Kronsteen's castle," Palatazin said. "That's where I
have to go, though God knows I don't want to. If there
was any other way . . . but there's not. So now I have to
ask you the question, Father. Will you go with me?"

Silvera tensed. An avalanche of thoughts began to
tumble through his brain, gathering force and speed. *I'm
not ready to believe this but*—Madre de Dios—*what if it's
true? I've got to tell the people in my parish, I've got to
help them get to safety. How can I make them understand? Stakes, caskets, vampires hiding in a castle? Surely
this is some kind of wild nightmare! Help him. You should
do as he asks. No, my parish comes first, I'm dying. I
need time, so much time. What should I do? I don't want
to die. Oh, God, I don't want to . . .*

"I would like to go today," Palatazin said, "while
there's still light. If you choose not to go, then I have another thing to ask of you. But in any event, I'll understand
your decision."

Silvera realized the palms of his hands were cold with
sweat. *What if this man is right?* he asked himself. *I've
never been afraid of anything, never! No,* he heard the
calm voice echo at the back of his brain. *No. You're
afraid of dying before your time. You're afraid of that
cold, dark place where God is going to send you because
you've done nothing for Him in this world but chase some
dope pushers and squeeze a few hands because that was
expected of you. You weren't called to the priesthood;
you drifted into it after everything else in your life went
bad. So what is it going to be?* "I . . . I'm going to have
to say no," he said, trying to keep his hands from shaking. "I have the people of my parish to think of. If you're
right, I'll have to find some way to . . . protect them. I'm
sorry."

Palatazin looked at him in silence for a moment, then
nodded. "All right." He stood up, opened the closet door,
and brought out a cardboard box filled with short wooden
stakes. "I bought these this morning," Palatazin said. "Ash
stakes, two feet long. There are two dozen. I also bought
a good strong hammer. I don't know if I'll ever get to use
them, but . . . I'd like for you to say some words for me.
Just . . . whatever you can. Will you do that?"

"Yes. Of course." Silvera stared at the cardboard box.

Then he said, "I'll pray for you." Palatazin nodded, clasped his hands together, and closed his eyes. Silvera bent his head and began to pray out loud, asking God to guide Palatazin's steps and to shield him from danger. But as he was praying, he was writhing inside. He felt as if his soul were shrinking, and very soon there would be nothing left at all. He suddenly thought of himself years ago, a punk kid in the drunk tank at the police station in Puerto Grande, a cramped place with obscene drawings on the walls and puddles of urine on the floor. He and two friends had been thrown in there, stinking drunk on tequila, after a fight with some sailors at the Navegar Club down on the docks. The sailors went to the hospital.

But there'd been another man in with them, an old man in tattered, dirty clothes with scabs all over his face. He had moaned for most of the night, twisting and turning in his bunk as if fighting off something that was coming down from the ceiling to smother him. Toward morning Silvera, a brash teen-ager with needle marks on his arms and a hunger for violence, realized the old man was dying. He'd sat on the floor, one of his eyes black and swollen and several teeth loose, watching that old man fight death. It was a brave struggle but a hideous mismatch. Silvera had found himself wondering where that man had been, what he had seen of the world, who he'd loved, and what he'd done.

Across the cell Silvera's friends slept, snoring like young bulls. He'd crept closer to that bunk, listening to the old man's hoarse mutterings as if they were radio transmissions from another world. ". . . he knows he should pay me that money, all of it like I asked . . . what am I gonna do? . . . sure, sure, *amigo*, you and me gonna tear this port apart . . . now that Giselle is a fine piece of ass, take your money and give you the best . . . the best . . . ohhhhh shit, that stuff'll fuck your head up . . . said I was gonna kill that bastard . . . dolphins. I love to watch them dolphins when they come flying up from the water . . . anchor's fucked up, won't hold a rowboat . . . WATCH THAT CABLE, DAMN IT! . . . one more drink, *amigo*, that's all I'm asking . . ."

Just before dawn the old man had opened his eyes and turned his head to look at the boy sitting beside him. He'd stared at Silvera for a long time with the whiskey-swollen slits he had for eyes. He coughed several times violently, and Silvera saw the flecks of blood on his lips. The old man had reached out and gripped his hand with a leathery, four-fingered paw.

"*Padre,*" the old man had whispered. "Help me . . . make it easy for me . . . please . . ."

"I . . . ain't a priest," he'd said. The grip had tightened.

"*Padre.* . . . I'm a sinner . . . I don't want to die!" A tear squeezed from one eye and trickled down through the dark folds of his face. "Help me . . ."

"How? I can't . . . do anything."

"Yes, you can. You can. Say something for me . . . some words . . ."

The man's grip was about to crush Silvera's hand. His eyes glistened, but the spark of life within was rapidly dying. "*Please,*" the old man whispered. *Me pray to God?* the boy had asked himself. *Shit, that's a laugh! Me on my knees like a peon, simpering and crying?* But the old guy was almost dead, he was drying up right there, so maybe he should at least try. But how to do it? What to say? "Uh, God," he said softly, "this man . . . uh, what's your name?"

"Gulf Star," he whispered, ". . . sailed on the Gulf Star . . ."

"Uh, yeah. God, this man sailed on the Gulf Star and I . . . guess he's a pretty good man." His knuckles cracked under the pressure of the man's grasp. "I don't know anything about him, but he's . . . uh, sick and he wanted me to say some words for him. I don't know if I'm doing this right or not, or if You're able to hear me. This man is really in bad shape, God, and I think he's going to . . . awwww, this is a lousy place for any man to be. A lousy place to die, God. Shit, what am I doing talking to myself!"

"Go on . . ." the man insisted. "Please, *padre.*"

"I told you I ain't no fuckin' priest!" he said sharply, but he knew the man hadn't heard. He was smiling, muttering some kind of prayer over and over again. "Okay," Silvera went on, looking at the ceiling. "If this man's got to die in this place, make it easy for him, God. I mean, don't let him suffer or anything like that, all right? Just . . . lay him down easy." He looked down at the old man. "That's all. I don't know anything else to say."

The old man was silent.

From across the cell his friend Chico lifted his head. "Hey, Ramon? Who you talkin' to, man?"

Father Silvera finished his prayer for Palatazin and then crossed himself. "I hope you're wrong," he told the cop. "But if you're not, God go with you."

"And with you," Palatazin said quietly. He got up, opened the door for the priest, and watched as Silvera walked to his Rambler. Silvera did not look back, and Palatazin noticed that he was trembling. He heard the rush of wind along the street and saw Silvera's coat flutter. The sky looked strange, pregnant with storm clouds. He'd never seen the sky over L.A. like that before.

Silvera was almost knocked down by the wind. He felt sharp grit strike his face and, as he climbed into his car, he noticed the residue of sand along the bottom of his windshield. He turned the key in the ignition and drove away, speared by shame.

Palatazin closed the door. "I have to go, Miss Clarke," he said, turning to Gayle. "Will you write the story for me?"

"Yes," she said, as she got to her feet. "But I'd like to go with you."

"Why?" he asked her. "If Father Silvera wouldn't go, why should you?"

"Let's say a . . . combination of professional and personal interests and leave it at that."

"No," Jo said suddenly. "If anyone is going to go with you, it must be me."

"You're staying here," he told her. He glanced at his wristwatch. "It's almost four. We'll have to hurry, Miss Clarke. Did your friend ever tell you how he got up to Kronsteen's castle?"

"Not exactly, but I remember something about Outpost Drive."

"We could lose more than an hour trying to find the way," Palatazin said grimly. "If we're there when the sun goes down . . ."

Jo said, "You didn't hear me, did you? I said I was going. Whatever happens to you happens to me . . ."

"Don't be foolish, Jo!"

"Foolish? I'm not staying in this house by myself! If you want to argue about it and waste more time, then that suits me fine, too." She stared at him, her eyes defiant and sure.

He met her gaze, then reached for her hand. "Gypsies!" he said with mock disgust. "You had to come from a family of them! All right. We'll have to hurry. But I warn both of you—this is not for the weak-hearted. Or the weak-stomached. When I ask for your help, you'll have to give it. There'll be no time for squeamishness. Understood?"

"Understood," Jo agreed.

"All right then." He leaned over and hefted the cardboard box full of stakes. "Let's go."

NINE

The Hell's Hole Hilton was trembling. Boards squealed as the wind, which had risen to almost forty miles an hour in the last thirty minutes, swept across the mountains from the east. The glass rattled in the window frame, and Bob Lampley could see handfuls of sand hitting it like buckshot. The eastern sky was veined with gold and gray, the clouds swirling together and breaking apart like fast-moving armies. Lampley felt his heart hammering. The wind-speed indicator was still climbing, passing forty now and rising to forty-two. The Hilton seemed to lurch suddenly on its rock and concrete base. *Jesus!* Lampley thought, his brain buzzing. *This whole place is going to give if the winds keep building!*

He'd made his last call to National less than an hour before. L.A. was getting twenty-five and th'rty mile-an-hour winds all the way from the San Fernando Valley south to Long Beach, and blowing sand had even been reported in Beverly Hills. The National Weather forecasters were going crazy trying to figure out what had kicked up this storm. It had started right in the middle of the Mojave and seemed to be moving in a direct line toward Los Angeles.

The black telephone rang. Lampley picked it up, trying to make out the tinny voice on the other end over the cracklings of electrical interference. Hal from Twentynine Palms was saying something about radar.

"What is it?" Lampley shouted. "I can't hear you, Hal!" The message was repeated, but Lampley could grasp only fragments. ". . . wind speed is up to . . . emergency procedure . . . watch your radar!" Wood cracked, the sound loud in Lampley's ear. Hal's voice was frantic, and it scared the shit out of Lampley. *Radar?* he thought. *What the hell's he talking about?* He glanced quickly at the sky and saw the undulating golden tendrils of sand whipping through the higher pines. He saw a tree branch crack and go tumbling away. The sand was beginning to build like a snowfall, covering every crevice of bare rock. "Hal!" he yelled. "What's your wind speed down there?"

The answer was a high, shrieking garble that was cut off in mid-sentence. The phone shrilled and crackled like mad laughter. *Lines down,* Lampley figured. *That's it, sure. Lines down between here and Twentynine Palms.* The Hilton lurched again, and now he seemed to be able to taste sand as it found its way through the chinks between the boards. *Better get my little ass out of here before this whole damned place caves in!* He checked his wind-speed indicator again. Forty-eight. The pressure gauge was going crazy, too. It would fall fast and rise, again and again. Right now it was taking a long, terrible tumble. He went quickly to the red phone and plucked it off the wall. He could hear the tones clicking like a combination lock. Then a familiar voice garbled slightly by static said, "National Weather, L.A."

"Eddie? This is Bob Lampley at . . ." And then he couldn't find his voice because he'd glanced down at the radar screen.

It was showing something that he just couldn't believe, as intensely as he examined it. The screen indicated a huge mass coming up from the east, bigger than anything Lampley had ever seen before. It seemed to be . . . *rolling.*

"What's that?" he said, his voice choked with fear. *"What's that?"*

"Bob? What . . . you . . . showing?" Static crackled and squealed.

Lampley dropped the phone and leaned over the radar screen. Whatever it was, it stretched for *miles.* His eyes almost bugged out of their sockets. His panic was complete when he saw the barometer hit rock bottom and hang there. The wind had stopped. He could hear the Hilton resettling, like broken bones meshing again. He stepped to the window and looked out.

Very high up the clouds were still racing. The light had turned a murky gold, the color of piss after an all-night drunk. Around the Hilton the trees were so still they could've been painted against the stone. *A vacuum,* he thought, *it's as still as a vacuum out there.* He glanced back at the mass on the radar screen and froze with the realization that something huge was sweeping in to fill that vacuum.

Lampley looked back out the window.

"Oh . . . my God . . ." he whimpered.

He could see it now, filling up the whole eastern horizon, churning and roiling and thrashing but still terribly silent. It was the Lucifer of sandstorms, a troubled monster of nature. Lampley couldn't see the ends of it at the north and south, but the radar indicated it was at least thirty miles thick. Lampley, his brain clutching at the edge of rational thought, estimated its speed at between forty and fifty miles an hour. It seemed as large as the Mojave itself, now screaming toward him on tortured winds with the mingled colors of white, gray, and yellow.

He stood transfixed as the thing rolled forward. In another moment he could hear a faint, terrible hissing.

The sound of bark and leaves being stripped from trees. In the wake of that storm, he knew, the earth would be skeletal.

Sand spattered against the window, streaming down to the sill with little rattlesnake hisses. Off to the right he saw the ranger tower consumed, as if into the maw of a grinning, yellow beast. He backed away from the window, bumped into the desk and knocked the pictures of his wife and child onto the floor. He caught a glimpse of the barometer; its needle was quickly rising. Then he was gripping the red phone again, placing the receiver to his ear. The line squealed with scrambled circuits.

Lampley looked back over his shoulder and saw with growing horror the storm about to descend upon the Hilton. There was no time to waste. He ran out the door into a hot and dry atmosphere—the breathable air thinned to a gasp—and out the fence toward his green International Scout. Sand ground beneath his boots and spun past him in dust-devil spirals twice as tall as himself. There was a light sheen of sand on the Scout, covering his windshield. He was six feet away from the door when he heard a thunderous freight-train roar and felt the first stinging lash of heavy sand. It whipped into his eyes, blinding him, and as he opened his mouth to cry out in pain, the sand was sucked into his lungs. He felt the hot weight of the storm pressing close, closer, closer. As he groped wildly for the door's handle, a furnace-blast of wind hit him, slamming him to his back. A yellow shadow fell upon him, and as he screamed with the agony of sand flailing the skin off his body, a torrent of sand filled his mouth and eyes and nostrils, choking him to death in less than a minute. The Hilton, all its white paint scraped off to bare wood, sagged and caved in under the next barrage of winds. Lampley's Scout was reduced to scarred metal.

The storm churned on toward Los Angeles, leaving the mountains little more than sand-heaped piles of bare rock. Like the vampires it was meant to shield, the storm was ravenous.

TEN

Outside his house on Charing Cross Road, Wes Richer was throwing suitcases into the trunk of his silver-blue Mercedes. He was aware of the building winds and the occasional sting of sand on his cheek, but time was his primary concern. He and Solange had to catch a Delta jet to Las Vegas at four-fifty.

They'd spent most of the day in police stations or being shuttled back and forth between them. Jane Dunne had cursed like a sailor when she was informed by the police that she couldn't leave L.A. yet, then asked if she would be so kind as to stop fighting the cops who were attempting to lift her out of the wheelchair and into their prowl car? Wes and Solange had seen her briefly at mid-morning, being wheeled along a corridor at the Beverly Hills police station, loudly demanding a drink. Wes figured her brain was so scorched she wasn't even frightened of what might happen to her if she found herself face-to-face with vampires again.

Wes and Solange had been taken into separate rooms at the Beverly Hills station and were patiently questioned by a couple of solid cops who tried to make them realize the difference between real vampires—ha-ha—and kids who might belong to some kind of weird vampire cult. Wes's interrogator was a chunky officer named Riccarda who chained-smoked Salems and kept saying, "Fangs? You're trying to tell me you really saw *fangs*, Wes? Well, you're a comic, right?" But Wes thought the cop believed him because he seemed to be just going through the motions and his eyes did look scared. Wes had seen a few people walking around the corridor in pajamas, robes, and slippers; they seemed shell-shocked, their eyes unfocused and blank. When Wes started asking one of them some questions, Riccarda came over and guided him away. There were a few reporters running around too, and one of them got a picture of Wes before the film was yanked out of his camera. The rest of the newsmen were herded into a room, and that was the last Wes saw of them.

Then Wes and Solange were put in a van with some more people and shuttled over to Parker Center where they were slipped in through a rear entrance. In the elevator a young girl from Beverly Hills suddenly began babbling about a Camaro that her mother had bought her and how she and her mother were going to fly down to Acapulco. But as she talked, her face grew paler and her voice higher until she was almost shrieking about how her mother had come home last night with her new boyfriend, Dave, and how Dave had said he wanted to kiss her good night. Then she'd seen the fangs, and her mother's face had been fish-belly white, the dark eyes gleaming. She had run out of the house and just kept on running. When the elevator doors opened, two cops took the girl away into a room where Wes could still hear her screaming.

Wes and Solange were left in a room together, and finally another cop came in to ask them basically the same questions they'd been asked in Beverly Hills. At the end of an hour, the cop, who looked like he could take on three or four Marines with no sweat, stood up from his chair and leaned over toward Wes. "You saw what were members of a vampire *cult*, didn't you, Mr. Richer?" he said quietly, but his voice was not very steady, and the lines in his forehead had deepened into trenches.

"We both know what we saw," Wes told him. "What's with this cult bullshit?"

"You saw kids who were dressed up as vampires, didn't you?" the cop said. "Like I said, a cult. That's what you saw. Isn't it?"

"Shit," Wes muttered. "Okay, okay. A cult, for Christ's sake! Now can we get out of here?"

The cop didn't reply for a while, but then he said simply, "I'll have an officer drive you home." And that was it.

Cult my ass, Wes thought as he slammed down the trunk. *I know what I saw, and by God I'm getting us out of this town right now! What's taking Solange so long to get ready for Christ's sake?* He was exhausted, but there would be time to grab some sleep on the plane. He was afraid of the nightmares he knew he was going to have for a long time to come—the way that vampiric ambulance attendant had grinned, those fangs glistening, and Jimmy's agonized scream piercing the night. He couldn't think of those things without feeling a little insane. He looked at his Rolex. It was almost four-fifteen.

"Damn it, Solange!" he said and started walking back to the house. She stepped out the front door then, wearing a long, white coat with a hood. She locked the door, glanced up at the sky, and hurried to the car. "What's the problem?" he asked her as she slipped into the passenger seat. "We're going to miss the plane."

"No, we won't," she said. "Where's all this sand coming from?"

"Who knows?" He slid behind the wheel, started the engine, and backed down the driveway. He drove up to Sunset and turned west to pick up the San Diego Freeway. Occasional blasts of wind rocked the car, and Wes had to use the windshield wipers several times to clear away the sand.

"I was making something for you," Solange said after they'd left Bel Air. She reached into a pocket and brought out a little ball of something wrapped in tissue paper and tied with a rubber band. Wes caught the sharp odor of garlic.

"What is it?" he asked, taking it in the palm of his hand and sniffing it.

"A *resguardo.* A good-luck talisman to keep away evil. It hasn't been dipped into holy water or blessed at seven churches so it won't be as powerful as it should be. You must keep it in a pocket, *always.*"

Wes glanced at her, then looked back at the thing again. A few days ago he would've laughed at something like this. Now things were different, the spirits and amulets and Solange's spells didn't seem so far-fetched. In fact, he felt relieved to have her with him. "What's in it?"

"Garlic. *Yerbabuena, perejil,* and a touch of camphor." She squinted as more sand hit the windshield in front of her face. "I had to make it quickly so I don't know how long its positive influences will last. Don't lose it."

He nodded and slipped it into his jacket. "How about yours?" he asked her, and when she remained silent, he said, "You *did* make one for yourself, didn't you?"

"No. There wasn't time."

"Keep this one then." He started to dig it out, but she stopped him with a slight grip on his wrist. "No," she said, "That one won't work for me. It has a few strands of your hair in it. Watch where you're going."

Wes looked back to the boulevard and swerved away from the center line as a Porsche swept past, horn blaring. He reached the freeway ramp and turned up onto it, heading south toward the airport. The sky was a strange dark gold color with grayish gold clouds racing from the east. Wes couldn't even tell where the sun was, and most of the cars on the freeway had already switched on their headlights. He heard a Bugs Bunny voice within him say, *Uhhhhh, ya wanna know what's up, doc? Dooooomsday!*

He increased his speed, whipping around slower cars. Wind hit the Mercedes and pushed it several feet to the right. He had to fight the wheel for a minute to steady the car. As they passed over West L.A. they could see spirals of sand dancing ahead and sheets of it being blown across the freeway. Solange's heart was pounding. She sensed something dark at work, an unexpected hand that had tipped the balance of power in favor of the vampires. *Not much time left,* she thought suddenly.

He put a hand on her thigh. "We're going to be fine," he told her. "We'll get ourselves a room at the Sands and lay out in the sun for about a week."

"What's going to happen to these people?" she asked quietly. "The ones who can't get out?"

He pretended not to hear her. "I've got some friends at the Sands. Maybe I can work up a show two or three nights 'a week. Yeah, that would be great. Just a nice, light show to keep the gamblers happy. I wouldn't even have to work very hard . . ."

"Wes," Solange repeated. "What is going to happen to these people?"

He didn't answer for a moment. "I don't know," he said. "I just know I want us to get far away from here . . ."

"How will we know if any place is ever far enough away?"

He didn't answer, couldn't answer. He pressed his foot further down on the accelerator.

Wes took the ramp that swung traffic off toward LAX and almost immediately found himself in a jam of cars, vans, cabs, and buses. With horns blowing, the traffic slowly inched forward toward the main terminal. Wes hammered the steering wheel in his impatience, as Solange watched the residue of sand slowly growing at the bottom of the windshield. Up ahead there were a couple of cops in orange slickers trying to direct traffic and at the same time keep their balance against the wind. As Wes neared them, he thought he heard one of the cops shout something like "All flights grounded," but he couldn't be sure. He rolled down his window and instantly caught grit in his eyes. He rolled the window back up to a slit and shouted frantically to the nearest cop. "Hey! Aren't the planes flying?"

"You kidding, man?" The officer kept his hand up in front of his face to shield his eyes and nose. "They can't even get off the ground in this!"

"Shit!" Wes muttered and started looking for a way to get out of the airport lane. He pounded the horn and slid in front of a bus, trying to edge out before he was caught in the vortex of traffic that swirled in a circle in front of the terminal. He hit the horn again as a black limo squeezed past, scraping paint off his side of the car; he caught a glimpse of a man in the rear seat, whose eyes were wide with terror. Wes swerved in front of a cab, hearing the wail of brakes and the responding discordant chorus of blaring horns. Then the Mercedes was climbing up and over a concrete median strip, almost slamming into a mad pack of cars racing back from the airport. Wes heard one of the cops shout something at him, but he sank his foot to the floor, heading north again back toward the San Diego Freeway.

"Where are you going?" Solange said. "Maybe we should just wait at the airport for the weather to clear."

"And when might that be? Damn it, where'd this storm come from?" He switched on the windshield wipers to clear away the sand; the glass was pocked and scratched in long arcs. He could see tiny glints of bare metal showing through the paint on the hood. "A sandstorm? Christ!" He took the freeway ramp at fifty, tires screeching. Another blast of wind hit the car, almost wrenching the wheel loose from Wes's grip. The sky had turned amber.

Oh, God, he thought, *night's coming fast!* "We're driving to Vegas," he said, trying to picture the serpentine twistings of the L.A. freeway system in his mind: Veer off onto the Santa Monica Freeway, curve north through the downtown district to the San Bernardino Freeway across East L.A. and Monterey Park, Interstate 15 out past Ontario. He'd drive to Vegas as if they were being chased by all the demons of Hell. Even Vegas might not be far enough away. Maybe they should just keep driving east and never look back.

Solange turned on the radio and searched for a station that wasn't drowned out by static. At the far end of the dial, she caught the faint sound of a newscaster's voice. "Today the president announced . . . gas rationing . . . members of Congress . . . denied . . . Los Angeles businessman . . . found guilty . . . tremor felt as far as . . . and registered four on the open-ended . . . the National Weather Service advises . . ."

"Turn that up," Wes said.

Solange did, but the crackle of static was overpowering. ". . . traveler's warnings extend as far north as Lancaster-Palmdale and to the south as . . . Weather Services advises all drivers . . ." Static squealed and chuckled, then the station was gone.

The Mercedes was rocketing through downtown L.A. Solange saw that the tops of several of the taller buildings —the Union Bank, the twin black Bank of America monoliths, the silver cylinders of the Bonaventure Hotel, the looming Arco Plaza—were shrouded in a shimmering golden mist. Sand was being blown in sheets back and forth ahead of them across the freeway; wind roared past the car. When she looked at Wes, she saw a slight sheen of sweat clinging to his face. He glanced at her and smiled grimly. "We'll be fine," he said, "as soon as we make it to Interstate 15 and start heading through the mountains. They'll cut this wind down to a . . ."

His eyes riveted on something in the road, and he slammed on the brakes. There were three cars locked together in the middle of the freeway. He felt the Mercedes begin to slip to the left and realized with a start of terror that the sand had covered the highway like ice. He quickly turned into the skid. The tangle of wrecked cars loomed up ahead, one of them with a red taillight still blinking. As the Mercedes swept past them, still skidding, Wes heard the loud grinding of metal, and the car pitched sideways, but then they were in the clear, and the car snapped itself steady. He increased the wiper speed, but now he could barely see where he was going. On the right side of the freeway, a car had smacked into the guardrail, and Solange thought she saw a body hanging out of the driver's door. But then they passed, and she didn't look back.

Not much time left, she thought. And went cold.

They crossed the sand-glutted ditch of the Los Angeles River and began to pass over the crowded houses and buildings of Boyle Heights. Wes switched on the air-conditioner because the temperature had risen sharply in the last five minutes. The air was stifling, and it was hard to draw a breath without tasting grit. They passed an overturned car that was burning fiercely, the flames fanned by the sweeping wind.

And then a dark brown cloud that seemed to shake the earth with its fury filled the sky, rolling forward like the dust kicked up from the heels of an advancing army. It engulfed the Mercedes, completely blinding them and smothering the windshield with sand. The wipers died under its weight. Wes cried out and steered the car to the right, his heart hammering. A pair of headlights came flying from his rearview mirror, and then a car spun around and around in front of them and disappeared into the dense curtain of sand.

"I can't see, I can't see!" Wes shouted. "We're going to have to pull off and stop, but Jesus Christ, I don't even know where I am!" He tried to graze the right guardrail, but he couldn't even find it. The engine coughed and stuttered. "Oh, Jesus," Wes whispered. "Don't go out on me now! Don't!" Coughed again. He stared at the lurching

rpms on his dash gauge. "Got enough sand in the engine
to choke a fucking camel!" he said. He pumped the accelerator as the Mercedes gave a last gasp and went dead. It
rolled perhaps ten yards and then stopped. Wes squeezed
the steering wheel until his knuckles cracked. "No!" he
said. "NO!"

With the end of the air-conditioner, the air had instantly become as stale as the inside of a desert tomb.
Wes turned on the ignition but the air that came through
the vents was searing—it seemed to be sucking oxygen
out instead of letting it in. Wes wiped his face with the
back of his hand and stared at the shining beads of sweat.
"So," he said quietly. "Here we sit."

They were silent for a long while, listening to the taunts
of the storm and the dry rasp of sand on metal.

"What time is it?" Solange finally asked.

He was afraid to look at his watch. "Almost five," he
said. "Maybe later."

"It's going to be dark soon . . ."

"I KNOW THAT!" Wes said sharply and was instantly
ashamed. Solange looked quickly away from him out the
window, but she couldn't see anything because the currents of sand were too thick. Wes switched on his emergency blinkers and prayed to God that any car coming up
behind them would see the lights in time. The soft *click
click click* sounded like a sepulchral metronome, ticking
away the few breaths of air they had left. Wes could see
Solange's profile—delicate, stoic, sad. "I'm sorry," he said
softly.

She nodded but didn't look at him.

*Hardy to Laurel: This is another fine mess you've got
us into!* Wes felt a grim smile spread across his face, but
it faded quickly. The car was still shuddering under riptides of wind, and now the windshield was almost completely covered. Wes could taste sand every time he inhaled; it gritted between his teeth. "We can't just sit here
and . . ." he let his voice trail off. "We can't. But, Jesus!
How long would we last out there?"

"Not very long," Solange said quietly.

"Yeah." He glanced at her and then away. "I guess
those sheikhs who bought houses up in Beverly Hills feel
right at home in this, huh? They can just open up their
two-camel garages and hit the trail. If they can find the
trail. Hmmm. I could do some material on that—a nice

five- or six-minute bit about Arabs buying up Beverly Hills. I can see the signs on Rodeo Drive—Chez Saudi, serving camelburgers around the clock. If you can't eat 'em, we'll sew you a nice coat . . . oh, shit." He'd suddenly gone very pale; he'd felt the presence of Death every time he took a shallow breath and sucked more grit into his lungs. He gripped the door handle and barely managed to stop himself before flinging it open. *Uh-uh*, he told himself. *No way. I sure as hell don't want to die, but I'd rather go slow than fast any old day.* He forced himself to release his grip and sit back.

"I haven't been very good to you, have I?"

She said nothing.

"I'm a taker," he said, "just like all the rest of them. Shark, barracuda, piranha . . . all those predatory-fish metaphors apply. I think I just wear a slightly better mask than most of them. Mine doesn't slip often because wearing a mask is what I do for a living. It *has* slipped, though, and I don't like what lies under it. Maybe the cops'll be along pretty soon. Maybe we can get towed out of this mess, huh?"

Solange looked at him. There were tears in her eyes. "I've seen behind your mask. There's a Bantu saying: You are what you are when you awaken. Before you open your eyes, before you swim up out of sleep, that's the real person. Many mornings I've watched you, and I've seen you curl up like a little boy needing protection or love or just . . . warmth. I think that's all you ever really needed. But you mistrust it. You push it away and look for it somewhere else, and so you never really find it at all."

He grunted and came up with a line from "Sheer Luck." " 'Elementary, Dr. Batson. Deucedly clever, what?' Shit! This fucking storm's not going to stop. I've never seen so much sand without a bottle of Coppertone in my hand and a transistor radio beside the chair." He told himself to start taking shallower breaths, maybe then she could get more air that way. "That's where I'd like to be right now. The beach at Acapulco. How'd you like that?"

"It would be . . . very nice."

"Damn straight. That's what we'll do when we get towed in. We'll make reservations at the Royal Aztec . . ." He stopped speaking as the car shuddered again.

"You're the best of them all," Solange said. "No one was ever any better to me than you are. I will take care of you—if I can." Then she hugged herself close to him, and he held her very tightly. He kissed her forehead, tasting her honey-pepper flavor, then listening to the moaning winds. He was starting to strain his breath through his teeth.

And around the stranded car the wind whispered like the voice of a little girl in a dream Wes had had a couple of nights ago. *Come out. Come outside and play with me. Come out, come out . . .*

. . . or I'll come in . . .

ELEVEN

Palatazin brought the Falcon to a halt. "Wait a minute," he said, staring up through the windshield; the wipers were turned to full-speed, the headlights on bright. "I thought I saw something." What he thought he'd seen was a huge, dark shape up there amidst the rocks and trees through a quick break in the swirling, amber clouds. Now there was nothing, just sand spinning against the glass.

"What was it?" Gayle leaned forward from the back seat. "The castle?"

"I'm not sure. I just saw it for a second before the clouds closed up. I couldn't tell very much except that it was big and way up on the mountain. It might've been a couple of miles from here, I don't know. Wait! There!" He pointed. The clouds had broken again, and for an instant they all could see it quite clearly, its high turrets standing against a darkening gold sky. From this distance it looked to Palatazin much like the ruins atop Mount Jaegar. *Yes,* he thought. *That's the place. That's where he's hiding.* At that height the vampire king would have an unobstructed panorama of L.A.; he could gloat as the lights went out in house after house. The castle looked as sturdy and impregnable as any fortress Palatazin had ever seen in the mountains of Hungary. *Seeing it was one thing,* he thought, *reaching it was quite another thing entirely.* The cold knot of tension that had formed in his stomach suddenly expanded, sending out chill tendrils into his arms and legs. He felt pitifully weak and frightened out of his wits.

"The wind's getting worse," Jo said in a tight, strained voice.

"Yes, I know." Sand had been spinning across the road for fifteen minutes now, and Palatazin could see piles of it collecting in pockets between rocks. Higher up the clouds tumbled over each other like great yellow dogs hearing the dinner whistle. They closed again, sealing off the Kronsteen castle. The Falcon's engine gave out a sudden wheeze and a tremble, and Palatazin revved it a couple of times. He looked at his watch and saw with horror that it was twenty minutes after five. With these thick clouds rolling in, darkness would fall within thirty minutes. The nagging thought that they would not make it to the castle in time now rang out in his brain like a clear clarion of warning. "We're going to have to turn back," he said finally.

There were no objections. Now the trick was finding a place to turn around. He drove on, conscious of the aged engine's sputtering. Suddenly a wall of wind came roaring through the scrub trees to the right, parting them like a comb through hair. It hit the car like a bulldozer, forcing it toward the rocky lip of the road. Palatazin fought for control. Jo screamed as the car shuddered to the left-hand shoulder and started to totter over the edge; she could see toy houses with their red roofs below and toy cars scattered on black and gold ribbons. Nothing moved down there for as far as she could see.

Palatazin slammed the gearshift into first and wrenched up the parking brake. The wind roared on, carrying wild, twisting coils of sand down into Hollywood. Very carefully Palatazin put the Falcon in reverse and backed away from the edge, slowly releasing the brake.

"We'll have to go up to find a place to turn," he heard himself say. His voice was dry and thin. "Neither one of you should've come. I was a fool to let you." He climbed further, looking for a cut in the trees or rocks that he could back the Falcon into. The storm was steadily worsening; another quarter-mile up the terrain was completely covered with blowing sand. It reminded him of the blizzards that had roared through Krajeck, particularly the storm that had been moaning outside the night his father had come home. A thought struck him like a blow to the temple, *Did the vampires have any measure of control over the weather? If they did, this freak sand-storm would be an effective way to immobilize the city's population. It would cut people off from each other, keep them confined to homes or offices. Planes wouldn't be flying, and the sea would be thrashed into a frenzy as well. And driving?* Palatazin realized they might not get down off this mountain alive. If the winds didn't take them crashing over the edge, if the sand didn't choke off the engine, if darkness didn't fall too soon . . . He could feel the castle crouched above them, perhaps less than a half-mile away along this twisting, sand-slick road.

Something huge and gray suddenly leaped up onto the hood, its snarling face pressed close to the glass. Gayle said "Jesus!" and Jo grasped Palatazin's arm. The thing looked more wolf than dog, but he could see the nail-studded collar and the tags around its neck. Its thick coat was full of sand, its eyes yellow and fierce. Over the sound of the wind, Palatazin could hear its low, menacing growls. The message was obvious. Palatazin saw other dogs slinking on the road ahead—a boxer, an Irish setter, a few mutts. They all shared the same glazed expressions of ferocity. *So,* he thought, *the vampire king has made sure his fortress is well protected. Even if we could reach the castle, we'd be mangled by these dogs when we got out of the car.* When Palatazin slowly drove on, the wolf-dog howled with rage and started scratching at the glass; it snapped repeatedly, as if trying to bite Palatazin's hands on the steering wheel. In another moment he saw a space on the right large enough to turn the Falcon around in. The wolf-dog stayed crouched on the hood, its baleful eyes glowering into Palatazin's until the car was turned back down the mountain. Then it leaped off and disap-peared with the rest of the pack.

The Falcon chugged like a weary locomotive, winds buffeting it from all directions. Once the engine rattled and quit, and they were rolling down to Hollywood, but Palatazin kept trying the key and finally it caught again, wheezing like an old man with emphysema. He raced the darkness back toward Romaine Street, threading his way across Hollywood and Sunset Boulevards—both dotted with stranded cars—and finding some streets blocked by wrecks or dunes. The Falcon crossed a deserted Santa Monica Boulevard and made it about three more blocks before it staggered and stopped dead. Palatazin tried the engine several times, but now the battery was groaning. Sand filled the engine. They were stranded almost five blocks from the house, and night was falling fast.

The interior of the car was already stifling. "Can we run for it?" Gayle asked softly.

"I don't know. It's five blocks. Not so far maybe. Maybe *too* far." He looked at Jo and then quickly turned away. Sand was already covering the windshield, sealing them in. It was as if they were being buried alive. "It's a long way," he said finally.

"What about these other houses?" Gayle asked. "Can't we ask for shelter?"

"We could, yes. But do you see any lights? Any life? How do we know we won't be stepping into a nest of vampires? How do we know some other poor souls won't mistake us for vampires and try to kill us? My house is protected with the garlic and the crucifixes. These are just . . . waiting for invasion."

"So what do we do? Sit here and suffocate?"

". . . or suffocate out there?" Palatazin pointed out. "The wind will slow us down. You'll get more sand into your lungs than air, just like this car did. Just like all these other cars did. But no. We definitely *cannot* stay here. The vampires won't be hampered by the storm because they don't breathe. So . . ." He looked at Jo again and smiled weakly. "Shall we flip a coin?"

"Hell no!" Gayle said. "I'm not staying here!"

Jo shook her head. "We try to make it back."

"All right then." *Five blocks,* he thought. *God, what a distance!* He was going to have to leave the stakes, mallet, and holy water in the trunk; there would be no way to carry them. No, he had to have the holy water at all costs. He took the keys out of the ignition and shrugged out of his coat, handing it to Jo. "Keep that up to your face," he told her. "Both of you, remember to breathe through your mouth with your teeth gritted. I'm going to get something out of the trunk. When I knock on your window, Jo, I want you to step out and grasp my hand. When you touch me, knock on Miss Clarke's window, and she'll take hold of your shoulder. Then we'll start to move. I doubt if we'll be able to see

very far out there. If one of us loses the others, don't
move from where you are. Just keep shouting and cover
your face with your hands. Okay?"

They nodded.

He started to open the door and then stopped. The
car vibrated with the force of the wind. He got the trunk
key in position so he wouldn't waste precious seconds
fumbling. "All right," he said. "I'm going." He sat there
for a few more seconds, then he stepped out of the car.

A blast of oven-hot wind seemed to suck him out. He
got the door closed and pulled himself along the side of
the car, his lower face tucked into the crook of his left
arm. He couldn't even take a fraction of a breath without
sucking in sand. A crosscurrent of wind hit him behind
the knees, knocking him to the ground. He began to
crawl, his face flayed raw. He pulled himself around to
the trunk, got the key in, and twisted. The trunk shot
open. He found the cloth-wrapped vial and used the
cloth to shield his mouth and nose, putting the vial in his
back pocket. Then he struggled around to the other side
of the car. The wind and sand nearly dragged him down.

When he rapped on the glass, Jo stepped out and almost fell, crying out as their hands slipped. When she
was ready, she knocked on the glass behind her and
Gayle came out. She grasped Jo's shoulder like a vise.
The short human chain started off being whipped and
shoved along the street. In another moment Palatazin felt
Jo's hand grinding his fingers together, and he knew she
couldn't get a breath. "NOT FAR!" he shouted, instantly
choking. She nodded, her slitted eyes weak and glazed.
All he could see of Gayle was a faint dark shape.

Jo fell. As he helped her to her feet, dark motes spun
before his eyes, and he knew they were all slowly suf-
focating to death. They weren't going to make it; there
were still three blocks to go. "COME ON!" he shouted
and pulled them toward the gray shapes on the right-hand
side of the street. The shapes slowly materialized into
wood-framed, two-storied houses not much different in
design from his own. They were all terribly dark, and
Palatazin was afraid of what they might be holding. He
tripped over something that lay on the sidewalk, half-
covered with sand. It was the corpse of a young man,
a bullet hole in his cheek. Palatazin stared dumbly at
the body for a few seconds and felt the hot waspish buzz

pass his face before he heard a muffled *crack!* He looked up in time to see the orange flash of the second shot fired from an upstairs window in the house that stood before him. The corpse at his feet shuddered. A man's voice rose to a frenzied wail, "Get away, ye heathen things of Satan! God Almighty shall strike you DEAD! And DEAD! And DEAD!" Palatazin pulled Jo after him, running toward the next house. The front door, its paint scoured down to the bare wood, was closed but unlocked. Palatazin plunged inside as the madman's shrieking turned into a sob of anguish.

When Gayle was through the door, Palatazin slammed it shut and bolted it. The air within the house was stale and heavy, but at least there were no torturing winds here. His face and hands felt raw, and he could see that Gayle's eyes were terribly bloodshot. Jo was gagging; she still held onto his coat, and sand was slithering off of it to the floor. He helped Jo over to a chair and wiped the beads of cold sweat off her face with his cloth. Her eyes were dark and vacant; she didn't seem to know where she was. "Jo?" he said. "We're all right now. We're safe." She began to cry very softly. Through the wind's howl Palatazin could hear the madman's scream. ". . . show yourselves! I know you're hiding in there, ye foul Satan spawn!" He began to sing in a high, croaking voice, "Shall we gather at the riiiiiver, the beautiful, the beautiful riiiiiiiver . . . ?"

Palatazin shut him out. Now he was wondering if they were alone in this house. The idea of being locked in here with another armed maniac filled him like sour wine. He was glad to have the reassuring weight of the .38 in its shoulder-holster, though from the size of the bullet hole in that corpse's face the man next door had to have a high-velocity rifle.

Gayle had the same idea at the same time. "What if we're not alone here?" she whispered.

"Anyone home?" he called out. There was no answer. Palatazin took his gun out of its holster and released the safety. He walked through the neatly furnished living room and into a short hallway where a flight of stairs led up to the second floor. "Anyone here?" he said, watching for the slightest movement. "We won't hurt you! We just wanted to get out of the storm!" He waited another moment, but there was still no reply. He put his gun away and went back to the living room. "I think we're alone," he told Gayle. "Maybe they got out before the storm hit."

Gayle looked around. There was a circular, red and blue braided rug on a hardwood floor, a large, comfortable-looking sofa with scrolled arms and legs, a dark-stained coffee table where a few copies of *Antique Monthly, National Geographic,* and *Horizon* magazines were neatly arranged, a couple of overstuffed chairs with clear plastic on the arms; and a brick fireplace over which hung an upside-down horseshoe. She could see ashes being stirred in the hearth by the wind's force. There were framed, sepia-toned prints on the walls and on the fireplace mantel a grouping of color photographs—a middle-aged couple smiling and hugging each other, kids and dogs at play.

The madman next door brayed with laughter.

"Jesus!" Gayle said softly. "That bastard tried to blow our heads off."

Palatazin nodded and stepped over to Jo, who'd regained at least some of her color. "You're better now?"

"Yes," she said and smiled weakly. "Better."

"Night's falling," Gayle said. "Very soon now." She pulled aside a curtain to look out at the street and could see very little but the swirling sand. The darkness was creeping. She turned and stared at Palatazin. "This storm will . . . keep them away too, won't it?"

"No. They don't breathe, and they have some kind of transparent eyelids that will keep the sand out. They have us where they want us."

"And where is that?" she asked.

"Trapped. All of us. Everyone in this city. No way out." He held her gaze for a moment and then looked away quickly because he'd realized they were in an unprotected house—no garlic smeared on the windowsills, no crucifixes on the doors and windows. He dropped his hand to his pocket to touch the bottle of holy water there; it seemed terribly small. "I'm afraid," he said softly, "that it's much too late for your story to do any good. The balance has shifted in their favor. They hold the power . . ."

"No!" she said. "There's still *something* we can do! We can call somebody, the police or the National Guard or . . . somebody . . ." She was silenced by the sand that spattered up against the window, hissing like hot fat at the bottom of a frying pan.

"I think you know better than that. I doubt if the phones are working. I'd try the lights if I wasn't afraid we'd stand out like a neon sign over a vampire diner. The air's none too good in here, is it?"

Gayle put her head in her hands. "Shit," she said in a faraway, dreamer's voice. "All I ever wanted to do was . . . be a good writer. That's all. Was that too much to ask?"

"I don't think so."

"I wanted to leave my mark. I wanted to . . . do something important. *Be* somebody important instead of a nobody . . . which—let's face it—I am." Her voice cracked a little bit, but she quickly cleared her throat, and then she was okay. "All mouth and fake guts," she said. "Will . . . what they do . . . be fast or slow?"

Palatazin pretended not to hear her.

The night closed in.

TWELVE

Father Silvera had reached his church before the worst of the storm hit, and now he opened the front door a crack and peered out. The street was deserted and already heaped with small sand drifts. There were no lights in any of the tenement windows simply because there was no electricity. Silvera had turned on the sanctuary lights for perhaps fifteen minutes before they flickered several times, dimming steadily with each flicker, and then went out. Darkness was filling up the church, deepening every minute. He looked out for a while longer, narrowing his eyes against flying grit, then went back to his room. He found several candles tucked away in a drawer, meant for either weddings or funerals, and he lit all of them, dripping wax onto saucers and sticking the candles into the hardening puddles. He took the candles out into the sanctuary and placed them around the gleaming brass crucifix on the altar. Looking at the Cross shamed him. He prayed that Palatazin would be safe in his journey and that when he found that castle, there would be no master there, no vampires there at all. He prayed that Palatazin was wrong, that he was suffering from fatigue or overwork. But at the back of his brain a shadow had begun to stir, and he was trying very hard to keep it from fully awakening. He had recalled something that an older priest had told him during his education in Mexico: "Some men are prisoners of rational thought." Perhaps he had been seeing the world through bars for a long time.

The sanctuary door creaked open. Silvera looked up from the altar to see a small figure come staggering out of the storm, whirlwinds of sand spinning around him. It was Leon LaPaz. Before Silvera could reach him, he fell, coughing violently, to the floor. Silvera helped him up onto a pew and then used all his strength against the door to keep the sand out.

"Are you all right, Leon?" he asked the boy, kneeling down beside him. Leon nodded, but he was pale and there were tear tracks down his cheeks. "I'll get you some water," Silvera said. He hurried back to his room, took a glass from a shelf over the sink, and turned on the cold water tap. The pipes stuttered for a few seconds, then let out a thin trickle of brownish water. *Damn it!* Silvera thought. *The sand's even getting into the water!* He sipped it, then spat it into the sink. The stuff was undrinkable.

"I'm sorry, Leon," he said when he went back out to the boy. "The water's going to have to wait." He put a finger under Leon's chin and tilted his face up. The boy's lips were wind-chapped, pulped, and swollen. "What were you doing out in that? You could've died out there!" Then he suddenly asked, "Where's Sandor? Your father hasn't come home yet?"

Leon shook his head, his eyes glimmering with tears. He was still breathless, and it was difficult for him to speak. "No . . . a man . . . came . . . a little while ago . . . for my sister . . ."

"A man? What man?"

"A . . . black man," Leon said. "To the apartment. He was tall and . . . mean and . . . he told me to come tell you . . . 'Cicero remembers' . . ."

"Cicero?" Silvera remembered the name of the black heroin dealer he'd stuffed into a garbage can. "When was this?"

"Maybe . . . maybe ten minutes." Leon gripped the priest's arms with small, trembling hands. "He took Juanita, Father! He said for me to come tell you he remembered and then he . . . took my sister and left! Where'd he take her, Father? What's he going to do to her?"

Silvera was stunned. *What was Cicero doing in this neighborhood during a raging sandstorm? Perhaps he'd been selling more horse and had been caught by the winds, unable to get out? And now that he had four-year-old Juanita, what would he do to her?*

"There are other people in my building, Father," Leon said. "A lot of the windows are broken, and the sand's getting in. They can't breathe too good."

"How many others?"

"Mrs. Rodriguez, the Garacas, Mr. and Mrs. Mendoza, Mr. Melazzo, maybe thirty more."

My God! Silvera thought. *What would happen to the hundred of others trapped in those flimsy tenements as the sand whipped through empty window frames and cracks that should've been repaired years ago? They would slowly suffocate if they couldn't find a better refuge!* Silvera paused, then made his decision. "Leon, you know where the staircase to the bell tower is, don't you?"

"*Sí.* Through that door over there."

"That's right. Now listen to me carefully. I want you to climb to the tower and crack open the shutters up there; you'll see the handles. The wind may get bad after that so you'll have to be very careful. Then I want you to take the rope that hangs down and pull on it as hard as you can. The bell may lift you off your feet, but that's all right, you'll come down again. Just don't let go of the rope, and keep ringing the bell. Can you do that?"

Leon nodded, his eyes bright with the importance of his mission.

"Good." Silvera squeezed his shoulder. Now he needed something to cover his face. As Leon scurried back through the door, Silvera took a towel from his bathroom and jammed most of it down into his coat so he could press the other end of it against his lower face and not worry about the wind carrying it away. As he approached the sanctuary door, he heard the first clear peal of Mary's Voice. It was an urgent, warning sound, metallic and determined. The bell's movement made the tower groan

over Silvera's head, and he could envision Leon's little
body being jerked upward. Silvera put his hand against
the door and then he stepped out. The wind screamed in
his ears.

Sand ripped into his face and hair. He was almost flung
to the ground, but he fought for his balance by leaning
against the wind. He could see absolutely nothing; the
darkness had conspired with the storm to isolate him inside a well with spinning, black walls. He struggled on
across the street, hearing tattered fragments of Mary's
Voice—it alternately pealed and moaned overhead.

Slowly, the line of buildings emerged from the murk.
He was gasping for a full breath by the time he
reached the door of Leon's building. Sand covered the
towel, and some of it had slipped through into his mouth
and nostrils. His face felt as if it were shredded. Shattered
glass from the building's door lay about his feet as he
stepped into the front corridor. He could hear tortured
winds wailing along the stairs, and they tried to pull him
in all directions at once. He tried to breathe without the
protective sieve of the towel; his nostrils and lungs instantly flamed.

He knocked on the first door he came to, and Carlos
Alva peered out, his dark eyes bugging above the gritty
handkerchief he had pressed to his face.

"Carlos!" Silvera shouted, though he stood less than a
foot away from the man. "Get your wife and children!
You're going to have to come to the church with me!"
Alva didn't seem to understand so Silvera put his mouth
next to the man's ear and shouted again. Alva nodded
and disappeared into the room for his family. Silvera
moved on to the next door.

It took him more than forty-five minutes to get them
all gathered together on the first floor—thirty-three people not counting the infants in their mothers' arms. Silvera had planned on getting them out in a human chain,
hand-to-hand, but the infants created a problem.

"Listen to me, all of you!" Silvera shouted at them.
"We're going to have to make it to the church! Can you
hear the bell ringing?" Now it sounded distant and muffled, and Silvera knew that Leon's arms would be about
ready to rip from their sockets. "We're going to follow
that sound!" he yelled, pointing in the direction of the
church. "Everyone clasp the shoulder of the person in

front of you and hold on tightly! I don't want the women to carry their babies. Give them to your husbands! The wind's very strong out there so we've got to walk carefully." He saw frightened eyes everywhere around him. There were cries for God and muttered prayers.

"We're going to be all right! Don't be afraid, just hold on! Be sure to cover the infants' faces! Is everyone protected? All right! Are we ready?" Someone starting sobbing. Carlos Alva, holding his baby son in one arm, gripped Silvera's shoulder. Silvera took a breath of flaming air and moved out into the street, the people trailing behind him.

He couldn't hear the bell for a few seconds. *Keep ringing it, Leon!* he called out mentally. Then he heard it, wailing for the lost. Behind him the human chain flailed against the wind, some of them falling and having to be helped up. The street had never seemed so wide or so wicked. Silvera felt he'd reached the middle of it because he couldn't see either side, but he couldn't be certain. Suddenly he heard a piercing scream behind him that went on and on. It reached a high crescendo and then rapidly faded. "What is it?" Silvera said over his shoulder to Alva. "Who screamed?"

Alva sent the question back. In another moment he told the priest, "Mrs. Mendoza is gone! Something pulled her out of the chain!"

"WHAT?" Silvera shouted. "STAY WHERE YOU ARE!" He felt his way back to the hole where Mrs. Mendoza had been between her husband and Mr. Sanchez. "What happened to her?" he asked her husband, whose face was pallid with shock. The man couldn't answer; he was muttering "Maria, Maria, Maria . . ." over and over again. Silvera looked around for her but couldn't see a thing. He peered at Sanchez. "What happened?"

Sanchez's teeth were chattering. "I don't know, Father!" he shouted. "She was holding onto my shoulder one second, then . . . she wasn't there! I heard her scream, and when I looked around, I thought I saw . . . I thought I saw . . ."

"What? What was it?"

"Something . . . a man maybe . . . dragging her off . . ."

Silvera stared into the darkness, sand slithering down his neck. There was nothing out there, nothing at all. He

heard himself say, "Close the hole," and then he felt his
way back to the front of the chain. His heart was thundering, his stomach roiled with fear. Alva clutched his
shoulder again, and they started off. Within ten seconds
there was another scream, fading into the distance. Silvera's head whipped around. "Felizia!" he heard a
woman wail. "What happen' to my little girl? FELIZIA-
AAAAA!" The woman started to leap out of the chain,
but Silvera shouted, "HOLD ONTO HER! WE KEEP
MOVING!"

A figure suddenly ran in front of him, and then was
quickly engulfed in the storm. He stopped so abruptly he
could feel the entire chain bump together. He'd gotten
the impression of a young boy in a black jacket, grinning
out of a silver-eyed skull. *Sweet Jesus, protect us!* he
thought. *Please help us get to that door! PLEASE!* He
began walking again; Alva's hand dug into his shoulder.
There was a scream from far behind, almost at the end
of the chain. "KEEP MOVING!" he shouted, though he
knew they couldn't possibly hear him back there. He
hoped they'd close the gap and stagger on. And now he
seemed to be aware of movement all around him—figures darting back and forth, shadowy shapes made formless by the blowing sand. He stepped onto the opposite
curb. The church door was only a few feet away at the
top of five steps.

"WE'RE HERE!" he shouted and realized at the same
instant that Alva's hand was gone. When he looked
back, he saw that both the man and his wife had been
taken out of the chain, leaving only their small daughter
frozen with terror, her hand outstretched where she'd
been clutching her mother's dress. Silvera grasped her
hand. The bell sang out furiously overhead. Silvera threw
open the church door and stood there, quickly herding
them in while he counted them. Of thirty-three who'd
left the building, twenty-six had made it. When the last
one had stepped across the threshold, Silvera slammed
the door shut and leaned against it, the breath rasping
through his lungs. Several people fell down before the
altar and began to pray; there were shrieks and sobs,
a wild tumult of noise.

He hadn't believed in vampires; he wasn't sure now if
he did or not, but he knew one thing for certain—whatever could exist in that storm wasn't human. He touched

Juan Romero on the shoulder. "Go up to the tower and take over the bell from Leon," Silvera said. "Keep ringing it until I send someone else up. Hurry!" Juan nodded and moved away. If anyone could hear that bell, Silvera reasoned, then maybe they could reach the church and safety. He put his face in his hands and prayed for strength. He was going to have to go back out there, into the dozens of other buildings that surrounded the church, to help as many people as he could find. He was afraid there would not be very many. But this time he wouldn't go out unprepared.

He walked to the altar and picked up the heavy brass crucifix; it caught the golden candlelight and shimmered. But it was so cold. Though it was a symbol of hope, he felt full of dark, bleak hopelessness. He gripped his hands around the crucifix's sharp edges, aware of how many eyes were watching him. He could use this to break into a grocery store for canned goods and bottled water. The stained-glass image of Jesus, occasionally shuddering with the violent wind, stared down at him through stern gray eyes. *You're dying anyway,* Silvera told himself, *so why should you be so afraid? Why should you want to cling to life like an old woman wringing drops out of a dishrag? Your days are numbered. Make them count.*

Then he gripped the crucifix, adjusted the towel over his face, and stepped back out into the maelstrom.

THIRTEEN

"Reminds me of the blizzards we used to have back home," Wes said softly, watching as the last clear square on the windshield was covered over. Now he and Solange sat in darkness. She had pressed against him, leaning her head on his shoulder, and though it was terribly hot, Wes didn't mind and neither did she. It was better somehow to be near one another. "One day Winter Hill would be a study in golds and browns, then when the storm passed through during the night and you looked out the window in the morning, the world would be white right up to the horizon. Trees, houses, fields . . . everything. People ride sleighs in Winter Hill when the snow falls like that, no kidding. Did I ever tell you I know how to snow-shoe?"

"No," Solange whispered.

"What'd I say I know how to do?"

"Snowshoe."

"Louder."

"Snowshoe!"

"Gesundheit! Now, what was I saying? Oh, yeah, about the sleighs. They were a terrific way to get around. The last time I went home for Christmas, everybody was using those damned snowmobiles. Progress, right? Well . . ." He decided he'd better shut up because he suddenly realized he couldn't breathe worth a damn. He finally managed to find a gulp of air. He wanted to comfort Solange, though, because when they were silent for too long she began to cry. Out of all the thousand or so jokes he had told before audiences in L.A., Las Vegas, and San Francisco he couldn't seem to remember a single one, just fragments of comedy bits that didn't make sense —*What's big, stiff, and belongs to Roy Rogers? Trigger; What'd the hung-over angel who'd visited earth overnight say to a furious St. Peter? Sorry, Pete, but I left my harp in Sam Frank's disco; Missionary in Africa's out walking one day and comes face-to-face with a lion. He sinks down to his knees and starts to pray for his life when the lion gets down on its knees beside him. "Dear brother lion," the missionary says, "how wonderful it is to see you join-ing me in Christian prayer when just a moment ago I feared for my life . . ." And the lion growls, "Don't in-terrupt while I'm sayin' grace!"*

Praying, Wes thought. *Now that might be an idea. What should I say? God please get us the hell out of here? God don't give up on old Wes and Solange just yet? God whose side are you on anyway?* The answer to that seemed painfully clear. *I've come a long way to die in a fucking sandstorm,* Wes thought. *From frat parties to bars to the Comedy Store to the big time, more or less, and all of it could now be just so much shit in a totebag. No agent to get the jobs now, no accountants to find the tax loopholes and the shelters, no fan mail pouring into the slot. Nobody saying how good I was and how much money I was going to make and that I was going to be King of Comedy Hill for a long, long time . . . nobody now but me and Solange.*

Well, he thought, *that would have to be enough.*

His brain felt feverish. *Where the hell are we? Sitting on the freeway, maybe right in the middle of it, somewhere over East L.A. Probably no shelter for blocks; the Mercedes stalled in what looked like a Sahara Desert sand dune. And vampires out there somewhere. Jimmy dead. Screaming in agony before he died. A bell ringing. Ambulance sirens wailing, lights flashing across a wide green lawn. A bell ringing. Crazy old lady in a wheelchair, grabbing my arm, scaring shit out of me. Blackberry brandy. Police car coming. A bell ringing. Parker Center, and a girl cracking up in the elevator. A bell . . . . . . RINGING . . . ?*

He opened his eyes, hadn't even felt himself starting to slip away. *What was that noise? Wait a minute, wait a minute! WAIT A MINUTE! A bell's ringing out there somewhere! Or is it my imagination?* He thought he heard it again, a soft distant moan that had a musical note to it, not like the shrill hissings of the wind at all. But now it was gone, if it had ever been there to begin with. He gently shook Solange. "What is it?" she said thickly, her breathing hoarse and uneven.

"Listen. Wait a minute . . . there! Did you hear that? A bell ringing?"

She shook her head. "No. It's the wind." Her eyes dropped, and she laid her head back on his shoulder.

"Don't go to sleep!" he said. "Wake up and listen! I'm telling you that's a bell ringing out there!"

"Bell . . . what bell . . . ?"

And now he heard it again, a distinct, low, musical note through the harsh discord of the storm. He thought it was coming from somewhere to the right, but he couldn't tell how far away. "Solange," he said, "I think maybe we're closer to shelter than we thought! We can make it there, I think! It won't be too far away!"

"No," she whispered. "I'm sleepy. We can't make it . . ."

"We can!" He shook her again, harder, trying to stave off the long, dark rolling waves that were beginning to spread through his body. "We're going to have to try, at least! Here, put your hood up. Cup your hands in front of your face to keep the sand out of your lungs. Can you do that?"

"I don't know . . . I'm so tired . . ."

"Me too, but we can't stay here if there's a safe place so close! We can sleep when we get there, okay? Come on. Put your hood up and try to shield your face with it." He did it for her. "There you go. Okay, I'm going to get out first and come around for you. Take a couple of deep breaths." When she tried, she winced w' h the effort; there was barely any air left to breathe. Wes's head was buzzing fiercely, the dark waves closing in. "I'm opening the door now. You ready?"

She nodded.

Wes pushed against the door and found it jammed shut. Panic exploded in his stomach. He shoved harder, the muscles in his shoulder straining. Sand began to stream off the window in thick rivulets, and it slithered into the car as Wes pushed. Then he'd opened it wide enough for them to slip out. He took Solange's hand as she slid across the seat and stepped out into a blinding flurry of sand, his feet sinking to the knees. A wall of sand came sliding over him, and as he tried to fight free of it, he almost lost Solange's grip. But then his face was clear, and he wrenched Solange after him through what he now realized had been a sand dune heaped up against the Mercedes's side.

It was dark now, and through the twisting currents of wind, he could see faint sparkles of light from across the river in downtown L.A. Behind him, Eas* L.A. and beyond lay in utter darkness. The wind seemed to have lessened somewhat since Wes had stopped the car; at least he could stand without having to struggle for balance. Sand still stung his face like hellish nettles and flamed the air he tried to draw between his teeth. There *was* air, though, and he found he could breathe fairly well if he kept his teeth gritted and remembered to spit every minute or so to clear his mouth. Above him he could hear howling currents of air; the worst of the storm seemed to have risen and was now circl'ng relentlessly over the city. Wes saw that the Mercedes was stripped of all its paint. There were more cars scattered on the freeway up ahead, all of them scoured down to shining metal. Dunes six and seven feet high had heaped up around them, collapsing over hoods and roofs. Most of the sodium-vapor lights along the freeway had gone out, but those few that remained cas* a cold, bluish glow down upon a scene of desolation that again reminded

Wes of the aftermath of a blizzard. One of the lightposts had gone down just ahead and lay stretched across the freeway, its bulb crackling like a dying meteor.

Wes heard the moaning of that bell again way off to the right. Somewhere down in the darkness of East L.A. He spat sand out of his mouth, shielding his eyes with one hand. "You okay?" he asked Solange, having to shout. She answered with a slight squeeze of his hand, and he began moving toward the nearest off-ramp, his shoes sinking into a couple of inches of sand. They passed a car with several bodies tumbling out of it, as if they'd died trying to dig their way out. Solange caught sight of one staring, blue-fleshed face and quickly looked away. Further on they came to a corpse, half-buried in the sand, that grinned up at them through a twisted death rictus; Wes could envision that thing sitting up, sand streaming off its body, and whispering, *"See? I got away from them. Oh, no, I wouldn't let them take me, so I just laid down and went to sleep. That's what you should've done, too. It would have been so much easier . . .*

The sound of that bell seemed nearer. Wes thought he saw an off-ramp just ahead under the pale glow of a sodium-vapor lamp. "You still with me?" he said.

"I'm fine! Don't worry about me!"

Wes almost stepped on two bodies, a man and a woman holding hands. He guided Solange around them, his nerve about to break.

They had started down the off-ramp when Wes heard a distant rumbling. He looked back over his shoulder and saw headlights moving quickly toward them from the west. Motorcycles, about fifteen or twenty of them. His heart leapt—*Highway Patrol cops!* He let go of Solange and started waving his arms, shouting, "Hey! Over here! Over here!"

"Wes," Solange said. "Wait . . . I don't think . . ."

The motorcycles curved toward them, sending up spinning tails of sand. Wes saw the face of the lead rider, white-fleshed and skeletal, red eyes burning with hunger. The thing grinned, then opened its mouth wide and motioned for the others to hurry. The fangs glinted with ghostly blue light.

Wes turned in horrid slow-motion and reached for Solange, but suddenly his vision was filled with a blinding

white light and the stuttering roar of the motorcycles
bore down on him. He was struck in the side by a booted
foot. Pain shot through him as he fell to the pavement.
He hung motionless for a few seconds over a dark void
and then slowly, slowly tumbled head-over-heels into its
maw. From its center he heard the shrilling of wind,
cracking and popping motorcycle exhaust, laughter, and
Solange calling to him. Her screaming soon stopped.
"Good-lookin' bitch . . . so good, so fiiine," someone said,
the voice echoing in Wes's head. "You can have what's
left of *him*, Viking. Oh yeah, baby, you're gonna be so
gooood to Kobra . . ."

The throbbing of his ribs roused Wes. He was being
turned over by rough, freezing hands. Through a mist of
pain Wes saw the face over him—broad and bearded,
pallid and vampiric. "He's alive," the biker said. "Ain't
much to him, but I figger he's worth a couple of swigs . . ."

"You said I could take the next one, man!" someone
else called out.

"Viking rates over you, Dicko," the one called Kobra
said. "Let him feed. You'll take the next one."

"Shit!" Dicko said. "Ain't nothing but dead meat
around here!"

"Take it easy, man. When we hook up with those
Ghost Riders and the rest of the Death Machine, we'll
flush 'em out like rats. Be plenty for everybody."

Viking bent over Wes, his mouth slowly opening. Wes
could see the bursts of silver in his eyes, and his own
face reflected in the merciless mirrors.

"Git some, Viking!" one of the others called out and
laughed.

Suddenly Viking blinked and jerked his head back.
"Shit! Burnin' my eyes!" He leaped up and away from
Wes, his large belly shaking as his body trembled. "Bastard's got somethin' in his clothes. Kobra! Got something
that burns my eyes!" He rubbed at them and backed
away.

Kobra shoved him aside and towered over Wes; he
leaned down, staring balefully at Wes, and seemed to be
sniffing the air. Almost instantly his eyes squeezed shut
with pain, and he scrambled away.

"What's he got, Kobra, huh?" Viking said. "What's
he got, what's he got?"

"Shut up!" Kobra rubbed his eyes and then glared at

Wes. "Don't matter what he's got. Bastard's ribs are caved. When the wind blows up again, he'll be lying under about two feet of sand. Forget about him."

Viking scooped up a handful of sand and flung it at Wes. "You're gonna die, motherfucker!" he said savagely. "And death is *cooolllddd . . .*"

"Come on." Kobra moved past him and out of Wes's field of vision. "I'm taking your black bitch with me, mister. She'll be nice and warm up at the castle, old Kobra'll see to that. You just lay there and think about that, okay?" Engines revved. Wes tried to pull himself to his feet, but pain exploded along his left side, where he'd been hurt in the crash of Jimmy's Cadillac. He fell back, panting. The motorcycles swept past him, roaring like wild animals. "Solange!" he tried to shout, but the name came out as a whisper.

And then they were gone, the sound of their cycles rapidly fading.

"Solange . . ." he whimpered, and curled up to die. Around him the wind began to chuckle.

The bell was still ringing, but now it seemed a world away.

Anger ached within him. *"Can't die!"* he shouted at himself. *"Got to find Solange! Can't let her be . . . like them!"* He lifted his head and whispered, "I'll find you!" After awhile he turned on his belly and started to crawl, sliding with the agonized movement of a crushed jack rabbit. He thanked God for the amulet Solange had given him; he didn't know how it had worked, but it had kept the vampires from biting him.

Now he counted the tolling of that bell to keep himself from slipping into darkness. "One . . . two . . . three . . . four . . . five . . ." Anger carried him along, and just behind him off in the shadows, he felt the presence of some grinning, scabrous thing with a vaudeville stage-hook, trying to catch hold of him and drag him back. He kept crawling.

FOURTEEN

Lights glowed dimly from the ceiling of a concrete-walled factory in Highland Park. Every so often they flickered out and, when they were gone, the conveyor belt would stop, too, and the workers had to pull the coffins along in the dark. But so far the electricity had been weak but fairly constant; the conveyor belt hummed, gears meshing perfectly. The gleaming coffins passed one after the other, faster and faster. Figures with shadowy faces grinned and nodded, pleased with their work. Soon they would be allowed to go out and feed, and another shift would take over. From now on, according to the Master, the factory would work from dusk until dawn, electricity or no. If the buzz saws went out, there were always hand saws and plenty of files and planes and other necessary tools.

At the end of the conveyor belt, where the big tractor-trailer trucks were lined up at the loading docks, there was a huge mound of sandy brown California soil the dump trucks had brought. Before the coffins were sealed and shoved into the trucks, the workers would lay down a good bed of dirt inside each of them. Then they were ready to go.

One of the workers, known as Mitchell Everett Gideon in his previous life, leaned on his shovel and waited for the next coffin to come down the line. His face was streaked with dirt, his eyes dark and sunken. He was cold with hunger but reassured by the knowledge that the plant whistle would blow in about an hour, and then he'd be allowed to feed. He wouldn't even have to spend time hunting, for one of the tractor-trailer trucks was loaded with humans, the Master's reward for work well done.

The next coffin came. He filled the bottom of it, pressed the dirt down with his shovel, and then it was carried away to a truck. Trucks were always coming and going, and it pleased him to see such efficiency. He was an important part of the machine now, much more important than he'd ever been in his life. He'd even met the Master and had told him everything he knew about the factory, about casket making, about getting the best possible effort out of a work crew. The Master was pleased and had asked Gideon if he could rely on him for help and suggestions. Gideon said yes, of course.

Another coffin came. Gideon filled it, working with a newfound strength, and watched it being carried away. Another truck moved out of its slot on the docks, and another backed in. He was ecstatically happy, ecstatic with his love for the Master. He had been granted the gift of eternal life . . . eternal *youth*.

It was all a dream come true.

FIFTEEN

At the end of two hours, Father Silvera had found more than fifty people and herded them back into the church Some of them were dazed, some were hysterical, others whimpered softly. The sanctuary teemed with life— people crying and praying, infants howling, people babbling, nearly insane. Silvera appointed four men to act as supervisors over the group; some of them wanted to go with him when he left again to continue his search, but he firmly told them no.

It was all he could do to keep himself steady out there. He didn't want to be responsible for losing anyone else. Stepping across that threshold and out into the dark sand-whipped street was the most terrible thing he'd ever asked himself to do. He was shaking very badly now his grip on the heavy brass crucifix so weak that several times he thought he couldn't continue holding onto it. But he did, mentally commanding those strained, deteriorating muscles to hold firm just a moment, just a second longer. His hands ached with his body's insidious betrayal.

Now out on the street again, he was alert for running shapes. He'd seen them several times. and once one of them had come dangerously close before it suddenly stopped and dodged away. Silvera presumed it was because of the crucifix. Perhaps they were afraid of it, just like in all the old vampire movies. He walked on, thankful that the wind had dropped enough for him to see the

buildings on either side of the street. His face was raw
and swollen from the sand's abrasion, and it was by
sheer habit now that he kept his eyes narrowed into tight,
protective slits. Mary's Voice called out behind him, the
sound echoing from street to street. He passed a grocery
store where the front window had been knocked out by a
wind-tossed garbage can; he made a mental note to come
back and get food and water for the people in the sanctuary. He was about to step into an apartment building
on Marquesa Street, just three blocks from his church,
when he heard a voice call, "Father Silvera! Help me!"

It was a little child's voice, and he didn't recognize it
at first. But then he heard "Please help me!" and a series
of broken sobs that faded away. He looked across the
street and up, and there in a broken, third-floor window
was Juanita LaPaz, her tiny face barely visible over the
sill. He could see her fingers grasping the wood tightly,
her eyes wide and terrified. "Please! I wan' my papa! I
wan' my . . ." She started to cry again, her hands going
to cover her eyes, and then she disappeared from the
window.

Silvera ran across the street, his shoes sinking down
into sand, and entered the building. It seemed deserted
and was as hot and dirty as a bowl of street-corner chili.
He took the stairs three at a time and was panting when
he got to the third-floor hallway, which was littered with
newspapers and old furniture and clothes. Graffiti covered the walls, along with splatters of what looked like
paint and dried blood. He paused, listening for the little
girl's crying. "Juanita?" he called out. "It's Father Silvera! Where are you, *querida?*"

He heard her muffled sobbing a couple of doors away.
When he opened the door, he found her standing barefoot in a room whose walls were covered with Power to
the People posters. Beneath her black bangs, her eyes
looked dull and glazed, as if—*oh, my God!* Silvera
thought—as if someone had given her drugs. She stood
staring at him and shivered.

"Thank God I've found you!" Silvera said, bending
down and hugging her. She didn't respond; her arms
hung limply at her sides. "Are you all right?"

"*Sí,*" she replied very softly. She seemed to be staring
right through him.

"Where's the man who took you, Juanita? Where did he go?"

"Gone far away. Please help me, I wan' my papa. Gone far away. Please help me, I wan' my . . ." Her eyes moved a fraction, staring over his right shoulder, and he saw a quicksilver glimmer of the terror frozen behind the doll-like mask of her face.

Silvera twisted his head around just as Cicero leaped through the doorway with a triumphant shriek.

They slammed together and crashed to the floor. Cicero hissed and tried to force the priest's chin back to get at the jugular vein. Silvera tried to gouge out the thing's eyes, but every time he struck, Cicero's head whipped to one side to evade the blow. Silvera clung to the crucifix with all his strength, and with his free hand he slammed an uppercut to the vampire's jaw. Cicero blinked but seemed unhurt. The vampire's head darted forward, fangs glistening. Silvera threw his arm across his neck and spat into the thing's eyes. Cicero recoiled, and Silvera struck out with his fist again, so hard he felt the vibration thrum up his shoulder. Before the thing could regain its grip, Silvera twisted and got a knee between them, then kicked out with tremendous, thigh-cracking effort. Cicero was flung back across the floor, but he quickly scrambled to his feet.

Silvera stood up, his lungs heaving. He grasped Juanita's shoulder and shook her hard to try to break the vampire's power over her. "Get behind me, Juanita! Hurry!" She was too dazed to understand.

Cicero grinned, the fangs sliding out of his upper and lower jaws. "Ain't gonna be so easy as that, Mr. Priest. Oh, nooooo. You in old Cicero's territory now. You got to play by *my* rules." The vampire stepped forward, hands curling into claws.

Silvera took a step backward. The crucifix felt leaden in his left hand. He held it up and thrust it forward at the vampire, his arm trembling. "Get back!" he commanded. "Your Master's dead, Cicero! He's destroyed!"

Cicero stopped, his face contorting. Then he threw back his head and laughed. " *'Get back'*? Ha! Man, you been watchin' too many old movies! Ha!" His eyes flamed. "Cicero Clinton ain't ashamed of what he is! I never believed in that re-ligion bullshit anyway, man, so that thing don't hurt me none now! And you're wrong.

The Master lives! He's in me right now, and I'm hungry, *reallll* hungry . . ." He came forward, his claws twitching, his face split by that leering, terrible grin.

Silvera grabbed the little girl and shoved her against the wall so he stood between her and the vampire. He heard her saying, like a broken record, ". . . gone far away. Please help me, I wan' my papa . . ."

"Gonna take you out slow, Mr. Priest," Cicero whispered. "Gonna make you hurt . . ." He tensed, knees bending for the leap. When he came for the priest's throat, he was a savage blur of motion.

But Silvera stood his ground. He swung the crucifix around in a vicious arc, aiming for the vampire's head. Cicero twisted slightly, but the sharp brass edge sliced a sizzling wound at the base of his neck. The dead flesh rippled and writhed, trying to close the smoking tear. There were yellowish-white tissues in the cut, but the vampire did not bleed. Silvera stepped forward quickly and struck again, aiming for the same place. The cut's edges now hissed and widened. Cicero staggered back, trying to shield the wound with his hands. Silvera's strength was weakening rapidly, and he felt his grip slipping. He feinted toward the thing's eyes, then struck again at the neck. Gray flesh ripped like rotten cheesecloth, exposing dead tissue and veins. The next blow of the crucifix almost severed Cicero's head from his body. The vampire staggered back, arms flailing in pain. Cicero's face hung at a right angle. It was contorted with fury; the fangs clicked together, seeking a hold on human flesh.

Then Cicero shrieked and rushed forward, trying to get the crucifix away from Silvera. The priest braced himself and swung out with the rest of his ebbing strength.

Cicero's head ripped from his body and tumbled into a corner. The headless body staggered on, its claws gripping Silvera's coat and hanging there; the fingers still writhed. Silvera could feel the waves of cold rolling off it, and he heard himself cry out in terror. He jerked away from the thing, and the body crumpled to the floor at his feet.

It was then that Juanita screamed and leaped into his arms. He hugged her close, pressing her head against his shoulder so she would not see any more of the horror. Across the room the fangs in the severed head kept clicking like dreadful castanets. The body at his feet suddenly shuddered, twisting like a dying snake. "God help us!" Silvera breathed. The body's limbs were still moving, it was pushing itself toward the head in the corner. Silvera didn't wait to see what would happen when it got there. With Juanita around his neck, Silvera raised the crucifix high over his head and slammed it down through the thing's spine. Bone and wood cracked; Silvera had dr'ven the crucifix through the body and into the floor. The vampire writhed, the feet trying to push it forward, but it was firmly pinned to the floor. The fangs began to grind together. Silvera left the crucifix where it was, put his arms around Juanita, and raced out of the building.

On the street he realized that he and the child were unprotected, but he felt certain that if he hadn't left Cicero's body pinned, it would have crawled across that floor and somehow made itself whole again. His stomach turned over at the thought. The moving shadows seemed to be on all sides. He was running now as hard as he could, his lungs pumping like bellows. He thought he heard something coming up from behind, but when he dared to look back, he saw nothing.

Less than a half-block from the church, he saw a corpse lying in the middle of the street. He was almost around it when the corpse's hand shot out, grabbing his ankle and almost tumbling him to the ground. The man raised his sand-caked face and whispered, "Help me . . ."

VII

Thursday, October 31
THE GHOST TOWN

ONE

Tommy Chandler stirred uneasily. The last bell was ringing, echoing down the long, silent halls of Fairfax High
School. He was running and trying to hold onto his books.
When he looked back, he could see the shadow that followed him relentlessly, its long arms swinging like the
orangutan's from "Murders in the Rue Morgue." And he
heard the guttural loathsome voice rolling down on him
like a tidal wave. *"I told you not to come back, fuckface
. . . told you not to . . . told you not toooooo . . . !"*

"Go away!" Tommy shouted, his voice cracking. "Leave
me alone!" And then he dropped his books all over the
hallway, which suddenly started changing shape, elongated
to incredible dimensions like a set from *The Thousand
Fingers of Dr. T.* He stopped to gather up his books, but
they kept slipping away from him, and he could hear the
muffled *boom boom boom* of Bull Thatcher's combat boots
coming up fast behind him. A shadow fell upon him like
a winter storm, and he looked up in terror . . .

. . . at the clock beside his bed. He could hear the
alarm ringing, and he reached out to shut it off. But before he could grasp it, the ringing stopped. He heard his
father's voice say, "Who is this? Why don't you say
something? Damn it, Cynthia, either someone's making
crank phone calls or . . ."

Tommy sat up in bed and fumbled for his extra pair
of eyeglasses on the table beside his bed. He put them on
and looked at the clock; it was a windup and hadn't
gone off at nine-forty when the electricity had died. It
was five minutes after midnight. *Who could be calling
now?* he wondered. The wind was still screaming at his
window, punctuated by the scatter-shots of sand on glass.
Before the television had gone black, the special KABC
weather report had said to expect winds of between thirty-

five and fifty miles per hour. And then the TV and lights had flickered out.

The telephone was ringing again. Tommy heard his father's muffled curse as he picked up the receiver.

Tommy had walked home from school that afternoon buffeted by hot western winds. He could look at the sky and tell a storm was coming because the clouds were thickening and cartwheeling for as far as he could see. He'd never seen anything quite like it before, not even in Denver. But the freak storm wasn't anything as incredible as the miracle at school yesterday. Of course, he'd had to return to the locker room, and as he was hurrying to gather up his books and get out, Mark Sturo told him not to worry, that Bull Thatcher and Ross Weir hadn't come to school, so he was safe. Buddy Carnes did come in while he was still at his locker, but Carnes hadn't even given him a sidelong glance. Now there might not even be any school today. That would be great, he thought, then he could watch Flash Gordon and Thriller on the Mexican stations . . . if the electricty came back on.

He got out of bed. From one wall a poster of Orlon Kronsteen, resplendent in his *King Vampire* makeup, glowered down at him. He went out into the hall and knocked on his parents' door. His father, a thin, pale man with thick eyeglasses like his son's, looked out.

"What are you doing out of bed, Tommy?"

"Woke up. Heard the phone ringing." He yawned, lifted his glasses, and rubbed his eyes. "Who's been calling?"

"I don't know. Some idiot who won't answer. I can hear a lot of static, but no voices. Why don't you try to go back to sleep?"

"The storm's still pretty bad, isn't it, Dad?"

"Yes. It is." He paused for a few seconds and then opened the door wider. "You want to come in and talk for a while?"

Tommy's mother, a sharp-chinned Radcliffe grad with dark, intense eyes, was sitting on the bed with her knees drawn up to her chest, making a mountain out of the covers. She was staring at the pale green curtains drawn across the window, watching them tremble every time an errant whisper of wind slipped through the casement. She looked at Tommy and smiled her tight, crooked smile. "Can't sleep either, huh?"

"Nope."

"Sounds like a hurricane, doesn't it? Gosh, who ever heard of a hurricane in California?"

"It's not as bad as it was a little while ago," his father said quietly. He sat on the edge of the bed and looked at the telephone. "I wonder who the hell that was? Somebody playing a joke?"

"Not very funny," Cynthia said.

Tommy stepped to the window, pushed aside the curtain, and looked out. For an instant he could've sworn he was back in Denver—*there was snow all over the place out there! Heaps and heaps of it, even beginning to cover over cars!* But then he saw a felled palm tree, all its fronds stripped away to leave a bare, ugly nub, and then he remembered this was California so that couldn't possibly be snow. It was sand, hot and thick, slowly piling up into mountainous dunes. "Where did all this sand come from, Dad?" he asked. His heart was beating a little faster.

"The Mojave Desert. The wind just carried it right over the mountains. That would be *our* luck, wouldn't it?"

"Yeah," Tommy said. "It sure would be." He strained his eyes to see across the street through the swirling, yellow sheets to the Vernon house.

"I never wanted to come to California," Tommy's father was saying. "I told Mr. Oakes I was an Achilles man all the way and, of course, I wanted the promotion, but . . ." He looked at his wife. "I wish we could've stayed in Scottsdale. That was a really beautiful city, and you didn't have to worry about traffic jams or smog or some crazy murderer running loose . . ."

"Dad." Tommy said very quietly. He wasn't sure what he was seeing, wasn't sure at all, but he thought he should say something.

"Now this," his dad said. "Christ! No electricity, no . . . where's that transistor radio, Cynthia?"

"Dad," Tommy said. "There's . . ."

"The one you bought at K-Mart? I think it's still packed away in a box, honey. Probably out in the hall closet. I doubt if the batteries are still working."

"I'll try to find it. Tommy, why don't you scare up some candles and matches if we're going to stay up? Okay?"

Tommy nodded and looked back out the window. What he thought he'd seen—a figure standing amidst the sand drifts on the Vernon's front yard, staring across at his house and seemingly right at him—was no longer there now. He craned his neck to either side but could see no one out there, if he had actually seen anyone at all. Still, a shiver ran up his spine. He went to get the candles and matches, passing his dad rummaging through the hall closet and feeling his way down the stairs to the kitchen. The wind shrilled and whistled around the house, trying to suck it off its foundations, but at the house's center there seemed to be a hole of unearthly darkness and silence, the stuff that had crept in when the electricity had gone. Tommy started opening drawers. He found a couple of candles and now he needed matches. He searched on a shelf above the sink and from the corner of his eye saw something move near the window that looked out over their tiny backyard. He wasn't sure what it was, but it had looked like someone . . . running. He stared out, his heart pumping ice water. "Hey, Mom!" he shouted. "Where are the matches?"

"Look under the sink!" she called down to him.

He opened a couple of cupboards down there and finally found a large pack of Fire Chiefs, the kind you could strike anywhere. And suddenly from the front of the house, there came an ugly-sounding *whump* and he could hear things crashing around in the living room. A whirl of wind and sand hit him as he raced out of the kitchen to the stairs. He could see the front door hanging on one hinge, and a coffee table had gone flying against a wall. His dad called out from upstairs, "Tommy? What was that?"

"Door's open!" he said. "The wind knocked it loose . . . I guess."

"Christ! If that sand gets inside . . . Tommy, can you prop it shut?"

"I'll try!" He moved across the room against the wail of wind and dragged a chair over to secure the door. It held, although the whistlings through the doorjamb had grown savage. Then he hurried upstairs, the flesh at the back of his neck beginning to creep.

His father had found the transistor radio and tuned it to KALA. A rock song was playing, the singer wailing something about everybody being part of a food chain. Tommy lit the candles and placed one on either side of the bed. The gruff-voiced dj came on after the song had

ended, his patter garbled by static. "Yeaaah! That was
Tonio K. and 'Life in the Foooooodchain!' Thass what it's
all about now, ain't it, brothers and sisters? Lemme
reeeelay to you what the scouts are tellin' old Tiger Eddie.
Got a whole lot of fine young ones trapped up in the Hollywood Recreation Center on Lexington Avenue. You get
yourself up there early for the best pickin's, you dig? Got
a few scattered all along Rosewood Avenue, you just got
to keep knockin' on them doors 'till you get lucky . . ."

"What's he talking about?" Tommy's dad asked nervously, looking at his son.

". . . old Tiger Eddie's gonna be with you right up 'til
night-night time about five-thirty this morning. Here's a
little note to make your mouths water. There are sixty
—count 'em, sixty—holed up over at the Westside Jewish
Center between Olympic and San Vicente. Just a reminder—the Master don't want 'em *old*, you dig? You
find some old coots, just do us all a favor and fling 'em
out in the wind, okay? Yeah! Dig it!"

"Christ! What's . . . what's that idiot talking about?"

And then something stepped through the open doorway into the bedroom.

It was Mr. Vernon. His eyes shone in a ghastly chalk-
white face. He was wearing a dirty white shirt and dark
trousers, and even in the dim candlelight Tommy could
see the brownish spots on his collar. Tommy's heart
leaped into his throat, almost choking him. His mom gave
out a little scream, and his dad whirled around so fast
his glasses almost flew off. "Pete!" his dad said in a
trembling voice. "What are you . . . I mean . . . why
are . . . ?"

"I've come to visit," Pete Vernon said, in a soft hiss
of a voice. "Oh, listen to that wind. Isn't it wonderful?"

"How did you . . . get in?"

"The front door, of course. As any visitor would enter.
I've brought my wife with me. Dianne?"

And then she was there, too, both of them blocking
the doorway, both of them pale and grinning.

"Don?" Tommy's mom said softly to his dad. Her
face had gone white, her eyes swimming with fear.

"*Don,*" Dianne Vernon whispered, gripping her mouth
around the name. Her eyes shifted very slowly and stared
into Tommy's face. Her gaze burned like hellfire. Then
she grinned and opened her mouth wide, and Tommy's

brain screamed with the terrible word—*VAMPIRE*—
he'd heard in a thousand monster movies—*VAMPIRE*
—when he was sitting in a safe chair at a safe distance
—*VAMPIRE*—in his own safe, private little world, but
now this was real—*VAMPIRE*—real, real, real . . .

"No!" he tried to shout, but it came out as a croak.
Mrs. Vernon swept past him like a dry wind, moving
inexorably upon his father. He cried out, "NO," and
leaped for her, trying to hold her back. She hissed and
twisted, and in the next instant Mr. Vernon's freezing
hands were on him, flinging him like a sack of rags out
into the hallway. He smacked against the wall hard and
slid to the floor, his brain reeling with pain and terror.
He heard his mother scream, then there was a high peal
of wicked laughter that was so terrible Tommy thought
he would go crazy before it stopped. But when it did
stop, the sucking sounds began, and those were much,
much worse.

And then a beautiful, terrible voice whispered,
"Tommy?"

He looked up, cold sweat breaking out on his face.

It was *her,* mounting the stairs now and coming down
the hallway toward him with slow, supple steps. He could
see the long, golden hair splashed over her bare shoulders. She was wearing a violet halter, the deep dish of
her navel exposed over tight denim cutoffs decorated
with different-colored patches—one showed Snoopy re-
clining atop his doghouse, another said Have a Nice
Day! Her thigh muscles tensed as she neared him, and
in the darkness he could see the awful sheen of her eyes.
That beautiful flesh would never again be touched by
the sun. "Tommy?" she whispered, and when she smiled,
she was still *so* pretty, even like this. She held out one
graceful hand to him. "How's about you and me gettin'
it on, huh?" she said softly.

"You're . . . *dead!*" Tommy said, the effort to speak
making sweat run down his face in rivulets. "You're not
Sandy Vernon anymore. You're not human . . ."

"You're wrong, Tommy. I'm still Sandy. And I know
how much you want me, Tommy. I could always tell.
That's why I liked to tease you and show off my legs for
you. I want you too, Tommy. I want you reeeeeeal
bad . . ." She stepped forward, about to touch him. Her
eyes blazed with wicked and soul-shaking promises. He

felt all on fire and yet so cold, as if he stood facing an
inferno while a blizzard raged at his back. His mind
slipped toward her, and he began to envision all the
wonderful possibilities, how he could just put his hand
into hers—NO!—and she would guide him right into
his own room to the bed—*NO, YOU CAN'T!*—and
then it would be better than anything he'd ever known,
better than a Mexican horror film festival—*SHE'S IN
YOUR MIND, GET HER OUT!*—or even three Orlon
Kronsteen films right in a row, all he would have to do
would be to lie back and let her—*GET HER OUT,
SHE'S COMING CLOSER!*—do everything to him,
everything, everyth . . .

"GET OUT!" he shrieked. "GET OUT!" He twisted
away from her grasp, from the fangs that were coming
down out from under her full, luscious lips, and raced
back along the hallway. He burst through a door into
the bathroom and locked it just before the beautiful vampire started battering on the wood. "Let me in!" she
shrieked in a frenzy. "You little bastard, let me in *right
now!*"

There was a tremendous blow, and the door shuddered; wood began to split. The blows followed one after
the other very rapidly now, and Tommy thought that
Mr. and Mrs. Vernon were probably out there too, helping to batter the door down. A great crevice suddenly
appeared in the wood; the door started to cave in.

Tommy realized he was still gripping the pack of
matches. But what good were they? What could he do
with them? He couldn't think; the noise outside was too
loud. Then he flung open the medicine cabinet and was
sweeping aside bottles of vitamins, cough medicine, and
cold capsules. There was nothing he could use. Suddenly
the door shattered, and they were on him, all three of
them ravenous and fighting over him, trying to tear him
to pieces. They started to drag him out of the bathroom.

His hand clutched a can of his mom's hair spray,
which was sitting on the sink. As Mr. Vernon's grip closed
on his throat, he shook a match into his hand and flailed
out, trying to scrape it across the wall. He missed, and
now Sandy was trying to grasp his arm, screaming shrilly,
"HE'S MINE! HE'S MINE! IT'S NOT FAIR!"

Tommy reached out, almost popping his shoulder out
of the socket, and dragged the match across plaster. It

sputtered and flared, illuminating the sudden burst of fear in the vampires' eyes. Tommy knocked the cap off the hair spray can, got his thumb on the button, and pushed. Immediately he could smell sweet flowers, and the image of his blood-drained mother lying in the next room streaked through his head. He held the match up in front of the spray just as Mr. Vernon made a guttural animal noise and leaped for his throat.

A two-foot jet of flames shot out of the spray can. He heard Mrs. Vernon scream, and he stuck that blue torch right in her husband's face.

Mr. Vernon roared in agony as the flame hit his eyes. He staggered back out of the bathroom, he and Sandy fighting for an instant as they jammed into each other in the doorway. Tommy charged them, keeping his thumb pressed down. The vampires stumbled over each other, trying to get away. "Come on back and fight!" Tommy screamed at them. "Come on, you dirty bastards!" He forgot and released his thumb. The flame instantly went out. Sandy's eyes gleamed, and she started back along the hallway for him. Tommy raced back to the bathroom where the matches lay scattered on the floor. He struck another one and lit his torch again; this time he kept more matches clutched in his hand. Sandy stopped just beyond the bathroom door and immediately backed away. "We'll get you!" she hissed from the head of the stairs. "We'll come back for you, you'll see!"

And then they were gone, sweeping down the stairs and away.

Tommy couldn't lift his thumb for another minute. The flame went out, and he stood in the midst of a stinking swirl of smoke. He was trembling, but he was afraid to cry because he knew if he started, he couldn't stop. He was sure those things meant what they said—they *would* be back.

It was a long time before he could make himself go into his parents' bedroom. On the floor Tiger Eddie's voice still growled from the transistor radio. "Oh yeaaaaah, brothers and sisters, got some real fine news for you if you happen to be huntin' out Santa Monica way. Seems there's a whole bunch of 'em stuck out at the Santa Monica Airport waitin' on planes that never took off, can ya dig it? You be first over there and have yourselves some fun for Tiger Eddie, okay? Gonna be keepin' you up to date 'til sign-off time. Right now here's a fine disc from the Motels . . ."

Tommy picked up the radio and flung it against the wall. It shattered into small bits of plastic and metal. Then he stood and looked down at his parents' bodies, a sob trying to work its way out of his throat.

He began to cry, but he kept his finger on the hair-spray button.

TWO

The madman next door was singing again, trying to out-shout the wind. "Onnnn Christ the solid rock I stand . . . alllll other ground is sinking sand, alllll other ground issssss sinking . . . I see you out there! You stay away, you hear me!" There was the quick *crack* of a shot fired at shadows. Then silence except for a few hoarse sobs.

You'd better save those bullets, Palatazin thought. *They may not be worth much, but I'm sure they're better than nothing.* He was sitting on the floor beside the window, his back against the wall. Jo lay on the sofa, drifting in and out of a troubled sleep.

Gayle came back from the kitchen, eating a slice of ham. "You sure you don't want any more of this?" she asked him quietly. "It's just going to go bad in that fridge."

He shook his head.

"There's fruit," she said. "Some apples and oranges."

"No. I don't want anything." He watched as she stepped cautiously to the window and peered out. "You'd better get some sleep while you can," he told her.

"How long until sunrise?"

"About three hours."

Softly, she said, "When is that wind going to stop?"

"The storm's died a little bit," he said, "but I wouldn't suggest our trying to leave this house. There's no telling what we might run into. I think we're about as safe here as we could possibly be."

"Some consolation. What happens at dawn?"

"What do you mean?"

"I know the vampires go crawling back into their

graves or holes or wherever, but what happens to us? Where do we go when the storm stops?"

Palatazin almost voiced his fears—that the storm had somehow been brought on by the vampires and would *not* stop, but would probably intensify during the daylight hours to keep the pockets of humanity isolated from each other—but he didn't. Instead he said quietly, "I want you and Jo to try to get out."

"Okay, I'll buy that. But what about you?"

"I'm going to finish what I began. I'm going to find a way up to the Kronsteen castle . . ."

"Alone? You're crazy if . . ."

"Yes, alone," he said firmly. "And I may be crazy, I admit it. But who else is there to do it? And if it's not done—if it's not at least tried—then from now on every night will be just like this one. People hiding in the dark, waiting for the vampires. When they're finished here, they're going to sweep eastward, town after town, city after city. Los Angeles is now, for all intens and purposes, theirs. How long do you think smaller cities would last? How long before they reach Chicago and New York? I think there are already vampires in those cities, placed there by their Master as advance scouts. But I think they're waiting to see how successful these vampires are here before they begin massing their armies."

"Surely some news is getting out to the rest of the country!" Gayle said. "Surely . . . somebody out there knows . . . what's happening to us! Don't they?"

Palatazin shook his head. "I doubt it. Right now all they know is that the sandstorm of the century has hit L.A. Other than that, what could they know? How could the news get out? No, Miss Clarke, I'm afraid we're quite isolated, which, of course, is exactly what the vampires want."

She was silent for a moment, wincing as a gust of wind blew sand against the glass. She sat down in a chair, drawing her legs up underneath her. "Why did they choose L.A.?" she asked him finally. "Why begin with us?"

"I'm not sure. Oh, I have my theories, but . . ." He shrugged. "Los Angeles may be one of the largest cities in the world, but it's really a gathering of villages, many of them having no real contact or intermingling with any of the others. I think the vampire king has had . . . much

experience in taking villages, and he began here because
he recognized that fact about L.A. Also, he probably realized how isolated this city already is from the rest of
the country, cut off by mountains and desert. And if you
hear about strange goings-on in L.A.—for instance that
Gravedigger thing—most people here and in other parts
of the country tend to simply shrug and say, 'Well, that's
life in Los Angeles.' Believe me, the vampire king has
studied this city thoroughly, and he saw how he could
take advantage of such attitudes. Also, to conquer a city
of this size . . . think of the confidence that's going to
give the vampires who are scattered all over this country,
waiting for their Master's command. They're going to
think they're invincible, that nothing can stand in their
way. They may be right."

"How are you going to get up that mountain with those
dogs standing guard?"

He looked at her and smiled grimly. "I don't know."

Gayle shivered. "Maybe I will try to get some sleep.
God knows I need it. I'm going to go scare up a pillow
and a blanket." She rose to her feet and started toward
the stairs.

"Will you bring a pillow for Jo, too, please?" he asked
her.

"Sure. Back in a minute." She climbed the stairs in the
dark, her hand gripping the banister hard. She opened a
door and peered in. It was a bedroom. There were a
couple of pillows on the bed, but the blanket and bedspread had been kicked off. She gathered up the pillows,
hurrying because the moan of the wind at the windows
sounded so ghastly, when her heart gave a violent kick.
She stared at the bed, an odd recollection ticking in her
brain.

There were no sheets. Just as in Jack's apartment before she'd found him . . .

"Palatazin," she said. It came out as a dry, throaty
whisper.

Something rustled in the room, shifting heavily. There
was the muffled noise of ripping cloth.

"Oh, God," Gayle whimpered, one hand going to her
mouth. "Oh, God, no, no, no . . ."

In the darkness the closet door began to open. Another
movement caught her eye, and now she could see a
cocooned shape writhing out from under the bed. It

jerked and stretched and, with the soft tearing of cloth, a grasping white hand protruded, fingers clawing at the sheet. A body came tumbling out of the closet. It was the gray-haired man in the mantel photographs, his legs still wrapped tightly. He fought to get free, and slowly his gaze turned upon Gayle. His eyes flamed.

Gayle screamed. She backed out of the bedroom, and as she did, she saw a woman's head appear out of the other shroud. "WHAT IS IT?" she heard Palatazin shout from downstairs. "GAYLE?"

She started down the stairs, tripped and fell headlong before she could grasp the banister. When she looked back, she saw the man coming at her, a black tongue licking his lower lip. He reached down and grasp^d her arm, his grip colder than the dead of winter. His grinning sickle of a mouth gaped, and Gayle almost fainted with horror as the fangs began to close in on her throat.

Palatazin stepped to the foot of the stairs with Jo behind him. The vampire, its fangs a half-inch from Gayle's jugular vein, looked up, its eyes narrowing as it sensed that something was not right.

Palatazin flung out his arm with the bottle of holy water clamped in his hand and saw the droplets spray across the vampire's face. Instantly the vampire shrieked in agony, trying to hold an arm over its eyes. It let go of Gayle and scurried up the stairs. Palatazin followed, his face gone gray.

In the bedroom the vampire whirled to face him, and Palatazin could see the smoking holes where the drops of water had struck. The female vampire had almost kicked free from her shroud, and now she began to crawl across the floor toward the scent of hot blood. The male vampire hissed and leaped toward Palatazin. He stepped back, slamming against the wall, and flung out with the bottle again. A machine-gun slash of holes crossed the vampire's forehead, putting out one eye. The thing screamed and fell to its knees, writhing in pain as if it had been sprayed with acid. When Palatazin stepped toward it, the vampire leaped up, shuddering with fear, and crashed through the window on the other side of the bedroom in a silvery shower of glass.

The female vampire gripped Palatazin's ankle, pulling herself toward him. He poured a little of the water in the palm of his hand and flung it quickly into her face.

She howled and contorted, pulling free of her cocoon, both hands pressed to her eyes. Then she was up and staggering blindly, trying to find the window. When her hand closed on the glass fragments on the sill, she pulled herself up and over, falling out of sight.

Palatazin looked through the window, wind whipping into his face. He saw the two figures, still running, and heard the madman's strident cry, "Ye foul spawn of Satan I strike the blow of God." There were three quick shots, and the vampires disappeared into the storm. Palatazin was stunned; he'd had no idea the holy water would have had that destructive an effect. His stomach heaved, dark motes spinning before his eyes. He could hear Gayle downstairs, babbling hysterically. When his dizziness passed, he looked at the bottle of holy water. It was a little less than half full now. *What was in this water that could've caused a reaction like that?* he wondered. There was a single drop remaining in the palm of his hand. He sniffed it, then licked it.

The water was salty.

Seawater? he asked himself. Then perhaps the salt had an immediate, corrosive effect on the vampires' dead flesh? He didn't know why Father Silvera had brought him seawater, but he was decidedly grateful for it.

"Andy?" Jo called from downstairs. Then in a panicked voice, "ANDY!"

He walked back down the stairs on trembling legs. "I'm all right," he assured her. "I'm fine. But now we have to check this house from top to bottom. I don't think there are any more of them hiding here, but we have to be certain." He looked into the living room where Gayle was huddled on the sofa, whimpering like a little girl. "You're going to be all right, Miss Clarke?" he asked her.

"Yeah," she said quickly. "Yeah. Yeah. Let me get my breath. Okay. Yeah."

He nodded, knowing there was very little that would keep her down for long. He squeezed Jo's hand. "We'll start with the basement," he said quietly.

THREE

Tommy was running. Behind him his house was on fire. He hadn't thought it would go up so quickly, but he figured the wind had helped fan the blaze. He'd stood over his parents' corpses for a long time, just looking at them and wondering what to do. He knew what was supposed to happen now. His mom and dad were supposed to sleep until the next nightfall, and then sometime in the darkness they would awaken to walk the streets with the rest of the Undead. That's what happened in all the movies.

The Undead.

That sounds so cold, Tommy had thought. *So final. Once you've stepped across that line, you don't come back, not ever. But this is my mom and dad lying here, not . . . vampires!* "Wake up," he whispered in the terrible darkness. "Both of you . . . please . . . wake up . . ."

But they hadn't even moved, and Tommy could see the deep punctures on their throats that told him they weren't ever going to wake up as Don and Cynthia Chandler again.

So after a long time of just standing there, he'd gone to his room, put on his jeans, a shirt, and his all-weather jacket, then looked in his closet for the old Army surplus backpack he'd used briefly when he was a Boy Scout in Scottsdale. He'd put some matches into his jacket pocket, then the rest of them went into the backpack along with an extra can of hair spray and his dad's Right Guard aerosol deodorant. He went downstairs and made himself a couple of peanut-butter-and-jelly sandwiches, wrapped them in waxed paper, and slipped them into the pack along with a meat cleaver he found in a drawer. The main question that faced him was whether he should try to make it to the ocean or head up into the mountains. He'd thought about staying here in the house until sunrise, but he couldn't bear the idea of letting his parents slip over that Undead line, and he couldn't stay with them lying in the bedroom all white and empty. The ocean was too far away so he decided on the mountains.

But one thing he couldn't be sure of was how many
real people there were in the houses around him, and how
many vampires waited out there for little boys running
in the night. He decided that if he saw anyone, he would
assume the worst. He folded the sheets around his parents
and stuffed newspapers under the bed. Then he cried a
little bit before he could muster the nerve to strike the
first match. He lit his spray-can torch and touched the
flame to the sheets; they crisped and caught fire very
quickly. There was no way he could wait to see if the
bodies caught or not. He turned and ran, his face
scorched by an agonizing lick of flame.

Now he was racing along the edge of Hancock Park,
sand stinging his cheeks, the wind bringing the odors
of oranges and cloves from the tar pits, the air metallic in
his gasping lungs. He could tell the storm had diminished
in force during the last several hours. Now sand dunes
lay scattered across the white field of the park, and broken branches littered his path. He was a good runner; he
knew he could last a long time because whenever he
jogged with his mom and dad in the evenings he always
left them behind and just kept on going until he looked
back and saw them as only two struggling dots. His heart
seemed jammed up in his throat. He turned and thought
he saw a faint, reddish glow in the sky where his house
was—had been—but he wasn't sure. He decided not to
look back again.

He was heading northeast toward the only wooded refuge he could think of that was anywhere near his house.
In August his dad had taken him up to the Nature Museum
and Bird Sanctuary on Mount Hollywood, then down into
the four-thousand acres (so the guidebook had said) of
Griffith Park. There were a lot of bridle paths crisscrossing the park but very few roads, and Tommy remembered being amazed at how close a really unspoiled
mountain area was to the winding residential streets of
Hollywood. So that was where he had to go. He knew
he could lose himself in that park, but getting there meant
crossing through the heart of Hollywood, and he was
bitterly afraid of what might be lurking there. He still
gripped the can of hair spray he'd repelled the Vernons
with, and there were good old dependable Fire Chiefs—
what I used to burn up my mom and dad with, he thought
suddenly—in his jacket pocket. As he ran, he saw the

wind rippling currents of sand before him, and he thought of that terrified kid in *Invaders from Mars*, running across a sand hill that whirlpooled beneath his feet to send him into a subterranean world of alien horrors.

And then he was aware of the figure running behind him about thirty yards off to the left. Tommy looked over his shoulder. There was a hideous, moon-white face floating toward him from the darkness. He increased his speed, zigzagging deeper into the park. When he dared to look back, the thing was gone.

The high fence around the largest of the tar pits had blown down; a sheen of sand, white mottled with black, covered the surface of a lake from which a huge, concrete mastodon struggled to escape. Tommy ran along its edge toward the eastern edge of the park. He passed benches stripped of paint where the old men played checkers on Saturday mornings; he passed long strips of pavement that would not be used by Sunday afternoon roller-skaters for a long time to come.

And then something slammed into the small of his back. A hand dug into his jacket, almost ripping it off his shoulders, and flung him to the ground with brutal force.

He lay there fighting for breath, a shrill alarm, *Don't let them bite you! Don't, don't, don't!* screaming in his head. He'd lost his grip on the spray can, and when he raised his head, he saw a couple of hulking boys standing over him, both of them leering in anticipation. The one who'd knocked him down was a fat-jowled Chicano with thick eyebrows and a spill of dirty, black hair on his forehead; he wore a blood-spattered, blue workshirt. The vampire looked at the can of hair spray at his feet and kicked it far out into the tar lake where it sank with a burst of bubbles. Then he advanced on Tommy, his eyes already glazed with pleasure.

But before the vampire could reach Tommy, a length of chain came snaking out of the darkness, cracking the Chicano across the face. He fell to his knees, howling with rage. The second vampire, a skinny, dark-haired kid with a scraggly mustache and goatee, whirled around to face the attacker. The chain whirred, striking him in the temple. He staggered and was about to rush forward when he saw who it was that had struck him.

Tommy's heart had leaped; now it fell again to a sickening depth. Bull Thatcher, armed with a three-foot chain,

had stepped between Tommy and the two vampires.
Tommy could see the bloodless, awful face of the Fairfax
High Horror.

"You're on my turf," Bull said menacingly. "I'm huntin' here. Get out."

"It's our kill, you . . ." the Chicano began. He was
silenced when the chain whistled across his face again.

"GET OUT!" Bull roared.

Tommy, his arms shaking so badly they moved like a
jerky marionette's, slowly began to slip off his backpack.

"Get out, both of you!" Bull repeated. "I'm hungry,
and I'm takin' this kill, you understand?" The vampires
glowered at each other hotly but began to retreat when
Bull lifted that chain and cracked it to the ground like a
whip.

"We'll get you!" the Chicano shouted. "We'll find you
when you're sleepin', and we'll fix you . . ."

Bull moved forward a few steps, the chain swinging
above his head. The vampires were running away now.
Tommy got his pack off, leaped to his feet, and ran in
the other direction. Bull Thatcher watched the vampires
run out of sight with a defiant smirk and then turned for
his prize. Running along the lake's edge, Tommy heard
his angered roar and flinched. He unsnapped a pocket
and reached in. Bull Thatcher was chasing him, coming
like the wind. Sweat popped up on Tommy's face; he
could hear the thing gaining on him, and he dared not
look back.

But then he heard the chain whistling toward his right
ear, and he ducked his head, spinning around to face
Bull and bringing out the meat cleaver in a tightly clenched
fist at the same time. Before Bull could stop, Tommy had
flung himself at the thing, burying that cleaver between
the vampire's eyes with all his strength. Bull, thrown off-
balance, staggered and fell into the tar pit on his back.
Instantly bubbles exploded around his body, and he
flailed at the air for something to grab. "NOOOO!" he
roared like a maddened animal. "NOOOOO! I WON'T
LET YOUUUUUU . . . !" Water and tar rushed into his
mouth. He began to sink, tar streaking his face in thick,
black lines. He fought wildly, but the tar had him and
he knew it. He began to scream, the meat cleaver buried
in his forehead but the wound bloodless.

Tommy knew the other vampires would hear and come

back. He started to run again, slipping his pack around
his trembling shoulders. He wanted to be sick, he wanted
to scream, he wanted to cry, but there wasn't time for
any of that baby stuff anymore. When he looked back, he
saw Bull's face disappear, and the scream bubbled away.

He ran on, breathing in great painful heaves. He left
the park and ran northward across Third Street and
through dark, silent residential streets where the merest
suggestion of movement was enough to make him whine
with fear. Then he was across Beverly Boulevard, still
going north. Sand whipped into his face; were it not for
his glasses, he would have been blinded. His lungs flamed,
and now he knew he couldn't go much further. The worst
part of it lay ahead, those main arteries through Hollywood. He was certain the vampires would be waiting
there. How many would there be? Dozens? Hundreds?
Thousands? He crossed Melrose and started to veer
toward the northeast; he saw a group of moving shadows
and dived beneath some hedges until they'd passed. He
made himself continue, staggering from street to street,
crossing through backyards and alleys. A gust of hot
wind hit him, almost stealing the last of his breath. Light-
headed, he tripped and almost fell over something that
he realized three strides later must have been a corpse.

And then a voice roared over his head. "I see you,
child of the devil! Ye legion of Lucifer . . . !" There was
a loud *crack!* right behind his ear, then a freight train
knocked him off his feet and rumbled on past, leaving
him crushed in the sand.

FOUR

"A boy!" Jo said, peering out the window through widened eyes. "That maniac shot a boy!"

Palatazin eased over beside her and looked out. He
could see the small figure lying prone in the sand right in
front of the house. At first he'd thought the boy must
be a vampire, but if that were so, a single bullet wouldn't
have stopped him. Palatazin paused, his heart beginning
to hammer, then took his .38 from its shoulder-holster.

Jo stared fearfully at the gun. "What are you going to do?"

"That boy may not be dead. I'll have to go out and see." He moved past her toward the door and, from the sofa, Gayle said, "For Christ's sake, be careful!"

Palatazin nodded and squeezed out the door onto the porch where a furnace breath of wind rocked him on his heels. Grit stung his eyes, and he had to wait a moment before he could see anything. Then he was moving down the porch steps his grip already sweaty on his .38. He was alert for any movement in the windows of that silent house next door, but so far he couldn't tell where the man was. He tensed and then ran out to the curb where that boy lay sprawled on his face. Palatazin could see a bleeding gash across the back of his head, the dark brown hair matted with blood. He got his arms under the boy and started to lift him.

"Heathen!" the voice shrieked. "God's blight on the wor'd!" A shot rang out, kicking up sand two feet away. Palatazin lifted the boy, struggled to his feet, and started to run back to the house. Another bullet screamed past Palaz'n's face, leaving what he thought was a burning red streak in the sullen air. Then he was on the porch, and Jo was opening the door to pull him in.

Gayle had brought a pillow and bedspread from upstairs, and now Palatazin laid the boy on the sofa, his forehead cradled against the pillow. "How badly is he hurt?" Gayle asked.

"I don't know. The bullet took off some scalp at the back of his head, probably gave him one hell of a knock, too." He took off the boy's backpack and laid it on the floor. It was heavy, and things clanked together inside. He unzipped and unsnapped several of the backpack's pockets, rummaging through them. "I'd say he was prepared for a little of everything," Palatazin said. "I wonder where he was trying to get to."

Jo was gingerly parting the boy's hair to look at the wound. In the darkness she couldn't see it very well, but her fingers were already sticky with warm blood. She reached over and grasped his wrist. The pulse seemed strong if erratic. "Can you find me some towels, Andy?" she said. "Maybe we can stop some of this bleeding."

He went upstairs to search the bathroom.

The boy suddenly stirred and moaned. He said in a

weary, old-man's voice, "You're dead . . . leave me alone!
. . . burned them up, I burned them, burned them . . ."
Then he was quiet again.

"Do you think he's going to die?" Gayle asked.

"I'm certainly no doctor," Jo said. "But he's a small
boy. I hope he's stronger than he looks."

Palatazin brought the towels, one of which he'd soaked
in cold water. Jo started cleaning the crusted blood away,
then pressed a towel against the wound.

Gayle watched for a few minutes and then turned away.
She could hear the wind's shriek outside, and it seemed
to her that it sounded much more savage than it had only
half an hour before. She stepped to the window and saw
sand corkscrewing in the middle of the street like a mini-
ature tornado. The window rattled in its frame. *Oh, my
God,* she thought. *Oh, no . . .* "How long until sunrise?"
she asked Palatazin.

"An hour or so."

"My God," she whispered. "I . . . I think the storm's
building again. The wind's getting stronger." Her control
broke, hot fear flooding out of her. "Why won't the storm
move out to sea? Why won't it just . . . go away or die
down or . . . leave us alone? *Why won't it?*" She turned
to stare at Palatazin.

"Because somehow *they* brought it here," he said quietly. Jo looked up at him from the boy. "It'll grow
stronger during the daylight hours to keep people isolated
and trapped. Then when night falls again, the vampires
will be out in full force."

"We can't . . . we can't last another night!" Jo's voice
was thick with dread.

"I know that. Somehow I've got to reach that castle today. I've got to find the vampire king and destroy him."

"How?" Gayle asked. "When the storm gets worse, you
won't even be able to get two blocks from here, much less
make it all the way across fucking Hollywood! And what
about those dogs up there? Do you think they'll step off
the road and just let you walk right on past?"

"No. I don't. I'm going to make it up the mountain
some way other than the road . . ."

"Climb it? Now you're really flipping out."

"What would you presume I do?" he shouted at her,
his face reddening. "What are my choices? There's Death
on every side now, but shall we just sit here and wait for

it to come grinning in the night? NO! I have to reach the
Kronsteen castle before sundown!"

The boy stirred again. "Kronsteen . . ." he moaned.
"Vampire. Bite you . . ."

Palatazin looked down at the small body in surprise.
What could this boy know of Orlon Kronsteen? But then
the boy was quiet, and whatever questions Palatazin had
for him would have to wait—if he could ever answer
them at all.

"You can't make it up to that castle," Gayle said. Behind her the wind gnawed at the glass.

"If I don't," he answered her coldly, "who will?"

Jo could see that Andy had already decided, and there
was nothing more to be said. She went back to work on
the boy, her eyes burning. *It was all hopeless, of course.
Everything was hopeless,* she thought, from his reaching
the castle to her being able to save this boy. But perhaps
in Andy's decision there was a spark of hope that might
keep them all alive for just one more day.

FIVE

Prince Vulkan sat at the head of his council table in his
attack command chamber, the same room in which he
had crushed Phillip Falco's skull and tossed him into
the fireplace. The stink of charred meat still clung to the
walls. Maps of Los Angeles were smoothed out before
him, and at the table sat his lieutenants, Kobra on his
right and Roach—the only human within a radius of more
than a mile—at his left.

It was almost time to sleep. Prince Vulkan could feel
the heavy weariness overtaking him fast, but he was
elated. From the reports of his lieutenants those areas
called Beverly Hills, West Los Angeles, Culver City, and
Highland Park had been completely overrun. The human
population of Boyle Heights had been reduced to a few
hidden groups, and the central part of Hollywood had all
but fallen as well. His lieutenants were as fat as ticks.
Like celebrants at a Roman orgy, they had fed, thrown
up blood, fed, thrown up again, and feverishly hunted
down more victims.

"Master," a young black vampire, who had in life been an administrative aide to the mayor, was saying, "the East Division needs more troops in Alhambra and Monterey Park. We can take those areas in one night if we're allowed another thousand." He wore the dirty remnants of what had been an expensive, gray vested suit; there were spatters of blood on his shirt.

"It's most important to concentrate on the canyon communities, Master," a vampire across the table said. He had curly, iron-gray hair and wore a profusion of silver chains spilling down the open vee of his Calvin Klein western shirt. Up until several nights ago he had been a major power at the Warner Brothers studios. "I've had reports from both Laurel and Coldwater canyons of scattered sightings. They're trying to escape across the Santa Monica Mountains."

Vulkan's gaze flared. "Were they stopped?"

"Yes. Most of them . . ."

"You didn't answer my question. They weren't stopped, were they?" Vulkan stared at him for a silent moment, his cat eyes blazing.

"We . . . we need more troops to patrol the . . . canyons," he protested softly, beginning to tremble.

Vulkan leaned forward. "I want none of them escaping, do you understand that? None of them. I don't care if the Central Division has to go without food. I want those gaps filled. And they *will* be filled. Won't they?"

The vampire nodded. "Immediately, Master."

"Perhaps Western Division can spare a thousand or so?" Vulkan looked across the table at a young vampire with shoulder-length, blond hair and the last yellow tinge of a surfer's tan.

"We can after we finish up in Venice," he said. "Lots of 'em are still hidin' in their basements over there. Then we'll go right through the condos at Marina Del Rey like shit through a goose, just slice 'em to pieces. I figure we can spare a thousand or so easy."

"Good." Vulkan's eyes were bright and giddy. He grinned and clasped his hands together, like a child at a carnival who sees so many lights he doesn't know where to turn first. He wished his father could see him now; he knew the Hawk would be very proud, perhaps even a bit envious. His father's greatest campaign—a war of revenge into the wild northland after rampaging barbarians had set two of the Hawk's villages to the torch—had lasted almost six months and resulted in a critical weakening of his army. Now here was Prince Conrad Vulkan, son of the Hawk, who would be young and strong forever. on the eve of conquering a city the size of which might have driven his father to madness. His army could never lose its strength; it would only grow in power, night after night, faster and faster, until the world trembled at its thunderous approach. *Oh, he thought, how good it was to be alive!* He looked at Kobra. "And the armored infantry? How many do you command now, Kobra?"

"The Death Machine, the Ghost Riders, most of the Angels, and the Undertakers—about thirty-five hundred able to ride right now, another fifteen hundred who'll be ready tomorrow night. We've got the hogs in a warehouse over near the river, but I don't know how long the engines are gonna last with all this sand blowin' around. That shit gets in the carbs and the fuel lines, and there's hell to pay. 'Course, we've got mechanics workin' on 'em. but . . ."

"You won't have to deal with the sand much longer," Vulkan said. "Once our objective is reached, the storm will pass. Until then you'll have to make do." He looked to the center of the table where the sand was beginning to corkscrew faster in the gleaming golden bowl. The others had stared at it fearfully when they'd come to the council, and none of them dared touch it.

"What powers that, Master?" Roach asked, his voice brimming with wonder. It looked to him like some gleaming jewel. a golden mechanism sent spinning by a force he couldn't even begin to understand.

"The hand that powers us all," Prince Vulkan said. "It's a holy object, and you would do well to remember that." He cast his gaze along the table. "Any more comments, reports, or suggestions? No? Then it is time to sleep The council is adjourned." They rose from their chairs and moved toward the door. "Sleep well," Vulkan told them and then looked up at Roach, who'd lagged behind. "Yes?"

"I just wanted to . . . say . . . I want to be like you someday. I want to . . . live forever, like you and the others. I want to know what it feels like, Master." His eyes were huge and shining behind his glasses, and he was almost panting. "Will you make me like you?"

Vulkan regarded him in silence for a moment. "Perhaps someday," he said finally. "Right now I need you as you are."

"I'll do anything for you, I'll follow you anywhere! Anything you ask, but please let me feel the power, too!"

Vulkan said, "Leave me. I want to be alone now."

Roach nodded and backed away. He stopped at the door. "Do you want me to go down and feed the dogs now?"

Someday, Vulkan thought, *you shall. Just as Falco did when his usefulness had ended.* "No, not yet. But make sure they're out at sunrise."

Roach left the room, his footsteps scuttling away down the stone-floored corridor. In the firelight the golden urn winked like a maleficent and beautiful eye. The sand had begun to spin with greater force. Vulkan watched it, mesmerized.

And now he could sense the presence of spirits around him, shades of beings who had lived and died in Los Angeles for scores of years. They were everywhere now, floating through the castle like silver cobwebs. His activity had stirred them up, brought them back from the dead in defiance. He recalled the night he'd intercepted the messages flowing between the spirit that had walked here when he first came and a house in that section of the city called Bel Air. The dead were restless and trying to halt his advance. But what should he care about them? They were phantoms, things that moved without shape or substance, and he was well beyond their grasp. Now he was Prince Conrad Vulkan, King of the Vampires, and no power on or of earth could ever stop him! He stared at the urn and thought he saw a specter moving toward it, trying to pass a shadowy grip through the spinning column of sand. Of course, that couldn't be done, and Prince Vulkan began to laugh with childish glee. The laughter grew, echoing in the rafters like a demonic chorus.

Nothing could stand in his way now; nothing could halt the advance of his army. When darkness fell again, the divisions would secure their own areas and then begin to radiate outward, like an exploding star, while the Central Division continued to explore the inner city in wider spirals, searching for stragglers. But Prince Vulkan knew there would not be many.

It was almost dawn. He could feel the coming sunlight —which this day would be no more than a faint glow in the thick, amber grain of the sky—with a sense of unease at the pit of his stomach. He left the chamber, left the swirling, helpless ghosts, and went down into the murky depths of the castle where his ebony casket filled with coarse Hungarian dirt waited.

SIX

Father Silvera was guiding a long chain of people toward his church from a decrepit, tottering tenement. The storm was furious, sand lashing his face like a cat-o'-nine-tails. He gripped the hand of the person behind him, and now he was stepping over half-buried corpses at his feet. He could see the church ahead, the vaguest dark outline in the yellow wind. When he reached the steps, he felt a shudder vibrate up his arm and looked back. They were all gone, all the people swept away either by the storm or by the vampires. He'd been gripping empty air, and his dead hand hadn't even registered the difference. In the distance he could hear people shrieking for his help, calling out his name, sobbing. He shouted "Where are you?" but then the sand whipped into his mouth and began to choke him, and he knew he could never find all of them, he knew he'd let them go, and there was nothing he could do for them, nothing . . . nothing. . . .

His head jerked upward. His eyes opened. He lay in deep blue light, the pounding of his heart making his entire body tremble. He was aware of three distinct sounds—the tolling of Mary's Voice above his head, the muffled sound of voices talking and weeping, and the steady roaring of the wind. He sat up from where he'd fallen asleep—*how long? An hour or more?*—on a pew and found that someone had spread a striped blanket across him. There was someone else asleep beside him, and at the end of the pew, a girl who looked no more than fifteen was nursing an infant. From the rear of the sanctuary, a woman began to weep in long, agonized moans; someone else whispered to her, trying to calm her. A baby began to wail. Father Silvera suddenly realized that there was a trace of light within the church from outside. He looked at the stained-glass window and saw some of the blue panes beginning to glow. On the altar most of the candles had burned themselves out.

Morning, he thought with a surge of relief. *Oh, thank God! We've survived the night!* He stood up, stepping over and around people huddled both on the pews and the floor, and peered out the front door. Sand whipped into his face; the wind had risen, and now it screamed violently around the church. The dunes had already shifted, and now they were building up eight and nine feet high against those walls that cut the wind's force. No one could go out in that and live very long, he knew. He closed the door and rebolted it, grit prickling the stubble of his beard.

He was walking back toward the altar when someone huddled on the end of a pew with a blanket draped around his shoulders said, "Father?"

Silvera stopped. It was the young man he'd found sprawled on the ground. He was shirtless, his broken ribs now bandaged with the torn strips of a woman's brown dress. "Did a woman come in last night?" the young man said, his eyes sunken and dark with hopelessness. "A black woman, very beautiful . . . ?"

"No," Silvera said. "No one else came in after I found you."

The young man nodded. There were deep lines around his eyes, as if he'd aged twenty years in one night. He looked dazed, on the verge of tears. Silvera had seen that look of shock often enough now to become familiar with it. "They took her," the young man said softly. "The ones on the motorcycles. I've got to find her, Father . . . I can't let them . . . make her one, too . . ."

"What's your name, son?"

"Name? Wes. Wes Richer. Where is this place?"

"My church is in East L.A. Where did you come from?"

Wes seemed to be trying to remember, but was having difficulty. "My car," he said. "The freeway . . ."

"The freeway? The nearest off-ramp is over a quarter-mile away!"

"I heard the bell," Wes said. "I knew if I kept going, I'd reach it. I wasn't aware of how far away it was, I just knew I . . . had to get there. Her name was . . . is . . .

Solange. The ones on the motorcycles took her." He pressed a hand against his side and winced. "Broken ribs, huh? I figured as much. How bad am I?"

"One of the women looked after you. She says you've got two fractured ribs on the left side. How bad do you feel?"

"Pretty fucking bad. Oops, sorry." He looked at the brightening window. "Is it morning?"

"Yes. Where did these motorcycle riders go?" The idea of vampires on motorcycles chilled him. It was bad enough that they were on foot, but vampires with vehicles was almost too terrible to think about.

"I don't know. East, I think. They were members of some kind of biker gang, and they said they were going to connect up with some others." He coughed a couple of times and winced. "Shit. My throat and lungs feel like they've been sandpapered. Do you have any water?"

"I'll get you some." Silvera went back to his room where he'd taken the case of bottled water and packs of paper cups that he'd gotten from the grocery store down the street. Two of the bottles were already empty. Silvera poured just a little into a cup and took it out to Wes. "Make it last," he told the young man, who nodded and drank gratefully.

"I've got to go," Wes said when he'd finished. "I've got to find Solange."

"No one's going anywhere. The storm's gotten stronger. You couldn't walk two blocks in it before you laid down and died."

"It was my fault they found us. I stood there and waved and shouted like an idiot, and then they swooped right down on us like fucking vultures. I should've known what they were! I should've known that only the . . . the vampires would be out there. Now they've got her, and God only knows what they've done to her!" His lower lip quivered. He crushed the cup and flung it aside. "I've got to find her!" he shouted, his eyes flaring with defiance.

"And where will you start looking?" Silvera asked him. "They could've taken her anywhere. And by now they've . . ." His voice trailed off because saying it would be unmerciful.

"NO!" Wes said. "I don't believe that!"

"You can't go out in this storm, Mr. Richer. Do you want to die so much?"

Wes smiled thinly. "Man, I'm half-dead already. So what does it matter, huh?"

Something about the cold logic of that pierced Silvera. It seemed to him that only the half-dead might have the courage to fight against the vampires because the living would have too much to lose. He had refused to help Palatazin, and that man had surely gone to his death. He remembered Cicero's triumphant shr'ek: "The Master lives!" Yes. Palatazin—or what had been Palatazin— was dead by now, and the Master's flock had increased. Only the half-dead, only those who had seen the limits of their lives and accepted that end as a fact, could hope to find the strength within themselves to fight back.

Silvera held his hands up before his face. They were shaking like the hands of an elderly man with the palsy.

How much longer could he hope to live? Two years? Three, possibly? Incurable, the doctors had said. Amyotrophic lateral sclerosis. Lou Gehrig's disease. First weakness and atrophy of the muscles in the hands coupled with fibrillations and spasticity. Muscular atrophy spreading to the forearms and shoulders. Wasting away week after week. Incurable. Lying in a hospital bed, probably in some charity ward, softening into a gray mass of jellied flesh. Nurses with grim lips hovering at his bedside. Incurable. Being fed through his nostrils. Time creeping. Messing his pants and being wiped clean by the nurses, trembling in bed, caged within a house that had gone rotten but refused to fall until all the dignity of its tenant had been thrown out into the garbage with the rubber diapers and the bibs and the nasal catheters.

Is that how I want to die? he asked himself. Now he saw his impending death as a gift from God. He had been given the opportunity to choose death with dignity or, as that quivering mass of flesh, the endless haunting of the realization that thousands—possibly millions—would be consumed by the vampires simply because he wanted two more years of life, because he wanted to die as a shriveled thing in a hospital bed.

The Master lives, Cicero had said. And Silvera knew it was true. In that castle somewhere in the Hollywood hills, the Master lived and plotted his moves for the next night's assault on the remaining humans of Los Angeles. A knot of dread was slowly gathering in his stomach. Palatazin had surely been killed. Who else but he knew that the Master had taken refuge in the Kronsteen Castle? Calm determination set in, but the fear kept jumping in his stomach like something trying to draw his attention. How could he get through the storm to the castle? He really didn't even know how to find it, and there were hundreds of roads, both paved and dirt, twisting through the hills. And what about the people here in the sanctuary? He couldn't just leave them to fend for themselves. But tonight the vampires would be back, maybe many times stronger than the night before. He was going to have to pray and seek guidance.

"I want to find Solange," Wes said grimly. "I don't care what I have to do or where I have to go."

"Don't be a fool. How far could you get with those broken ribs? You don't even know where you'd be going. You'd wind up suffocated on some East L.A. side street." He paused because he could see the anger in Wes's eyes quickly giving way to pain. "I'm sorry," Silvera said quietly. "How about some more water?"

Wes shook his head. "No. I . . . I just want to try to sleep . . ."

"All right. And I have some thinking to do. If you'll excuse me." He moved away from Wes without looking back, because he'd seen the young man's face and heard his first strangled, hopeless sob.

SEVEN

The boy on the sofa suddenly screamed and jerked his head up.

Jo, sitting in a chair beside him, leaned forward and put a hand on his shoulder. "It's all right," she said soothingly. "No one's going to hurt you. Come on, lie back."

"No! House is on fire! They're burning up, both of them!" His eyes were wild, and he was fighting the bedspread that covered him.

"It's morning," Jo said, putting more pressure on his shoulder to keep him still. "Whatever happened to you last night is over. Everything's going to be all right now."

"Huh?" He looked at her as if he was seeing her for the first time. "Who are you?"

"I'm Jo, and that's Gayle over there. What's your name?"

"It's . . . uh . . ." He squinted and touched the back of his head. The wound had been covered with a couple of large, square Band-Aids. "Head hurts," he said. "My name is . . . uh . . . *Tommy!*" Everything but his own name seemed dark and jumbled together. Strange backward images of things were caught in his brain like distorted reflections in a hall of mirrors. "Head hurts bad," he said.

"It should. But I guess that's a good sign. You've been shot."

"Shot? Like with a bullet?"

"Well, grazed is the right word, I suppose. Come on, lie back down. You don't want to start bleeding again, do you?"

He allowed her to push him back down on the pillow. Thunder crashed between his temples, and he felt sick to his stomach. He was trying to remember his last name and where he lived and what he was doing on this sofa with this woman sitting next to him. He concentrated on making sense out of one of the funhouse mirror reflections. There was a bed, and on that bed there were shapes covered with the sheets. They were lying very still. Something painful struck him across the top of the head, making him wince and whimper, and that mirror shattered to pieces. He decided not think about any more reflections, not just yet.

"He's been gone a long time," Gayle said, standing next to the window. Her voice was as taut as overstretched cable, and all she could see out there were blowing currents of white and yellow.

"He knows what he's doing," Jo answered. Something cold leaped up around her heart; she forced it away and smoothed the spread up under the boy's chin. Tommy was as pale as death, and now she could hear him whimpering softly. *What kind of hell did he go through last night?* she wondered.

In another moment Gayle said, "There he is!" and opened the front door. A swirl of wind and sand blew in, and at the center of it Palatazin, a sheet around his head and face like an Arabian headdress, stepped across the threshold, carrying the cardboard box of stakes he'd just retrieved from the Falcon. Gayle quickly closed the door, having to push hard against it. Palatazin laid the box on the floor and unwrapped his protective shroud. It had strained the air enough for him to breathe through his teeth, but walking out there was like struggling through glue while being struck in the face with buckets of sand. His shirt was soaked with sweat.

"Could you see anything moving out there?" Gayle asked him.

"I could hardly see five feet in front of me," he said. "I walked right past the car before I realized where I was. But there's one blessing. Our friend with the rifle can't see either. How's the boy?"

"He was awake a few minutes ago," Jo said. "He says his name is Tommy."

Palatazin came over beside the sofa and looked down at him. "Do you think he's going to be all right? He's so pale!"

"You would be too if you'd taken a bullet across the back of your head." She lifted the cold washrag and felt his forehead for perhaps the twentieth time in an hour. "He doesn't have a fever, but I wouldn't know whether he had a concussion or not. At least he was coherent when he spoke."

Palatazin nodded, his brow furrowed in concern, and then turned back to the window. He was glad this boy was alive, of course, but now he was responsible for the life of one more person. What was going to happen to them after he'd gone? Taking them with him was out of the question. If Jo protested, he would remind her that she'd almost died in the storm last night, and having to keep three other people together out there would be more than he could handle. He gravely doubted his own chances of making it across Hollywood. "The car's completely covered over now," he said to Gayle. "The dunes are piling up almost as tall as the house."

"And you still think you can make it up to the Kronsteen castle?"

He didn't look at her. "I have to try."

"It's over four miles! If you say you can't see more than five feet in front of you, how the hell will you even know where you're going?"

Palatazin motioned toward the gun and shoulder-holster lying across the back of a chair. "I want you to keep that. I'm going to leave you the rest of the holy water, too. If I get up there . . . *when* I get up there . . . I won't need anything more th⌐n the hammer and stakes. I think the vampire king is somehow controlling this storm. When he dies, I think the storm will blow itself out to sea. Until then it's going to circle over the city and possibly get worse before nightfall . . ."

"Wait a minute!" Jo said, rising from her chair. "Do you think you can climb up that mountain *alone?*"

"You're staying here, Jo. All of you are. Don't argue because the decision's been made."

"Like hell it has! We'll take a vote on it!"

"No, we won't!" he said angrily. "Yes, I'm going up alone to the Kronsteen castle. You and Gayle and the boy are staying right here. You'll have the holy water and the gun. I suggest you go down to the basement after dusk and lock yourselves in. Save the holy water as long as you can. If you have to use the gun, aim for the vampires' eyes. With any luck and the help of God, I can reach the castle much faster than if I had to take care of the two of you and an injured boy . . ."

"We can take care of ourselves!" Jo said. "You won't have to worry about us!"

"You're staying here," he told her, his voice stern.

"The Kronsteen castle? Orlon Kronsteen's castle?"

Palatazin looked past Jo. The boy sat up from the sofa; he still looked dazed and weak, but his voice was clear. "Is that where you're going?" the boy asked.

"That's right," Palatazin said. "How are you feeling?"

"Better, I guess. My head keeps ringing."

Palatazin smiled and walked over to the sofa. "Young man, you should be grateful you *have* a head. If that wound were perhaps a fraction of an inch deeper, you might not. Tommy, is it?"

"Yes, sir."

"Tommy what?"

The boy started to speak, but then his eyes seemed to lose their focus. He winced and shook his head. "Tommy . . . Tommy . . . Ch . . ."

"Take your time." Palatazin glanced quickly at Jo, then back to the boy. "Do you remember anything of what happened to you last night?"

Tommy closed his eyes. He was trying to look into the funhouse mirrors that stood along the distorted corridor in his mind. There was a girl in one of them, a very pretty girl with long, blond hair. She was reaching out for him and smiling, but suddenly her smile turned hideous, and he could see the glistening fangs slowly protruding from her jaws. That mirror abruptly shattered. There was a fire burning in the next one, but he couldn't bear to look into it. The mirror after that rippled with darkness; there seemed to be figures in it, chasing after him, getting closer and closer. There was someone with a chain, shouting. The mirror cracked with the same loud sound he remembered hearing before he'd slid down a sandy maw into the belly of a toadish, squatting monster. "Can't think," he said. He backed out of that corridor and opened his eyes. "My head hurts too much."

Palatazin reached down and picked up the backpack. "You were wearing this."

"Uhhhh, sure! I know that! From the Scouts. My dad used to take me when we lived in . . . in . . ." The chain of dim memories suddenly collapsed. Tears sprang to his eyes.

"Your father? What happened to your parents?"

"Can't," Tommy said very softly. "Can't."

Palatazin realized they were probably dead, or worse. He could see the pain etched across the boy's face so he put the backpack down on the floor. "It's okay," he said. "You don't have to remember just this minute. My name's Andy. I guess you must be hungry, huh? I think we can find you something from the refrigerator if it hasn't all gone bad by now."

"There are some cans of Vienna sausage in the pantry," Jo said. "And sardines."

"Ugh," Tommy said. "I don't think I can eat anything just right now anyway, thanks. My stomach doesn't feel so good." He looked up and held Palatazin's gaze. "Why do you want to go to Orlon Kronsteen's castle?"

"Because of the vampires," Palatazin said quietly. "I suppose you do know about them?"

"Yeah." Another mirror shattered in Tommy's head. He'd seen vampires in the movies. No, no, that wasn't right. They were here in L.A., and one of them looked like the blond girl in tight denim cutoffs who'd lived across the street. Her name was . . . Sandra . . . Susie . . . something. . . .

"I don't know how many there are now, but I'm sure they number in the thousands. They're trying to take over this city, Tommy. Somehow they brought this sand-storm here and they don't want any of us to get out." His eyes had gotten very dark, reflecting the state of his spirit. "I think their leader is hiding up in the Kronsteen castle. Someone has to find him and kill him before sundown, or . . . what happened last night will happen again, only ten times worse. There are probably other vampires hiding there with him, and they're all going to have to be destroyed."

"You? You're going to do it?"

Palatazin nodded.

"I know all about the castle!" Tommy said excitedly. "Last year *Famous Monsters*—that's a magazine—did a story about it. Forry Ackerman and Vincent Price toured it on the tenth anniversary of Orlon Kronsteen's murder! They took a psychic up there and everything! She said she could feel his ghost walking around . . ."

"That's fine," Palatazin said, "but . . ."

"They had a lot of pictures of the place," Tommy continued, "and a diagram that showed most of the rooms. A couple of months ago my . . . dad . . ." he frowned suddenly, memories streaked through his brain and vanishing into darkness. He tried to grasp some of them before they were gone. "My dad . . . drove me up there on a . . . on a Sunday afternoon, I think. We couldn't go all the way to the top because there was a . . . chain and a No Trespassing sign across the road. But I . . . remember seeing it through the trees way up in the distance." He blinked suddenly as if startled. "A blue Pacer! My dad drove a blue Pacer!" Images started to come back to him, like bright red explosions in the blackest of all black nights. A stucco house on a long street lined with similar houses. The flaring of a match, illuminating hideously pale faces. A concrete mastodon struggling to free itself from a lake of tar. A grinning, dark-haired boy standing over him. Someone else—another boy, larger than the first one—staggering backward, falling into that clinging, black ooze and screaming. Tommy felt cold sweat on his face. He said, "I think . . . something bad happened to my mom and dad. I think I left them because . . . be-cause . . . there were vampires and . . ." His face sud-denly crumpled. Whatever had happened was too terrible for him to think about.

Palatazin put his hand on the boy's shoulder. "It's over, son."

Tommy looked up at him grimly, his face streaked with tears. "No, it's not. The vampires got my mom and dad. I know they did! You're going after the king vampire, aren't you?"

Palatazin nodded. He knew he'd never seen any harder, more determined eyes than those in the face of this skinny boy.

"He's the one who holds them together," Tommy said. "If you can kill him and the ones around him, the others won't know what to do. They'll be too disorganized to think for themselves. That's what happened in *Midnight Hour*, the one where Orlon Kronsteen played Count Du-Pre. Professor Van Dorn found him in the abbey ruins and . . ." His voice trailed off. "But that was just a movie, wasn't it?" he said softly. "That wasn't real at all."

"I'm going to have to use your backpack, okay?" Palatazin said after another moment. "To carry the stakes."

Tommy nodded. Palatazin dumped everything out of the pack and started putting the stakes in. "The matches and the spray can," Tommy said. "You can make a torch out of them."

Palatazin thought that over and returned them to the pack. He stuffed six stakes into the largest pocket, and three more in the others. There was barely enough room for the hammer.

"You won't be able to find him so easily," Tommy said. "He'll be hidden, probably down in one of the basements."

Palatazin looked up and frowned. *"One* of the basements?"

"There are two. That place has more than a hundred rooms. It'll be easy to get lost once you've gotten inside. You might not even be able to find your way out again."

Palatazin glanced over at Jo. She looked dazed, and he didn't know how much more of this she could take. Outside the light was a thick, dusky amber. He looked at his watch and saw that the crystal had been cracked and grains of sand clung to the face. He remembered checking it when he'd awakened from two hours of sleep just after sunrise, and now he thought he must've broken it in getting the stakes out of the car. The frozen time was ten-fifty

"I can help you get in and out," Tommy said. "You won't be able to kill all of them. If the others find you, they'll tear you to pieces."

"No."

"I can *help* you!" Tommy suddenly stood up. His head spun, his vision going in and out of focus, but he forced himself to stand steady. "I know what the castle looks like inside!"

"Lie back down, son," Palatazin said firmly. "You're in no condition to go anywhere." He slipped the backpack over one shoulder, then over his head so it hung down at his side within easy reach. It was time to go now.

"How are you going?" Gayle asked him.

"The fastest route I can," he said. "I'll walk to LaBrea Avenue—that's only a couple of blocks west—and head northward across Hollywood."

"It's a long way up there," Gayle said. "Four or five miles at least."

"Please." He smiled grimly. "No pep talks, okay?" He looked at Jo and knew she was trying very hard to be brave for him. "Well," he shrugged in mock incredulity. "Who would've ever thought this fat, bald, middle-aged cop would turn out to be a vampire hunter, huh?" He put his arms around her and held her close. "I'm going to be all right," he whispered into her ear. "You'll see. I am going to finish it, and then I'll be back for you." He looked at Gayle. "Will you help me wrap that cloth around my mouth and nose?"

When she'd finished, there was just the narrowest of slits left for his eyes. He turned up the collar of his coat and buttoned his shirt all the way. Then he went to the door. He stopped, his hand gripping the knob, and looked back at them.

"I want you all to remember this. If I come to the door in the night, don't let me in, no matter what I say or do. My . . . mother opened the door on that last night in Krajeck, and I don't want any of you doing the same thing. Keep the holy water close at hand. If I'm still on the porch at daylight, then you'll know I'm . . . the same man I was when I left. Is that understood?" He waited for Jo to nod, then he said, "I love you."

"I love *you*," she answered; her voice cracked.

Palatazin walked out into the wind. Jo stepped to the

window and watched him vanish into the yellow swirl.
She put a hand over her mouth to stifle a sob.

Tommy stood beside her. *He's going to die*, Tommy
thought. *Or worse, just like my parents. He's going to get
lost in that castle, and then the vampires will have him.*

Jo reached out and took his hand. Her touch was very
cold.

EIGHT

The sanctuary was tumultuous with noise. From the end
of a pew, Wes watched Father Silvera trying to cope with
all of them. It seemed he was always bending or kneeling
down beside somebody to pray with them, or trying to
comfort someone who was weeping inconsolably. *That's
got to be one of the toughest gigs there is*, Wes thought.
But Silvera seemed to be handling everything okay; only
once in a while did Wes see him falter when a quick
weary expression swept over his face. Then he was talking with someone else, kneeling down beside them, or simply listening while they poured out their terrors distilled
from the night before. Wes saw that it had been rough on
everybody. There were children who looked as forlorn as
war orphans, their dark eyes confused and terrified. One
little girl had curled up in a corner, sucking her thumb
and staring straight ahead. Father Silvera and others had
gone over several times to talk quietly with her, but she
never answered and never moved. A few of the men had
brought guns into the sanctuary with them, and it was
only with much effort that Silvera persuaded them to
give their guns up. The priest had taken the weapons
into the back of the church and put them away. Good
thing too, Wes thought, because one of those men had
snapped about an hour ago and had to be forcibly restrained from running out into the storm by three others.
A gray-haired woman with deep wrinkles in her face
came over to check on him, babbling in Spanish while she
unwrapped the bandages and tenderly pressed at his side.
He kept saying "*Sí, sí,*" even though he didn't understand
a word she was saying. When she was finished, she
wrapped the bandages back very tightly and left him.

He couldn't keep his mind off Solange for very long. Her last scream had drilled a hole straight through his brain, and it felt as if his life-force were slowly leaking out. Was it possible she was still alive? And more importantly, was it possible she was still . . . *human?* That remark the one called Kobra—that grinning, murderous albino—had made about a castle still puzzled him, though he tried attacking it from all angles. What castle had the vampire meant? Or had it just been a figure of speech? The only place he could think of that could really be referred to as a castle was that monstrosity Orlon Kronsteen had put together up in the hills. He recalled the night—*God, how long ago that seemed!*—Solange had asked questions over her Ouija board and the spectral reply that he'd first thought was one of Martin Blue's parlor tricks—*They Thirst.* Now he saw the actual meaning of that message, and it chilled his blood. Even then the spirits had been trying to warn them of the hideous force, gathering strength over L.A.

Had Kobra meant the Kronsteen castle? Wes could see how that would be a perfect refuge for the vampires. It was fairly isolated yet at a strategic height that overlooked the entire city in all directions. The place was as huge as an old medieval fortress, and it had been empty since Kronsteen's death about eleven or so years ago. The vampires might even have found it quite homey. That phrase spelled off the Ouija board thudded into his brain. If they *had* contacted Kronsteen that night, then perhaps it was the old man himself trying to let them know that the Undead had made themselves uninvited guests in his desolate old castle. . . .

Yes. It was a place, at least, to begin looking. Solange might still be alive. Maybe they'd bitten her but hadn't . . . killed her yet . . . or whatever they did to make you as they were. She might be alive up there at the Kronsteen castle!

Overhead the church bell tolled intermittently. He could hear the shriek of the wind outside, and every so often the beautiful stained-glass window trembled, as if about to cave in. The eyes of Jesus seemed fixed upon him, urging him to be strong. And suddenly the answer to a frequently asked question seemed very clear indeed— *God is on the side of those who don't give up.*

Wes turned toward the door. He thought he'd heard

another sound at the center of the storm, a deep rumbling that seemed to shake the church. *What is this?* he thought. *An earthquake?* Now others had heard it, too, and for a moment absolute silence hung within the sanctuary. The rumbling intensified, became the muffled thunder of . . . machinery.

"That's an engine!" Wes said. He stood up painfully, moving past a knot of people near the door. As he hurriedly unbolted it, Silvera joined him, and together they looked out into an eye-stinging swirl of sand.

Blinding, white headlights were approaching very slowly. In another moment they could see a large, grayish green shape, a scoop pushing aside mountains of sand. It was some kind of military vehicle, and when it came to the gleaming metal hulk of an abaondoned car, its massive treads reared up and over, smashing the car flat. Silvera could see wipers and spray working at a frantic pace across a high windshield. Printed across the driver's door was: United States Marines, Camp Pendleton, Ca.

Silvera stepped out into the storm and started waving his arms, oblivious to the sand lashing into his face. The vehicle, some sort of huge tractorlike troop carrier, hardly needed to veer toward the curb since it took up most of the street. Hydraulic brakes hissed, the most beautiful sound Silvera had ever heard. From behind the troop carrier another smaller vehicle, a jeeplike thing with an enclosed cab and large, solid rubber tires like those used on dune buggies, came up over the curb onto the sidewalk and stopped just in front of the priest. Two marines inside slipped gray hoods over their heads, covering their noses and mouths, and stepped out of the cab. One of them motioned toward the church and followed Silvera in.

"I'm Lieutenant Rutledge," the first marine said when they'd gotten inside. He took his hood off and shook the sand out of it. He was a tall man with regulation-cut brown hair and glacial blue eyes. Wes caught the glint of a .45 in a waist holster beneath his poplin jacket.

"Ramon Silvera," the priest said and shook his hand. "To say we're glad to see you would be quite an understatement."

"I'll bet," Rutledge said. He looked around the sanctuary quickly and returned his gaze to Silvera. "We've moved into the area from Camp Pendleton with about thirty-five tractors. Another fifty are on the way. We're evacuating as many as we can up to the Red Cross facilities at Crystal Lake. How many do you have here?"

"Fifty-eight," Silvera said.

Rutledge glanced back at the other marine, who Wes figured must be his driver. "That's pretty strange, sir," the lieutenant said. "In a six mile grid we've only found nine people. Just where *is* everybody?"

"Don't you know?" Silvera looked at him incredulously, feeling a ripple of dark laughter vibrate through him.

"No, sir. I'm afraid I don't . . ."

Wes, who'd put on his shirt and dark brown leather jacket, glanced again at that .45 and moved away. He turned his back on them, his heart pounding, and walked toward the rear of the sanctuary. He knew he was going to have to be very careful because never in his entire life had he done anything like what he was about to try. He only knew that he needed a way to get up to that castle. He slipped through the door into the priest's meager living quarters.

"All right, everyone!" Silvera called out in Spanish. "We're going to be leaving in a few minutes! Everyone's going to be moving through the door single file! There's a truck outside that will take us all out of here . . ."

Wes was frantically hunting for the weapons Silvera had confiscated. It took him a few minutes, but he found them—three pistols and a couple of switchblades—at the bottom of a chest of drawers. He picked up one of the knives and flicked it open; a nine-inch blade flashed out. He closed it and put it into his jacket. Of the three guns, only one of them—a .22 with a carving of Jesus on the white ivory handle—looked fit to use. The others were rusty things that might fall to pieces or explode in his hand. He only wanted to put a scare into the marines, but he knew he'd need a gun he could depend on later It felt obscene and oily in his grip. He'd never liked guns, but now this one would help him find Solange. The ugly thought that he might have to use this gun surfaced within him, like something nasty floating on a slimy pool. His gaze fell upon the small ceramic crucifix next to the door. He didn't know how much good it would do, but he lifted it off its nail and went out into the sanctuary.

People were gathering up their children and belong-

ings, linking hands, and crossing the threshold into the
wind. No one was in the bell tower now, but the storm's
force made the bell shudder every few minutes, and the
clapper gave out a muffled, tentative moan. Wes saw Silvera standing at the doorway, herding the people out; he
didn't see the marines and assumed they were already
outside, helping with the loading of the troop transport.

Wes waited for most of them to step across and, as he
neared the door, the priest suddenly looked first at his
face, then at the crucifix in his left hand and the gun in
his right. "What do you think you're going to do, *amigo?*"
Silvera asked him quietly.

"Just stay out of my way, Father. I appreciate your
help and all that, but now I've got to do this." He started
to step past the priest, but Silvera's hand came up and
grasped his collar.

"What are you planning? To take their jeep?"

Wes nodded. "I've asked you to stay out of my way."

Silvera looked over his shoulder out at the transport
truck. The rear gate had dropped down, and Lieutenant
Rutledge was hustling people inside. In another few minutes everyone was going to be aboard. Silvera glanced at
the jeeplike vehicle, then back to Wes. "Where do you
think you're going? There are several thousand places the
vampires could've taken your friend."

"I know where I'm going. I think they may have taken
her up into the Hollywood hills, to . . ."

"The Kronsteen castle?" Silvera asked.

Wes's eyes widened. "That's right. What do you know
about it?"

"Enough." He let go of the man's collar. "Give me
the gun."

"Father, I told you I . . ."

"Give me the gun," Silvera repeated evenly.

"You haven't heard a word I've said, have you? This
may be the only chance I get and I've got to take it!"

"Chance?" Silvera frowned and shook his head. "What
chance?" He gripped Wes's wrist and pried the gun loose
from his fingers. "You didn't even know enough to release
the safety, did you? Are you sure it's loaded?"

"I'm not going to any goddamned Crystal Lake!" Wes
said, his face reddening. "I'm taking that jeep if I have
to . . ."

"What?" the priest asked blandly. "Fight for it bare-

handed? Kill for it? No, I don't think you want to do that."
He glanced over and saw the last of his people filing into
the transport. "I don't want anyone else getting hurt. So
do you think you're going to be able to drive right up to
that place—through this storm—and take on a hoard of
vampires with a gun and a crucifix? What else did you
take?"

"A knife," Wes said. "Sorry, I didn't see any stakes
lying around here."

Silvera regarded him for a moment in silence "You
must love that woman very much."

"I've . . . always been there when she needed me. She
needs me now."

"She may be like them by now. You know that, don't
you?"

"And maybe she's not," Wes said. "I have to know for
sure before I . . . leave her behind."

Silvera nodded. "You surprise me. But regardless of
whatever rage you're feeling, you're going to need more
than these implements. Much more." He turned his head
and saw Lieutenant Rutledge waving him over. Then he
said to Wes, "You wait here. Understand?"

"Why?"

"Just wait." Silvera left Wes, walking across the
church to his room. He took a small, clear flask from a
silk-lined black case resting at the top shelf of his closet.
The flask was identical to the one he'd taken to Palatazin. Then he went out to the font of holy water in the
vestibule, and dipped the flask down into the small,
white ceramic basin. The flask filled quickly, with a little
more than two ounces. He wasn't sure how much effect
holy water would actually have on the vampires, but he
figured—he hoped—Palatazin had known that it would
have *some* effect, even if just to frighten them. Silvera
lifted the flask, capped it, and thought of something his
mentor Father Raphael had said back in the tiny village
of Puerto Grande. "Now, my son. You ask me why I dip
up water from the Pacific Ocean for the rituals. The answer is both simple and complex. Well water is too precious here to deprive humans of it, no matter how holy
the ritual. God saw human needs long before he saw the
need for ritual. Secondly, what holier water is there
than water from the cradle of life? God's blessing only
makes it more so, *but the strength is already there.*

You've seen how saltwater heals wounds and sores, how it cleanses and purifies. Any water can be holy; it needs only to be blessed. But this—seawater—is twice blessed . . ."

Silvera had kept Father Raphael's tradition alive, though now it was more difficult to bring jugs of water back from the Pacific. But now he needed a purifier, something to wash away this unholy evil that gnawed like a cancer at human flesh. He held the flask up; it felt slightly warm in his hand, and the warmth seemed to spread up his forearm. He was ready now. He returned to where Wes waited and put the flask in his inside coat pocket. "All right," he said. "We can go now."

" 'We'?" Wes said. "What are you talking about?"

"I'm going with you. The holy water may help even up the odds. And that man won't shoot *me*." He motioned toward Lieutenant Rutledge, who shouted, "Let's go, Father!" and waved impatiently. Silvera dropped the gun down to his side and, shielding his face with his forearm, walked toward the tractor with Wes right behind him. Lieutenant Rutledge and his driver stepped back to allow them up into the dark cavity, but suddenly Silvera turned toward him and thrust out the gun.

Rutledge stared incredulously at it, then looked into Silvera's face. "What's this shit?" the man shouted.

"My friend and I are taking your jeep, and we don't have time to argue! Tell your driver there to give us the keys!"

"You want the Crab? What are you, crazy or something? We're trying to get you out of this mess!"

"You can help us by giving us the keys! Come on!"

"Man, you take the cake, you know that? You and I both know you're not going to shoot anybody, so let's just forget this . . ."

Silvera yanked the hood off the marine's face and put the barrel alongside his nose. "I don't have time for a debate!" the priest said. "Hand them over!"

"Shit!" Rutledge lifted his hands now and glanced fearfully at the other marine. "Okay, okay! Whitehurst, give these maniacs the keys to the Crab! Look, you! Priest or not, you steal a military vehicle and your holy ass is going *under* the stockade!"

"Wes, take his keys! And the .45, too. You've got clips for that?"

Rutledge patted his inside jacket pocket. Silvera reached in, took out two clips, and handed them to Wes. Then he stepped away from Rutledge and backed toward the jeep. Wes slipped into the driver's seat and started the engine.

"You're crazy!" Rutledge shouted, pulling his hood back down. "Both of you!" Whitehurst grasped at his arm and guided him up into the transport vehicle, then in another few seconds the rear gate began to swing shut.

Silvera had a last glimpse of Rutledge's furious face before he climbed into the jeep. Wes put it into reverse, backed along the sidewalk, and then swung out into the street. The vehicle's tires gripped hard, carrying them between monstrous dunes and away from Silvera's church. The priest turned to look back through the Plexiglass rear windshield. The tractor was moving away in the opposite direction, lumbering like a huge metallic beetle. He put the two guns down on the floorboard. "Can you drive this thing?" he asked.

"Handles like a dune buggy," Wes answered. "Steering's tighter, though." The headlights were cutting clear yellow paths in the storm ahead, and the instrumentation panel—which curved slightly around Wes like a plane's cockpit—glowed a faint green. He changed gears, noting the gearshift pattern depicted on a small metal plate on the dashboard—there were four forward gears and two reverse. The interior seemed to be stripped down to the bare minimum but was comfortable enough. It smelled slightly oily, just as Wes thought the interior of a tank might smell. He could feel a powerful engine behind him, pushing them along now at about ten miles per hour; he was afraid to drive any faster because of the dunes and wrecked cars that littered the street ahead, coming up swiftly out of the gloom. "I hope you know what you've gotten yourself into, Father," Wes said quietly.

"I do." Silvera leaned over and looked at the gas gauge—there was a little more than half a tank. He looked behind the seats into a roomy storage compartment, finding a full three-gallon can of gasoline, a coiled rope, maps of the city, and a couple of small red cylinders of oxygen in green backpack carriers. Near the oxygen bottles there were two green, rubber masks complete with wide-vision goggles. Those, he thought, might be

especially useful, and he silently gave thanks for Rutledge's careful preparations.

Wes put the knife and crucifix on top of the dashboard. Sand was beginning to pile up on the windshield
so he turned the wipers on at their highest speed. The
jeep thumped and jubbled over rapidly shifting sand
dunes, but the thick tires gave them enough traction to
get through without sinking. When Silvera looked back
again, he couldn't see his church or the troop carrier,
just a solid sheet of blowing yellow. In another moment
Wes turned a corner, the jeep barely sliding around two
cars that had crashed together in the middle of the street,
and found himself at the bottom of the freeway ramp
he'd crawled down. He slowed and peered up. The ramp
was blocked by a mountainous sand dune that had built
up over another stalled car. Wes cursed softly.

"We'll run into fewer of those if we stay off the freeway," Silvera told him. "I think I know the way from
here. Across the river and around L.A. Back up a block
and turn left." Wes did, the tires slipping with a sickening lurch but always catching just when he thought they
were about to start digging a grave.

The air was getting bad. Silvera reached back, opened
the nozzle on one of the oxygen tanks, and let some bleed
out. He was sweating profusely, beads of moisture dap-
pling his cheeks.

"You wouldn't have shot that lieutenant, would you?"
Wes asked as they turned onto the stark yellow desolation of Brooklyn Avenue in dead Boyle Heights.

"No one would die for a set of keys. He doesn't care
about the vehicle."

"Why did you help me?"

"Not because I think we can find your friend. I don't.
But if you're willing to go to that place, knowing what's
probably waiting up there, then I am too. Let's leave it
at that."

"Fine with me." The engine suddenly sputtered, then
coughed out a wad of sand. Wes checked the temperature
gauge; it was running hot, but what the hell. If the
damned marines couldn't build a vehicle that could plow
through this fucking storm, then nobody could. Wes hoped
their luck and good old American machinery would hold
out just a while longer. If it didn't, they would die; it was
as simple as that.

A fierce wind struck them broadside, shivering the jeep as if it were made of cardboard. The vehicle slipped to the left, tires digging for a purchase, and then darted forward like a land crab scrambling away from a shadow across a wind-rippled beach. Wes remembered Rutledge calling it a Crab. That was probably one of those cute names the military stuck on everything, but it described the tenacity and responsiveness of the vehicle pretty well. A Crab it was.

Nothing moved on Brooklyn Avenue except the dunes, sliding like hot, yellow dancers to a mad maestro's shrilling tune. Everywhere there were stranded cars, and Wes didn't see the almost mummified corpses until the Crab had gone right over them, snapping them like twigs. His hands tightened around the wheel. Death was very close.

The boulevard stretched on out of sight. Behind them the way back had already closed.

NINE

Palatazin had been gone for almost twenty minutes when Tommy turned away from the window and said to Jo, "He's going to die up there." He said it quite calmly, without emotion and very seriously, because he knew it to be true.

"Why don't you sit down, kid?" Gayle said. She didn't want Jo to start crying again. There was a look in the boy's eyes that scared the hell out of her. They were like an old man's eyes, filled with pain and bitter wisdom. "Okay?" she urged. "Why don't you?"

"He doesn't know anything about the castle! *I* do! He'll get lost in there!"

"Please . . ." Jo said weakly and collapsed in a chair.

"I could help him," Tommy said, his gaze moving from Jo to Gayle. "I know I could!"

"Oh, Christ!" Gayle said, anger leaping in her eyes. "Why don't you shut up? He's going to be all right!"

Tommy stood motionless, staring at her. She looked out the window quickly, but she could still see him reflected in the glass. He walked back to the sofa and took the case off the pillow. "What are you doing?" Jo asked, but he didn't answer. He put on his jacket, zipped it up to the neck, and raised the collar. "No!" Jo said. "You're not!"

He folded the pillowcase into a square. "I guess you both think I'm a stupid little kid, don't you? Well, I may be little . . . but I'm sure as hell not stupid! That man who just left here is stupid because he thinks he can get into the Kronsteen castle, find the king vampire, and get out again just like that." He snapped his fingers. "Or he may just be trying to fool himself into believing that, I don't know. Well, he won't be coming back . . . at least not as what he was when he left, I don't help him. If I hurry, I can catch him . . ."

"You're not going anywhere!" Gayle said firmly, taking a step toward him.

Tommy stood his ground. His eyes were like chunks of ice. "My parents are gone," he said quietly. "They're dead. I'm not a little boy anymore."

Gayle stopped suddenly, realizing that he was right, he wasn't a child anymore. Whatever had happened to him last night had changed him forever. And wouldn't he have the same chances out there as Palatazin? Probably better. Certainly he could move faster, and his lungs were probably in much better shape. She glanced at Jo, then back at Tommy. "Do you think you can get him in and out of there safely?"

"I know I can." He stepped past her toward the door. "I'll have to hurry. If I can't find him, I'll have to come back, but I'll look as long as I can." He put the square of cloth up in front of his face like a mask. "Wish me luck," he said and slipped out through the door.

"That's a very brave little boy," Gayle said after he'd gone.

"No," Jo answered. "A very brave young man."

Tommy ran in the direction he'd seen Palatazin take. He was hoping he'd see footprints in the sand, but they'd already been blown away. He was half-blind, trapped within a cubicle of swirling yellowish-brown walls, his lungs scorched. His head was beginning to throb, but he welcomed the pain because it would keep him alert. He ran on, realizing that he might pass within ten feet of Palatazin and never know the man was there. Panic hit him—for a few seconds he couldn't draw a breath. He made himself slow down to a walk and breathe through his mouth at a regular pace. Sand scraped his cheeks and forehead, and now he realized that even if he did want to go back, he'd never find the way.

Huge dunes stood all around him, most of them towering over the hulks of cars. They shifted and slithered down as he passed, threatening to collapse over him. The world was dim amber light, a shriek of wind, and the coarse hissing of sand. The wind whipped around him, almost throwing him to his knees. He thought he heard a high whining voice at the center of it, whispering *Little boy, little boy, lie down and sleep....*

He went on and in another moment a dark shape emerged from the twisting currents. It was a Lincoln Continental, the paint stripped down to the bare metal, most of the car covered over by a dune. He decided to get inside it for a few minutes to clear the sand out of his eyes and mouth. When he pulled the driver's door open, a withered, blue-faced corpse came sliding out, its arms outstretched toward him. He swallowed a cry, spat out sand, and continued on. The wind whispered around his head—*Lie down and sleep, lie down and sleeeeeep ...* "No!" he heard himself shout. "NO, I WON'T!"

In another three steps he tripped over something and fell to the ground. His legs had gotten tangled in the frozen arms of a dead woman, the flesh over her skull stretched as tight as old leather. Tommy kicked free and crawled away, tears stinging his eyes. *Sleeeeep*, the wind moaned. *Close your eyes now, and sleep ...*

It was so tempting. *Maybe I should*, Tommy thought. *Just for a little while. Close my eyes and rest, and when I get my strength back, I can keep on looking for him. Yeah. That's the thing to do.* He wondered if Mr. Palatazin was also sleeping somewhere, all curled up and comfortable. A yellow blanket began to drift over him.

And then he realized what he was doing and kicked off the blanket. He struggled to his feet, his heart pounding. *I was lying down to die*, he realized. *Old Death almost got me that time, and it slipped up so softly ...* "NO, I WON'T!" he shouted, though the words were ripped to shreds by the wind. He began to run again, past more stranded cars and half-covered things that were probably bodies, but he was afraid to look at them too

closely. He ran past a street sign that said LaBrea Avenue,
and now there were indentations on the ground that might
have been scattered footprints or just deep-rippled places
—he couldn't tell. In the shadow of a towering dune,
there was an imprint that might have been made by a
falling body. Panic flared within him. He knew he had
to hurry; he might already be too late.

Ahead, at the corner of LaBrea and Lexington avenues, Tommy saw Palatazin's body sprawled in the wind-
break of a stranded car. There was a long groove where
the man had dragged himself for several yards.

Tommy ran to him and bent down. He could hear
Palatazin's tortured breathing. "Wake up!" Tommy said,
shaking him. "Don't go to sleep! WAKE UP!"

Palatazin moved, lifted a hand, and grasped his shoulder. He tried to focus on Tommy, but his eyes were bloodshot and watery. Sand had filled the cracks in his face,
giving it the look of a dried-up riverbed. "Who . . . ?"
he whispered hoarsely. He let his head fall back. "Oh,
God," he breathed. "Go back . . . go back . . ."

"NO! YOU'VE GOT TO WAKE UP!"

"Can't make it . . . too far . . ."

"We'll find our way back together!" Tommy said, but
he knew they couldn't, not really. The man was too weak
and so was he, the wind too strong, the sand too dense.
"Stand up! Come on!" He pulled at Palatazin's arm with
both hands; his unprotected face felt as if it was being
flayed. Palatazin stirred and tried to rise, the effort showing in the grim set of his eyes, but he only got up on one
knee and leaned against the car, his breath coming in
heaving gasps.

"What are . . . you . . . doing out here?" Palatazin
shouted at him. "I told you . . . told you to stay at the
house!"

"Can you walk?" Tommy shouted back.

Palatazin tried to stand up again, but he didn't seem
to have any strength left in his legs. His heart was racing,
his lungs pumping like bellows but only drawing in short,
burning gasps of air. He felt dizzy and about to pass out,
and he clung to the boy for support. "I guess . . . I'm not
in as . . . good a shape as I thought I was. Lungs are
hurting."

"You have to stand up!" Tommy shouted. "I'll help
you! Hold onto me and . . ."

"No," Palatazin said. "Just let me lie down and rest for a little while . . . just a little while . . ."

"YOU HAVE TO STAND UP!" Tommy shook him, but now the man was sliding down into the sand. His eyes were closing, and he was just a heavy mass of flesh without consciousness or will. And suddenly Tommy realized there was someone standing a few feet away from them, just behind his left shoulder. He whirled around to face a lean, leathery-looking man with long, grayish brown hair and a wild gray beard that flowed down over his chest in tattered, dirty strands. He wore filthy blue jeans and a yellow T-shirt that said Timothy Leary for President across the front under a picture of Leary sitting atop the White House and smoking a joint. Tommy was afraid to move. The man stared at him through keen electric-blue eyes, barely seeming to mind the storm. Then the man looked around quickly and fell to his knees beside Tommy. He oozed with the odors of grime, sweat, and sewage. "You're not one of *them*, are you, man? I mean, you can't be one of *them* because you're out here in the daylight, aren't you? I mean, what daylight there is, right? What's ailing this dude?"

"He's going to die!" Tommy shouted. "Help me make him wake up!"

The man dug a dirty hand into his pocket, fished around for a few seconds, and then brought out a clear plastic capsule and popped it open under Palatazin's nose. Palatazin immediately sputtered and opened his eyes, and Tommy smelled the heavy odor of ammonia. "Peace, brother," the man said, holding up two fingers in a *V* before Palatazin's face. "Amyl nitrate does it again!"

Tommy realized the man had no protection, nothing to mask his face, not even a jacket. "Where did you come from?"

"Me? I come from everywhere, man! From under the hot earth where the cool streams run! From where the babbling brooks play in the concrete night! That's where I live!" He pointed a skinny finger, and Tommy looked over his shoulder. He could see the open manhole.

"The vibes aren't right up here, man! Not right at all! Gimme a hand and let's get this dude downstairs!" The man started dragging Palatazin toward the open hole in the center of the street, and Tommy pulled as best he could. Palatazin was conscious but dazed, his breathing still forced and ragged. The bearded man clambered down a few metal rungs with familiar ease, then helped Palatazin down into the darkness. Tommy followed. At the bottom of the metal rungs, in a large, circular concrete tunnel with pipes and cables running along its sides, the man eased Palatazin to a sitting position, picked up a bull's-eye lantern from the floor, and then scurried back up to pull the manhole cover into place. Tommy watched the daylight disappear and with it went the scream of the wind. When it was gone, the man switched on his lantern and climbed down again. He shone the light at Palatazin, who was weakly pulling the rest of the sheet away from his face. "You need another popper, man?"

Palatazin shook his head. "One's enough." His nostrils felt as if they were still on fire, but at least his brain was working again. Finding shelter from that savage wind was a blessing, no matter how foul the mingled odors of human excrement were down there.

"Damn straight." The man sat on his haunches, his face whitened by the backwash of the light, and looked from Palatazin to Tommy with quick, animal-like jerks of his head. "Bad vibes up there these days," he said finally, motioning with a tilt of his chin. "You want to be careful. Dig it!" He grinned, showing a mouthful of teeth that would've driven a dentist mad.

"Who *are* you?" Tommy asked.

"Me? I'm the Big R, the Hollywood Creeper. I'm Johnny Ratkins. My friends call me Ratty."

"You . . . live down here?"

"No, man, not *here!*" He scowled and pointed a finger down. "Here!" Now he made a broad, expansive movement with the same hand. "Everywhere. This is my mansion, safe from all the bad vibes there ever was or ever will be. Got a million rooms down here, a million corridors. Got babbling brooks and sweet streams and lakes . . . yeah! Real lakes, man! If I could just figure out how to get a Chris-Craft through that little hole, I'd be one happy dude! Dig it! What are you two dudes doing out in those bad vibes?"

Palatazin coughed a couple of times, spat out phlegm thickened with sand, and said, "Trying to get across Hollywood. I thought I could make it, but . . ." He looked at Tommy. "Why did you leave the house? I told you to stay back there!"

"You'd be dead now if I had! I said I could help you, and I still can!"

"You're a little fool!"

Tommy glowered at him, and when he spoke, his voice carried a cutting edge. "You're not my father so don't try to tell me what I can or can't do."

Ratty whistled through the nubs of his front teeth. "Heaaaavy! That's the center, man. That's Truth in a teacup!" He grinned at Palatazin. "The little dude's telling it like it is. If I hadn't heard him shouting, I wouldn't have stuck my head out to see what was going down. What was going down was *you*, man, so you'd better cool it."

"I suppose I should say thank you for getting us out of that."

"No need. Ratty does what he can. Oh, I've come across other folks like you two, stumbling around and lost with all those bad vibes sucking the air right out of their lungs. Some of them I helped." His gaze darkened. "Some of them I couldn't. The poppers wouldn't even bring them around. You feeling okay now?"

"Better," Palatazin said. What he was breathing was not the sweetest air possible, but at least he didn't have to sift it through his teeth, and for that he was grateful. His lungs felt raspy and raw.

"You want something to pick you up?" Ratty dug into his jeans again and this time brought out a handful of ampules, pills, and capsules in a variety of colors. "I've got whatever you need. Speed, yellowjackets, reds . . . got a microdot here somewhere that'll fuck up your head for a week!" He giggled and offered them to Palatazin.

"No, thank you."

"How about some angel dust? Or . . ." He reached into another pocket and brought out a clear cellophane packet containing what looked to Palatazin like sliced mushrooms. Ratty gazed at it lovingly. "Magic," he said.

Palatazin shook his head, and Ratty looked offended, as if his greatest offering had been refused. "What are you?" Palatazin asked him. "A dealer?"

"A dealer? Me? Listen, do you call John Travolta a *dancer?* I'm an artist, man! Look at these!" He shook the packet in front of Palatazin's face. "All meat and pure magic, the finest you can buy on the whole fuckin' Coast! Magic mushrooms! No additives, no preservatives, just pure homegrown, farmed by yours truly using all natural elements in the sod . . ."

"That's fine," Palatazin said and waved the packet away.

"This other stuff is junk compared to my mushrooms," Ratty said. He put the rest of his cache away, opened the packet, and sniffed at it. He closed his eyes and thrust the packet out toward Palatazin, who caught the heady odor of sewage. "I grow 'em down here," Ratty said. "I just got to figure out a way to get rid of the smell, then I'll be in the high cotton . . ."

Palatazin grunted and moved a few feet away from the man because he'd caught a whiff from him that was less than delicate. *What kind of lunatic was this?* he wondered. *Some hippie holdover who'd been living in these sewers for years perhaps, happy just to pop pills and grow "magic mushrooms" on . . . God! . . . did he say "natural elements in the sod"? Surely he had to go out sometime, if just to get batteries for his flashlight. And what did he eat?* His mind quickly shunted that thought away.

But then Ratty leaned forward and said, "Hey, what's in the bag? You don't have a can opener in there, do you? I sure could use one. I lost mine a couple of days ago. You don't have a ham sandwich in there, do you?"

Palatazin unsnapped one of the pockets and brought out a stake. Ratty was immediately silent. He took it and shone the light on it as if it were some relic from a lost civilization. "What's this for?" he said quietly. "The bloodsuckers?"

"The vampires."

"Bad vibes. Baaaad vibes!" He handed the stake back and wiped his hand on the leg of his filthy jeans. "I've seen them, man. They're everywhere, multiplying like flies on a fruitcake. You look in their eyes, and they get you—*pow!*—just like that." He lowered his voice to a conspiratorial whisper. "Couple of them chased me last night. I broke into Hoffman's Deli and got myself some food. On the way out there they were, right on the corner. I didn't know what they were at first, but then one of them flashed his chompers and I said, 'Uh-oh, old Ratty may have had some bad dreams in his time, but never like this!' So I took off, and they came after me. I was flying high on speed, and I was making moves like O.J. Simpson, but I still couldn't shake 'em. And all the time I was hearing these crazy voices, shrieking and screaming in my head." A nervous grin flickered across his face. His eyes were bright, scorched blue. "They chased me down into the line that runs underneath Hollywood Boulevard. I tried to hide in the dark. They move so . . . *quiet*. They don't even breathe. They can come up behind you, and you'd never know it until it was too late. I stayed where I was for a long time, until finally I heard somebody scream way on down the line. I figured there were other people hiding in the sewers too, and the vampires found them instead of Ratty. Lucky Ratty, huh?"

"Yes," Palatazin said. "Very lucky." But now a terrible uncertainty struck him—what if there were more vampires down here? Could they move around freely in this dark world, or would they still be bound by their unholy fear of sunlight? He wondered where the sun was now. God! he thought. *What time is it?* "We've got to hurry," he told Tommy.

"How? We can't go anywhere up there!"

Palatazin paused. He glanced at Ratty, then back at the boy. "You're right. We . . . can't go anywhere *up there.*"

"Huh?" Tommy said.

"How far do these sewers go?" he asked Ratty. There was an anxious excitement in his voice.

The man shrugged. "Everywhere. Across Hollywood, L.A., Beverly Hills, up into the canyons . . ." He stopped and narrowed his eyes slightly. "Where are you trying to get to?"

"Up above the Hollywood Bowl, just this side of Mulholland Drive . . ."

"Jesus! What's this, an expedition?"

"Of a kind."

"Yeah, well, too bad you didn't bring your wadin' boots," Ratty said, " 'cause you'd sure as hell need 'em! That's a long way to go, man."

"But could it be done?"

Ratty was silent. He sat on his haunches and seemed to be thinking it over for a few minutes. Then he said, "Where—exactly—do you want to go?"

"Across Hollywood to Outpost Drive, then up into the hills. There's another road branching off from Outpost, up higher, but I doubt if a sewer runs underneath it."

"I know where Outpost starts. On the other side of Franklin Avenue. Goes straight up the mountain, doesn't it?"

"That's right."

"Means a lot of shit pouring down the line, too. Hard going. Be like climbing a mountain covered with ice. 'Course now, not all the lines are the same size. Some of them you can walk in, some of them you crawl through, some of them . . . you hope you can get out of without gettin' stuck tight as a cork. It's about a three-mile hike from here to Franklin. You didn't answer my question. Where do you want to go?"

"The Kronsteen castle. Do you know where that is?"

"Nope, but it sure as hell sounds like a place with bad vibes. You say it's up close to Mulholland? You're takin' about another couple of miles almost straight up. *If* you can get through the tunnels. *If* you don't take a wrong turn and get lost, because all the lines aren't laid down exactly underneath the streets. I've got a nose for direction, man. I've been down here ever since I got back from Nam." Something sharp and brittle passed across Ratty's gaze. "I'd rather be down here where it's safe. The world up there has gone nuts, you dig? Bad vibes all over the place! Anyway, I know the line system like you know the way back and forth from your boob tube to the john. But even *I* get lost sometimes, and there are a lot of places I ain't been. Got the picture?"

"You're saying it can't be done?"

"Nope. I'm saying *you* can't do it."

"I know that," Palatazin answered.

Ratty looked from him to Tommy and back again. Tommy could hear the muffled roaring of the storm through the manhole cover above his head; it sounded like some huge animal gnawing at the iron, trying to get in at them. "What's the deal?" Ratty asked.

"We're going after the vampires," Palatazin said quietly. "At best we've got only four hours of real daylight left because when the sun drops low enough the storm cover will bring early darkness. We can't make it to the castle up there. We could make it by using the sewers. Couldn't we?"

"Maybe," Ratty said. "Don't like screwing with the bloodsuckers, man. That gives Ratty the creeps. You . . . going up to this place to give them the shaft, huh?"

"That's where their leader—their king—is sleeping. I think if I can destroy him, it might throw the rest of them into confusion . . ."

"Like Indians, huh? You get rid of the chief, and the rest of them are scared shitless?"

"Sort of like that, yes."

"Yeah. I can dig that." Ratty nodded and looked down into the stygian darkness of the tunnel. "I mean, this could be like . . . the end of the world or something, couldn't it? Those bloodsuckers keep getting stronger all the time, more and more of them . . . less of us. Right?"

"Yes." Palatazin held Ratty's gaze. "I have to get up to that castle. We have to start now. Will you help me?"

Ratty chewed his fingernail for a minute. His eyes kept getting larger and larger. He giggled suddenly. "Why not, man? I'm a crazy patriot. Shit! Why not?" He grinned into the darkness with all the good humor and courage his pills could give him. Then he stood up, his knees popping, and shone the light ahead along what looked to be an endless tunnel. "This is the way." He waited for Palatazin to stand and then start moving, his back seemingly permanently bent. Palatazin followed with Tommy bringing up the rear. The stink of sewage was getting stronger, but it was certainly preferable to the hellish wasteland above. Water trickled at their feet.

Time was their enemy now, and time lay on the vampires' side. Palatazin felt freighted with responsibility, not only for Jo and Gayle and Tommy but for the hundreds of thousands of people still trapped in L.A. What might happen to them tonight and all the nights to come if the king vampire couldn't be found? He felt as if he were going to do battle with an ancient adversary, a nightmare that had ripped away his childhood and plunged him into a world where all shadows were suspect, where every twilight was a terrifying reminder that somewhere the *vampir* were awakening.

He saw something move out of the corner of his eye, an indistinct shape touched briefly by the lantern's back-wash. His first thought was that a vampire had gotten Tommy and was now coming up behind him, but when he looked over his shoulder, there was nothing there and

Tommy was fine. And then he heard the faint whisper of a remembered voice brushing past his ear. He was quite sure of what it said. *André, I won't leave you . . .*

That made him feel better. But there was such a long way to go, and nothing could stop the relentless descent of the sun.

TEN

The Crab had slowed to a crawl. Brooklyn Avenue at Soto Street in the center of Boyle Heights was blocked by towering dunes that had built up around a horrendous traffic accident, nine or ten cars slammed together right at the intersection. Wes stopped the Crab. The visibility was so bad now that even the high-intensity headlights couldn't pierce the dark, amber gloom, and he had to drive as slowly as possible without stalling the engine to avoid crashing into a dune or a twisted, wrecked car. The worst of the storm, he knew, had hit yesterday at rush hour, so there would be thousands of wrecked and stranded cars—all of them now scrap metal for the dunes to grasp and grow over like pregnant yellow leeches. He wondered what had happened to the drivers of these cars. Had they found shelter before they suffocated? Or had the vampires found them first?

"Dead end," he said to Silvera. "We can't get around that."

"Turn right on Soto. There's a Hollywood Freeway entrance ramp about eight blocks ahead."

Wes was relieved to find that the ramp was clear, but when the Crab had crested it, the headlights picked out one wrecked or stalled car after another. The dunes shifted restlessly, threatening to spill over and bury the Crab. There were many corpses caught in the airless cars and many who had been caught out in the open as well. Some of them looked as if they were simply sleeping; others had died in agony, eyes and mouths filled with sand. Wes felt his nerve breaking. The Crab made it about fifteen yards before it was halted by another mass of sand and metal. The wind sucked and pulled wildly at the vehicle.

"Back down the ramp," Silvera said tersely. He reached back and leaked some oxygen into the cab. "We'll have to find another way."

"THERE'S NOT ANOTHER WAY!" Wes shouted. "Jesus Christ! Everything's blocked!"

Silvera waited for him to calm down and said, "Take it easy. That's not going to solve anything and it's sure as hell not going to get us across L.A."

Wes was trembling. If he'd ever needed a joint or a plain old cigarette before, this was the time, but he had neither and there was no air to spare, anyway. *Do you want to give up?* he asked himself. *No! I can't! Like the priest says, we'll have to find another way . . .*

"Back up," Silvera said.

"I can't see a thing." The rear windwhield was layered with sand, and he could envision backing into one of those huge dunes. It would be good-bye with a slither and a moan. The engine kicked a couple of times, and Wes's heart started to pound.

"All right." Silvera got one of the oxygen masks from the rear compartment and slipped it on. The second of the oxygen tanks was in a backpack carrier that would allow it to fit right between the shoulder blades. Silvera fumbled for a moment while he attached the rubber line from the mask into the tank's small feed-out nozzle; there was a soft *click* as the male and female joints connected. He turned on the oxygen and took a breath of sweet, cold air, then shrugged the backpack over his shoulders. "I'll go out to guide you down," he said, his voice muffled by the mask. "I'll be right behind you. I'll slam on the right side when I want you to turn right, left for left. Got that?"

"Yeah," Wes said. "For Christ's sake be careful!"

Silvera stepped out and the wind almost threw him to the ground. He moved like an astronaut in an alien atmosphere, cabled to his life-support system. There were two half-obscured corpses right beside the Crab, a woman clutching a little girl. He shivered and went around to the back as Wes put the Crab into reverse and started moving. Several times Silvera had to hammer against the sides to keep Wes from backing into either a dune or a wrecked car. When they reached the ramp, cold sweat clung to his face, and he was dizzy from hyperventilating. He quickly climbed in, took his seat, and removed the mask. "You're clear," he said. "But I think we can rule out the freeways from now on."

They passed under the freeway and turned left on Marengo, moving past the dark buildings of the County General Hospital complex where a doctor named Doran had told Silvera he was dying. Now he wondered if Doran had beat him there, or whether the good doctor might now be making a totally different kind of midnight house call. They curved slowly around the complex to North Main Street, which Silvera knew would take them across the river and through downtown L.A.

The Crab was almost across the North Main bridge when its headlights picked out the monstrous cluster of yellow dunes blocking their way.

Rats in a maze, Wes thought as he braked the Crab. *Thats what we are.* The headlights gleamed off the grillwork of a Cadillac caught under a mountain of sand. The dunes loomed up like the mountains of the moon.

"Back up," Silvera said, tension crackling in his voice. His face had turned the color of dried clay.

It took them over another hour of starts and stops at the dead-ends of mangled wreckage and blowing dunes before they found a clear way across the river at 7th Street, more than five miles south of the place where they'd first tried to cross. Factories and warehouses stood on the other side of the river, all of them dead and dark. Chain link fences had been blown down, and they lay tangled across 7th Street like barbed wire. About a block further was an overturned truck in the center of the street.

Wes slowed and turned right, driving along a narrower street with warehouses on each side. He thought he knew where he was now. Downtown L.A. lay just a few streets over, and from the center of town he could wind his way up into Hollywood. It would be a fearful trip, but nothing compared to what might be waiting for them in Kronsteen's old fortress. The Crab still seemed to be in pretty good shape, though the engine continued to sputter. Wes figured it had been built for rough duty, though, and probably had a system of air filters that trapped most of the sand. Still, he recalled that it had been traveling very close behind the massive troop carrier, presumably so that the bigger vehicle would take the brunt of the storm. The Crab might shudder and die at any minute, or it might carry them all the way without a whimper. He just didn't know.

Suddenly Silvera looked at him oddly. "Stop," he ordered.

"What?" Wes said. "Stop where?"

"Here."

Wes braked the vehicle; it slid a couple of feet and then halted. "What is it?"

"I don't know. I . . . thought I saw something back there. We passed a warehouse on the right about fifty feet. I don't know what it was I saw, but . . . something was stacked on the loading dock and . . ." He looked back over his shoulder but couldn't see anything. "Caskets," he said softly. "I think there were caskets stacked on that loading dock."

Wes put the Crab into reverse. The dark outline of a metal-walled warehouse came up into Silvera's window. The remnants of a chain link fence stuck up out of the sand like picket-fence slats on a New England beach. There was a break in the blowing, grayish-yellow sheets, and through a clear hole they both saw a row of big trucks lined up before a long loading dock, and on that dock something covered over with a dark green tarpaulin. The tarpaulin fluttered and fell back once, then again. The second time Silvera said. "There!" and Wes could see the oblong, brown boxes, stacked in neat rows as if awaiting shipment.

Silvera said, "I'm going out." He put on the oxygen mask and the tank and left the Crab, walking hurriedly and at an angle against the wind. Wes worked with the other mask and tank for a few minutes, finally got them together, and slipped the tank into another of the backpack carriers. The mask clung as tight as a second skin, but the goggle lenses gave him a wide-angle view, and the first breath of air he drew was shockingly sweet. He got out of the vehicle and followed Silvera, climbing up the dunes and stepping over the collapsed fence.

On the loading dock Silvera pulled off the tarpaulin and let the wind whip it away. Then he opened the lid of a coffin and peered inside. It was filled with dirt, but there was no one in it, not even the impression of a body. As Wes struggled up onto the dock and walked along it, he realized the warehouse was at least as long as a football field, possibly longer; its far end disappeared in whirling yellow. He looked into the empty coffin, then at Silvera. He had to shout to make himself heard. "What did you expect to find in there?"

"I'm not sure." Silvera opened the next coffin and the next one after that. They were all filled with dirt, but no vampires. *Why would they be?* he asked himself suddenly. The vampires wouldn't sleep exposed to the weather; they'd sleep enclosed. His gaze fell upon a large sliding door set in the wall. He went over to it and slid it back several feet. A wave of rancid chill came rolling out of the warehouse; it was the same feeling he'd had in the Dos Terros tenement. Silvera glanced at Wes, his eyes wary behind the mask, before he stepped through the opening.

At first he couldn't see a thing. Then he gradually made out high, crisscrossed metal rafters, rows of fluorescent lights, metal rungs leading up to a catwalk that stretched the length of the building, a few electric carts and yellow forklifts. But then he saw what lay before him, what lay all around him, what lay in neat rows from wall to wall and on out of sight. He caught his breath with shock.

The warehouse was filled with what must have been over a thousand coffins. They were all lying closed on the concrete floor, and Silvera realized why those caskets had been left stacked on the loading dock. There was simply no more room in this huge warehouse.

"Jesus Christ!" Wes said softly, standing behind the priest.

"This is where they sleep," Silvera heard himself say. "Not all of them . . . not anywhere near all of them, but . . . my God! Every warehouse in the entire industrial district may be full of them!" He took a tentative step forward, then leaned down and opened the coffin nearest him.

On its bed of brown California soil, a young male vampire wearing a light blue shirt spotted with blood lay with its arms crossed over its chest. The eyes seemed to be staring right through the milky-lids with a dull, hateful gaze. Those lids, Silvera realized, were very similar to those found in most reptiles; they would be natural protection against the sand. The vampire lay still, a killing machine awaiting full darkness. Silvera stared at the thing and thought he heard in his brain a soft, terrible

whisper—*Lean over here, man, just a little bit closer. . . .*
He quickly closed the coffin lid with his foot and
stepped around it carefully, his own breathing suddenly
too loud and harsh within the mask.

He opened the next coffin and found a little black
girl—her flesh faded to a sick, pasty gray—lying there.
He sensed her longing for his blood even in sleep. She
shifted suddenly, and the movement made Silvera step
back a few paces. She gripped the casket's sides, then
lay still again. He closed the lid, a chill skittering up his
spine.

Wes walked along the first row of coffins. He opened
one of them, his hand shaking. A small boy—no more
than four or five—lay there. As Wes watched, stunned.
the child's hand slowly lifted, fingers grasping at air, and
then fell back on his chest. The mouth opened, a red
slash in the yellowish face, and the fangs clicked together
like the snapping of a bear trap. *Was it dreaming?* Wes
wondered. *Of what? Seeing me in its dreams, and dreaming that it's sinking its fangs into my throat?* He leaned
forward to close the casket, and a shimmering little child's
voice wafted through his brain—*Danny don't want you
to go . . . Danny want you to stay here for always.* Wes
paused, his head thundering. Silvera leaned across him,
closed the lid quickly and pulled him away.

"Thanks," Wes said, blinking. "They're strong even
when . . . they're sleeping."

"Help me drag that one out into the light," Silvera
said. He gripped the edge of the first casket he'd opened.
Wes got on the other side, and together they pushed and
pulled the thing out onto the loading dock into the murky
light. "I'm going to open it now," the priest said. Before
Wes could respond, he did, then backpedaled away several feet, ready for anything.

The vampire instantly stared writhing, clawing at the
coffin's sides, its mouth opening in a grimace. The fangs
clicked together with terrible force. Wes saw awareness
and pain flood into the eyes, then pure agony. The vampire screamed, an unearthly wail that was unlike anything Wes had ever heard.

Then the thing sat up violently, flinging clumps of dirt
from the coffin. Its murderous gaze fell upon Silvera.
and it started to rise, its head twisted at an angle away
from the sunlight.

Silvera knew it was going to try to get back inside the warehouse into the cool darkness. He shoved Wes through the doorway, leaped inside, and started sliding the door shut as the vampire hurtled forward, screaming in rage and pain. As the door closed, the vampire flung itself frantically against the metal. Both men together could hardly hold it shut. The door shuddered as the vampire hammered on it, then began to scratch at it like a mindless animal. Wes held back a scream; he was standing in total darkness with a thousand or more vampires at his back, and one outside trying to get in. He thought he heard furtive movement behind him, the creaking of a few hundred casket lids.

Then the clawing noises stopped.

Silvera waited a moment more, then started to pull the door open. "It's a trick!" Wes shouted. Silvera opened the door a few inches and peered out. The coffin on the loading dock was closed again. When Silvera opened the door wider, Wes heard quick, scuttling sounds behind him, lids being closed hastily. Silvera stepped out onto the dock, leaned down slowly, and threw back the lid again.

The vampire—now hideously bloated like a three-day-old corpse—sat up and snapped at Silvera's face; the fangs sank into the rubber mask, then withdrew. Before Silvera's eyes, fluids bubbled up beneath the thing's flesh, the arms, legs, and face blowing up like the sausage appendages of a freakish carnival fat man. The blue shirt stretched, buttons popping off; fluids leaked from the mouth, nostrils, and eyes, pooling around the head. Then rapidly, the form shriveled into something as thin and frail as a dead leaf; the gums sank, the eyes fell inward and seemed to melt away, the nose flattened and collapsed. The vampire curled up into an *S*, shivered violently, and then was still. Now it looked like a month-old corpse, which, Silvera realized, it probably was.

Wes barely got his mask off before his stomach heaved. After he was finished, his ribs hurt as if Satan himself had kicked them with his cloven hoof.

"Wait here," Silvera said and walked quickly along the dock back toward the Crab. Wes put his mask back on and sat down far away from the dead vampire. *There are too many of them!* he thought. *Thousands!* His mind slipped back to Solange; surely she was one of them by now. He couldn't bear to think about that, not just yet.

The priest came back carrying the gasoline can and the ceramic crucifix. The .45 was jammed down in his waistband. He gave Wes the crucifix and then went back into the warehouse. Wes followed, his legs unsteady. Silvera uncapped the gasoline can and started dousing as many caskets as he could. The three gallons didn't stretch very far, though, and Silvera poured the last quarter gallon or so in a shimmering pool on the floor at the foot of the first few caskets. Then he flung the can away and walked back to the door. Taking the .45, he unclicked the safety and aimed at the puddle of gas. The shot sounded like a cannon going off. Wes saw sparks fly. The puddle burst into blue flames and started crawling in snakelike tendrils across several coffins, following the gasoline trails. In another moment they started charring, and black smoke whirled. Reflections and shadows glimmered off the metal walls. A few of the coffin lids shivered and started to open. Silvera said tersely, "Get out! Hurry!"

Before they slid the doorway shut completely, Silvera took the crucifix from Wes and jammed it at an angle through the inside door handle. Then they ran.

In the Crab they took off their gear. Wes started the engine. Above the shriek of the wind, he heard other screams that made him want to clap his hands to his ears. "Drive. Fast," Silvera said. Wes pushed the vehicle through a small dune that had built up in front of the Crab during the time they'd been gone. When they had left the warehouse district behind, Wes said, "Do you think they'll all burn?"

"No. But some of them will. The inside of that place, with those metal walls, will get hot pretty quickly, and the crucifix may keep them away from the door. If they get out, the sunlight will kill them. But I don't think all of them will burn, no."

"My God! I didn't know there were . . . so many . . ."

"And many thousands more than those, I'm sure." Silvera laid the .45 back on the floorboard. He squeezed his hands into fists to try to stop their trembling. Fear had filled him up as if he were an old cracked jug, and it was beginning to leak out. Suddenly he realized that he couldn't tell where the sun was anymore. The entire sky seemed the same dirty brown color, streaked with gray and yellow. "What time is it?" he asked.

Wes glanced at his watch and thanked Rolex for their
airtight, shockproof cases. "Almost three." He took off
his watch and laid it on the dashboard so they could both
see it.

"We have to hurry," Silvera said quietly. A voice
within him shrieked, TOO LATE! TOO LATE! IT'S
GOING TO BE DARK SOON AND IT'LL BE TOO
LATE!

The towers of L.A. loomed up out of the murky sky
like tombstones in a graveyard for giants. Then they
were gone, obscured by new curtains of sand. Before
Wes's face the wipers shuddered and groaned. The Crab's
engine stuttered, gasping for air. Darkness seemed to be
creeping in all around them, brown veined with gray.
Near the white, drift-covered plain of Pershing Square,
tumbleweeds came flying out of nowhere, scraping across
the windshield, and were gone. Wes came to one blocked
street after another, having to back up carefully and retrace his path. The gas gauge's needle was beginning to
fall, the engine temperature gauge at the danger line.

L.A. could have been a ghost town chewed to shreds
by the ravaging Mojave, Wes thought. A bright and glittering Xanadu laid to waste, a city of dreams gone bad,
a stately pleasure-domed place that the desert and Evil
had finally marched upon in tandem to conquer and
destroy. Evil had always lived here, Wes knew, in the
back rooms, in the sweltering tenements, in the meeting
rooms and palaces. It had always watched and waited,
using a Manson here, a Hillside Strangler there, a Roach
thrown in for good measure, like hideous ingredients in
a dreadful cauldron brew. And now this perhaps was
Evil's main course, the *pièce de résistance* poured out of
that cauldron like a stew of rattlesnake heads and human
blood. When darkness fell, the dinner bell would start
ringing again. And Evil would shout through a hundred-
thousand unholy, triumphant throats, *Feast! Feast! For
the banquet is spread and we are so very hungry . . .*

Wes realized that they had little to fight the vampires
with now, just some water in a vial, the guns and that
switchblade. What good would bullets and a knife be?
Wes had hoped for some kind of protection from the
crucifix, but now that they'd left it behind, they'd have
to go on with what remained. He still had the little ball

of stuff Solange had made for him; it had worked against the bikers, but what protection would the priest have?

He thrust those fears aside, but they kept trying to gnaw their way back in like little ravenous weasels. He would have to deal with them later, but not now. Just looking at the fuel gauge told him they'd crossed the point of no return, probably way back when they'd come over the L.A. River. So there was nothing to do now but keep going, he thought, nothing to do now but give it the best shot Wesley Richer had ever given anything in his life. His palms were as cold and sweaty as the first night he'd stepped up on that stage at the Comedy Store, but this stage was a far more important one, and the hook that yanked you off would take you to your death . . . or worse.

But death wouldn't be so bad, he thought, not really, not when the alternative was to be like those things in the coffins. He'd already decided how to do it if that was the only way out—.45 barrel into the mouth and up, quick squeeze on the trigger, and *boom!* Jump the night train. Pull a Freddie Prinze. Hitchhike home in the hard rain. Suicide.

He only hoped he could take Solange with him.

ELEVEN

Tommy's head was aching, and Palatazin had to stop to catch his breath. He sat beside the boy in the dark, foul clamminess of the tunnel while Ratty took the lantern and scuttled on ahead. In another few minutes they saw the light coming back, just a yellow dot at first and then a spreading beam. Ratty knelt down beside Palatazin. "We're almost under Hollywood Boulevard. You okay, little dude?"

"Yeah. I'm fine," Tommy said.

"How much further to Outpost Drive?" Palatazin asked him.

"Not far. Then we start climbing if the tunnel's big enough. And you got to remember, I can squeeze into a whole lot of places *you* can't. You two ready?"

"Ready," Tommy said and rose to his feet.

Since crossing under DeLongpre Avenue the water at
the bottom of the tunnel had increased from a slow trickle
to what now seemed like a thick, muddy creek. The tunnel that Ratty had said ran underneath Sunset Boulevard
was large and high, and it had amazed Palatazin that the
lantern picked out spray-painted graffiti on the walls. At
their feet slow currents moved around islands of brown
sludge. Now they came to two tunnels splitting off in opposite directions. Ratty paused for a minute, shining his
light around, and chose the right one. The ceiling dropped
dramatically here, and they moved on with their backs
bent. Occasional currents swirled over their shoes; the
odors of sewage were nothing short of gruesome. Ratty
splashed through the mess like a trout fisherman. "Not
far!" he called back, waiting for them to catch up. "It's
just through here. Hey! Watch it, little dude!" He shone
the lights at gray rats scurrying protectively around a
nest in a crack between two sections of pipe just above
Tommy's head. All but two or three of the largest rats
squealed and ran; they stared back defiantly, their eyes
pink pinpoints. "Sometimes they jump for your face,"
Ratty said when they'd gone on past. "They grab hold,
you can't shake 'em off for shit. One time I woke up
after I'd crashed on yellows and found two of the little
bastards tryin' to dig a nest in my beard!"

Ratty stopped suddenly and sniffed the air. "That's it.
The big one under Hollywood." They came to the end of
the narrow tunnel and stepped out into another large one.
At the bottom of this tunnel, the water was deeper, perhaps a foot or so, and swirled around every manner of
dank, unidentifiable debris. Rats chittered in the darkness,
and Palatazin could hear them splashing in the water like
birds in a birdbath. Ratty sloshed forward without hesitation, aiming his light along the far wall; there were
more tunnel entrances over there, each one bleeding out
little streams of water. "Let's see now," Ratty said, narrowing his eyes in thought. The light moved from one
tunnel to the next. "It's that one," he said, holding steady
on the center entrance. "Yeah. I'm pretty sure."

Tommy said, "Don't you know?" His voice crackled
with tension. Being down here reminded him of the movie
Them, about the giant ants that had made a nest underneath L.A.

"Sure I know," Ratty replied and tapped his skull.

"Got the map right up in here. Just sometimes I tend to get a little confused, that's all." He giggled suddenly, his eyes burning like blue lamps from the pills he'd popped.

"Let's go," Palatazin said irritably. "Come on!"

Ratty shrugged and started forward. Tommy took three steps and felt his right foot slide over something softly hideous. He screamed and jerked his leg away, stumbling into Palatazin. "What is it?" Palatazin said sharply. Ratty turned and shone his light down. A man's corpse was being laboriously pushed along by the westward currents. The rats were astride it, leaping and nibbling. Palatazin took Tommy's shoulder and pulled him away. They crossed the tunnel, walking faster, and entered the tunnel opening Ratty had indicated.

The tunnel crooked to the right and grew steadily narrower. Palatazin walked bent over, his lungs rasping, and realized that Ratty's lantern was losing power. The beam of light had now dulled to a soft yellow. He could hear rats chittering behind them, closing up in their wake; he wondered how much more the boy could stand. But Tommy had made a man's choice, and now there was no turning back for him. More tunnels, some only holes a foot or less in diameter, branched off from the one they moved through. Water trickled and dripped, the echoes as disconcertingly loud as footsteps. They came to a metal-runged ladder. Ratty aimed the light up at a manhole cover perhaps twelve feet overhead. "I better go up to find out for sure where we are," he said, and gave Palatazin the lantern. Palatazin nodded, and Ratty scuttled up quickly, shoving the cover aside. A weak amber light came down from the opening, and then Ratty had disappeared into the storm.

After a few minutes Palatazin said, "Tommy, I don't think we're going to make it before they start waking up. It's already very dark up there. *Too* dark. When the sun's rays get weak enough, I'm afraid they'll start . . . prowling again."

"We can't go back," Tommy said.

"I know."

"Will they all . . . wake up at the same time?"

Palatazin shook his head. "I'm not sure. Possibly not. There are so many things I don't know about them. The oldest ones may wake up first, or possibly the ones who are hungriest. My God, I hate to leave Jo unprotected . . ." He stopped suddenly because he thought he'd heard a sliding movement behind them. He shone the light in that direction. The light was too weak to reach very far, and the tunnel seemed layered with impenetrable shadows.

"What is it?" Tommy asked nervously, looking over his shoulder.

"I . . . don't know. I thought I heard something, but . . ."

Ratty appeared overhead and came down quickly. "Okay," he said, breathing heavily, his beard and hair full of sand. "We're under Franklin Avenue, but we've got to go east a little ways to pick up the tunnel under Outpost. I'm not sure how big it's gonna be."

"Just get us there," Palatazin said and gave him back the lantern.

They moved on, the uneasy tick of time hammering at the back of Palatazin's skull. The tunnel crooked to the left, then to the right again, and grew narrower still. Seepage from the canyons sloshed noisily underfoot. Several times Palatazin said, "Wait," and they stood motionless while he listened. When Ratty aimed the light back, the tunnel was clear for as far as they could see.

They came to a metal screen blocking their way. Palatazin took the mallet from the pack and spent a few minutes hammering it to one side. Further on the tunnel began to angle upward perceptibly; it veered again to the right, then straightened out and seemed endless. The ceiling dropped once again, and now even Tommy walked bent over. Palatazin, his spine already aching, stepped carefully to keep from slipping in the morass at the tunnel's bottom as water and debris flowed over his shoes.

And now he heard that noise again and turned, straining to see through the utter darkness. He was quite sure this time that he'd heard the muffled noise of cold laughter, quickly fading away. He made Tommy walk between himself and Ratty. The hairs at the back of his neck were standing on end now, because he feared that there were vampires down here who were already awake, sealed off from any hint of the sun. Possibly they were terribly hungry, and their hunger had kept them from sleeping; possibly they roamed the sewers in packs looking for victims. He remembered the matches and the aerosol can in the pack and, as he walked, he slipped his hand in and touched the can. Ratty's lantern was getting steadily weaker.

The tunnel angled upward sharply. They started climbing.

TWELVE

The house was filling up with darkness. It had come insidiously, relentlessly, and early. It was the hazed light that frightened Jo so much because she was so uncertain of when the vampires would awaken and from where they'd attack—the little house across the street? the one next to that? Over an hour earlier she and Gayle had heard the man next door crying out garbled prayers, then there'd been a long silence broken by a single shot. After that they didn't hear him anymore.

Now Jo sat in a chair away from the window, her face a grim mask. Her fingers moved around the small crucifix that hung from her neck, the gift from Andy. Gayle had pulled the curtains closed, but every few minutes she would interrupt her nervous wandering around the room to peer out at the thickening gloom. Sand scraped the glass like fingernails across a blackboard. Gayle kept Palatazin's .38 close at hand. "Going to be dark soon," she kept saying as if forcing herself to accept that inevitability. Every time she pulled back the curtains to look out, she steeled herself to expect a pallid, grinning face looking in.

Jo found herself drifting into memories—she could recall the first time she'd met Andy's mother, on their third date the night after a St. Stephen's Day festival. The woman had been friendly enough, but so quiet and withdrawn; her eyes had seemed washed-out and blank, and they'd seemed to stare right through Jo at something coming up from behind. Now she understood why.

And then something knocked at the door.

Gayle's heart leaped. She grasped the .38 and pulled it out of the shoulder-holster. She stared at Jo, her eyes widened into fearful circles.

The knock came again, two fast raps on the door.

"Don't answer it!" Jo whispered. "Don't make a sound!"

"It might be Palatazin!" Gayle said and turned toward the door, one hand going out for the knob and the other gripped white-knuckled around the gun.

"NO!" Jo said. "DON'T!"

Silence but for the hissing of the wind. Gayle slowly unlocked the door, turned the knob, and opened it enough to look out. At first she couldn't see a thing, so she opened the door a little wider.

And then something from a Jules Verne nightmare stepped in front of her, a green-garbed monstrosity with huge bug eyes and a hoglike snout. Gayle cried out and brought the gun up to fire, but the thing reached in and grasped her wrist. "Whoa, Miss!" the thing said with a pronounced Texas drawl. "I'm Corporal Preston, US Marines. I'd take it kindly if you'd remove your finger from that trigger."

Relief flooded through her, weakening her knees. She realized the man was wearing an oxygen mask and goggles, and as he stepped into the house, she could see the tank on his back. The man closed the door behind him and pulled his mask up. He was just a kid, really, with a lantern jaw and acne scars on his cheeks. He nodded toward Jo, who'd risen to her feet in amazement. "How many people you got in here, Miss?" he asked Gayle.

"Two. Just us."

"Okay. There's a unit vehicle about three blocks from here. We're going to be getting you out. I couldn't find anybody in the house next door. Anybody live over there?" He motioned toward the madman's house.

"No," Gayle said. "Not anymore."

"Okay. You two ladies just hang on awhile longer, you'll hear the truck coming. You want to watch where you point that pop gun, Miss." He slid his mask back down and started for the door, taking a small can of orange Day-Glo paint from the inside of his jacket.

"We can't leave!" Jo said suddenly. "We're . . . waiting . . ."

The marine studied her through his goggles. "Ma'am," he said patiently, "everybody who can git is already gone, making tracks to high ground. I've got orders to evacuate all the folks I can find, and let me tell you, I can't find very many of 'em. What are you waiting for?"

Gayle said, "There are two more of us. A man and a boy."

"Oh. They went out in this storm, did they?"

Gayle nodded. Jo's eyes were reddening.

"I wouldn't worry," Preston said. "They probably got picked up by another unit by now. The trucks are all over the area. And nobody could get very far out there without . . . uh . . . ." He trailed off. "The truck'll be here in a few minutes."

He opened the door, letting in a hot swirl of wind and sand. On the outside of the door he sprayed a large numeral two, glaring orange against the bare, pocked wood. "You ladies just sit tight for a while," he called over his shoulder before he shut the door. Struggling against the wind, he went on to the next house. The fire tracks where Royce had taken the Crab on up ahead were already gone. Preston could look back and see the faint yellow glow of the tractor's high-intensity headlights approaching. *At least,* he thought, *most of these folks have already gotten out one way or another. Nobody answered their doors, so they must've gotten to safety.* But he wondered how, since there seemed to be a lot of abandoned cars, all of them covered over with blowing dunes. He was following orders, though, and searching door-to-door, and he didn't have time to think about anything else. Nobody answered next door so he went on. His spray can hadn't seen much use today.

THIRTEEN

It was almost five o'clock when Wes found the turnoff onto Blackwood Road. The sky had turned the texture of hard leather, as dull brown as the ox-blood shoes the pimps used to wear as they watched their low-rent merchandise parade on Whore's Walk. It seemed low enough to scrape across the Crab's roof. On either side of the road, trees bent and shivered, limbs ripping away and flying off down the hillside. The Crab's tires fought for a sure purchase on the incline; it seemed to slip three feet for every two it gained. The wheel shuddered in Wes's grip.

"This is the way up?" Silvera asked him. "You're sure?"

"I'm sure."

Silvera could only see walls of blowing sand all around them. Still, he had a *feeling* that the castle was somewhere close, looming overhead like a huge stone vulture hanging to the cliff. Fear had coiled in his belly, a cold serpent undulating as it crawled up to enclose his heart in a freezing grasp. His nerve was slipping as badly as the Crab's tires. But there was no turning back now, there had never been. He saw his way clearly and knew he was following it as it had been laid down, stone for stone, all the way from the Dos Terros tenement he'd gone into with Rico Esteban. It was meant for him to be here, as surely as Wes was meant to commandeer this vehicle. This moment had been ordained for him during the tick of the clock in which Dr. Doran had told him he was dying. It was all part of the mysterious jigsaw puzzle that, when viewed close up, seemed to be nothing but meaningless colors and angles of movement. But when viewed from far away, perhaps over the shoulder, it became as tightly constructed and meaningful as the stained-glass window in his own church. He didn't know what the future would bring; he dared not guess. But neither would he let fear strangle him.

A howling gust of wind hit the Crab, almost tearing the wheel out of Wes's hands. The engine whirred as sand shifted beneath the wheels, and the Crab hung motionless for a few seconds. The tires gripped and pulled, then lost traction again. Wes looked at Silvera.

"The road's too steep! Tires can't get a . . . *Christ!*" The Crab skidded sideways toward a dropoff on the left side of the road. Wes pumped the brakes frantically, but the vehicle was being pushed by the wind faster and faster, as if shoved by a Satanic hand. "We're going over!" he shouted, twisting the wheel.

The rear slipped over, tires spinning in empty air. Wes glanced to the left, saw dashing currents and a shrub-stubbled ravine forty feet below. For an agonizing few seconds he felt the Crab tipping. He sank his foot to the floorboard; the front tires dug down through shifting sand. The Crab suddenly lurched as the right front tire scrabbled across concrete. It leaped away from the dropoff and met another wailing torrent of wind head-on. Then it was thrown to the side like a roller coaster that had jumped the tracks.

It crashed into a tree at the edge of the road and hung there, perhaps six feet away from the dropoff. The wind whirled past, roaring in fury. The Crab's engine gave a little moan and died. Wes stared straight ahead, afraid to move for fear of rocking the vehicle over. His eyes were glassy, his lips as white as newly-cut marble.

"We're okay," Silvera said shakily. "The wind's got us pinned against that tree. We're not going anywhere."

"God," Wes breathed. "I thought . . . we were . . . it's a hell of a long way down . . ." When he forced himself to let go of the wheel, the blood came back into his fingers with a tingling rush.

"We're going to have to make it on foot the rest of the way. How far up is it?"

"I don't know. It's right at the top, but . . . I don't know."

"You all right?"

"Yeah. Will be. Just give me a minute."

Silvera reached back for his gear. "I don't know how much air we've got left in these, but it'll have to be enough."

"Listen, if that fucking wind could throw a car over the cliff, it could pick us up and toss us right onto that spindle on top of the Capitol Records building!"

"Yes, I know. So we'll have to be careful, won't we? The wind may be worse higher up. Now *you* listen to me. We're going to have to move damned fast out there, and we'll have to be lucky. I don't know how we're going to get inside that place yet, and I really don't know what we *can* do when and if we do get in. I feel like I . . . have to go. You don't. You can stay here if you like."

"Stay here?" Wes frowned, gazed out at the storm for a few seconds, and then back to Silvera. "No. I'm scared so bad I'm about to piss nickels, but I've come too far to stay here. Solange is up there somewhere. I want to find her."

"You may not be able to. And what you find may not be the person you knew."

"I understand that," Wes said quietly.

"Then you also understand that once we get in there, we may not be coming out?"

Wes nodded.

"I want you to do what I say when I say it," Silvera said. "No balking." He reached down to the floorboard for the guns, handed Wes the .45, and slipped the .22 into his own waistband. He touched the small bottle of holy water in his side coat pocket. "I don't know much about these things," Silvera said. "The water may not have any effect. Neither may the guns, but aim for their eyes. That should make them think twice."

"Don't fire till you see the whites of their eyes, huh?" Wes said nervously.

"I don't think I'd wait that long. Once we get inside, I'm going to be searching for one in particular, and I pray to God that the water has some effect on him. Or the bullets. And . . ." He took out the switchblade. "If he's sleeping I'm going to cut out his heart with this. Now you'd better get ready."

Wes geared up. Silvera slipped his oxygen mask on, and then it was time to go.

Silvera had to push to get the door open. He squeezed out, and Wes followed him out the passenger's side because the driver's door was jammed against that tree. They began to climb the road, their feet slipping and sinking. Occasional strong blasts of wind staggered them, pushing them dangerously close to the rock-rimmed drop-offs on the left side of the road before they could regain their balance. It was almost fully dark now, and Silvera knew that if the vampires weren't already prowling they soon would be. The road stretched up into whirling black, as if it led over the edge of the world and when they fell, they would keep falling through the dark forever.

They had been walking for perhaps fifteen minutes when Silvera saw something move ahead—a quick, furtive movement, something that seemed smaller than a man but still indistinguishable in the gloom. It seemed to vanish, sucked up by the storm. He had the feeling they were being watched by something coming up fast from behind. He slid the gun out and whirled around. Nothing there but darkness, ghostly patterns of sand hissing and dancing and breaking apart, whirling out over the great dark plain where a glittering city had once been. He kept moving, keeping right beside Wes. Now there was another quick movement off in the thick shrubs to the left at the road's edge. Then another on the right.

He couldn't tell yet what they were, but they disappeared as quickly as he saw them.

And then from out of the storm curtain that fluttered in their faces leaped a huge reddish brown mongrel, its eyes burning like yellow lamps.

Silvera saw the bared teeth. He lifted his arm and fired but never heard the two shots. The dog leaped past his shoulder, almost knocking him to the ground, and was swallowed up in the darkness. Silvera didn't know whether he'd hit it or not.

Another dog, smaller than the first one but coal black so they didn't see it until it was right there at their feet, jumped for Wes's face, jaws snapping shut as Wes shouted and dodged. The dog tensed for another leap, but Silvera stepped forward and kicked it in the ribs. It howled and whirled, snapping at the priest's leg. Wes fired a shot; the bullet splintered the dog's skull and flung it away like a rag. Something struck at the back of Silvera's knees, staggering him. He felt teeth ripping into his right calf, gnawing for the bone. He twisted and wrenched his leg away and, as the collie came at him again, he shot it between the eyes. The collie fell, kicked a few times, and then was still. "I'll watch the rear!" Silvera shouted. His leg was bleeding, but he barely felt the pain. Now there seemed to be a hundred shapes all around them, leaping and feinting, coming in to draw their shots before darting away. Silvera held his fire, but twice Wes shot at shadows. "Save it!" Silvera told him. "Make it count!"

Something that looked like a gray bull mastiff came charging out of the storm, rearing up on powerful, muscle-corded hind legs. It towered as high as Wes, showing teeth that could rip his throat out. Wes was about to fire when the dog vanished off to his right. He looked up and could see shapes gathered on the boulders that hung over the road. They crouched low, like wolves about to leap. Dogs came snapping at Silvera's legs, backed away, and charged again. A black mongrel with dull, deadly eyes leaped high from the pack, fangs closing on the sleeve of his gun hand. He almost lost the .22, but then he kicked the dog with his uninjured leg, heard cloth rip, and his arm was free. He fired a shot into the snapping pack and instantly they split apart, leaping to both sides and scurrying away. "Keep moving!" he shouted to Wes. "Don't let them stop you!"

There was a brown blur in the corner of Wes's eye. A slat-ribbed mongrel was tracking him, looking for an opening. He shot at it and heard it yip. The dogs began coming down from the rocks, circling the two men. Silvera saw a huge, bluish-gray dog that could have been a Siberian husky or some kind of wolf. It wore a nail-studded collar, and when its eyes caught the priest's, they burned with demonic hunger. The wolf-dog was stalking him, letting the smaller dogs rush in first and waiting to see what would happen. When a couple of them came at Silvera's left and he whirled to meet them, the wolf-dog leaped from the right, soundlessly, its jaws opening wide to crush the human's gun arm.

Silvera saw the gray streak and pulled his arm back, but the massive dog hit him so hard he was thrown to the ground on his side, the breath whistling painfully from between his teeth. The dog straddled him, fangs going up under the mask to rip his throat. He could feel the hot wetness of its muzzle and saw the glittering eyes pressed right up to his own with triumphant defiance.

In the next instant the dog's face caved in, teeth and bone disintegrating; blood splattered across Silvera's mask and goggles. He heard Wes's second shot, the .45's barrel less than three feet away, and then there wasn't much left of the wolf-dog's head but ooze and broken bone. Silvera pushed the heavy corpse aside and staggered to his feet, wiping the blood off his goggles so he could see the next attackers. The shapes darted and danced around them, but they wouldn't come in close. Silvera thought the wolf-dog might've been the pack's leader, and now they seemed disorganized and much less confident. The circle of snapping animals slowly widened, and then they were swallowed up by the storm. Wes and Silvera could hear the animals howling up in the rocks, like subjects mourning their dead king. "They may be back!" Silvera said. "We've got to hurrry!" He only had two bullets left and, as they walked, Silvera took the .45 and slapped in a new clip, then handed it back to Wes.

The road began to level off. They sensed the castle before they saw it, a huge turreted thing of dark stone just beyond the storm's whirling curtain. The wind was terrible, ripping past Wes and Silvera with a vengeance, almost casting them off the cliff's edge and down into a series of rocky ravines below. They moved carefully, making sure one step was firm before they tried the next. Mountains of sand grew and fell all around them, hissing and sliding and then finally falling off the cliff, leaving diaphanous trails across the muddy sky. At first Silvera thought he was looking at an extension of the mountain, a jumble of stones that loomed up in fearsome peaks, but as he moved closer, he saw the high wall, and the chinks between the gray blocks like rough scales on the hide of a leviathan. He saw towers, parapets, sloping roofs whitened with sand, saw teeth of glass glittering in high window frames, dunce-cap spires spiking the sky. The castle looked like a grinning stone skull capped with Satanic horns. The place was huge, as dark and forbidding as a nightmare. Silvera stopped in his tracks, overwhelmed. *Go on,* he told himself. *This has to be faced. It has to be done.*

As they neared the wall, the wind stopped, blocked off by the mass of stone. Mounds of sand had heaped up against the enormous wooden gate and covered the driveway as well to a depth of perhaps six inches. Wes and Silvera looked up, dwarfed by the structure; the parapets and towers seemed to be leaning slightly, the windows set at odd angles and none of them quite the same size. Some of the stones protruded and some of them were recessed, cracked, and crumbling.

"What are we going to do?" Wes asked. "How do we get over that wall?"

Silvera moved along the driveway toward the gate, stopped, and looked up at the tangle of barbed wire six feet above. "I think I can climb over that if you'll help me," he said.

Wes paused, looking at the balconies and windows for a sign of activity; the place looked dead, deceptively so. *Maybe they're still sleeping!* he thought. *If we hurry, we can get in, find Solange, and get out before they're up!* He watched Silvera walk to the gate. In the distance he could hear a chorus of howls, as if the dogs were gathering for another attack. Silvera looked over his shoulder into the darkness, the flesh at the back of his neck crawling.

And with his next step he heard the quiet *click!* of a

disengaging spring. He realized what it was a split-second before the trap's gleaming, serrated jaws burst up from the sand around his left foot and snapped shut on his ankle. There was no pain at first, just the brittle sound of cracking bone, and he then knew what he should've guessed before he started along the driveway. The sand had been spread thickly and deliberately here to hide the iron traps that lay in wait for intruders. Now the pain hit, a white-hot wave that made him cry out in the mask. He was staggering backward, but slowly—so slowly—like in a nightmare where all motion seems crazy and useless. He tried to brace his fall with a hand and saw with horror another trap's jaws snapping shut, missing his wrist by several inches. He hit the ground on his side; a third trap cracked together just beside his face. Then it seemed he could see the castle from the corner of his eye, and he was watching the towers tumble toward him. The towers fell, smothering him in agonizing darkness.

FOURTEEN

Prince Vulkan's eyes opened. At once he was fully alert, like any wild animal eager to hunt. Tonight, he'd decided, he would go down into Los Angeles and join his troops rather than wait for food to be brought up to the castle. He would hunt with his soldiers and race with the wind, seeking out the scent of warm blood, the noises of humans whimpering in their attics and basements. He was chilled with the need for food, though the cold wasn't yet painful.

Uneasiness ached within him, a strange kind of confusion and uncertainty that he hadn't known in a very long time. In his dreams he'd stood at the center of a huge stadium, even larger than the Coliseum in Rome, with high banks of bright lights shining down. He was on a platform, the green field marked off in columns on each side, and the waves of frantic adulation had swept down, crashing on him, hot and sweet, from the thousands who filled the stadium around him. They were all calling him *Master*, and when they started leaping onto the field and running toward him to kiss his hands, his lieutenants and their

attack dogs had formed a ring around him for protection.
It was at that moment that he knew the city had fallen.
Los Angeles was theirs, the first conquest of the invincible
vampiric army. The first of many.

The shouting swelled. His name cracked through the
sky like thunder, rolling ominously in all directions. His
hour was at hand; next would be the fall of San Francisco
and San Diego, securing a hold on the West. Then the
army would begin crawling eastward, advance parties
moving into the major cities, one wing swinging north
into Canada and one south into Mexico. It was the beginning of a new age, and he would be its rising star.

But amid the joyful celebration, he felt a gnarled hand
fall upon his shoulder, and he turned to face the Headmaster.

But a different Headmaster. Its eyes had dimmed
somewhat, the black lips were tightly drawn. "Beware,
Conrad," the Headmaster had said. "Be careful, and
guard yourself."

"My hour has come!" Vulkan said. "Beware of what?
Listen to them scream my name! *My* name!"

"You stand in a dream," the Headmaster whispered,
the hand gripping the prince's shoulder. "You lie at sleep,
and these things have not yet come to pass . . ."

"They *will!* I know they will! Listen to them shouting!"

"I hear the wind." The Headmaster blinked, and when
its eyes opened again, Vulkan sensed a weariness about
his old teacher, a . . . weakness. "My opponent moves
His pieces, Conrad. We've not yet won the game."

"Game?" Vulkan asked. The shouting died to a whisper
and was swept away. Now he stood alone in the center of
the stadium with the Headmaster, and the glaring lights
were beginning to hurt his eyes. "What pieces do you
mean?"

"They're strong, Conrad, don't you understand that?
They refuse to accept defeat! They refuse to be broken!
You've barely scratched the surface of humanity in this
city, and you think the whole world is already yours! It
is *not!*" The Headmaster's voice came out as a growl,
rumbling down the length of the field. "They're escaping
by the thousands, Conrad . . ."

"NO! The storm won't let them!"

The Headmaster's eyes flared. "There are limits to all

things, Conrad, even to the powers *I* possess. And the power you have as well. But it is endurance that will win the game. And if nothing else they know how to endure."

"I've crushed them!" Vulkan shouted. "The city is mine!"

The Headmaster shook its dark head and stared at him sadly. "You've learned all the lessons but one, and that is the most important. Never consider your position safe. *Never!* You may destroy a knight or a bishop, and be struck down by a pawn."

"Nothing can touch me!" Vulkan cried out defiantly. "I'm not . . . *weak!*"

"There are four who would destroy you," the Headmaster said. "They approach even now, as you lie dreaming of glory. Four pieces—one is a knight, another is a bishop, a third is a rook, and the fourth is a pawn. Without fully realizing it they have come together in a deadly combination, Conrad. I've done all I can to stop them, but they *endure.* And they advance. We can still destroy them. We can still win the game, but you must know them and beware . . ."

"We?" Vulkan shook free of the Headmaster's grip. *"We?* Didn't you hear them shouting? Whose name did they call? Mine! Prince Conrad Vulkan, King of the Vampires! They call me *Master.* They recognize me as the highest power!"

"I have given you and your kind life. I have taught you the secrets of power, the sorcery of Aba-aner, Nectanebus, and Solomon. I have taught you what it means to be a king. But you're not invincible, Conrad . . ."

Vulkan stared at him for a long time, then said coldly, "Who would dare to test me?"

"Four humans," the Headmaster replied.

"Four humans!" Vulkan said disdainfully, and when he grinned he showed his fangs. "Don't you understand the size of my army now? Before the sun rises again, they'll number twice a million! And tomorrow night . . ." He lifted a hand and curled it into a fist, his eyes wild and bright green. And then his grin suddenly contorted with the realization. "You're . . . afraid, aren't you? You're scared! Of what? Those *four?* Why don't you find them? Why don't you tear them to pieces for me?"

"Because," the Headmaster said softly, "our enemy is

using them, working through them just as we work through all the others. I can't . . . touch them . . ."

"You're afraid!" the prince shouted. "Well, I'm not! I've learned all the lessons now, my troops call out for me, and we still advance! Nothing can stop us now. Are you afraid because . . ." He stopped, thinking the unutterable, but now he knew the truth, and the words burst from his throat. "That's it, isn't it? You're afraid of *me*. You don't want me to get too strong, do you? You're afraid of what I've learned!"

The Headmaster watched him silently. Its eyes began to burn like pools of slag flowing out of a volcanic furnace.

"I'm going to live forever," Vulkan said, "and I'll always be young, always! So you've seen what I can do, and you've come to make me doubt myself, haven't you? You've come to make me afraid of four humans, just like you are!"

"Forever is too long," the Headmaster said, "and never long enough. I came to warn you, Conrad. I've done all I can for you, the rest will have to be . . ."

"I don't need you anymore!" the prince said. "School's out!"

The Headmaster seemed to tremble with rage. Its body began to gather into a hulking mass, like a thick blight of shadow. It neared Vulkan, covering him over with the force of a freezing wind. "Fool," it whispered. "Little boy. Little fool . . ."

"I'm not a little boy, I'm not, I'm not, I'm NOT!" Vulkan shouted, but when he tried to step away from the Headmaster, he felt locked into its shadow.

"Did you think you were my only pupil, Conrad? You're not. I have other ones with the potential to be even stronger than you. It's not your strength I fear, Conrad, but your weakness. I see this city falling before your kind, but not by their power. You've done what we wanted to do; now time has come to retreat . . ."

"Retreat?" Vulkan repeated incredulously. "No! This is *my* city now, my Babylon! I won't run from four humans . . ."

"Taking ground is one thing," the Headmaster said, "keeping it is another. Take your lieutenants and as many others as you can, and leave this place right now. Cross the mountains to the west. Start again. I can help you just as I did before . . ."

"WHY?" Vulkan shouted. "WHY ARE YOU AFRAID?"

"Because of what our enemy will use against us. This city . . ."

Vulkan clapped his hands to his ears. "GET OUT!" he shouted. "You won't make me afraid! You won't make me lose! Nothing can hurt me!"

The Headmaster stared at him for a long moment, and when it spoke again, there was an edge of sadness and anger in its rasping voice. "I treated you as a . . . a special son, Conrad. My hope for a new beginning." The thick shadow hovered, dark folds enclosing the prince. "So you would deny me, wouldn't you? After all these hundreds of years, you would deny me in a moment?" The eyes began to burn with savage ferocity.

"I have taught you well, perhaps too well, but now I see what was beyond my power to give you. I could never make you grow up. You will be seventeen years old forever, filled with the childish needs and fantasies of youth. You haven't taken a kindgom, Conrad, I've given it to you. So be it. What is forever to you is to me . . . an episode. Now you have your kingdom. Protect it as you will. But you're correct in one thing, my pupil. School *is* out."

The shadow began to turn like a whirlwind, while above it the two blazing yellow lamps of its eyes continued to burn into Vulkan's skull. Vulkan shuddered, the cold rippling through his veins. The shadow twisted itself into a frenzy, then began to roll up upon itself like a black scroll of ancient parchment; in another moment it had begun to fade. The merciless eyes were the last to disappear, darkening like unplugged lamps. When the Headmaster was gone, the stadium around Prince Vulkan swirled away, shimmering like a mirage, the bright banks of lights going out one by one.

And then Prince Vulkan's eyes opened in darkness.

He lay still for a few moments, wondering about the implications of his dream. He felt uneasy, chilled, unprotected. They were old feelings, and they stirred up memories of his human existence like dark debris from the bottom of a pond. Four humans? Coming to challenge the king of the vampires? It was absurd.

After a while he raised his arms, threw the coffin lid back, and stepped out of his bed of warm, protective dirt. He stood in the first-level basement, a large network of corridors and rooms that had been filled with old, broken furniture, cardboard boxes, crates, and stacks of ancient newspapers and magazines bound together with rotting twine. In one of those boxes Prince Vulkan had found yellowing glossies and old placards advertising the films of Orlon Kronsteen. There had been a picture of the man in vampire makeup, hovering over a young blond girl who slept unaware. It had greatly amused Prince Vulkan to see the Hollywood impression of his kind. The face in that photograph looked stupid and lethargic, not nearly hungry enough. Once while walking the streets of Chicago's Southside near Cornell Square after nightfall, Prince Vulkan had stopped with Falco—dear, departed. traitorous Falco—before a blinking marquee that said DAMEN SOUTH THEATER and beneath that, DOUBLE CHILLS! CURSE OF THE VA PIRE—Chr stopher Lee & COU TESS DRAC LA—Ingrid Pitt. Of course, he'd had to see them, two old vampire movies scratched to shreds, really quite humorous. He'd seen silent movies before in London, but now not only did they talk, but they were in color too! Some of the people in the sparse theater audience laughed at the vampires on the screen. Prince Vulkan, acting more out of impulse than hunger, had moved across the balcony and sat behind a man who was snoring with his mouth wide open. Vulkan could peer through the balding skull at the inner workings of the brain and see that man's entire life—wife named Cecilia, two children named Mike and Lisa, images of a small apartment with a Swiss-style cuckoo clock on the wall, piles of papers and bills on a desk beneath a small, yellow-shaded lamp, buddies crowded around in a dark tavern with swords crossed above the bar, a glass of beer on a napkin that said McDougall's. That man wanted very much to be young again, carefree, hot-rodding along a street called Brezina in a red car with a foxtail on the antenna. In less than twelve minutes, from the bite to the ingestion of the blood, Prince Vulkan had altered that man's destiny. And now that man, Corcoran by name, was one of the several hundred vampires in Chicago who awaited the Master's triumphant return.

It was time to call the dogs in for the night. Prince

Vulkan concentrated on finding the largest of them, the gray-blue wolf that had taken control of the pack. His eyes rolled back in his head as he searched, but he couldn't find the dog. Like a wisp of cold wind or an errant shadow, he went beyond his body, casting his mental eye like a fiery globe out into the storm. He couldn't *feel* that dog anymore; the link between them had been inexplicably severed. Now he could feel some of them out there, but it was a confusion of pain and dumb rage. He searched among them, touching their minds. They were out of control and afraid. Vulkan picked up mental impressions of thunder and lightning, dreaded fire, a pain that crushed and scorched. Quickly he allowed himself to come back. His eyes rolled back in their sockets, their pupils narrowed into tight slits. Something had happened to the pack's leader. The dog must be dead. But what—and who—had killed it?

He hurried along the corridor, past the rooms where Kobra and his other lieutenants would just be drifting up out of sleep. He climbed a long, curving, stone stairway that led to a three-inch-thick oak door and, beyond that, to the castle's main floor. He unbolted the door and stepped out into a wide central corridor that ran the width of the castle. Beside the door, at the foot of another curving, stone stairway, stood Kobra's motorcycle, most of the black paint now scoured away by the force of the storm.

"Roach!" Vulkan shouted, his voice roaring through the castle's hallways, alcoves, and chambers. "ROACH!"

He hurried upstairs, shoes clattering on the rough stones. The second-floor corridors whispered with turbulent winds that had found their way in through chinks and cracks. There were many windowless rooms here that also held coffins, and already many of the vampires were drifting from chamber to chamber like specters. They moved quickly out of his path as he approached. One of them, a beautiful blond woman wearing a blood-splattered black dress, fell to her knees and tried to kiss his hand, but he hissed at her and wrenched away. His mind was on more urgent matters.

"Roach!" he screamed again, and in another moment he saw a bright spot of light ahead of him, getting nearer. Roach had a flashlight in his hand. "I called for you!" Vulkan said, his eyes blazing. "Where were you?"

"I heard, Master, but I was . . . starting the fire in the council chamber. It's ready for you, Master . . ."

Vulkan looked beyond the man's eyes; it was simple because Roach's mentality was so childlike, so pliable. He saw what Roach had seen just a moment earlier: That corkscrew of sand in the golden urn, twisting around and around with its hypnotic rhythm. Roach had prepared the fire and the maps, but he'd been entranced by the urn. He was oblivious to anything else, like a child with a strange toy. He got out of Roach's mind quickly because it teemed with dark shapes and shadows, the memory of hands around the throat of a woman whose facial features kept shifting, a body rolling down a dimly lit staircase and coming to rest at the bottom like a broken-necked doll, swarms of rats and roaches kicking in their death agonies. "Something's happened to the dogs!" Vulkan said, then recalled the Headmaster's voice: *"There are four who would come to destroy you."* "Someone may have gotten past them!"

Roach looked startled. "Who? Someone . . . past the dogs . . . ?"

"Come with me." He moved past Roach along the corridor to yet another narrow stairway that curved up to a double-bolted oak door. He unlocked and opened it, stepping out on a wide balcony that stood perhaps fifty feet above the ground. He strode across to the stone parapet and looked out into the night; he heard quite clearly the distant, confused howling of the pack. Yes. He was certain now. His first line of defense had been broken. But what of the second? He leaned over and looked down.

At first he saw nothing out of the ordinary; the main gate was still closed, the courtyard fortified. But then he caught a glimpse of movement just on the other side of the gate, and he saw two men—two *humans* wearing some kind of masks and breathing apparatus—down where the iron traps had been laid. One of them was injured—he could see the trap clamped around the figure's left ankle—and the other one was trying to pull him away from the gate toward the line of dead trees a few yards away, where darkness and the terrain might give them concealment.

Vulkan grinned. When he'd realized that his initial defense had been broken, that someone had actually man-

aged to come both through the storm and past the dogs
to reach him, he'd been filled with uneasy concern and a
sort of dreadful wonder. *"Four are coming,"* the Headmaster had said. *"They endure."* But the Headmaster
had been wrong. There were only two, both of them already weak. One lay prone, and the other looked as if he
might fall at any moment. There were only two, and
they had come up this mountain to their deaths. The
Headmaster had been wrong.

"Wrong!" the prince shouted. "Beware of what? Of
you?" He began to laugh, his mouth opening and the
long fangs sliding out of their sockets in his jaws. The
laughter—a cold, harsh chuckling—went on for another
moment, then stopped abruptly. Vulkan's eyes narrowed.
He watched the man struggling with his wounded—or
dead—companion. "Go down and find Kobra," he said
to Roach. "You and he bring those two—what's left of
them—to the council chamber. And understand—I don't
want them touched. Not yet."

Roach nodded eagerly and scurried across the balcony
through the door.

Prince Vulkan leaned over the parapet, watching the
two men with great interest. How did these two manage
to find him? he wondered. What had brought them up
the mountain? Did other humans know where he was
hidden? If so, his refuge was not quite as safe as he had
thought. The Headmaster's warning echoed in his head,
but he brushed it aside. Some sport was what he needed
to take his mind off the Headmaster. Yes! Sport! Fun
and games, like the rapier contests, the bear versus boar
fights, the battles between dogs and rats that his father
the Hawk had enjoyed so. If these two humans could
endure the journey up the mountain in this storm, if indeed they were so good at enduring hardships, then
surely they could endure a little more for the pleasure of
the vampire king and his court. *Surely.*

FIFTEEN

Ratty probed ahead with the lantern. Its weakening yellow glow stiched patches of shadow together like a golden needle through dense cloth. The tunnel still climbed, as it had for the last two miles, its floor slick with seepage.

Palatazin's legs and back were weary, and several times he'd had to lean against a wall to rest, so their progress had been drastically slowed. Droplets of sweat gleamed on his face, and now he was fighting claustrophobia and the continual feeling that something was stalking them from behind, perhaps allowing them to continue as a cat might allow a mouse to exhaust itself in a futile effort. He could feel something *cold* back there, and several times—when he sensed the chill closing in at the back of his neck—he'd taken a box of matches and a spray can from the pack, lit it, and turned to protect the rear. He'd never seen them back there, but he could hear scuttlings and angered hisses just beyond the light. The flame was keeping them away. For now.

They'd passed beneath more manhole covers, and Palatazin had climbed up to look out, to see if he recognized anything from his earlier drive to Kronsteen's castle. Sand and wind slapped his face, but the storm didn't seem quite as fierce up here as it had below. Visibility was a little better, and he could make out the dark shapes of white stucco and redwood-frame houses perched on the hillside. They kept climbing. Palatazin was fearful of missing the turnoff altogether. Perhaps they'd already missed it. He couldn't be certain.

His spine started crawling again. He was aware of the noises behind him; he lit a match. In its reddish flare, he could see several pairs of dead, bullet-hole eyes perhaps ten feet away. The vampires—there were at least three—scattered into the darkness, anticipating the lick of flame from the spray-can torch. He took the spray can out of the pack, popped its cap off, and pressed the button down, spraying it toward the match. The flame erupted in a dart of red and blue. The vampires hastily retreated into the

461

shadows, and Palatazin could hear their angered hissing and curses.

They continued climbing, Palatazin guarding the rear. When the flame began to sputter, he could see the vampires creeping toward them, faces vulpine and hideous, just beyond the limit of the fire. There were three, two young men and a girl, anger exploding in their eyes with swirls of silver and red.

"Put it down, old man," one of them whispered. Palatazin heard the voice quite clearly, echoing through his head, but it didn't seem as if the boy had moved his lips.

"Go on," the female vampire whispered, a cold grin across her face. "Put down the fire like a nice boy ..."

"NO!" Palatazin shouted. His vision seemed to be fogging over, the darkness creeping up on all sides to consume him.

"They're in your mind!" Tommy said sharply. "Don't listen to them!"

"Please," the female said and licked her lips with a black tongue. "Pretty please." One of the others feinted for Palatazin's arm, and Palatazin almost released the button. The can was getting hot in his hand, and he knew the propellant would only last a minute or so longer.

Suddenly Ratty stopped. "Hey? You hear that?" he demanded, his voice cracking with tension.

Palatazin tried to listen over the voices whispering in his head. The three vampires were getting bolder now, darting in toward the flame, and trying to knock it from his hand. "I hear it!" Tommy answered. "Dogs howling up there!" Palatazin tried to concentrate over the tauntings of the vampires, and immediately he could hear it too—a ghostly chorus of wails floating somewhere above them.

"We've got to find a way up!" he shouted, and then he heard the female whisper, "No you don't. You want to put that down and stay with us, don't you?" The flame sputtered once, twice. Now the tunnel seemed filled with the reek of burning aerosol and oily smoke. One of the other vampires lunged for Palatazin, but he thrust the weakening flame in an arc across the boy's face; the thing screamed shrilly and staggered back.

Ratty found a ladder and pulled himself up. When he pushed the cover aside, the merest hint of muddy brown light filtered down into the tunnel, but it seemed enough to keep the vampires away. They stood clustered together hissing like rattlers in the shadows, and Palatazin heard a silvery, sweet voice in his mind say, "We need you here with us. Please stay . . . please stay . . ."

And for an instant he wanted to.

"We've got to go up here!" he shouted as the wind churned around him and off down the tunnel with a faint whistling. The flame went out. Behind him, Tommy was just on his way up the ladder to Ratty waiting at the top. The vampires stood beyond the limits of the light, but when Palatazin started up the ladder, one of them darted in and grabbed his ankle, trying to pull him back down. He kicked free and saw a pair of hideous fangs exposed in the thing's mouth as it tried to bite his ankle, then it screamed from exposure to the fractional light and scurried away. As Palatazin reached the top and squeezed through, he heard a distant, weakening whisper, "Don't go . . . don't go . . . don't . . ."

The storm thrashed around him, and now he heard the howling somewhere off to his left, terrible and shrill. The three of them moved forward, the wind about to throw them off balance from all directions. In another moment Palatazin saw a couple of houses that he thought he recognized, though he couldn't be sure. Then out of the gloom rose the familiar dead trees and the narrow road snaking up Outpost Drive.

"We're close enough!" he shouted to Ratty, shielding his face with his arm. "The castle's at the top of this road!"

"I'm scared shitless of the bloodsuckers, man," Ratty shouted back, "but I'm sure as hell not going back into that tunnel! You dig?"

Palatazin nodded. "You okay?" he asked Tommy.

"Okay!" the boy answered, keeping his hands cupped in front of his mouth and nose. He staggered, nearly knocked over by the wind's force.

"Then we go up!" Palatazin took the lead, with Ratty bringing up the rear. They linked hands, fighting upward. The wind was fierce, and Tommy fell a couple of times, almost being swept away before either Palatazin or Ratty could help him. They passed a low-slung vehicle that looked like a jeep but a little larger crashed against a tree on the left-hand side of the road. A little further ahead they came to the partly obscured carcasses of several

dogs. There was howling all around them now, and Palatazin could feel eyes watching them from the overhang
of rocks above the road. When he peered up through
slitted eyes, he could just barely make out the shapes of
dogs crouched there, crying into the storm. Several times
a dog would leap out of the darkness to snap at their heels,
then it would vanish just as quickly. One of them, a
collie, bounded up behind Ratty and yanked at his leg,
throwing him to the ground, then leaped away.

Palatazin knew they'd be within sight of the castle in a
few minutes. He was certain some of the vampires—if
not all—were already awake. Soon the castle would be
crawling with them, as would the city below. The
backpack full of stakes weighed heavily on him, and ants
of fear scurried in his stomach. He hoped he could catch
some of the vampires still in their caskets, particularly
the king, although logically he might be among the first
to awaken. Theirs was still the element of surprise,
though, and that was vitally important. This was what
the army would call a suicide mission, Palatazin told
himself. Getting there is not the difficult part of it; coming back safely is. But he'd known that all along and
accepted it just as he was certain his father had accepted
the fact before him. It was the boy he was sorry for.

When the castle loomed up before them, Palatazin
stopped in his tracks and whispered, "My God, help us!"
He looked from towers to parapets to battlements, and he
could see the tangled barbed-wire at the top of the protective walls. "How do we get inside *that?*" Panic boiled in
his stomach. Had they come all this way to be stopped at
the castle's walls of this monument to an eccentric
horror film star? *No!* Palatazin told himself. *We can't go
back now!* They neared it, the force of wind and sand
abating somewhat. Palatazin looked to the huge front
gate and could see a few iron-jawed traps clamped together on the sand-heaped drive. Another driveway split
off from the main one and circled around the right side
of the castle.

Suddenly Tommy jerked his arm. He looked over his
shoulder and saw Ratty running for the safety of the
line of dead, shriveled trees several yards away. Tommy
pulled at him and motioned upward, his face a pale,
fearful mask. Palatazin turned and looked up. A man
stood on a high balcony, staring off into the night; his

face was turned toward L.A., which the vampire army was now devastating. Palatazin ran for the trees and crouched down between Tommy and Ratty. The man on the parapet swept his gaze across the horizon, then seemed to stare right at their hiding place. It was hard to tell because of the distance, but Palatazin thought that it might be Walter Benefield up there. The man looked away and lifted his hand to his mouth once, then again. The howling faded and stopped. Then the man disappeared, and Palatazin grasped a breath.

"Almost cooked our asses," Ratty said, his voice shaking. "Truth in a teacup!"

In another few minutes a couple of dogs came running past their hiding-place, following the cobblestoned drive around the other side of the castle. They were followed by others, some of them snarling and fighting. The pack seemed scattered and confused, but within it Palatazin saw several dogs who looked as large as panthers. A couple of the mammoth ones stopped and turned toward the trees, showing their teeth in low, menacing growls, but then they ran on, vanishing around the curve of the rough-stoned wall. Ratty cringed, but Palatazin thought the dogs had ceased to care about them. He thought they were hurrying to be fed. And that meant there was another way through that wall to the castle. A service entrance, perhaps? He tried to remember back to his brief association with the Kronsteen murder case. He recalled reading Lieutenant Summerford's outline on how the killers had gotten in. There was something about a service entrance, yes. A service entrance, a gate, and . . . a wine cellar.

"Let's find out where those dogs are going," Palatazin said to Tommy when most of them had passed. When Ratty scowled, Palatazin said, "You can stay here if you like."

"Yeah, man. I can dig that. Old Ratty'll just burrow himself in right here and lay low like he did in Nam." He started scooping out great handfuls of dirt and sand at the trunk of a gnarled tree. When Palatazin and Tommy left the tree-line, Ratty looked up. "Git some!" he said and returned to his work.

They hurried up the drive, moving close along to the massive wall. Palatazin heard the dogs up ahead, a melee of whining and barking. Then there was another noise—

machinery, clattering gears and chains. The barking
started to die down. Tommy ran on ahead and saw the
dogs scurrying in where the driveway turned under a stone
arch and into the castle's rear courtyard. The gate, an
iron-barred, medieval contraption that was opened and
lowered by a chain and pulley, had been hoisted open just
enough for the dogs to get through.

"Hurry, you bastards!" he heard a man shout. "Come
on! Inside!"

Tommy squeezed himself against the wall, his heart
pounding. When the dogs were all inside, the chain clicked
through gears, and the iron gate was slowly lowered to the
ground. Tommy waited another moment before sliding
over to the gate. He peered in; there were a few U-Haul
vans parked in the courtyard along with a bright yellow
John Deere bulldozer and a black Lincoln Continental.
The castle rose up as abruptly as a black-walled mesa.
At its base Tommy saw that the man—short and squat
with cropped dark hair—had thrown back a thick-looking
wooden door recessed into the stone; the dogs were
scrambling over each other in their haste to get through.
A couple of them snarled and snapped at the man, who
lifted a wicked-looking wooden staff and whacked it into
their midst. "Get down there!" he shouted. "Bastards!"
When the dogs were gone, he stepped down into the opening and the door closed behind him.

"Benefield," Palatazin whispered, peering over Tommy's
head. "My God!" He stepped forward and curled his
hands around the bars, trying to shake the gate; it wouldn't
budge. "This is where the killers got inside years ago," he
murmured. "But how?" He seemed to recall something
in Summerford's report about Kronsteen's murderers being small men, possibly teen-agers thin enough to . . . He
bent down, scooping away double handfuls of sand from
the bottom of the gate. His heart leapt. This was where
the killers had dug eleven years ago; the earth had
never been replaced. There was room for someone very
thin to crawl under. He looked at Tommy, and the boy
understood.

Even Tommy, minus his jacket, sucking in his dia-
phragm, had trouble. He crawled and contorted his
small body, and once he thought he was stuck, but then
at last he was under and standing on the other side. He
stepped over to the chain that hung down from a couple

of iron pulleys along the wall and pulled. His shoulder muscles cracked, and the gate only rose a couple of feet before he had to let it down again. The next time he tried harder, and he discovered that the chain was just like a big venetian blind cord; by pulling it at an angle he could lock the chain in the lower pulley and hold the gate steady. He got the gate up four feet and could lift it no further. Palatazin slipped under, and together they hurried past the bulldozer and U-Haul trucks to the door Benefield had entered.

It was latched from the inside, but three hard blows from Palatazin's hammer was enough to break the lock. He shoved the door open. They faced a long flight of stone stairs that disappeared into inky depths. They started down, feeling their way along cold, wet stone walls veined with cracks. Rats squealed from their holes and skittered underfoot. Palatazin could hear the barking of the dogs very far below them. Other corridors branched off from the stairway, some of them sealed off by iron bars like the gate Tommy had crawled under. Palatazin was afraid there might be traps in those corridors—more iron-jawed leg-breakers, guns rigged up to doorknobs, a scattering of poison-soaked nails, a central stone that might pivot and shatter their ankles—so he thought it best to follow the path the dogs had taken. "Do you have any idea where this goes?" he whispered to Tommy.

"I think the wine cellar in the lower basement. Orlon Kronsteen had about a million bottles down there."

"The vampires won't sleep on the level where the dogs are kept," Palatazin said. "They might wake up with an arm or a leg chewed off. What's on the upper basement?"

"Just big rooms."

"That's probably where some of the caskets are." The noise of the dogs was much louder now. "I expect we won't catch many of them sleeping, though."

They heard the muffled sound of blows. "Get back!" Benefield shouted. "I'll knock your ribs in!" A dog growled fiercely; there was another blow and a yelp.

The stairs ended at a closed door. Beyond it, Palatazin knew, lay the wine cellar and the dogs, Benefield and his wooden staff. He didn't think Benefield had become a vampire yet, not if the king was using him as a human servant. But did Benefield have a gun or knife as well as that staff? Palatazin pushed against the door; it creaked open a few inches. He saw a series of large rooms that seemed full of empty-shelved wine racks. A flashlight was set on one of the shelves, its beam playing over a frenzy of snarling, leaping dogs. Then Benefield stepped into view, cracking his staff on the floor to keep the dogs back while he tossed bits of raw meat at them from a leather pouch he had slung under his shoulder. A German shepherd rushed in, trying to steal a piece of bloody meat out of his hand before he threw it. Benefield shouted "GET BACK!" and cracked the animal across the head with his weapon. It yelped and staggered, and others scrambled over its body. "I'd fix you if I had the dust!" Benefield said quietly and chuckled. In the dim light his eyes were black holes in a pale skull. "Oh, yeah, if I had the dust, I'd spray it in your faces and fix you all real good. Get back, there! Here, you shit!" He was standing with his back to the door, about fifteen feet away.

Palatazin steeled himself and came through the door into the chamber, raising the hammer.

A gray mongrel whose muzzle was already bloody snapped its eyes toward the intruder and bared its teeth, emitting a series of ear-cracking barks. Benefield started to turn his head and Palatazin saw he wasn't going to reach the man in time. He leaped, and Benefield's eyes widened with recognition. The staff came whirling out of the darkness toward Palatazin's face, but he got his left arm in the way and took the blow just below the wrist. Then he crashed headlong into Benefield, and they staggered through the baying, hungry dogs to the floor. They rolled, Palatazin trying to strike at the other man's temple with the hammer, but Benefield clamped one viselike hand around his right wrist and started squeezing. Benefield had lost his staff; his free hand snaked up and found Palatazin's throat.

The dogs snarled around them, leaping in and grabbing at cuffs and sleeves, snapping at faces. Several of them starting fighting among themselves over the scraps of meat; one grabbed the leather pouch, trying to rip it from Benefield's shoulder. Palatazin struck the man's face with a fist that was rapidly going numb; blood began streaming from Benefield's nose, but he grinned and kept squeezing. A dog lunged for Palatazin's sleeve. Another bit Benefield's ear and tore a hunk of it away, but the man was beyond pain now, beyond everything but the lust to kill. He rolled over on top of Palatazin, got a knee on his hammer-hand, and started squeezing his throat with both hands. Palatazin fought for air; his temples were pounding, he could feel teeth gnawing at his left ankle, while another dog's fetid breath blew in his face. The animals swirled around the two combatants in a frenzy, leaping and howling with bloodlust.

Tommy picked up the staff, jumping away from another dog that snarled and rushed at him. He thrust the staff at it, catching the animal in the throat and driving it back. A hole opened around him as the animals avoided the familiar weapon. Tommy took aim and swung into the back of Benefield's head. The man grunted but didn't loosen his hold. "LET HIM GO!" Tommy shouted, and struck again. The staff broke off in the middle, leaving Tommy with a jagged, three-foot shard of wood.

Benefield pitched to the side. His head hit the floor with a soft *thunk,* and Palatazin worked the frozen fingers out of their grooves in his throat. He stood up, backing away from the dogs that leaped and snarled on all sides. They didn't care about him anymore; now they went after Benefield's leather pouch with fierce passion, straddling the body and fighting each other off. One of them ripped the pouch off and ran with it, the others right on its heels, some of them stopping to gobble up chunks that had scattered on the floor. They vanished into the far recesses of the chamber among the hundreds of high wine racks. Palatazin looked down at Benefield for a moment, then rolled him over, and felt for a heartbeat.

"Is he dead?" Tommy asked him, breathing hard. "Did I . . . kill him?"

Palatazin stood up and took the flashlight off the shelf. "No," he said hoarsely. His knees were shaking, and when he wiped the sweat from the side of his face, he saw that it was streaked with red. He straightened the pack across his shoulder, his fingers clenching and unclenching the hammer's handle. If he didn't kill Benefield, the man would warn the vampires. It was as simple, and terrible, as that. He knelt down beside the man, studying his toadish face, and raised the hammer to smash his forehead. At its zenith his hand stopped and hung there; his strength was gathered but not his stomach. It was one thing to kill a vampire, or to kill a human who was trying to kill you;

it was quite something else to kill a helpless man in cold blood. *Captain Palatazin,* he thought, *ex-Captain that is, do you want the boy to see you do this?* He looked at Tommy and saw his glazed, sickened eyes. *A vampire, yes. A man, no.* Palatazin stood up. He had no way of knowing when Benefield would come around, or if he ever would. "And I wanted you to stay home, didn't I?" Palatazin asked the boy, trying to smile. He failed miserably. "Where do we go from here?"

"There'll be . . ." Tommy looked away from Benefield with an effort. "There'll be another stairway here somewhere, leading to the upper basement. I don't really know where it is, but . . ."

"We'll find it. Let's get out of here before those dogs come back. I don't think they feed them very well around here." Gripping the hammer in one hand and the flashlight in the other, Palatazin plowed into the darkness with Tommy right at his side.

SIXTEEN

"Clever toys," Prince Vulkan said, picking up one of the air tanks from the pile of equipment that lay at the center of the council-chamber table. He studied the nozzle for a moment with deep concentration, then turned its release lever and listened to the quiet hissing for a few seconds. He smiled and closed it off, setting the bottle down carefully beside the golden bowl. He picked up a mask, looked at it, and then dropped it back down. "Clever," he said. "Aren't these humans clever, Kobra?"

Kobra grinned. He was standing near the fireplace where Father Silvera and Wes crouched on the floor. In his hand was his prized Mauser pistol, though it was hardly necessary. The priest's face was a study in pain, covered with bright beads of sweat that slowly dripped down onto his shirt. The trap was still clamped around his cracked left ankle, the iron teeth grating on bone. He lay on his side, his leg all but useless, and every few seconds he shivered with agony. But he didn't make a sound. Beside him Wes sat on the floor, the fire crackling behind him. Outside, when Roach and Kobra had unbolted the front gate and stepped out, Kobra following as Roach probed at the ground with his staff for the traps he'd laid out during the day, Wes had instantly recognized the albino. When Roach ripped Wes's oxygen mask off, Kobra had whipped that pistol from the inside of his black jacket with lightning speed.

"I've seen that sonofabitch before! Where do I know you from, fucker?" The albino's eyes narrowed. "Oh, yeah. Last night? Little party out in East L.A.? That's a fine black piece you had there, man. I fang-fucked her alllll night long . . ."

Wes had leaped to his feet, rage flaming in his eyes, but Roach had prodded him back with the staff. Kobra had laughed out loud, showing his fangs. "Man, you're crazy. You know that? Uh-uh now, no quick moves. The Master says I can't have you . . . yet, but I sure could blow away your kneecap real fast!" Kobra had stepped forward across several sprung traps lying in the sand, abruptly stopping a few feet from Wes. He hissed and thrust a black-gloved hand before his face. "He's got something on him that burns me, Roach! Find it and get rid of it! Hurry!"

Roach had smiled and dug the staff into Wes's stomach, dangerously close to his broken ribs. "You want to take your clothes off, don't you?"

Wes had known it was no use. He started to reach into his inside jacket pocket for the *resguardo,* hoping to at least fling it in the vampire's face, but Kobra said sharply, "Stop him!" At once Roach was on him, tearing his coat off him and throwing it out for the wind to catch; it sailed up and up, then disappeared over the cliff's edge. "Yeah," Kobra had said quietly. "It's gone now. Take his gun."

The .45 was pulled from Wes's waistband. Now all hope, even the hope of suicide, was gone.

Kobra had torn Silvera's mask off and knelt down to stare at the man's face, tracing the angle of his jaw with the Mauser's barrel. Silvera moaned, coming around from the shock. Wes had hoped he was dead, for the priest's own sake. Silvera's gun was also taken away. Kobra found the blade—whistled at it as he snapped it open—and then dug the bottle of holy water from a pocket. "What's this shit?" he asked Wes. But Wes refused to answer, and Kobra stared at the liquid for a few seconds, slowly drawing his lips back into a snarl.

"Don't like it," he'd whispered. "Shit! Burning my hands! Don't like it! DON'T LIKE IT!" He'd screamed suddenly, whether in rage or pain Wes couldn't tell, and flung the bottle far out into the night. Wes had thought he'd heard shattering glass, but he wasn't sure. At once Kobra had been grinning into Wes's face, the Mauser right at his throat. Those two hot, horrible eyes bored into Wes's skull. "Thought you'd trick me, didn't you? Thought I'd take that shit, whatever it was, right on up to the Master, didn't you? Huh? Your kind can't hurt us, man. We hurt *you!*" When Wes didn't speak, Kobra stepped back, blinking and uncertain; he'd stared at the gloved hand that had touched the bottle of holy water, and Wes could tell that even through the glove and the glass, the water must've scorched his flesh.

"Carry him!" Roach motioned with the staff toward Father Silvera. "Move!"

And so they'd gone through the gate into the castle's courtyard. Wes, supporting the priest so he wouldn't step on that injured leg, had winced when he'd heard Roach draw the bolt shut again. The castle stood high over them, a Bald Mountain in which horrors danced and partied. They climbed another wide stairway to the massive front door, surrounded by grinning stone faces and bracketed by two hideous gargoyles in Thinker poses atop stone obelisks. Kobra pushed the door open and shoved the two men inside. The door was closed, and two bolts clanked into place.

As they walked along a wide, cold corridor, Wes was aware of figures moving around them, shapes scurrying across their path, glittering eyes staring hungrily from arched doorways, hideous pallid faces hanging like death masks in the darkness, whispers and chuckling and an occasional knife-blade pierce of freezing laughter. Figures shambled out and plucked at their clothes; there were many young girls—black, white, and Chicano—who had the sad and ravenous eyes of street prostitutes but whose need now, Wes knew, was of a more terrible kind.

Kobra herded them up a long, twisting stairway. On an upper corridor something leaped for Wes out of the darkness. A cold hand gripped his shoulder, fingers digging into the flesh, but immediately Kobra barked, "The Master wants them!" and the thing scurried back to whatever hole it had crawled from. Another figure—a very beautiful, blond woman in a black dress—stepped from a doorway and took Wes's hand. She smiled at him seductively and nipped at his knuckles with her fangs, then slipped away and was gone.

"Here," Roach had said.

They had waited almost an hour, guarded by Kobra and Roach, before the door opened again. When the black-garbed figure stepped into the orange glow of the firelight—Halloween colors around a face as sharply cut as an alabaster sculpture but strangely, in its own way, angelic—Wes had known that this was the thing they'd come to find. The Dark Angel. The Master. But . . . a boy, hardly older than an adolescent. The vampire's eyes sparkled like emerald chips, his mouth twisted to one side in a mocking sort of smile. Beside him, Wes had heard Silvera catch his breath with a shudder. The vampire stared at them for a moment in silence, then his gaze had shifted toward Roach. "Go to the balcony and call the dogs in. Feed them and lock them away for the night."

Roach had taken a metallic, high-pitched, dog whistle from a back pocket and left the room. Wes had noticed how Roach had stepped back, his shoulders slumping in deference, when the boy vampire had come in. Even Kobra had made a slight bowing motion with his shoulders. *Royalty*, Wes had thought. *We're in the presence of vampiric royalty. And power.*

Now Prince Vulkan picked up the .45 from the table examined it, and set it back down. "What my father would've given for weapons like that," he said quietly. "Ah! That's the thunder and lightning the dogs feared, isn't it? A theoretical question for you—if Alexander the Great had possessed such thunder, how long would it have been before the world fell at his feet? But then again, he made his own thunder, didn't he? The thunder of an unstoppable army."

The vampire sat in a chair, crossing his legs under him as any boy might do. "When Alexander's enemies heard that sound, they knew all was lost. Oh, they fought, of course they did. But they fought like trapped dogs, without plan or purpose. They ran to the four winds, but they couldn't get away." He smiled, his eyes glittering.

"The world is about to hear Prince Vulkan's thunder. It's going to roll eastward across this land, and then . . .

they'll run, but they can't get away. This city is my Babylon. The noise of its falling will cause the world to tremble. And then they'll know the king of the vampires is on the march with an army no power on this planet can stop." He sat back, looking from Wes to Silvera, and stared at the priest's grimy white collar. "You!" he said sharply. "What's your name?"

Silvera didn't answer. Kobra stepped forward and thrust down with his boot on the trap's edge. The priest screamed in agony, the beads of sweat growing larger and streaming down his face. "That's enough," Vulkan said, and instantly Kobra stepped back.

"He was carrying something, Master," Kobra said. "A bottle of water that . . . burned my fingers when I held it."

"And where is this bottle now?"

"I threw it away, over the cliff."

Vulkan nodded. "Good. So we have a *lelkesz* among us. A priest. You won't be the first to join our ranks, I promise you. Nor the last." He giggled suddenly with high, childish glee and clapped his hands together. "They're falling, left and right, up and down! Thousands and thousands of your kind down there right at this moment! All the humans are dying, and all the *vampir* are being born!" His gaze darkened like an approaching storm cloud, and Wes realized with a sudden start that he could see the shadow of the chair cast by the firelight on the opposite wall, but the boy vampire himself did not throw one. "How did you find me?" Vulkan asked him. "How many others know where I am?"

"I don't know," Wes said. "I came here to find someone else."

"You came to kill *me!*" Vulkan said. "Why else was the *lelkesz* carrying his holy water?"

"I'm looking for the woman he took from me," Wes said and motioned with a tilt of his head toward Kobra.

"Woman? What woman?"

"The black bitch," Kobra explained.

"I see." Vulkan regarded Wes for a moment and grinned. "Human loyalty, is it? The dumb concern of one lower species for another?" He concentrated on Wes, his eyes flaming, and Wes felt as if two drills were spinning at his forehead, slowly cutting through his skull and probing deep into the brain. A chill rippled through him; he felt filthy and violated, utterly helpless. He could not force himself to look away from Prince Vulkan until the vampire nodded and released him. "Love?" the vampire said. "Yes. Love." He savored that word on the tips of his forked tongue. "Your conception of that is very different from mine. Is she here, Kobra?"

"Downstairs, still sleeping."

"Bring her here. And find Roach as well. He's taken much too long."

Kobra nodded, put the Mauser into his jacket, and left the room.

"I like courage," Vulkan said to Wes. "You'll be fine hunters, both of you." He stared at Father Silvera for a moment and then glanced toward the iron trap. "The Bite of Life heals all wounds and sicknesses," he said softly. "It stops all time forever. You'll see."

Silvera raised his head and spat.

The vampire threw back his chin and laughed, and Wes could see the gleaming fangs in his sickle-mouth. When Vulkan looked at them again, his cat eyes glowed with an unholy spark. "What else could I expect of a *lelkesz!* I've always found them quite unreasonable and stupid." His eyes narrowed now, and Wes could hardly stand to look at them. *"You,"* he said to Silvera. "You came to kill me, didn't you? What were you going to do, splash me with that *aqua pura?* Drive a crucifix through my heart? It's been tried before, by better men than you. And where are they now? *They're part of my army.* Or they're dead. No man—no *one*—can kill the king of the vampires!"

Silvera crossed himself, his head pounded. He felt dangerously close to passing out. "My God," he whispered. "My God, help us . . ."

"NO!" Vulkan shouted, rattling the rafters high above. In a leap too fast for Wes to follow, the vampire was there, bent over the priest, one clawlike hand gripped around the man's face. The fingers dug deeply into the flesh. Vulkan's eyes were blazing.

"Priest!" he hissed. "Fool! With one hand I could peel your face away like the skin from a grape! I could squeeze your skull until your brains ooze out! And you dare to use that name in my presence? You're close to death now, priest. Be very careful, very careful indeed! If you use that name again, I'll twist the head from your body, and I'll do it very slowly, do you understand?"

Wes could see the fingers tighten, and Silvera's eyes began to bulge. He moaned once, very softly. When his eyes had closed, the vampire loosened his grip and stepped back, his gaze moving toward Wes. Vulkan blinked and rubbed his temple. It seemed to Wes that he'd been hurt in some way, but he wasn't sure how. Wes crawled over to Silvera. The priest was still alive, but his nose was bleeding from the pressure of Vulkan's grip.

Prince Vulkan sat cross-legged on the table near the golden urn with its spinning column of sand. The firelight flickered across him, transforming him into an unholy orange-fleshed icon with green-jeweled eyes. "The Headmaster was wrong," he said to Wes in a steel-and-velvet voice. "I'm stronger than he is now. I've learned all the lessons, and there's nothing else to learn. He was wrong. Nothing can hurt me. I'll be young forever and ever and ever . . ." He clasped his hands together and began to laugh. The sound of that chilling, childlike laughter pushed Wes further toward the dark edge of madness.

SEVENTEEN

Palatazin and Tommy moved through shadowy catacombs, following the flashlight's beam. They'd climbed another series of stone stairs, leaving the barking of the dogs far below them, and now found themselves in a maze of large, high-ceilinged rooms. Some of them were empty, but some held assorted debris- -boxes, piles of newspapers where rats nested, old discarded furniture, scattered pictures and posters from Kronsteen's glory days. In one of the rooms the flashlight picked out large wooden crates, all of them empty and stenciled LAX . . . FRAGILE . . . THIS SIDE UP.

Then they began to find the caskets.

Some of them were already open, the bed of dirt holding the impression of the body that had been lying there. When they found the first closed casket, Palatazin stiffened with disgust; his stomach gave a quick lurch, and he knew he'd have to hurry before either his nerve gave out or Benefield started screaming from below. He handed Tommy the light, laid the pack on the floor, and took out a stake. When he spoke in a whisper, he could see the white curls of his breath in the cold room.

"Some are still sleeping. That one may awaken as soon as I open 'he casket lid, so I'll have to strike quickly. I don't know what'll happen after that. Just hold the light steady, all right?"

Tommy nodded. His eyes were as shiny as new quarters, and he was trying hard to keep his hand from shaking. *They're brave in the movies,* he told himself as Palatazin, gripping the hammer and stake, stepped forward. His heart was racing. There were no klieg lights up in the rafters, no dry-ice smog floating at their feet, no Peter Cushing looking wise and courageous, just Palatazin, his face filthy and sweaty, one hand trembling now as he reached out to open the coffin lid.

A very handsome young man lay inside, arms folded protectively across his chest. The light brown eyes, veined with red, stared balefully through the milky lids at Palatazin. He was bare-chested, a gold ankh on a chain around his neck, and wore tight brown corduroys: Tommy recognized him almost at once as the star of a CBS-TV movie on drag racers called *Thunder City*. At any other time, Tommy realized, he might be ask'ng for this man's autograph. Except he wasn't a man anymore, he was one of *them*.

Palatazin pushed the lid all the way back. When the flashlight beam touched his face, the vampire, just between sleep and waking, shifted away from it, his mouth coming open in a silent snarl. Palatazin saw with a start of dread that the vampire's hands were locked firmly on his biceps, the arms drawn up so that getting to the heart was impossible. Something moved behind those transparent lids—a flicker of awareness, as quick and cold as mercury. The vampire was about to awaken.

Palatazin saw his striking point. He placed the stake's sharp tip at the hollow of the young man's throat. Then he braced his legs and swung the hammer with all his strength. Instantly a freezing hand came up and grabbed Palatazin's left wrist, crushing it, but too late. The hammer struck with a terrible wet sound, and the stake ripped through vampiric flesh, pinning the head down. The eyes came open, blazing with a hatred that might have gnawed the marrow out of Palatazin's bones. A black, forked tongue snaked out of the mouth with a hideous rasping noise. The body thrashed, both hands gripping the stake and now . . . starting to pull it out of the bloodless wound.

Quickly Palatazin took another stake from the pack, aimed its point over the thing's heart and drove it deep with one strike of the hammer, like sinking a blade through rotten cheese. A foul, graveyard odor bubbled up; the entire chest seemed to cave inward, and for an instant Palatazin thought he could see through the satiny flesh a black, malignant lump pierced by the stake. The body thrashed wildly, mouth opening wide and snapping shut with a noise like a gunshot. A reddish-black ooze that smelled of crypts and evil and all the things that lurked in shadows or cut the throats of children or raped babies began to rise out of the wound, and Palatazin stepped back as the black tendrils of liquid streamed down the heaving chest and stomach. He didn't want any of that stuff to get on him, afraid that if it did, he would be forever cursed. It was the vampire's hideous ichor, Lucifer's wine flowing from a cracked cask. The body suddenly stiffened, both hands straining to reach Palatazin. The staring, vengeful eyes caught fire, blue flames eating deep into the skull. Tommy made a low, gasping sound of sickness and turned away, but Palatazin felt compelled to watch. The blackening face collapsed as if it were a waxen Halloween mask; fire glowed through the empty eyesockets for a few seconds more, then abruptly burned itself out. Something dark and dreadful passed through Palatazin—a dank breath of cold wind that carried in its wake a whispered scream, then whirled itself away. The vampire's dead body had already started to shrivel like a November leaf.

"*My God,*" Palatazin whispered hoarsely. His right arm, the arm that had struck the killing blow, seemed to be full of power, tingling with it. His hand wanted to strike again. He picked up the pack, then turned toward Tommy. The boy's face was as gray as a ninety-year-old man's. "Are you ready to go on?" he asked the boy.

"Yeah," Tommy said. He was weaving slightly and dared not look at the thing in the coffin, but he handed Palatazin the flashlight and followed, holding up the broken staff like a spear.

They found two more sleeping vampires and killed them the same way. The first was a young black man, the second a dark-haired little girl who must have been about the same age as Tommy. The child was awakening when Palatazin opened the coffin, stretching like a cat, but she was still dazed from sleep and too slow to stop the descending hammer. When it was over, Palatazin's stomach heaved, and he stood retching in a corner for a moment, trying to get something up. But they had to go on. The supply of stakes was dwindling fast.

The next closed coffin they found was in a room that contained two others, but both of those were open. Tommy put the staff aside and held the light. Palatazin readied his implements, leaned down, and flung the lid open. Inside lay a very beautiful black woman, her arms at her sides. She wore a white silk blouse, black pants, and a belt with a half-moon of diamonds on the buckle. Palatazin looked into those stunning, terrible eyes and shuddered; he could feel his resolve quickly seeping away. He bent to strike.

But before he could lift his arm to its zenith, the beautiful vampire came up out of her coffin, her eyes burning him to the bone. He heard the word "NO!" shouted in his brain and allowed it to stun him, allowed his will to be sapped. She gripped his other wrist and grinned, starting to rise toward him, that beautiful unholy face split by the seeking fangs.

"STRIKE HER!" Tommy screamed.

Palatazin heard himself cry out as he tried to pull free of her. He swung the hammer toward her head, but she reached out and caught his hand.

As her grip tightened around his wrist, she could feel the tides of blood flowing within him, and she was ravaged by total, hungry need. She could see everything so clearly now—*this* was life, not that other, former existence. It was all so simple this way—nothing mattered but the blood and warming the urgent freeze that gnawed at her. Solange drew him closer, and when the smell of his fear washed over her, she heard her own small, frantic voice calling from the flipside of her soul—*don't let them have you, don't, don't, don't . . .*

But oh, the need . . . oh, the sweet, freezing need was so strong . . .

"You don't want to destroy me," she whispered. You want me to . . . kiss you. Like this . . ."

"NOOOO!" Tommy backpedaled, turned, and picked

up the split staff he'd laid on the floor so he could grip
the flashlight with both hands.

The vampire drew Palatazin's head down. His eyes
swam with helpless tears and stupid rage. She pressed her
frigid lips to his throat, opened her mouth wide, and
plunged the fangs deeply. Palatazin felt an instant of
searing, white-hot pain, followed by a dull thundering in
his head that he knew must be the sound of blood being
sucked from his veins.

Tommy stepped forward, his eyes wild, and started to
strike with the staff.

Suddenly a hand closed around the back of his neck and
flung him like a rag against the far wall. He fell, all the
breath squeezed out of his lungs, and tried to crawl for
the staff. A booted foot came down on his arm. He
looked up into the scorching red eyes of the albino vampire who grinned down at him. Tommy could hear the
female vampire's hideous sucking, her grunts of pleasure,
and Palatazin's soft whimpering.

The albino picked up the staff and started breaking
it into small, useless pieces. "Where's Roach, you little
shit?" he said quietly, his voice brimming with menace.
"This was his! Did you and the man kill him?"

When Tommy didn't answer, the albino gripped his
hair and wrenched him to his feet. He withdrew a pistol
from his jacket and jammed the barrel into Tommy's
mouth. "I'll ask one more time, then your brains go on
the wall . . ."

Palatazin, his veins filling with arctic cold as his blood
emptied into Solange's body, was falling into a dark crevasse that had suddenly split the earth at his feet. He
could hear high, freezing winds, silvery laughter, moans,
and guttural screams. His soul was dying, falling from
light into darkness, from life to the terrible kingdom of
the Undead. He could feel his own hand at his throat,
ineffectually trying to push her head away. The fangs
were fastened tight. His fingers moved slowly . . . so
slowly . . .

Until they closed on the chain of the $19.99, jewelry-
store crucifix that dangled down in his shirt.

He tore it off his neck. His arm fell, weighed down by
the thing. Then he lifted it again, thunder hammering between his temples, and pressed it against the vampire's
cheek.

Instantly there was a hiss of blue flame, and the black flesh blistered. She shrieked and pulled away from him, dragging four furrows across his throat. He fell on his side, curling up like a fetus for warmth against the frost that had filled a quarter of his body. He put the crucifix to his lips and fought the shivers that raged through him like cold, conflicting currents.

Solange was still shrieking, holding her injured cheek and cowering in a corner.

Kobra's eyes widened slightly, then he began to grin again. "I'll blow this little shit's head off, old man!"

Palatazin writhed on the floor, pressing the crucifix against the ragged, bloody bites on his throat. Blue flames hissed, searing the wounds closed. Pain shook him, twisting him inside out. He hung on to consciousness by a thread and saw Solange throwing up his blood into a steaming puddle. Then he lifted his head and saw the albino holding the gun's barrel between Tommy's teeth.

"Eat it," Kobra snarled. "Right now! Want to see his brains?"

"Oh, God," Palatazin breathed, fighting dark waves that crashed within him. "Oh, my God in Heaven . . ."

"Eat it!" Kobra shrieked.

Palatazin looked into Tommy's eyes and saw the boy shake his head *no*. Very slowly, with numbed hands, he worked the tiny crucifix off its chain and put it in his mouth. Tears streamed down his cheeks.

"Put it down, fucker! Lemme see that throat work!"

Palatazin tried to swallow, but the crucifix, as small as it was, caught in his throat and choked him. He coughed it up. Kobra's eyes were blazing. Tommy staggered, about to fall, but the albino wrenched him upright again. "Either *that* goes down," Kobra whispered, "or the boy gets blown away. Your choice. Make it FAST!"

Palatazin looked into Tommy's glazing eyes for a few seconds, took a deep breath, and swallowed. The crucifix scraped the back of his throat going down, hung in his esophagus. He swallowed again, harder, and felt it sink to his stomach like a infant must feel a penny or a metal button going down, cold and coppery. He felt shamed, blighted . . . but at least Tommy was still alive.

"Reallll good!" Kobra crowed and flung the boy aside. Tommy slithered to the floor and lay still. Kobra looked at Solange and shouted, "Stop whining! Your pretty

face'll heal soon enough! Stupid bitch, you should've
seen that chain around his neck!" She slid down into the
corner, clasping her arms around herself and rocking,
her eyes wide with terror. Then Kobra stared at Palatazin and stepped forward. "How do you like the pain,
fucker? Get up!"

"Can't . . ." Palatazin said, shaking his head. "No."

"She just bit you enough to give you a good buzz. Now
get on your feet!"

Palatazin staggered up, then fell back to his knees.
He was terribly weak and only wanted to find a warm
place to sleep.

"How'd you and the kid get in here? You kill Roach?
I hope you did. I didn't like him anyway." His gaze fell
upon the backpack and the fallen hammer. "Brought the
heavy artillery, didn't you?" He grinned widely, the fangs
giving his lean face the look of walking death. "Yeah.
Sure did. The Master's going to want to find out more
about you two. And now that Roach's dead, Kobra don't
have a fuckin' thing to worrry about. You!" He glared at
the whimpering female vampire. "You're going before
the Master, too! Get yourself up!"

Kobra nudged Palatazin in the ribs with his boot and
motioned with the gun. "Man, you must *crave* pain,"
he said softly. "You're going to get it soon as the Master
finds out what you've done. I wouldn't want to be in
your shoes, no way!" He reached down, grasped Palatazin's shoulder, and hauled him to his feet. Palatazin
staggered, so dizzy from loss of blood he was about to
pass out. Bright motes of dust seemed to be floating before his face, exploding like multicolored novas. He still
felt slimed by the vampire's kiss, but the wounds on his
throat had been cauterized. They were achingly raw, and
he could smell the faint charred odor of his own burnt
flesh.

"Get the kid," Kobra said.

Palatazin walked over shakily to where Tommy had
curled himself up into a ball on the floor. Tommy's teeth
were chattering; his eyes were dull and glassy. Palatazin
figured he might have gone into shock. But then Tommy
recognized him and allowed himself to be helped up.

Kobra felt an icy spear of hunger pierce him. He could
smell Palatazin's spilled blood; the delicious odor made
him shiver. Double needs twisted through him. He'd

always been a death junkie when he was human, and now he needed human blood to stop the mounting pain. But he also knew that the Master would want to see these two humans, would want to find out how they'd gotten into the castle and where they'd come from. He hoped that the Master would reward him for his self-control with these two when the interrogation was done. "Upstairs," Kobra said. "The Master's waiting."

EIGHTEEN

Palatazin was shoved into the council room first. He stopped, frozen with dread and wonder, when he saw the king vampire—a young boy with green cat eyes—sitting atop the table. Prince Vulkan stared at him, betraying neither concern nor surprise. Palatazin heard Tommy's stunned gasp, and then Kobra shoved Palatazin forward, brought Solange in, and closed the chamber door. "Found these two in the basement," Kobra said. "They got past Roach, must've killed him because the kid had the stick he used to work the dogs with. The man was carrying a packful of stakes, a hammer, the whole fuckin' number . . ."

Vulkan's eyes began to scorch Palatazin's skull with their intensity, but he didn't move.

Wes, his heart pounding, slowly rose from the floor. "Solange?" he whispered.

She looked at him through frightened, feral eyes and took a step backward. Kobra's hand snaked out and clamped around her waist. She tried to cringe away, to turn her head away from Wes, but Kobra laughed and grabbed the back of her neck, forcing her to look at him.

"There's your lover, baby. Like what you see? Can you see the veins running through his body, the sweet, hot blood flowing like a hundred fountains? That's *life*, baby. Your life from now on."

"Leave her alone!" Wes shrieked. He started to move forward, but Prince Vulkan stopped him with a single glance. He heard the command in his head like a shout about to split his brain: "SIT DOWN." He had no choice

but to obey and, when he had, he began to shake uncontrollably, the tears burning his eyes. He couldn't bear
to look at her again because there was nothing left of
Solange anymore.

Palatazin had seen Father Silvera lying on his side
near the hearth. He didn't know how the priest had gotten
up here, or why he'd decided to come, but the man
looked weak and haggard and . . . yes, very near death.
As they all were. Silvera lifted his head and looked
at him, but no recognition flickered in his dazed eyes. His
head sank back down, and he lay still like a wounded dog.
Palatazin saw the trap clamped around the man's leg.

Now Prince Vulkan, the king of the vampires that
Palatazin had dreaded all his life, uncoiled himself from
his sitting position and came across the room, his face
caught between black shadow and flickering orange light.
Vulkan examined the seared wounds on Palatazin's throat
with an almost clinical interest. Then he lifted his gaze
and said, "You know our kind, don't you? Yes. You do. I
see it in your eyes. You know . . . *me*. How is that?"

"I know of you," Palatazin replied, trying hard to keep
his voice steady. He was caught between the burning eyes
of Kobra and Vulkan, his head filled with fiery torment.

"How?"

"I was . . . a boy in Krajeck . . ."

The king vampire's face was expressionless, a carved
thing of flawless white stone. Palatazin could imagine
the ancient, dark secrets that lay behind his eyes; they
were hideous things, secrets from Satan's black magic
box. "Krajeck," the vampire said and nodded. "Yes. I
remember Krajeck. And you were one of those who
escaped."

"My father didn't," Palatazin said softly.

"Your father? His name?"

"Emil Palatazin."

"So. You came to destroy me because I gave your father the gift of eternal life? I don't think he'd like that,
do you?"

"Where . . . where is he?"

Prince Vulkan smiled and touched the wounds on Palatazin's throat. Palatazin jerked his head back. "Don't you
know you're in the presence of?" Vulkan whispered,
his voice like a cold night breeze through silk curtains.
"I'm a king. The greatest king this world has ever known

or ever will know. I can stop time. I can . . . do magic. I can end all Death. Your father is one of my servants now, in the monastery atop Mount Jaeger. Oh, he's in good hands. They all are. The Countess sees to that. But time is so cruel to the human kind, so terribly cruel. Here stands a son who is older than the father, who fears Death as an enemy while his father has learned to use it as a friend. And now the son has come to put an end to me." He grinned and grasped Palatazin's collar, pulling his face forward. "It's not to be!" he hissed. "Your kind is slow and stupid and weak! The *vampir* will win!"

Vulkan suddenly blinked, released Palatazin, and stepped back. There were four now, he realized, just as the Headmaster had warned. An ancient emotion that might have been fear began to crawl within him. *No! The Headmaster was wrong! These four couldn't hurt him!*

"Why here?" Palatazin asked him. "Why this city?"

"Why?" Vulkan hissed. He wanted to grab this human and shake him until his neck snapped, but now he feared stepping too near. The Headmaster's warning was echoing within him; he was confused and couldn't think. "Because this is the city of youth!" he said. "They worship youth here, in their clothes and cars and dreams! Their youth gives my army eternal strength. I don't want the old, I don't want the infirm. Only the ones who can be of use to me! And what better place to conquer than this . . . young, shining citadel? We'll live forever, don't you see that? Never age, never, never, never!"

"Shit," Wes muttered. "Peter Pan."

"What?" Vulkan said, staring at him.

"A fucking black-as-sin Peter Pan," Wes said. "You're going to fly everybody away to some vampire Never-Never Land. Step right up, sell your souls, and come on in. That's not the way the world works. That's not the way it should be."

"That's the way it shall be," Prince Vulkan said softly, stepping menacingly toward Wes.

"Death isn't an enemy," Wes said. "It makes things new again, and anything that doesn't die just . . . rots and mummifies. Or becomes like *you* are."

"Like you will be," the vampire whispered. "If I choose to let you."

Wes stood up. He looked across the room at Solange for a few seconds, then back at Prince Vulkan. "Nope,"

he said quietly, "I don't think so." And then he threw
himself at that table, reaching for the '45. A voice
cracked through his head like a whip—"NO, YOU WILL
NOT," and he was flung aside by some intangible, terrible force as his hand closed on the gun. He was thrown
to the floor as Prince Vulkan swept forward like a black
wind, all claws and teeth, in a whirl of rage.

Wes wheeled around, aimed upward, and fired.

The bullet passed through Prince Vulkan's chest and
struck stone on the opposite wall, spraying sparks past
Solange's head. Wes fired again; there was a metallic
crack! and then he felt Prince Vulkan lifting him up by
the throat with both hands. The vampire shook him violently. Wes dropped the gun, his eyes bulging from their
sockets. Bone cracked. Tommy clutched Palatazin's arms,
trying to hide his eyes from the sight of Wes's face. Palatazin held him tightly.

Prince Vulkan shrieked and threw Wes to the floor.
Wes was trembling like a shattered marionette, his head
twisted at a hideous angle. Vulkan began to kick him,
each kick breaking another bone. Kobra came forward,
his eyes bright with the prospect of death. He whined,
"Let me kill him, Master. Let me, let me, please . . ."

Vulkan kicked Wes again and stepped back. Kobra
grinned widely and shot Wes twice in the head from
less than three feet away.

Across the room Solange screamed and sank to her
knees, burying her face in her hands.

"Now you're three!" Vulkan said, grinning at Palatazin.
"You can't hurt me! The Headmaster was . . ." He
stopped suddenly, his head cocking to one side. His eyes
widened.

Palatazin's heart thumped. In the distance he could
hear the great whine of the storm, slowly—very slowly—
winding down like the dying of a huge, infernal engine.

"NO!" Prince Vulkan shouted. He looked at the table
and saw the shattered gold urn. Wes's second bullet had
hit it as it passed through the vampire's stomach.

The funnel of sand had stopped, and where the sand
hissed out onto the table it burned with a faint blue flame.
Prince Vulkan picked up the urn, his face contorted with
rage, and flung it against a wall. It hit a gilt-edged painting before clanging to the floor.

"No!" the vampire shrieked, shaking the rafters with

his fury. He overturned the table in a frenzy; the maps fluttered down like dead leaves in a hurricane, and the table shattered, splitting into pieces like a gleaming black mirror. The vampire turned his burning gaze upon Palatazin and Tommy.

"The *vampir* shall win!" he shouted at them in a voice that cracked from a man's to a boy's. "I don't need the Headmaster anymore! I don't need his protection, I don't!" He scooped up maps and flung them at Palatazin. "I'll have it all, every bit of it!" He looked at Kobra. "Won't I? SAY IT!"

"Yeah," Kobra nodded, but now his voice was uncertain. "You will."

Vulkan swept over to Father Silvera and roughly pulled him to his feet. Silvera bit his lip to hold back a scream. He could feel the cold radiating out of the vampire. "*You!* Death is so close for you . . . so *close!* I can feel it in you now, chewing through your body! I can stop it! I can make you whole if you will serve me!"

Someone knocked at the door. Vulkan called, "Enter!" and two vampires—one a young boy with long blond hair and the other a husky man with curly gray hair—stepped into the room. They glanced around at the wreckage, and Vulkan snapped, "What is it?"

"The trucks, Master," the boy said. "They're ready to go down."

"All right! Go ahead!"

The boy hesitated, glancing at Wes's corpse and then back to the vampire king.

"Well? What else?"

"Some of the others . . . are afraid, Master," the boy said. "They want to know why the . . . storm's dying down."

"Tell them not to fear," the vampire king said quietly, green embers glowing in his gaze. "Tell them Prince Vulkan is in control. And one other thing—bring back enough to feed everyone in the castle tonight. I want a celebration!" Vulkan released Father Silvera and stepped back from the blazing hearth. "I want a report from the factory as soon as possible. Send a courier. And you, Asher!" The husky vampire looked up fearfully, the golden chains around his neck catching red light. "Those holes are to be filled tonight, do you understand that? I want none of them escaping! Either cut them off or . . ."

He let the alternative hang in the air like a sword suspended by a hair. "Can West supp'y Central with another thousand?" he asked the younger vampire.

"My sergeants are already moving the Western Division into Marina Del Rey, Master. When we secure that area, Central can have the extra troops."

"Good. Now go, both of you. And good hunting." When they'd left the room, Prince Vulkan stared at Palatazin and Tommy for a few seconds, then back at Silvera. "You see?" he said softly. "It's happening. Street by street, house by house . . ."

"You'll be stopped . . ." Silvera began weakly, trying to keep his weight off his cracked ankle, but then the vampire king's face pressed toward his, his lip curling with disgust. "By *whom?*" Vulkan sneered. "By you? By them? By that dead man there on the floor? I think . . . not. Oh, priest, I can feel the blood roaring through your veins. I can *see* it! I'm going to have it inside me, warming me like a sweet flame. And tomorrow night you will have forgotten everything and everyone but me."

Vulkan glanced quickly at Kobra. "The priest is mine. You and the female can have those two." He motioned toward Palatazin and Tommy. "When you're finished, take that dead filth and feed him to the dogs. Now, priest, you come with me." He clamped a hand around Silvera's arm and pushed him across the room to the door. Silvera, grinding his teeth with the pain, had no choice but to follow. As he passed Palatazin, he recognized the man but only hazily, and as he started to speak, Vulkan opened the chamber door and shoved Silvera through into the corridor. The door closed with a solid, terrible finality.

Instantly Kobra moved in front of it and slid a bolt across to lock it. Palatazin began to back away from him, trying to shield Tommy. From the far corner Solange's eyes seemed to shine, faintly and malevolently. Kobra grinned and slid his Mauser back into his jacket. He would be happy to take his time now. "Nowhere to go," he taunted. "Nowhere to run. Ain't that a shame? You're gonna live forever, old man. And if you're realllll good, tomorrow night I might even let you lick my boots clean. How about that?" He started to move forward, his black-gloved hands twisted into claws.

Palatazin and Tommy kept backing away, stepping

through a puddle of blood that had seeped from what was left of Wes Richer's head. "You! Solange!" Kobra said. "You can have the kid. I'm taking old Palatazin."

Solange rose to her feet. Her gaze was fixed on the corpse, and she walked toward it as if in a dream, one unsteady step after the next.

Palatazin stumbled over the splintered remnants of the council table. One intricately-scrolled black leg stuck up like a bull's horn; it was almost cracked away so when Palatazin wrenched it with his last wave of ebbing strength, it came loose in his grip, a formidable, two-foot club with one splintered end. Still Kobra came, more cautiously now, sidestepping and feinting, low laughter bubbling in his throat. His eyes bored into Palatazin's, and Palatazin could feel his nerve being scorched away. His hands were slippery with sweat on the table leg.

Behind Kobra, Solange bent down over the corpse. The scent of the spilled blood, fiery sweet, was driving her mad. She hadn't drunk enough of Palatazin to warm her, and now she had to drink—she *had* to—and stop the freezing in her veins. She put her head down into the puddle and lapped at it with closed eyes, like a starved animal. She knew the odor of this one. Memories welled up in her head like iridescent bubbles from a black pool of stagnant water. She thought she was about to wake up from a nightmare in a sun-filled room that smelled of flowers, and when she rolled over in bed, she would put her arms around Wes and press very close to his body. She lifted her head, blood dripping from her lips, and realized she couldn't see her reflection in the shimmering puddle. There were memories in the blood, and they made her cold, very cold. She touched his head, the familiar tangle of hair on a dead skull. Currents twisted and raged within her, armies battling over a single foot of earth. She was dead. Dead but not dead, not living. Darkly existing. That one had done this to her, the one who now laughed and moved toward the two humans. That one had taken her from light into dark. That one had killed Wes. Not dead. Not living. Not dead. Not. Not. She put her hands to her head and screamed.

Kobra, startled, looked back at her.

And Palatazin plunged the jagged end of that table leg toward his heart.

The point struck, but, deflected by the Mauser in it

jacket holster, only staggered Kobra. At once Kobra gripped the makeshift stake and wrenched it from Palatazin's grip, flinging it aside. "Not that way, Van Helsing," Kobra sneered. "Can't finish off old Kobra that way!" His hands struck, lightning fast, pushing back Palatazin's chin and exposing the scarred throat. Kobra bore him down to the floor. Tommy grabbed Kobra's hair and tried to gouge out his eyes, but Kobra struck him a backhanded blow across the cheek, as if he were swatting at a fly. Tommy fell, dazed.

Kobra's mouth opened. Palatazin struggled, knowing that now he was only an instant away from joining the ranks of the Undead. Kobra's head lowered, the fangs sliding out and ready.

And suddenly Solange's fingernails were digging into the flesh above his gaunt cheekbones. They sank deep, ripping away hunks of meat that did not bleed. Kobra's face contorted; he shrieked and threw himself backward from Palatazin, trying to crush the female vampire who clung to his back. They rolled on the floor, hissing and shrieking. Palatazin staggered to his feet and saw Solange plunge her fingers into Kobra's eye sockets. The eyeballs burst, leaking great spurts of black fluid. Kobra howled in agony, twisted around, and got his hands on Solange's throat. They rolled through Wes's blood and across the floor, into the maw of the raging fireplace.

NINETEEN

"Look over, priest," Prince Vulkan commanded. He grasped Silvera's collar and thrust him against the balcony's parapet. Silvera could hear the growl of engines in the holes of the storm's fading scream. A yellow bulldozer was pushing mounds of sand to each side as it moved away down the mountain, followed by three orange U-Haul trucks.

"They're taking my lieutenants down to the battle," Vulkan said. "They'll be returning with food—humans to feed the king's court. We'll have a good celebration. Now look out there." He pointed into the far darkness, and Silvera's heavy-lidded gaze followed. "That's where your city lies, from horizon to horizon. Do you see any lights? Any cars? Any blinking neon signs that shout the names of your idols on billboards and marquees? No. My army marches the streets and boulevards, and your kind hides in holes. I've already won. The world has begun to bow to me, starting right here. Did you really think you could destroy the king of the vampires?"

Silvera didn't answer. He was so terribly tired, so beaten. His head pounded, and he had no feeling in his arms or in that injured leg. It was all over now; a better man, a better servant of God, would have to carry on the fight. He looked down and saw his own body in his mind, spinning down after he'd jumped. Because that was the only escape now.

The storm was winding down. The wind had stilled to a soft moan, and the sand had stopped blowing. Prince Vulkan looked uneasily at the sky. He felt alone. The Headmaster's protection was gone, the final gift lying broken on the council chamber's floor. He felt vulnerable now, a soldier without armor. But no! He'd learned all the lessons, he'd sat too long at the Headmaster's knee. It was time to put his mark upon the world, and the Headmaster be damned! "I am Prince Conrad Vulkan, king of the vampires!" he shouted into the darkness, his eyes blazing. The wind whispered around him in an empty reply.

And then the wind died.

Silvera peered out over the city. The storm had stopped. Now from the darkness he seemed to hear the screaming and shrieking of vast multitudes of the Undead down in the city that had once been known as Los Angeles, as they danced and celebrated to the strains of a Luciferian symphony heard only by vampiric ears. The shrieking went on and on, hideous and obscene, echoing through the hills like mad laughter. Silvera put his hands to his ears. "Listen to them sing!" Prince Vulkan shouted. "They sing for me!"

In the distance, over the ocean, lightning streaked through the night.

Silvera grasped the edge of the parapet. He couldn't even feel the cold stone. When the next flash of lightning came, much closer, he could see the streets and buildings of the metropolis below him illuminated for a split second, like rows of stones in a graveyard. There was a faint rumble of thunder from the west. *Now,* he told himself. *Go now!* He tensed to leap.

And suddenly the castle shook beneath his feet.

Thunder rumbled. In its wake there was no sound but the fading echoes of the vampires' shouting. Then total, utter silence. The world stood motionless.

And then again, the rasping of stones rubbing together as the castle trembled. Silvera could feel the vibrations rippling up his uninjured leg, hammering into his body.

Prince Vulkan gripped the edge. *"No!"* he hissed. His eyes were wild, the pupils narrowed into slits.

Silence. Lightning flashing in the distance, its flare illuminating the naked fear etched across the king vampire's face. He was watching the ebony sky, his head cocked to one side as if he had heard a terrifying, long-dreaded voice. Thunder welled, rolling through the hills, and when the castle trembled again, a great black slab of stone broke away from an upper parapet and pitched downward, crashing into the balcony just behind Father Silvera. The balcony shuddered, cracks zigzagging in all directions.

Silvera could see earth and boulders sliding off the edge of the cliff just underneath the castle. Part of the wall sagged and disappeared in a tumble of stones. From somewhere there was a terrible splitting sound, a rending of the earth that seemed to Silvera like the noise of a thick telephone book being torn by muscular hands. He clung to the parapet as the balcony began to heave and buck beneath him. Mounds of earth pitched off the cliff, rolling down in an avalanche toward Hollywood. More of the wall vanished, and now the courtyard itself was beginning to slide away. The castle started leaning toward the precipice, ancient stones groaning in agony.

Earth cracked, opening huge fissures that snaked beneath the castle. In the next bright gleam of lightning, seemingly directly overhead, Silvera saw a stunning and terrible sight. The entire basin of Hollywood and L.A. was pitching, heaving like a Doomsday bellows. He saw buildings sagging, splitting apart, and falling one after the other, at first silently, but then the roar of destruction swept up into the hills like the shouting of an advancing army. A fissure had begun to run the length of Sunset Boulevard, and in the intermittent flashes of lightning Silvera saw its advance, swift and relentless, sucking down entire blocks in its wake. He could hear screaming now, coming from the guts of the castle. When he looked down, he saw several vampires trying to run across the courtyard to the main gate vanish into a fissure than ran along at their feet just before overtaking them.

"NOOOOOOOO!" Prince Vulkan wailed, his voice drowning out the next drum roll of thunder. His fingers dug into the parapet, his eyes glowing with green fire. His mouth worked with silent rage. From above came a loud grinding noise, and when he looked up, he saw a dunce-capped tower fall like a head being lopped off. The stones and slate struck the parapet, knocking great chunks out of it. Father Silvera threw himself back as a stone struck the parapet just in front of him, collapsing it. Prince Vulkan stood in a rain of slate, the pieces striking his back and shoulders. Silvera pressed himself against the wall for safety.

"NO!" Vulkan shouted into the night. "I WON'T . . . I WON'T LET IT HAPPEN . . . !" A chunk of masonry struck him between the shoulder blades, driving him to his knees.

The tremors went on for another moment, then stopped abruptly. The castle seemed to be balanced at an angle, and blocks of stone kept falling from above, crashing down into the courtyard or off the mountain's side. Between the peals of thunder Silvera heard the high shrieking of the vampire hordes down in the city, except now that shrieking was pained and terrified, lost and confused. And then another sound, one that came to him only faintly but with an impact that wrenched at him.

The sound of bells.

Church bells. Ringing in Beverly Hills, in Hollywood, in Los Angeles and East L.A., in Santa Monica and Culver City and Inglewood. Stirred by the tremor, they were singing to Father Silvera, and their song sounded like victory. He knew that Mary's Voice was singing loudest of all, and tears suddenly filled his eyes.

"You've lost!" he shouted to Prince Vulkan. "It's the earthquake! The Big One that's going to sink this city beneath the sea! You've lost it all!"

Vulkan whirled, his face mad with rage. "LIAR!" he shrieked. "Nothing can . . . nothing can stop . . . nothing can . . ."

And the earth reared up, a chain of mountains rising abruptly across lower Hollywood, black peaks pushing up through avenues and boulevards three hundred feet high, then dropping again into gaping holes that sucked the city down like a whirlpools of brick and concrete. Buildings tumbled like huge chessmen across a shattering board. The castle pitched and shivered and started to fall to pieces. Vulkan, his eyes wide circles of terror, screamed in a boy's cracking voice, "Headmaster, help meeeeee! Help meeeeeee . . . !" His cry was lost in the din of thunder and falling stone.

Silvera fell to his knees on the sagging balcony. Between the thunder and the bells, he could hear the voice of God, and he understood the message. Whatever power that had protected these vampires was gone; the pendulum of power had swung back now, and it was time for the evil to die. The city was going to fall, yes, but it would fall by the will of God and for His purposes. Not for the vampires but *upon* them, a vampiric Sodom and Gomorrah.

Vulkan stood at the shattered edge of the balcony, wailing in a language that Silvera couldn't understand. He lifted his hands in supplication and was struck down again by a chunk of stone. The L.A. basin dipped and heaved. Mountains split the earth, rising to tremendous heights—their crumbling sides stubbled with palm trees, broken sections of freeways, houses and buildings— and then sank rapidly down below sea level. Hideous screams, like those of the tormented in Dante's *Inferno*, echoed through the shifting hills, a hundred thousand screams rippling, mingling, intertwining. And above them the great clamor of the thunder and the bells.

The vampire king whirled to face Father Silvera, his face contorted with hatred. "I haven't lost!" he shrieked. "Not yet! I can still win!" The balcony pitched beneath his feet, and he struggled for balance. And suddenly he began to change, his body lengthening and darkening like a shadow. His face became vulpine, the fangs jutting from a mouth that was a blood-red slash in a dark, green-eyed horror. He lifted his arms to the sky, and Father Silvera saw them split the sleeves of his velvet coat. They became black, leathery wings that flailed at the air, reaching for height. The thing hissed at Silvera in triumph, turned, and threw itself from the balcony. Its wings moved powerfully, muscles rippling along the shoulders, and hovered for an instant in mid-air. Then with a last defiant glance backward, Prince Vulkan began to move away from the crumbling castle, the wings beating a hard, steady rhythm.

And Silvera knew what must be done. The only choice, and what God had put him in this position to do.

He leaped across the balcony and threw himself into space, his hands grasping for Prince Vulkan's ankles. Behind him, the balcony gave and dropped away. He got hold of Vulkan's right leg just below the knee, but his hands had no strength, and instantly he started to slip. Vulkan shrieked, more an animal's cry than anything else, and tried to kick the priest loose, but Silvera threw his arms around the ankle and held on with his last reserves of strength. A black-clawed hand raked across his skull once, then again, but now they were falling together in a slow spiral, and Vulkan stopped his attack to concentrate on gaining altitude.

For a moment they swept across the tops of dead pines, then Silvera was aware of cold air on his face, and they were climbing over the shattered city. Streets and buildings were being swallowed by the earth less than a hundred feet below them. Vulkan started to turn north. Silvera gritted his teeth and reached up, grasping the thing's waist. He fought to crawl up over the king vampire's body, straining to reach and pin down those powerful wings. A claw flashed out, taking away most of Silvera's cheek to the bone. He screamed in agony, but now he had both arms around Vulkan's waist, and he was trying to force his numbed hands up onto the shoulders. Vulkan twisted around to fight, almost flinging the priest off, and they plummeted more than forty feet before the wings started beating again.

Silvera was aware of a loud roaring below them now. When he looked to the west, he could see a two-hundred-foot wall of Pacific Ocean, white foam churning atop a gleaming black and green sea that looked as solid as fine Venetian marble, a monstrous tidal wave sweeping across the city, carrying with it yachts, cars, billboards, theater marquees, chunks of boardwalk, roofs, coffins, shattered sections of freeway, airplanes, palm trees, and entire buildings that reared up from the depths like the prows of gigantic, sinking ships. And now Father Silvera remembered what his mentor Father Raphael had told him about the holy water in Puerto Grande, where fresh well water had been as precious as life itself. "Use water from the cradle of life, Ramon. The salt heals and cleanses . . ."

Below him Los Angeles was being flooded. It was a cauldron of holy water blessed by God Himself, and tonight all the evil would be cleansed, every bit of it.

Silvera blinked the blood out of his eyes and hauled himself upward, grasping for the king vampire's wings. He caught and trapped one shoulder, throwing his other arm around Vulcan's neck.

They fell, spiraling in a long arc over West L.A. Prince Vulkan fought wildly, getting one winged arm free and struggling for altitude. Silvera hung onto his neck, wrenching downward to throw Vulkan out of control. But now they were rising again, very rapidly.

And then something huge loomed into their path—a wall of glass and steel that seemed to fill up the horizon. It was an office building, now starting to tremble and pitch forward as the tidal wave swept it from its foundations. Vulkan threw himself to the left, trying to veer over and away. Silvera saw that they were barely going to skim the roof as the building crashed down before them. Clasping his legs around the thing's waist, he let go of Vulkan's neck and grasped for his shoulders, pinning the leathery wings back in an effort that almost ripped his own arms from their sockets. He felt electric with power, filled with renewed strength. They tumbled forward, caught in a whirlwind, and Silvera shouted in Prince Vulkan's batlike ear, "You've lost, you've lost, you've . . . !"

They crashed through a plate-glass window. The building fell upon them like a massive tombstone, shattering as the sea roared up into it and through its hundred cubicles. The pieces were swept under, boiled to the surface, swept under and over again, and finally vanished beneath the littered foam.

TWENTY

The council chamber pitched at an angle, paintings falling from the walls to the floor, stones grinding and loosening, rafters crashing around Palatazin and Tommy. A great jagged crack split the floor and started to widen between them and the bolted door.

From the massive fireplace one of the scorched, burning figures slowly rose from the other and, roaring with hatred and bloodlust, came shambling across the room with its hands outthrust. Tommy could see the black eye-sockets in Kobra's face, the flesh dangling from yellow bone, the lips and cheeks burned away to expose those hideous, snapping fangs. From the smoking rags of his jacket, he wrenched the scorched Mauser and screamed "WHERE ARE YOU!" The barrel swung toward Palatazin; Kobra's finger twitched on the trigger.

And in the next instant the antique weapon, its magazine heated to an explosive level, blew up in Kobra's face, red-hot bullets glowing like tracers. Kobra's headless body was flung backward to the floor where it lay writhing, the stub of a hand still gripping the mangled lump of iron.

Palatazin gripped Tommy's arm and threw him across the widening chasm in the floor. Then he jumped, scrambling for a grip on the other side as the entire room heaved, great chunks of stone cracking loose from the walls and rolling like deadly pinwheels. The door was jammed shut, and Palatazin had to throw his shoulder against it to break it open. The corridor was filled with screams, falling rafters, and dust. Vampires came out of the darkness, bumping into Palatazin and Tommy, then racing away in a panicked frenzy. The corridor bucked, rippling beneath their feet. "This way!" Tommy shouted to him. They ran toward the corridor's far end where a pack of vampires fought to get down the stairway. Behind them the floor split and collapsed, sending a half-dozen of the Undead plunging through. Palatazin almost tripped over the female vampire in black who now crawled on the stairs, screaming "Master! Master help me!" A cloud of dust came welling up the stairway, almost blinding him. Vampires were fighting all around him in their frenzy to get out of the castle, some stumbling and falling over the struggling, gnashing bodies of others. Palatazin reached back and grasped Tommy's arm, and together they fought their way through. In the lower corridor vampires ran back and forth, calling for their Master and wailing for help. Stones and rafters fell from above, crashing to the floor and often crushing one or more vampires underneath. The corridor was filled with dust, struggling shapes, screams, and moans. Three huge blocks fell with a tangle of rafters, blocking the corridor ahead of Palatazin and Tommy. They found the door leading downward, stepped through it, and bolted it. And now they knew they had to hurry because the castle was pitching and swaying above them, sending chunks of stone hurtling into the basements. They passed through the rooms where coffins lay with their beds of dirt and descended the stone stairs in almost total darkness, into the lower basement where the dogs bayed and fought to escape, running back and forth like the vampires above, lost without a guiding hand.

They retraced their way through the wine racks, twice coming to solid walls and having to go back and start over. "This way!" Tommy said, pulling at him. "There's blood on the floor!" Palatazin looked down and saw smeared droplets of blood that might have been either his or Benefield's, but Benefield himself was gone. The shattered half of the man's staff lay a couple of feet away. They found the door, almost hidden in the darkness, and started up the long stairway to the outside.

The night was filled with screams. Fissures veined the courtyard, splitting even wider as the man and the boy ran for the iron-barred gate. Beyond Palatazin the black Lincoln Continental pitched into a crevice, metal crumpling like tinfoil as the earth ground it under. Vampires were running across the courtyard, their dazed eyes recognizing Tommy and Palatazin as humans, but their primary need now was for escape and safety. Some of them were walking, holding out their arms, and screaming for their Master. Palatazin saw several plunge through fissures and disappear.

He hauled up the gate and locked the chain in place, then they went through, running along the cobblestone, driveway. From the forest a sand-whitened figure ran toward them, arms waving like a scarecrow's. "Hey! Don't leave old Ratty up here, man! This fuckin' mountain's coming apart!"

Palatazin heard a hideous grinding and cracking sound, and when he looked back over his shoulder, he saw the castle's uppermost towers sway, then crumple in an explosion of stone. The earth under his feet heaved, throwing him off balance. Half of the castle buckled and slowly began to give way, sliding over the cliff's edge like a huge melting candle. Cracks split the ground at his feet, and now he knew the enormity of this earthquake would destroy Los Angeles. There was no way they could escape on foot. Going back into the tunnels, which had been his first idea, would be suicide. He remembered the stalled vehicle further down the road. If it had enough gas, if it hadn't already gone over the side! But now they had no choice, for the mountain was shaking itself to pieces beneath them.

They started down, Ratty's face stark white with terror beneath the grime. Tommy fell, almost sliding into a fissure that hissed open at his feet; Palatazin pulled him away and now half-carried, half-dragged him. From behind there was a growing thunderous rumble that made Ratty whirl around and shout "Jesus!"

Palatazin looked. The rest of the castle was going over, stones churning and boiling, rafters exploding into the air. It had vanished in less than three seconds, nothing left of it but a section of wall and the front gate. Above the noise of the castle's destruction, Palatazin could hear a hideous chorus of screams and shrieks—the dreadful, agonized song of the damned. Looking out over the black plain of L.A., he saw with frightening clarity the ripple of green phosphorescence atop a wave that must have been at least 300 feet high, rolling across the city from the west. He heard himself cry out, more of a moan than anything else, as he watched that wave sweep onward across avenue and boulevard and freeway. The towers of buildings jutted up like new reefs before they were either covered over or broken off.

Behind the main wave were others coming in at angles across the backwash, breaking together in thunderclaps of water that shot foam another hundred feet into the air. The L.A. basin was filling up, zigzagged with froth

and green wake. And still the earth shook. Even larger
waves were churning in from the ruined Santa Monica
breakwaters over ten miles away. Palatazin knew Westwood Village, Venice, Century City, West L.A., and most
of Beverly Hills would already be underwater. Under
salt water, he realized, remembering the effect that had
on the vampires. The vampires weren't drowning down
there because they couldn't drown; they were being
burned up. Palatazin shouted jubilantly to the sky. They
were dying, most if not all of them trapped beneath fallen
houses and buildings while the seawater roared in around
them, searing them to the bone, blinding them, killing
them.

In another moment they saw the jeeplike vehicle. They
started running for it, and suddenly the world gave a
great heave beneath Palatazin's feet that sent him spinning out into space. He heard Tommy cry out and grab
his arm, and then they were both falling, sliding down
into the crevasse where the road had been. Palatazin
scrambled for a handhold on loose rocks and clumps of
exposed roots. Suddenly there was someone above him,
leaning over the precipice with an extended hand. Palatazin had just an instant to recognize who it was—his
mother, her eyes dark and determined in a heavily
creased, almost pellucid face. He reached up and caught
her hand, feeling flesh against flesh, and then he was
holding onto a gnarled root that looked like a closed fist.
Tommy was gripping his other sleeve, both of them dangling over a black abyss.

A rope came snaking down beside Palatazin. "Grab
it!" he told Tommy. When the boy had transferred his
weight to the rope, there was the noise of an engine starting, and Tommy was pulled quickly to the top. In another moment the rope was dropped again, and Palatazin
grasped it, then was hauled up the same way. At the top
he saw that Ratty had tied it to the front fender of that
jeep, then started the engine—thank God it *would* start,
he breathed—and backed it away to pull them up. "Saw
that in a cowboy movie once," Ratty said as Tommy
climbed into the back and Palatazin took the passenger
seat. "God bless old Hopalong Cassidy, man! Ain't been
in one of these bastards since Nam. Dig it!" He whooped
and threw the thing into reverse, backing away from the
deep pit. He was driving in the trench that the bulldozer

had cleared out, moving faster in reverse than Palatazin could have driven in a forward gear.

"You all right?" Palatazin asked Tommy.

"Yeah," the boy said, but he looked pale and stunned, and he was shaking very badly. Tears suddenly filled his eyes and streamed down his cheeks, but his lips remained drawn in a grim, gray line. "Yeah," he said softly.

"Thought your asses were cooked," Ratty said. "You were in there a long time, man. Too fucking long! Then the bulldozer and the trucks came out, and Ratty dug himself a deeeep hole." The ground shook. Sand and boulders were falling onto the road, the larger rocks rolling on off the edge and vanishing. Ratty, still driving in reverse, dodged the smaller ones as best he could with a skill that Palatazin thought might have shown how he'd gotten out of Viet Nam alive. He found a place to turn and spun the vehicle around violently, then headed down the mountain at breakneck speed. "We've got to get our asses out of here, man. Shit! Ain't much gas, but I don't think we're going to find a station that's open, do you? Christ Almighty!" He stomped on the brakes because water was churning over the road just ahead. The single yellow-glowing headlight picked out frothy waves littered with planks, roof tiles, a bright red lawn chair, and smoking shapes that looked like large snails after they'd been doused with salt. Palatazin realized with a shudder that those were what remained of the vampires. The jeep plowed through water that lapped up to the doors. A melted shape rubbed up against Palatazin's door, then was swept away in the tides behind the jeep. The water climbed steadily toward the hood, but then they were out of the flooded area and ascending again. They passed a green road sign that said Mulholland Drive—½ m.

"Where do we go from there?" Ratty asked.

"High ground. I think we should follow Mulholland west into the mountains and find a place to wait through the aftershocks up there."

The earth trembled suddenly, and Ratty yelped. "Shit! You feel that? This whole place is coming apart, man. Just splitting up into little pieces and going down like Atlantis!"

"What happens if we run into any more flooded areas? Can we get through?"

"I think so. This ain't just an ordinary jeep, man. I drove something like this in Nam, but I guess this is an improved version. It's an amphibious buggy, made for swamps, rice paddies, I guess even deserts. Sure don't know what it was doing up there, but if the gas holds out long enough, we'll be okay. Providing we don't get swallowed up in a hole or covered over with a big wave. I think the aftershocks are gonna be rough." He looked at Palatazin as if he suddenly realized the significance of what had happened. "The vampires," he said. "What's going to happen to them?"

"It's over for them," Palatazin said.

"Over. Yeah. The whole city is over, man. Kaput! There must've been a . . . a whole lot of people trapped down there, too."

And now Palatazin admitted to himself what must be true and felt a sick, heavy sense of loss at the pit of his stomach. Jo was dead by now, and Gayle Clarke as well. So were possibly thousands of other people who'd been trapped by the storm and the earthquake. It had all happened so fast; certainly there was no chance they could've escaped. The vampires had been destroyed, yes, but at a terrible cost. His old apartment building, his house on Romaine Street, the house where they'd taken refuge must now be under at least seventy-five feet of water. The entire L.A. basin was gone, a new coastline scooped out. The aftershocks would probably send the water further inland all through the night as more earth collapsed. He was speared with agony and put his hands to his face. First it had been his father and, in a way, his mother. Now the vampires had taken his wife as well.

He began to cry, emotions thrashing within him. The hot tears ran down his cheeks and softly dripped onto his shirt. Very soon he was wracked with sobs.

Ratty and Tommy averted their eyes. When they reached Mulholland Drive, right at the crest of the Santa Monica Mountains, Ratty turned to the northeast and sank his foot to the floorboard.

VIII

Friday, November 1
THE BASE

ONE

When Gayle woke up screaming the second time, it was morning, and bright hot sunlight was streaming through the venetian blinds into the barracks.

Almost at once a tall, middle-aged man with close-cropped silvery hair and brown eyes that. glowed warmly behind a pair of aviator glasses was standing beside her bunk. He wore sharply pressed, dark blue trousers with scarlet and gold stripes down the sides and a light brown shirt with a crucifix pinned to each lapel. Gayle looked up at him fearfully, her mind still filled with shrouded shapes that writhed and contorted like hideous worms.

"You're going to be fine now, M¡ss," the man said quietly. "There's nothing to be afraid of anymore."

"Nightmare," she said. "I was . . . dreaming . . . about them . . ."

The man's face seemed to pale slightly, his gaze sharpening. "I'm Chaplain Lott, Miss . . ." He waited for her to reply, carefully studying her face.

"Gayle Clarke. I saw you last night, didn't I? At the airstrip?" Her gaze rested on the crucifix on his left lapel. She was comforted by its presence, safe from danger, safe from the night and the things that lurked within it.

"Yes, probably." He glanced around. Most of the bunks were occupied or had suitcases and clothes thrown across them. It was one of the largest barracks on the Twenty-nine Palms Marine Corps Base in the Mojave Desert, about 150 miles from the submerged ruin of L.A. The barracks and most of the base's buildings were filled with people of all ages and descriptions. There was very little talking, and no laughter at all. Those who had spent the night here or had been airlifted out of the Marine rescue centers at Palmdale and Adelanto had brought their own horror stories with them, and no one could take more than their share. The night had been filled with crying and sudden screams. The tales that Chaplain Lott had heard babbled from feverish lips had been enough to gray his hair and stoop him over as if shouldering a terrible, unholy burden. When the first groups had started coming in—just an hour or so after the beginning of the series of earthquakes that had pushed Los Angeles beneath the sea and left Santa Ana, Riverside, Redlands. and Pasadena as ghost towns on the edge of the Pacific—Lott had rationalized those tales as mass hysteria. But then as the cargo and troop planes came in, bringing hundreds of survivors every hour, he had seen in those shocked and haunted faces a truth that shook him to the center of his soul. These were not simply people who believed in raw head and bloody bones tales, these were people who had lived through them. The other base chaplains and Father Allison were hearing the same things. Then there were the marines who looked as close to madness as a man can be without going over the edge. They wanted to talk to Lott, wanted to touch the crucifix, wanted to be prayed for. They'd seen things, they said, and then they'd told him what those things were.

The base had been closed off to the reporters, who flocked at the gates trying to wheedle, bribe, or threaten their way in. Someone said the governor had been there last night before boarding a jet bound for Washington, but Lott hadn't seen him. Now there were rumors that the vice-president was due very soon.

Lott sat down on the empty cot to Gayle's left, where Jo had slept uneasily and for only a few minutes at a time. Jo had calmed Gayle when she'd screamed herself awake the first time, around five in the morning, but now Jo was gone, and Gayle didn't know where she could be. The barracks smelled of fear, like sweat and scorched flesh. She noticed that most of the blinds had been pulled up to let in the golden, desert sunlight. The light had never seemed as important or as beautiful as it did at this moment.

"Who were you brought in with?" Lott asked Gayle. "A relative?"

"No. A friend."

"I see. Is there anything I can do for you?"

She smiled grimly. "I'm sure there are others who need you more."

"That's nice," Lott said.

"What's nice?"

"You smiled. Not a very big smile, nor even a good one. But a smile all the same. That's about the first smile I've seen since all this began."

"So what do I get, a medal?"

He laughed. It felt fine and seemed to push back some of the shadows that had gathered within him. "Good, that's good. At least you're not catatonic like some of them are." He opened his breast pocket and brought out a pack of Winstons. When he offered it, Gayle took a cigarette, almost biting through the filter, and leaned toward the lighter flame Lott offered. He lit one for himself and then put the pack down on the cot beside her. "Here you are," he said. "In lieu of a medal."

"Thanks." Gayle slipped her shoes on and laced them up. "How many have come in so far?"

"Classified information," Lott said.

"You don't know?"

"They won't tell me. But all the extra barracks are filled up, there are people jammed into the gym like sardines, and I understand there are just as many at Fort Irwin and Edwards Air Force Base. The planes are still landing, two or three every hour, and the Seabees are putting up a hundred or so prefab Quonset huts. Offhand, I'd guess there are upwards of fifty thousand here."

"The quake's over?"

"For now, yes. I understand all the coastal areas are being evacuated. San Diego was hit pretty hard, and I imagine the topography of San Francisco has been altered a bit, but the quake seemed to be centered right in L.A. It wasn't as devastating as the experts had been predicting for years, thank God, but it turned Los Angeles into a hundred-foot-deep tidal pool." His eyes darkened, and he regarded the ash of his cigarette. "It could've been worse. Things always can be worse."

Gayle looked around at the other people crammed into the barracks. Babies were crying, their mothers and fathers trying to console them or each other. There were sleeping bags on the floor with exhausted people still curled up in them. A few cots down from Gayle a pretty

Chicano girl with amber eyes had wrapped her arms around herself and was staring off into space, her face totally blanked with shock; beyond her a little boy was playing on the floor with a plastic dump truck, occasionally stopping to look up at his mother, who stood staring out a window with red, swollen eyes.

"The mess hall's open," Lott said. "You can get some breakfast there if you'd like."

"What's going to happen now? Can I get a ride out of here?"

"No. The base has been closed off indefinitely. And a good thing, too. The reporters are snarling around outside. You wouldn't want to have to answer any questions now, would you?"

She grunted. "I was . . . I *am* a reporter myself."

"Oh. Well, I'm sure you understand then."

"Who ordered the base closed?"

"Classified," Lott said and smiled faintly. "But I imagine everyone will have to stay here until some kind of official investigation or statement or . . . whatever . . . is released. Which could be a long while."

"So nobody out there knows about the vampires yet, do they?"

Lott drew deeply on his cigarette and started looking around for something to put the ashes in. He found a paper cup beside another empty cot, then glanced back at Gayle. "No," he said quietly. "They don't. I've been briefed on my official stance. The United States Marine Corps does not believe in vampires, nor do we wish to verify any of the rumors that will be created out of mass hysteria. Those are the key words, Miss Clarke. Mass hysteria."

"Bullshit," Gayle said and rose to her feet. "It's that kind of attitude, that disbelief, that made them so strong! We laughed at the legends, we called them old wives' tales that came about because of some childish fear of the things in the night, but they were there all the time, just waiting to strike. We *helped* them because we refused to believe in what we couldn't see. Well, I'll tell you— I've seen enough in these past few days to last a lifetime, and from now on I'll be real careful in deciding what not to believe . . ."

"Just a minute," Lott said. "I've told you my official stance. Unofficially, I . . . have to wonder."

"There are more of them out there, hiding in other
cities. People have to know. They have to learn to believe and to fight before what happened in L.A. happens
all over again."

Lott looked at her for a moment, his jaw working.
"And you want to teach them, is that it?"

"I want to write the story. I think I can. I don't know
where I'll sell it—I don't know if it can be sold—but I
have to get out of here first . . ."

"Excuse me, please," he said uneasily. "There are
others I have to attend to." He started to move away,
but Gayle said, "I'm not asking you to help me," and he
stopped. "I'm asking you if it can be done."

"You've never served in the military, have you?"

"Screw it! I don't want to hear about who ordered
what, or what's classified and what isn't. All that I can
get on my own. I'm talking to you as one human being
to another, and don't try to put the military between us.
Believe me, I won't be doing any talking to the reporters
outside." Her eyes gleamed fiercely. "I've lived this story,
and it's *mine*."

Lott paused, started to walk away again, and then
looked back at her. He drew once more on his cigarette,
and then crushed it out in the cup. His brow deeply furrowed, he walked back toward Gayle, set the cup on the
windowsill, and pulled up the venetian blind. Gayle saw
a startlingly clear azure sky, the sun blazing down on
white sands, gray mountains, stucco buildings, and concrete roadways. Three large green and brown variegated
trucks loaded with people bound for other barracks across
the base moved past the window. Gayle caught some of
their haggard, dazed expressions. She could see a couple
of helicopters sweeping in across the desert from the east;
they passed overhead, rotors faintly chukking.

Lott was quiet for a very long time, his eyes deep-set
and brooding. "I've been a marine for almost twenty
years, Miss. The corps is my life. I have a duty to obey
orders. If the base is secured, I have to do my best to
keep it secured. Do you understand that?" He looked
at Gayle, waiting for a reply.

"Yeah," Gayle said. "But I'd say you had a duty to
something else, wouldn't you? Or do you wear those for
show?"

"Of course," he continued without any hint that he'd

ever heard what she'd just said, "this is a very large base, almost 930 square miles of desert, mountains, and lava rock. There are supply sheds, warehouses, garages, dozens of places to hide. A stockade, too. That's a place of interest where the Shore Patrol puts all the marines who go AWOL, and I've counseled quite a few. Well, with L.A. on one side and Las Vegas on the other, what can you expect? I remember a boy who went AWOL, I think his name was Patterson, from . . . oh, Indiana, Ohio, somewhere like that. He'd gone over the hill because his girl of two or three years was getting married, and he wanted to stop the wedding. He didn't make it home, and he didn't stop the wedding, but he did get off the base. He stole a jeep and headed east, across twenty-five miles of country so hostile even the snakes avoid it. Helicopters patrol that area during the day, and there are observation towers equipped with searchlights. Some of that eastern area's too rough even to run a fence across, and in other places the wind keeps the sand piled up into dunes so high that somebody who wanted to go AWOL could just walk right out and away. Nearest road wouldn't be too far, maybe two or three miles. Patterson went at night. Of course, he had a map and a compass, and I imagine he drove with his lights out. It's dangerous country. If he'd gotten lost out there, the Shore Patrol might not've found anything but his bones. I don't know how he got that jeep, but . . . well, there are so many vehicles here, sometimes a single jeep can go missing for a couple of days without anyone knowing. Hercules coming in." He pointed toward the sky, and Gayle saw a lumbering aircraft, the kind that had brought her and Jo to the base last night, dropping smoothly toward the airstrip a few miles away. "Beautiful plane," Lott said. "Works like a mule. Sometimes people get careless and forget where they've left their jeeps, even leave the keys in the ignition. With all the confusion and civilians here right now, I wouldn't be surprised if someone parked a jeep behind this barracks tonight and completely forgot about it until tomorrow morning. Of course, the SPs will be patrolling tonight. They'd probably find it and tow it in if it wasn't gone after 2200 hours. That's ten o'clock, civilian time. Check?" He looked at her, his gaze deliberately vacant.

"Check," she said. "And thank you."

He seemed puzzled. "For what? Oh, the cigarettes.

You're very welcome. Now if you'll excuse me, there are others I'd better see to. If you're hungry, the nearest mess hall is just over on Flag Square. You'll see the signs." He left her without a backward glance, moving through the bunks to where a man sat with his hands to his face, his back stooped like a question mark.

TWO

In the crowded, noisy mess hall, Jo peeled the top off a paper cup of orange juice that had Red Cross stenciled across the side and forced herself to drink it. It tasted weak and chalky, but it was the first thing in her stomach since the slice of ham between two pieces of moldy bread she'd eaten during the night when she, Andy, and Gayle had been trapped in that house. The orange juice churned in her stomach; she thought it might come up. She doubted if anything would ever taste the same again, if anything would ever *be* the same again. The world had tilted, and everything she'd ever believed in had gone sliding off into black nothingness. Her eyes burned with tears and the need for sleep, but she was all cried out, and trying to sleep was a torment.

She couldn't believe that Andy was dead. She refused to believe it. When she had finally slept last night, she'd had a strange dream in which she'd been walking along a dark twisting road, just the faintest glimmer of reddish light on the horizon. She'd walked alone for what seemed like miles, then suddenly she was aware of someone walking with her. It was Nina Palatazin, her face gray and wrinkled but her eyes more sharp and alert than Jo ever remembered seeing them. The old woman walked with difficulty, but her spine was straight, and she held her chin high. Finally she'd spoken in a voice that seemed faint and faraway, like the soft murmur of a cool desert wind.

"This road goes on, child," she'd said. "It's not an easy road; it's not a safe road. But you can't step off it, and you can't stop. It goes both ways—out of the past and into the future. There's more ahead for Andy. Much more. You'll have to be prepared, and you'll have to be strong. Can you be?" The old woman looked at her sharply, and Jo saw that her form seemed to be undulating, shimmering like silk.

"He's dead. The vampires took him, or the storm, or the earthquake . . ."

"Do you really believe that?"

"I . . . don't want to believe it."

"Then *hope*," the old woman insisted. "And don't ever stop because once that's gone, you might as well sit down right here and never move again."

"He's dead," Jo said quietly. "Isn't he? Can't *you* tell me?"

"I can tell you that he lives, that he's hurt and tired, that he's coming to you soon. But isn't that only what you want to hear?"

"Yes," Jo said uneasily.

"The road goes on," the old woman said. "It promises nothing except a journey, from birth to death. He's not going to need me anymore. It's you who'll have to go the rest of the way with him, by the will of God. Oh, look at that!" She stared off toward the horizon, her gaunt face lit by the soothing, reddish glow, like the warming touch of a distant, comforting hearth. "The night's almost over," she said. "It's going to be daylight soon, very soon. Oh, I'm tired now . . ." She looked past Jo, out across a dark plain. "I think I want to rest for a while, in that peaceful place. But you have to keep going, Jo. Both of you do." The old woman stared at her for a few seconds, then stepped off the road and began walking away into the distance. Jo watched her disappear out of sight, and at the last moment, she broke up into fragments of white light that pulsated and then vanished, whipped away by the wind. Jo walked on, shivering. But now the light had gotten stronger, and she knew she couldn't stop, couldn't turn back. Darkness lapped at her heels, and there was nothing to do but meet the sun. Soon after that she'd awakened.

Since dawn Jo had stood at the airstrip with a few hundred other people, watching the big planes come in. Trucks and ambulance vans rolled across the tarmac to carry away both the survivors and the injured. Jo knew that many thousands had been taken to Fort Irwin and Edwards Air Force Base too, and that the names of all the survivors would be a long time coming. If Fate had swept Andy's life away, she chose to believe that he'd found the vampire king after all and had plunged an ash stake deep into its u~holy heart. She reached up to her throat and touched the tiny crucifix Andy had bought for her. It seemed very important that she wear it now.

She'd heard the rumors circulating from the new ar-rivals—a million dead, possibly more. L.A. under one hundred feet of ocean. The waves littered with bodies and debris. The vampires shriveled, burned, gone, melted into hideous black forms that smoked and sizzled like hot fat in a huge frying pan. But there were the rumors of miracles as well. Houses ripped up and washed to safety on the boiling crests of tidal waves. Hundreds of survi-vors found by the Marine helicopters and Navy rescue craft, clinging to the remnants of roofs, wooden planks, overturned boats, and the barely exposed islands of L.A.'s tallest buildings. The thousands who had braved the vam-pires and the choking sand to head across the canyons on foot, escaping into the Santa Monica Mountains be-fore the earthquake struck. Rumors of premonitions, her-oism, breaks of luck that had saved hundreds from certain death. Encounters with strange figures in the sandstorm who had led families and groups of survivors to safety at higher elevations and then had inexplicably disappeared. Raw, rugged endurance and an anger that had kept people going, one step at a time, until the danger was past.

Now, sitting at a table with a young couple and an older family who looked as shell-shocked as any war veterans, Jo drank down the rest of her orange juice and looked out the window beside her. She could see one of those large transport planes coming in for a landing, and another starting to circle the field, the sun shining off it like a silver coin. *The survivors were still coming in, thank God,* she told herself. Hope was beginning to gather within her again, crackling like a fire that had al-most burned out. She mustn't let it. Now she had to hope and pray that Andy was aboard one of those planes and was somehow, somewhere safe.

A woman with curly brown hair and very tired-looking dark eyes sat down across from Jo. She had a cup of black coffee, and she was wearing a spotted white smock. Her name tag with a red cross on it said OWENS. The woman—a Red Cross doctor or nurse, Jo reasoned—

sipped at her coffee, closed her eyes for a few seconds, and then opened them again, staring out the window at the incoming planes.

"I know it must be difficult," Jo said.

The woman looked at her and nodded. "Yes. Very. Red Cross medical personnel are here from four different states, but still . . . we're low on whole blood, metaraminol, dextran . . . well, a lot of things. We're seeing a lot of shock cases. You're from the L.A. area?"

"That's right, yes."

"I can see it in your eyes. Was it . . . bad for you?"

Jo nodded.

"I'm sorry." The woman cleared her throat and looked around the crowded mess hall, then back at Jo. "I flew in from Arizona last night. I had no idea there would be this many people."

"I hope there are more," Jo said. "I suppose you've . . . heard everything by now?"

"Uh-uh." She lifted a warning hand. "I'm not supposed to discuss anything I might have overheard. Orders."

"Oh, of course." Jo smiled wanly and looked away. The military didn't want any information or rumors or old wives' tales getting off the base. Of course. The rest of the nation had to be protected from hearing about the things in the night. Anger flamed her face, but she was too weary to let it out.

"That's very pretty," the woman said.

"Pardon me?"

She touched her throat. "Your chain and crucifix. I've been seeing a lot of those today. As a matter of fact, I just came out of surgery on a man who'd swallowed one of them. It was giving his lower intestine fits, and it wasn't going to come out the easy way. Yours is about the same size."

"Oh." Jo turned in her chair. A Red Cross helicopter chattered over the mess hall, bound for the airstrip. It was time for her to get back there now, to maintain her vigil. She had to know, one way or the other. "Well," she said and rose to her feet, "I'd better make room for someone else."

"It was good talking with you, Mrs. . . . ."

"Palatazin," she said. "It's Hungarian." She started to turn away and then stopped. "Thank you for being here. Thank you for helping."

"I hope I *have* helped," the woman said.

Jo left the table and moved toward the mess hall door. She stepped outside into the clear sunlight, and in the distance she could see the huge, sprawling tent city that had been set up to house more survivors and most of the Marine personnel. Trucks and jeeps drove among them, stirring up lazy whirls of dust. More planes were circling the airstrip, and now she felt the need to hurry.

"Just a minute," someone said behind her. Jo turned to face the Red Cross lady. "What did you say your name was?"

Her heart began beating a little harder. "Palatazin."

"My God," the woman said softly. "I just . . . I . . . thought that crucifix looked the same. That man . . . he's . . . your husband?"

Jo was shocked speechless. Her lips worked for a few seconds before she could get the name out. "Andy?" she whispered. She began to cry, and Dr. Owens put an arm around her shoulder and quickly led her to a parked jeep. They drove to a white stucco building being used as a Red Cross facility. The first room that Jo—trembling, afraid that the doctor had made a terrible mistake and that this wasn't her Andy at all—entered was full of chairs and tables, cots and sleeping bags, a makeshift waiting room crammed with people. She heard Tommy's high, clear voice shout "HEY!" before she saw him, and when he stood up from a chair across the room, her knees went weak. And then she was running toward him, laughing and crying at the same time. She hugged him tightly, unable to say a word. Someone else, a man with a dirty beard and a filthy T-shirt, stood up, too. The waves of stench that he exuded had kept people away from him in a ten-foot radius.

"We thought you were dead!" Tommy said, his eyes brimming with tears. He looked fine to Jo, just fine, but there were lines in his face that had no business being there. "We thought the earthquake had gotten both of you!"

"No, no. How did *you* get out?"

"Our gas ran out. We had to spend the night up in a cave in the mountains. There were about twenty others there too. The shocks kept coming, all night. Then we heard helicopters, and they found us with their searchlights just before dawn. Then we . . . God, I'm glad to see you!"

"Andy," Jo said and looked at Dr. Owens. "Is he all right?"

The woman's eyes darkened. "We got that obstruction out of him about an hour ago, but he was . . . very despondent. It was a relatively simple operation, but he wanted to give up on us a couple of times there." She glanced at Tommy, then back to Jo. "I think he went through a very rough time."

"We found *him*," Tommy said, his voice knotted with new tension. A chill skittered quickly up his spine. Ever since they'd been flown in on a C-130 Hercules several hours before, when Palatazin's stomach had started cramping, he couldn't get over the feeling that something with burning eyes was still stalking them, staying just behind them and out of sight. He was sure his days of watching horror movies were over. Now he was going to be a comedy freak. "Up in the castle," he said. "The Master."

"Truth in a teacup!" the bearded man said. "The bloodsuckers were swarmin' up there!"

"Is it over?" she asked Tommy, but the boy couldn't reply.

A Red Cross nurse and a stocky man in a white uniform came through a pair of doors behind Jo and approached them. The nurse said, "This is the one, right here," and pointed toward the bearded man. "He's dirty enough to start a lice farm and he refuses to take a shower. I've told him he can't stay in the infirmary area, Dr. Whitcombe, but . . . ."

"A *shower?*" the bearded man said and looked helplessly at Tommy.

"You heard her. Jesus, you're rank!" The doctor clamped a large hand on Ratty's shoulder. "Listen, we've got enough problems here without plague. You coming along or do I call the SPs?"

"A *shower?*" he repeated incredulously.

"Yep. With Lava Soap. Let's go."

Ratty muttered and started walking, his shoulders slumped in resignation. At the doors he stopped and said to Tommy, "Keep the faith, little dude." When the doctor gripped his arm again, Ratty looked haughtily at him, pulled free, and then was gone through the doors.

"I want to see my husband," Jo said finally to Dr. Owens. "Right now."

"All right. He's upstairs." She nodded toward a stairway that had a desk pulled beside it where a couple of nurses were sorting folders. A sign on the desk read No Admittance Beyond This Point.

When Jo looked back at him, Tommy said, "I'll wait. I won't go anywhere." Jo nodded and followed Dr. Owens up the stairs. Her heart was pounding as they walked along a concrete-floor corridor with a series of large rooms on either side. The place looked like it had been used for classes because there were a lot of desks piled out in the hallway. Now the building had been turned into a makeshift hospital. Jo could see the beds through the open doors, six or more to a room. Nurses and doctors hurried about, pushing gurneys or carts filled with equipment.

"He'll still be pretty groggy," Dr. Owens warned her, "and I doubt if he'll make much sense. But I'm sure seeing you will make him feel a whole lot better." She stopped, checking a sheet of paper taped to the wall beside one of the doors. On it was a list of six names. "A. Palatazin," Dr. Owens read. "Good thing your name is one of those that you don't for . . ." She turned, realizing that Jo had already stepped past her into the room. Dr. Owens saw no need to linger. There was still a lot of work to do.

Jo stood in the room, looking from bed to bed. In the dim light that filtered through drawn blinds, she saw only strangers, people asleep, a couple of them wearing casts. One of them, a young woman, moaned softly in her sleep. She had a sudden crazy thought—*What if Andy wasn't here at all? What if the records had been mixed up? The doctor wrong? Everything gone topsy-turvy in the confusion?*

And then she looked over at the bed across the room just underneath the window and took a tentative step forward. *No. That couldn't be Andy lying there, hooked up to IV tubes and a bag of blood. That was a much older man, his face ashen white against the pillow.* She took another step. He was covered over by a dark blue blanket, but she could see a crisscrossing of bandages at his throat just under the chin, and she put a hand to her mouth to stifle a cry. In another bed a young black man stirred uneasily, his arm and leg in casts connected to a series of lines and pulleys. He opened his eyes, stared at her for a few seconds, then closed them again with a soft sigh.

Jo stood over Andy and traced a finger across his cheek. His face, as pale as it was, seemed beautiful to her. There seemed to be much more gray in his curly halo of hair. She reached under the blanket and sheet, found his wrist, and felt the pulse beating there. It was weak, as fragile as the preciousness of life itself. But what a marvelous thing it was, what a wonder. Life was achingly short, but that was the challenge of it—to do the best with it in the time allowed, to age and change and grow. And that was something the Undead could never do. That was a gift denied them.

Andy's fingers moved. She grasped his hand, wouldn't let go. His eyes slowly opened. He stared at the ceiling for a moment, then turned his head toward her with obvious effort. When he focused on her, he said in a hoarse whisper, "Jo?"

"It's me. It's me," she said. "I'm here, Andy. Everything's all right now. I'm alive. Gayle's alive. And thank God, so are you . . ."

"Alive?" he whispered. "No, it's a dream . . ."

She shook her head, tears brimming from her eyes. "It's real, Andy. The marines came and took us out before the earthquake started. Tommy told me what happened."

"Tommy? Where is he?" He blinked, unsure whether he was dreaming or not.

"Downstairs. He's fine."

Palatazin stared at her for a long moment, then his face collapsed like the shattering of a mirror. He took her hand in both of his and pressed it to his lips. "Oh, God," he whispered. "You're not dead . . . you're not dead . . ."

"It's all right," Jo said softly and ran a hand over his forehead and into his hair. "Everything's going to be fine now, you'll see . . ."

It was another minute or so before he could speak again, and then only in a quiet, faraway voice that told her he was trying desperately to hang on to consciousness. "The vampires," he said. "They're gone."

"Gone? How?"

"The ocean. The saltwater. It roared in and . . . I

think some of them must've gotten out, but not many . . .
not many. I think—I hope—their king is dead. I didn't
see him after the quake started, but . . ." He remembered
Father Silvera and the young man and the female vampire who had found the strength to deny her own existence and thus had saved both he and Tommy. He would
pray for all of them because they'd all been brave, and
the combination of their actions had helped stop the advance of the vampiric army. He thought that Father Silvera
might have survived, but he doubted it. He was certain
the priest had died fighting, and that the king vampire
had been destroyed either in the collapse of the castle or
by that huge, swirling cauldron of saltwater. If not . . .
Palatazin closed his eyes. He couldn't think about that
possibility, not yet. But for now the cancerous spread of
them had been halted.

"What are we going to do now?" Jo asked him.

He opened his eyes. "We go on," he said. "We find
another place to live. We put what's happened behind us.
But we *don't* forget. They didn't think we were so strong.
They didn't think we could even fight back. But we did.
And we can again if we have to." He paused, then
smiled slightly. "Think I can find that chief of police job
in some little town now? A very long way from here."

"Yes," she said softly and returned his smile. "I know
you can."

He nodded. "I'm . . . not going to be the same for a
while, Jo. You're going to have to help me understand
and . . . deal with what's happened . . ."

"I will."

"And Tommy, too," he said. "His parents are gone,
he's still not even sure what happened to him that night,
or how he got to us. Maybe it's . . . best that he never
remembers, but I think someday he will. We'll both have
to be strong for him."

"Yes," she promised.

He squeezed her hand and kissed it. "My good Jo,"
he whispered. "Strong like a rock."

"I won't leave you," she told him. "I'll sleep downstairs
on the floor if I have to, but I won't leave until you're
on your feet again."

"God save the doctor who tries to throw you out,"
Palatazin said. And looking up at her shining face, he
knew there were things he should tell her, but he couldn't,

not yet. He knew the vampires were gone, yes, but the Evil that had created them and given them power lived on, somewhere in the darkest limits where the world trembled between night and day, where the things that ruled the court of midnight held sway. The Evil would be back, in some different form perhaps, but with the same terrible purpose. It had learned a lesson this time and was not likely to repeat its mistake.

And his father stalked the monastery ruins atop Mount Jaeger along with the other grinning things from his boyhood village. Someday his father would have to find release, all of them would, and Palatazin felt sure that if it were not his own hand that guided the stake, then it would be someone else's, perhaps . . . Tommy's hand grown older and stronger and wiser. But those were all things of the future, and he didn't want to think about them just yet.

Palatazin's vision was blurring around the edges. Jo had never looked more beautiful; life had never seemed more precious a gift.

"I love you," he said.

"I love *you*." She leaned over and kissed his cheek, a tear falling from her face onto his, and when she lifted her head, she saw he'd gone back to sleep.

THREE

At exactly ten o'clock Gayle quietly left her bunk in the barracks and made her way to the door. There were still people awake and whispering in the darkness, but they paid her no attention. A child cried out suddenly, awakened from a nightmare, and Gayle heard a woman's voice whispering soothingly as she reached the door and slipped out into the cool desert darkness.

Stars blazed in the sky, but there was no moon, a fact Gayle was grateful for. Only a few figures moved along the road. Spare lights burned in other barracks, and an occasional cigarette glowed in the night. She was rounding the far side of the building when she was caught by the bright, white glow of headlights. A jeep carrying two

SPs rolled to a halt beside her, and she stopped immediately.

"Ten o'clock curfew, Miss," one of them said. "Hadn't you heard?"

"Oh, a curfew? I'm sorry, I didn't know I was breaking any rules. I've just been out walking for a while, to think."

"Uh-huh. What barracks are you assigned to, please?"

"That one, way over there." She pointed to a building about sixty yards beyond them and across the road.

"You'd best get in for the night, miss. Climb in and we'll take you over."

"No, really I . . ." She paused, frowning, and tried her best to summon up some tears. All she got was a glazed expression, but she figured it was probably good enough. "I . . . need to be alone. Please. I need to think."

"Ten o'clock curfew, Miss," the SP said. He checked his wristwatch. "It's ten-oh-eight right now."

"I . . . lost my husband in the earthquake," Gayle said softly. "I just needed to get out and walk. The walls were closing in on me."

The first SP nodded, glanced over at the other one, and then back to Gayle. His face had softened a fraction, but his eyes were still hard. "I'm sorry to hear about your husband, ma'am, but I'm afraid you'll have to obey the curfew like everyone else. Of course, I don't suppose it would hurt if you finished your walk, do you, Roy?"

"Nope," the other SP said and gunned the engine.

"Okay, then. But afterward, straight to your barracks, Ma'am. Good night." He gave her a quick salute and then the jeep had rolled on past her, its red taillights flaring briefly before it turned to the left and disappeared.

Shit! Gayle thought. *Have to watch out for those cops!* She walked quickly around the barracks, the noise of her footsteps disquietingly loud on the pavement. She kept looking back over her shoulder, but the SPs didn't return. *Why would they?* she asked herself. *They bought my story.*

She found the jeep parked on the other side of a large green dumpster. The keys were in the ignition, and under the passenger seat there was a canteen and a few items rolled up in cellophane. She tore the packet open and found a small penlight, a compass, and a map of the base that showed the desert terrain and lava rock that lay to the east. It looked like hard country, but she had no choice. Chaplain Lott had helped her as much as he could—now getting there was her responsibility.

Okay, she told herself. *Time to go.* She flicked on the light and studied the map for a minute, then found an easterly heading on the compass and started the engine. The noise seemed loud enough to wake up every marine within ten miles. She saw a light come on in a building just a few yards away and, with fear galloping through her, she pushed down on the accelerator. She was determined to head as near due east as she could, but several times she saw the lights of an oncoming truck or jeep ahead, and she either turned off onto another road or stopped behind a building for a few minutes to wait and muster her courage. The further east she went, the more scattered and dark the buildings became. Finally she could look back over her shoulder at most of the base. Ahead of her, like black hulks in the starlight, loomed a ridge of mountains directly in her path. The pavement ended at a group of sheds surrounded by a high barbed-wire fence. Gayle turned off the road and started across the desert, the jeep's tires jubbling over rocks and sage-brush.

A monstrous apparition suddenly came sweeping over the mountains, red and green and white lights flashing. It was another Hercules transport plane, coming in low toward the airstrip. She could see the green cockpit glow, and the noise of the plane's passage deafened her. Then it had passed over, a wave of scorched air churning behind it, the roar slowly receding. Gayle recalled what Lott had said about the observation towers and immediately cut her headlights. The night enveloped her, but soon she could see fairly well just by the starlight. The desert stretched out on all sides, the mountains coming up to meet her. Several times she had to risk flicking on the penlight to check the compass.

An observation tower came up on her right frighteningly close, like an oil derrick topped by a black square of glass. Gayle angled away from it, expecting a piercing shaft of light, but none came. Cactus-strewn foothills began to rise out of the earth, carrying her into the mountains. She found what seemed to be no more than a rutted, boulder-strewn goat track, hardly wide enough for the jeep, but she started up along it. She became aware of a faint *chuck-chuck-chuck* that seemed to be steadily drawing closer. She stopped the jeep's engine. A helicopter passed overhead, flying slowly, and vanished toward the west.

Soon she passed near a second observation tower perched high on the mountain. The other side of the mountain was far rougher terrain—deep gullies, cracked earth, a scattering of high, soft dunes. She wondered where she'd go when—and if—she made it off the base. Las Vegas? Flagstaff? Phoenix? She had no money nor ID, nothing left in the world but the clothes she wore. She couldn't even prove she was a survivor of the quake, much less a reporter. If she went ambling into some small newspaper office talking about vampires, they'd either kick her ass out or call the men in white coats. But she had to try. Surely there were a lot of stragglers who'd made it out of L.A. on their own, who had gotten to telephones and started calling friends and relatives with chilling stories to tell. There was going to be a lot of scoffing—mass hysteria, had Lott said?—but if the stories were repeated often enough, by hundreds of people, every editor in the nation would have to start paying attention. It would first be a matter of convincing somebody to loan her a typewriter and some desk space in a newspaper office, and if that place didn't take the story, she'd go on to the next, and the next, and the next one after that. *Hell,* she thought, she could wash dishes and live in a fleabag motel if she had to, but she was determined to be at the forefront when the story broke. Eventually somebody would buy it, and she could work her way up from there. In a year she thought she'd be able to write her own ticket, possibly with the *New York Times* or *Rolling Stone.* In any case, a publication based as far away from California as she could get.

A helicopter suddenly came out of the night from the south, flying less than fifty feet from the ground. It passed over her with a thunderous racket, frightening Gayle so much she hit the brakes. The helicopter immediately started veering back, and Gayle realized they must've seen the brake lights flash. She pressed her foot to the floorboard, knowing there was no place to hide out here. The land was miserably bare, a series of sand dunes and red rock ridges ahead of her. The helicopter swept back over her again. Grit blinded her for a few seconds, and when she cleared her eyes, she saw the copter coming back for a third pass. A searchlight blazed down from the copter's underbelly and began a long, slow sweep.

Gayle zigzagged desperately. Then the searchlight had crept up behind her, glancing off the jeep. It came back and held, blinding her with its intensity. Over the combined roar of the jeep's engine and the copter's blades, she heard a voice amplified through a loudspeaker command, "Pull over! You're in violation of martial law! Halt immediately."

Gayle spun the wheel to the side and veered out of the light. If they stopped her, she knew she wouldn't have another chance to get off the base. Hot and dazzling, the light found her again. Above her the voice took on new menace. ". . . in violation of martial law. If you don't stop right now, you will *be* stopped."

Christ! she thought. *What are they going to do, shoot me? Maybe a warning shot, or perhaps they'd try to hit the tires, but surely they wouldn't shoot a civilian!* She was going to have to call their bluff. The wind whipped into her face, a maelstrom of dust and sand churning around her from the copter's rotors. She was going up over a cactus-stubbled ridge, the tires shuddering over purple rock. She heard a high thrumming sound and winced. About five yards to the left she'd seen sparks and dust fly in an orderly line—bullets. She was filled with rage, and when the next row of bullets fired from a machine gun with pinpoint accuracy struck the ground just ahead of her, she realized they were trying to make her turn. She kept going straight ahead.

At the crest of the ridge, she felt the jeep shudder madly. The wheel shook free from her hands, and she knew the bastards had hit a tire. She fought for control as the jeep hurtled over the ridge and down. It fishtailed to the right, and through the churn of sand she saw what the helicopter had been trying to turn her away from—a high barbed-wire fence at the bottom of the ridge and beyond it a flat plain stubbled with scrub and cactus. The limits of the base. She spun the wheel back, having an instant to fear that the fence might be electrified, then the jeep had crashed into it, flattening and roaring over it. The copter screamed past, trying to hover in her path. Unintimidated, Gayle drove straight ahead and underneath it, leaving the copter whirling like an angered insect. It found her again and stayed with her for another few minutes until she passed a large sign on a post driven deep into the sand. She glanced back at it and saw in the backwash of the copter's light the words U.S. GOVERNMENT PROPERTY—NO TRESPASSING BEYOND THIS POINT. The copter came down low on her, the searchlight striking her savagely in the eyes. Then it veered away slowly, in defeat. The light went out.

Gayle didn't reduce her speed. Less than a mile later the left rear tire spun off the wheel, ripped to shreds, and the bare wheel dug a trench in the sand before the jeep came to a halt. She cut the engine and sat there for a few minutes until she could stop shaking. Then she began to study the map. According to it—and she hoped she'd read the compass right so far—there should be a road a couple of miles ahead that would take her to a white dot called Amboy. She took the map, flashlight, and canteen, checked her compass again and started walking.

By the time she'd reached the narrow black line of road, a chill wind had kicked up. Her legs ached fiercely, but she had no time to rest. She'd seen more helicopters flying around in the distance, and she expected a truck full of soldiers to come roaring across the desert after her at any moment. She walked north toward whatever Amboy was. Something slithered across the road in front of her, and she realized with a shudder that it must've been a sidewinder. She started watching her step and was surprised when headlights appeared on the flat horizon ahead. She started to wave her arms, then realized that it could very well be a jeep or a truck sent out after her from the base. She moved quickly off the road and crouched down in a gully about twenty feet away.

The headlights brightened, the vehicle took form. It was a white van, and as it passed, Gayle saw NBC NEWS printed on its side above the peacock logo. She stood up and shouted, "HEY!" but the van went on without even slowing, heading south.

Well, Gayle thought, *it was headed in the wrong direction anyway.* After another mile her legs felt like taut springs, and the ground seemed to be crawling with rattlers. She wondered if there was a telephone in Amboy. She hadn't seen or talked with her parents in a long time, but she figured they were still up in Susanville, watching the grass grow. Her brother Jeff would be sixteen now and probably hanging out at the roller rink while her folks ran their little corner drugstore. Though she'd had her differences with her parents, she knew she should call them, if just to let them know she was still alive. If they asked her to come home or even volunteered to come pick her up, she would say no. Definitely.

Headlights came up very fast behind her, scrawling her shadow across the pavement. A dark blue, late model Buick passed her and went on perhaps fifty yards before it slowed and stopped. Then it reversed, and the driver was looking out through his window. "You need a ride?" he asked.

"Sure do," Gayle said without hesitation. He waved her over, and she got in, putting her map and canteen on the seat between them. The man drove on, and Gayle rubbed her aching calves. "Where are you headed?"

"East," the man said.

"Yeah, me too. How far east?"

"As far as I can."

"Good." Gayle took the pack of Winstons out of her pocket and offered him one. He shook his head, and she punched in the cigarette lighter. "Lucky for me you came along. I would've had a long walk."

"What are you doing out here?" the man asked her. "All alone, I mean?"

"I was . . . uh . . . my car broke down a few miles back. I got out of L.A. before the quake hit, and all I want to do is put a lot of miles between me and that place." The lighter popped out, and Gayle lit her cigarette. In its glow she studied the man. He was chunky with large shoulders and hands; he wore a red-checked shirt and dark trousers, one knee was torn, exposing a raw-looking wound. There were cuts on his knuckles too, and the one ear that Gayle could see looked absolutely mangled. He wore thick eyeglasses, held together in the middle with black electrical tape, and behind those glasses his small darting eyes looked watery and . . . spooky. He seemed to be trying to watch her without turning his head. There was a bruise on his chin, another cut on his cheek. His face, lit by the green glow of the dashboard, was large-jawed and thin-lipped. He carried an air of determination about him, an urgency, and when Gayle glanced at the speedometer, she saw that they were moving at just under eighty. The man finally turned his head and looked at her, then back to the road. Under his gaze Gayle felt . . . slimed.

She shifted uneasily in her seat and blew out a lungful of smoke. The headlights picked out a green road sign. Amboy—3. "Amboy," Gayle said. "That's where you can let me out."

He was silent. His huge hands tightened on the wheel, and Gayle thought that if he exerted an ounce more of pressure, it might break off in his grip. "Were you in L.A. too?" she asked him.

"Yes," he said quietly. A thin smile flickered across his face, then was gone.

"Then you know about *them?* The vampires?"

He watched the road.

"I hear they're all dead," Gayle continued. "Most of them, at least. Maybe a few got out, but they can't hide forever. They'll make mistakes. The sun'll catch them if it hasn't already. And I'm going to do my damned best to make sure everybody else knows about them, too."

The man glanced at her quickly. "How?"

"I'm a reporter," she said. "I'm going to write the hummingest story you ever read, once I find someone who'll give me the chance. It'll just be a matter of time. Hey, you're passing . . ." But then they were roaring through a cluster of dark, white-washed buildings, the speedometer still hovering at eighty. "That was Amboy." Gayle said anxiously. "That's where I wanted to get out."

"No. That's not where you're going."

"What do you mean?" Her eyes narrowed, and she felt a sharp needle of fear pierce her.

"Not Amboy. You're a liar. I didn't pass any car on the side of the road. So you're a liar, aren't you?"

"Listen, I . . ."

"I don't want to listen," the man said. He touched his forehead and winced as if in pain. "I've heard too many lies. And now you're going to go out and write some more lies, aren't you? About *them.*" He spoke that word with reverence. "I know . . . I know what kind of person you are." His gaze darkened, his lips curled in bitterness. "You're all the same, every one of you. You're all like *she* was . . ."

"She? Who?"

"Her," the man said softly. "She did things to make my

head hurt. She said she was never going to leave me, never going to let them take me away. But she lied. She said she was wrong, that I was crazy and she was leaving. That's who."

Gayle squeezed herself against the door, her eyes wide with terror.

"Can't fool Waltie," he said. "Can't laugh behind his back anymore, no. Because *I've* got the power now! It's inside me!"

"Yeah, okay. Why don't you just pull off up here and I'll . . ."

"I'm not stupid!" he said loudly. "I never was!" He glared at her with a burning gaze that seemed to shrivel her into a cinder. "That one thought I was stupid. He wanted to take me to the police. I knew what he was doing all the time! Go on, look. LOOK, I SAID!" He motioned with a jerk of his head toward the backseat.

Gayle looked, her heart pounding. Jammed down on the rear floorboard was a dead man, shirtless, with black bruises on his throat. His face had been pulped by heavy blows. Her stomach lurched. She gripped the door handle and saw desert flatlands blurring by at eighty miles an hour.

"I stopped her from leaving," the man said, "but they took her away in an ambulance. Then the *doctors* came. They all kept . . . picking at me. Picking . . . picking my brain apart," the man groaned. "But they won't laugh anymore. Nobody will. I've got the power . . ."

"What . . . power . . . ?"

"*His* power!" the man hissed. "He's gone now, they're all gone, but I've got to carry the message to the ones who are waiting! I've got to . . . got to tell them that it's time to strike!" His eyes were wild, like cracked black saucers behind the magnifying lenses. "They will. They'll do anything I say because I was the Master's pupil and I sat at his feet and worshipped him and I . . . I *touched* him . . . !"

"Nooooo," Gayle whispered hoarsely, cringing away.

"I'm the one, it's me who has to go on for him. I've got to find them in all the cities and tell them it's time to find a new Master, to band together." He rubbed at a spot on his forehead. "They'll win next time," he whispered. "And they'll make me like them so I can live forever . . ." He giggled, then his face immediately clouded over.

The Buick flashed past a sign that said Junction Interstate 40—5. The man began slowing the car. He turned off the road and started across the desert. Gayle looked around desperately, but there was nothing—just flatland, cactus, sagebrush. The stars burned with cold indifference. When the speedometer had dropped to under thirty, Gayle tried to leap out, but the man grabbed her by the hair and dragged her across the seat. She whirled, striking him with the lit cigarette, but he gripped her wrist and shook it out of her hand. The car stopped, and he clamped a hand around the base of her neck. The terrible pressure numbed her. He opened his door and dragged her out, flinging her to the rock-stubbled ground.

She started crawling frantically. He followed, his lips wet and gleaming, and kicked her down when she tried to rise. "I can't let you live," he said quietly. "You want to hurt them, don't you? You want to hurt *me* . . ."

"No . . ." Gayle said quickly. "No . . . I wouldn't . . ."

"LIAR!" he snarled and kicked her in the side. She cried out in pain and curled up, trying to shield her face with her hands. He stood over her, a dark shape against the night, his breathing quick and harsh. At his sides his hands clenched and unclenched, tendons standing out in the wrists as if he were squeezing a pair of invisible grips. "You have to die. Right now."

And then he was on her, pressing a knee into her stomach. He gripped her throat and started to squeeze. She fought and thrashed, trying to roll away, but his weight had her pinned, and now her head was filling up with blood. She struck him across the face, knocking his glasses off. "Go on," he said and grinned. "Yeah. Fight. Go on . . ."

Gayle pushed against his chin, whimpering like an animal. He moaned in ecstasy as her body shuddered. Her hands clawed at the air, then fell back to the earth. His eyes closed, his breath coming out in a rasp.

Her right hand touched a rough-edged rock lying just above her head. She concentrated on making her fingers close around it as black and red motes spun before her eyes.

Then she brought her hand up in a savage arc, smashing the rock against the side of his head. He grunted,

his eyes opening in surprise. She struck him again, right
at the temple, and he fell to one side. Gayle kicked away
from him, panting for breath. When she tried to stand
up, a tidal wave of dizziness sent her crashing back to
her knees, and it was all she could do to crawl. When
she looked back over her shoulder, she saw him lying
there, one hand clenching like an automaton.

Then he abruptly sat up. His head twitched to the side,
as if the blows to his skull had scrambled his nerve im-
pulses.

She crawled away madly, still clutching that rock.
"I'll find you!" he shrieked. "You can't get away! Got to
serve the Master . . . got to . . . serve . . ." He rose to
his feet, fell again, stood up unsteadily, and started coming after her, his hands searching before him.

And then Gayle found herself on the edge of a five-
foot gulley stubbled at the bottom with brush and flat
rocks. She stared down into it and thought she saw something move very slowly in there. Another movement.
Something coiled on a rock. A third one, slithering
through the brush into a hole. She saw a diamond design
on leathery hide, a flat head with a flicking tongue. Three
or more snakes coiled over each other. Another lifted its
head toward the human scent. The rattlings began, soft
and insistent.

Bellowing with rage, the man was on her. He gripped
for her throat again, his face shiny with sweat.

Gayle hooked a foot into his crotch and struck him in
the head with the rock as hard as she could. His bellowing was abruptly silenced. She reached up, fingers digging
into his shoulders, and shoved him toward the gully. He
stood balanced on the edge for a few seconds, hands flailing, then the sand collapsed beneath his feet and he toppled over, falling right into the midst of the rattlesnake
nest. There was an enraged cacophony of rattlings and
quick, slithering sounds, and then the man began screaming. The screaming went on for a long time. When it had
died down to a low, guttural moan, Gayle forced herself
to look over the edge.

A four-foot rattler lay coiled on his chest. It struck,
hitting him in the cheek; it withdrew and struck again.
The man's graying face was covered with punctures. The
snakes swarmed around and over him, striking everywhere. They coiled around his arms and legs like brace-

lets. His left hand had caught one, and the head was
crushed, but the tail still writhed. The man's eyes were
open, transfixed with horror, and seemed to have sunk
back into his head. As Gayle watched, he started shuddering as if electricity rippled through him. The snakes
gathered and struck again.

Gayle crawled away and threw up in the sand. After a
long time she crawled toward the car, but before she
could get there, the pain in her throat and head flared.
She put her cheek down against the cool sand and closed
her eyes. When she could lift her head again, she saw that
the car's headlights had dimmed. A cold wind rustled
past her, whispering through the brush. A terrible urge
to sleep almost overcame her; she wanted to lie there
forever, listening to the wind. If she closed her eyes and
slept, she'd be all right, she thought, and she wouldn't
have to worry about anything anymore.

But the story. She had a job to do now, an important
task to carry out. Her voice might be the first of hundreds,
warning others to check their basements, their root cel-
lars and their abandoned buildings, to watch for the track
of the vampire. It would take time to find all of them, but
they were out there . . . waiting. It would have to be
done; *she* had to do it.

There was no time for sleep. She looked up again and
saw the first pink traces of dawn on the eastern horizon.
There were headlights in the distance, coming along the
road. Gayle crawled to the Buick and pulled herself up
painfully to sit in the driver's seat. The car was moving
past. Gayle hit the horn, but the battery was so weak it
only gave out a muffled squawk. The car was driving
away now, probably headed toward Interstate 40. She
found the headlight switch and started punching it on and
off as fast as she could. The lights burned low, casting a
dim, brownish/light that she knew would hardly be noticed from the road. "Stop," she whispered hoarsely.
"Please stop, please stop, please . . ."

The car's brake lights flared. It stopped and sat there
for a moment or more. Then, slowly, it began to back up.
Gayle watched as a man got out. He stood beside his
car, as if uncertain. Then he started walking toward the
Buick as a woman in the passenger seat rolled down her
window. The round faces of two children peered out the
rear windshield.

The man was middle-aged and looked terribly haggard.
There was a bandage on his forehead. His eyes were wide
and fearful and, as he approached the Buick, Gayle saw
that he had something in his hand. "What's wrong?" he
said in a trembling voice. "Miss? You okay?" He stopped
several yards from the car, as if he might decide to run
at any second.

"Need help," Gayle whispered. "Need . . . ride . . ."
She stepped out of the car toward him, and as her knees
buckled and she fell to the ground, she saw him thrust
his hand forward. The object he held gleamed with dawn's
faint light, and it was the most beautiful thing Gayle had
ever seen.

A crucifix.

Graham
Masterton
Mirror

On the other side of the mirror lies a world beyond your darkest nightmares . . .

Screen writer Martin Williams is a man possessed. His obsession – 'Boofuls', the darling boy-angel of 30s Hollywood, whose horrific death was more spectacular than anything Hollywood ever dreamed up . . .

Now fifty years later all Martin wants is to make the movie that will bring Boofuls back to life. He can't believe his luck when he manages to buy a mirror from his idol's house. But that mirror was there when Boofuls died, and it has seen many things, more than the human eye can imagine . . .

Strange things happen in the mirror. Stranger things happen to the people who try to probe its secrets. And Martin is about to enter the gateway through which all hell will break loose . . .

Also by Graham Masterton in Sphere Books:

REVENGE OF THE MANITOU   THE WELLS OF HELL
THE DEVILS OF D-DAY   THE HEIRLOOM
CHARNEL HOUSE   TENGU
NIGHT WARRIORS   DEATH TRANCE

0 7474 0191 8   HORROR   £3.50

Guy N. Smith

While the forces of nature create a white hell outside, a satanic force from beyond the grave is at work inside . . .

Into this world step three unwitting travellers, driven by the blizzard to seek refuge at a country house hotel. A 'hotel' where the 'guests' live in a diabolical world of lunacy and madness, where demented creatures prowl the corridors, where putrefying flesh lies in the cellar and blood-curdling screams echo from the bedrooms . . .

And, amidst the horrors, the monstrous spawn of a subnormal girl awaits a virgin sacrifice to bring the Prince of Evil to life . . .

Also by Guy N. Smith in Sphere Books:
FIEND

0 7474 0057 1   HORROR   £2.99

A selection of bestsellers from SPHERE

FICTION

THE PALACE	Paul Erdman	£3.50
KALEIDOSCOPE	Danielle Steel	£3.50
AMTRAK WARS VOL. 4	Patrick Tilley	£3.50
TO SAIL BEYOND THE SUNSET	Robert A. Heinlein	£3.50
JUBILEE: THE POPPY CHRONICLES 1	Claire Rayner	£3.50

FILM AND TV TIE-IN

WILLOW	Wayland Drew	£2.99
BUSTER	Colin Shindler	£2.99
COMING TOGETHER	Alexandra Hine	£2.99
RUN FOR YOUR LIFE	Stuart Collins	£2.99
BLACK FOREST CLINIC	Peter Heim	£2.99

NON-FICTION

MARLON BRANDO	David Shipman	£3.50
MONTY: THE MAN BEHIND THE LEGEND	Nigel Hamilton	£3.99
BURTON: MY BROTHER	Graham Jenkins	£3.50
BARE-FACED MESSIAH	Russell Miller	£3.99
THE COCHIN CONNECTION	Alison and Brian Milgate	£3.50

All Sphere books are available at your local bookshop or newsagent, or can be ordered direct from the publisher. Just tick the titles you want and fill in the form below.

Name_____

Address_____

_____

Write to Sphere Books, Cash Sales Department, P.O. Box 11, Falmouth, Cornwall TR10 9EN

Please enclose a cheque or postal order to the value of the cover price plus:

UK: 60p for the first book, 25p for the second book and 15p for each additional book ordered to a maximum charge of £1.90.

OVERSEAS & EIRE: £1.25 for the first book, 75p for the second book and 28p for each subsequent title ordered.

BFPO: 60p for the first book, 25p for the second book plus 15p per copy for the next 7 books, thereafter 9p per book.

Sphere Books reserve the right to show new retail prices on covers which may differ from those previously advertised in the text elsewhere, and to increase postal rates in accordance with the P.O.